Library of America, a nonprofit organization, champions our nation's cultural heritage by publishing America's greatest writing in authoritative new editions and providing resources for readers to explore this rich, living legacy.

RAY BRADBURY

Ray Bradbury

NOVELS & STORY CYCLES

The Martian Chronicles

Fahrenheit 451

Dandelion Wine

Something Wicked This Way Comes

Jonathan R. Eller, *editor*

THE LIBRARY OF AMERICA

Published in the United States by Library of America.
Visit our website at www.loa.org.

This paper exceeds the requirements of
ANSI/NISO Z39.48–1992 (Permanence of Paper).

Distributed to the trade in the United States
by Penguin Random House Inc.
and in Canada by Penguin Random House Canada Ltd.

Library of Congress Control Number: 2021933605
ISBN 978-1-59853-700-0

Second Printing
The Library of America—347

Manufactured in the United States of America

Ray Bradbury:
Novels & Story Cycles
is kept in print by a gift from

JOHN LOGAN

to the Guardians of American Letters Fund,
established by Library of America
to ensure that every volume in the series
will be permanently available.

Contents

THE MARTIAN CHRONICLES

for my wife MARGUERITE with all of my love.

And for Walter I. Bradbury,
editor and friend, who was midwife to this book, a long time ago . . . with gratitude.

"It is good to renew one's wonder," said the philosopher. "Space travel has again made children of us all."

Chronology

January 1999: ROCKET SUMMER

ONE MINUTE it was Ohio winter, with doors closed, windows locked, the panes blind with frost, icicles fringing every roof, children skiing on slopes, housewives lumbering like great black bears in their furs along the icy streets.

And then a long wave of warmth crossed the small town. A flooding sea of hot air; it seemed as if someone had left a bakery door open. The heat pulsed among the cottages and bushes and children. The icicles dropped, shattering, to melt. The doors flew open. The windows flew up. The children worked off their wool clothes. The housewives shed their bear disguises. The snow dissolved and showed last summer's ancient green lawns.

Rocket summer. The words passed among the people in the open, airing houses. *Rocket summer.* The warm desert air changing the frost patterns on the windows, erasing the art work. The skis and sleds suddenly useless. The snow, falling from the cold sky upon the town, turned to a hot rain before it touched the ground.

Rocket summer. People leaned from their dripping porches and watched the reddening sky.

The rocket lay on the launching field, blowing out pink clouds of fire and oven heat. The rocket stood in the cold winter morning, making summer with every breath of its mighty exhausts. The rocket made climates, and summer lay for a brief moment upon the land. . . .

February 1999: YLLA

THEY HAD a house of crystal pillars on the planet Mars by the edge of an empty sea, and every morning you could see Mrs. K eating the golden fruits that grew from the crystal walls, or cleaning the house with handfuls of magnetic dust which, taking all dirt with it, blew away on the hot wind. Afternoons, when the fossil sea was warm and motionless, and the wine trees stood stiff in the yard, and the little distant Martian bone town was all enclosed, and no one drifted out their doors, you could see Mr. K himself in his room, reading from a metal book with raised hieroglyphs over which he brushed his hand, as one might play a harp. And from the book, as his fingers stroked, a voice sang, a soft ancient voice, which told tales of when the sea was red steam on the shore and ancient men had carried clouds of metal insects and electric spiders into battle.

Mr. and Mrs. K had lived by the dead sea for twenty years, and their ancestors had lived in the same house, which turned and followed the sun, flower-like, for ten centuries.

Mr. and Mrs. K were not old. They had the fair, brownish skin of the true Martian, the yellow coin eyes, the soft musical voices. Once they had liked painting pictures with chemical fire, swimming in the canals in the seasons when the wine trees filled them with green liquors, and talking into the dawn together by the blue phosphorous portraits in the speaking room.

They were not happy now.

This morning Mrs. K stood between the pillars, listening to the desert sands heat, melt into yellow wax, and seemingly run on the horizon.

Something was going to happen.

She waited.

She watched the blue sky of Mars as if it might at any moment grip in on itself, contract, and expel a shining miracle down upon the sand.

Nothing happened.

Tired of waiting, she walked through the misting pillars.

A gentle rain sprang from the fluted pillar tops, cooling the scorched air, falling gently on her. On hot days it was like walking in a creek. The floors of the house glittered with cool streams. In the distance she heard her husband playing his book steadily, his fingers never tired of the old songs. Quietly she wished he might one day again spend as much time holding and touching her like a little harp as he did his incredible books.

But no. She shook her head, an imperceptible, forgiving shrug. Her eyelids closed softly down upon her golden eyes. Marriage made people old and familiar, while still young.

She lay back in a chair that moved to take her shape even as she moved. She closed her eyes tightly and nervously.

The dream occurred.

Her brown fingers trembled, came up, grasped at the air. A moment later she sat up, startled, gasping.

She glanced about swiftly, as if expecting someone there before her. She seemed disappointed; the space between the pillars was empty.

Her husband appeared in a triangular door. "Did you call?" he asked irritably.

"No!" she cried.

"I thought I heard you cry out."

"Did I? I was almost asleep and had a dream!"

"In the daytime? You don't often do that."

She sat as if struck in the face by the dream. "How strange, how very strange," she murmured. "The dream."

"Oh?" He evidently wished to return to his book.

"I dreamed about a man."

"A man?"

"A tall man, six feet one inch tall."

"How absurd; a giant, a misshapen giant."

"Somehow"—she tried the words—"he looked all right. In spite of being tall. And he had—oh, I know you'll think it silly—he had *blue* eyes!"

"Blue eyes! Gods!" cried Mr. K. "What'll you dream next? I suppose he had *black* hair?"

"How did you *guess?*" She was excited.

"I picked the most unlikely color," he replied coldly.

"Well, black it was!" she cried. "And he had a very white

skin; oh, he was *most* unusual! He was dressed in a strange uniform and he came down out of the sky and spoke pleasantly to me." She smiled.

"Out of the sky; what nonsense!"

"He came in a metal thing that glittered in the sun," she remembered. She closed her eyes to shape it again. "I dreamed there was the sky and something sparkled like a coin thrown into the air, and suddenly it grew large and fell down softly to land, a long silver craft, round and alien. And a door opened in the side of the silver object and this tall man stepped out."

"If you worked harder you wouldn't have these silly dreams."

"I rather enjoyed it," she replied, lying back. "I never suspected myself of such an imagination. Black hair, blue eyes, and white skin! What a strange man, and yet—quite handsome."

"Wishful thinking."

"You're unkind. I didn't think him up on purpose; he just came in my mind while I drowsed. It wasn't like a dream. It was so unexpected and different. He looked at me and he said, 'I've come from the third planet in my ship. My name is Nathaniel York——'"

"A stupid name; it's no name at all," objected the husband.

"Of course it's stupid, because it's a dream," she explained softly. "And he said, 'This is the first trip across space. There are only two of us in our ship, myself and my friend Bert.'"

"*Another* stupid name."

"And he said, 'We're from a city on *Earth*; that's the name of our planet,'" continued Mrs. K. "That's what he said. 'Earth' was the name he spoke. And he used another language. Somehow I understood him. With my mind. Telepathy, I suppose."

Mr. K turned away. She stopped him with a word. "Yll?" she called quietly. "Do you ever wonder if—well, if there *are* people living on the third planet?"

"The third planet is incapable of supporting life," stated the husband patiently. "Our scientists have said there's far too much oxygen in their atmosphere."

"But wouldn't it be fascinating if there were people? And they traveled through space in some sort of ship?"

"Really, Ylla, you know how I hate this emotional wailing. Let's get on with our work."

* * *

It was late in the day when she began singing the song as she moved among the whispering pillars of rain. She sang it over and over again.

"What's that song?" snapped her husband at last, walking in to sit at the fire table.

"I don't know." She looked up, surprised at herself. She put her hand to her mouth, unbelieving. The sun was setting. The house was closing itself in, like a giant flower, with the passing of light. A wind blew among the pillars; the fire table bubbled its fierce pool of silver lava. The wind stirred her russet hair, crooning softly in her ears. She stood silently looking out into the great sallow distances of sea bottom, as if recalling something, her yellow eyes soft and moist. "'Drink to me only with thine eyes, and I will pledge with mine,'" she sang, softly, quietly, slowly. "'Or leave a kiss within the cup, and I'll not ask for wine.'" She hummed now, moving her hands in the wind ever so lightly, her eyes shut. She finished the song.

It was very beautiful.

"Never heard that song before. Did you compose it?" he inquired, his eyes sharp.

"No. Yes. No, I don't know, really!" She hesitated wildly. "I don't even know what the words are; they're another language!"

"What language?"

She dropped portions of meat numbly into the simmering lava. "I don't know." She drew the meat forth a moment later, cooked, served on a plate for him. "It's just a crazy thing I made up, I guess. I don't know why."

He said nothing. He watched her drown meats in the hissing fire pool. The sun was gone. Slowly, slowly the night came in to fill the room, swallowing the pillars and both of them, like a dark wine poured to the ceiling. Only the silver lava's glow lit their faces.

She hummed the strange song again.

Instantly he leaped from his chair and stalked angrily from the room.

Later, in isolation, he finished supper.

When he arose he stretched, glanced at her, and suggested,

yawning, "Let's take the flame birds to town tonight to see an entertainment."

"You don't *mean* it?" she said. "Are you feeling well?"

"What's so strange about that?"

"But we haven't gone for an entertainment in six months!"

"I think it's a good idea."

"Suddenly you're so solicitous," she said.

"Don't talk that way," he replied peevishly. "Do you or do you not want to go?"

She looked out at the pale desert. The twin white moons were rising. Cool water ran softly about her toes. She began to tremble just the least bit. She wanted very much to sit quietly here, soundless, not moving until this thing occurred, this thing expected all day, this thing that could not occur but might. A drift of song brushed through her mind.

"I——"

"Do you good," he urged. "Come along now."

"I'm tired," she said. "Some other night."

"Here's your scarf." He handed her a phial. "We haven't gone anywhere in months."

"Except you, twice a week to Xi City." She wouldn't look at him.

"Business," he said.

"Oh?" She whispered to herself.

From the phial a liquid poured, turned to blue mist, settled about her neck, quivering.

The flame birds waited, like a bed of coals, glowing on the cool smooth sands. The white canopy ballooned on the night wind, flapping softly, tied by a thousand green ribbons to the birds.

Ylla laid herself back in the canopy and, at a word from her husband, the birds leaped, burning, toward the dark sky. The ribbons tautened, the canopy lifted. The sand slid whining under; the blue hills drifted by, drifted by, leaving their home behind, the raining pillars, the caged flowers, the singing books, the whispering floor creeks. She did not look at her husband. She heard him crying out to the birds as they rose higher, like ten thousand hot sparkles, so many red-yellow fireworks in the heavens, tugging the canopy like a flower petal, burning through the wind.

She didn't watch the dead, ancient bone-chess cities slide under, or the old canals filled with emptiness and dreams. Past dry rivers and dry lakes they flew, like a shadow of the moon, like a torch burning.

She watched only the sky.

The husband spoke.

She watched the sky.

"Did you hear what I said?"

"What?"

He exhaled. "You might pay attention."

"I was thinking."

"I never thought you were a nature lover, but you're certainly interested in the sky tonight," he said.

"It's very beautiful."

"I was figuring," said the husband slowly. "I thought I'd call Hulle tonight. I'd like to talk to him about us spending some time, oh, only a week or so, in the Blue Mountains. It's just an idea——"

"The Blue Mountains!" She held to the canopy rim with one hand, turning swiftly toward him.

"Oh, it's just a suggestion."

"When do you want to go?" she asked, trembling.

"I thought we might leave tomorrow morning. You know, an early start and all that," he said very casually.

"But we *never* go this early in the year!"

"Just this once, I thought——" He smiled. "Do us good to get away. Some peace and quiet. You know. You haven't anything *else* planned? We'll go, won't we?"

She took a breath, waited, and then replied, "No."

"What?" His cry startled the birds. The canopy jerked.

"No," she said firmly. "It's settled. I won't go."

He looked at her. They did not speak after that. She turned away.

The birds flew on, ten thousand firebrands down the wind.

In the dawn the sun, through the crystal pillars, melted the fog that supported Ylla as she slept. All night she had hung above the floor, buoyed by the soft carpeting of mist that poured from the walls when she lay down to rest. All night she had slept on this silent river, like a boat upon a soundless tide. Now the fog burned away, the mist level lowered until she was deposited upon the shore of wakening.

She opened her eyes.

Her husband stood over her. He looked as if he had stood there for hours, watching. She did not know why, but she could not look him in the face.

"You've been dreaming again!" he said. "You spoke out and kept me awake. I *really* think you should see a doctor."

"I'll be all right."

"You talked a lot in your sleep!"

"Did I?" She started up.

Dawn was cold in the room. A gray light filled her as she lay there.

"What was your dream?"

She had to think a moment to remember. "The ship. It came from the sky again, landed, and the tall man stepped out and talked with me, telling me little jokes, laughing, and it was pleasant."

Mr. K touched a pillar. Founts of warm water leaped up, steaming; the chill vanished from the room. Mr. K's face was impassive.

"And then," she said, "this man, who said his strange name was Nathaniel York, told me I was beautiful and—and kissed me."

"Ha!" cried the husband, turning violently away, his jaw working.

"It's only a dream." She was amused.

"Keep your silly, feminine dreams to yourself!"

"You're acting like a child." She lapsed back upon the few remaining remnants of chemical mist. After a moment she laughed softly. "I thought of some *more* of the dream," she confessed.

"Well, what is it, what *is* it?" he shouted.

"Yll, you're so bad-tempered."

"Tell me!" he demanded. "You can't keep secrets from me!" His face was dark and rigid as he stood over her.

"I've never seen you this way," she replied, half shocked, half entertained. "All that happened was this Nathaniel York person told me—well, he told me that he'd take me away into his ship, into the sky with him, and take me back to his planet with him. It's really quite ridiculous."

"Ridiculous, is it!" he almost screamed. "You should have heard yourself, fawning on him, talking to him, singing with him, oh gods, all night; you should have *heard* yourself!"

"Yll!"

"When's he landing? Where's he coming down with his damned ship?"

"Yll, lower your voice."

"Voice be damned!" He bent stiffly over her. "And in this dream"—he seized her wrist—"didn't the ship land over in Green Valley, *didn't* it? Answer me!"

"Why, yes—"

"And it landed this afternoon, didn't it?" he kept at her.

"Yes, yes, I think so, yes, but only in a dream!"

"Well"—he flung her hand away stiffly—"it's good you're truthful! I heard every word you said in your sleep. You mentioned the valley and the time." Breathing hard, he walked between the pillars like a man blinded by a lightning bolt. Slowly his breath returned. She watched him as if he were quite insane. She arose finally and went to him. "Yll," she whispered.

"I'm all right."

"You're sick."

"No." He forced a tired smile. "Just childish. Forgive me, darling." He gave her a rough pat. "Too much work lately. I'm sorry. I think I'll lie down awhile——"

"You were so excited."

"I'm all right now. Fine." He exhaled. "Let's forget it. Say, I heard a joke about Uel yesterday, I meant to tell you. What do you say you fix breakfast, I'll tell the joke, and let's not talk about all this."

"It was only a dream."

"Of course." He kissed her cheek mechanically. "Only a dream."

At noon the sun was high and hot and the hills shimmered in the light.

"Aren't you going to town?" asked Ylla.

"Town?" He raised his brows faintly.

"This is the day you *always* go." She adjusted a flower cage on its pedestal. The flowers stirred, opening their hungry yellow mouths.

He closed his book. "No. It's too hot, and it's late."

"Oh." She finished her task and moved toward the door. "Well, I'll be back soon."

"Wait a minute! Where are you going?"

She was in the door swiftly. "Over to Pao's. She invited me!"

"Today?"

"I haven't seen her in a long time. It's only a little way."

"Over in Green Valley, isn't it?"

"Yes, just a walk, not far, I thought I'd——" She hurried.

"I'm sorry, really sorry," he said, running to fetch her back, looking very concerned about his forgetfulness. "It slipped my mind. I invited Dr. Nlle out this afternoon."

"Dr. Nlle!" She edged toward the door.

He caught her elbow and drew her steadily in. "Yes."

"But Pao——"

"Pao can wait, Ylla. We must entertain Nlle."

"Just for a few minutes——"

"No, Ylla."

"No?"

He shook his head. "No. Besides, it's a terribly long walk to Pao's. All the way over through Green Valley and then past the big canal and down, isn't it? And it'll be very, very hot, and Dr. Nlle would be delighted to see you. Well?"

She did not answer. She wanted to break and run. She wanted to cry out. But she only sat in the chair, turning her fingers over slowly, staring at them expressionlessly, trapped.

"Ylla?" he murmured. "You *will* be here, won't you?"

"Yes," she said after a long time. "I'll be here."

"All afternoon?"

Her voice was dull. "All afternoon."

Late in the day Dr. Nlle had not put in an appearance. Ylla's husband did not seem overly surprised. When it was quite late he murmured something, went to a closet, and drew forth an evil weapon, a long yellowish tube ending in a bellows and a trigger. He turned, and upon his face was a mask, hammered from silver metal, expressionless, the mask that he always wore when he wished to hide his feelings, the mask which curved and hollowed so exquisitely to his thin cheeks and chin and brow. The mask glinted, and he held the evil weapon in his hands, considering it. It hummed constantly, an insect hum. From it hordes of golden bees could be flung out with a high shriek. Golden, horrid bees that stung, poisoned, and fell lifeless, like seeds on the sand.

"Where are you going?" she asked.

"What?" He listened to the bellows, to the evil hum. "If Dr. Nlle is late, I'll be damned if I'll wait. I'm going out to hunt a bit. I'll be back. You be sure to stay right here now, won't you?" The silver mask glimmered.

"Yes."

"And tell Dr. Nlle I'll return. Just hunting."

The triangular door closed. His footsteps faded down the hill.

She watched him walking through the sunlight until he was gone. Then she resumed her tasks with the magnetic dusts and the new fruits to be plucked from the crystal walls. She worked with energy and dispatch, but on occasion a numbness took hold of her and she caught herself singing that odd and memorable song and looking out beyond the crystal pillars at the sky.

She held her breath and stood very still, waiting.

It was coming nearer.

At any moment it might happen.

It was like those days when you heard a thunderstorm coming and there was the waiting silence and then the faintest pressure of the atmosphere as the climate blew over the land in shifts and shadows and vapors. And the change pressed at your ears and you were suspended in the waiting time of the coming storm. You began to tremble. The sky was stained and coloured; the clouds were thickened; the mountains took on an iron taint. The caged flowers blew with faint sighs of warning. You felt your hair stir softly. Somewhere in the house the voice-clock sang, "Time, time, time, time . . ." ever so gently, no more than water tapping on velvet.

And then the storm. The electric illumination, the engulfments of dark wash and sounding black fell down, shutting in, forever.

That's how it was now. A storm gathered, yet the sky was clear. Lightning was expected, yet there was no cloud.

Ylla moved through the breathless summer house. Lightning would strike from the sky any instant; there would be a thunderclap, a boll of smoke, a silence, footsteps on the path, a rap on the crystalline door, and her *running* to answer. . . .

Crazy Ylla! she scoffed. Why think these wild things with your idle mind?

And then it happened.

There was a warmth as of a great fire passing in the air. A whirling, rushing sound. A gleam in the sky, of metal.

Ylla cried out.

Running through the pillars, she flung wide a door. She faced the hills. But by this time there was nothing.

She was about to race down the hill when she stopped herself. She was supposed to stay here, go nowhere. The doctor was coming to visit, and her husband would be angry if she ran off.

She waited in the door, breathing rapidly, her hand out.

She strained to see over toward Green Valley, but saw nothing.

Silly woman. She went inside. You and your imagination, she thought. That was nothing but a bird, a leaf, the wind, or a fish in the canal. Sit down. Rest.

She sat down.

A shot sounded.

Very clearly, sharply, the sound of the evil insect weapon.

Her body jerked with it.

It came from a long way off. One shot. The swift humming distant bees. One shot. And then a second shot, precise and cold, and far away.

Her body winced again and for some reason she started up, screaming, and screaming, and never wanting to stop screaming. She ran violently through the house and once more threw wide the door.

The echoes were dying away, away.

Gone.

She waited in the yard, her face pale, for five minutes.

Finally, with slow steps, her head down, she wandered about the pillared rooms, laying her hand to things, her lips quivering, until finally she sat alone in the darkening wine room, waiting. She began to wipe an amber glass with the hem of her scarf.

And then, from far off, the sound of footsteps crunching on the thin, small rocks.

She rose up to stand in the center of the quiet room. The glass fell from her fingers, smashing to bits.

The footsteps hesitated outside the door.

Should she speak? Should she cry out, "Come in, oh, come in"?

She went forward a few paces.

The footsteps walked up the ramp. A hand twisted the door latch.

She smiled at the door.

The door opened. She stopped smiling.

It was her husband. His silver mask glowed dully.

He entered the room and looked at her for only a moment. Then he snapped the weapon bellows open, cracked out two dead bees, heard them spat on the floor as they fell, stepped on them, and placed the empty bellows gun in the corner of the room as Ylla bent down and tried, over and over, with no success, to pick up the pieces of the shattered glass. "What were you doing?" she asked.

"Nothing," he said with his back turned. He removed the mask.

"But the gun—I heard you fire it. Twice."

"Just hunting. Once in a while you like to hunt. Did Dr. Nlle arrive?"

"No."

"Wait a minute." He snapped his fingers disgustedly. "Why, I remember *now*. He was supposed to visit us *tomorrow* afternoon. How stupid of me."

They sat down to eat. She looked at her food and did not move her hands. "What's wrong?" he asked, not looking up from dipping his meat in the bubbling lava.

"I don't know. I'm not hungry," she said.

"Why not?"

"I don't know; I'm just not."

The wind was rising across the sky; the sun was going down. The room was small and suddenly cold.

"I've been trying to remember," she said in the silent room, across from her cold, erect, golden-eyed husband.

"Remember what?" He sipped his wine.

"That song. That fine and beautiful song." She closed her eyes and hummed, but it was not the song. "I've forgotten it. And, somehow, I don't want to forget it. It's something I want always to remember." She moved her hands as if the rhythm might help her to remember all of it. Then she lay back in her chair. "I can't remember." She began to cry.

"Why are you crying?" he asked.

"I don't know, I don't know, but I can't help it. I'm sad and I don't know why, I cry and I don't know why, but I'm crying."

Her head was in her hands; her shoulders moved again and again.

"You'll be all right tomorrow," he said.

She did not look up at him; she looked only at the empty desert and the very bright stars coming out now on the black sky, and far away there was a sound of wind rising and canal waters stirring cold in the long canals. She shut her eyes, trembling.

"Yes," she said. "I'll be all right tomorrow."

August 1999: THE SUMMER NIGHT

IN THE stone galleries the people were gathered in clusters and groups filtering up into shadows among the blue hills. A soft evening light shone over them from the stars and the luminous double moons of Mars. Beyond the marble amphitheater, in darknesses and distances, lay little towns and villas; pools of silver water stood motionless and canals glittered from horizon to horizon. It was an evening in summer upon the placid and temperate planet Mars. Up and down green wine canals, boats as delicate as bronze flowers drifted. In the long and endless dwellings that curved like tranquil snakes across the hills, lovers lay idly whispering in cool night beds. The last children ran in torchlit alleys, gold spiders in their hands throwing out films of web. Here or there a late supper was prepared in tables where lava bubbled silvery and hushed. In the amphitheaters of a hundred towns on the night side of Mars the brown Martian people with gold coin eyes were leisurely met to fix their attention upon stages where musicians made a serene music flow up like blossom scent on the still air.

Upon one stage a woman sang.

The audience stirred.

She stopped singing. She put her hand to her throat. She nodded to the musicians and they began again.

The musicians played and she sang, and this time the audience sighed and sat forward, a few of the men stood up in surprise, and a winter chill moved through the amphitheater. For it was an odd and a frightening and a strange song this woman sang. She tried to stop the words from coming out her lips, but the words were these:

"She walks in beauty, like the night
Of cloudless climes and starry skies;
And all that's best of dark and bright
Meet in her aspect and her eyes . . ."

The singer clasped her hands to her mouth. She stood, bewildered.

"What words are those?" asked the musicians.

"What song is that?"

"What *language* is that!"

And when they blew again upon their golden horns the strange music came forth and passed slowly over the audience, which now talked aloud and stood up.

"What's wrong with you?" the musicians asked each other.

"What tune is that you played?"

"What tune did *you* play?"

The woman wept and ran from the stage. And the audience moved out of the amphitheater. And all around the nervous towns of Mars a similar thing had happened. A coldness had come, like white snow falling on the air.

In the black alleys, under the torches, the children sang:

"—and when she got there, the cupboard was bare,
And so her poor dog had none!"

"Children!" voices cried. "What was that rhyme? Where did you learn it?"

"We just *thought* of it, all of a sudden. It's just words we don't understand."

Doors slammed. The streets were deserted. Above the blue hills a green star rose.

All over the night side of Mars lovers awoke to listen to their loved ones who lay humming in the darkness.

"What is that tune?"

And in a thousand villas, in the middle of the night, women awoke, screaming. They had to be soothed while the tears ran down their faces. "There, there. Sleep. What's wrong? A dream?"

"Something terrible will happen in the morning."

"Nothing can happen, all is well with us."

A hysterical sobbing. "It is coming nearer and nearer and *nearer*!"

"Nothing can happen to us. What could? Sleep now. Sleep."

It was quiet in the deep morning of Mars, as quiet as a cool and black well, with stars shining in the canal waters, and, breathing in every room, the children curled with their spiders in closed hands, the lovers arm in arm, the moons gone, the torches cold, the stone amphitheaters deserted.

The only sound, just before dawn, was a night watchman, far away down a lonely street, walking along in the darkness, humming a very strange song. . . .

August 1999: THE EARTH MEN

WHOEVER WAS knocking at the door didn't want to stop. Mrs. Ttt threw the door open. "Well?"

"You speak *English*!" The man standing there was astounded.

"I speak what I speak," she said.

"It's wonderful *English*!" The man was in uniform. There were three men with him, in a great hurry, all smiling, all dirty.

"What do you want?" demanded Mrs. Ttt.

"You are a *Martian*!" The man smiled. "The word is not familiar to you, certainly. It's an Earth expression." He nodded at his men. "We are from Earth. I'm Captain Williams. We've landed on Mars within the hour. Here we are, the *Second* Expedition! There was a First Expedition, but we don't know what happened to it. But here we are, anyway. And you are the first Martian we've met!"

"Martian?" Her eyebrows went up.

"What I mean to say is, you live on the fourth planet from the sun. Correct?"

"Elementary," she snapped, eying them.

"And we"—he pressed his chubby pink hand to his chest—"we are from Earth. Right, men?"

"Right, sir!" A chorus.

"This is the planet Tyrr," she said, "if you want to use the proper name."

"Tyrr, Tyrr." The captain laughed exhaustedly. "What a *fine* name! But, my good woman, how is it you speak such perfect English?"

"I'm not speaking, I'm thinking," she said. "Telepathy! Good day!" And she slammed the door.

A moment later there was that dreadful man knocking again.

She whipped the door open. "What now?" she wondered.

The man was still there, trying to smile, looking bewildered. He put out his hands. "I don't think you *understand*——"

"What?" she snapped.

The man gazed at her in surprise. "We're from *Earth*!"

"I haven't time," she said. "I've a lot of cooking today and there's cleaning and sewing and all. You evidently wish to see Mr. Ttt; he's upstairs in his study."

"Yes," said the Earth Man confusedly, blinking. "By all means, let us see Mr. Ttt."

"He's busy." She slammed the door again.

This time the knock on the door was most impertinently loud.

"See here!" cried the man when the door was thrust open again. He jumped in as if to surprise her. "This is no way to treat visitors!"

"All over my clean floor!" she cried. "Mud! Get out! If you come in my house, wash your boots first."

The man looked in dismay at his muddy boots. "This," he said, "is no time for trivialities. I think," he said, "we should be celebrating." He looked at her for a long time, as if looking might make her understand.

"If you've made my crystal buns fall in the oven," she exclaimed, "I'll hit you with a piece of wood!" She peered into a little hot oven. She came back, red, steamy-faced. Her eyes were sharp yellow, her skin was soft brown, she was thin and quick as an insect. Her voice was metallic and sharp. "Wait here. I'll see if I can let you have a moment with Mr. Ttt. What was your business?"

The man swore luridly, as if she'd hit his hand with a hammer. "Tell him we're from Earth and it's never been done before!"

"What hasn't?" She put her brown hand up. "Never mind. I'll be back."

The sound of her feet fluttered through the stone house.

Outside, the immense blue Martian sky was hot and still as a warm deep sea water. The Martian desert lay broiling like a prehistoric mud pot, waves of heat rising and shimmering. There was a small rocket ship reclining upon a hilltop nearby. Large footprints came from the rocket to the door of this stone house.

Now there was a sound of quarreling voices upstairs. The men within the door stared at one another, shifting on their boots, twiddling their fingers, and holding onto their hip belts. A man's voice shouted upstairs. The woman's voice replied. After fifteen minutes the Earth men began walking in and out the kitchen door, with nothing to do.

"Cigarette?" said one of the men.

Somebody got out a pack and they lit up. They puffed slow streams of pale white smoke. They adjusted their uniforms, fixed their collars. The voices upstairs continued to mutter and chant. The leader of the men looked at his watch.

"Twenty-five minutes," he said. "I wonder what they're up to up there." He went to a window and looked out.

"Hot day," said one of the men.

"Yeah," said someone else in the slow warm time of early afternoon. The voices had faded to a murmur and were now silent. There was not a sound in the house. All the men could hear was their own breathing.

An hour of silence passed. "I hope we didn't cause any trouble," said the captain. He went and peered into the living room.

Mrs. Ttt was there, watering some flowers that grew in the center of the room.

"I knew I had forgotten something," she said when she saw the captain. She walked out to the kitchen. "I'm sorry." She handed him a slip of paper. "Mr. Ttt is much too busy." She turned to her cooking. "Anyway, it's not Mr. Ttt you want to see; it's Mr. Aaa. Take that paper over to the next farm, by the blue canal, and Mr. Aaa'll advise you about whatever it is you want to know."

"We don't want to know anything," objected the captain, pouting out his thick lips. "We already *know* it."

"You have the paper, what more do you want?" she asked him straight off. And she would say no more.

"Well," said the captain, reluctant to go. He stood as if waiting for something. He looked like a child staring at an empty Christmas tree. "Well," he said again. "Come on, men."

The four men stepped out into the hot silent day.

Half an hour later, Mr. Aaa, seated in his library sipping a bit of electric fire from a metal cup, heard the voices outside in the stone causeway. He leaned over the window sill and gazed at the four uniformed men who squinted up at him.

"Are you Mr. Aaa?" they called.

"I am."

"Mr. Ttt sent us to see you!" shouted the captain.

"Why did he do that?" asked Mr. Aaa.

"He was busy!"

"Well, that's a shame," said Mr. Aaa sarcastically. "Does he think I have nothing else to do but entertain people he's too busy to bother with?"

"That's not the important thing, sir," shouted the captain.

"Well, it is to me. I have much reading to do. Mr. Ttt is inconsiderate. This is not the first time he has been this thoughtless of me. Stop waving your hands, sir, until I finish. And pay attention. People usually listen to me when I talk. And you'll listen courteously or I won't talk at all."

Uneasily the four men in the court shifted and opened their mouths, and once the captain, the veins on his face bulging, showed a few little tears in his eyes.

"Now," lectured Mr. Aaa, "do you think it fair of Mr. Ttt to be so ill-mannered?"

The four men gazed up through the heat. The captain said, "We're from Earth!"

"I think it very ungentlemanly of him," brooded Mr. Aaa.

"A *rocket* ship. We came in it. Over there!"

"Not the first time Ttt's been unreasonable, you know."

"All the way from Earth."

"Why, for half a mind, I'd call him up and tell him off."

"Just the four of us; myself and these three men, my crew."

"I'll call him up, yes, that's what I'll do!"

"Earth. Rocket. Men. Trip. Space."

"Call him and give him a good lashing!" cried Mr. Aaa. He vanished like a puppet from a stage. For a minute there were angry voices back and forth over some weird mechanism or other. Below, the captain and his crew glanced longingly back at their pretty rocket ship lying on the hillside, so sweet and lovely and fine.

Mr. Aaa jerked up in the window, wildly triumphant. "Challenged him to a duel, by the gods! A duel!"

"Mr. Aaa——" the captain started all over again, quietly.

"I'll shoot him dead, do you hear!"

"Mr. Aaa, I'd like to *tell* you. We came sixty million miles."

Mr. Aaa regarded the captain for the first time. "Where'd you say you were from?"

The captain flashed a white smile. Aside to his men he

whispered, "*Now* we're getting someplace!" To Mr. Aaa he called, "We traveled sixty million miles. From Earth!"

Mr. Aaa yawned. "That's only *fifty* million miles this time of year." He picked up a frightful-looking weapon. "Well, I have to go now. Just take that silly note, though I don't know what good it'll do you, and go over that hill into the little town of Iopr and tell Mr. Iii all about it. *He's* the man you want to see. Not Mr. Ttt, he's an idiot; I'm going to kill him. Not me, because you're not in my line of work."

"Line of work, line of work!" bleated the captain. "Do you have to be in a certain line of work to welcome Earth men!"

"Don't be silly, everyone knows *that*!" Mr. Aaa rushed downstairs. "Good-by!" And down the causeway he raced, like a pair of wild calipers.

The four travelers stood shocked. Finally the captain said, "We'll find someone yet who'll listen to us."

"Maybe we could go out and come in again," said one of the men in a dreary voice. "Maybe we should take off and land again. Give them time to organize a party."

"That might be a good idea," murmured the tired captain.

The little town was full of people drifting in and out of doors, saying hello to one another, wearing golden masks and blue masks and crimson masks for pleasant variety, masks with silver lips and bronze eyebrows, masks that smiled or masks that frowned, according to the owners' dispositions.

The four men, wet from their long walk, paused and asked a little girl where Mr. Iii's house was.

"There." The child nodded her head.

The captain got eagerly, carefully down on one knee, looking into her sweet young face. "Little girl, I want to talk to you."

He seated her on his knee and folded her small brown hands neatly in his own big ones, as if ready for a bedtime story which he was shaping in his mind slowly and with a great patient happiness in details.

"Well, here's how it is, little girl. Six months ago another rocket came to Mars. There was a man named York in it, and his assistant. Whatever happened to them, we don't know. Maybe they crashed. They came in a rocket. So did we. You should see it! A *big* rocket! So we're the *Second* Expedition, following up the First. And we came all the way from Earth. . . ."

The little girl disengaged one hand without thinking about it, and clapped an expressionless golden mask over her face. Then she pulled forth a golden spider toy and dropped it to the ground while the captain talked on. The toy spider climbed back up to her knee obediently, while she speculated upon it coolly through the slits of her emotionless mask and the captain shook her gently and urged his story upon her.

"We're Earth Men," he said. "Do you believe me?"

"Yes." The little girl peeped at the way she was wiggling her toes in the dust.

"Fine." The captain pinched her arm, a little bit with joviality, a little bit with meanness to get her to look at him. "We built our own rocket ship. Do you believe *that*?"

The little girl dug in her nose with a finger. "Yes."

"And—take your finger out of your nose, little girl—*I* am the captain, and——"

"Never before in history has anybody come across space in a big rocket ship," recited the little creature, eyes shut.

"Wonderful! How did you know?"

"Oh, telepathy." She wiped a casual finger on her knee.

"Well, aren't you just *ever* so excited?" cried the captain. "Aren't you glad?"

"You just better go see Mr. Iii right away." She dropped her toy to the ground. "Mr. Iii will like talking to you." She ran off, with the toy spider scuttling obediently after her.

The captain squatted there looking after her with his hand out. His eyes were watery in his head. He looked at his empty hands. His mouth hung open. The other three men stood with their shadows under them. They spat on the stone street. . . .

Mr. Iii answered his door. He was on his way to a lecture, but he had a minute, if they would hurry inside and tell him what they desired. . . .

"A little attention," said the captain, red-eyed and tired. "We're from Earth, we have a rocket, there are four of us, crew and captain, we're exhausted, we're hungry, we'd like a place to sleep. We'd like someone to give us the key to the city or something like that, and we'd like somebody to shake our hands and say 'Hooray' and say 'Congratulations, old man!' That about sums it up."

Mr. Iii was a tall, vaporous, thin man with thick blind blue crystals over his yellowish eyes. He bent over his desk and brooded upon some papers, glancing now and again with extreme penetration at his guests.

"Well, I haven't the forms with me here, I don't *think*." He rummaged through the desk drawers. "Now, where *did* I put the forms?" He mused. "Somewhere. Somewhere. Oh, *here* we are! Now!" He handed the papers over crisply. "You'll have to sign these papers, of course."

"Do we have to go through all this rigmarole?"

Mr. Iii gave him a thick glassy look. "You say you're from Earth, don't you? Well, then there's nothing for it but you sign."

The captain wrote his name. "Do you want my crew to sign also?"

Mr. Iii looked at the captain, looked at the three others, and burst into a shout of derision. "*Them* sign! Ho! How marvelous! Them, oh, *them* sign!" Tears sprang from his eyes. He slapped his knee and bent to let his laughter jerk out of his gaping mouth. He held himself up with the desk. "*Them* sign!"

The four men scowled. "What's funny?"

"Them sign!" sighed Mr. Iii, weak with hilarity. "So very funny. I'll have to tell Mr. Xxx about this!" He examined the filled-out form, still laughing. "Everything *seems* to be in order." He nodded. "Even the agreement for euthanasia if final decision on such a step is necessary." He chuckled.

"Agreement for *what*?"

"Don't talk. I have something for you. Here. Take this key."

The captain flushed. "It's a great honor."

"Not the key to the city, you fool!" snapped Mr. Iii. "Just a key to the House. Go down that corridor, unlock the big door, and go inside and shut the door tight. You can spend the night there. In the morning I'll send Mr. Xxx to see you."

Dubiously the captain took the key in hand. He stood looking at the floor. His men did not move. They seemed to be emptied of all their blood and their rocket fever. They were drained dry.

"What is it? What's wrong?" inquired Mr. Iii. "What are you waiting for? What do you want?" He came and peered up into the captain's face, stooping. "Out with it, you!"

"I don't suppose you could even——" suggested the captain. "I mean, that is, try to, or think about . . ." He hesitated. "We've worked hard, we've come a long way, and maybe you could just shake our hands and say 'Well done!' do you—think?" His voice faded.

Mr. Iii stuck out his hand stiffly. "Congratulations!" He smiled a cold smile. "Congratulations." He turned away. "I must go now. Use that key."

Without noticing them again, as if they had melted down through the floor, Mr. Iii moved about the room packing a little manuscript case with papers. He was in the room another five minutes but never again addressed the solemn quartet that stood with heads down, their heavy legs sagging, the light dwindling from their eyes. When Mr. Iii went out the door he was busy looking at his fingernails. . . .

They straggled along the corridor in the dull, silent afternoon light. They came to a large burnished silver door, and the silver key opened it. They entered, shut the door, and turned.

They were in a vast sunlit hall. Men and women sat at tables and stood in conversing groups. At the sound of the door they regarded the four uniformed men.

One Martian stepped forward, bowing. "I am Mr. Uuu," he said.

"And I am Captain Jonathan Williams, of New York City, on Earth," said the captain without emphasis.

Immediately the hall exploded!

The rafters trembled with shouts and cries. The people, rushing forward, waved and shrieked happily, knocking down tables, swarming, rollicking, seizing the four Earth Men, lifting them swiftly to their shoulders. They charged about the hall six times, six times making a full and wonderful circuit of the room, jumping, bounding, singing.

The Earth Men were so stunned that they rode the toppling shoulders for a full minute before they began to laugh and shout at each other:

"Hey! This is more *like* it!"

"This is the life! Boy! Yay! Yow! Whoopee!"

They winked tremendously at each other. They flung up their hands to clap the air. "Hey!"

"Hooray!" said the crowd.

They set the Earth Men on a table. The shouting died.

The captain almost broke into tears. "Thank you. It's good, it's good."

"Tell us about yourselves," suggested Mr. Uuu.

The captain cleared his throat.

The audience ohed and ahed as the captain talked. He introduced his crew; each made a small speech and was embarrassed by the thunderous applause.

Mr. Uuu clapped the captain's shoulder. "It's good to see another man from Earth. I am from Earth also."

"How was that again?"

"There are many of us here from Earth."

"You? From Earth?" The captain stared. "But is that possible? Did you come by rocket? Has space travel been going on for centuries?" His voice was disappointed. "What—what country are you from?"

"Tuiereol. I came by the spirit of my body, years ago."

"Tuiereol." The captain mouthed the word. "I don't know that country. What's this about spirit of body?"

"And Miss Rrr over here, she's from Earth, too, *aren't* you, Miss Rrr?"

Miss Rrr nodded and laughed strangely.

"And so is Mr. Www and Mr. Qqq and Mr. Vvv!"

"I'm from Jupiter," declared one man, preening himself.

"I'm from Saturn," said another, eyes glinting slyly.

"Jupiter, Saturn," murmured the captain, blinking.

It was very quiet now; the people stood around and sat at the tables which were strangely empty for banquet tables. Their yellow eyes were glowing, and there were dark shadows under their cheekbones. The captain noticed for the first time that there were no windows; the light seemed to permeate the walls. There was only one door. The captain winced. "This is confusing. Where on Earth is this Tuiereol? Is it near America?"

"What is America?"

"You never heard of America! You say you're from Earth and yet you don't know!"

Mr. Uuu drew himself up angrily. "Earth is a place of seas and nothing but seas. There is no land. I am from Earth, and know."

"Wait a minute." The captain sat back. "You look like a regular Martian. Yellow eyes. Brown skin."

"Earth is a place of all *jungle*," said Miss Rrr proudly. "I am from Orri, on Earth, a civilization built of silver!"

Now the captain turned his head from and then to Mr. Uuu and then to Mr. Www and Mr. Zzz and Mr. Nnn and Mr. Hhh and Mr. Bbb. He saw their yellow eyes waxing and waning in the light, focusing and unfocusing. He began to shiver. Finally he turned to his men and regarded them somberly.

"Do you realize what this is?"

"What, sir?"

"This is no celebration," replied the captain tiredly. "This is no banquet. These aren't government representatives. This is no surprise party. Look at their eyes. Listen to them!"

Nobody breathed. There was only a soft white move of eyes in the close room.

"Now I understand"—the captain's voice was far away—"why everyone gave us notes and passed us on, one from the other, until we met Mr. Iii, who sent us down a corridor with a key to open a door and shut a door. And here we are. . . ."

"Where are we, sir?"

The captain exhaled. "In an insane asylum."

It was night. The large hall lay quiet and dimly illumined by hidden light sources in the transparent walls. The four Earth Men sat around a wooden table, their bleak heads bent over their whispers. On the floors, men and women lay huddled. There were little stirs in the dark corners, solitary men or women gesturing their hands. Every half-hour one of the captain's men would try the silver door and return to the table. "Nothing doing, sir. We're locked in proper."

They think we're really insane, sir?"

"Quite. That's why there was no hullabaloo to welcome us. They merely tolerated what, to them, must be a constantly recurring psychotic condition." He gestured at the dark sleeping shapes all about them. "Paranoids, every single one! What a welcome they gave us! For a moment there"—a little fire rose and died in his eyes—"I thought we were getting our true reception. All the yelling and singing and speeches. Pretty nice, wasn't it—while it lasted?"

"How long will they keep us here, sir?"

"Until we prove we're not psychotics."

"That should be easy."

"I *hope* so."

"You don't sound very certain, sir."

"I'm not. Look in that corner."

A man squatted alone in darkness. Out of his mouth issued a blue flame which turned into the round shape of a small naked woman. It flourished on the air softly in vapors of cobalt light, whispering and sighing.

The captain nodded at another corner. A woman stood there, changing. First she was embedded in a crystal pillar, then she melted into a golden statue, finally a staff of polished cedar, and back to a woman.

All through the midnight hall people were juggling thin violet flames, shifting, changing, for nighttime was the time of change and affliction.

"Magicians, sorcerers," whispered one of the Earth Men.

"No, hallucination. They pass their insanity over into us so that we see their hallucinations too. Telepathy. Autosuggestion and telepathy."

"Is that what worries you, sir?"

"Yes. If hallucinations can appear this 'real' to us, to anyone, if hallucinations are catching and almost believable, it's no wonder they mistook us for psychotics. If that man can produce little blue fire women and that woman there melt into a pillar, how natural if normal Martians think we produce our rocket ship with *our* minds."

"Oh," said his men in the shadows.

Around them, in the vast hall, flames leaped blue, flared, evaporated. Little demons of red sand ran between the teeth of sleeping men. Women became oily snakes. There was a smell of reptiles and animals.

In the morning everyone stood around looking fresh, happy, and normal. There were no flames or demons in the room. The captain and his men waited by the silver door, hoping it would open.

Mr. Xxx arrived after about four hours. They had a suspicion that he had waited outside the door, peering in at them for at least three hours before he stepped in, beckoned, and led them to his small office.

He was a jovial, smiling man, if one could believe the mask he wore, for upon it was painted not one smile, but three. Behind it, his voice was the voice of a not so smiling psychologist. "What seems to be the trouble?"

"You think we're insane, and we're not," said the captain.

"Contrarily, I do not think *all* of you are insane." The psychologist pointed a little wand at the captain. "No. Just *you*, sir. The others are secondary hallucinations."

The captain slapped his knee. "So *that's* it! That's why Mr. Iii laughed when I suggested my men sign the papers too!"

"Yes, Mr. Iii told me." The psychologist laughed out of the carved, smiling mouth. "A good joke. Where was I? Secondary hallucinations, yes. Women come to me with snakes crawling from their ears. When I cure them, the snakes vanish."

"We'll be glad to be cured. Go right ahead."

Mr. Xxx seemed surprised. "Unusual. Not many people want to be cured. The cure is drastic, you know."

"Cure ahead! I'm confident you'll find we're all sane."

"Let me check your papers to be sure they're in order for a 'cure.'" He checked a file. "Yes. You know, such cases as yours need special 'curing.' The people in that hall are simpler forms. But once you've gone this far, I must point out, with primary, secondary, auditory, olfactory, and labial hallucinations, as well as tactile and optical fantasies, it is pretty bad business. We have to resort to euthanasia."

The captain leaped up with a roar. "Look here, we've stood quite enough! Test us, tap our knees, check our hearts, exercise us, ask questions!"

"You are free to speak."

The captain raved for an hour. The psychologist listened.

"Incredible," he mused. "Most detailed dream fantasy I've ever heard."

"God damn it, we'll show you the rocket ship!" screamed the captain.

"I'd like to see it. Can you manifest it in this room?"

"Oh, certainly. It's in that file of yours, under *R*."

Mr. Xxx peered seriously into his file. He went "Tsk" and

shut the file solemnly. "Why did you tell me to look? The rocket isn't there."

"Of course not, you idiot! I was joking. Does an insane man joke?"

"You find some odd senses of humor. Now, take me out to your rocket. I wish to see it."

It was noon. The day was very hot when they reached the rocket.

"So." The psychologist walked up to the ship and tapped it. It gonged softly. "May I go inside?" he asked slyly.

"You may."

Mr. Xxx stepped in and was gone for a long time.

"Of all the silly, exasperating things." The captain chewed a cigar as he waited. "For two cents I'd go back home and tell people not to bother with Mars. What a suspicious bunch of louts."

"I gather that a good number of their population are insane, sir. That seems to be their main reason for doubting."

"Nevertheless, this is all so damned irritating."

The psychologist emerged from the ship after half an hour of prowling, tapping, listening, smelling, tasting.

"*Now* do you believe!" shouted the captain, as if he were deaf.

The psychologist shut his eyes and scratched his nose. "This is the most incredible example of sensual hallucination and hypnotic suggestion I've ever encountered. I went through your 'rocket,' as you call it." He tapped the hull. "I hear it. Auditory fantasy." He drew a breath. "I smell it. Olfactory hallucination, induced by sensual telepathy." He kissed the ship. "I taste it. Labial fantasy!"

He shook the captain's hand. "May I congratulate you? You are a psychotic genius! You have done a most complete job! The task of projecting your psychotic image life into the mind of another via telepathy and keeping the hallucinations from becoming sensually weaker is almost impossible. Those people in the House usually concentrate on visuals or, at the most, visuals and auditory fantasies combined. You have balanced the whole conglomeration! Your insanity is beautifully complete!"

"My insanity." The captain was pale.

"Yes, yes, what a lovely insanity. Metal, rubber, gravitizers, foods, clothing, fuel, weapons, ladders, nuts, bolts, spoons. Ten thousand separate items I checked on your vessel. Never have I seen such a complexity. There were even *shadows* under the bunks and under *everything*! Such concentration of will! And everything, no matter how or when tested, had a smell, a solidity, a taste, a sound! Let me embrace you!"

He stood back at last. "I'll write this into my greatest monograph! I'll speak of it at the Martian Academy next month! *Look* at you! Why, you've even changed your eye color from yellow to blue, your skin to pink from brown. And those clothes, and your hands having five fingers instead of six! Biological metamorphosis through psychological imbalance! And your three friends——"

He took out a little gun. "Incurable, of course. You poor, wonderful man. You will be happier dead. Have you any last words?"

"Stop, for God's sake! Don't shoot!"

"You sad creature. I shall put you out of this misery which has driven you to imagine this rocket and these three men. It will be most engrossing to watch your friends and your rocket vanish once I have killed you. I will write a neat paper on the dissolvement of neurotic images from what I perceive here today."

"I'm from Earth! My name is Jonathan Williams, and these——"

"Yes, I know," soothed Mr. Xxx, and fired his gun.

The captain fell with a bullet in his heart. The other three men screamed.

Mr. Xxx stared at them. "You continue to exist? This is superb! Hallucinations with time and spatial persistence!" He pointed the gun at them. "Well, I'll scare you into dissolving."

"No!" cried the three men.

"An auditory appeal, even with the patient dead," observed Mr. Xxx as he shot the three men down.

They lay on the sand, intact, not moving.

He kicked them. Then he rapped on the ship.

"*It* persists! *They* persist!" He fired his gun again and again at the bodies. Then he stood back. The smiling mask dropped from his face.

Slowly the little psychologist's face changed. His jaw sagged. The gun dropped from his fingers. His eyes were dull and vacant. He put his hands up and turned in a blind circle. He fumbled at the bodies, saliva filling his mouth.

"Hallucinations," he mumbled frantically. "Taste. Sight. Smell. Sound. Feeling." He waved his hands. His eyes bulged. His mouth began to give off a faint froth.

"Go away!" he shouted at the bodies. "Go away!" he screamed at the ship. He examined his trembling hands. "Contaminated," he whispered wildly. "Carried over into me. Telepathy. Hypnosis. Now *I'm* insane. Now *I'm* contaminated. Hallucinations in all their sensual forms." He stopped and searched around with his numb hands for the gun. "Only one cure. Only one way to make them go away, vanish."

A shot rang out. Mr. Xxx fell.

The four bodies lay in the sun. Mr. Xxx lay where he fell.

The rocket reclined on the little sunny hill and didn't vanish.

When the town people found the rocket at sunset they wondered what it was. Nobody knew, so it was sold to a junkman and hauled off to be broken up for scrap metal.

That night it rained all night. The next day was fair and warm.

March 2000: THE TAXPAYER

HE WANTED to go to Mars on the rocket. He went down to the rocket field in the early morning and yelled in through the wire fence at the men in uniform that he wanted to go to Mars. He told them he was a taxpayer, his name was Pritchard, and he had a right to go to Mars. Wasn't he born right here in Ohio? Wasn't he a good citizen? Then why couldn't *he* go to Mars? He shook his fists at them and told them that he wanted to get away from Earth; anybody with any sense wanted to get away from Earth. There was going to be a big atomic war on Earth in about two years, and he didn't want to be here when it happened. He and thousands of others like him, if they had any sense, would go to Mars. See if they wouldn't! To get away from wars and censorship and statism and conscription and government control of this and that, of art and science! You could have Earth! He was offering his good right hand, his heart, his head, for the opportunity to go to Mars! What did you have to do, what did you have to sign, whom did you have to know, to get on the rocket?

They laughed out through the wire screen at him. He didn't want to go to Mars, they said. Didn't he know that the First and Second Expeditions had failed, had vanished; the men were probably dead?

But they couldn't prove it, they didn't know for *sure*, he said, clinging to the wire fence. Maybe it was a land of milk and honey up there, and Captain York and Captain Williams had just never bothered to come back. Now were they going to open the gate and let him in to board the Third Expeditionary Rocket, or was he going to have to kick it down?

They told him to shut up.

He saw the men walking out to the rocket.

Wait for me! he cried. Don't leave me here on this terrible world, I've got to get away; there's going to be an atom war! Don't leave me on Earth!

They dragged him, struggling, away. They slammed the police-wagon door and drove him off into the early morning, his face pressed to the rear window, and just before they sirened over a hill, he saw the red fire and heard the big sound and felt the huge tremor as the silver rocket shot up and left him behind on an ordinary Monday morning on the ordinary planet Earth.

April 2000: THE THIRD EXPEDITION

THE SHIP came down from space. It came from the stars and the black velocities, and the shining movements, and the silent gulfs of space. It was a new ship; it had fire in its body and men in its metal cells, and it moved with a clean silence, fiery and warm. In it were seventeen men, including a captain. The crowd at the Ohio field had shouted and waved their hands up into the sunlight, and the rocket had bloomed out great flowers of heat and color and run away into space on the *third* voyage to Mars!

Now it was decelerating with metal efficiency in the upper Martian atmospheres. It was still a thing of beauty and strength. It had moved in the midnight waters of space like a pale sea leviathan; it had passed the ancient moon and thrown itself onward into one nothingness following another. The men within it had been battered, thrown about, sickened, made well again, each in his turn. One man had died, but now the remaining sixteen, with their eyes clear in their heads and their faces pressed to the thick glass ports, watched Mars swing up under them.

"Mars!" cried Navigator Lustig.

"Good old Mars!" said Samuel Hinkston, archaeologist.

"Well," said Captain John Black.

The rocket landed on a lawn of green grass. Outside, upon this lawn, stood an iron deer. Further up on the green stood a tall brown Victorian house, quiet in the sunlight, all covered with scrolls and rococo, its windows made of blue and pink and yellow and green colored glass. Upon the porch were hairy geraniums and an old swing which was hooked into the porch ceiling and which now swung back and forth, back and forth, in a little breeze. At the summit of the house was a cupola with diamond leaded-glass windows and a dunce-cap roof! Through the front window you could see a piece of music titled "Beautiful Ohio" sitting on the music rest.

Around the rocket in four directions spread the little town, green and motionless in the Martian spring. There were white houses and red brick ones, and tall elm trees blowing in the wind, and tall maples and horse chestnuts. And church steeples with golden bells silent in them.

The rocket men looked out and saw this. Then they looked at one another and then they looked out again. They held to each other's elbows, suddenly unable to breathe, it seemed. Their faces grew pale.

"I'll be damned," whispered Lustig, rubbing his face with his numb fingers. "I'll be damned."

"It just can't be," said Samuel Hinkston.

"Lord," said Captain John Black.

There was a call from the chemist. "Sir, the atmosphere is thin for breathing. But there's enough oxygen. It's safe."

"Then we'll go out," said Lustig.

"Hold on," said Captain John Black. "How do we know what this is?"

"It's a small town with thin but breathable air in it, sir."

"And it's a small town the like of Earth towns," said Hinkston, the archaeologist. "Incredible. It can't be, but it *is*."

Captain John Black looked at him idly. "Do you think that the civilizations of two planets can progress at the same rate and evolve in the same way, Hinkston?"

"I wouldn't have thought so, sir."

Captain Black stood by the port. "Look out there. The geraniums. A specialized plant. That specific variety has only been known on Earth for fifty years. Think of the thousands of years it takes to evolve plants. Then tell me if it is logical that the Martians should have: one, leaded-glass windows; two, cupolas; three, porch swings; four, an instrument that looks like a piano and probably *is* a piano; and five, if you look closely through this telescopic lens here, is it logical that a Martian composer would have published a piece of music titled, strangely enough, 'Beautiful Ohio'? All of which means that we have an Ohio River on Mars!"

"Captain Williams, of course!" cried Hinkston.

"What?"

"Captain Williams and his crew of three men! Or Nathaniel York and his partner. That would explain it!"

"That would explain absolutely nothing. As far as we've been able to figure, the York expedition exploded the day it reached Mars, killing York and his partner. As for Williams and his three men, their ship exploded the second day after their arrival. At least the pulsations from their radios ceased at that time, so we figure that if the men were alive after that they'd have contacted us. And anyway, the York expedition was only a year ago, while Captain Williams and his men landed here some time during last August. Theorizing that they are still alive, could they, even with the help of a brilliant Martian race, have built such a town as this and *aged* it in so short a time? Look at that town out there; why, it's been standing here for the last seventy years. Look at the wood on the porch newel; look at the trees, a century old, all of them! No, this isn't York's work or Williams'. It's something else. I don't like it. And I'm not leaving the ship until I know what it is."

"For that matter," said Lustig, nodding, "Williams and his men, as well as York, landed on the *opposite* side of Mars. We were very careful to land on *this* side."

"An excellent point. Just in case a hostile local tribe of Martians killed off York and Williams, we have instructions to land in a further region, to forestall a recurrence of such a disaster. So here we are, as far as we know, in a land that Williams and York never saw."

"Damn it," said Hinkston, "I want to get out into this town, sir, with your permission. It may be there *are* similar thought patterns, civilization graphs on every planet in our sun system. We may be on the threshold of the greatest psychological and metaphysical discovery of our age!"

"I'm willing to wait a moment," said Captain John Black.

"It may be, sir, that we're looking upon a phenomenon that, for the first time, would absolutely prove the existence of God, sir."

"There are many people who are of good faith without such proof, Mr. Hinkston."

"I'm one myself, sir. But certainly a town like this could not occur without divine intervention. The *detail.* It fills me with such feelings that I don't know whether to laugh or cry."

"Do neither, then, until we know what we're up against."

"Up against?" Lustig broke in. "Against nothing, Captain. It's a good, quiet green town, a lot like the old-fashioned one I was born in. I like the looks of it."

"When were you born, Lustig?"

"Nineteen-fifty, sir."

"And you, Hinkston?"

"Nineteen fifty-five, sir. Grinnell, Iowa. And this looks like home to me."

"Hinkston, Lustig, I could be either of your fathers. I'm just eighty years old. Born in 1920 in Illinois, and through the grace of God and a science that, in the last fifty years, knows how to make *some* old men young again, here I am on Mars, not any more tired than the rest of you, but infinitely more suspicious. This town out here looks very peaceful and cool, and so much like Green Bluff, Illinois, that it frightens me. It's too *much* like Green Bluff." He turned to the radioman. "Radio Earth. Tell them we've landed. That's all. Tell them we'll radio a full report tomorrow."

"Yes, sir."

Captain Black looked out the rocket port with his face that should have been the face of a man eighty but seemed like the face of a man in his fortieth year. "Tell you what we'll do, Lustig; you and I and Hinkston'll look the town over. The other men'll stay aboard. If anything happens they can get the hell out. A loss of three men's better than a whole ship. If something bad happens, our crew can warn the next rocket. That's Captain Wilder's rocket, I think, due to be ready to take off next Christmas. If there's something hostile about Mars we certainly want the next rocket to be well armed."

"So are we. We've got a regular arsenal with us."

"Tell the men to stand by the guns then. Come on, Lustig, Hinkston."

The three men walked together down through the levels of the ship.

It was a beautiful spring day. A robin sat on a blossoming apple tree and sang continuously. Showers of petal snow sifted down when the wind touched the green branches, and the blossom scent drifted upon the air. Somewhere in the town someone was playing the piano and the music came and went, came and went, softly, drowsily. The song was "Beautiful Dreamer." Somewhere else a phonograph, scratchy and faded, was hissing out a record of "Roamin' in the Gloamin'," sung by Harry Lauder.

The three men stood outside the ship. They sucked and gasped at the thin, thin air and moved slowly so as not to tire themselves.

Now the phonograph record being played was:

"Oh, give me a June night
The moonlight and you . . ."

Lustig began to tremble. Samuel Hinkston did likewise.

The sky was serene and quiet, and somewhere a stream of water ran through the cool caverns and tree shadings of a ravine. Somewhere a horse and wagon trotted and rolled by, bumping.

"Sir," said Samuel Hinkston, "it must be, it *has* to be, that rocket travel to Mars began in the years before the first World War!"

"No."

"How else can you explain these houses, the iron deer, the pianos, the music?" Hinkston took the captain's elbow persuasively and looked into the captain's face. "Say that there were people in the year 1905 who hated war and got together with some scientists in secret and built a rocket and came out here to Mars——"

"No, no, Hinkston."

"Why not? The world was a different world in 1905; they could have kept it a secret much more easily."

"But a complex thing like a rocket, no, you couldn't keep it secret."

"And they came up here to live, and naturally the houses they built were similar to Earth houses because they brought the culture with them."

"And they've lived here all these years?" said the captain.

"In peace and quiet, yes. Maybe they made a few trips, enough to bring enough people here for one small town, and then stopped for fear of being discovered. That's why this town seems so old-fashioned. I don't see a thing, myself, older than the year 1927, do you? Or maybe, sir, rocket travel is older than we think. Perhaps it started in some part of the world centuries ago and was kept secret by the small number of men who came to Mars with only occasional visits to Earth over the centuries."

"You make it sound almost reasonable."

"It has to be. We've the proof here before us; all we have to do is find some people and verify it."

Their boots were deadened of all sound in the thick green grass. It smelled from a fresh mowing. In spite of himself, Captain John Black felt a great peace come over him. It had been thirty years since he had been in a small town, and the buzzing of spring bees on the air lulled and quieted him, and the fresh look of things was a balm to the soul.

They set foot upon the porch. Hollow echoes sounded from under the boards as they walked to the screen door. Inside they could see a bead curtain hung across the hall entry, and a crystal chandelier and a Maxfield Parrish painting framed on one wall over a comfortable Morris chair. The house smelled old, and of the attic, and infinitely comfortable. You could hear the tinkle of ice in a lemonade pitcher. In a distant kitchen, because of the heat of the day, someone was preparing a cold lunch. Someone was humming under her breath, high and sweet.

Captain John Black rang the bell.

Footsteps, dainty and thin, came along the hall, and a kind-faced lady of some forty years, dressed in the sort of dress you might expect in the year 1909, peered out at them.

"Can I help you?" she asked.

"Beg your pardon," said Captain Black uncertainly. "But we're looking for—that is, could you help us——" He stopped. She looked out at him with dark, wondering eyes.

"If you're selling something——" she began.

"No, wait!" he cried. "What town is this?"

She looked him up and down. "What do you mean, what town is it? How could you be in a town and not know the name?"

The captain looked as if he wanted to go sit under a shady apple tree. "We're strangers here. We want to know how this town got here and how you got here."

"Are you census takers?"

"No."

"Everyone knows," she said, "this town was built in 1868. Is this a game?"

"No, not a game!" cried the captain. "We're from Earth."

"Out of the *ground*, do you mean?" she wondered.

"No, we came from the third planet, Earth, in a ship. And we've landed here on the fourth planet, Mars—"

"This," explained the woman, as if she were addressing a child, "is Green Bluff, Illinois, on the continent of America, surrounded by the Atlantic and Pacific oceans, on a place called the world, or, sometimes, the Earth. Go away now. Good-by."

She trotted down the hall, running her fingers through the beaded curtains.

The three men looked at one another.

"Let's knock the screen door in," said Lustig.

"We can't do that. This is private property. Good God!"

They went to sit down on the porch step.

"Did it ever strike you, Hinkston, that perhaps we got ourselves somehow, in some way, off track, and by accident came back and landed on Earth?"

"How could we have done that?"

"I don't know, I don't know. Oh God, let me think."

Hinkston said, "But we checked every mile of the way. Our chronometers said so many miles. We went past the Moon and out into space, and here we are. I'm *positive* we're on Mars."

Lustig said, "But suppose, by accident, in space, in time, we got lost in the dimensions and landed on an Earth that *is* thirty or forty years ago."

"Oh, go away, Lustig!"

Lustig went to the door, rang the bell, and called into the cool dim rooms: "What year is this?"

"Nineteen twenty-six, of course," said the lady, sitting in a rocking chair, taking a sip of her lemonade.

"Did you hear that?" Lustig turned wildly to the others. "Nineteen twenty-six! We *have* gone back in time! This *is* Earth!"

Lustig sat down, and the three men let the wonder and terror of the thought afflict them. Their hands stirred fitfully on their knees. The captain said, "I didn't ask for a thing like this. It scares the hell out of me. How can a thing like this happen? I wish we'd brought Einstein with us."

"Will anyone in this town believe us?" said Hinkston. "Are we playing with something dangerous? Time, I mean. Shouldn't we just take off and go home?"

"No. Not until we try another house."

They walked three houses down to a little white cottage under an oak tree. "I like to be as logical as I can be," said the captain. "And I don't believe we've put our finger on it yet. Suppose, Hinkston, as you originally suggested, that rocket travel occurred years ago? And when the Earth people lived here a number of years they began to get homesick for Earth. First a mild neurosis about it, then a full-fledged psychosis. Then threatened insanity. What would you do as a psychiatrist if faced with such a problem?"

Hinkston thought. "Well, I think I'd rearrange the civilization on Mars so it resembled Earth more and more each day. If there was any way of reproducing every plant, every road, and every lake, and even an ocean, I'd do so. Then by some vast crowd hypnosis I'd convince everyone in a town this size that this really *was* Earth, not Mars at all."

"Good enough, Hinkston. I think we're on the right track now. That woman in that house back there just *thinks* she's living on Earth. It protects her sanity. She and all the others in this town are the patients of the greatest experiment in migration and hypnosis you will ever lay eyes on in your life."

"That's *it*, sir!" cried Lustig.

"Right!" said Hinkston.

"Well." The captain sighed. "Now we've got somewhere. I feel better. It's all a bit more logical. That talk about time and going back and forth and traveling through time turns my stomach upside down. But *this* way——" The captain smiled. "Well, well, it looks as if we'll be fairly popular here."

"Or will we?" said Lustig. "After all, like the Pilgrims, these people came here to escape Earth. Maybe they won't be too happy to see us. Maybe they'll try to drive us out or kill us."

"We have superior weapons. This next house now. Up we go."

But they had hardly crossed the lawn when Lustig stopped and looked off across the town, down the quiet, dreaming afternoon street. "Sir," he said.

"What is it, Lustig?"

"Oh, sir, *sir*, what I *see*——" said Lustig, and he began to cry. His fingers came up, twisting and shaking, and his face was all wonder and joy and incredulity. He sounded as if at any moment he might go quite insane with happiness. He looked down the street and began to run, stumbling awkwardly, falling, picking himself up, and running on. "Look, look!"

"Don't let him get away!" The captain broke into a run.

Now Lustig was running swiftly, shouting. He turned into a yard halfway down the shady street and leaped up upon the porch of a large green house with an iron rooster on the roof.

He was beating at the door, hollering and crying, when Hinkston and the captain ran up behind him. They were all gasping and wheezing, exhausted from their run in the thin air. "Grandma! Grandpa!" cried Lustig.

Two old people stood in the doorway.

"David!" their voices piped, and they rushed out to embrace and pat him on the back and move around him. "David, oh, David, it's been so many years! How you've grown, boy; how big you are, boy. Oh, David boy, how are you?"

"Grandma, Grandpa!" sobbed David Lustig. "You look fine, fine!" He held them, turned them, kissed them, hugged them, cried on them, held them out again, blinking at the little old people. The sun was in the sky, the wind blew, the grass was green, the screen door stood wide.

"Come in, boy, come in. There's iced tea for you, fresh, lots of it!"

"I've got friends here." Lustig turned and waved at the captain and Hinkston frantically, laughing. "Captain, come on up."

"Howdy," said the old people. "Come in. Any friends of David's are our friends too. Don't stand there!"

In the living room of the old house it was cool, and a grandfather clock ticked high and long and bronzed in one corner. There were soft pillows on large couches and walls filled with books and a rug cut in a thick rose pattern, and iced tea in the hand, sweating, and cool on the thirsty tongue.

"Here's to our health." Grandma tipped her glass to her porcelain teeth.

"How long you been here, Grandma?" said Lustig.

"Ever since we died," she said tartly.

"Ever since you what?" Captain John Black set down his glass.

"Oh yes." Lustig nodded. "They've been dead thirty years."

"And you sit there calmly!" shouted the captain.

"Tush." The old woman winked glitteringly. "Who are you to question what happens? Here we are. What's life, anyway? Who does what for why and where? All we know is here we are, alive again, and no questions asked. A second chance." She toddled over and held out her thin wrist. "Feel." The captain felt. "Solid, ain't it?" she asked. He nodded. "Well, then," she said triumphantly, "why go around questioning?"

"Well," said the captain, "it's simply that we never thought we'd find a thing like this on Mars."

"And now you've found it. I dare say there's lots on every planet that'll show you God's infinite ways."

"Is this Heaven?" asked Hinkston.

"Nonsense, no. It's a world and we get a second chance. Nobody told us why. But then nobody told us why we were on Earth, either. That other Earth, I mean. The one you came from. How do we know there wasn't *another* before *that* one?"

"A good question," said the captain.

Lustig kept smiling at his grandparents. "Gosh, it's good to see you. Gosh, it's good."

The captain stood up and slapped his hand on his leg in a casual fashion. "We've got to be going. Thank you for the drinks."

"You'll be back, of course," said the old people. "For supper tonight?"

"We'll try to make it, thanks. There's so much to be done. My men are waiting for me back at the rocket and——"

He stopped. He looked toward the door, startled.

Far away in the sunlight there was a sound of voices, a shouting and a great hello.

"What's that?" asked Hinkston.

"We'll soon find out." And Captain John Black was out the front door abruptly, running across the green lawn into the street of the Martian town.

He stood looking at the rocket. The ports were open and his crew was streaming out, waving their hands. A crowd of people had gathered, and in and through and among these people the members of the crew were hurrying, talking, laughing, shaking hands. People did little dances. People swarmed. The rocket lay empty and abandoned.

A brass band exploded in the sunlight, flinging off a gay tune from upraised tubas and trumpets. There was a bang of drums and a shrill of fifes. Little girls with golden hair jumped up and down. Little boys shouted, "Hooray!" Fat men passed around ten-cent cigars. The town mayor made a speech. Then each member of the crew, with a mother on one arm, a father or sister on the other, was spirited off down the street into little cottages or big mansions.

"Stop!" cried Captain Black.

The doors slammed shut.

The heat rose in the clear spring sky, and all was silent. The brass band banged off around a corner, leaving the rocket to shine and dazzle alone in the sunlight.

"Abandoned!" said the captain. "They abandoned the ship, they did! I'll have their skins, by God! They had orders!"

"Sir," said Lustig, "don't be too hard on them. Those were all old relatives and friends."

"That's no excuse!"

"Think how they felt, Captain, seeing familiar faces outside the ship!"

"They had their orders, damn it!"

"But how would you have felt, Captain?"

"I would have obeyed orders——" The captain's mouth remained open.

Striding along the sidewalk under the Martian sun, tall, smiling, eyes amazingly clear and blue, came a young man of some twenty-six years. "John!" the man called out, and broke into a trot.

"What?" Captain John Black swayed.

"John, you old son of a bitch!"

The man ran up and gripped his hand and slapped him on the back.

"It's you," said Captain Black.

"Of course, who'd you *think* it was?"

"Edward!" The captain appealed now to Lustig and Hinkston, holding the stranger's hand. "This is my brother Edward. Ed, meet my men, Lustig, Hinkston! My brother!"

They tugged at each other's hands and arms and then finally embraced. "Ed!" "John, you bum, you!" "You're looking fine, Ed, but, Ed, what *is* this? You haven't changed over the years. You died, I remember, when you were twenty-six and I was nineteen. Good God, so many years ago, and here you are and, Lord, what goes on?"

"Mom's waiting," said Edward Black, grinning.

"Mom?"

"And Dad too."

"Dad?" The captain almost fell as if he had been hit by a mighty weapon. He walked stiffly and without co-ordination. "Mom and Dad alive? Where?"

"At the old house on Oak Knoll Avenue."

"The old house." The captain stared in delighted amazement. "Did you hear that, Lustig, Hinkston?"

Hinkston was gone. He had seen his own house down the street and was running for it. Lustig was laughing. "You see, Captain, what happened to everyone on the rocket? They couldn't help themselves."

"Yes. Yes." The captain shut his eyes. "When I open my eyes you'll be gone." He blinked. "You're still there. God, Ed, but you look *fine*!"

"Come on, lunch's waiting. I told Mom."

Lustig said, "Sir, I'll be with my grandfolks if you need me."

"What? Oh, fine, Lustig. Later, then."

Edward seized his arm and marched him. "There's the house. Remember it?"

"Hell! Bet I can beat you to the front porch!"

They ran. The trees roared over Captain Black's head; the earth roared under his feet. He saw the golden figure of Edward Black pull ahead of him in the amazing dream of reality. He saw the house rush forward, the screen door swing wide. "Beat you!" cried Edward. "I'm an old man," panted the captain, "and you're still young. But then, you *always* beat me, I remember!"

In the doorway, Mom, pink, plump, and bright. Behind her, pepper-gray, Dad, his pipe in his hand.

"Mom, Dad!"

He ran up the steps like a child to meet them.

* * *

It was a fine long afternoon. They finished a late lunch and they sat in the parlor and he told them all about his rocket and they nodded and smiled upon him and Mother was just the same and Dad bit the end off a cigar and lighted it thoughtfully in his old fashion. There was a big turkey dinner at night and time flowing on. When the drumsticks were sucked clean and lay brittle upon the plates, the captain leaned back and exhaled his deep satisfaction. Night was in all the trees and coloring the sky, and the lamps were halos of pink light in the gentle house. From all the other houses down the street came sounds of music, pianos playing, doors slamming.

Mom put a record on the victrola, and she and Captain John Black had a dance. She was wearing the same perfume he remembered from the summer when she and Dad had been killed in the train accident. She was very real in his arms as they danced lightly to the music. "It's not every day," she said, "you get a second chance to live."

"I'll wake in the morning," said the captain. "And I'll be in my rocket, in space, and all this will be gone."

"No, don't think that," she cried softly. "Don't question. God's good to us. Let's be happy."

"Sorry, Mom."

The record ended in a circular hissing.

"You're tired, Son." Dad pointed with his pipe. "Your old bedroom's waiting for you, brass bed and all."

"But I should report my men in."

"Why?"

"Why? Well, I don't know. No reason, I guess. No, none at all. They're all eating or in bed. A good night's sleep won't hurt them."

"Good night, Son." Mom kissed his cheek. "It's good to have you home."

"It's good to *be* home."

He left the land of cigar smoke and perfume and books and gentle light and ascended the stairs, talking, talking with Edward. Edward pushed a door open, and there was the yellow brass bed and the old semaphore banners from college and a

very musty raccoon coat which he stroked with muted affection. "It's too much," said the captain. "I'm numb and I'm tired. Too much has happened today. I feel as if I'd been out in a pounding rain for forty-eight hours without an umbrella or a coat. I'm soaked to the skin with emotion."

Edward slapped wide the snowy linens and flounced the pillows. He slid the window up and let the night-blooming jasmine float in. There was moonlight and the sound of distant dancing and whispering.

"So this is Mars," said the captain, undressing.

"This is it." Edward undressed in idle, leisurely moves, drawing his shirt off over his head, revealing golden shoulders and the good muscular neck.

The lights were out; they were in bed, side by side, as in the days how many decades ago? The captain lolled and was nourished by the scent of jasmine pushing the lace curtains out upon the dark air of the room. Among the trees, upon a lawn, someone had cranked up a portable phonograph and now it was playing softly, "Always."

The thought of Marilyn came to his mind.

"Is Marilyn here?"

His brother, lying straight out in the moonlight from the window, waited and then said, "Yes. She's out of town. But she'll be here in the morning."

The captain shut his eyes. "I want to see Marilyn very much."

The room was square and quiet except for their breathing.

"Good night, Ed."

A pause. "Good night, John."

He lay peacefully, letting his thoughts float. For the first time the stress of the day was moved aside; he could think logically now. It had all been emotion. The bands playing, the familiar faces. But now . . .

How? he wondered. How was all this made? And why? For what purpose? Out of the goodness of some divine intervention? Was God, then, really that thoughtful of his children? How and why and what for?

He considered the various theories advanced in the first heat of the afternoon by Hinkston and Lustig. He let all kinds of new theories drop in lazy pebbles down through his

mind, turning, throwing out dull flashes of light. Mom. Dad. Edward. Mars. Earth. Mars. Martians.

Who had lived here a thousand years ago on Mars? Martians? Or had this always been the way it was today?

Martians. He repeated the word idly, inwardly.

He laughed out loud almost. He had the most ridiculous theory quite suddenly. It gave him a kind of chill. It was really nothing to consider, of course. Highly improbable. Silly. Forget it. Ridiculous.

But, he thought, just *suppose* . . . Just suppose, now, that there were Martians living on Mars and they saw our ship coming and saw us inside our ship and hated us. Suppose, now, just for the hell of it, that they wanted to destroy us, as invaders, as unwanted ones, and they wanted to do it in a very clever way, so that we would be taken off guard. Well, what would the best weapon be that a Martian could use against Earth Men with atomic weapons?

The answer was interesting. Telepathy, hypnosis, memory, and imagination.

Suppose all of these houses aren't real at all, this bed not real, but only figments of my own imagination, given substance by telepathy and hypnosis through the Martians, thought Captain John Black. Suppose these houses are really some *other* shape, a Martian shape, but, by playing on my desires and wants, these Martians have made this seem like my old home town, my old house, to lull me out of my suspicions. What better way to fool a man, using his own mother and father as bait?

And this town, so old, from the year 1926, long before *any* of my men were born. From a year when I was six years old and there *were* records of Harry Lauder, and Maxfield Parrish paintings *still* hanging, and bead curtains, and "Beautiful Ohio," and turn-of-the-century architecture. What if the Martians took the memories of a town *exclusively* from *my* mind? They say childhood memories are the clearest. And after they built the town from *my* mind, they populated it with the most-loved people from all the minds of the people on the rocket!

And suppose those two people in the next room, asleep, are not my mother and father at all. But two Martians, incredibly brilliant, with the ability to keep me under this dreaming hypnosis all of the time.

And that brass band today? What a startlingly wonderful plan it would be. First, fool Lustig, then Hinkston, then gather a crowd; and all the men in the rocket, seeing mothers, aunts, uncles, sweethearts, dead ten, twenty years ago, naturally, disregarding orders, rush out and abandon ship. What more natural? What more unsuspecting? What more simple? A man doesn't ask too many questions when his mother is suddenly brought back to life; he's much too happy. And here we all are tonight, in various houses, in various beds, with no weapons to protect us, and the rocket lies in the moonlight, empty. And wouldn't it be horrible and terrifying to discover that all of this was part of some great clever plan by the Martians to divide and conquer us, and kill us? Sometime during the night, perhaps, my brother here on this bed will change form, melt, shift, and become another thing, a terrible thing, a Martian. It would be very simple for him just to turn over in bed and put a knife into my heart. And in all those other houses down the street, a dozen other brothers or fathers suddenly melting away and taking knives and doing things to the unsuspecting, sleeping men of Earth. . . .

His hands were shaking under the covers. His body was cold. Suddenly it was not a theory. Suddenly he was very afraid.

He lifted himself in bed and listened. The night was very quiet. The music had stopped. The wind had died. His brother lay sleeping beside him.

Carefully he lifted the covers, rolled them back. He slipped from bed and was walking softly across the room when his brother's voice said, "Where are you going?"

"What?"

His brother's voice was quite cold. "I said, where do you think you're going?"

"For a drink of water."

"But you're not thirsty."

"Yes, yes, I am."

"No, you're not."

Captain John Black broke and ran across the room. He screamed. He screamed twice.

He never reached the door.

* * *

In the morning the brass band played a mournful dirge. From every house in the street came little solemn processions bearing long boxes, and along the sun-filled street, weeping, came the grandmas and mothers and sisters and brothers and uncles and fathers, walking to the churchyard, where there were new holes freshly dug and new tombstones installed. Sixteen holes in all, and sixteen tombstones.

The mayor made a little sad speech, his face sometimes looking like the mayor, sometimes looking like something else.

Mother and Father Black were there, with Brother Edward, and they cried, their faces melting now from a familiar face into something else.

Grandpa and Grandma Lustig were there, weeping, their faces shifting like wax, shimmering as all things shimmer on a hot day.

The coffins were lowered. Someone murmured about "the unexpected and sudden deaths of sixteen fine men during the night——"

Earth pounded down on the coffin lids.

The brass band, playing "Columbia, the Gem of the Ocean," marched and slammed back into town, and everyone took the day off.

June 2001: —AND THE MOON BE STILL AS BRIGHT

IT WAS so cold when they first came from the rocket into the night that Spender began to gather the dry Martian wood and build a small fire. He didn't say anything about a celebration; he merely gathered the wood, set fire to it, and watched it burn.

In the flare that lighted the thin air of this dried-up sea of Mars he looked over his shoulder and saw the rocket that had brought them all, Captain Wilder and Cheroke and Hathaway and Sam Parkhill and himself, across a silent black space of stars to land upon a dead, dreaming world.

Jeff Spender waited for the noise. He watched the other men and waited for them to jump around and shout. It would happen as soon as the numbness of being the "first" men to Mars wore off. None of them said anything, but many of them were hoping, perhaps, that the other expeditions had failed and that this, the Fourth, would be *the* one. They meant nothing evil by it. But they stood thinking it, nevertheless, thinking of the honor and fame, while their lungs became accustomed to the thinness of the atmosphere, which almost made you drunk if you moved too quickly.

Gibbs walked over to the freshly ignited fire and said, "Why don't we use the ship chemical fire instead of that wood?"

"Never mind," said Spender, not looking up.

It wouldn't be right, the first night on Mars, to make a loud noise, to introduce a strange, silly bright thing like a stove. It would be a kind of imported blasphemy. There'd be time for that later; time to throw condensed-milk cans in the proud Martian canals; time for copies of the New York *Times* to blow and caper and rustle across the lone gray Martian sea bottoms; time for banana peels and picnic papers in the fluted, delicate ruins of the old Martian valley towns. Plenty of time for that. And he gave a small inward shiver at the thought.

He fed the fire by hand, and it was like an offering to a dead giant. They had landed on an immense tomb. Here a civilization had died. It was only simple courtesy that the first night be spent quietly.

"This isn't my idea of a celebration." Gibbs turned to Captain Wilder. "Sir, I thought we might break out rations of gin and meat and whoop it up a bit."

Captain Wilder looked off toward a dead city a mile away. "We're all tired," he said remotely, as if his whole attention was on the city and his men forgotten. "Tomorrow night, perhaps. Tonight we should be glad we got across all that space without getting a meteor in our bulkhead or having one man of us die."

The men shifted around. There were twenty of them, holding to each other's shoulders or adjusting their belts. Spender watched them. They were not satisfied. They had risked their lives to do a big thing. Now they wanted to be shouting drunk, firing off guns to show how wonderful they were to have kicked a hole in space and ridden a rocket all the way to Mars.

But nobody was yelling.

The captain gave a quiet order. One of the men ran into the ship and brought forth food tins which were opened and dished out without much noise. The men were beginning to talk now. The captain sat down and recounted the trip to them. They already knew it all, but it was good to hear about it, as something over and done and safely put away. They would not talk about the return trip. Someone brought that up, but they told him to keep quiet. The spoons moved in the double moonlight; the food tasted good and the wine was even better.

There was a touch of fire across the sky, and an instant later the auxiliary rocket landed beyond the camp. Spender watched as the small port opened and Hathaway, the physician-geologist—they were all men of twofold ability, to conserve space on the trip—stepped out. He walked slowly over to the captain.

"Well?" said Captain Wilder.

Hathaway gazed out at the distant cities twinkling in the starlight. After swallowing and focusing his eyes he said, "That city there, Captain, is dead and has been dead a good many thousand years. That applies to those three cities in the hills also. But that fifth city, two hundred miles over, sir——"

"What about it?"

"People were living in it last week, sir."

Spender got to his feet.

"Martians," said Hathaway.

"Where are they now?"

"Dead," said Hathaway. "I went into a house on one street. I thought that it, like the other towns and houses, had been dead for centuries. My God, there were bodies there. It was like walking in a pile of autumn leaves. Like sticks and pieces of burnt newspaper, that's all. And *fresh.* They'd been dead ten days at the outside."

"Did you check other towns? Did you see *anything* alive?"

"Nothing whatever. So I went out to check the other towns. Four out of five have been empty for thousands of years. What happened to the original inhabitants I haven't the faintest idea. But the fifth city always contained the same thing. Bodies. Thousands of bodies."

"What did they die of?" Spender moved forward.

"You won't believe it."

"What killed them?"

Hathaway said simply, "Chicken pox."

"My God, no!"

"Yes. I made tests. Chicken pox. It did things to the Martians it never did to Earth Men. Their metabolism reacted differently, I suppose. Burnt them black and dried them out to brittle flakes. But it's chicken pox, nevertheless. So York and Captain Williams and Captain Black must have got through to Mars, all three expeditions. God knows what happened to them. But we at least know what *they* unintentionally did to the Martians."

"You saw no other life?"

"Chances are a few of the Martians, if they were smart, escaped to the mountains. But there aren't enough, I'll lay you money, to be a native problem. This planet is through."

Spender turned and went to sit at the fire, looking into it. Chicken pox, God, chicken pox, think of it! A race builds itself for a million years, refines itself, erects cities like those out there, does everything it can to give itself respect and beauty, and then it dies. Part of it dies slowly, in its own time, before our age, with dignity. But the rest! Does the rest of Mars die of a disease with a fine name or a terrifying name or a majestic name? No, in the name of all that's holy, it has to be chicken pox, a child's disease, a disease that doesn't even kill *children* on Earth! It's not right and it's not fair. It's like saying the Greeks died of mumps, or the proud Romans died on their beautiful hills of athlete's foot! If only we'd given the Martians time to arrange their death robes, lie down, look fit, and think up some *other* excuse for dying. It can't be a dirty, silly thing like chicken pox. It doesn't fit the architecture; it doesn't fit this entire world!

"All right, Hathaway, get yourself some food."

"Thank you, Captain."

And as quickly as that it was forgotten. The men talked among themselves.

Spender did not take his eyes off them. He left his food on his plate under his hands. He felt the land getting colder. The stars drew closer, very clear.

When anyone talked too loudly the captain would reply in a low voice that made them talk quietly from imitation.

The air smelled clean and new. Spender sat for a long time just enjoying the way it was made. It had a lot of things in it he couldn't identify: flowers, chemistries, dusts, winds.

"Then there was that time in New York when I got that blonde, what's her name?—Ginnie!" cried Biggs. "*That* was it!"

Spender tightened in. His hand began to quiver. His eyes moved behind the thin, sparse lids.

"And Ginnie said to me——" cried Biggs.

The men roared.

"So I smacked her!" shouted Biggs with a bottle in his hand.

Spender set down his plate. He listened to the wind over his ears, cool and whispering. He looked at the cool ice of the white Martian buildings over there on the empty sea lands.

"What a woman, what a woman!" Biggs emptied his bottle in his wide mouth. "Of all the women I ever knew!"

The smell of Biggs's sweating body was on the air. Spender let the fire die. "Hey, kick her up there, Spender!" said Biggs, glancing at him for a moment, then back to his bottle. "Well, one night Ginnie and me——"

A man named Schoenke got out his accordion and did a kicking dance, the dust springing up around him.

"Ahoo—I'm alive!" he shouted.

"Yay!" roared the men. They threw down their empty plates.

Three of them lined up and kicked like chorus maidens, joking loudly. The others, clapping hands, yelled for something to happen. Cheroke pulled off his shirt and showed his naked chest, sweating as he whirled about. The moonlight shone on his crew-cut hair and his young, clean-shaven cheeks.

In the sea bottom the wind stirred along faint vapors, and from the mountains great stone visages looked upon the silvery rocket and the small fire.

The noise got louder, more men jumped up, someone sucked on a mouth organ, someone else blew on a tissue-papered comb. Twenty more bottles were opened and drunk. Biggs staggered about, wagging his arms to direct the dancing men.

"Come on, sir!" cried Cheroke to the captain, wailing a song.

The captain had to join the dance. He didn't want to. His face was solemn. Spender watched, thinking: You poor man, what a night this is! They don't know what they're doing. They should have had an orientation program before they came to Mars to tell them how to look and how to walk around and be good for a few days.

"That does it." The captain begged off and sat down, saying he was exhausted. Spender looked at the captain's chest. It wasn't moving up and down very fast. His face wasn't sweaty, either.

Accordion, harmonica, wine, shout, dance, wail, roundabout, clash of pan, laughter.

Biggs weaved to the rim of the Martian canal. He carried six empty bottles and dropped them one by one into the deep blue canal waters. They made empty, hollow, drowning sounds as they sank.

"I christen thee, I christen thee, I christen thee——" said Biggs thickly. "I christen thee Biggs, Biggs, Biggs Canal——"

Spender was on his feet, over the fire, and alongside Biggs before anyone moved. He hit Biggs once in the teeth and once in the ear. Biggs toppled and fell down into the canal water. After the splash Spender waited silently for Biggs to climb back up onto the stone bank. By that time the men were holding Spender.

"Hey, what's eating you, Spender? Hey?" they asked.

Biggs climbed up and stood dripping. He saw the men holding Spender. "Well," he said, and started forward.

"That's enough," snapped Captain Wilder. The men broke away from Spender. Biggs stopped and glanced at the captain.

"All right, Biggs, get some dry clothes. You men, carry on your party! Spender, come with me!"

The men took up the party. Wilder moved off some distance and confronted Spender. "Suppose you explain what just happened," he said.

Spender looked at the canal. "I don't know. I was ashamed. Of Biggs and us and the noise. Christ, what a spectacle."

"It's been a long trip. They've got to have their fling."

"Where's their respect, sir? Where's their sense of the right thing?"

"You're tired, and you've a different way of seeing things, Spender. That's a fifty-dollar fine for you."

"Yes, sir. It was just the idea of Them watching us make fools of ourselves."

"Them?"

"The Martians, whether they're dead or not."

"Most certainly dead," said the captain. "Do you think They know we're here?"

"Doesn't an old thing always know when a new thing comes?"

"I suppose so. You sound as if you believe in spirits."

"I believe in the things that were done, and there are evidences of many things done on Mars. There are streets and houses, and there are books, I imagine, and big canals and clocks and places for stabling, if not horses, well, then some domestic animal, perhaps with twelve legs, who knows? Everywhere I look I see things that were *used*. They were touched and handled for centuries.

"Ask me, then, if I believe in the spirit of the things as they were used, and I'll say yes. They're all here. All the things which had uses. All the mountains which had names. And we'll never be able to use them without feeling uncomfortable. And somehow the mountains will never sound right to us; we'll give them new names, but the old names are there, somewhere in time, and the mountains were shaped and seen under those names. The names we'll give to the canals and mountains and cities will fall like so much water on the back of a mallard. No matter how we touch Mars, we'll never touch it. And then we'll get mad at it, and you know what we'll do? We'll rip it up, rip the skin off, and change it to fit ourselves."

"We won't ruin Mars," said the captain. "It's too big and too good."

"You think not? We Earth Men have a talent for ruining big, beautiful things. The only reason we didn't set up hot-dog stands in the midst of the Egyptian temple of Karnak is because it was out of the way and served no large commercial purpose. And Egypt is a small part of Earth. But here, this whole thing is ancient and different, and we have to set down somewhere and start fouling it up. We'll call the canal the Rockefeller Canal and the mountain King George Mountain and the sea the Dupont Sea, and there'll be Roosevelt and Lincoln and Coolidge cities and it won't ever be right, when there are the *proper* names for these places."

"That'll be your job, as archaeologist, to find out the old names, and we'll use them."

"A few men like us against all the commercial interests." Spender looked at the iron mountains. "*They* know we're here tonight, to spit in their wine, and I imagine they hate us."

The captain shook his head. "There's no hatred here." He listened to the wind. "From the look of their cities they were a graceful, beautiful, and philosophical people. They accepted what came to them. They acceded to racial death, that much we know, and without a last-moment war of frustration to tumble down their cities. Every town we've seen so far has been flawlessly intact. They probably don't mind us being here any more than they'd mind children playing on the lawn, knowing and understanding children for what they are. And, anyway, perhaps all this will change us for the better.

"Did you notice the peculiar quiet of the men, Spender, until Biggs forced them to get happy? They looked pretty humble and frightened. Looking at all this, we know we're not so hot; we're kids in rompers, shouting with our play rockets and atoms, loud and alive. But one day Earth will be as Mars is today. This will sober us. It's an object lesson in civilizations. We'll learn from Mars. Now suck in your chin. Let's go back and play happy. That fifty-dollar fine still goes."

* * *

The party was not going too well. The wind kept coming in off the dead sea. It moved around the men and it moved around the captain and Jeff Spender as they returned to the group. The wind pulled at the dust and the shining rocket and pulled at the accordion, and the dust got into the vamped harmonica. The dust got in their eyes and the wind made a high singing sound in the air. As suddenly as it had come the wind died.

But the party had died too.

The men stood upright against the dark cold sky.

"Come on, gents, come on!" Biggs bounded from the ship in a fresh uniform, not looking at Spender even once. His voice was like someone in an empty auditorium. It was alone. "Come on!"

Nobody moved.

"Come on, Whitie, your harmonica!"

Whitie blew a chord. It sounded funny and wrong. Whitie knocked the moisture from his harmonica and put it away.

"What kinda party *is* this?" Biggs wanted to know.

Someone hugged the accordion. It gave a sound like a dying animal. That was all.

"Okay, me and my bottle will go have our own party." Biggs squatted against the rocket, drinking from a flask.

Spender watched him. Spender did not move for a long time. Then his fingers crawled up along his trembling leg to his holstered pistol, very quietly, and stroked and tapped the leather sheath.

"All those who want to can come into the city with me," announced the captain. "We'll post a guard here at the rocket and go armed, just in case."

The men counted off. Fourteen of them wanted to go, including Biggs, who laughingly counted himself in, waving his bottle. Six others stayed behind.

"Here we go!" Biggs shouted.

The party moved out into the moonlight, silently. They made their way to the outer rim of the dreaming dead city in the light of the racing twin moons. Their shadows, under them, were double shadows. They did not breathe, or seemed not to, perhaps, for several minutes. They were waiting for something to stir in the dead city, some gray form to rise, some ancient, ancestral shape to come galloping across the vacant sea bottom on an ancient, armored steed of impossible lineage, of unbelievable derivation.

Spender filled the streets with his eyes and his mind. People moved like blue vapor lights on the cobbled avenues, and there were faint murmurs of sound, and odd animals scurrying across the gray-red sands. Each window was given a person who leaned from it and waved slowly, as if under a timeless water, at some moving form in the fathoms of space below the moon-silvered towers. Music was played on some inner ear, and Spender imagined the shape of such instruments to evoke such music. The land was haunted.

"Hey!" shouted Biggs, standing tall, his hands around his open mouth. "Hey, you people in the city there, you!"

"Biggs!" said the captain.

Biggs quieted.

They walked forward on a tiled avenue. They were all whispering now, for it was like entering a vast open library or a mausoleum in which the wind lived and over which the stars shone. The captain spoke quietly. He wondered where the people had gone, and what they had been, and who their kings were, and how they had died. And he wondered, quietly aloud, how they had built this city to last the ages through, and had they ever come to Earth? Were they ancestors of Earth Men ten thousand years removed? And had they loved and hated similar loves and hates, and done similar silly things when silly things were done?

Nobody moved. The moons held and froze them; the wind beat slowly around them.

"Lord Byron," said Jeff Spender.

"Lord who?" The captain turned and regarded him.

"Lord Byron, a nineteenth-century poet. He wrote a poem a long time ago that fits this city and how the Martians must feel, if there's anything left of them to feel. It might have been written by the last Martian poet."

The men stood motionless, their shadows under them.

The captain said, "How does the poem go, Spender?"

Spender shifted, put out his hand to remember, squinted

silently a moment; then, remembering, his slow quiet voice repeated the words and the men listened to everything he said:

"So we'll go no more a-roving
So late into the night,
Though the heart be still as loving,
And the moon be still as bright."

The city was gray and high and motionless. The men's faces were turned in the light.

"For the sword outwears its sheath,
And the soul wears out the breast,
And the heart must pause to breathe,
And love itself must rest.

"Though the night was made for loving,
And the day returns too soon,
Yet we'll go no more a-roving
By the light of the moon."

Without a word the Earth Men stood in the center of the city. It was a clear night. There was not a sound except the wind. At their feet lay a tile court worked into the shapes of ancient animals and peoples. They looked down upon it.

Biggs made a sick noise in his throat. His eyes were dull. His hands went to his mouth; he choked, shut his eyes, bent, and a thick rush of fluid filled his mouth, spilled out, fell to splash on the tiles, covering the designs. Biggs did this twice. A sharp winy stench filled the cool air.

No one moved to help Biggs. He went on being sick.

Spender stared for a moment, then turned and walked off into the avenues of the city, alone in the moonlight. Never once did he pause to look back at the gathered men there.

They turned in at four in the morning. They lay upon blankets and shut their eyes and breathed the quiet air. Captain Wilder sat feeding little sticks into the fire.

McClure opened his eyes two hours later. "Aren't you sleeping, sir?"

"I'm waiting for Spender." The captain smiled faintly.

McClure thought it over. "You know, sir, I don't think he'll ever come back. I don't know how I know, but that's the way I feel about him, sir; he'll never come back."

McClure rolled over into sleep. The fire crackled and died.

Spender did not return in the following week. The captain sent searching parties, but they came back saying they didn't know where Spender could have gone. He would be back when he got good and ready. He was a sorehead, they said. To the devil with him!

The captain said nothing but wrote it down in his log. . . .

It was a morning that might have been a Monday or a Tuesday or any day on Mars. Biggs was on the canal rim; his feet hung down into the cool water, soaking, while he took the sun on his face.

A man walked along the bank of the canal. The man threw a shadow down upon Biggs. Biggs glanced up.

"Well, I'll be damned!" said Biggs.

"I'm the last Martian," said the man, taking out a gun.

"What did you say?" asked Biggs.

"I'm going to kill you."

"Cut it. What kind of joke's that, Spender?"

"Stand up and take it in the stomach."

"For Christ's sake, put that gun away."

Spender pulled the trigger only once. Biggs sat on the edge of the canal for a moment before he leaned forward and fell into the water. The gun had made only a whispering hum. The body drifted with slow unconcern under the slow canal tides. It made a hollow bubbling sound that ceased after a moment.

Spender shoved his gun into its holster and walked soundlessly away. The sun was shining down upon Mars. He felt it burn his hands and slide over the sides of his tight face. He did not run; he walked as if nothing were new except the daylight. He walked down to the rocket, and some of the men were eating a freshly cooked breakfast under a shelter built by Cookie.

"Here comes The Lonely One," someone said.

"Hello, Spender! Long time no see!"

The four men at the table regarded the silent man who stood looking back at them.

"You and them goddamn ruins," laughed Cookie, stirring a black substance in a crock. "You're like a dog in a bone yard."

"Maybe," said Spender, "I've been finding out things. What would you say if I said I'd found a Martian prowling around?"

The four men laid down their forks.

"Did you? Where?"

"Never mind. Let me ask you a question. How would you feel if you were a Martian and people came to your land and started tearing it up?"

"I know exactly how I'd feel," said Cheroke. "I've got some Cherokee blood in me. My grandfather told me lots of things about Oklahoma Territory. If there's a Martian around, I'm all for him."

"What about you other men?" asked Spender carefully.

Nobody answered; their silence was talk enough. Catch as catch can, finder's keepers, if the other fellow turns his cheek slap it hard, etc. . . .

"Well," said Spender, "I've found a Martian."

The men squinted at him.

"Up in a dead town. I didn't think I'd find him. I didn't intend looking him up. I don't know what he was doing there. I've been living in a little valley town for about a week, learning how to read the ancient books and looking at their old art forms. And one day I saw this Martian. He stood there for a moment and then he was gone. He didn't come back for another day. I sat around, learning how to read the old writing, and the Martian came back, each time a little nearer, until on the day I learned how to decipher the Martian language—it's amazingly simple and there are picturegraphs to help you—the Martian appeared before me and said, 'Give me your boots.' And I gave him my boots and he said, 'Give me your uniform and all the rest of your apparel.' And I gave him all of that, and then he said, 'Give me your gun,' and I gave him my gun. Then he said, 'Now come along and watch what happens.' And the Martian walked down into camp and he's here now."

"I don't see any Martian," said Cheroke.

"I'm sorry."

Spender took out his gun. It hummed softly. The first bullet got the man on the left; the second and third bullets took the men on the right and the center of the table. Cookie turned in horror from the fire to receive the fourth bullet. He fell back into the fire and lay there while his clothes caught fire.

The rocket lay in the sun. Three men sat at breakfast, their hands on the table, not moving, their food getting cold in front of them. Cheroke, untouched, sat alone, staring in numb disbelief at Spender.

"You can come with me," said Spender.

Cheroke said nothing.

"You can be with me on this." Spender waited.

Finally Cheroke was able to speak. "You killed them," he said, daring to look at the men around him.

"They deserved it."

"You're crazy!"

"Maybe I am. But you can come with me."

"Come with you, for what?" cried Cheroke, the color gone from his face, his eyes watering. "Go on, get out!"

Spender's face hardened. "Of all of them, I thought *you* would understand."

"Get out!" Cheroke reached for his gun.

Spender fired one last time. Cheroke stopped moving.

Now Spender swayed. He put his hand to his sweating face. He glanced at the rocket and suddenly began to shake all over. He almost fell, the physical reaction was so overwhelming. His face held an expression of one awakening from hypnosis, from a dream. He sat down for a moment and told the shaking to go away.

"Stop it, stop it!" he commanded of his body. Every fiber of him was quivering and shaking. "Stop it!" He crushed his body with his mind until all the shaking was squeezed out of it. His hands lay calmly now upon his silent knees.

He arose and strapped a portable storage locker on his back with quiet efficiency. His hand began to tremble again, just for a breath of an instant, but he said, "No!" very firmly, and the trembling passed. Then, walking stiffly, he moved out between the hot red hills of the land, alone.

* * *

The sun burned farther up the sky. An hour later the captain climbed down out of the rocket to get some ham and eggs. He was just saying hello to the four men sitting there when he stopped and noticed a faint smell of gun fumes on the air. He saw the cook lying on the ground, with the campfire under him. The four men sat before food that was now cold.

A moment later Parkhill and two others climbed down. The captain stood in their way, fascinated by the silent men and the way they sat at their breakfast.

"Call the men, all of them," said the captain.

Parkhill hurried off down the canal rim.

The captain touched Cheroke. Cheroke twisted quietly and fell from his chair. Sunlight burned in his bristled short hair and on his high cheekbones.

The men came in.

"Who's missing?"

"It's still Spender, sir. We found Biggs floating in the canal."

"Spender!"

The captain saw the hills rising in the daylight. The sun showed his teeth in a grimace. "Damn him," he said tiredly. "Why didn't he come and talk to me?"

"He should've talked to *me*," cried Parkhill, eyes blazing. "I'd have shot his bloody brains out, that's what I'd have done, by God!"

Captain Wilder nodded at two of his men. "Get shovels," he said.

It was hot digging the graves. A warm wind came from over the vacant sea and blew the dust into their faces as the captain turned the Bible pages. When the captain closed the book someone began shoveling slow streams of sand down upon the wrapped figures.

They walked back to the rocket, clicked the mechanisms of their rifles, put thick grenade packets on their backs, and checked the free play of pistols in their holsters. They were each assigned a certain part of the hills. The captain directed them without raising his voice or moving his hands where they hung at his sides.

"Let's go," he said.

* * *

Spender saw the thin dust rising in several places in the valley and he knew the pursuit was organized and ready. He put down the thin silver book that he had been reading as he sat easily on a flat boulder. The book's pages were tissue-thin, pure silver, hand-painted in black and gold. It was a book of philosophy at least ten thousand years old he had found in one of the villas of a Martian valley town. He was reluctant to lay it aside.

For a time he had thought, What's the use? I'll sit here reading until they come along and shoot me.

The first reaction to his killing the six men this morning had caused a period of stunned blankness, then sickness, and now, a strange peace. But the peace was passing, too, for he saw the dust billowing from the trails of the hunting men, and he experienced the return of resentment.

He took a drink of cool water from his hip canteen. Then he stood up, stretched, yawned, and listened to the peaceful wonder of the valley around him. How very fine if he and a few others he knew on Earth could be here, live out their lives here, without a sound or a worry.

He carried the book with him in one hand, the pistol ready in his other. There was a little swift-running stream filled with white pebbles and rocks where he undressed and waded in for a brief washing. He took all the time he wanted before dressing and picking up his gun again.

The firing began about three in the afternoon. By then Spender was high in the hills. They followed him through three small Martian hill towns. Above the towns, scattered like pebbles, were single villas where ancient families had found a brook, a green spot, and laid out a tile pool, a library, and a court with a pulsing fountain. Spender took half an hour, swimming in one of the pools which was filled with the seasonal rain, waiting for the pursuers to catch up with him.

Shots rang out as he was leaving the little villa. Tile chipped up some twenty feet behind him, exploded. He broke into a trot, moved behind a series of small bluffs, turned, and with his first shot dropped one of the men dead in his tracks.

They would form a net, a circle; Spender knew that. They would go around and close in and they would get him. It was a strange thing that the grenades were not used. Captain Wilder could easily order the grenades tossed.

But I'm much too nice to be blown to bits, thought Spender. That's what the captain thinks. He wants me with only one hole in me. Isn't that odd? He wants my death to be clean. Nothing messy. Why? Because he understands me. And because he understands, he's willing to risk good men to give me a clean shot in the head. Isn't that it?

Nine, ten shots broke out in a rattle. Rocks around him jumped up. Spender fired steadily, sometimes while glancing at the silver book he carried in his hand.

The captain ran in the hot sunlight with a rifle in his hands. Spender followed him in his pistol sights but did not fire. Instead he shifted and blew the top off a rock where Whitie lay, and heard an angry shout.

Suddenly the captain stood up. He had a white handkerchief in his hands. He said something to his men and came walking up the mountain after putting aside his rifle. Spender lay there, then got to his feet, his pistol ready.

The captain came up and sat down on a warm boulder, not looking at Spender for a moment.

The captain reached into his blouse pocket. Spender's fingers tightened on the pistol.

The captain said, "Cigarette?"

"Thanks." Spender took one.

"Light?"

"Got my own."

They took one or two puffs in silence.

"Warm," said the captain.

"It is."

"You comfortable up here?"

"Quite."

"How long do you think you can hold out?"

"About twelve men's worth."

"Why didn't you kill all of us this morning when you had the chance? You could have, you know."

"I know. I got sick. When you want to do a thing badly enough you lie to yourself. You say the other people are all wrong. Well, soon after I started killing people I realized they were just fools and I shouldn't be killing them. But it was too late. I couldn't go on with it then, so I came up here where I could lie to myself some more and get angry, to build it all up again."

"Is it built up?"

"Not very high. Enough."

The captain considered his cigarette. "Why did you do it?"

Spender quietly laid his pistol at his feet. "Because I've seen that what these Martians had was just as good as anything we'll ever hope to have. They stopped where we should have stopped a hundred years ago. I've walked in their cities and I know these people and I'd be glad to call them my ancestors."

"They have a beautiful city there." The captain nodded at one of several places.

"It's not that alone. Yes, their cities are good. They knew how to blend art into their living. It's always been a thing apart for Americans. Art was something you kept in the crazy son's room upstairs. Art was something you took in Sunday doses, mixed with religion, perhaps. Well, these Martians have art and religion and everything."

"You think they knew what it was all about, do you?"

"For my money."

"And for that reason you started shooting people."

"When I was a kid my folks took me to visit Mexico City. I'll always remember the way my father acted—loud and big. And my mother didn't like the people because they were dark and didn't wash enough. And my sister wouldn't talk to most of them. I was the only one really liked it. And I can see my mother and father coming to Mars and acting the same way here.

"Anything that's strange is no good to the average American. If it doesn't have Chicago plumbing, it's nonsense. The thought of that! Oh God, the thought of that! And then—the war. You heard the congressional speeches before we left. If things work out they hope to establish three atomic research and atom bomb depots on Mars. That means Mars is finished; all this wonderful stuff gone. How would you feel if a Martian vomited stale liquor on the White House floor?"

The captain said nothing but listened.

Spender continued: "And then the other power interests coming up. The mineral men and the travel men. Do you remember what happened to Mexico when Cortez and his very fine good friends arrived from Spain? A whole civilization destroyed by greedy, righteous bigots. History will never forgive Cortez."

"You haven't acted ethically yourself today," observed the captain.

"What could I do? Argue with you? It's simply me against the whole crooked grinding greedy setup on Earth. They'll be flopping their filthy atom bombs up here, fighting for bases to have wars. Isn't it enough they've ruined one planet, without ruining another; do they have to foul someone else's manger? The simple-minded windbags. When I got up here I felt I was not only free of their so-called culture, I felt I was free of their ethics and their customs. I'm out of their frame of reference, I thought. All I have to do is kill you all off and live my own life."

"But it didn't work out," said the captain.

"No. After the fifth killing at breakfast, I discovered I wasn't all new, all Martian, after all. I couldn't throw away everything I had learned on Earth so easily. But now I'm feeling steady again. I'll kill you all off. That'll delay the next trip in a rocket for a good five years. There's no other rocket in existence today, save this one. The people on Earth will wait a year, two years, and then when they hear nothing from us, they'll be very afraid to build a new rocket. They'll take twice as long and make a hundred extra experimental models to insure themselves against another failure."

"You're correct."

"A good report from you, on the other hand, if you returned, would hasten the whole invasion of Mars. If I'm lucky I'll live to be sixty years old. Every expedition that lands on Mars will be met by me. There won't be more than one ship at a time coming up, one every year or so, and never more than twenty men in the crew. After I've made friends with them and explained that our rocket exploded one day—I intend to blow it up after I finish my job this week—I'll kill them off, every one of them. Mars will be untouched for the next half century. After a while, perhaps the Earth people will give up trying. Remember how they grew leery of the idea of building Zeppelins that were always going down in flames?"

"You've got it all planned," admitted the captain.

"I have."

"Yet you're outnumbered. In an hour we'll have you surrounded. In an hour you'll be dead."

"I've found some underground passages and a place to live you'll never find. I'll withdraw there to live for a few weeks. Until you're off guard. I'll come out then to pick you off, one by one."

The captain nodded. "Tell me about your civilization here," he said, waving his hand at the mountain towns.

"They knew how to live with nature and get along with nature. They didn't try too hard to be all men and no animal. That's the mistake we made when Darwin showed up. We embraced him and Huxley and Freud, all smiles. And then we discovered that Darwin and our religions didn't mix. Or at least we didn't think they did. We were fools. We tried to budge Darwin and Huxley and Freud. They wouldn't move very well. So, like idiots, we tried knocking down religion.

"We succeeded pretty well. We lost our faith and went around wondering what life was for. If art was no more than a frustrated outflinging of desire, if religion was no more than self-delusion, what good was life? Faith had always given us answers to all things. But it all went down the drain with Freud and Darwin. We were and still are a lost people."

"And these Martians are a *found* people?" inquired the captain.

"Yes. They knew how to combine science and religion so the two worked side by side, neither denying the other, each enriching the other."

"That sounds ideal."

"It was. I'd like to show you how the Martians did it."

"My men are waiting."

"We'll be gone half an hour. Tell them that, sir."

The captain hesitated, then rose and called an order down the hill.

Spender led him over into a little Martian village built all of cool perfect marble. There were great friezes of beautiful animals, white-limbed cat things and yellow-limbed sun symbols, and statues of bull-like creatures and statues of men and women and huge fine-featured dogs.

"There's your answer, Captain."

"I don't see."

"The Martians discovered the secret of life among animals. The animal does not question life. It lives. Its very reason for living is life; it enjoys and relishes life. You see—the statuary, the animal symbols, again and again."

"It looks pagan."

"On the contrary, those are God symbols, symbols of life. Man had become too much man and not enough animal on Mars too. And the men of Mars realized that in order to survive they would have to forgo asking that one question any longer: *Why live?* Life was its own answer. Life was the propagation of more life and the living of as good a life as possible. The Martians realized that they asked the question 'Why live at all?' at the height of some period of war and despair, when there was no answer. But once the civilization calmed, quieted, and wars ceased, the question became senseless in a new way. Life was now good and needed no arguments."

"It sounds as if the Martians were quite naïve."

"Only when it paid to be naïve. They quit trying too hard to destroy everything, to humble everything. They blended religion and art and science because, at base, science is no more than an investigation of a miracle we can never explain, and art is an interpretation of that miracle. They never let science crush the aesthetic and the beautiful. It's all simply a matter of degree. An Earth Man thinks: 'In that picture, color does not exist, really. A scientist can prove that color is only the way the cells are placed in a certain material to reflect light. Therefore, color is not really an actual part of things I happen to see.' A Martian, far cleverer, would say: 'This is a fine picture. It came from the hand and the mind of a man inspired. Its idea and its color are from life. This thing is good.'"

There was a pause. Sitting in the afternoon sun, the captain looked curiously around at the little silent cool town.

"I'd like to live here," he said.

"You may if you want."

"You ask *me* that?"

"Will any of those men under you ever really understand all this? They're professional cynics, and it's too late for them. Why do you want to go back with them? So you can keep up with the Joneses? To buy a gyro just like Smith has? To listen to music with your pocketbook instead of your glands? There's a little patio down here with a reel of Martian music in it at least fifty thousand years old. It still plays. Music you'll never hear in your life. You could hear it. There are books. I've gotten on well in reading them already. You could sit and read."

"It all sounds quite wonderful, Spender."

"But you won't stay?"

"No. Thanks, anyway."

"And you certainly won't let me stay without trouble. I'll have to kill you all."

"You're optimistic."

"I have something to fight for and live for; that makes me a better killer. I've got what amounts to a religion, now. It's learning how to breathe all over again. And how to lie in the sun getting a tan, letting the sun work into you. And how to hear music and how to read a book. What does your civilization offer?"

The captain shifted his feet. He shook his head. "I'm sorry this is happening. I'm sorry about it all."

"I am too. I guess I'd better take you back now so you can start the attack."

"I guess so."

"Captain, I won't kill you. When it's all over, you'll still be alive."

"What?"

"I decided when I started that you'd be untouched."

"Well . . ."

"I'll save you out from the rest. When they're dead, perhaps you'll change your mind."

"No," said the captain. "There's too much Earth blood in me. I'll have to keep after you."

"Even when you have a chance to stay here?"

"It's funny, but yes, even with that. I don't know why. I've never asked myself. Well, here we are." They had returned to their meeting place now. "Will you come quietly, Spender? This is my last offer."

"Thanks, no." Spender put out his hand. "One last thing. If you win, do me a favor. See what can be done to restrict tearing this planet apart, at least for fifty years, until the archaeologists have had a decent chance, will you?"

"Right."

"And last—if it helps any, just think of me as a very crazy fellow who went berserk one summer day and never was right again. It'll be a little easier on you that way."

"I'll think it over. So long, Spender. Good luck."

"You're an odd one," said Spender as the captain walked back down the trail in the warm-blowing wind.

The captain returned like something lost to his dusty men. He kept squinting at the sun and breathing hard.

"Is there a drink?" he said. He felt a bottle put cool into his hand. "Thanks." He drank. He wiped his mouth.

"All right," he said. "Be careful. We have all the time we want. I don't want any more lost. You'll have to kill him. He won't come down. Make it a clean shot if you can. Don't mess him. Get it over with."

"I'll blow his damned brains out," said Sam Parkhill.

"No, through the chest," said the captain. He could see Spender's strong, clearly determined face.

"His bloody brains," said Parkhill.

The captain handed him the bottle jerkingly. "You heard what I said. Through the chest."

Parkhill muttered to himself.

"Now," said the captain.

They spread again, walking and then running, and then walking on the hot hillside places where there would be sudden cool grottoes that smelled of moss, and sudden open blasting places that smelled of sun on stone.

I hate being clever, thought the captain, when you don't really feel clever and don't want to *be* clever. To sneak around and make plans and feel big about making them. I hate this feeling of thinking I'm doing right when I'm not really certain I am. Who are we, anyway? The majority? Is that the answer? The majority is always holy, is it not? Always, always; just never wrong for one little insignificant tiny moment, is it? Never ever wrong in ten million years? He thought: What is this majority and who are in it? And what do they think and how did they get that way and will they ever change and how the devil did I get caught in this rotten majority? I don't feel comfortable. Is it claustrophobia, fear of crowds, or common sense? Can one man be right, while all the world thinks they are right? Let's not think about it. Let's crawl around and act exciting and pull the trigger. There, and *there*!

The men ran and ducked and ran and squatted in shadows and showed their teeth, gasping, for the air was thin, not meant for running; the air was thin and they had to sit for five minutes at a time, wheezing and seeing black lights in their eyes, eating at the thin air and wanting more, tightening their eyes, and at last getting up, lifting their guns to tear holes in that thin summer air, holes of sound and heat.

Spender remained where he was, firing only on occasion.

"Damned brains all over!" Parkhill yelled, running uphill.

The captain aimed his gun at Sam Parkhill. He put it down and stared at it in horror. "What were you doing?" he asked of his limp hand and the gun.

He had almost shot Parkhill in the back.

"God help me."

He saw Parkhill still running, then falling to lie safe.

Spender was being gathered in by a loose, running net of men. At the hilltop, behind two rocks, Spender lay, grinning with exhaustion from the thin atmosphere, great islands of sweat under each arm. The captain saw the two rocks. There was an interval between them of some four inches, giving free access to Spender's chest.

"Hey, you!" cried Parkhill. "Here's a slug for your head!"

Captain Wilder waited. Go on, Spender, he thought. Get out, like you said you would. You've only a few minutes to escape. Get out and come back later. Go on. You said you would. Go down in the tunnels you said you found, and lie there and live for months and years, reading your fine books and bathing in your temple pools. Go on, now, man, before it's too late.

Spender did not move from his position.

"What's wrong with him?" the captain asked himself.

The captain picked up his gun. He watched the running, hiding men. He looked at the towers of the little clean Martian village, like sharply carved chess pieces lying in the afternoon. He saw the rocks and the interval between where Spender's chest was revealed.

Parkhill was charging up, screaming in fury.

"No, Parkhill," said the captain. "I can't let you do it. Nor the others. No, none of you. Only me." He raised the gun and sighted it.

Will I be clean after this? he thought. Is it right that it's me who does it? Yes, it is. I know what I'm doing for what reason and it's right, because I think I'm the right person. I hope and pray I can live up to this.

He nodded his head at Spender. "Go on," he called in a loud whisper which no one heard. "I'll give you thirty seconds more to get away. Thirty seconds!"

The watch ticked on his wrist. The captain watched it tick. The men were running. Spender did not move. The watch ticked for a long time, very loudly in the captain's ears. "Go on, Spender, go on, get away!"

The thirty seconds were up.

The gun was sighted. The captain drew a deep breath. "Spender," he said, exhaling.

He pulled the trigger.

All that happened was that a faint powdering of rock went up in the sunlight. The echoes of the report faded.

The captain arose and called to his men: "He's dead."

The other men did not believe it. Their angles had prevented their seeing that particular fissure in the rocks. They saw their captain run up the hill, alone, and thought him either very brave or insane.

The men came after him a few minutes later.

They gathered around the body and someone said, "In the chest?"

The captain looked down. "In the chest," he said. He saw how the rocks had changed color under Spender. "I wonder why he waited. I wonder why he didn't escape as he planned. I wonder why he stayed on and got himself killed."

"Who knows?" someone said.

Spender lay there, his hands clasped, one around the gun, the other around the silver book that glittered in the sun.

Was it because of me? thought the captain. Was it because I refused to give in myself? Did Spender hate the idea of killing me? Am I any different from these others here? Is that what did it? Did he figure he could trust me? What other answer is there?

None. He squatted by the silent body.

I've got to live up to this, he thought. I can't let him down now. If he figured there was something in me that was like himself and couldn't kill me because of it, then what a job I have ahead of me! That's it, yes, that's it. I'm Spender all over again, but I think before I shoot. I don't shoot at all, I don't kill. I do things with people. And he couldn't kill me because I was himself under a slightly different condition.

The captain felt the sunlight on the back of his neck. He heard himself talking: "If only he had come to me and talked it over before he shot anybody, we could have worked it out somehow."

"Worked what out?" said Parkhill. "What could we have worked out with *his* likes?"

There was a singing of heat in the land, off the rocks and off the blue sky. "I guess you're right," said the captain. "We could never have got together. Spender and myself, perhaps. But Spender and you and the others, no, never. He's better off now. Let me have a drink from that canteen."

It was the captain who suggested the empty sarcophagus for Spender. They had found an ancient Martian tomb yard. They put Spender into a silver case with waxes and wines which were ten thousand years old, his hands folded on his chest. The last they saw of him was his peaceful face.

They stood for a moment in the ancient vault. "I think it would be a good idea for you to think of Spender from time to time," said the captain.

They walked from the vault and shut the marble door.

The next afternoon Parkhill did some target practice in one of the dead cities, shooting out the crystal windows and blowing the tops off the fragile towers. The captain caught Parkhill and knocked his teeth out.

August 2001: THE SETTLERS

THE MEN of Earth came to Mars.

They came because they were afraid or unafraid, because they were happy or unhappy, because they felt like Pilgrims or did not feel like Pilgrims. There was a reason for each man. They were leaving bad wives or bad jobs or bad towns; they were coming to find something or leave something or get something, to dig up something or bury something or leave something alone. They were coming with small dreams or large dreams or none at all. But a government finger pointed from four-color posters in many towns: THERE'S WORK FOR YOU IN THE SKY: SEE MARS! and the men shuffled forward, only a few at first, a double-score, for most men felt the great illness in them even before the rocket fired into space. And this disease was called The Loneliness, because when you saw your home town dwindle the size of your fist and then lemon-size and then pin-size and vanish in the fire-wake, you felt you had never been born, there was no town, you were nowhere, with space all around, nothing familiar, only other strange men. And when the state of Illinois, Iowa, Missouri, or Montana vanished into cloud seas, and, doubly, when the United States shrank to a misted island and the entire planet Earth became a muddy baseball tossed away, then you were alone, wandering in the meadows of space, on your way to a place you couldn't imagine.

So it was not unusual that the first men were few. The number grew steadily in proportion to the census of Earth Men already on Mars. There was comfort in numbers. But the first Lonely Ones had to stand by themselves. . . .

December 2001: THE GREEN MORNING

WHEN THE sun set he crouched by the path and cooked a small supper and listened to the fire crack while he put the food in his mouth and chewed thoughtfully. It had been a day not unlike thirty others, with many neat holes dug in the dawn hours, seeds dropped in, and water brought from the bright canals. Now, with an iron weariness in his slight body, he lay and watched the sky color from one darkness to another.

His name was Benjamin Driscoll, and he was thirty-one years old. And the thing that he wanted was Mars grown green and tall with trees and foliage, producing air, more air, growing larger with each season; trees to cool the towns in the boiling summer, trees to hold back the winter winds. There were so many things a tree could do: add color, provide shade, drop fruit, or become a children's playground, a whole sky universe to climb and hang from; an architecture of food and pleasure, that was a tree. But most of all the trees would distill an icy air for the lungs, and a gentle rustling for the ear when you lay nights in your snowy bed and were gentled to sleep by the sound.

He lay listening to the dark earth gather itself, waiting for the sun, for the rains that hadn't come yet. His ear to the ground, he could hear the feet of the years ahead moving at a distance, and he imagined the seeds he had placed today sprouting up with green and taking hold on the sky, pushing out branch after branch, until Mars was an afternoon forest, Mars was a shining orchard.

In the early morning, with the small sun lifting faintly among the folded hills, he would be up and finished with a smoky breakfast in a few minutes and, trodding out the fire ashes, be on his way with knapsacks, testing, digging, placing seed or sprout, tamping lightly, watering, going on, whistling, looking at the clear sky brightening toward a warm noon.

"You need the air," he told his night fire. The fire was a ruddy, lively companion that snapped back at you, that slept close by with drowsy pink eyes warm through the chilly night. "We all need the air. It's a thin air here on Mars. You get tired so soon. It's like living in the Andes, in South America, high. You inhale and don't get anything. It doesn't satisfy."

He felt his rib case. In thirty days, how it had grown. To take in more air, they would all have to build their lungs. Or plant more trees.

"That's what I'm here for," he said. The fire popped. "In school they told a story about Johnny Appleseed walking across America planting apple trees. Well, I'm doing more. I'm planting oaks, elms, and maples, every kind of tree, aspens and deodars and chestnuts. Instead of making just fruit for the stomach, I'm making air for the lungs. When those trees grow up some year, *think* of the oxygen they'll make!"

He remembered his arrival on Mars. Like a thousand others, he had gazed out upon a still morning and thought, How do I fit here? What will I do? Is there a job for me?

Then he had fainted.

Someone pushed a vial of ammonia to his nose and, coughing, he came around.

"You'll be all right," said the doctor.

"What happened?"

"The air's pretty thin. Some can't take it. I think you'll have to go back to Earth."

"No!" He sat up and almost immediately felt his eyes darken and Mars revolve twice around under him. His nostrils dilated and he forced his lungs to drink in deep nothingnesses. "I'll be all right. I've got to stay here!"

They let him lie gasping in horrid fishlike motions. And he thought, Air, air, air. They're sending me back because of air. And he turned his head to look across the Martian fields and hills. He brought them to focus, and the first thing he noticed was that there were no trees, no trees at all, as far as you could look in any direction. The land was down upon itself, a land of black loam, but nothing on it, not even grass. Air, he thought, the thin stuff whistling in his nostrils. Air, air. And on top of hills, or in their shadows, or even by little creeks, not a tree and not a single green blade of grass. Of course! He felt the answer came not from his mind, but his lungs and his throat. And the thought was like a sudden gust of pure oxygen, raising him up. Trees and grass. He looked down at his hands and turned them over. He would plant trees and grass. That would be his job, to fight against the very thing that might prevent his staying here. He would have a private horticultural war with Mars. There lay the old soil, and the plants of it so ancient they had worn themselves out. But what if new forms were introduced? Earth trees, great mimosas and weeping willows and magnolias and magnificent eucalyptus. What then? There was no guessing what mineral wealth hid in the soil, untapped because the old ferns, flowers, bushes, and trees had tired themselves to death.

"Let me up!" he shouted. "I've got to see the Co-ordinator!"

He and the Co-ordinator had talked an entire morning about things that grew and were green. It would be months, if not years, before organized planting began. So far, frosted food was brought from Earth in flying icicles; a few community gardens were greening up in hydroponic plants.

"Meanwhile," said the Co-ordinator, "it's your job. We'll get what seed we can for you, a little equipment. Space on the rockets is mighty precious now. I'm afraid, since these first towns are mining communities, there won't be much sympathy for your tree planting——"

"But you'll let me do it?"

They let him do it. Provided with a single motorcycle, its bin full of rich seeds and sprouts, he had parked his vehicle in the valley wilderness and struck out on foot over the land.

That had been thirty days ago, and he had never glanced back. For looking back would have been sickening to the heart. The weather was excessively dry; it was doubtful if any seeds had sprouted yet. Perhaps his entire campaign, his four weeks of bending and scooping were lost. He kept his eyes only ahead of him, going on down this wide shallow valley under the sun, away from First Town, waiting for the rains to come.

Clouds were gathering over the dry mountains now as he drew his blanket over his shoulders. Mars was a place as unpredictable as time. He felt the baked hills simmering down into frosty night, and he thought of the rich, inky soil, a soil so black and shiny it almost crawled and stirred in your fist, a rank soil from which might sprout gigantic beanstalks from which, with bone-shaking concussion, might drop screaming giants.

The fire fluttered into sleepy ash. The air tremored to the distant roll of a cartwheel. Thunder. A sudden odor of water.

Tonight, he thought, and put his hand out to feel for rain. Tonight.

He awoke to a tap on his brow.

Water ran down his nose into his lips. Another drop hit his eye, blurring it. Another splashed his chin.

The rain.

Raw, gentle, and easy, it mizzled out of the high air, a special elixir, tasting of spells and stars and air, carrying a peppery dust in it, and moving like a rare light sherry on his tongue.

Rain.

He sat up. He let the blanket fall and his blue denim shirt spot, while the rain took on more solid drops. The fire looked as though an invisible animal were dancing on it, crushing it, until it was angry smoke. The rain fell. The great black lid of sky cracked in six powdery blue chips, like a marvelous crackled glaze, and rushed down. He saw ten billion rain crystals, hesitating long enough to be photographed by the electrical display. Then darkness and water.

He was drenched to the skin, but he held his face up and let the water hit his eyelids, laughing. He clapped his hands together and stepped up and walked around his little camp, and it was one o'clock in the morning.

It rained steadily for two hours and then stopped. The stars came out, freshly washed and clearer than ever.

Changing into dry clothes from his cellophane pack, Mr. Benjamin Driscoll lay down and went happily to sleep.

The sun rose slowly among the hills. It broke out upon the land quietly and wakened Mr. Driscoll where he lay.

He waited a moment before arising. He had worked and waited a long hot month, and now, standing up, he turned at last and faced the direction from which he had come.

It was a green morning.

As far as he could see the trees were standing up against the sky. Not one tree, not two, not a dozen, but the thousands he had planted in seed and sprout. And not little trees, no, not saplings, not little tender shoots, but great trees, huge trees, trees as tall as ten men, green and green and huge and round and full, trees shimmering their metallic leaves, trees whispering, trees in a line over hills, lemon trees, lime trees, redwoods and mimosas and oaks and elms and aspens, cherry, maple, ash, apple, orange, eucalyptus, stung by a tumultuous rain, nourished by alien and magical soil and, even as he watched, throwing out new branches, popping open new buds.

"Impossible!" cried Mr. Benjamin Driscoll.

But the valley and the morning were green.

And the air!

All about, like a moving current, a mountain river, came the new air, the oxygen blowing from the green trees. You could see it shimmer high in crystal billows. Oxygen, fresh, pure, green, cold oxygen turning the valley into a river delta. In a moment the town doors would flip wide, people would run out through the new miracle of oxygen, sniffing, gusting in lungfuls of it, cheeks pinking with it, noses frozen with it, lungs revivified, hearts leaping, and worn bodies lifted into a dance.

Mr. Benjamin Driscoll took one long deep drink of green water air and fainted.

Before he woke again five thousand new trees had climbed up into the yellow sun.

February 2002: THE LOCUSTS

THE ROCKETS set the bony meadows afire, turned rock to lava, turned wood to charcoal, transmuted water to steam, made sand and silica into green glass which lay like shattered mirrors reflecting the invasion, all about. The rockets came like drums, beating in the night. The rockets came like locusts, swarming and settling in blooms of rosy smoke. And from the rockets ran men with hammers in their hands to beat the strange world into a shape that was familiar to the eye, to bludgeon away all the strangeness, their mouths fringed with nails so they resembled steel-toothed carnivores, spitting them into their swift hands as they hammered up frame cottages and scuttled over roofs with shingles to blot out the eerie stars, and fit green shades to pull against the night. And when the carpenters had hurried on, the women came in with flowerpots and chintz and pans and set up a kitchen clamor to cover the silence that Mars made waiting outside the door and the shaded window.

In six months a dozen small towns had been laid down upon the naked planet, filled with sizzling neon tubes and yellow electric bulbs. In all, some ninety thousand people came to Mars, and more, on Earth, were packing their grips. . . .

August 2002: NIGHT MEETING

BEFORE GOING on up into the blue hills, Tomás Gomez stopped for gasoline at the lonely station.

"Kind of alone out here, aren't you, Pop?" said Tomás.

The old man wiped off the windshield of the small truck. "Not bad."

"How do you like Mars, Pop?"

"Fine. Always something new. I made up my mind when I came here last year I wouldn't expect nothing, nor ask nothing, nor be surprised at nothing. We've got to forget Earth and how things were. We've got to look at what we're in here, and how *different* it is. I get a hell of a lot of fun out of just the weather here. It's *Martian* weather. Hot as hell daytimes, cold as hell nights. I get a big kick out of the different flowers and different rain. I came to Mars to retire and I wanted to retire in a place where everything is different. An old man needs to have things different. Young people don't want to talk to him, other old people bore hell out of him. So I thought the best thing for me is a place so different that all you got to do is open your eyes and you're entertained. I got this gas station. If business picks up too much, I'll move on back to some other old highway that's not so busy, where I can earn just enough to live on and still have time to feel the *different* things here."

"You got the right idea, Pop," said Tomás, his brown hands idly on the wheel. He was feeling good. He had been working in one of the new colonies for ten days straight and now he had two days off and was on his way to a party.

"I'm not surprised at anything any more," said the old man. "I'm just looking. I'm just experiencing. If you can't take Mars for what she is, you might as well go back to Earth. Everything's crazy up here, the soil, the air, the canals, the natives (I never saw any yet, but I hear they're around), the clocks. Even my clock acts funny. Even *time* is crazy up here. Sometimes I feel I'm here all by myself, no one else on the whole damn planet. I'd take bets on it. Sometimes I feel about eight years old, my body squeezed up and everything else tall. Jesus, it's just the place for an old man. Keeps me alert and keeps me happy. You know what Mars is? It's like a thing I got for Christmas seventy years ago—don't know if you ever had one—they called them kaleidoscopes, bits of crystal and cloth and beads and pretty junk. You held it up to the sunlight and looked in through at it, and it took your breath away. All the patterns! Well, that's Mars. Enjoy it. Don't ask it to be nothing else but what it is. Jesus, you know that highway right there, built by the Martians, is over sixteen centuries old and still in good condition? That's one dollar and fifty cents, thanks and good night."

Tomás drove off down the ancient highway, laughing quietly.

It was a long road going into darkness and hills and he held to the wheel, now and again reaching into his lunch bucket and taking out a piece of candy. He had been driving steadily for an hour, with no other car on the road, no light, just the road going under, the hum, the roar, and Mars out there, so quiet. Mars was always quiet, but quieter tonight than any other. The deserts and empty seas swung by him, and the mountains against the stars.

There was a smell of Time in the air tonight. He smiled and turned the fancy in his mind. There was a thought. What did Time smell like? Like dust and clocks and people. And if you wondered what Time sounded like it sounded like water running in a dark cave and voices crying and dirt dropping down upon hollow box lids, and rain. And, going further, what did Time look like? Time looked like snow dropping silently into a black room or it looked like a silent film in an ancient theater, one hundred billion faces falling like those New Year balloons, down and down into nothing. That was how Time smelled and looked and sounded. And tonight—Tomás shoved a hand into the wind outside the truck—tonight you could almost *touch* Time.

He drove the truck between hills of Time. His neck prickled and he sat up, watching ahead.

He pulled into a little dead Martian town, stopped the engine, and let the silence come in around him. He sat, not breathing, looking out at the white buildings in the moonlight. Uninhabited for centuries. Perfect, faultless, in ruins, yes, but perfect, nevertheless.

He started the engine and drove on another mile or more before stopping again, climbing out, carrying his lunch bucket, and walking to a little promontory where he could look back at that dusty city. He opened his thermos and poured himself a cup of coffee. A night bird flew by. He felt very good, very much at peace.

Perhaps five minutes later there was a sound. Off in the hills, where the ancient highway curved, there was a motion, a dim light, and then a murmur.

Tomás turned slowly with the coffee cup in his hand.

And out of the hills came a strange thing.

It was a machine like a jade-green insect, a praying mantis, delicately rushing through the cold air, indistinct, countless green diamonds winking over its body, and red jewels that glittered with multifaceted eyes. Its six legs fell upon the ancient highway with the sounds of a sparse rain which dwindled away, and from the back of the machine a Martian with melted gold for eyes looked down at Tomás as if he were looking into a well.

Tomás raised his hand and thought Hello! automatically but did not move his lips, for this *was* a Martian. But Tomás had swum in blue rivers on Earth, with strangers passing on the road, and eaten in strange houses with strange people, and his weapon had always been his smile. He did not carry a gun. And he did not feel the need of one now, even with the little fear that gathered about his heart at this moment.

The Martian's hands were empty too. For a moment they looked across the cool air at each other.

It was Tomás who moved first.

"Hello!" he called.

"Hello!" called the Martian in his own language.

They did not understand each other.

"Did you say hello?" they both asked.

"What did you say?" they said, each in a different tongue.

They scowled.

"Who are you?" said Tomás in English.

"What are you doing here?" In Martian; the stranger's lips moved.

"Where are you going?" they said, and looked bewildered.

"I'm Tomás Gomez."

"I'm Muhe Ca."

Neither understood, but they tapped their chests with the words and then it became clear.

And then the Martian laughed. "Wait!" Tomás felt his head touched, but no hand had touched him. "There!" said the Martian in English. "That is better!"

"You learned my language, so quick!"

"Nothing at all!"

They looked, embarrassed with a new silence, at the steaming coffee he had in one hand.

"Something different?" said the Martian, eying him and the coffee, referring to them both, perhaps.

"May I offer you a drink?" said Tomás.

"Please."

The Martian slid down from his machine.

A second cup was produced and filled, steaming. Tomás held it out.

Their hands met and—like mist—fell through each other.

"Jesus Christ!" cried Tomás, and dropped the cup.

"Name of the Gods!" said the Martian in his own tongue.

"Did you see what happened?" they both whispered.

They were very cold and terrified.

The Martian bent to touch the cup but could not touch it.

"Jesus!" said Tomás.

"Indeed." The Martian tried again and again to get hold of the cup, but could not. He stood up and thought for a moment, then took a knife from his belt. "Hey!" cried Tomás. "You misunderstand, catch!" said the Martian, and tossed it. Tomás cupped his hands. The knife fell through his flesh. It hit the ground. Tomás bent to pick it up but could not touch it, and he recoiled, shivering.

Now he looked at the Martian against the sky.

"The stars!" he said.

"The stars!" said the Martian, looking, in turn, at Tomás.

The stars were white and sharp beyond the flesh of the Martian, and they were sewn into his flesh like scintillas swallowed into the thin, phosphorescent membrane of a gelatinous sea fish. You could see stars flickering like violet eyes in the Martian's stomach and chest, and through his wrists, like jewelry.

"I can see through you!" said Tomás.

"And I through you!" said the Martian, stepping back.

Tomás felt of his own body and, feeling the warmth, was reassured, *I* am real, he thought.

The Martian touched his own nose and lips. "*I* have flesh," he said, half aloud. "*I* am alive."

Tomás stared at the stranger. "And if *I* am real, then *you* must be dead."

"No, you!"

"A ghost!"

"A phantom!"

They pointed at each other, with starlight burning in their limbs like daggers and icicles and fireflies, and then fell to judging their limbs again, each finding himself intact, hot, excited, stunned, awed, and the other, ah yes, that other over there, unreal, a ghostly prism flashing the accumulated light of distant worlds.

I'm drunk, thought Tomás. I won't tell anyone of this tomorrow, no, no.

They stood there on the ancient highway, neither of them moving.

"Where are you from?" asked the Martian at last.

"Earth."

"What is that?"

"There." Tomás nodded to the sky.

"When?"

"We landed over a year ago, remember?"

"No."

"And all of you were dead, all but a few. You're rare, don't you *know* that?"

"That's not true."

"Yes, dead. I saw the bodies. Black, in the rooms, in the houses, dead. Thousands of them."

"That's ridiculous. We're *alive*!"

"Mister, you're invaded, only you don't know it. You must have escaped."

"I haven't escaped; there was nothing to escape. What do you mean? I'm on my way to a festival now at the canal, near the Eniall Mountains. I was there last night. Don't you see the city there?" The Martian pointed.

Tomás looked and saw the ruins. "Why, that city's been dead thousands of years."

The Martian laughed. "Dead. I slept there yesterday!"

"And I was in it a week ago and the week before that, and I just drove through it now, and it's a heap. See the broken pillars?"

"Broken? Why, I see them perfectly. The moonlight helps. And the pillars are upright."

"There's dust in the streets," said Tomás.

"The streets are clean!"

"The canals are empty right there."

"The canals are full of lavender wine!"

"It's dead."

"It's alive!" protested the Martian, laughing more now. "Oh, you're quite wrong. See all the carnival lights? There are beautiful boats as slim as women, beautiful women as slim as boats, women the color of sand, women with fire flowers in their hands. I can see them, small, running in the streets there. That's where I'm going now, to the festival; we'll float on the waters all night long; we'll sing, we'll drink, we'll make love. Can't you *see* it?"

"Mister, that city is dead as a dried lizard. Ask any of our party. Me, I'm on my way to Green City tonight; that's the new colony we just raised over near Illinois Highway. You're mixed up. We brought in a million board feet of Oregon lumber and a couple dozen tons of good steel nails and hammered together two of the nicest little villages you ever saw. Tonight we're warming one of them. A couple rockets are coming in from Earth, bringing our wives and girl friends. There'll be barn dances and whisky——"

The Martian was now disquieted. "You say it is over *that* way?"

"There are the rockets." Tomás walked him to the edge of the hill and pointed down. "See?"

"No."

"Damn it, there they *are*! Those long silver things."

"No."

Now Tomás laughed. "You're blind!"

"I see very well. You are the one who does not see."

"But you see the new *town*, don't you?"

"I see nothing but an ocean, and water at low tide."

"Mister, that water's been evaporated for forty centuries."

"Ah, now, now, that *is* enough."

"It's true, I tell you."

The Martian grew very serious. "Tell me again. You do not see the city the way I describe it? The pillars very white, the boats very slender, the festival lights—oh, I see them *clearly*! And listen! I can hear them singing. It's no space away at all."

Tomás listened and shook his head. "No."

"And I, on the other hand," said the Martian, "cannot see what you describe. Well."

Again they were cold. An ice was in their flesh.

"Can it be . . . ?"

"What?"

"You say 'from the sky'?"

"Earth."

"Earth, a name, nothing," said the Martian. "*But* . . . as I came up the pass an hour ago . . ." He touched the back of his neck. "I felt . . ."

"Cold?"

"Yes."

"And now?"

"Cold again. Oddly. There was a thing to the light, to the hills, the road," said the Martian. "I felt the strangeness, the road, the light, and for a moment I felt as if I were the last man alive on this world. . . ."

"So did I!" said Tomás, and it was like talking to an old and dear friend, confiding, growing warm with the topic.

The Martian closed his eyes and opened them again. "This can only mean one thing. It has to do with Time. Yes. You are a figment of the Past!"

"No, you are from the Past," said the Earth Man, having had time to think of it now.

"You are so *certain*. How can you prove who is from the Past, who from the Future? What year is it?"

"Two thousand and one!"

"What does that mean to *me*?"

Tomás considered and shrugged. "Nothing."

"It is as if I told you that it is the year 4462853 S.E.C. It is nothing and more than nothing! Where is the clock to show us how the stars stand?"

"But the ruins prove it! They prove that *I* am the Future, *I* am alive, *you* are dead!"

"Everything in me denies this. My heart beats, my stomach hungers, my mouth thirsts. No, no, not dead, not alive, either of us. More alive than anything else. Caught between is more like it. Two strangers passing in the night, that is it. Two strangers passing. Ruins, you say?"

"Yes. You're afraid?"

"Who wants to see the Future, who *ever* does? A man can face the Past, but to think—the pillars *crumbled*, you say? And the sea empty, and the canals dry, and the maidens dead, and the flowers withered?" The Martian was silent, but then he looked on ahead. "But there they are. I see them. Isn't that enough for me? They wait for me now, no matter *what* you say."

And for Tomás the rockets, far away, waiting for *him*, and the town and the women from Earth. "We can never agree," he said.

"Let us agree to disagree," said the Martian. "What does it matter who is Past or Future, if we are both alive, for what follows will follow, tomorrow or in ten thousand years. How do you know that those temples are not the temples of your own civilization one hundred centuries from now, tumbled and broken? You do not know. Then don't ask. But the night *is* very short. There go the festival fires in the sky, and the birds."

Tomás put out his hand. The Martian did likewise in imitation.

Their hands did not touch; they melted through each other.

"Will we meet again?"

"Who knows? Perhaps some other night."

"I'd like to go with you to that festival."

"And I wish I might come to your new town, to see this ship you speak of, to see these men, to hear all that has happened."

"Good-by," said Tomás.

"Good night."

The Martian rode his green metal vehicle quietly away into the hills. The Earth Man turned his truck and drove it silently in the opposite direction.

"Good lord, what a dream that was," sighed Tomás, his

hands on the wheel, thinking of the rockets, the women, the raw whisky, the Virginia reels, the party.

How strange a vision was that, thought the Martian, rushing on, thinking of the festival, the canals, the boats, the women with golden eyes, and the songs.

The night was dark. The moons had gone down. Starlight twinkled on the empty highway where now there was not a sound, no car, no person, nothing. And it remained that way all the rest of the cool dark night.

October 2002: THE SHORE

MARS WAS a distant shore, and the men spread upon it in waves. Each wave different, and each wave stronger. The first wave carried with it men accustomed to spaces and coldness and being alone, the coyote and cattlemen, with no fat on them, with faces the years had worn the flesh off, with eyes like nailheads, and hands like the material of old gloves, ready to touch anything. Mars could do nothing to them, for they were bred to plains and prairies as open as the Martian fields. They came and made things a little less empty, so that others would find courage to follow. They put panes in hollow windows and lights behind the panes.

They were the first men.

Everyone knew who the first women would be.

The second men should have traveled from other countries with other accents and other ideas. But the rockets were American and the men were American and it stayed that way, while Europe and Asia and South America and Australia and the islands watched the Roman candles leave them behind. The rest of the world was buried in war or the thoughts of war.

So the second men were Americans also. And they came from the cabbage tenements and subways, and they found much rest and vacation in the company of the silent men from the tumbleweed states who knew how to use silences so they filled you up with peace after long years crushed in tubes, tins, and boxes in New York.

And among the second men were men who looked, by their eyes, as if they were on their way to God. . . .

November 2002: THE FIRE BALLOONS

FIRE EXPLODED over summer night lawns. You saw sparkling faces of uncles and aunts. Sky-rockets fell up in the brown shining eyes of cousins on the porch, and the cold charred sticks thumped down in dry meadows far away.

The Most Reverend Father Joseph Daniel Peregrine opened his eyes. What a dream: he and his cousins with their fiery play at his grandfather's ancient Ohio home so many years ago!

He lay listening to the great hollow of the church, the other cells where other Fathers lay. Had they, too, on the eve of the flight of the rocket *Crucifix*, lain with memories of the Fourth of July? Yes. This was like those breathless Independence dawns when you waited for the first concussion and rushed out on the dewy sidewalks, your hands full of loud miracles.

So here they were, the Episcopal Fathers, in the breathing dawn before they pin-wheeled off to Mars, leaving their incense through the velvet cathedral of space.

"Should we go at all?" whispered Father Peregrine. "Shouldn't we solve our own sins on Earth? Aren't we running from our lives here?"

He arose, his fleshy body, with its rich look of strawberries, milk, and steak, moving heavily.

"Or is it sloth?" he wondered. "Do I dread the journey?"

He stepped into the needle-spray shower.

"But I shall take you to Mars, body." He addressed himself. "Leaving old sins here. And on to Mars to find new sins?" A delightful thought, almost. Sins no one had ever thought of. Oh, he himself had written a little book: *The Problem of Sin on Other Worlds*, ignored as somehow not serious enough by his Episcopal brethren.

Only last night, over a final cigar, he and Father Stone had talked of it.

"On Mars sin might appear as virtue. We must guard against virtuous acts there that, later, might be found to be sins!" said Father Peregrine, beaming. "How exciting! It's been centuries since so much adventure has accompanied the prospect of being a missionary!"

"*I* will recognize sin," said Father Stone bluntly, "*even* on Mars."

"Oh, we priests pride ourselves on being litmus paper, changing color in sin's presence," retorted Father Peregrine, "but what if Martian chemistry is such we do not color *at all*! If there are new senses on Mars, you must admit the possibility of unrecognizable sin."

"If there is no malice aforethought, there is no sin or punishment for same—the Lord assures us that," Father Stone replied.

"On Earth, yes. But perhaps a Martian sin might inform the subconscious of its evil, telepathically, leaving the conscious mind of man free to act, seemingly without malice! What *then*?"

"What *could* there be in the way of new sins?"

Father Peregrine leaned heavily forward. "Adam *alone* did not sin. Add Eve and you add temptation. Add a second man and you make adultery possible. With the addition of sex or people, you add sin. If men were harmless, they could not strangle with their hands. You would not have that particular sin of murder. Add arms, and you add the possibility of a new violence. Amoebas cannot sin because they reproduce by fission. They do not covet wives or murder each other. Add sex to amoebas, add arms and legs, and you would have murder and adultery. Add an arm or leg or person, or take away each, and you add or subtract possible evil. On Mars, what if there are five new senses, organs, invisible limbs we can't conceive of—then mightn't there be five new *sins*?"

Father Stone gasped. "I think you *enjoy* this sort of thing!"

"I keep my mind alive, Father; just alive, is all."

"Your mind's always juggling, isn't it?—mirrors, torches, plates."

"Yes. Because sometimes the Church seems like those posed circus tableaux where the curtain lifts and men, white, zinc-oxide, talcum-powder statues, freeze to represent abstract Beauty. Very wonderful. But I hope there will always be room for me to dart about among the statues, don't you, Father Stone?"

Father Stone had moved away. "I think we'd better go to bed. In a few hours we'll be jumping up to see your *new* sins, Father Peregrine."

* * *

The rocket stood ready for the firing.

The Fathers walked from their devotions in the chilly morning, many a fine priest from New York or Chicago or Los Angeles—the Church was sending its best—walking across town to the frosty field. Walking, Father Peregrine remembered the Bishop's words:

"Father Peregrine, you will captain the missionaries, with Father Stone at your side. Having chosen you for this serious task, I find my reasons deplorably obscure, Father, but your pamphlet on planetary sin did not go unread. You are a flexible man. And Mars is like that uncleaned closet we have neglected for millenniums. Sin has collected there like bric-a-brac. Mars is twice Earth's age and has had double the number of Saturday nights, liquor-baths, and eye-poppings at women as naked as white seals. When we open that closet door, things will fall on us. We need a quick, flexible man—one whose mind can dodge. Anyone a little dogmatic might break in two. I feel you'll be resilient. Father, the job is yours."

The Bishop and the Fathers knelt.

The blessing was said and the rocket given a little shower of holy water. Arising, the Bishop addressed them:

"I know you will go with God, to prepare the Martians for the reception of His Truth. I wish you all a *thoughtful* journey."

They filed past the Bishop, twenty men, robes whispering, to deliver their hands into his kind hands before passing into the cleansed projectile.

"I wonder," said Father Peregrine, at the last moment, "if Mars is hell? Only waiting for our arrival before it bursts into brimstone and fire."

"Lord, be with us," said Father Stone.

The rocket moved.

Coming out of space was like coming out of the most beautiful cathedral they had ever seen. Touching Mars was like touching the ordinary pavement outside the church five minutes after having *really* known your love for God.

The Fathers stepped gingerly from the steaming rocket and knelt upon Martian sand while Father Peregrine gave thanks.

"Lord, we thank Thee for the journey through Thy rooms. And, Lord, we have reached a new land, so we must have new eyes. We shall hear new sounds, and must needs have new ears. And there will be new sins, for which we ask the gift of better and firmer and purer hearts. Amen."

They arose.

And here was Mars like a sea under which they trudged in the guise of submarine biologists, seeking life. Here the territory of hidden sin. Oh, how carefully they must all balance, like gray feathers, in this new element, afraid that walking *itself* might be sinful; or breathing, or simple fasting!

And here was the mayor of First Town come to meet them with outstretched hand. "What can I do for you, Father Peregrine?"

"We'd like to know about the Martians. For only if we know about them can we plan our church intelligently. Are they ten feet tall? We will build large doors. Are their skins blue or red or green? We must know when we put human figures in the stained glass so we may use the right skin color. Are they heavy? We will build sturdy seats for them."

"Father," said the mayor, "I don't think you should worry about the Martians. There are two races. One of them is pretty well dead. A few are in hiding. And the second race—well, they're not quite human."

"Oh?" Father Peregrine's heart quickened.

"They're round luminous globes of light, Father, living in those hills. Man or beast, who can say? But they act intelligently, I hear." The mayor shrugged. "Of course, they're not men, so I don't think you'll care——"

"On the contrary," said Father Peregrine swiftly. "Intelligent, you say?"

"There's a story. A prospector broke his leg in those hills and would have died there. The blue spheres of light came at him. When he woke, he was down on a highway and didn't know how he got there."

"Drunk," said Father Stone.

"That's the story," said the mayor. "Father Peregrine, with most of the Martians dead, and only these blue spheres, I frankly think you'd be better off in First City. Mars is opening up. It's a frontier now, like in the old days on Earth, out West, and in Alaska. Men are pouring up there. There're a couple thousand black Irish mechanics and miners and day laborers in First Town who need saving, because there're too many wicked women came with them, and too much ten-century-old Martian wine——"

Father Peregrine was gazing into the soft blue hills.

Father Stone cleared his throat. "Well, Father?"

Father Peregrine did not hear. "Spheres of blue *fire*?"

"Yes, Father."

"Ah," Father Peregrine sighed.

"Blue balloons." Father Stone shook his head. "A circus!"

Father Peregrine felt his wrists pounding. He saw the little frontier town with raw, fresh-built sin, and he saw the hills, old with the oldest and yet perhaps an even newer (to him) sin.

"Mayor, could your black Irish laborers cook one more day in hellfire?"

"I'd turn and baste them for you, Father."

Father Peregrine nodded to the hills. "Then that's where we'll go."

There was a murmur from everyone.

"It would be so simple," explained Father Peregrine, "to go into town. I prefer to think that if the Lord walked here and people said, 'Here is the beaten path,' He would reply, "Show me the weeds. I will *make* a path.'"

"But——"

"Father Stone, think how it would weigh upon us if we passed sinners by and did not extend our hands."

"But globes of fire!"

"I imagine man looked funny to other animals when we first appeared. Yet he has a soul, for all his homeliness. Until we prove otherwise, let us assume that these fiery spheres have souls."

"All right," agreed the mayor, "but you'll be back to town."

"We'll see. First, some breakfast. Then you and I, Father Stone, will walk alone into the hills. I don't want to frighten those fiery Martians with machines or crowds. Shall we have breakfast?"

The Fathers ate in silence.

* * *

At nightfall Father Peregrine and Father Stone were high in the hills. They stopped and sat upon a rock to enjoy a moment of relaxation and waiting. The Martians had not as yet appeared, and they both felt vaguely disappointed.

"I wonder——" Father Peregrine mopped his face. "Do you think if we called 'Hello!' they might answer?"

"Father Peregrine, won't you ever be serious?"

"Not until the good Lord is. Oh, don't look so terribly shocked, please. The Lord is not serious. In fact, it is a little hard to know just what else He is except loving. And love has to do with humor, doesn't it? For you cannot love someone unless you put up with him, can you? And you cannot put up with someone constantly unless you can laugh at him. Isn't that true? And certainly we are ridiculous little animals wallowing in the fudge-bowl, and God must love us all the more because we appeal to his humor."

"*I* never thought of God as humorous," said Father Stone.

"The Creator of the platypus, the camel, the ostrich, and man? Oh, come now!" Father Peregrine laughed.

But at this instant, from among the twilight hills, like a series of blue lamps lit to guide their way, came the Martians.

Father Stone saw them first. "Look!"

Father Peregrine turned, and the laughter stopped in his mouth.

The round blue globes of fire hovered among the twinkling stars, distantly trembling.

"Monsters!" Father Stone leaped up.

But Father Peregrine caught him. "Wait!"

"We should've gone to town!"

"No, listen, look!" pleaded Father Peregrine.

"I'm afraid!"

"Don't be. This is God's work!"

"The devil's!"

"No, now, quiet!" Father Peregrine gentled him and they crouched with the soft blue light on their upturned faces as the fiery orbs drew near.

And again, Independence Night, thought Father Peregrine, tremoring. He felt like a child back in those July Fourth evenings, the sky blowing apart, breaking into powdery stars and burning sound, the concussions jingling house-windows like the ice on a thousand thin ponds. The aunts, uncles, cousins crying, "Ah!" as to some celestial physician. The summer sky colors. And the Fire Balloons, lit by an indulgent grandfather, steadied in his massively tender hands. Oh, the memory of those lovely Fire Balloons, softly lighted, warmly billowed bits of tissue, like insect wings, lying like folded wasps in boxes, and last of all, after the day of riot and fury, at long last from their boxes, delicately unfolded, blue, red, white, patriotic—the Fire Balloons! He saw the dim faces of dear relatives long dead and mantled with moss as Grandfather lit the tiny candle and let the warm air breathe up to form the balloon plumply luminous in his hands, a shining vision which they held, reluctant to let it go; for, once released, it was yet another year gone from life, another Fourth, another bit of Beauty vanished. And then up, up, still up through the warm summer night constellations, the Fire Balloons had drifted, while red-white-and-blue eyes followed them, wordless, from family porches. Away into deep Illinois country, over night rivers and sleeping mansions, the Fire Balloons dwindled, forever gone. . . .

Father Peregrine felt tears in his eyes. Above him the Martians, not one but a *thousand* whispering Fire Balloons, it seemed, hovered. Any moment he might find his long-dead and blessed grandfather at his elbow, staring up at Beauty.

But it was Father Stone.

"Let's go, please, Father!"

"I must speak to them." Father Peregrine rustled forward, not knowing what to say, for what had he ever said to the Fire Balloons of time past except with his mind: *you are beautiful, you are beautiful,* and that was not enough now. He could only lift his heavy arms and call upward, as he had often wished to call after the enchanted Fire Balloons, "Hello!"

But the fiery spheres only burned like images in a dark mirror. They seemed fixed, gaseous, miraculous, forever.

"We come with God," said Father Peregrine to the sky.

"Silly, silly, silly." Father Stone chewed the back of his hand. "In the name of God, Father Peregrine, stop!"

But now the phosphorescent spheres blew away into the hills. In a moment they were gone.

Father Peregrine called again, and the echo of his last cry shook the hills above. Turning, he saw an avalanche shake out dust, pause, and then, with a thunder of stone wheels, crash down the mountain upon them.

"Look what you've done!" cried Father Stone.

Father Peregrine was almost fascinated, then horrified. He turned, knowing they could run only a few feet before the rocks crushed them into ruins. He had time to whisper, *Oh, Lord!* and the rocks fell!

"Father!"

They were separated like chaff from wheat. There was a blue shimmering of globes, a shift of cold stars, a roar, and then they stood upon a ledge two hundred feet away watching the spot where their bodies would have been buried under tons of stone.

The blue light evaporated.

The two Fathers clutched each other. "What happened?"

"The blue fires lifted us!"

"We ran, *that* was it!"

"No, the globes saved us."

"They couldn't!"

"They *did*."

The sky was empty. There was a feel as if a great bell had just stopped tolling. Reverberations lingered in their teeth and marrows.

"Let's get away from here. You'll have us killed."

"I haven't feared death for a good many years, Father Stone."

"We've proved nothing. Those blue lights ran off at the first cry. It's useless."

"No." Father Peregrine was suffused with a stubborn wonder. "Somehow, they saved us. That proves they have souls."

"It proves only that they *might* have saved us. Everything was confused. We might have escaped, ourselves."

"They are not animals, Father Stone. Animals do not save lives, especially of strangers. There is mercy and compassion here. Perhaps, tomorrow, we may prove more."

"Prove what? How?" Father Stone was immensely tired now; the outrage to his mind and body showed on his stiff face. "Follow them in helicopters, reading chapter and verse? They're not human. They haven't eyes or ears or bodies like ours."

"But I feel something about them," replied Father Peregrine. "I know a great revelation is at hand. They saved us. They *think*. They had a choice; let us live or die. That proves free will!"

Father Stone set to work building a fire, glaring at the sticks in his hands, choking on the grey smoke. "I myself will open a convent for nursling geese, a monastery for sainted swine, and I shall build a miniature apse in a microscope so that paramecia can attend services and tell their beads with their flagella."

"Oh, Father Stone."

"I'm sorry." Father Stone blinked redly across the fire. "But this is like blessing a crocodile before he chews you up. You're risking the entire missionary expedition. We belong in First Town, washing liquor from men's throats and perfume off their hands!"

"Can't you recognize the human in the inhuman?"

"I'd much rather recognize the inhuman in the human."

"But if I prove these things sin, know sin, know a moral life, have free will and intellect, Father Stone?"

"That will take much convincing."

The night grew rapidly cold and they peered into the fire to find their wildest thoughts, while eating biscuits and berries, and soon they were bundled for sleep under the chiming stars. And just before turning over one last time Father Stone, who had been thinking for many minutes to find something to bother Father Peregrine about, stared into the soft pink charcoal bed and said, "Not Adam and Eve on Mars. No original sin. Maybe the Martians live in a state of God's grace. Then we can go back down to town and start work on the Earth Men."

Father Peregrine reminded himself to say a little prayer for Father Stone, who got so mad and who was now being vindictive, God help him. "Yes, Father Stone, but the Martians killed some of our settlers. That's sinful. There must have been an Original Sin and a Martian Adam and Eve. We'll find them. Men are men, unfortunately, no matter what their shape, and inclined to sin."

But Father Stone was pretending sleep.

Father Peregrine did not shut his eyes.

Of course they couldn't let these Martians go to hell, could they? With a compromise to their consciences, could they go back to the new colonial towns, those towns so full of sinful gullets and women with scintilla eyes and white oyster bodies rollicking in beds and with lonely laborers? Wasn't that the place for the Fathers? Wasn't this trek into the hills merely a personal whim? Was he really thinking of God's Church, or was he quenching the thirst of a spongelike curiosity? Those blue round globes of St. Anthony's fire—how they burned in his mind! What a challenge, to find the man behind the mask, the human behind the inhuman. Wouldn't he be proud if he could say, even to his secret self, that he had converted a rolling huge pool-table full of fiery spheres! What a sin of pride! Worth doing penance for! But then one did many prideful things out of Love, and he loved the Lord so much and was so happy at it that he wanted everyone else to be happy too.

The last thing he saw before sleep was the return of the blue fires, like a flight of burning angels silently singing him to his worried rest.

The blue round dreams were still there in the sky when Father Peregrine awoke in the early morning.

Father Stone slept like a stiff bundle, quietly. Father Peregrine watched the Martians floating and watching him. They were human—he *knew* it. But he must prove it or face a dry-mouthed, dry-eyed Bishop telling him kindly to step aside.

But how to prove humanity if they hid in the high vaults of the sky? How to bring them nearer and provide answers to the many questions?

"They saved us from the avalanche."

Father Peregrine arose, moved off among the rocks, and began to climb the nearest hill until he came to a place where a cliff dropped sheerly to a floor two hundred feet below. He was choking from his vigorous climb in the frosty air. He stood, getting his breath.

"If I fell from here, it would surely kill me."

He let a pebble drop. Moments later it clicked on the rocks below.

"The Lord would never forgive me."

He tossed another pebble.

"It wouldn't be suicide, would it, if I did it out of Love . . . ?"

He lifted his gaze to the blue spheres. "But first, another try." He called to them: "Hello, hello!"

The echoes tumbled upon each other, but the blue fires did not blink or move.

He talked to them for five minutes. When he stopped, he peered down and saw Father Stone, still indignantly asleep, below in the little camp.

"I must prove everything." Father Peregrine stepped to the cliff rim. "I am an old man. I am not afraid. Surely the Lord will understand that I am doing this for Him?"

He drew a deep breath. All his life swam through his eyes, and he thought, In a moment shall I die? I am afraid that I love living much too much. But I love things more.

And, thinking thus, he stepped off the cliff.

He fell.

"Fool!" he cried. He tumbled end over end. "You were wrong!" The rocks rushed up at him, and he saw himself dashed on them and sent to glory. "Why did I do this thing?" But he knew the answer, and an instant later was calm as he fell. The wind roared around him and the rocks hurtled to meet him.

And then there was a shift of stars, a glimmering of blue light, and he felt himself surrounded by blueness and suspended. A moment later he was deposited, with a gentle bump, upon the rocks, where he sat a full moment, alive, and touching himself, and looking up at those blue lights that had withdrawn instantly.

"You saved me!" he whispered. "You wouldn't let me die. You knew it was wrong."

He rushed over to Father Stone, who still lay quietly asleep. "Father, Father, wake up!" He shook him and brought him round. "Father, they saved me!"

"Who saved you?" Father Stone blinked and sat up.

Father Peregrine related his experience.

"A dream, a nightmare; go back to sleep," said Father Stone irritably. "You and your circus balloons."

"But I was awake!"

"Now, now, Father, calm yourself. There now."

"You don't believe me? Have you a gun? Yes, there, let me have it."

"What are you going to do?" Father Stone handed over

the small pistol they had brought along for protection against snakes or other similar and unpredictable animals.

Father Peregrine seized the pistol. "I'll prove it!"

He pointed the pistol at his own hand and fired.

"Stop!"

There was a shimmer of light, and before their eyes the bullet stood upon the air, poised an inch from his open palm. It hung for a moment, surrounded by a blue phosphorescence. Then it fell, hissing, into the dust.

Father Peregrine fired the gun three times—at his hand, at his leg, at his body. The three bullets hovered, glittering, and, like dead insects, fell at their feet.

"You see?" said Father Peregrine, letting his arm fall, and allowing the pistol to drop after the bullets. "They know. They understand. They are not animals. They think and judge and live in a moral climate. What animal would save me from myself like this? There is no animal would do that. Only another man, Father. Now, do you believe?"

Father Stone was watching the sky and the blue lights, and now, silently, he dropped to one knee and picked up the warm bullets and cupped them in his hand. He closed his hand tight.

The sun was rising behind them.

"I think we had better go down to the others and tell them of this and bring them back up here," said Father Peregrine.

By the time the sun was up, they were well on their way back to the rocket.

Father Peregrine drew the round circle in the center of the blackboard.

"This is Christ, the son of the Father."

He pretended not to hear the other Fathers' sharp intake of breath.

"This is Christ, in all his Glory," he continued.

"It looks like a geometry problem," observed Father Stone.

"A fortunate comparison, for we deal with symbols here. Christ is no less Christ, you must admit, in being represented by a circle or a square. For centuries the cross has symbolized his love and agony. So this circle will be the Martian Christ. This is how we shall bring him to Mars."

The Fathers stirred fretfully and looked at each other.

"You, Brother Mathias, will create, in glass, a replica of this circle, a globe, filled with bright fire. It will stand upon the altar."

"A cheap magic trick," muttered Father Stone.

Father Peregrine went on patiently: "On the contrary. We are giving them God in an understandable image. If Christ had come to us on Earth as an octopus, would we have accepted him readily?" He spread his hands. "Was it then a cheap magic trick of the Lord's to bring us Christ through Jesus, in man's shape? After we bless the church we build here and sanctify its altar and this symbol, do you think Christ would refuse to inhabit the shape before us? You know in your hearts he would not refuse."

"But the body of a soulless animal!" said Brother Mathias.

"We've already gone over that, many times since we returned this morning, Brother Mathias. These creatures saved us from the avalanche. They realized that self-destruction was sinful, and prevented it, time after time. Therefore we must build a church in the hills, live with them, to find their own special ways of sinning, the alien ways, and help them to discover God."

The Fathers did not seem pleased at the prospect.

"Is it because they are so odd to the eye?" wondered Father Peregrine. "But what is a shape? Only a cup for the blazing soul that God provides us all. If tomorrow I found that sea-lions suddenly possessed free will, intellect, knew when not to sin, knew what life was and tempered justice with mercy and life with love, then I would build an undersea cathedral. And if the sparrows should, miraculously, with God's will gain everlasting souls tomorrow, I would freight a church with helium and take after them, for all souls, in any shape, if they have free will and are aware of their sins, will burn in hell unless given their rightful communions. I would not let a Martian sphere burn in hell, either, for it is a sphere only in mine eyes. When I close my eyes it stands before me, an intelligence, a love, a soul—and I must not deny it."

"But that glass globe you wish placed on the altar," protested Father Stone.

"Consider the Chinese," replied Father Peregrine imperturbably.

"What sort of Christ do Christian Chinese worship? An oriental Christ, naturally. You've all seen oriental Nativity scenes. How is Christ dressed? In Eastern robes. Where does he walk? In Chinese settings of bamboo and misty mountain and crooked tree. His eyelids taper, his cheekbones rise. Each country, each race adds something to our Lord. I am reminded of the Virgin of Guadalupe, to whom all Mexico pays its love. Her skin? Have you noticed the paintings of her? A dark skin, like that of her worshipers. Is that blasphemy? Not at all. It is not logical that men should accept a God, no matter how real, of another color. I often wonder why our missionaries do well in Africa, with a snow-white Christ. Perhaps because white is a sacred color, in albino, or any other form, to the African tribes. Given time, mightn't Christ darken there too? The form does not matter. Content is everything. We cannot expect these Martians to accept an alien form. We shall give them Christ in their own image."

"There's a flaw in your reasoning, Father," said Father Stone. "Won't the Martians suspect us of hypocrisy? They will realize that we don't worship a round, globular Christ, but a man with limbs and a head. How do we explain the difference?"

"By showing there is none. Christ will fill any vessel that is offered. Bodies or globes, he is there, and each will worship the same thing in a different guise. What is more, we must *believe* in this globe we give the Martians. We must believe in a shape which is meaningless to us as to form. This spheroid *will* be Christ. And we must remember that we ourselves, and the shape of our Earth Christ, would be meaningless, ridiculous, a squander of material to these Martians."

Father Peregrine laid aside his chalk. "Now let us go into the hills and build our church."

The Fathers began to pack their equipment.

The church was not a church, but an area cleared of rocks, a plateau on one of the low mountains, its soil smoothed and brushed, and an altar established whereon Brother Mathias placed the fiery globe he had constructed.

At the end of six days of work the "church" was ready.

"What shall we do with this?" Father Stone tapped an iron bell they had brought along, "What does a bell mean to *them*?"

"I imagine I brought it for our own comfort," admitted

Father Peregrine. "We need a few familiarities. This church seems so little like a church. And we feel somewhat absurd here—even I; for it is something new, this business of converting the creatures of another world. I feel like a ridiculous play-actor at times. And then I pray to God to lend me strength."

"Many of the Fathers are unhappy. Some of them joke about all this, Father Peregrine."

"I know. We'll put this bell in a small tower, for their comfort, anyway."

"What about the organ?"

"We'll play it at the first service, tomorrow."

"But, the Martians——"

"I know. But again, I suppose, for our own comfort, our own music. Later we may discover theirs."

They arose very early on Sunday morning and moved through the coldness like pale phantoms, rime tinkling on their habits; covered with chimes they were, shaking down showers of silver water.

"I wonder if it *is* Sunday here on Mars?" mused Father Peregrine, but seeing Father Stone wince, he hastened on, "It might be Tuesday or Thursday—who knows? But no matter. My idle fancy. It's Sunday to us. Come."

The Fathers walked into the flat, wide area of the "church" and knelt, shivering and blue-lipped.

Father Peregrine said a little prayer and put his cold fingers to the organ keys. The music went up like a flight of pretty birds. He touched the keys like a man moving his hands among the weeds of a wild garden, startling up great soarings of beauty into the hills.

The music calmed the air. It smelled the fresh smell of morning. The music drifted into the mountains and shook down mineral powders in a dusty rain.

The Fathers waited.

"Well, Father Peregrine." Father Stone eyed the empty sky where the sun was rising, furnace-red. "I don't see our friends."

"Let me try again." Father Peregrine was perspiring.

He built an architecture of Bach, stone by exquisite stone, raising a music cathedral so vast that its farthest chancels were in Nineveh, its farthest dome at St. Peter's left hand. The music stayed and did not crash in ruin when it was over, but partook of a series of white clouds and was carried away among other lands.

The sky was still empty.

"They'll come!" But Father Peregrine felt the panic in his chest, very small, growing. "Let us pray. Let us ask them to come. They read minds; they *know*."

The Fathers lowered themselves yet again, in rustlings and whispers. They prayed.

And to the East, out of the icy mountains of seven o'clock on Sunday morning or perhaps Thursday morning or maybe Monday morning on Mars, came the soft, fiery globes.

They hovered and sank and filled the area around the shivering priests. "Thank you; oh, thank you, Lord." Father Peregrine shut his eyes tight and played the music, and when it was done he turned and gazed upon his wondrous congregation.

And a voice touched his mind, and the voice said:

"We have come for a little while."

"You may stay," said Father Peregrine.

"For a little while only," said the voice quietly. "We have come to tell you certain things. We should have spoken sooner. But we had hoped that you might go on your way if left alone."

Father Peregrine started to speak, but the voice hushed him.

"We are the Old Ones," the voice said, and it entered him like a blue gaseous flare and burned in the chambers of his head. "We are the old Martians, who left our marble cities and went into the hills, forsaking the material life we had lived. So very long ago we became these things that we now are. Once we were men, with bodies and legs and arms such as yours. The legend has it that one of us, a good man, discovered a way to free man's soul and intellect, to free him of bodily ills and melancholies, of deaths and transfigurations, of ill humors and senilities, and so we took on the look of lightning and blue fire and have lived in the winds and skies and hills forever after that, neither prideful nor arrogant, neither rich nor poor, passionate nor cold. We have lived apart from those we left behind, those other men of this world, and how we came to be has been forgotten, the process lost; but we shall never die, nor do harm. We have put away the sins of the body and live in God's grace. We covet no other property; we have no property. We do not steal, nor kill, nor lust, nor hate. We live in happiness.

We cannot reproduce; we do not eat or drink or make war. All the sensualities and childishnesses and sins of the body were stripped away when our bodies were put aside. We have left sin behind, Father Peregrine, and it is burned like the leaves in the autumn wicker, and it is gone like the soiled snow of an evil winter, and it is gone like the sexual flowers of a red-and-yellow spring, and it is gone like the panting nights of hottest summer, and our season is temperate and our clime is rich in thought."

Father Peregrine was standing now, for the voice touched him at such a pitch that it almost shook him from his senses. It was an ecstasy and a fire washing through him.

"We wish to tell you that we appreciate your building this place for us, but we have no need of it, for each of us is a temple unto himself and we need no place wherein to cleanse ourselves. Forgive us for not coming to you sooner, but we are separate and apart and have talked to no one for ten thousand years, nor have we interfered in any way with the life of this planet. It has come into your mind now that we are the lilies of the field; we toil not, neither do we spin. You are right. And so we suggest that you take the parts of this temple into your own new cities and there cleanse them. For, rest assured, we are happy, and at peace."

The Fathers were on their knees in the vast blue light, and Father Peregrine was down, too, and they were weeping, and it did not matter that their time had been wasted; it did not matter to them at all.

The blue spheres murmured and began to rise once more, on a breath of cool air.

"May I"—cried Father Peregrine, not daring to ask, eyes closed—"may I come again, someday, that I may learn from you?"

The blue fires blazed. The air trembled.

Yes. Someday he might come again. Someday.

And then the Fire Balloons blew away and were gone, and he was like a child, on his knees, tears streaming from his eyes, crying to himself, "Come back, come back!" And at any moment Grandfather might lift him and carry him upstairs to his bedroom in a long-gone Ohio town. . . .

* * *

They filed down out of the hills at sunset. Looking back, Father Peregrine saw the blue fires burning. No, he thought, we couldn't build a church for the likes of you. You're Beauty itself. What church could compete with the fireworks of the pure soul?

Father Stone moved in silence beside him. And at last he spoke:

"The way I see it is there's a Truth on every planet. All parts of the Big Truth. On a certain day they'll all fit together like the pieces of a jigsaw. This has been a shaking experience. I'll never doubt again, Father Peregrine. For this Truth here is as true as Earth's Truth, and they lie side by side. And we'll go on to other worlds, adding the sum of the parts of the Truth until one day the whole Total will stand before us like the light of a new day."

"That's a lot, coming from you, Father Stone."

"I'm sorry now, in a way, we're going down to the town to handle our own kind. Those blue lights now. When they settled about us, and that *voice* . . ." Father Stone shivered.

Father Peregrine reached out to take the other's arm. They walked together.

"And you know," said Father Stone finally, fixing his eyes on Brother Mathias, who strode ahead with the glass sphere tenderly carried in his arms, that glass sphere with the blue phosphorus light glowing forever inside it, "you know, Father Peregrine, that globe there——"

"Yes?"

"It's Him. It *is* Him, after all."

Father Peregrine smiled, and they walked down out of the hills towards the new town.

February 2003: INTERIM

THEY BROUGHT in fifteen thousand lumber feet of Oregon pine to build Tenth City, and seventy-nine thousand feet of California redwood and they hammered together a clean, neat little town by the edge of the stone canals. On Sunday nights you could see red, blue, and green stained-glass light in the churches and hear the voices singing the numbered hymns. "We will now sing 79. We will now sing 94." And in certain houses you heard the hard clatter of a typewriter, the novelist at work; or the scratch of a pen, the poet at work; or no sound at all, the former beachcomber at work. It was as if, in many ways, a great earthquake had shaken loose the roots and cellars of an Iowa town, and then, in an instant, a whirlwind twister of Oz-like proportions had carried the entire town off to Mars to set it down without a bump. . . .

April 2003: THE MUSICIANS

THE BOYS would hike far out into the Martian country. They carried odorous paper bags into which from time to time upon the long walk they would insert their noses to inhale the rich smell of the ham and mayonnaised pickles, and to listen to the liquid gurgle of the orange soda in the warming bottles. Swinging their grocery bags full of clean watery green onions and odorous liverwurst and red catsup and white bread, they would dare each other on past the limits set by their stern mothers. They would run, yelling:

"First one there gets to kick!"

They hiked in summer, autumn, or winter. Autumn was most fun, because then they imagined, like on Earth, they were scuttering through autumn leaves.

They would come like a scatter of jackstones on the marble flats beside the canals, the candy-cheeked boys with blue-agate eyes, panting onion-tainted commands to each other. For now that they had reached the dead, forbidden town it was no longer a matter of "Last one there's a girl!" or "First one gets to play Musician!" Now the dead town's doors lay wide and they thought they could hear the faintest crackle, like autumn leaves, from inside. They would hush themselves forward, by each other's elbows, carrying sticks, remembering their parents had told them, "Not there! No, to none of the old towns! Watch where you hike. You'll get the beating of your life when you come home. We'll check your shoes!"

And there they stood in the dead city, a heap of boys, their hiking lunches half devoured, daring each other in shrieky whispers.

"Here goes nothing!" And suddenly one of them took off, into the nearest stone house, through the door, across the living room, and into the bedroom where, without half looking, he would kick about, thrash his feet, and the black leaves would fly through the air, brittle, thin as tissue cut from midnight sky. Behind him would race six others, and the first boy there would be the Musician, playing the white xylophone bones beneath the outer covering of black flakes. A great skull would roll to view, like a snowball; they shouted! Ribs, like spider legs, plangent as a dull harp, and then the black flakes of mortality blowing all about them in their scuffling dance; the boys pushed and heaved and fell in the leaves, in the death that had turned the dead to flakes and dryness, into a game played by boys whose stomachs gurgled with orange pop.

And then out of one house into another, into seventeen houses, mindful that each of the towns in its turn was being burned clean of its horrors by the Firemen, antiseptic warriors with shovels and bins, shoveling away at the ebony tatters and peppermint-stick bones, slowly but assuredly separating the terrible from the normal; so they must play very hard, these boys, the Firemen would soon be here!

Then, luminous with sweat, they gnashed at their last sandwiches. With a final kick, a final marimba concert, a final autumnal lunge through leaf stacks, they went home.

Their mothers examined their shoes for black flakelets which, when discovered, resulted in scalding baths and fatherly beatings.

By the year's end the Firemen had raked the autumn leaves and white xylophones away, and it was no more fun.

May 2003: THE WILDERNESS

OH, THE Good Time has come at last—

It was twilight and Janice and Leonora packed steadily in their summer house, singing songs, eating little, and holding to each other when necessary. But they never glanced at the window where the night gathered deep and the stars came out bright and cold.

"Listen!" said Janice.

A sound like a steamboat down the river, but it was a rocket in the sky. And beyond that—banjos playing? No, only the summer night crickets in this year 2003. Ten thousand sounds breathed through the town and the weather. Janice, head bent, listened. Long, long ago, 1849, this very street had breathed the voices of ventriloquists, preachers, fortune-tellers, fools, scholars, gamblers, gathered at this self-same Independence, Missouri. Waiting for the moist earth to bake and the great tidal grasses to come up heavy enough to hold the weight of their carts, their wagons, their indiscriminate destinies, and their dreams.

Oh, the Good Time has come at last,
To Mars we are a-going, Sir,
Five Thousand Women in the sky,
That's quite a springtime sowing, Sir!

"That's an old Wyoming song," said Leonora. "Change the words and it's fine for 2003."

Janice lifted a matchbox of food pills, calculating the totals of things carried in those high-axled, tall-bedded wagons. For each man, each woman, incredible tonnages! Hams, bacon slabs, sugar, salt, flour, dried fruits, pilot bread, citric acid, water, ginger, pepper—a list as big as the land! Yet here, today, pills that fit a wristwatch fed you not from Fort Laramie to Hangtown, but all across a wilderness of stars.

Janice threw wide the closet door and almost screamed.

Darkness and night and all the spaces between the stars looked out at her.

Long years ago two things had happened. Her sister had

locked her, shrieking, in a closet. And, at a party, playing hide-and-seek, she had run through the kitchen and into a long dark hall. But it wasn't a hall. It was an unlit stair-well, a swallowing blackness. She had run out upon empty air. She had pedalled her feet, screamed, and fallen! Fallen in midnight blackness. Into the cellar. It took a long while, a heartbeat, to fall. And she had smothered in that closet a long, long time without daylight, without friends, no one to hear her screamings. Away from everything, locked in darkness. Falling in darkness. Shrieking!

The two memories.

Now, with the closet door wide, with darkness like a velvet shroud hung before her to be stroked by a trembling hand, with the darkness like a black panther breathing there, looking at her with unlit eyes, the two memories rushed out. Space and a falling. Space and being locked away, screaming. She and Leonora working steadily, packing, being careful not to glance out the window at the frightening Milky Way and the vast emptiness. Only to have the long-familiar closet, with its private night, remind them at last of their destiny.

This was how it would be, out there, sliding towards the stars, in the night, in the great hideous black closet, screaming, but no one to hear. Falling forever among meteor clouds and godless comets. Down the elevator shaft. Down the nightmare coal-chute into nothingness.

She screamed. None of it came out of her mouth. It collided upon itself in her chest and head. She screamed. She slammed the closet door! She lay against it! She felt the darkness breathe and yammer at the door and she held it tight, eyes watering. She stood there a long time, until the trembling vanished, watching Leonora work. And the hysteria, thus ignored, drained away and away, and at last was gone. A wristwatch ticked, with a clean sound of normality, in the room.

"Sixty *million* miles." She moved at last to the window as if it were a deep well. "I can't believe that men on Mars, tonight, are building towns, waiting for us."

"The only thing to believe is catching our Rocket tomorrow."

Janice raised a white gown like a ghost in the room.

"Strange, strange. To marry—on another world."

"Let's go to bed."

"No! The call comes at midnight. I couldn't sleep, thinking how to tell Will I've decided to take the Mars Rocket. Oh, Leonora, think of it, my voice travelling sixty million miles on the light-phone to him. I changed my mind so quick—I'm scared!"

"Our *last* night on Earth."

Now they really knew and accepted it, now the knowledge had found them out. They were going away, and they might never come back. They were leaving the town of Independence in the state of Missouri on the continent of North America, surrounded by one ocean which was the Atlantic and another the Pacific, none of which could be put in their travelling cases. They had shrunk from this final knowledge. Now it was facing them. And they were struck numb.

"Our children, they won't be Americans, or Earth people at all. We'll all be Martians, the rest of our lives."

"I don't want to go!" cried Janice, suddenly.

The panic rose in her, with ice and fire.

"I'm afraid! The space, the darkness, the rocket, the meteors! *Everything* gone! Why should I go out there!"

Leonora took hold of her shoulders and held her close, rocking her. "It's a New World. It's like the old days. The men first and the women following."

"Why, why should I go, tell me!"

"Because," said Leonora, at last, quietly, seating her on the bed, "Will is up there."

His name was good to hear. Janice quieted.

"These men make it so hard," said Leonora. "Used to be if a woman ran two hundred miles after a man it was something. Then they made it a thousand miles. And now they put a whole universe between us. But that can't stop us, can it?"

"I'm afraid I'll be a fool on the Rocket."

"I'll be a fool with you." Leonora got up. "Now, let's walk around town, let's see everything one last time."

Janice stared out at the town. "Tomorrow night, this'll all be here, but we won't. People'll wake up, eat, work, sleep, wake again, but we won't know it, and they'll never miss us."

Leonora and Janice moved around each other as if they couldn't find the door.

"Come on."

They opened the door, switched off the lights, stepped out, and shut the door behind them.

In the sky there was a great coming-in and coming-in. Vast flowering motions, huge whistlings and whirlings, snowstorms falling. Helicopters, white flakes, dropping quietly. From west and east and north and south the women were arriving, arriving, their hearts neatly tissue-papered in their suitcases. Through all of the night sky you saw helicopters blizzard down. The hotels were full, private homes were making accommodations, tent cities rose in meadows and pastures like strange, ugly flowers, and the town and the country were warm with more than summer tonight. Warm with women's pink faces and the sunburnt faces of new men watching the sky. Beyond the hills rockets tried their fire, and a sound like a giant organ pressed upon all its keys at once, shuddered every crystal window and every hidden bone. You felt it in your jaw, your toes, your fingers, a shivering.

Leonora and Janice sat in the drugstore among strange women.

"You ladies look pretty, but you sure look sad," said the soda fountain man.

"Two chocolate malteds." Leonora smiled for both of them, as if Janice were mute.

They gazed at the chocolate drink as if it was a rare museum painting. Malts would be scarce, for many years, on Mars.

Janice fussed in her purse and took out an envelope, reluctantly, and laid it on the marble counter.

"This is from Will to me. It came in the rocket mail two days ago. It was this that made up my mind for me, made me decide to go. I didn't tell you. I want you to see it now. Go ahead, read the note."

Leonora shook the note out of the envelope and read it aloud:

"'Dear Janice: This is *our* house if you decide to come to Mars. Will.'"

Leonora tapped the envelope again and a color photograph dropped out, glistening, on the counter. It was a picture of a house, a dark, mossy, ancient, caramel-brown, comfortable house with red flowers and green cool ferns bordering it, and a disreputably hairy ivy on the porch.

"But, Janice!"

"What?"

"This is a picture of *your* house, here on Earth, here on Elm Street!"

"No. Look close."

And they looked again, together, and on both sides of the comfortable dark house and behind it was scenery that was not Earth scenery. The soil was a strange color of violet, and the grass was the faintest bit red, and the sky glowed like a grey diamond, and a strange crooked tree grew to one side, looking like an old woman with crystals in her white hair.

"That's the house Will's built for me," said Janice, "on Mars. It helps to look at it. All yesterday, when I had the chance, alone, and was most afraid and panicky, I took out this picture and looked at it."

They both gazed at the dark comfortable house sixty million miles away, familiar but unfamiliar, old but new, a yellow light shining in the right front parlor window.

"That man Will," said Leonora, nodding her head, "knows just what he's doing."

They finished their drinks. Outside, a vast warm crowd of strangers wandered by and the "snow" fell steadily in the summer sky.

They bought many silly things to take with them, bags of lemon candy, glossy women's magazines, fragile perfumes (let the take-off weighers worry later about what constitutes "essential load"); and then they walked out into the town and, not minding the expense, rented two belted jackets—two small machines that refused gravity and imitated the butterfly—and touched the delicate controls and felt themselves whispered like white blossom petals over the town. "Anywhere," said Leonora, "anywhere at all."

They let the wind blow them where it would, they let the wind take them through the night of summer apple trees and the night of warm preparation, over the lovely town, over the houses of childhood and other days, over schools and avenues, over creeks and meadows and farms so familiar that each grain of wheat was a golden coin. They blew as leaves must blow before the threat of a fire-wind, with warning whispers and summer lightning crackling among the folded hills. They saw the milk-dust country roads where not so long ago they had drifted in moonlit helicopters in great whorls of sound spiraling down to touch beside cool night streams with the young men who were now gone.

They floated in an immense sigh above a town already made remote by the little space between themselves and the earth, a town receding behind them in a black river and coming up in a tidal wave of lights and color ahead, untouchable and a dream now, already smeared in their eyes with nostalgia, with a panic of memory that began before the thing was gone.

Blown quietly, eddying, they gazed secretly at a hundred faces of dear friends they were leaving behind, the lamplit people held and framed by windows which slid by on the wind, it seemed; all of Time breathing them along. There was no tree they did not examine for old confessions of love carved and whittled there, no sidewalk they did not skim across as over fields of mica-snow. For the first time they knew that their town was beautiful and the lonely lights and the ancient bricks beautiful, and they both felt their eyes grow large with the beauty of this feast they were giving themselves. All floated upon an evening carousel, with fitful drifts of music wafting up here and there, and voices calling and murmuring from houses that were whitely haunted by television.

The two women passed like needles, sewing one tree to the next with their perfume. Their eyes were too full, and yet they kept putting away each detail, each shadow, each solitary oak and elm, each passing car upon the small snaking streets below, until not only their eyes but their heads and then their hearts were too full.

I feel like I'm dead, thought Janice, and in the graveyard on a spring night and everything alive but me and everyone moving and ready to go on with life without me. It's like I felt each spring when I was very young, passing the graveyard and weeping for them because they were dead and it didn't seem fair, on nights as soft as that, that I was alive. I was guilty of living. And now here, tonight, I feel they have taken me from the graveyard and let me go above the town just once more to see what it is like to be living, to be a town and a people, before they slam the black door on me again.

Softly, softly, like two white paper lanterns on a night wind, the women moved over their lifetime and their past, and over the meadows where the tent cities glowed and the highways where supply trucks would be clustered and running until dawn. They hovered above it all for a long time.

The courthouse clock was booming eleven-forty-five when they came like spider webs floating from the stars, touching on the moonlit pavement before Janice's old house. The city was asleep, and Janice's house waited for them to come in searching for *their* sleep, which was not there.

"Is this *us*, here?" asked Janice. "Janice Smith and Leonora Holmes, in the year 2003?"

"Yes."

Janice licked her lips and stood straight. "I wish it was some other year."

"1492? 1612?" Leonora sighed and the wind in the trees sighed with her, moving away. "It's always Columbus Day or Plymouth Rock Day, and I'll be darned if I know what we women can do about it."

"Be old maids."

"Or, do just what we're doing."

They opened the door of the warm night house, the sounds of the town dying slowly in their ears. As they shut the door, the phone began to ring.

"The call!" cried Janice, running.

Leonora came into the bedroom after her and already Janice had the receiver up and was saying, "Hello, hello!" And the operator in a far city was readying the immense apparatus which would tie two worlds together, and the two women waited, one sitting and pale, the other standing but just as pale, bent towards her.

There was a long pause, full of stars and time, a waiting pause not unlike the last three years for all of them. And now the moment had arrived, and it was Janice's turn to phone through millions upon millions of miles of meteors and comets, running away from the yellow sun which might boil or burn her words or scorch the meaning from them, her voice like a silver needle through everything, in stitches of talking, across the big night, reverberating from the moons of Mars and rushing on. And then her voice found its way to a man in a room in a city there on another world, five minutes by radio away. And her message was this:

"Hello, Will. This is Janice!"

She swallowed.

"They say I haven't much time. A minute."

She closed her eyes.

"I want to talk slow but they say talk fast and get it all in. So, I want to say—I've decided. I will come up there. I'll go on the Rocket tomorrow. I *will* come up there to you, after all. And I love you. I hope you can hear me. I love you. It's been so long . . ."

Her voice motioned on its way to that unseen world. Now, with her message sent, the words said, she wanted to call them back, to censor, to rearrange them, to make a prettier sentence, a fairer explanation of her soul. But already the words were hung between planets and if, by some cosmic radiation, they could have been illuminated, caught fire in vaporous wonder there, her love would have lit a dozen worlds and startled the night side of Earth into a premature dawn, she thought. Now the words were not hers at all, they belonged to space, they belonged to no one until they arrived, and they were travelling at 186,000 miles a second to their target.

What will he say to me? What will he say back in *his* minute of time? she wondered. She fussed with and twisted the watch on her wrist, and the light-phone receiver on her ear crackled and space talked to her with electrical jigs and dances and audible auroras.

"Has he replied?" whispered Leonora.

"Shhh!" said Janice, bending, as if sick.

Then the voice came through space from him.

"I hear him!" cried Janice.

"What does he say?"

The voice called out from Mars and took itself through the places where there was no sunrise or sunset, but always the night with a sun in the middle of the blackness. And somewhere between Mars and Earth everything of the message was lost, perhaps in a sweep of electrical gravity rushing by on the floodtides of a meteor, or interfered with by a rain of silver meteors. In any event, the small words and the unimportant words of the message were washed away. And his voice came through saying only one word:

". . . love . . ."

After that, there was the huge night again and the sound of stars turning and suns whispering to themselves and the sound of her heart, like another world in space, filling her earphones.

"Did you *hear* him?" asked Leonora.

Janice could only nod.

"What did he say, what did he say?" cried Leonora.

But Janice could not tell anyone, it was much too good to tell. She sat, listening to that one word again and again, as her memory played it back to her. She sat listening, while Leonora took the phone away from her without her knowing it, and put it back upon its hook.

Then they were in bed and the lights out and the night wind blowing through the rooms a smell of the long journey in darkness and stars, and their voices talking of tomorrow, and the days after tomorrow which would not be days at all, but day-nights of timeless time; their voices faded away into sleep or wakeful thinking, and Janice lay alone in her bed.

Is this how it was over a century ago, she wondered, when the women, the night before, lay ready for sleep, or not ready, in the small towns of the East, and heard the sound of horses in the night and the creak of the Conestoga wagons ready to go, and the brooding of oxen under the trees, and the cry of children already lonely before their time? All the sounds of arrivals and departures into the deep forests and fields, the blacksmiths working in their own red hells through midnight? And the smell of bacons and hams ready for the journeying, and the heavy feel of the wagons like ships foundering with goods, with water in the wooden kegs to tilt and slop across prairies, and the chickens hysterical in their slung-beneath-the-wagon crates, and the dogs running out to the wilderness ahead and, fearful, running back with a look of empty space in their eyes? Is this then how it was so long ago? On the rim of the precipice, on the edge of the cliff of stars. In their time the smell of buffalo, and in our time the smell of the Rocket. Is this then how it was?

And she decided, as sleep assumed the dreaming for her, that yes, yes indeed, very much so, irrevocably, this was as it had always been and would forever continue to be.

June 2003: WAY IN THE MIDDLE OF THE AIR

"DID YOU hear about it?"

"About what?"

"The niggers, the niggers!"

"What about 'em?"

"Them leaving, pulling out, going away; did you hear?"

"What you mean, pulling out? How can they do that?"

"They can, they will, they are."

"Just a couple?"

"Every single one here in the South!"

"No."

"Yes!"

"I got to see that. I don't believe it. Where they going —Africa?"

A silence.

"Mars."

"You mean the *planet* Mars?"

"That's right."

The men stood up in the hot shade of the hardware porch. Someone quit lighting a pipe. Somebody else spat out into the hot dust of noon.

"They can't leave, they can't do that."

"They're doing it, anyways."

"Where'd you hear this?"

"It's everywhere, on the radio a minute ago, just come through."

Like a series of dusty statues, the men came to life.

Samuel Teece, the hardware proprietor, laughed uneasily. "I *wondered* what happened to Silly. I sent him on my bike an hour ago. He ain't come back from Mrs. Bordman's yet. You think that black fool just pedaled off to Mars?"

The men snorted.

"All I say is, he better bring back my bike. I don't take stealing from no one, by God."

"Listen!"

The men collided irritably with each other, turning.

Far up the street the levee seemed to have broken. The black warm waters descended and engulfed the town. Between the blazing white banks of the town stores, among the tree silences, a black tide flowed. Like a kind of summer molasses, it poured turgidly forth upon the cinnamon-dusty road. It surged slow, slow, and it was men and women and horses and barking dogs, and it was little boys and girls. And from the mouths of the people partaking of this tide came the sound of a river. A summer-day river going somewhere, murmuring and irrevocable. And in that slow, steady channel of darkness that cut across the white glare of day were touches of alert white, the eyes, the ivory eyes staring ahead, glancing aside, as the river, the long and endless river, took itself from old channels into a new one. From various and uncountable tributaries, in creeks and brooks of color and motion, the parts of this river had joined, become one mother current, and flowed on. And brimming the swell were things carried by the river: grandfather clocks chiming, kitchen clocks ticking, caged hens screaming, babies wailing; and swimming among the thickened eddies were mules and cats, and sudden excursions of burst mattress springs floating by, insane hair stuffing sticking out, and boxes and crates and pictures of dark grandfathers in oak frames—the river flowing it on while the men sat like nervous hounds on the hardware porch, too late to mend the levee, their hands empty.

Samuel Teece wouldn't believe it. "Why, hell, where'd they get the transportation? How they goin' to get to Mars?"

"Rockets," said Grandpa Quartermain.

"All the damn-fool things. Where'd they get rockets?"

"Saved their money and built them."

"I never heard about it."

"Seems these niggers kept it secret, worked on the rockets all themselves, don't know where—in Africa, maybe."

"Could they *do* that?" demanded Samuel Teece, pacing about the porch. "Ain't there a law?"

"It ain't as if they're declarin' war," said Grandpa quietly.

"Where do they get off, God damn it, workin' in secret, plottin'?" shouted Teece.

"Schedule is for all this town's niggers to gather out by Loon Lake. Rockets be there at one o'clock, pick 'em up, take 'em to Mars."

"Telephone the governor, call out the militia," cried Teece. "They should've given notice!"

"Here comes your woman, Teece."

The men turned again.

As they watched, down the hot road in the windless light first one white woman and then another arrived, all of them with stunned faces, all of them rustling like ancient papers. Some of them were crying, some were stern. All came to find their husbands. They pushed through barroom swing doors, vanishing. They entered cool, quiet groceries. They went in at drug shops and garages. And one of them, Mrs. Clara Teece, came to stand in the dust by the hardware porch, blinking up at her stiff and angry husband as the black river flowed full behind her.

"It's Lucinda, Pa; you got to come home!"

"I'm not comin' home for no damn darkie!"

"She's leaving. What'll I do without her?"

"Fetch for yourself, maybe. I won't get down on my knees to stop her."

"But she's like a family member," Mrs. Teece moaned.

"Don't shout! I won't have you blubberin' in public this way about no goddamn——"

His wife's small sob stopped him. She dabbed at her eyes. "I kept telling her, 'Lucinda,' I said, 'you stay on and I raise your pay, and you get *two* nights off a week, if you want,' but she just looked set! I never seen her so set, and I said, 'Don't you *love* me, Lucinda?' and she said yes, but she had to go because that's the way it was, is all. She cleaned the house and dusted it and put luncheon on the table and then she went to the parlor door and—and stood there with two bundles, one by each foot, and shook my hand and said, 'Good-by, Mrs. Teece.' And she went out the door. And there was her luncheon on the table, and all of us too upset to even eat it. It's still there now, I know; last time I looked it was getting cold."

Teece almost struck her. "God damn it, Mrs. Teece, you get the hell home. Standin' there makin' a sight of yourself!"

"But, Pa . . ."

He strode away into the hot dimness of the store. He came back out a few seconds later with a silver pistol in his hand.

His wife was gone.

The river flowed black between the buildings, with a rustle and a creak and a constant whispering shuffle. It was a very quiet thing, with a great certainty to it; no laughter, no wildness, just a steady, decided, and ceaseless flow.

Teece sat on the edge of his hardwood chair. "If one of 'em so much as laughs, by Christ, I'll kill 'em."

The men waited.

The river passed quietly in the dreamful noon.

"Looks like you goin' to have to hoe your own turnips, Sam," Grandpa chuckled.

"I'm not bad at shootin' white folks neither." Teece didn't look at Grandpa. Grandpa turned his head away and shut up his mouth.

"Hold on there!" Samuel Teece leaped off the porch. He reached up and seized the reins of a horse ridden by a tall Negro man. "You, Belter, come down off there!"

"Yes, sir." Belter slid down.

Teece looked him over. "Now, just what you think you're doin'?"

"Well, Mr. Teece . . ."

"I reckon you think you're goin', just like that song—what's the words? 'Way up in the middle of the air'; ain't *that* it?"

"Yes, sir." The Negro waited.

"You recollect you owe me fifty dollars, Belter?"

"Yes, sir."

"You tryin' to sneak out? By God, I'll horsewhip you!"

"All the excitement, and it slipped my mind, sir."

"It slipped his mind." Teece gave a vicious wink at his men on the hardware porch. "God damn, mister, you know what you're goin' to do?"

"No, sir."

"You're stayin' here to work out that fifty bucks, or my name ain't Samuel W. Teece." He turned again to smile confidently at the men in the shade.

Belter looked at the river going along the street, that dark river flowing and flowing between the shops, the dark river on wheels and horses and in dusty shoes, the dark river from which he had been snatched on his journey. He began to shiver. "Let me go, Mr. Teece. I'll send your money from up there, I promise!"

"Listen, Belter." Teece grasped the man's suspenders like two harp strings, playing them now and again, contemptuously, snorting at the sky, pointing one bony finger straight at God. "Belter, you know anything about what's up there?"

"What they tells me."

"What they tells him! Christ! Hear that? What they tells him!" He swung the man's weight by his suspenders, idly, ever so casual, flicking a finger in the black face. "Belter, you fly up and up like a July Fourth rocket, and bang! There you are, cinders, spread all over space. Them crackpot scientists, they don't know nothin', they kill you all off!"

"I don't care."

"Glad to hear that. Because you know what's up on that planet Mars? There's monsters with big raw eyes like mushrooms! You seen them pictures on those future magazines you buy at the drugstore for a dime, ain't you? Well! Them monsters jump up and suck marrow from your bones!"

"I don't care, don't care at all, don't care." Belter watched the parade slide by, leaving him. Sweat lay on his dark brow. He seemed about to collapse.

"And it's cold up there; no air, you fall down, jerk like a fish, gaspin', dyin', stranglin', stranglin' and dyin'. You *like* that?"

"Lots of things I don't like, sir. Please, sir, let me go. I'm late."

"I'll let you go when I'm *ready* to let you go. We'll just talk here polite, until I say you can leave, and you know it damn well. You want to travel, do you? Well, Mister Way up in the Middle of the Air, you get the hell home and work out that fifty bucks you owe me! Take you two months to do that!"

"But if I work it out, I'll miss the rocket, sir!"

"Ain't that a shame now?" Teece tried to look sad.

"I give you my horse, sir."

"Horse ain't legal tender. You don't move until I get my money." Teece laughed inside. He felt very warm and good.

A small crowd of dark people had gathered to hear all this. Now as Belter stood, head down, trembling, an old man stepped forward.

"Mister?"

Teece flashed him a quick look. "Well?"

"How much this man owe you, mister?"

"None of your damn business!"

The old man looked at Belter. "How much, son?"

"Fifty dollars."

The old man put out his black hands at the people around him. "There's twenty-five of you. Each give two dollars; quick now, this no time for argument."

"Here, now!" cried Teece, stiffening up, tall, tall.

The money appeared. The old man fingered it into his hat and gave the hat to Belter. "Son," he said, "you ain't missin' no rocket."

Belter smiled into the hat. "No, sir, I guess I ain't!"

Teece shouted: "You give that money back to them!"

Belter bowed respectfully, handing the money over, and when Teece would not touch it he set it down in the dust at Teece's feet. "There's your money, sir," he said. "Thank you kindly." Smiling, he gained the saddle of his horse and whipped his horse along, thanking the old man, who rode with him now until they were out of sight and hearing.

"Son of a bitch," whispered Teece, staring blind at the sun. "Son of a bitch."

"Pick up the money, Samuel," said someone from the porch.

It was happening all along the way. Little white boys, barefoot, dashed up with the news. "Them that has helps them that hasn't! And that way they *all* get free! Seen a rich man give a poor man two hundred bucks to pay off some'un! Seen some'un else give some'un else ten bucks, five bucks, sixteen, lots of that, all over, everybody!"

The white men sat with sour water in their mouths. Their eyes were almost puffed shut, as if they had been struck in their faces by wind and sand and heat.

The rage was in Samuel Teece. He climbed up on the porch and glared at the passing swarms. He waved his gun. And after a while when he had to do something, he began to shout at anyone, any Negro who looked up at him. "Bang! There's another rocket out in space!" he shouted so all could hear. "Bang! By God!" The dark heads didn't flicker or pretend to hear, but their white eyes slid swiftly over and back. "Crash! All them rockets fallin'! Screamin', dyin'! Bang! God Almighty, I'm glad *I'm* right here on old terra firma. As they says in that old joke, the more firma, the less terra! Ha, ha!"

Horses clopped along, shuffling up dust. Wagons bumbled on ruined springs.

"Bang!" His voice was lonely in the heat, trying to terrify the dust and the blazing sun sky. "Wham! Niggers all over space! Jerked outa rockets like so many minnows hit by a meteor, by God! Space fulla meteors. You know that? Sure! Thick as buckshot; powie! Shoot down them tin-can rockets like so many ducks, so many clay pipes! Ole sardine cans full of black cod! Bangin' like a stringa ladyfingers, bang, bang, bang! Ten thousand dead here, ten thousand there. Floatin' in space, around and around earth, ever and ever, cold and way out, Lord! You hear that, *you* there!"

Silence. The river was broad and continuous. Having entered all cotton shacks during the hour, having flooded all the valuables out, it was now carrying the clocks and the washboards, the silk bolts and curtain rods on down to some distant black sea.

High tide passed. It was two o'clock. Low tide came. Soon the river was dried up, the town silent, the dust settling in a film on the stores, the seated men, the tall hot trees.

Silence.

The men on the porch listened.

Hearing nothing, they extended their thoughts and their imaginations out and out into the surrounding meadows. In the early morning the land had been filled with its usual concoctions of sound. Here and there, with stubborn persistence to custom, there had been voices singing, the honey laughter under the mimosa branches, the pickaninnies rushing in clear water laughter at the creek, movements and bendings in the fields, jokes and shouts of amusement from the shingle shacks covered with fresh green vine.

Now it was as if a great wind had washed the land clean of sounds. There was nothing. Skeleton doors hung open on leather hinges. Rubber-tire swings hung in the silent air, uninhibited. The washing rocks at the river were empty, and the watermelon patches, if any, were left alone to heat their hidden liquors in the sun. Spiders started building new webs in abandoned huts; dust started to sift in from unpatched roofs in golden spicules. Here and there a fire, forgotten in the last rush, lingered and in a sudden access of strength fed upon the dry bones of some littered shack. The sound of a gentle feeding burn went up through the silenced air.

The men sat on the hardware porch, not blinking or swallowing.

"I can't figure why they left *now*. With things lookin' up. I mean, every day they got more rights. What they *want*, anyway? Here's the poll tax gone, and more and more states passin' anti-lynchin' bills, and all kinds of equal rights. What *more* they want? They make almost as good money as a white man, but there they go."

Far down the empty street a bicycle came.

"I'll be goddamned, Teece, here comes your Silly now."

The bicycle pulled up before the porch, a seventeen-year-old colored boy on it, all arms and feet and long legs and round watermelon head. He looked up at Samuel Teece and smiled.

"So you got a guilty conscience and came back," said Teece.

"No, sir, I just brought the bicycle."

"What's wrong, couldn't get it on the rocket?"

"That wasn't it, sir."

"Don't tell me what it was! Get off, you're not goin' to steal my property!" He gave the boy a push. The bicycle fell. "Get inside and start cleaning the brass."

"Beg pardon?" The boy's eyes widened.

"You heard what I said. There's guns need unpacking there, and a crate of nails just come from Natchez——"

"Mr. Teece."

"And a box of hammers need fixin'——"

"Mr. Teece, sir?"

"You *still* standin' there!" Teece glared.

"Mr. Teece, you don't mind I take the day off," he said apologetically.

"And tomorrow and day after tomorrow and the day after the day after that," said Teece.

"I'm afraid so, sir."

"You *should* be afraid, boy. Come here." He marched the boy across the porch and drew a paper out of a desk. "Remember this?"

"Sir?"

"It's your workin' paper. You signed it, there's your X right there, ain't it? Answer me."

"I didn't sign that, Mr. Teece." The boy trembled. "Anyone can make an X."

"Listen to this, Silly. Contract: 'I will work for Mr. Samuel Teece two years, starting July 15, 2001, and if intending to leave will give four weeks' notice and continue working until my position is filled.' There." Teece slapped the paper, his eyes glittering. "You cause trouble, we'll take it to court."

"I can't do that," wailed the boy, tears starting to roll down his face. "If I don't go today, I don't go."

"I know just how you feel, Silly; yes, sir, I sympathize with you, boy. But we'll treat you good and give you good food, boy. Now you just get inside and start working and forget all about that nonsense, eh, Silly? Sure." Teece grinned and patted the boy's shoulder.

The boy turned and looked at the old men sitting on the porch. He could hardly see now for his tears. "Maybe—maybe one of these gentlemen here . . ." The men looked up in the hot, uneasy shadows, looking first at the boy and then at Teece.

"You meanin' to say you think a *white man* should take your place, boy?" asked Teece coldly.

Grandpa Quartermain took his red hands off his knees. He looked out at the horizon thoughtfully and said, "Teece, what about me?"

"What?"

"I'll take Silly's job."

The porch was silent.

Teece balanced himself in the air. "Grandpa," he said warningly.

"Let the boy go. I'll clean the brass."

"Would you, would you, really?" Silly ran over to Grandpa, laughing, tears on his cheeks, unbelieving.

"Sure."

"Grandpa," said Teece, "keep your damn trap outa this."

"Give the kid a break, Teece."

Teece walked over and seized the boy's arm. "He's mine. I'm lockin' him in the back room until tonight."

"Don't, Mr. Teece!"

The boy began to sob now. His crying filled the air of the porch. His eyes were tight. Far down the street an old tin Ford was choking along, approaching, a last load of colored people in it. "Here comes my family, Mr. Teece, oh, please, please, oh God, please!"

"Teece," said one of the other men on the porch, getting up, "let him go."

Another man rose also. "That goes for me too."

"And me," said another.

"What's the use?" The men all talked now. "Cut it out, Teece."

"Let him go."

Teece felt for his gun in his pocket. He saw the men's faces. He took his hand away and left the gun in his pocket and said, "So that's how it is?"

"That's how it is," someone said.

Teece let the boy go. "All right. Get out." He jerked his hand back in the store. "But I hope you don't think you're gonna leave any trash behind to clutter my store."

"No, sir!"

"You clean everything outa your shed in back; burn it."

Silly shook his head. "I'll take it with."

"They won't let you put it on that damn rocket."

"I'll take it with," insisted the boy softly.

He rushed back through the hardware store. There were sounds of sweeping and cleaning out, and a moment later he appeared, his hands full of tops and marbles and old dusty kites and junk collected through the years. Just then the old tin Ford drove up and Silly climbed in and the door slammed. Teece stood on the porch with a bitter smile. "What you goin' to do *up there*?"

"Startin' new," said Silly, "Gonna have my *own* hardware."

"God damn it, you been learnin' my trade so you could run off and use it!"

"No, sir, I never thought one day *this'd* happen, sir, but it did. I can't help it if I learned, Mr. Teece."

"I suppose you got names for your rockets?"

They looked at their one clock on the dashboard of the car.

"Yes, sir."

"Like Elijah and the Chariot, The Big Wheel and The Little Wheel, Faith, Hope, and Charity, eh?"

"We got names for the ships, Mr. Teece."

"God the Son and the Holy Ghost, I wouldn't wonder? Say, boy, you got one named the First Baptist Church?"

"We got to leave now, Mr. Teece."

Teece laughed. "You got one named Swing Low, and another named Sweet Chariot?"

The car started up. "Good-by, Mr. Teece."

"You got one named Roll Dem Bones?"

"Good-by, mister!"

"And another called Over Jordan! Ha! Well, tote that rocket, boy, lift that rocket, boy, go on, get blown up, see if *I* care!"

The car churned off into the dust. The boy rose and cupped his hands to his mouth and shouted one last time at Teece: "Mr. Teece, Mr. Teece, what *you* goin' to do nights from now on? What you goin' to *do* nights, Mr. Teece?"

Silence. The car faded down the road. It was gone. "What in hell did he mean?" mused Teece. "What am I goin' to *do* nights?"

He watched the dust settle, and it suddenly came to him.

He remembered nights when men drove to his house, their knees sticking up sharp and their shotguns sticking up sharper, like a carful of cranes under the night trees of summer, their eyes mean. Honking the horn and him slamming his door, a gun in his hand, laughing to himself, his heart racing like a ten-year-old's, driving off down the summer-night road, a ring of hemp rope coiled on the car floor, fresh shell boxes making every man's coat look bunchy. How many nights over the years, how many nights of the wind rushing in the car, flopping their hair over their mean eyes, roaring, as they picked a tree, a good strong tree, and rapped on a shanty door!

"So *that's* what the son of a bitch meant?" Teece leaped out into the sunlight. "Come back, you bastard! What am I goin' to do nights? Why, that lousy, insolent son of a . . ."

It was a good question. He sickened and was empty. Yes. What *will* we do nights? he thought. Now *they're* gone, what? He was absolutely empty and numb.

He pulled the pistol from his pocket, checked its load.

"What you goin' to do, Sam?" someone asked.

"Kill that son of a bitch."

Grandpa said, "Don't get yourself heated."

But Samuel Teece was gone around behind the store. A moment later he drove out the drive in his open-top car. "Anyone comin' with me?"

"I'd like a drive," said Grandpa, and got up.

"Anyone else?"

Nobody replied.

Grandpa got in and slammed the door. Samuel Teece gutted the car out in a great whorl of dust. They didn't speak as they rushed down the road under the bright sky. The heat from the dry meadows was shimmering.

They stopped at a crossroad. "Which way'd they go, Grandpa?"

Grandpa squinted. "Straight on ahead, I figure."

They went on. Under the summer trees their car made a lonely sound. The road was empty, and as they drove along they began to notice something. Teece slowed the car and bent out, his yellow eyes fierce.

"God damn it, Grandpa, you see what them bastards did?"

"What?" asked Grandpa, and looked.

Where they had been carefully set down and left, in neat bundles every few feet along the empty country road, were old roller skates, a bandanna full of knickknacks, some old shoes, a cartwheel, stacks of pants and coats and ancient hats, bits of oriental crystal that had once tinkled in the wind, tin cans of pink geraniums, dishes of waxed fruit, cartons of Confederate money, washtubs, scrubboards, wash lines, soap, somebody's tricycle, someone else's hedge shears, a toy wagon, a jack-in-the-box, a stained-glass window from the Negro Baptist Church, a whole set of brake rims, inner tubes, mattresses, couches, rocking chairs, jars of cold cream, hand mirrors. None of it flung down, no, but deposited gently and with feeling, with decorum, upon the dusty edges of the road, as if a whole city had walked here with hands full, at which time a great bronze trumpet had sounded, the articles had been relinquished to the quiet dust, and one and all, the inhabitants of the earth had fled straight up into the blue heavens.

"Wouldn't burn them, they said," cried Teece angrily. "No, wouldn't burn them like I said, but had to take them along and leave them where they could see them for the last time, on the road, all together and whole. Them niggers think they're smart."

He veered the car wildly, mile after mile, down the road, tumbling, smashing, breaking, scattering bundles of paper, jewel boxes, mirrors, chairs. "There, by damn, and *there*!"

The front tire gave a whistling cry. The car spilled crazily off the road into a ditch, flinging Teece against the glass.

"Son of a bitch!" He dusted himself off and stood out of the car, almost crying with rage.

He looked at the silent, empty road. "We'll never catch them now, never, never." As far as he could see there was nothing but bundles and stacks and more bundles neatly placed like little abandoned shrines in the late day, in the warm-blowing wind.

Teece and Grandpa came walking tiredly back to the hardware store an hour later. The men were still sitting there, listening, and watching the sky. Just as Teece sat down and eased his tight shoes off someone cried, "Look!"

"I'll be *damned* if I will," said Teece.

But the others looked. And they saw the golden bobbins rising in the sky, far away. Leaving flame behind, they vanished.

In the cotton fields the wind blew idly among the snow clusters. In still farther meadows the watermelons lay, unfingerprinted, striped like tortoise cats lying in the sun.

The men on the porch sat down, looked at each other, looked at the yellow rope piled neat on the store shelves, glanced at the gun shells glinting shiny brass in their cartons, saw the silver pistols and long black metal shotguns hung high and quiet in the shadows. Somebody put a straw in his mouth. Someone else drew a figure in the dust.

Finally Samuel Teece held his empty shoe up in triumph, turned it over, stared at it, and said, "Did you notice? Right up to the very last, by God, he said 'Mister'!"

2004–05: THE NAMING OF NAMES

THEY CAME to the strange blue lands and put their names upon the lands. Here was Hinkston Creek and Lustig Corners and Black River and Driscoll Forest and Peregrine Mountain and Wilder Town, all the names of people and the things that the people did. Here was the place where Martians killed the first Earth Men, and it was Red Town and had to do with blood. And here where the second expedition was destroyed, and it was named Second Try, and each of the other places where the rocket men had set down their fiery caldrons to burn the land, the names were left like cinders, and of course there was a Spender Hill and a Nathaniel York Town. . . .

The old Martian names were names of water and air and hills. They were the names of snows that emptied south in stone canals to fill the empty seas. And the names of sealed and buried sorcerers and towers and obelisks. And the rockets struck at the names like hammers, breaking away the marble into shale, shattering the crockery milestones that named the old towns, in the rubble of which great pylons were plunged with new names: IRON TOWN, STEEL TOWN, ALUMINUM CITY, ELECTRIC VILLAGE, CORN TOWN, GRAIN VILLA, DETROIT II, all the mechanical names and the metal names from Earth.

And after the towns were built and named, the graveyards were built and named, too: Green Hill, Moss Town, Boot Hill, Bide 'a Wee; and the first dead went into their graves. . . .

But after everything was pinned down and neat and in its place, when everything was safe and certain, when the towns were well enough fixed and the loneliness was at a minimum, then the sophisticates came in from Earth. They came on parties and vacations, on little shopping trips for trinkets and photographs and the "atmosphere"; they came to study and apply sociological laws; they came with stars and badges and rules and regulations, bringing some of the red tape that had crawled across Earth like an alien weed, and letting it grow on Mars wherever it could take root. They began to plan people's lives and libraries; they began to instruct and push about the very people who had come to Mars to get away from being instructed and ruled and pushed about.

And it was inevitable that some of these people pushed back. . . .

April 2005: USHER II

"'DURING THE whole of a dull, dark, and soundless day in the autumn of the year, when the clouds hung oppressively low in the heavens, I had been passing alone, on horseback, through a singularly dreary tract of country, and at length found myself, as the shades of evening drew on, within view of the melancholy House of Usher. . . .'"

Mr. William Stendahl paused in his quotation. There, upon a low black hill, stood the House, its cornerstone bearing the inscription 2005 A.D.

Mr. Bigelow, the architect, said, "It's completed. Here's the key, Mr. Stendahl."

The two men stood together silently in the quiet autumn afternoon. Blueprints rustled on the raven grass at their feet.

"The House of Usher," said Mr. Stendahl with pleasure. "Planned, built, bought, paid for. Wouldn't Mr. Poe be *delighted*?"

Mr. Bigelow squinted. "Is it everything you wanted, sir?"

"Yes!"

"Is the color right? Is it *desolate* and *terrible*?"

"*Very* desolate, *very* terrible!"

"The walls are—*bleak*?"

"Amazingly so!"

"The tarn, is it 'black and lurid' enough?"

"Most incredibly black and lurid."

"And the sedge—we've dyed it, you know—is it the proper gray and ebon?"

"Hideous!"

Mr. Bigelow consulted his architectural plans. From these he quoted in part: "Does the whole structure cause an 'iciness, a sickening of the heart, a dreariness of thought'? The House, the lake, the land, Mr. Stendahl?"

"Mr. Bigelow, it's worth every penny! My God, it's beautiful!"

"Thank you. I had to work in total ignorance. Thank the Lord you had your own private rockets or we'd never have been allowed to bring most of the equipment through. You notice, it's always twilight here, this land, always October, barren, sterile, dead. It took a bit of doing. We killed everything. Ten thousand tons of DDT. Not a snake, frog, or Martian fly left! Twilight always, Mr. Stendahl; I'm proud of that. There are machines, hidden, which blot out the sun. It's always properly 'dreary.'"

Stendahl drank it in, the dreariness, the oppression, the fetid vapors, the whole "atmosphere," so delicately contrived and fitted. And that House! That crumbling horror, that evil lake, the fungi, the extensive decay! Plastic or otherwise, who could guess?

He looked at the autumn sky. Somewhere above, beyond, far off, was the sun. Somewhere it was the month of April on the planet Mars, a yellow month with a blue sky. Somewhere above, the rockets burned down to civilize a beautifully dead planet. The sound of their screaming passage was muffled by this dim, soundproofed world, this ancient autumn world.

"Now that my job's done," said Mr. Bigelow uneasily, "I feel free to ask what you're going to do with all this."

"With Usher? Haven't you guessed?"

"No."

"Does the name Usher mean nothing to you?"

"Nothing."

"Well, what about *this* name: Edgar Allan Poe?"

Mr. Bigelow shook his head.

"Of course," Stendahl snorted delicately, a combination of dismay and contempt. "How could I expect you to know blessed Mr. Poe? He died a long while ago, before Lincoln. All of his books were burned in the Great Fire. That's thirty years ago—1975."

"Ah," said Mr. Bigelow wisely. "One of *those*!"

"Yes, one of those, Bigelow. He and Lovecraft and Hawthorne and Ambrose Bierce and all the tales of terror and fantasy and horror and, for that matter, tales of the future were burned. Heartlessly. They passed a law. Oh, it started very small. In 1950 and '60 it was a grain of sand. They began by controlling books of cartoons and then detective books and, of course, films, one way or another, one group or another, political bias, religious prejudice, union pressures; there was always a minority afraid of something, and a great majority afraid of the dark, afraid of the future, afraid of the past, afraid of the present, afraid of themselves and shadows of themselves."

"I see."

"Afraid of the word 'politics' (which eventually became a synonym for Communism among the more reactionary elements, so I hear, and it was worth your life to use the word!), and with a screw tightened here, a bolt fastened there, a push, a pull, a yank, art and literature were soon like a great twine of taffy strung about, being twisted in braids and tied in knots and thrown in all directions, until there was no more resiliency and no more savor to it. Then the film cameras chopped short and the theaters turned dark, and the print presses trickled down from a great Niagara of reading matter to a mere innocuous dripping of 'pure' material. Oh, the word 'escape' was radical, too, I tell you!"

"Was it?"

"It was! Every man, they said, must face reality. Must face the Here and Now! Everything that was *not so* must go. All the beautiful literary lies and flights of fancy must be shot in mid-air! So they lined them up against a library wall one Sunday morning thirty years ago, in 1975; they lined them up, St. Nicholas and the Headless Horseman and Snow White and Rumpelstiltskin and Mother Goose—oh, what a wailing!—and shot them down, and burned the paper castles and the fairy frogs and old kings and the people who lived happily ever after (for of course it was a fact that *nobody* lived happily ever after!), and Once Upon A Time became No More! And they spread the ashes of the Phantom Rickshaw with the rubble of the Land of Oz; they filleted the bones of Glinda the Good and Ozma and shattered Polychrome in a spectroscope and served Jack Pumpkinhead with meringue at the Biologists' Ball! The Beanstalk died in a bramble of red tape! Sleeping Beauty awoke at the kiss of a scientist and expired at the fatal puncture of his syringe. And they made Alice drink something from a bottle which reduced her to a size where she could no longer cry 'Curiouser and curiouser,' and they gave the Looking Glass one hammer blow to smash it and every Red King and Oyster away!"

He clenched his fists. Lord, how immediate it was! His face was red and he was gasping for breath.

As for Mr. Bigelow, he was astounded at this long explosion. He blinked and at last said, "Sorry. Don't know what you're talking about. Just names to me. From what I hear, the Burning was a good thing."

"Get out!" screamed Stendahl. "You've done your job, now let me alone, you idiot!"

Mr. Bigelow summoned his carpenters and went away.

Mr. Stendahl stood alone before his House.

"Listen here," he said to the unseen rockets. "I came to Mars to get away from you Clean-Minded people, but you're flocking in thicker every day, like flies to offal. So I'm going to show you. I'm going to teach you a fine lesson for what you did to Mr. Poe on Earth. As of this day, beware. The House of Usher is open for business!"

He pushed a fist at the sky.

The rocket landed. A man stepped out jauntily. He glanced at the House, and his gray eyes were displeased and vexed. He strode across the moat to confront the small man there.

"Your name Stendahl?"

"Yes."

"I'm Garrett, Investigator of Moral Climates."

"So you finally got to Mars, you Moral Climate people? I wondered when you'd appear."

"We arrived last week. We'll soon have things as neat and tidy as Earth." The man waved an identification card irritably toward the House. "Suppose you tell me about that place, Stendahl?"

"It's a haunted castle, if you like."

"I don't like, Stendahl, I *don't* like. The sound of that word 'haunted.'"

"Simple enough. In this year of our Lord 2005 I have built a mechanical sanctuary. In it copper bats fly on electronic beams, brass rats scuttle in plastic cellars, robot skeletons dance; robot vampires, harlequins, wolves, and white phantoms, compounded of chemical and ingenuity, live here."

"That's what I was afraid of," said Garrett, smiling quietly. "I'm afraid we're going to have to tear your place down."

"I knew you'd come out as soon as you discovered what went on."

"I'd have come sooner, but we at Moral Climates wanted to be sure of your intentions before we moved in. We can have the

Dismantlers and Burning Crew here by supper. By midnight your place will be razed to the cellar. Mr. Stendahl, I consider you somewhat of a fool, sir. Spending hard-earned money on a folly. Why, it must have cost you three million dollars——"

"Four million! But, Mr. Garrett, I inherited twenty-five million when very young. I can afford to throw it about. Seems a dreadful shame, though, to have the House finished only an hour and have you race out with your Dismantlers. Couldn't you possibly let me play with my Toy for just, well, twenty-four hours?"

"You know the law. Strict to the letter. No books, no houses, nothing to be produced which in any way suggests ghosts, vampires, fairies, or any creature of the imagination."

"You'll be burning Babbitts next!"

"You've caused us a lot of trouble, Mr. Stendahl. It's in the record. Twenty years ago. On Earth. You and your library."

"Yes, me and my library. And a few others like me. Oh, Poe's been forgotten for many years now, and Oz and the other creatures. But I had my little cache. We had our libraries, a few private citizens, until you sent your men around with torches and incinerators and tore my fifty thousand books up and burned them. Just as you put a stake through the heart of Halloween and told your film producers that if they made anything at all they would have to make and remake Ernest Hemingway. My God, how many times have I seen *For Whom the Bell Tolls* done! Thirty different versions. All realistic. Oh, realism! Oh, here, oh, now, oh hell!"

"It doesn't pay to be bitter!"

"Mr. Garrett, you must turn in a full report, mustn't you?"

"Yes."

"Then, for curiosity's sake, you'd better come in and look around. It'll take only a minute."

"All right. Lead the way. And no tricks. I've a gun with me."

The door to the House of Usher creaked wide. A moist wind issued forth. There was an immense sighing and moaning, like a subterranean bellows breathing in the lost catacombs.

A rat pranced across the floor stones. Garrett, crying out, gave it a kick. It fell over, the rat did, and from its nylon fur streamed an incredible horde of metal fleas.

"Amazing!" Garrett bent to see.

An old witch sat in a niche, quivering her wax hands over some orange-and-blue tarot cards. She jerked her head and hissed through her toothless mouth at Garrett, tapping her greasy cards.

"Death!" she cried.

"Now *that's* the sort of thing I mean," said Garrett. "Deplorable!"

"I'll let you burn her personally."

"Will you, really?" Garrett was pleased. Then he frowned. "I must say you're taking this all so well."

"It was enough just to be able to create this place. To be able to say I did it. To say I nurtured a medieval atmosphere in a modern, incredulous world."

"I've a somewhat reluctant admiration for your genius myself, sir." Garrett watched a mist drift by, whispering and whispering, shaped like a beautiful and nebulous woman. Down a moist corridor a machine whirled. Like the stuff from a cotton-candy centrifuge, mists sprang up and floated, murmuring, in the silent halls.

An ape appeared out of nowhere.

"Hold on!" cried Garrett.

"Don't be afraid." Stendahl tapped the animal's black chest. "A robot. Copper skeleton and all, like the witch. See?" He stroked the fur, and under it metal tubing came to light.

"Yes." Garrett put out a timid hand to pet the thing. "But why, Mr. Stendahl, why all *this*? What obsessed you?"

"Bureaucracy, Mr. Garrett. But I haven't time to explain. The government will discover soon enough." He nodded to the ape. "All right. *Now.*"

The ape killed Mr. Garrett.

"Are we almost ready, Pikes?"

Pikes looked up from the table. "Yes, sir."

"You've done a splendid job."

"Well, I'm paid for it, Mr. Stendahl," said Pikes softly as he lifted the plastic eyelid of the robot and inserted the glass eyeball to fasten the rubberoid muscles neatly. "There."

"The spitting image of Mr. Garrett."

"What do we do with him, sir?" Pikes nodded at the slab where the real Mr. Garrett lay dead.

"Better burn him, Pikes. We wouldn't want two Mr. Garretts, would we?"

Pikes wheeled Mr. Garrett to the brick incinerator. "Good-by." He pushed Mr. Garrett in and slammed the door.

Stendahl confronted the robot Garrett. "You have your orders, Garrett?"

"Yes, sir." The robot sat up. "I'm to return to Moral Climates. I'll file a complementary report. Delay action for at least forty-eight hours. Say I'm investigating more fully."

"Right, Garrett. Good-by."

The robot hurried out to Garrett's rocket, got in, and flew away.

Stendahl turned. "Now, Pikes, we send the remainder of the invitations for tonight. I think we'll have a jolly time, don't you?"

"Considering we waited twenty years, quite jolly!"

They winked at each other.

Seven o'clock. Stendahl studied his watch. Almost time. He twirled the sherry glass in his hand. He sat quietly. Above him, among the oaken beams, the bats, their delicate copper bodies hidden under rubber flesh, blinked at him and shrieked. He raised his glass to them. "To our success." Then he leaned back, closed his eyes, and considered the entire affair. How he would savor this in his old age. This paying back of the antiseptic government for its literary terrors and conflagrations. Oh, how the anger and hatred had grown in him through the years. Oh, how the plan had taken a slow shape in his numbed mind, until that day three years ago when he had met Pikes.

Ah yes, Pikes. Pikes with the bitterness in him as deep as a black, charred well of green acid. Who was Pikes? Only the greatest of them all! Pikes, the man of ten thousand faces, a fury, a smoke, a blue fog, a white rain, a bat, a gargoyle, a monster, that was Pikes! Better than Lon Chaney, the father? Stendahl ruminated. Night after night he had watched Chaney in the old, old films. Yes, better than Chaney. Better than that other ancient mummer? What was his name? Karloff? Far better! Lugosi? The comparison was odious! No, there was only one Pikes, and he was a man stripped of his fantasies now, no place on Earth to go, no one to show off to. Forbidden even to perform for himself before a mirror!

Poor impossible, defeated Pikes! How must it have felt, Pikes, the night they seized your films, like entrails yanked from the camera, out of your guts, clutching them in rolls and wads to stuff them up a stove to burn away? Did it feel as bad as having some fifty thousand books annihilated with no recompense? Yes. Yes. Stendahl felt his hands grow cold with the senseless anger. So what more natural than they would one day talk over endless coffeepots into innumerable midnights, and out of all the talk and the bitter brewings would come—the House of Usher.

A great church bell rang. The guests were arriving.

Smiling, he went to greet them.

Full grown without memory, the robots waited. In green silks the color of forest pools, in silks the color of frog and fern, they waited. In yellow hair the color of the sun and sand, the robots waited. Oiled, with tube bones cut from bronze and sunk in gelatin, the robots lay. In coffins for the not dead and not alive, in planked boxes, the metronomes waited to be set in motion. There was a smell of lubrication and lathed brass. There was a silence of the tomb yard. Sexed but sexless, the robots. Named but unnamed, and borrowing from humans everything but humanity, the robots stared at the nailed lids of their labeled F.O.B. boxes, in a death that was not even a death, for there had never been a life. And now there was a vast screaming of yanked nails. Now there was a lifting of lids. Now there were shadows on the boxes and the pressure of a hand squirting oil from a can. Now one clock was set in motion, a faint ticking. Now another and another, until this was an immense clock shop, purring. The marble eyes rolled wide their rubber lids. The nostrils winked. The robots, clothed in hair of ape and white of rabbit, arose: Tweedledum following Tweedledee, Mock-Turtle, Dormouse, drowned bodies from the sea compounded of salt and whiteweed, swaying; hanging blue-throated men with turned-up, clam-flesh eyes, and creatures of ice and burning tinsel, loam-dwarfs and pepper-elves, Tik-Tok, Ruggedo, St. Nicholas with a self-made snow flurry blowing on before him, Bluebeard with whiskers like acetylene flame, and sulphur clouds from which green fire snouts protruded, and, in scaly and gigantic serpentine, a dragon with a furnace in its belly reeled out the door with a scream, a tick, a bellow, a silence, a rush, a wind. Ten thousand lids fell back. The clock shop moved out into Usher. The night was enchanted.

A warm breeze came over the land. The guest rockets, burning the sky and turning the weather from autumn to spring, arrived.

The men stepped out in evening clothes and the women stepped out after them, their hair coiffed up in elaborate detail.

"So *that's* Usher!"

"But where's the door?"

At this moment Stendahl appeared. The women laughed and chattered. Mr. Stendahl raised a hand to quiet them. Turning, he looked up to a high castle window and called:

"Rapunzel, Rapunzel, let down your hair."

And from above, a beautiful maiden leaned out upon the night wind and let down her golden hair. And the hair twined and blew and became a ladder upon which the guests might ascend, laughing, into the House.

What eminent sociologists! What clever psychologists! What tremendously important politicians, bacteriologists, and neurologists! There they stood, within the dank walls.

"Welcome, all of you!"

Mr. Tryon, Mr. Owen, Mr. Dunne, Mr. Lang, Mr. Steffens, Mr. Fletcher, and a double-dozen more.

"Come in, come in!"

Miss Gibbs, Miss Pope, Miss Churchil, Miss Blunt, Miss Drummond, and a score of other women, glittering.

Eminent, eminent people, one and all, members of the Society for the Prevention of Fantasy, advocators of the banishment of Halloween and Guy Fawkes, killers of bats, burners of books, bearers of torches; good clean citizens, every one, who had waited until the rough men had come up and buried the Martians and cleansed the cities and built the towns and repaired the highways and made everything safe. And then, with everything well on its way to Safety, the Spoil-Funs, the people with mercurochrome for blood and iodine-colored eyes, came now to set up their Moral Climates and dole out goodness to everyone. And they were his friends! Yes, carefully, carefully, he had met and befriended each of them on Earth in the last year!

"Welcome to the vasty halls of Death!" he cried.

"Hello, Stendahl, what *is* all this?"

"You'll see. Everyone off with their clothes. You'll find booths to one side there. Change into costumes you find there. Men on this side, women on that."

The people stood uneasily about.

"I don't know if we should stay," said Miss Pope. "I don't like the looks of this. It verges on—blasphemy."

"Nonsense, a *costume* ball!"

"Seems quite illegal." Mr. Steffens sniffed about.

"Come off it." Stendahl laughed. "Enjoy yourselves. Tomorrow it'll be a ruin. Get in the booths!"

The House blazed with life and color; harlequins rang by with belled caps and white mice danced miniature quadrilles to the music of dwarfs who tickled tiny fiddles with tiny bows, and flags rippled from scorched beams while bats flew in clouds about gargoyle mouths which spouted down wine, cool, wild, and foaming. A creek wandered through the seven rooms of the masked ball. Guests sipped and found it to be sherry. Guests poured from the booths, transformed from one age into another, their faces covered with dominoes, the very act of putting on a mask revoking all their licenses to pick a quarrel with fantasy and horror. The women swept about in red gowns, laughing. The men danced them attendance. And on the walls were shadows with no people to throw them, and here or there were mirrors in which no image showed. "All of us vampires!" laughed Mr. Fletcher. "Dead!"

There were seven rooms, each a different color, one blue, one purple, one green, one orange, another white, the sixth violet, and the seventh shrouded in black velvet. And in the black room was an ebony clock which struck the hour loud. And through these rooms the guests ran, drunk at last, among the robot fantasies, amid the Dormice and Mad Hatters, the Trolls and Giants, the Black Cats and White Queens, and under their dancing feet the floor gave off the massive pumping beat of a hidden and telltale heart.

"Mr. Stendahl!"

A whisper.

"Mr. Stendahl!"

A monster with the face of Death stood at his elbow. It was Pikes. "I must see you alone."

"What is it?"

"Here." Pikes held out a skeleton hand. In it were a few half-melted, charred wheels, nuts, cogs, bolts.

Stendahl looked at them for a long moment. Then he drew Pikes into a corridor. "Garrett?" he whispered.

Pikes nodded. "He sent a robot in his place. Cleaning out the incinerator a moment ago, I found these."

They both stared at the fateful cogs for a time.

"This means the police will be here any minute," said Pikes. "Our plan will be ruined."

"I don't know." Stendahl glanced in at the whirling yellow and blue and orange people. The music swept through the misting halls. "I should have guessed Garrett wouldn't be fool enough to come in person. But wait!"

"What's the matter?"

"Nothing. There's nothing the matter. Garrett sent a robot to us. Well, we sent one back. Unless he checks closely, he won't notice the switch."

"Of course!"

"Next time he'll come *himself.* Now that he thinks it's safe. Why, he might be at the door any minute, in *person*! More wine, Pikes!"

The great bell rang.

"There he is now, I'll bet you. Go let Mr. Garrett in."

Rapunzel let down her golden hair.

"Mr. Stendahl?"

"Mr. Garrett. The *real* Mr. Garrett?"

"The same." Garrett eyed the dank walls and the whirling people. "I thought I'd better come see for myself. You can't depend on robots. Other people's robots, especially. I also took the precaution of summoning the Dismantlers. They'll be here in one hour to knock the props out from under this horrible place."

Stendahl bowed. "Thanks for telling me." He waved his

hand. "In the meantime, you might as well enjoy this. A little wine?"

"No, thank you. What's going on? How low can a man sink?"

"See for yourself, Mr. Garrett."

"Murder," said Garrett.

"Murder most foul," said Stendahl.

A woman screamed. Miss Pope ran up, her face the color of a cheese. "The most horrid thing just happened! I saw Miss Blunt strangled by an ape and stuffed up a chimney!"

They looked and saw the long yellow hair trailing down from the flue. Garrett cried out.

"Horrid!" sobbed Miss Pope, and then ceased crying. She blinked and turned. "Miss Blunt!"

"Yes," said Miss Blunt, standing there.

"But I just saw you crammed up the flue!"

"No," laughed Miss Blunt. "A robot of myself. A clever facsimile!"

"But, but . . ."

"Don't cry, darling. I'm quite all right. Let me look at myself. Well, so there I *am*! Up the chimney. Like you said. Isn't that funny?"

Miss Blunt walked away, laughing.

"Have a drink, Garrett?"

"I believe I will. That unnerved me. My God, what a place. This *does* deserve tearing down. For a moment there . . ."

Garrett drank.

Another scream. Mr. Steffens, borne upon the shoulders of four white rabbits, was carried down a flight of stairs which magically appeared in the floor. Into a pit went Mr. Steffens, where, bound and tied, he was left to face the advancing razor steel of a great pendulum which now whirled down, down, closer and closer to his outraged body.

"Is that me down there?" said Mr. Steffens, appearing at Garrett's elbow. He bent over the pit. "How strange, how odd, to see yourself die."

The pendulum made a final stroke.

"How realistic," said Mr. Steffens, turning away.

"Another drink, Mr. Garrett?"

"Yes, please."

"It won't be long. The Dismantlers will be here."

"Thank God!"

And for a third time, a scream.

"What now?" said Garrett apprehensively.

"It's my turn," said Miss Drummond. "Look."

And a second Miss Drummond, shrieking, was nailed into a coffin and thrust into the raw earth under the floor.

"Why, I remember *that*," gasped the Investigator of Moral Climates. "From the old forbidden books. The Premature Burial. And the others. The Pit, the Pendulum, and the ape, the chimney, the Murders in the Rue Morgue. In a book I burned, yes!"

"Another drink, Garrett. Here, hold your glass steady."

"My lord, you *have* an imagination, haven't you?"

They stood and watched five others die, one in the mouth of a dragon, the others thrown off into the black tarn, sinking and vanishing.

"Would you like to see what we have planned for you?" asked Stendahl.

"Certainly," said Garrett. "What's the difference? We'll blow the whole damn thing up, anyway. You're nasty."

"Come along then. This way."

And he led Garrett down into the floor, through numerous passages and down again upon spiral stairs into the earth, into the catacombs.

"What do you want to show me down here?" said Garrett.

"Yourself killed."

"A duplicate?"

"Yes. And also something else."

"What?"

"The Amontillado," said Stendahl, going ahead with a blazing lantern which he held high. Skeletons froze half out of coffin lids. Garrett held his hand to his nose, his face disgusted.

"The what?"

"Haven't you ever heard of the Amontillado?"

"No!"

"Don't you recognize this?" Stendahl pointed to a cell.

"Should I?"

"Or this?" Stendahl produced a trowel from under his cape smiling.

"What's that thing?"

"Come," said Stendahl.

They stepped into the cell. In the dark, Stendahl affixed the chains to the half-drunken man.

"For God's sake, what are you doing?" shouted Garrett, rattling about.

"I'm being ironic. Don't interrupt a man in the midst of being ironic, it's not polite. There!"

"You've locked me in chains!"

"So I have."

"What are you going to do?"

"Leave you here."

"You're joking."

"A very good joke."

"Where's my duplicate? Don't we see him killed?"

"There is no duplicate."

"But the *others*!"

"The others are dead. The ones you saw killed were the real people. The duplicates, the robots, stood by and watched."

Garrett said nothing.

"Now you're supposed to say, 'For the love of God, Montresor!'" said Stendahl. "And I will reply, 'Yes, for the love of God.' Won't you say it? Come on. *Say* it."

"You fool."

"Must I coax you? Say it. Say 'For the love of God, Montresor!'"

"I won't, you idiot. Get me out of here." He was sober now.

"Here. Put this on." Stendahl tossed in something that belled and rang.

"What is it?"

"A cap and bells. Put it on and I might let you out."

"Stendahl!"

"Put it on, I said!"

Garrett obeyed. The bells tinkled.

"Don't you have a feeling that this has all happened before?" inquired Stendahl, setting to work with trowel and mortar and brick now.

"What're you doing?"

"Walling you in. Here's one row. Here's another."

"You're insane!"

"I won't argue that point."

"You'll be prosecuted for this!"

He tapped a brick and placed it on the wet mortar, humming.

Now there was a thrashing and pounding and a crying out from within the darkening place. The bricks rose higher. "More thrashing, please," said Stendahl. "Let's make it a good show."

"Let me out, let me out!"

There was one last brick to shove into place. The screaming was continuous.

"Garrett?" called Stendahl softly. Garrett silenced himself. "Garrett," said Stendahl, "do you know why I've done this to you? Because you burned Mr. Poe's books without really reading them. You took other people's advice that they needed burning. Otherwise you'd have realized what I was going to do to you when we came down here a moment ago. Ignorance is fatal, Mr. Garrett."

Garrett was silent.

"I want this to be perfect," said Stendahl, holding his lantern up so its light penetrated in upon the slumped figure. "Jingle your bells softly." The bells rustled. "Now, if you'll please say, 'For the love of God, Montresor,' I might let you free."

The man's face came up in the light. There was a hesitation. Then grotesquely the man said, "For the love of God, Montresor."

"Ah," said Stendahl, eyes closed. He shoved the last brick into place and mortared it tight. "*Requiescat in pace*, dear friend."

He hastened from the catacomb.

In the seven rooms the sound of a midnight clock brought everything to a halt.

The Red Death appeared.

Stendahl turned for a moment at the door to watch. And then he ran out of the great House across the moat, to where a helicopter waited.

"Ready, Pikes?"

"Ready."

"There it goes!"

They looked at the great House, smiling. It began to crack down the middle, as with an earthquake, and as Stendahl watched the magnificent sight he heard Pikes reciting behind him in a low, cadenced voice:

"'. . . my brain reeled as I saw the mighty walls rushing asunder—there was a long tumultuous shouting sound like the voice of a thousand waters—and the deep and dank tarn at my feet closed sullenly and silently over the fragments of the House of Usher.'"

The helicopter rose over the steaming lake and flew into the west.

August 2005: THE OLD ONES

AND WHAT more natural than that, at last, the old people come to Mars, following in the trail left by the loud frontiersmen, the aromatic sophisticates, and the professional travelers and romantic lecturers in search of new grist.

And so the dry and crackling people, the people who spent their time listening to their hearts and feeling their pulses and spooning syrups into their wry mouths, these people who once had taken chair cars to California in November and third-class steamers to Italy in April, the dried-apricot people, the mummy people, came at last to Mars. . . .

September 2005: THE MARTIAN

THE BLUE mountains lifted into the rain and the rain fell down into the long canals and old LaFarge and his wife came out of their house to watch.

"First rain this season," LaFarge pointed out.

"It's good," said his wife.

"Very welcome."

They shut the door. Inside, they warmed their hands at a fire. They shivered. In the distance, through the window, they saw rain gleaming on the sides of the rocket which had brought them from Earth.

"There's only one thing," said LaFarge, looking at his hands.

"What's that?" asked his wife.

"I wish we could have brought Tom with us."

"Oh, now, Lafe!"

"I won't start again; I'm sorry."

"We came here to enjoy our old age in peace, not to think of Tom. He's been dead so long now, we should try to forget him and everything on Earth."

"You're right," he said, and turned his hands again to the heat. He gazed into the fire. "I won't speak of it any more. It's just I miss driving out to Green Lawn Park every Sunday to put flowers on his marker. It used to be our only excursion."

The blue rain fell gently upon the house.

At nine o'clock they went to bed and lay quietly, hand in hand, he fifty-five, she sixty, in the raining darkness.

"Anna?" he called softly.

"Yes?" she replied.

"Did you hear something?"

They both listened to the rain and the wind.

"Nothing," she said.

"Someone whistling," he said.

"No, I didn't hear it."

"I'm going to get up to see anyhow."

He put on his robe and walked through the house to the front door. Hesitating, he pulled the door wide, and rain fell cold upon his face. The wind blew.

In the dooryard stood a small figure.

Lightning cracked the sky, and a wash of white color illumined the face looking in at old LaFarge there in the doorway.

"Who's there?" called LaFarge, trembling.

No answer.

"Who is it? What do you want!"

Still not a word.

He felt very weak and tired and numb. "Who are you?" he cried.

His wife entered behind him and took his arm. "Why are you shouting?"

"A small boy's standing in the yard and won't answer me," said the old man, trembling. "He looks like Tom!"

"Come to bed, you're dreaming."

"But he's there; see for yourself."

He pulled the door wider to let her see. The cold wind blew and the thin rain fell upon the soil and the figure stood looking at them with distant eyes. The old woman held to the doorway.

"Go away!" she said, waving one hand. "Go away!"

"Doesn't it look like Tom?" asked the old man.

The figure did not move.

"I'm afraid," said the old woman. "Lock the door and come to bed. I won't have anything to do with it."

She vanished, moaning to herself, into the bedroom.

The old man stood with the wind raining coldness on his hands.

"Tom," he called softly. "Tom, if that's you, if by some chance it is you, Tom, I'll leave the door unlatched. And if you're cold and want to come in to warm yourself, just come in later and lie by the hearth; there're some fur rugs there."

He shut but did not lock the door.

His wife felt him return to bed, and shuddered. "It's a terrible night. I feel so old," she said, sobbing.

"Hush, hush," he gentled her, and held her in his arms. "Go to sleep."

After a long while she slept.

And then, very quietly, as he listened, he heard the front door open, the rain and wind come in, the door shut. He heard soft footsteps on the hearth and a gentle breathing. "Tom," he said to himself.

Lightning struck in the sky and broke the blackness apart.

In the morning the sun was very hot.

Mr. LaFarge opened the door into the living room and glanced all about, quickly.

The hearthrugs were empty.

LaFarge sighed. "I'm getting old," he said.

He went out to walk to the canal to fetch a bucket of clear water to wash in. At the front door he almost knocked young Tom down carrying in a bucket already filled to the brim. "Good morning, Father!"

"Morning, Tom." The old man fell aside. The young boy, barefooted, hurried across the room, set the bucket down, and turned, smiling. "It's a fine day!"

"Yes, it is," said the old man incredulously. The boy acted as if nothing was unusual. He began to wash his face with the water.

The old man moved forward. "Tom, how did you get here? You're alive?"

"Shouldn't I be?" The boy glanced up.

"But, Tom, Green Lawn Park, every Sunday, the flowers and . . ." LaFarge had to sit down. The boy came and stood before him and took his hand. The old man felt of the fingers, warm and firm. "You're really here, it's not a dream?"

"You *do* want me to be here, don't you?" The boy seemed worried.

"Yes, yes, Tom!"

"Then why ask questions? Accept me!"

"But your mother; the shock . . ."

"Don't worry about her. During the night I sang to both of you, and you'll accept me more because of it, especially her. I know what the shock is. Wait till she comes, you'll see." He laughed, shaking his head of coppery, curled hair. His eyes were very blue and clear.

"Good morning, Lafe, Tom." Mother came from the bedroom, putting her hair up into a bun. "Isn't it a fine day?"

Tom turned to laugh in his father's face. "You *see*?"

They ate a very good lunch, all three of them, in the shade behind the house. Mrs. LaFarge had found an old bottle of sunflower wine she had put away, and they all had a drink of that. Mr. LaFarge had never seen his wife's face so bright. If there was any doubt in her mind about Tom, she didn't voice it. It was a completely natural thing to her. And it was also becoming natural to LaFarge himself.

While Mother cleared the dishes LaFarge leaned toward his son and said confidentially, "How old are you now, Son?"

"Don't you know, Father? Fourteen, of course."

"Who are you, *really*? You can't be Tom, but you are *someone*. Who?"

"Don't." Startled, the boy put his hands to his face.

"You can tell me," said the old man. "I'll understand. You're a Martian, aren't you? I've heard tales of the Martians; nothing definite. Stories about how rare Martians are and when they come among us they come as Earth Men. There's something about you—you're Tom and yet you're not."

"Why can't you accept me and stop talking?" cried the boy. His hands completely shielded his face. "Don't doubt, please don't doubt me!" He turned and ran from the table.

"Tom, come back!"

But the boy ran off along the canal toward the distant town.

"Where's Tom going?" asked Anna, returning for more dishes. She looked at her husband's face. "Did you say something to bother him?"

"Anna," he said, taking her hand. "Anna, do you remember anything about Green Lawn Park, a market, and Tom having pneumonia?"

"What *are* you talking about?" She laughed.

"Never mind," he said quietly.

In the distance the dust drifted down after Tom had run along the canal rim.

At five in the afternoon, with the sunset, Tom returned. He looked doubtfully at his father. "Are you going to ask me anything?" he wanted to know.

"No questions," said LaFarge.

The boy smiled his white smile. "Swell."

"Where've you been?"

"Near the town. I almost didn't come back. I was almost"—the boy sought for a word—"trapped."

"How do you mean, 'trapped'?"

"I passed a small tin house by the canal and I was almost made so I couldn't come back here ever again to see you. I don't know how to explain it to you, there's no way, I can't tell you, even *I* don't know; it's strange, I don't want to talk about it."

"We won't then. Better wash up, boy. Suppertime."

The boy ran.

Perhaps ten minutes later a boat floated down the serene surface of the canal, a tall lank man with black hair poling it along with leisurely drives of his arms. "Evening, Brother LaFarge," he said, pausing at his task.

"Evening, Saul, what's the word?"

"All kinds of words tonight. You know that fellow named Nomland who lives down the canal in the tin hut?"

LaFarge stiffened. "Yes?"

"You know what sort of rascal he was?"

"Rumor had it he left Earth because he killed a man."

Saul leaned on his wet pole, gazing at LaFarge. "Remember the name of the man he killed?"

"Gillings, wasn't it?"

"Right. Gillings. Well, about two hours ago Mr. Nomland came running to town crying about how he had seen Gillings, alive, here on Mars, today, this afternoon! He tried to get the jail to lock him up safe. The jail wouldn't. So Nomland went home, and twenty minutes ago, as I get the story, blew his brains out with a gun. I just came from there."

"Well, well," said LaFarge.

"The darnedest things happen," said Saul. "Well, good night, LaFarge."

"Good night."

The boat drifted on down the serene canal waters.

"Supper's hot," called the old woman.

Mr. LaFarge sat down to his supper and, knife in hand, looked over at Tom. "Tom," he said, "what did you do this afternoon?"

"Nothing," said Tom, his mouth full. "Why?"

"Just wanted to know." The old man tucked his napkin in.

At seven that night the old woman wanted to go to town. "Haven't been there in months," she said. But Tom desisted. "I'm afraid of the town," he said. "The people. I don't want to go there."

"Such talk for a grown boy," said Anna. "I won't listen to it. You'll come along. *I* say so."

"Anna, if the boy doesn't want to . . ." started the old man.

But there was no arguing. She hustled them into the canal-boat and they floated up the canal under the evening stars, Tom lying on his back, his eyes closed; asleep or not, there was no telling. The old man looked at him steadily, wondering. Who is this, he thought, in need of love as much as we? Who is he and what is he that, out of loneliness, he comes into the alien camp and assumes the voice and face of memory and stands among us, accepted and happy at last? From what mountain, what cave, what small last race of people remaining on this world when the rockets came from Earth? The old man shook his head. There was no way to know. This, to all purposes, was Tom.

The old man looked at the town ahead and did not like it, but then he returned to thoughts of Tom and Anna again and he thought to himself: Perhaps this is wrong to keep Tom but a little while, when nothing can come of it but trouble and sorrow, but how are we to give up the very thing we've wanted, no matter if it stays only a day and is gone, making the emptiness emptier, the dark nights darker, the rainy nights wetter? You might as well force the food from our mouths as take this one from us.

And he looked at the boy slumbering so peacefully at the bottom of the boat. The boy whimpered with some dream. "The people," he murmured in his sleep. "Changing and changing. The trap."

"There, there, boy." LaFarge stroked the boy's soft curls and Tom ceased.

LaFarge helped wife and son from the boat.

"Here we are!" Anna smiled at all the lights, listening to the music from the drinking houses, the pianos, the phonographs, watching people, arm in arm, striding by in the crowded streets.

"I wish I was home," said Tom.

"You never talked that way before," said the mother. "You always liked Saturday nights in town."

"Stay close to me," whispered Tom. "I don't want to get trapped."

Anna overheard. "Stop talking that way; come along!"

LaFarge noticed that the boy held his hand. LaFarge squeezed it. "I'll stick with you, Tommy-boy." He looked at the throngs coming and going, and it worried him also. "We won't stay long."

"Nonsense, we'll spend the evening," said Anna.

They crossed a street, and three drunken men careened into them. There was much confusion, a separation, a wheeling about, and then LaFarge stood stunned.

Tom was gone.

"Where is he?" asked Anna irritably. "Him always running off alone any chance he gets. Tom!" she called.

Mr. LaFarge hurried through the crowd, but Tom was gone.

"He'll come back; he'll be at the boat when we leave," said Anna certainly, steering her husband back toward the motion-picture theater. There was a sudden commotion in the crowd, and a man and woman rushed by LaFarge. He recognized them. Joe Spaulding and his wife. They were gone before he could speak to them.

Looking back anxiously, he purchased the tickets for the theater and allowed his wife to draw him into the unwelcome darkness.

Tom was not at the landing at eleven o'clock. Mrs. LaFarge turned very pale.

"Now, Mother," said LaFarge, "don't worry. I'll find him. Wait here."

"Hurry back." Her voice faded into the ripple of the water.

He walked through the night streets, hands in pockets. All about, lights were going out one by one. A few people were still leaning out their windows, for the night was warm, even though the sky still held storm clouds from time to time among the stars. As he walked he recalled the boy's constant references to being trapped, his fear of crowds and cities. There was no sense in it, thought the old man tiredly. Perhaps the boy was gone forever, perhaps he had never been. LaFarge turned in at a particular alley, watching the numbers.

"Hello there, LaFarge."

A man sat in his doorway, smoking a pipe.

"Hello, Mike."

"You and your woman quarrel? You out walking it off?"

"No. Just walking."

"You look like you lost something. Speaking of lost things," said Mike, "somebody got found this evening. You know Joe Spaulding? You remember his daughter Lavinia?"

"Yes." LaFarge was cold. It all seemed a repeated dream. He knew which words would come next.

"Lavinia came home tonight," said Mike, smoking. "You recall, she was lost on the dead sea bottoms about a month ago? They found what they thought was her body, badly deteriorated, and ever since the Spaulding family's been no good. Joe went around saying she wasn't dead, that wasn't really her body. Guess he was right. Tonight Lavinia showed up."

"Where?" LaFarge felt his breath come swiftly, his heart pounding.

"On Main Street. The Spauldings were buying tickets for a show. And there, all of a sudden, in the crowd, was Lavinia. Must have been quite a scene. She didn't know them first off. They followed her half down a street and spoke to her. Then she remembered."

"Did you see her?"

"No, but I heard her singing. Remember how she used to sing 'The Bonnie Banks of Loch Lomond'? I heard her trilling out for her father a while ago over there in their house. It was good to hear; her such a beautiful girl. A shame, I thought, her dead; and now with her back again it's fine. Here now, you look weak yourself. Better come in for a spot of whisky. . . ."

"Thanks, no, Mike." The old man moved away. He heard Mike say good night and did not answer, but fixed his eyes upon the two-story building where rambling clusters of crimson Martian flowers lay upon the high crystal roof. Around back, above the garden, was a twisted iron balcony, and the windows above were lighted. It was very late, and still he thought to himself: What will happen to Anna if I don't bring Tom home with me? This second shock, this second death, what will it do to her? Will she remember the first death, too, and this dream, and the sudden vanishing? Oh God, I've got to find Tom, or what will come of Anna? Poor Anna, waiting there at the landing. He paused and lifted his head. Somewhere above, voices bade other soft voices good night, doors turned and shut, lights dimmed, and a gentle singing continued. A moment later a girl no more than eighteen, very lovely, came out upon the balcony.

LaFarge called up through the wind that was blowing.

The girl turned and looked down. "Who's there?" she cried.

"It's me," said the old man, and, realizing this reply to be silly and strange, fell silent, his lips working. Should he call out, "Tom, my son, this is your father"? How to speak to her? She would think him quite insane and summon her parents.

The girl bent forward in the blowing light. "I know you," she replied softly. "Please go; there's nothing you can do."

"You've got to come back!" It escaped LaFarge before he could prevent it.

The moonlit figure above drew into shadow, so there was no identity, only a voice. "I'm not your son any more," it said. "We should never have come to town."

"Anna's waiting at the landing!"

"I'm sorry," said the quiet voice. "But what can I do? I'm happy here, I'm loved, even as you loved me. I am what I am, and I take what can be taken; it's too late now, they've caught me."

"But Anna, the shock to her. Think of that."

"The thoughts are too strong in this house; it's like being imprisoned. I can't change myself back."

"You are Tom, you *were* Tom, weren't you? You aren't joking with an old man; you're not really Lavinia Spaulding?"

"I'm not anyone, I'm just myself; wherever I am, I am something, and now I'm something you can't help."

"You're not safe in the town. It's better out on the canal where no one can hurt you," pleaded the old man.

"That's true." The voice hesitated. "But I must consider these people now. How would they feel if, in the morning, I was gone again, this time for good? Anyway, the mother knows what I am; she guessed, even as you did. I think they all guessed but didn't question. You don't question Providence. If you can't have the reality, a dream is just as good. Perhaps I'm not their dead one back, but I'm something almost better to them; an ideal shaped by their minds. I have a choice of hurting them or your wife."

"They're a family of five. They can stand your loss better!"

"Please," said the voice. "I'm tired."

The old man's voice hardened. "You've got to come. I can't let Anna be hurt again. You're our son. You're my son, and you belong to us."

"No, please!" The shadow trembled.

"You don't belong to this house or these people!"

"No, don't do this to me!"

"Tom, Tom, Son, listen to me. Come back, slip down the vines, boy. Come along, Anna's waiting; we'll give you a good home, everything you want." He stared and stared upward, willing it to be.

The shadows drifted, the vines rustled.

At last the quiet voice said, "All right, Father."

"Tom!"

In the moonlight the quick figure of a boy slid down through the vines. LaFarge put up his arms to catch him.

The room lights above flashed on. A voice issued from one of the grilled windows. "Who's down there?"

"Hurry, boy!"

More lights, more voices. "Stop, I have a gun! Vinny, are you all right?" A running of feet.

Together the old man and the boy ran across the garden.

A shot sounded. The bullet struck the wall as they slammed the gate.

"Tom, you that way; I'll go here and lead them off! Run to the canal; I'll meet you there in ten minutes, boy!"

They parted.

The moon hid behind a cloud. The old man ran in darkness.

"Anna, I'm here!"

The old woman helped him, trembling, into the boat. "Where's Tom?"

"He'll be here in a minute," panted LaFarge.

They turned to watch the alleys and the sleeping town. Late strollers were still out: a policeman, a night watchman, a rocket pilot, several lonely men coming home from some nocturnal rendezvous, four men and women issuing from a bar, laughing. Music played dimly somewhere.

"Why doesn't he come?" asked the old woman.

"He'll come, he'll come." But LaFarge was not certain. Suppose the boy had been caught again, somehow, someway, in his travel down to the landing, running through the midnight streets between the dark houses. It was a long run, even for a young boy. But he should have reached here first.

And now, far away, along the moonlit avenue, a figure ran.

LaFarge cried out and then silenced himself, for also far away was another sound of voices and running feet. Lights blazed on in window after window. Across the open plaza leading to the landing, the one figure ran. It was not Tom; it was only a running shape with a face like silver shining in the light of the globes clustered about the plaza. And as it rushed nearer, nearer, it became more familiar, until when it reached the landing it was Tom! Anna flung up her hands. LaFarge hurried to cast off. But already it was too late.

For out of the avenue and across the silent plaza now came one man, another, a woman, two other men, Mr. Spaulding, all running. They stopped, bewildered. They stared about, wanting to go back because this could be only a nightmare, it was quite insane. But they came on again, hesitantly, stopping, starting.

It was too late. The night, the event, was over. LaFarge twisted the mooring rope in his fingers. He was very cold and lonely. The people raised and put down their feet in the moonlight, drifting with great speed, wide-eyed, until the crowd, all ten of them, halted at the landing. They peered wildly down into the boat. They cried out.

"Don't move, LaFarge!" Spaulding had a gun.

And now it was evident what had happened. Tom flashing through the moonlit streets, alone, passing people. A policeman seeing the figure dart past. The policeman pivoting, staring at the face, calling a name, giving pursuit. "*You*, stop!" Seeing a criminal face. All along the way, the same thing, men here, women there, night watchmen, rocket pilots. The swift figure meaning everything to them, all identities, all persons, all names. How many different names had been uttered in the last five minutes? How many different faces shaped over Tom's face, all wrong?

All down the way the pursued and the pursuing, the dream and the dreamers, the quarry and the hounds. All down the way the sudden revealment, the flash of familiar eyes, the cry of an old, old name, the remembrances of other times, the crowd multiplying. Everyone leaping forward as, like an image reflected from ten thousand mirrors, ten thousand eyes, the running dream came and went, a different face to those ahead, those behind, those yet to be met, those unseen.

And here they all are now, at the boat, wanting the dream for their own, just as we want him to be Tom, not Lavinia or William or Roger or any other, thought LaFarge. But it's all done now. The thing has gone too far.

"Come up, all of you!" Spaulding ordered them.

Tom stepped up from the boat. Spaulding seized his wrist. "You're coming home with me. I *know*."

"Wait," said the policeman. "He's my prisoner. Name's Dexter; wanted for murder."

"No!" a woman sobbed. "It's my husband! I guess I know my husband!"

Other voices objected. The crowd moved in.

Mrs. LaFarge shielded Tom. "This is my son; you have no right to accuse him of anything. We're going home right now!"

As for Tom, he was trembling and shaking violently. He looked very sick. The crowd thickened about him, putting out their wild hands, seizing and demanding.

Tom screamed.

Before their eyes he changed. He was Tom and James and a man named Switchman, another named Butterfield; he was the town mayor and the young girl Judith and the husband William and the wife Clarisse. He was melting wax shaping to their minds. They shouted, they pressed forward, pleading. He screamed, threw out his hands, his face dissolving to each demand. "Tom!" cried LaFarge. "Alice!" another. "William!" They snatched his wrists, whirled him about, until with one last shriek of horror he fell.

He lay on the stones, melted wax cooling, his face all faces, one eye blue, the other golden, hair that was brown, red, yellow, black, one eyebrow thick, one thin, one hand large, one small.

They stood over him and put their fingers to their mouths. They bent down.

"He's dead," someone said at last.

It began to rain.

The rain fell upon the people, and they looked up at the sky.

Slowly, and then more quickly, they turned and walked away and then started running, scattering from the scene. In a minute the place was desolate. Only Mr. and Mrs. LaFarge remained, looking down, hand in hand, terrified.

The rain fell upon the upturned, unrecognizable face.

Anna said nothing but began to cry.

"Come along home, Anna, there's nothing we can do," said the old man.

They climbed down into the boat and went back along the canal in the darkness. They entered their house and lit a small fire and warmed their hands. They went to bed and lay together, cold and thin, listening to the rain returned to the roof above them.

"Listen," said LaFarge at midnight. "Did you hear something?"

"Nothing, nothing."

"I'll go look anyway."

He fumbled across the dark room and waited by the outer door for a long time before he opened it.

He pulled the door wide and looked out.

Rain poured from the black sky upon the empty dooryard, into the canal and among the blue mountains.

He waited five minutes and then softly, his hands wet, he shut and bolted the door.

November 2005: THE LUGGAGE STORE

IT WAS a very remote thing, when the luggage-store proprietor heard the news on the night radio, received all the way from Earth on a light-sound beam. The proprietor felt how remote it was.

There was going to be a war on Earth.

He went out to peer into the sky.

Yes, there it was. Earth, in the evening heavens, following the sun into the hills. The words on the radio and that green star were one and the same.

"I don't believe it," said the proprietor.

"It's because you're not there," said Father Peregrine, who had stopped by to pass the time of evening.

"What do you mean, Father?"

"It's like when I was a boy," said Father Peregrine. "We heard about wars in China. But we never believed them. It was too far away. And there were too many people dying. It was impossible. Even when we saw the motion pictures we didn't believe it. Well, that's how it is now. Earth *is* China. It's so far away it's unbelievable. It's not here. You can't touch it. You can't even see it. All you see is a green light. Two billion people living on that light? Unbelievable! War? We don't hear the explosions."

"We will," said the proprietor. "I keep thinking about all those people that were going to come to Mars this week. What was it? A hundred thousand or so coming up in the next month or so. What about *them* if the war starts?"

"I imagine they'll turn back. They'll be needed on Earth."

"Well," said the proprietor, "I'd better get my luggage dusted off. I got a feeling there'll be a rush sale here any time."

"Do you think everyone now on Mars will go back to Earth if this *is* the Big War we've all been expecting for years?"

"It's a funny thing, Father, but yes, I think we'll *all* go back. I know, we came up here to get away from things—politics, the atom bomb, war, pressure groups, prejudice, laws—I know. But it's still home there. You wait and see. When the first bomb drops on America the people up here'll start thinking. They haven't been here long enough. A couple years is all. If they'd been here forty years, it'd be different, but they got relatives down there, and their home towns. Me, I can't believe in Earth any more; I can't imagine it much. But I'm old. I don't count. I might stay on here."

"I doubt it."

"Yes, I guess you're right."

They stood on the porch watching the stars. Finally Father Peregrine pulled some money from his pocket and handed it to the proprietor. "Come to think of it, you'd better give me a new valise. My old one's in pretty bad condition. . . ."

November 2005: THE OFF SEASON

SAM PARKHILL motioned with the broom, sweeping away the blue Martian sand.

"Here we are," he said. "Yes, sir, look at that!" He pointed. "Look at that sign. SAM'S HOT DOGS! Ain't that beautiful, Elma?"

"Sure, Sam," said his wife.

"Boy, what a change for me. If the boys from the Fourth Expedition could see me now. Am I glad to be in business myself while all the rest of them guys're off soldiering around still. We'll make thousands, Elma, thousands."

His wife looked at him for a long time, not speaking. "Whatever happened to Captain Wilder?" she asked finally. "That captain that killed that guy who thought he was going to kill off every other Earth Man, what was his name?"

"Spender, that nut. He was too damn particular. Oh, Captain Wilder? He's off on a rocket to Jupiter, I hear. They kicked him upstairs. I think he was a little batty about Mars too. Touchy, you know. He'll be back down from Jupiter and Pluto in about twenty years if he's lucky. That's what he gets for shooting off his mouth. And while he's freezing to death, look at me, look at this place!"

This was a crossroads where two dead highways came and went in darkness. Here Sam Parkhill had flung up this riveted aluminum structure, garish with white light, trembling with juke-box melody.

He stooped to fix a border of broken glass he had placed on the footpath. He had broken the glass from some old Martian buildings in the hills. "Best hot dogs on two worlds! First man on Mars with a hot-dog stand! The best onions and chili and mustard! You can't say I'm not alert. Here's the main highways, over there is the dead city and the mineral deposits. Those trucks from Earth Settlement 101 will have to pass here twenty-four hours a day! Do I know my locations, or don't I?"

His wife looked at her fingernails.

"You think those ten thousand new-type work rockets will come through to Mars?" she said at last.

"In a month," he said loudly. "Why you look so funny?"

"I don't trust those Earth people," she said. "I'll believe it when I see them ten thousand rockets arrive with the one hundred thousand Mexicans and Chinese on them."

"Customers." He lingered on the word. "One hundred thousand hungry people."

"If," said his wife slowly, watching the sky, "there's no atomic war. I don't trust no atom bombs. There's so many of them on Earth now, you never can tell."

"Ah," said Sam, and went on sweeping.

From the corners of his eyes he caught a blue flicker. Something floated in the air gently behind him. He heard his wife say, "Sam. A friend of yours to see you."

Sam whirled to see the mask seemingly floating in the wind.

"So you're back again!" And Sam held his broom like a weapon.

The mask nodded. It was cut from pale blue glass and was fitted above a thin neck, under which were blowing loose robes of thin yellow silk. From the silk two mesh silver hands appeared. The mask mouth was a slot from which musical sounds issued now as the robes, the mask, the hands increased to a height, decreased.

"Mr. Parkhill, I've come back to speak to you again," the voice said from behind the mask.

"I thought I told you I don't want you near here!" cried Sam. "Go on, I'll give you the Disease!"

"I've already had the Disease," said the voice. "I was one of the few survivors. I was sick a long time."

"Go on and hide in the hills, that's where you belong, that's where you've been. Why you come on down and bother *me*? Now, all of a sudden. Twice in one day."

"We mean you no harm."

"But I mean you harm!" said Sam, backing up. "I don't like strangers. I don't like Martians. I never seen one before. It ain't natural. All these years you guys hide, and all of a sudden you pick on me. Leave me alone."

"We come for an important reason," said the blue mask.

"If it's about this land, it's mine. I built this hot-dog stand with my own hands."

"In a way it *is* about the land."

"Look here," said Sam. "I'm from New York City. Where I come from there's ten million others just like me. You Martians are a couple dozen left, got no cities, you wander around in the hills, no leaders, no laws, and now you come tell me about this land. Well, the old got to give way to the new. That's the law of give and take. I got a gun here. After you left this morning I got it out and loaded it."

"We Martians are telepathic," said the cold blue mask. "We are in contact with one of your towns across the dead sea. Have you listened on your radio?"

"My radio's busted."

"Then you don't know. There's big news. It concerns Earth——"

A silver hand gestured. A bronze tube appeared in it.

"Let me show you this."

"A gun," cried Sam Parkhill.

An instant later he had yanked his own gun from his hip holster and fired into the mist, the robe, the blue mask.

The mask sustained itself a moment. Then, like a small circus tent pulling up its stakes and dropping soft fold on fold, the silks rustled, the mask descended, the silver claws tinkled on the stone path. The mask lay on a small huddle of silent white bones and material.

Sam stood gasping.

His wife swayed over the huddled pile.

"That's no weapon," she said, bending down. She picked up the bronze tube. "He was going to show you a message. It's all written out in snake-script, all the blue snakes. I can't read it. Can you?"

"No, that Martian picture writing, it wasn't anything. Let it go!" Sam glanced hastily around. "There may be others! We've got to get him out of sight. Get the shovel!"

"What're you going to do?"

"Bury him, of course!"

"You shouldn't have shot him."

"It was a mistake. Quick!"

Silently she fetched him the shovel.

At eight o'clock he was back sweeping the front of the hot-dog stand self-consciously. His wife stood, arms folded, in the bright doorway.

"I'm sorry what happened," he said. He looked at her, then away. "You know it was purely the circumstances of Fate."

"Yes," said his wife.

"I hated like hell to see him take out that weapon."

"What weapon?"

"Well, I thought it was one! I'm sorry, I'm sorry! How many times do I say it!"

"Ssh," said Elma, putting one finger to her lips. "Ssh."

"I don't care," he said. "I got the whole Earth Settlements, Inc., back of me!" He snorted. "These Martians won't dare——"

"Look," said Elma.

He looked out onto the dead sea bottom. He dropped his broom. He picked it up and his mouth was open, a little free drop of saliva flew on the air, and he was suddenly shivering.

"Elma, Elma, Elma!" he said.

"Here they come," said Elma.

Across the ancient sea floor a dozen tall, blue-sailed Martian sand ships floated, like blue ghosts, like blue smoke.

"Sand ships! But there aren't any more, Elma, no more sand ships."

"Those seem to be sand ships," she said.

"But the authorities confiscated all of them! They broke them up, sold some at auction! I'm the only one in this whole damn territory's got one and knows how to run one."

"Not any more," she said, nodding at the sea.

"Come on, let's get out of here!"

"Why?" she asked slowly, fascinated with the Martian vessels.

"They'll kill me! Get in our truck, quick!"

Elma didn't move.

He had to drag her around back of the stand where the two machines stood, his truck, which he had used steadily until a month ago, and the old Martian sand ship which he had bid for at auction, smiling, and which, during the last three weeks, he had used to carry supplies back and forth over the glassy sea floor. He looked at his truck now and remembered. The engine was out on the ground; he had been puttering with it for two days.

"The truck don't seem to be in running condition," said Elma.

"The sand ship. Get in!"

"And let you drive me in a sand ship? Oh no."

"Get in! I can do it!"

He shoved her in, jumped in behind her, and flapped the tiller, let the cobalt sail up to take the evening wind.

The stars were bright and the blue Martian ships were skimming across the whispering sands. At first his own ship would not move, then he remembered the sand anchor and yanked it in.

"There!"

The wind hurled the sand ship keening over the dead sea bottom, over long-buried crystals, past upended pillars, past deserted docks of marble and brass, past dead white chess cities, past purple foothills, into distance. The figures of the Martian ships receded and then began to pace Sam's ship.

"Guess I showed them, by God!" cried Sam. "I'll report to the Rocket Corporation. They'll give me protection! I'm pretty quick."

"They could have stopped you if they wanted," Elma said tiredly. "They just didn't bother."

He laughed. "Come off it. Why should they let me get off? No, they weren't quick enough, is all."

"Weren't they?" Elma nodded behind him.

He did not turn. He felt a cold wind blowing. He was afraid to turn. He felt something in the seat behind him, something as frail as your breath on a cold morning, something as blue as hickory-wood smoke at twilight, something like old white lace, something like a snowfall, something like the icy rime of winter on the brittle sedge.

There was a sound as of a thin plate of glass broken—laughter. Then silence. He turned.

The young woman sat at the tiller bench quietly. Her wrists were thin as icicles, her eyes as clear as the moons and as large, steady and white. The wind blew at her and, like an image on cold water, she rippled, silk standing out from her frail body in tatters of blue rain.

"Go back," she said.

"No." Sam was quivering, the fine, delicate fear-quivering of a hornet suspended in the air, undecided between fear and hate. "Get off my ship!"

"This isn't your ship," said the vision. "It's old as our world. It sailed the sand seas ten thousand years ago when the seas were whispered away and the docks were empty, and you came and took it, stole it. Now turn it around, go back to the crossroad place. We have need to talk with you. Something important has happened."

"Get off my ship!" said Sam. He took a gun from his holster with a creak of leather. He pointed it carefully. "Jump off before I count three or——"

"Don't!" cried the girl. "I won't hurt you. Neither will the others. We came in peace!"

"One," said Sam.

"Sam!" said Elma.

"Listen to me," said the girl.

"Two," said Sam firmly, cocking the gun trigger.

"Sam!" cried Elma.

"Three," said Sam.

"We only——" said the girl.

The gun went off.

In the sunlight, snow melts, crystals evaporate into a steam, into nothing. In the firelight, vapors dance and vanish. In the core of a volcano, fragile things burst and disappear. The girl, in the gunfire, in the heat, in the concussion, folded like a soft scarf, melted like a crystal figurine. What was left of her, ice, snowflake, smoke, blew away in the wind. The tiller seat was empty.

Sam holstered his gun and did not look at his wife.

"Sam," she said after a minute more of traveling, whispering over the moon-colored sea of sand, "stop the ship."

He looked at her and his face was pale. "No, you don't. Not after all this time, you're not pulling out on me."

She looked at his hand on his gun. "I believe you would," she said. "You actually would."

He jerked his head from side to side, hand tight on the tiller bar. "Elma, this is crazy. We'll be in town in a minute, we'll be okay!"

"Yes," said his wife, lying back cold in the ship.

"Elma, listen to me."

"There's nothing to hear, Sam."

"Elma!"

They were passing a little white chess city, and in his frustration, in his rage, he sent six bullets crashing among the crystal towers. The city dissolved in a shower of ancient glass and splintered quartz. It fell away like carved soap, shattered. It was no more. He laughed and fired again, and one last tower, one last chess piece, took fire, ignited, and in blue flinders went up to the stars.

"I'll show them! I'll show everybody!"

"Go ahead, show us, Sam." She lay in the shadows.

"Here comes another city!" Sam reloaded his gun. "Watch me fix it!"

The blue phantom ships loomed up behind them, drawing steadily apace. He did not see them at first. He was only aware of a whistling and a high windy screaming, as of steel on sand, and it was the sound of the sharp razor prows of the sand ships preening the sea bottoms, their red pennants, blue pennants unfurled. In the blue light ships were blue dark images, masked men, men with silvery faces, men with blue stars for eyes, men with carved golden ears, men with tinfoil cheeks and ruby-studded lips, men with arms folded, men following him, Martian men.

One, two, three. Sam counted. The Martian ships closed in.

"Elma, Elma, I can't hold them all off!"

Elma did not speak or rise from where she had slumped.

Sam fired his gun eight times. One of the sand ships fell apart, the sail, the emerald body, the bronze hull points, the moon-white tiller, and all the separate images in it. The masked men, all of them, dug into the sand and separated out into orange and then smoke-flame.

But the other ships closed in.

"I'm outnumbered, Elma!" he cried. "They'll kill me!"

He threw out the anchor. It was no use. The sail fluttered down, folding unto itself, sighing. The ship stopped. The wind stopped. Travel stopped. Mars stood still as the majestic vessels of the Martians drew around and hesitated over him.

"Earth Man," a voice called from a high seat somewhere. A silverine mask moved. Ruby-rimmed lips glittered with the words.

"I didn't do anything!" Sam looked at all the faces, one hundred in all, that surrounded him. There weren't many Martians left on Mars—one hundred, one hundred and fifty, all told. And most of them were here now, on the dead seas, in their resurrected ships, by their dead chess cities, one of which had just fallen like some fragile vase hit by a pebble. The silverine masks glinted.

"It was all a mistake," he pleaded, standing out of his ship, his wife slumped behind him in the deeps of the hold, like a dead woman. "I came to Mars like any honest enterprising businessman. I took some surplus material from a rocket that crashed and I built me the finest little stand you ever saw right there on that land by the crossroads—you know where it is. You've got to admit it's a good job of building." Sam laughed, staring around. "And that Martian—I know he was a friend of yours—came. His death was an accident, I assure you. All I wanted to do was have a hot-dog stand, the only one on Mars, the first and most important one. You understand how it is? I was going to serve the best darned hot dogs there, with chili and onions and orange juice."

The silver masks did not move. They burned in the moonlight. Yellow eyes shone upon Sam. He felt his stomach clench in, wither, become a rock. He threw his gun in the sand.

"I give up."

"Pick up your gun," said the Martians in chorus.

"What?"

"Your gun." A jeweled hand waved from the prow of a blue ship. "Pick it up. Put it away."

Unbelieving, he picked up the gun.

"Now," said the voice, "turn your ship and go back to your stand."

"Now?"

"Now," said the voice. "We will not harm you. You ran away before we were able to explain. Come."

Now the great ships turned as lightly as moon thistles. Their wing-sails flapped with a sound of soft applause on the air. The masks were coruscating, turning, firing the shadows.

"Elma!" Sam tumbled into the ship. "Get up, Elma. We're going back." He was excited. He almost gibbered with relief. "They aren't going to hurt me, kill me, Elma. Get up, honey, get up."

"What—what?" Elma blinked around and slowly, as the ship was sent into the wind again, she helped herself, as in a dream, back up to a seat and slumped there like a sack of stones, saying no more.

The sand slid under the ship. In half an hour they were back at the crossroads, the ships planted, all of them out of the ships.

The Leader stood before Sam and Elma, his mask beaten of polished bronze, the eyes only empty slits of endless blue-black, the mouth a slot out of which words drifted into the wind.

"Ready your stand," said the voice. A diamond-gloved hand waved. "Prepare the viands, prepare the foods, prepare the strange wines, for tonight is indeed a great night!"

"You mean," said Sam, "you'll let me stay on here?"

"Yes."

"You're not mad at me?"

The mask was rigid and carved and cold and sightless.

"Prepare your place of food," said the voice softly. "And take this."

"What is it?"

Sam blinked at the silver-foil scroll that was handed him, upon which, in hieroglyph, snake figures danced.

"It is the land grant to all of the territory from the silver mountains to the blue hills, from the dead salt sea there to the distant valleys of moonstone and emerald," said the Leader.

"M-mine?" said Sam, incredulous.

"Yours."

"One hundred thousand miles of territory?"

"Yours."

"Did you hear that, Elma?"

Elma was sitting on the ground, leaning against the aluminum hot-dog stand, eyes shut.

"But why, why—why are you giving me all this?" asked Sam, trying to look into the metal slots of the eyes.

"That is not all. Here." Six other scrolls were produced. The names were declared, the territories announced.

"Why, that's half of Mars! I own half of Mars!" Sam rattled the scrolls in his fists. He shook them at Elma, insane with laughing. "Elma, did you hear?"

"I heard," said Elma, looking at the sky.

She seemed to be watching for something. She was becoming a little more alert now.

"Thank you, oh, thank you," said Sam to the bronze mask.

"Tonight is the night," said the mask. "You must be ready."

"I will be. What is it—a surprise? Are the rockets coming through earlier than we thought, a month earlier from Earth? All ten thousand rockets, bringing the settlers, the miners, the workers and their wives, all hundred thousand of them? Won't that be swell, Elma? You see, I told you. I told you, that town there won't always have just one thousand people in it. There'll be fifty thousand more coming, and the month after that a hundred thousand more, and by the end of the year five million Earth Men. And me with the only hot-dog stand staked out on the busiest highway to the mines!"

The mask floated on the wind. "We leave you. Prepare. The land is yours."

In the blowing moonlight, like metal petals of some ancient flower, like blue plumes, like cobalt butterflies immense and quiet, the old ships turned and moved over the shifting sands, the masks beaming and glittering, until the last shine, the last blue color, was lost among the hills.

"Elma, why did they do it? Why didn't they kill me? Don't they know anything? What's wrong with them? Elma, do you understand?" He shook her shoulder. "I own half of Mars!"

She watched the night sky, waiting.

"Come on," he said. "We've got to get the place fixed. All the hot dogs boiling, the buns warm, the chili cooking, the onions peeled and diced, the relish laid out, the napkins in the clips, the place spotless! Hey!" He did a little wild dance, kicking his heels. "Oh boy, I'm happy; yes, sir, I'm happy," he sang, off key. "This is my lucky day!"

He boiled the hot dogs, cut the buns, sliced the onions in a frenzy.

"Just think, that Martian said a surprise. That can only mean one thing, Elma. Those hundred thousand people coming in ahead of schedule, tonight, of all nights! We'll be flooded! We'll work long hours for days, what with tourists riding around seeing things, Elma. Think of the money!"

He went out and looked at the sky. He didn't see anything.

"In a minute, maybe," he said, snuffing the cool air gratefully, arms up, beating his chest. "Ah!"

Elma said nothing. She peeled potatoes for French fries quietly, her eyes always on the sky.

"Sam," she said half an hour later. "There it is. Look."

He looked and saw it.

Earth.

It rose full and green, like a fine-cut stone, above the hills.

"Good old Earth," he whispered lovingly. "Good old wonderful Earth. Send me your hungry and your starved. Something, something—how does that poem go? Send me your hungry, old Earth. Here's Sam Parkhill, his hot dogs all boiled, his chili cooking, everything neat as a pin. Come on, you Earth, send me your rockets!"

He went out to look at his place. There it sat, perfect as a fresh-laid egg on the dead sea bottom, the only nucleus of light and warmth in hundreds of miles of lonely wasteland. It was like a heart beating alone in a great dark body. He felt almost sorrowful with pride, gazing at it with wet eyes.

"It sure makes you humble," he said among the cooking odors of wieners, warm buns, rich butter. "Step up," he invited the various stars in the sky. "Who'll be the first to buy?"

"Sam," said Elma.

Earth changed in the black sky.

It caught fire.

Part of it seemed to come apart in a million pieces, as if a gigantic jigsaw had exploded. It burned with an unholy dripping glare for a minute, three times normal size, then dwindled.

"What was that?" Sam looked at the green fire in the sky.

"Earth," said Elma, holding her hands together.

"That can't be Earth, that's not Earth! No, that ain't Earth! It can't be."

"You mean it couldn't be Earth," said Elma, looking at him. "That just isn't Earth. No, that's not Earth; is that what you mean?"

"Not Earth—oh no, it *couldn't* be," he wailed.

He stood there, his hands at his sides, his mouth open, his eyes wide and dull, not moving.

"Sam." She called his name. For the first time in days her eyes were bright. "Sam?"

He looked up at the sky.

"Well," she said. She glanced around for a minute or so in silence. Then briskly she flapped a wet towel over her arm. "Switch on more lights, turn up the music, open the doors. There'll be another batch of customers along in about a million years. Gotta be ready, yes, sir."

Sam did not move.

"What a swell spot for a hot-dog stand," she said. She reached over and picked a toothpick out of a jar and put it between her front teeth. "Let you in on a little secret, Sam," she whispered, leaning toward him. "This looks like it's going to be an off season."

November 2005: THE WATCHERS

THEY ALL came out and looked at the sky that night. They left their suppers or their washing up or their dressing for the show and they came out upon their now-not-quite-as-new porches and watched the green star of Earth there. It was a move without conscious effort; they all did it, to help them understand the news they had heard on the radio a moment before. There was Earth and there the coming war, and there hundreds of thousands of mothers or grandmothers or fathers or brothers or aunts or uncles or cousins. They stood on the porches and tried to believe in the existence of Earth, much as they had once tried to believe in the existence of Mars; it was a problem reversed. To all intents and purposes, Earth now was dead; they had been away from it for three or four years. Space was an anesthetic; seventy million miles of space numbed you, put memory to sleep, depopulated Earth, erased the past, and allowed these people here to go on with their work. But now, tonight, the dead were risen, Earth was reinhabited, memory awoke, a million names were spoken: What was so-and-so doing tonight on Earth? What about this one and that one? The people on the porches glanced sidewise at each other's faces.

At nine o'clock Earth seemed to explode, catch fire, and burn.

The people on the porches put up their hands as if to beat the fire out.

They waited.

By midnight the fire was extinguished. Earth was still there. There was a sigh, like an autumn wind, from the porches.

"We haven't heard from Harry for a long time."

"He's all right."

"We should send a message to Mother."

"She's all right."

"*Is* she?"

"Now, don't worry."

"Will she be all right, do you think?"

"Of course, of course; now come to bed."

But nobody moved. Late dinners were carried out onto the night lawns and set upon collapsible tables, and they picked at these slowly until two o'clock and the light-radio message flashed from Earth. They could read the great Morse-code flashes which flickered like a distant firefly:

AUSTRALIAN CONTINENT ATOMIZED IN PREMATURE EXPLOSION OF ATOMIC STOCKPILE. LOS ANGELES, LONDON BOMBED. WAR. COME HOME. COME HOME. COME HOME.

They stood up from their tables.

COME HOME. COME HOME. COME HOME.

"Have you heard from your brother Ted this year?"

"You know. With mail rates five bucks a letter to Earth, I don't write much."

COME HOME.

"I've been wondering about Jane; you remember Jane, my kid sister?"

COME HOME.

At three in the chilly morning the luggage-store proprietor glanced up. A lot of people were coming down the street.

"Stayed open late on purpose. What'll it be, mister?"

By dawn the luggage was gone from his shelves.

December 2005: THE SILENT TOWNS

THERE WAS a little white silent town on the edge of the dead Martian sea. The town was empty. No one moved in it. Lonely lights burned in the stores all day. The shop doors were wide, as if people had run off without using their keys. Magazines, brought from Earth on the silver rocket a month before, fluttered, untouched, burning brown, on wire racks fronting the silent drugstores.

The town was dead. Its beds were empty and cold. The only sound was the power hum of electric lines and dynamos, still alive, all by themselves. Water ran in forgotten bathtubs, poured out into living rooms, onto porches, and down through little garden plots to feed neglected flowers. In the dark theaters, gum under the many seats began to harden with tooth impressions still in it.

Across town was a rocket port. You could still smell the hard, scorched smell where the last rocket blasted off when it went back to Earth. If you dropped a dime in the telescope and pointed it at Earth, perhaps you could see the big war happening there. Perhaps you could see New York explode. Maybe London could be seen, covered with a new kind of fog. Perhaps then it might be understood why this small Martian town is abandoned. How quick was the evacuation? Walk in any store, bang the NO SALE key. Cash drawers jump out, all bright and jingly with coins. That war on Earth must be very bad. . . .

Along the empty avenues of this town, now, whistling softly, kicking a tin can ahead of him in deepest concentration, came a tall, thin man. His eyes glowed with a dark, quiet look of loneliness. He moved his bony hands in his pockets, which were tinkling with new dimes. Occasionally he tossed a dime to the ground. He laughed temperately, doing this, and walked on, sprinkling bright dimes everywhere.

His name was Walter Gripp. He had a placer mine and a remote shack far up in the blue Martian hills and he walked to town once every two weeks to see if he could marry a quiet and intelligent woman. Over the years he had always returned to his shack, alone and disappointed. A week ago, arriving in town, he had found it this way!

That day he had been so surprised that he rushed to a delicatessen, flung wide a case, and ordered a triple-decker beef sandwich.

"Coming up!" he cried, a towel on his arm.

He flourished meats and bread baked the day before, dusted a table, invited himself to sit, and ate until he had to go find a soda fountain, where he ordered a bicarbonate. The druggist, being one Walter Gripp, was astoundingly polite and fizzed one right up for him!

He stuffed his jeans with money, all he could find. He loaded a boy's wagon with ten-dollar bills and ran lickety-split through town. Reaching the suburbs, he suddenly realized how shamefully silly he was. He didn't need money. He rode the ten-dollar bills back to where he'd found them, counted a dollar from his own wallet to pay for the sandwiches, dropped it in the delicatessen till, and added a quarter tip.

That night he enjoyed a hot Turkish bath, a succulent filet carpeted with delicate mushrooms, imported dry sherry, and strawberries in wine. He fitted himself for a new blue flannel suit, and a rich gray Homburg which balanced oddly atop his gaunt head. He slid money into a juke box which played "That Old Gang of Mine." He dropped nickels in twenty boxes all over town. The lonely streets and the night were full of the sad music of "That Old Gang of Mine" as he walked, tall and thin and alone, his new shoes clumping softly, his cold hands in his pockets.

But that was a week past. He slept in a good house on Mars Avenue, rose mornings at nine, bathed, and idled to town for ham and eggs. No morning passed that he didn't freeze a ton of meats, vegetables, and lemon cream pies, enough to last ten years, until the rockets came back from Earth, if they ever came.

Now, tonight, he drifted up and down, seeing the wax women in every colorful shop window, pink and beautiful. For the first time he knew how dead the town was. He drew a glass of beer and sobbed gently.

"Why," he said, "I'm all *alone*."

He entered the Elite Theater to show himself a film, to distract his mind from his isolation. The theater was hollow, empty, like a tomb with phantoms crawling gray and black on the vast screen. Shivering, he hurried from the haunted place.

Having decided to return home, he was striking down the middle of a side street, almost running, when he heard the phone.

He listened.

"Phone ringing in someone's house."

He proceeded briskly.

"Someone should answer that phone," he mused.

He sat on a curb to pick a rock from his shoe, idly.

"Someone!" he screamed, leaping. "Me! Good lord, what's wrong with me!" he shrieked. He whirled. Which house? That one!

He raced over the lawn, up the steps, into the house, down a dark hall.

He yanked up the receiver.

"Hello!" he cried.

Buzzzzzzzzz.

"Hello, hello!"

They had hung up.

"Hello!" he shouted, and banged the phone. "You stupid idiot!" he cried to himself. "Sitting on that curb, you fool! Oh, you damned and awful fool!" He squeezed the phone. "Come on, ring again! Come *on*!"

He had never thought there might be others left on Mars. In the entire week he had seen no one. He had figured that all other towns were as empty as this one.

Now, staring at this terrible little black phone, he trembled. Interlocking dial systems connected every town on Mars. From which of thirty cities had the call come?

He didn't know.

He waited. He wandered to the strange kitchen, thawed some iced huckleberries, ate them disconsolately.

"There wasn't anyone on the other end of that call," he murmured. "Maybe a pole blew down somewhere and the phone rang by itself."

But hadn't he heard a click, which meant someone had hung up far away?

He stood in the hall the rest of the night. "Not because of the phone," he told himself. "I just haven't anything else to do."

He listened to his watch tick.

"She won't phone back," he said. "She won't *ever* call a number that didn't answer. She's probably dialing other houses in town right *now*! And here I sit—— Wait a minute!" He laughed. "Why do I keep saying 'she'?"

He blinked. "It could as easily be a 'he,' couldn't it?"

His heart slowed. He felt very cold and hollow.

He wanted very much for it to be a "she."

He walked out of the house and stood in the center of the early, dim morning street.

He listened. Not a sound. No birds. No cars. Only his heart beating. Beat and pause and beat again. His face ached with strain. The wind blew gently, oh so gently, flapping his coat.

"Sh," he whispered. "*Listen.*"

He swayed in a slow circle, turning his head from one silent house to another.

She'll phone more and more numbers, he thought. It must be a woman. Why? Only a woman would call and call. A man wouldn't. A man's independent. Did I phone anyone? No! Never thought of it. It must be a woman. It *has* to be, by God!

Listen.

Far away, under the stars, a phone rang.

He ran. He stopped to listen. The ringing, soft. He ran a few more steps. Louder. He raced down an alley. Louder still! He passed six houses, six more. Much louder! He chose a house and its door was locked.

The phone rang inside.

"Damn you!" He jerked the doorknob.

The phone screamed.

He heaved a porch chair through the parlor window, leaped in after it.

Before he even touched the phone, it was silent.

He stalked through the house then and broke mirrors, tore down drapes, and kicked in the kitchen stove.

Finally, exhausted, he picked up the thin directory which listed every phone on Mars. Fifty thousand names.

He started with number one.

Amelia Ames. He dialed her number in New Chicago, one hundred miles over the dead sea.

No answer.

Number two lived in New New York, five thousand miles across the blue mountains.

No answer.

He called three, four, five, six, seven, eight, his fingers jerking, unable to grip the receiver.

A woman's voice answered, "Hello?"

Walter cried back at her, "Hello, oh lord, hello!"

"This is a recording," recited the woman's voice. "Miss Helen Arasumian is not home. Will you leave a message on the wire spool so she may call you when she returns? Hello? This is a recording. Miss Arasumian is not home. Will you leave a message——"

He hung up.

He sat with his mouth twitching.

On second thought he redialed that number.

"When Miss Helen Arasumian comes home," he said, "tell her to go to hell."

He phoned Mars Junction, New Boston, Arcadia, and Roosevelt City exchanges, theorizing that they would be logical places for persons to dial from; after that he contacted local city halls and other public institutions in each town. He phoned the best hotels. Leave it to a woman to put herself up in luxury.

Suddenly he stopped, clapped his hands sharply together, and laughed. Of course! He checked the directory and dialed a long distance call through to the biggest beauty parlor in New Texas City. If ever there was a place where a woman would putter around, patting mud packs on her face and sitting under a drier, it would be a velvet-soft, diamond-gem beauty parlor!

The phone rang. Someone at the other end lifted the receiver.

A woman's voice said, "Hello?"

"If this is a recording," announced Walter Gripp, "I'll come over and blow the place up."

"This isn't a record," said the woman's voice. "Hello! Oh, hello, there *is* someone alive! Where are you?" She gave a delighted scream.

Walter almost collapsed. "*You!*" He stood up jerkily, eyes wild. "Good lord, what luck, what's your name?"

"Genevieve Selsor!" She wept into the receiver. "Oh, I'm so glad to hear from you, whoever you are!"

"Walter Gripp!"

"Walter, hello, Walter!"

"Hello, Genevieve!"

"Walter. It's such a nice name. Walter, Walter!"

"Thank you."

"Walter, where *are* you?"

Her voice was so kind and sweet and fine. He held the phone tight to his ear so she could whisper sweetly into it. He felt his feet drift off the floor. His cheeks burned.

"I'm in Marlin Village," he said. "I——"

Buzz.

"Hello?" he said.

Buzz.

He jiggled the hook. Nothing.

Somewhere a wind had blown down a pole. As quickly as she had come, Genevieve Selsor was gone.

He dialed, but the line was dead.

"I know where she is, anyway." He ran out of the house. The sun was rising as he backed a beetle-car from the stranger's garage, filled its back seat with food from the house, and set out at eighty miles an hour down the highway, heading for New Texas City.

A thousand miles, he thought. Genevieve Selsor, sit tight, you'll hear from me!

He honked his horn on every turn out of town.

At sunset, after an impossible day of driving, he pulled to the roadside, kicked off his tight shoes, laid himself out in the seat, and slid the gray Homburg over his weary eyes. His breathing became slow and regular. The wind blew and the stars shone gently upon him in the new dusk. The Martian mountains lay all around, millions of years old. Starlight glittered on the spires of a little Martian town, no bigger than a game of chess, in the blue hills.

He lay in the half-place between awakeness and dreams. He whispered. Genevieve. *Oh, Genevieve, sweet Genevieve*, he sang softly, *the years may come, the years may go. But Genevieve, sweet Genevieve* . . . . There was a warmth in him. He heard her quiet sweet cool voice sighing. *Hello, oh, hello, Walter! This is no record. Where are you, Walter, where are you?*

He sighed, putting up a hand to touch her in the moonlight. Long dark hair shaking in the wind; beautiful, it was. And her lips like red peppermints. And her cheeks like fresh-cut wet roses. And her body like a clear vaporous mist, while her soft cool sweet voice crooned to him once more the words to the old sad song, *Oh, Genevieve, sweet Genevieve, the years may come, the years may go* . . .

He slept.

He reached New Texas City at midnight.

He halted before the Deluxe Beauty Salon, yelling.

He expected her to rush out, all perfume, all laughter.

Nothing happened.

"She's asleep." He walked to the door. "Here I am!" he called. "Hello, Genevieve!"

The town lay in double moonlit silence. Somewhere a wind flapped a canvas awning.

He swung the glass door wide and stepped in.

"Hey!" He laughed uneasily. "Don't hide! I know you're here!"

He searched every booth.

He found a tiny handkerchief on the floor. It smelled so good he almost lost his balance. "Genevieve," he said.

He drove the car through the empty streets but saw nothing. "If this is a practical joke . . ."

He slowed the car. "Wait a minute. We were cut off. Maybe she drove to Marlin Village while I was driving here! She probably took the old Sea Road. We missed each other during the day. How'd she know I'd come get her? I didn't *say* I would. And she was so afraid when the phone died that she rushed to Marlin Village to find me! And here I am, by God, what a fool *I* am!"

Giving the horn a blow, he shot out of town.

He drove all night. He thought, What if she isn't in Marlin Village waiting, when I arrive?

He wouldn't think of that. She *must* be there. And he would run up and hold her and perhaps even kiss her, once, on the lips.

Genevieve, sweet Genevieve, he whistled, stepping it up to one hundred miles an hour.

Marlin Village was quiet at dawn. Yellow lights were still burning in several stores, and a juke box that had played steadily for one hundred hours finally, with a crackle of electricity, ceased, making the silence complete. The sun warmed the streets and warmed the cold and vacant sky.

Walter turned down Main Street, the car lights still on, honking the horn a double toot, six times at one corner, six times at another. He peered at the store names. His face was white and tired, and his hands slid on the sweaty steering wheel.

"Genevieve!" he called in the empty street.

The door to a beauty salon opened.

"Genevieve!" He stopped the car.

Genevieve Selsor stood in the open door of the salon as he ran across the street. A box of cream chocolates lay open in her arms. Her fingers, cuddling it, were plump and pallid. Her face, as she stepped into the light, was round and thick, and her eyes were like two immense eggs stuck into a white mess of bread dough. Her legs were as big around as the stumps of trees, and she moved with an ungainly shuffle. Her hair was an indiscriminate shade of brown that had been made and remade, it appeared, as a nest for birds. She had no lips at all and compensated this by stenciling on a large red, greasy mouth that now popped open in delight, now shut in sudden alarm. She had plucked her brows to thin antenna lines.

Walter stopped. His smile dissolved. He stood looking at her.

She dropped her candy box to the sidewalk.

"Are you—Genevieve Selsor?" His ears rang.

"Are you Walter Griff?" she asked.

"Gripp."

"Gripp," she corrected herself.

"How do you do," he said with a restrained voice.

"How do you do." She shook his hand.

Her fingers were sticky with chocolate.

"Well," said Walter Gripp.

"What?" asked Genevieve Selsor.

"I just said, 'Well,'" said Walter.

"Oh."

It was nine o'clock at night. They had spent the day picnicking, and for supper he had prepared a filet mignon which she didn't like because it was too rare, so he broiled it some more and it was too much broiled or fried or something. He laughed and said, "We'll see a movie!" She said okay and put her chocolaty fingers on his elbow. But all she wanted to see was a fifty-year-old film of Clark Gable. "Doesn't he just kill you?" She giggled. "Doesn't he *kill* you, now?" The film ended. "Run it off again," she commanded. "Again?" he asked. "Again," she said. And when he returned she snuggled up and put her paws all over him. "You're not quite what I expected, but you're nice," she admitted. "Thanks," he said, swallowing. "Oh, that Gable," she said, and pinched his leg. "Ouch," he said.

After the film they went shopping down the silent streets. She broke a window and put on the brightest dress she could find. Dumping a perfume bottle on her hair, she resembled a drowned sheep dog. "How old are you?" he inquired. "Guess." Dripping, she led him down the street. "Oh, thirty," he said. "Well," she announced stiffly, "I'm only twenty-seven, so there!"

"Here's another candy store!" she said. "Honest, I've led the life of Reilly since everything exploded. I never liked my folks, they were fools. They left for Earth two months ago. I was supposed to follow on the last rocket, but I stayed on; you know why?"

"Why?"

"Because everyone picked on me. So I stayed where I could throw perfume on myself all day and drink ten thousand malts and eat candy without people saying, 'Oh, that's full of calories!' So here I *am*!"

"Here you are." Walter shut his eyes.

"It's getting late," she said, looking at him.

"Yes."

"I'm tired," she said.

"Funny. I'm wide awake."

"Oh," she said.

"I feel like staying up all night," he said. "Say, there's a good record at Mike's. Come on, I'll play it for you."

"I'm tired." She glanced up at him with sly, bright eyes.

"I'm very alert," he said. "Strange."

"Come back to the beauty shop," she said. "I want to show you something."

She took him in through the glass door and walked him over to a large white box. "When I drove from Texas City," she said, "I brought this with me." She untied the pink ribbon. "I thought: Well, here I am, the only lady on Mars, and here is the only man, and, well . . ." She lifted the lid and folded back crisp layers of whispery pink tissue paper. She gave it a pat. "There."

Walter Gripp stared.

"What is it?" he asked, beginning to tremble.

"Don't you know, silly? It's all lace and all white and all fine and everything."

"No, I don't know what it is."

"It's a wedding dress, silly!"

"Is it?" His voice cracked.

He shut his eyes. Her voice was still soft and cool and sweet, as it had been on the phone. But when he opened his eyes and looked at her . . .

He backed up. "How nice," he said.

"Isn't it?"

"Genevieve." He glanced at the door.

"Yes?"

"Genevieve, I've something to tell you."

"Yes?" She drifted toward him, the perfume smell thick about her round white face.

"The thing I have to say to you is . . ." he said.

"Yes?"

"Good-by!"

And he was out the door and into his car before she could scream.

She ran and stood on the curb as he swung the car about.

"Walter Griff, come back here!" she wailed, flinging up her arms.

"Gripp," he corrected her.

"Gripp!" she shouted.

The car whirled away down the silent street, regardless of her stompings and shriekings. The exhaust from it fluttered the white dress she crumpled in her plump hands, and the stars shone bright, and the car vanished out onto the desert and away into blackness.

He drove all night and all day for three nights and days. Once he thought he saw a car following, and he broke into a shivering sweat and took another highway, cutting off across the lonely Martian world, past little dead cities, and he drove and drove for a week and a day, until he had put ten thousand miles between himself and Marlin Village. Then he pulled into a small town named Holtville Springs, where there were some tiny stores he could light up at night and restaurants to sit in, ordering meals. And he's lived there ever since, with two deep freezes packed with food to last him one hundred years, and enough cigars to last ten thousand days, and a good bed with a soft mattress.

And when once in a while over the long years the phone rings—he doesn't answer.

April 2026: THE LONG YEARS

WHENEVER THE wind came through the sky, he and his small family would sit in the stone hut and warm their hands over a wood fire. The wind would stir the canal waters and almost blow the stars out of the sky, but Mr. Hathaway would sit contented and talk to his wife, and his wife would reply, and he would speak to his two daughters and his son about the old days on Earth, and they would all answer neatly.

It was the twentieth year after the Great War. Mars was a tomb planet. Whether or not Earth was the same was a matter for much silent debate for Hathaway and his family on the long Martian nights.

This night one of the violent Martian dust storms had come over the low Martian graveyards, blowing through ancient towns and tearing away the plastic walls of the newer, American-built city that was melting down into the sand, desolated.

The storm abated. Hathaway went out into the cleared weather to see Earth burning green on the windy sky. He put his hand up as one might reach to adjust a dimly burning globe in the ceiling of a dark room. He looked across the long-dead sea bottoms. Not another living thing on this entire planet, he thought. Just myself. And *them*. He looked back within the stone hut.

What was happening on Earth now? He had seen no visible sign of change in Earth's aspect through his thirty-inch telescope. Well, he thought, I'm good for another twenty years if I'm careful. Someone might come. Either across the dead seas or out of space in a rocket on a little thread of red flame.

He called into the hut, "I'm going to take a walk."

"All right," his wife said.

He moved quietly down through a series of ruins. "Made in New York," he read from a piece of metal as he passed. "And all these things from Earth will be gone long before the old Martian towns." He looked toward the fifty-centuries-old village that lay among the blue mountains.

He came to a solitary Martian graveyard, a series of small hexagonal stones on a hill swept by the lonely wind.

He stood looking down at four graves with crude wooden crosses on them, and names. Tears did not come to his eyes. They had dried long ago.

"Do you forgive me for what I've done?" he asked of the crosses. "I was very much alone. You do understand, don't you?"

He returned to the stone hut and once more, just before going in, shaded his eyes, searching the black sky.

"You keep waiting and waiting and looking," he said, "and one night, perhaps——"

There was a tiny red flame on the sky.

He stepped away from the light of the hut.

"—and you look *again*," he whispered.

The tiny red flame was still there.

"It wasn't there last night," he whispered.

He stumbled and fell, picked himself up, ran behind the hut, swiveled the telescope, and pointed it at the sky.

A minute later, after a long, wild staring, he appeared in the low door of the hut. The wife and the two daughters and the son turned their heads to him. Finally he was able to speak.

"I have good news," he said. "I have looked at the sky. A rocket is coming to take us all home. It will be here in the early morning."

He put his hands down and put his head into his hands and began to cry gently.

He burned what was left of New New York that morning at three.

He took a torch and moved into the plastic city and with the flame touched the walls here or there. The city bloomed up in great tosses of heat and light. It was a square mile of illumination, big enough to be seen out in space. It would beckon the rocket down to Mr. Hathaway and his family.

His heart beating rapidly with pain, he returned to the hut. "See?" He held up a dusty bottle into the light. "Wine I saved, just for tonight. I knew that someday someone would find us! We'll have a drink to celebrate!"

He poured five glasses full.

"It's been a long time," he said, gravely looking into his drink. "Remember the day the war broke? Twenty years and seven months ago. And all the rockets were called home from Mars. And you and I and the children were out in the mountains, doing archaeological work, research on the ancient surgical methods of the Martians. We ran our horses, almost killing them, remember? But we got here to the city a week late. Everyone was gone. America had been destroyed; every rocket had left without waiting for stragglers, remember, remember? And it turned out we were the *only* ones left? Lord, Lord, how the years pass. I couldn't have stood it without you here, all of you. I'd have killed myself without you. But with you, it was worth waiting. Here's to us, then." He lifted his glass. "And to our long wait together." He drank.

The wife and the two daughters and the son raised their glasses to their lips.

The wine ran down over the chins of all four of them.

By morning the city was blowing in great black soft flakes across the sea bottom. The fire was exhausted, but it had served its purpose; the red spot on the sky grew larger.

From the stone hut came the rich brown smell of baked gingerbread. His wife stood over the table, setting down the hot pans of new bread as Hathaway entered. The two daughters were gently sweeping the bare stone floor with stiff brooms, and the son was polishing the silverware.

"We'll have a huge breakfast for them," laughed Hathaway. "Put on your best clothes!"

He hurried across his land to the vast metal storage shed. Inside was the cold-storage unit and power plant he had repaired and restored with his efficient, small, nervous fingers over the years, just as he had repaired clocks, telephones, and spool recorders in his spare time. The shed was full of things he had built, some senseless mechanisms the functions of which were a mystery even to himself now as he looked upon them.

From the deep freeze he fetched rimed cartons of beans and strawberries, twenty years old. Lazarus come forth, he thought, and pulled out a cool chicken.

The air was full of cooking odors when the rocket landed.

Like a boy, Hathaway raced down the hill. He stopped once because of a sudden sick pain in his chest. He sat on a rock to regain his breath, then ran all the rest of the way.

He stood in the hot atmosphere generated by the fiery rocket. A port opened. A man looked down.

Hathaway shielded his eyes and at last said, "Captain Wilder!"

"Who is it?" asked Captain Wilder, and jumped down and stood there looking at the old man. He put his hand out. "Good lord, it's Hathaway!"

"That's right." They looked into each other's faces.

"Hathaway, from my old crew, from the Fourth Expedition."

"It's been a long time, Captain."

"Too long. It's good to see you."

"I'm old," said Hathaway simply.

"I'm not young myself any more. I've been out to Jupiter and Saturn and Neptune for twenty years."

"I heard they had kicked you upstairs so you wouldn't interfere with colonial policy here on Mars." The old man looked around. "You've been gone so long you don't know what's happened——"

Wilder said, "I can guess. We've circled Mars twice. Found only one other man, name of Walter Gripp, about ten thousand miles from here. We offered to take him with us, but he said no. The last we saw of him he was sitting in the middle of the highway in a rocking chair, smoking a pipe, waving to us. Mars is pretty well dead, not even a Martian alive. What about Earth?"

"You know as much as I do. Once in a while I get the Earth radio, very faintly. But it's always in some other language. I'm sorry to say I only know Latin. A few words come through. I take it most of Earth's a shambles, but the war goes on. Are you going back, sir?"

"Yes. We're curious, of course. We had no radio contact so far out in space. We'll want to see Earth, no matter what."

"You'll take us with you?"

The captain started. "Of course, your wife, I remember her. Twenty-five years ago, wasn't it? When they opened First Town and you quit the service and brought her up here. And there were children——"

"My son and two daughters."

"Yes, I remember. They're here?"

"Up at our hut. There's a fine breakfast waiting all of you up the hill. Will you come?"

"We would be honored, Mr. Hathaway." Captain Wilder called to the rocket, "Abandon ship!"

They walked up the hill, Hathaway and Captain Wilder, the twenty crew members following, taking deep breaths of the thin, cool morning air. The sun rose and it was a good day.

"Do you remember Spender, Captain?"

"I've never forgotten him."

"About once a year I walk up past his tomb. It looks like he got his way at last. He didn't want us to come here, and I suppose he's happy now that we've all gone away."

"What about—what was his name?—Parkhill, Sam Parkhill?"

"He opened a hot-dog stand."

"It sounds just *like* him."

"And went back to Earth the next week for the war." Hathaway put his hand to his chest and sat down abruptly upon a boulder. "I'm sorry. The excitement. Seeing you again after all these years. Have to rest." He felt his heart pound. He counted the beats. It was very bad.

"We've a doctor," said Wilder. "Excuse me, Hathaway, I know you are one, but we'd better check you with our own——" The doctor was summoned.

"I'll be all right," insisted Hathaway. "The waiting, the excitement." He could hardly breathe. His lips were blue. "You know," he said as the doctor placed a stethoscope to him, "it's as if I kept alive all these years just for this day, and now you're here to take me back to Earth, I'm satisfied and I can just lie down and quit."

"Here." The doctor handed him a yellow pellet. "We'd better let you rest."

"Nonsense. Just let me sit a moment. It's good to see all of you. Good to hear new voices again."

"Is the pellet working?"

"Fine. Here we go!"

They walked on up the hill.

"Alice, come see who's here!"

Hathaway frowned and bent into the hut. "Alice, did you hear?"

His wife appeared. A moment later the two daughters, tall and gracious, came out, followed by an even taller son.

"Alice, you remember Captain Wilder?"

She hesitated and looked at Hathaway as if for instructions and then smiled. "Of course, Captain Wilder!"

"I remember, we had dinner together the night before I took off for Jupiter, Mrs. Hathaway."

She shook his hand vigorously. "My daughters, Marguerite and Susan. My son, John. You remember the captain, surely?"

Hands were shaken amid laughter and much talk.

Captain Wilder sniffed the air. "Is that *gingerbread*?"

"Will you have some?"

Everyone moved. Folding tables were hurried out while hot foods were rushed forth and plates and fine damask napkins and good silverware were laid. Captain Wilder stood looking first at Mrs. Hathaway and then at her son and her two tall, quiet-moving daughters. He looked into their faces as they darted past and he followed every move of their youthful hands and every expression of their wrinkleless faces. He sat upon a chair the son brought. "How old are you, John?"

The son replied, "Twenty-three."

Wilder shifted his silverware clumsily. His face was suddenly pale. The man next to him whispered, "Captain Wilder, that can't be right."

The son moved away to bring more chairs.

"What's that, Williamson?"

"I'm forty-three myself, Captain. I was in school the same time as young John Hathaway there, twenty years ago. He says he's only twenty-three now; he only *looks* twenty-three. But that's wrong. He should be forty-two, at least. What's it mean, sir?"

"I don't know."

"You look kind of sick, sir."

"I don't feel well. The daughters, too, I saw them twenty years or so ago; they haven't changed, not a wrinkle. Will you do me a favor? I want you to run an errand, Williamson. I'll tell you where to go and what to check. Late in the breakfast, slip away. It should take you only ten minutes. The place isn't far from here. I saw it from the rocket as we landed."

"Here! What are you talking about so seriously?" Mrs. Hathaway ladled quick spoons of soup into their bowls. "Smile now; we're all together, the trip's over, and it's like home!"

"Yes." Captain Wilder laughed. "You certainly look very well and young, Mrs. Hathaway!"

"Isn't that like a man!"

He watched her drift away, drift with her pink face warm, smooth as an apple, unwrinkled and colorful. She chimed her laugh at every joke, she tossed salads neatly, never once pausing for breath. And the bony son and curved daughters were brilliantly witty, like their father, telling of the long years and their secret life, while their father nodded proudly to each.

Williamson slipped off down the hill.

"Where's *he* going?" asked Hathaway.

"Checking the rocket," said Wilder. "But, as I was saying, Hathaway, there's nothing on Jupiter, nothing at all for men. That includes Saturn and Pluto." Wilder talked mechanically, not hearing his words, thinking only of Williamson running down the hill and climbing back to tell what he had found.

"Thanks." Marguerite Hathaway was filling his water glass. Impulsively he touched her arm. She did not even mind. Her flesh was warm and soft.

Hathaway, across the table, paused several times, touched his chest with his fingers, painfully, then went on listening to the murmuring talk and sudden loud chattering, glancing now and again with concern at Wilder, who did not seem to like chewing his gingerbread.

Williamson returned. He sat picking at his food until the captain whispered aside to him, "Well?"

"I found it, sir."

"And?"

Williamson's cheeks were white. He kept his eyes on the laughing people. The daughters were smiling gravely and the son was telling a joke. Williamson said, "I went into the graveyard."

"The four crosses were there?"

"The four crosses were there, sir. The names were still on them. I wrote them down to be sure." He read from a white paper: "Alice, Marguerite, Susan, and John Hathaway. Died of unknown virus. July 2007."

"Thank you, Williamson." Wilder closed his eyes.

"Nineteen years ago, sir." Williamson's hand trembled.

"Yes."

"Then who are *these*!"

"I don't know."

"What are you going to do?"

"I don't know that either."

"Will we tell the other men?"

"Later. Go on with your food as if nothing happened."

"I'm not very hungry now, sir."

The meal ended with wine brought from the rocket. Hathaway arose. "A toast to all of you; it's good to be with friends again. And to my wife and children, without whom I couldn't have survived alone. It is only through their kindness in caring for me that I've lived on, waiting for your arrival." He moved his wineglass toward his family, who looked back self-consciously, lowering their eyes at last as everyone drank.

Hathaway drank down his wine. He did not cry out as he fell forward onto the table and slipped to the ground. Several men eased him to rest. The doctor bent to him and listened. Wilder touched the doctor's shoulder. The doctor looked up and shook his head. Wilder knelt and took the old man's hand. "Wilder?" Hathaway's voice was barely audible. "I spoiled the breakfast."

"Nonsense."

"Say good-by to Alice and the children for me."

"Just a moment, I'll call them."

"No, no, don't!" gasped Hathaway. "They wouldn't understand. I wouldn't want them to understand! Don't!"

Wilder did not move.

Hathaway was dead.

Wilder waited for a long time. Then he arose and walked away from the stunned group around Hathaway. He went to Alice Hathaway, looked into her face, and said, "Do you know what has just happened?"

"Something about my husband?"

"He's just passed away; his heart," said Wilder, watching her.

"I'm sorry," she said.

"How do you feel?" he asked.

"He didn't want us to feel badly. He told us it would happen one day and he didn't want us to cry. He didn't teach us how, you know. He didn't want us to know. He said it was the worst thing that could happen to a man to know how to be lonely and know how to be sad and then to cry. So we're not to know what crying is, or being sad."

Wilder glanced at her hands, the soft warm hands and the fine manicured nails and the tapered wrists. He saw her slender, smooth white neck and her intelligent eyes. Finally he said, "Mr. Hathaway did a fine job on you and your children."

"He would have liked to hear you say that. He was so proud of us. After a while he even forgot that he had made us. At the end he loved and took us as his real wife and children. And, in a way, we *are*."

"You gave him a good deal of comfort."

"Yes, for years on end we sat and talked. He so much loved to talk. He liked the stone hut and the open fire. We could have lived in a regular house in the town, but he liked it up here, where he could be primitive if he liked, or modern if he liked. He told me all about his laboratory and the things he did in it. He wired the entire dead American town below with sound speakers. When he pressed a button the town lit up and made noises as if ten thousand people lived in it. There were airplane noises and car noises and the sounds of people talking. He would sit and light a cigar and talk to us, and the sounds of the town would come up to us, and once in a while the phone would ring and a recorded voice would ask Mr. Hathaway scientific and surgical questions and he would answer them. With the phone ringing and us here and the sounds of the town and his cigar, Mr. Hathaway was quite happy. There's only one thing he couldn't make us do," she said. "And that was to grow old. He got older every day, but we stayed the same. I guess he didn't mind. I guess he wanted us this way."

"We'll bury him down in the yard where the other four crosses are. I think he would like that."

She put her hand on his wrist, lightly. "I'm sure he would."

Orders were given. The family followed the little procession down the hill. Two men carried Hathaway on a covered stretcher. They passed the stone hut and the storage shed where Hathaway, many years before, had begun his work. Wilder paused within the workshop door.

How would it be, he wondered, to live on a planet with a wife and three children and have them die, leaving you alone with the wind and silence? What would a person do? Bury them with crosses in the graveyard and then come back up to the workshop and, with all the power of mind and memory and accuracy of finger and genius, put together, bit by bit, all those things that were wife, son, daughter. With an entire American city below from which to draw needed supplies, a brilliant man might do anything.

The sound of their footsteps was muffled in the sand. At the graveyard, as they turned in, two men were already spading out the earth.

They returned to the rocket in the late afternoon.

Williamson nodded at the stone hut. "What are we going to do about *them*?"

"I don't know," said the captain.

"Are you going to turn them off?"

"Off?" The captain looked faintly surprised. "It never entered my mind."

"You're not taking them back with us?"

"No, it would be useless."

"You mean you're going to leave them here, like *that*, as they *are*!"

The captain handed Williamson a gun. "If you can do anything about this, you're a better man than I."

Five minutes later Williamson returned from the hut, sweating. "Here, take your gun. I understand what you mean now. I went in the hut with the gun. One of the daughters smiled at me. So did the others. The wife offered me a cup of tea. Lord, it'd be murder!"

Wilder nodded. "There'll never be anything as fine as them again. They're built to last; ten, fifty, two hundred years. Yes, they've as much right to—to life as you or I or any of us." He knocked out his pipe. "Well, get aboard. We're taking off. This city's done for, we'll not be using it."

It was late in the day. A cold wind was rising. The men were aboard. The captain hesitated. Williamson said, "Don't tell me you're going back to say—good-by—to them?"

The captain looked at Williamson coldly. "None of your business."

Wilder strode up toward the hut through the darkening wind. The men in the rocket saw his shadow lingering in the stone-hut doorway. They saw a woman's shadow. They saw the captain shake her hand.

Moments later he came running back to the rocket.

On nights when the wind comes over the dead sea bottoms and through the hexagonal graveyard, over four old crosses and one new one, there is a light burning in the low stone hut, and in that hut, as the wind roars by and the dust whirls and the cold stars burn, are four figures, a woman, two daughters, a son, tending a low fire for no reason and talking and laughing.

Night after night for every year and every year, for no reason at all, the woman comes out and looks at the sky, her hands up, for a long moment, looking at the green burning of Earth, not knowing why she looks, and then she goes back and throws a stick on the fire, and the wind comes up and the dead sea goes on being dead.

August 2026: THERE WILL COME SOFT RAINS

IN THE living room the voice-clock sang, *Tick-tock, seven o'clock, time to get up, time to get up, seven o'clock!* as if it were afraid that nobody would. The morning house lay empty. The clock ticked on, repeating and repeating its sounds into the emptiness. *Seven-nine, breakfast time, seven-nine!*

In the kitchen the breakfast stove gave a hissing sigh and ejected from its warm interior eight pieces of perfectly browned toast, eight eggs sunnyside up, sixteen slices of bacon, two coffees, and two cool glasses of milk.

"Today is August 4, 2026," said a second voice from the kitchen ceiling, "in the city of Allendale, California." It repeated the date three times for memory's sake. "Today is Mr. Featherstone's birthday. Today is the anniversary of Tilita's marriage. Insurance is payable, as are the water, gas, and light bills."

Somewhere in the walls, relays clicked, memory tapes glided under electric eyes.

Eight-one, tick-tock, eight-one o'clock, off to school, off to work, run, run, eight-one! But no doors slammed, no carpets took the soft tread of rubber heels. It was raining outside. The weather box on the front door sang quietly: "Rain, rain, go away; rubbers, raincoats for today . . ." And the rain tapped on the empty house, echoing.

Outside, the garage chimed and lifted its door to reveal the waiting car. After a long wait the door swung down again.

At eight-thirty the eggs were shriveled and the toast was like stone. An aluminum wedge scraped them into the sink, where hot water whirled them down a metal throat which digested and flushed them away to the distant sea. The dirty dishes were dropped into a hot washer and emerged twinkling dry.

Nine-fifteen, sang the clock, *time to clean*.

Out of warrens in the wall, tiny robot mice darted. The rooms were acrawl with the small cleaning animals, all rubber and metal. They thudded against chairs, whirling their mustached runners, kneading the rug nap, sucking gently at hidden dust. Then, like mysterious invaders, they popped into their burrows. Their pink electric eyes faded. The house was clean.

Ten o'clock. The sun came out from behind the rain. The house stood alone in a city of rubble and ashes. This was the one house left standing. At night the ruined city gave off a radioactive glow which could be seen for miles.

Ten-fifteen. The garden sprinklers whirled up in golden founts, filling the soft morning air with scatterings of brightness. The water pelted windowpanes, running down the charred west side where the house had been burned evenly free of its white paint. The entire west face of the house was black, save for five places. Here the silhouette in paint of a man mowing a lawn. Here, as in a photograph, a woman bent to pick flowers. Still farther over, their images burned on wood in one titanic instant, a small boy, hands flung into the air; higher up, the image of a thrown ball, and opposite him a girl, hands raised to catch a ball which never came down.

The five spots of paint—the man, the woman, the children, the ball—remained. The rest was a thin charcoaled layer.

The gentle sprinkler rain filled the garden with falling light.

Until this day, how well the house had kept its peace. How carefully it had inquired, "Who goes there? What's the password?" and, getting no answer from lonely foxes and whining cats, it had shut up its windows and drawn shades in an old-maidenly preoccupation with self-protection which bordered on a mechanical paranoia.

It quivered at each sound, the house did. If a sparrow brushed a window, the shade snapped up. The bird, startled, flew off! No, not even a bird must touch the house!

The house was an altar with ten thousand attendants, big, small, servicing, attending, in choirs. But the gods had gone away, and the ritual of the religion continued senselessly, uselessly.

Twelve noon.

A dog whined, shivering, on the front porch.

The front door recognized the dog voice and opened. The dog, once huge and fleshy, but now gone to bone and covered with sores, moved in and through the house, tracking mud. Behind it whirred angry mice, angry at having to pick up mud, angry at inconvenience.

For not a leaf fragment blew under the door but what the wall panels flipped open and the copper scrap rats flashed swiftly out. The offending dust, hair, or paper, seized in miniature steel jaws, was raced back to the burrows. There, down tubes which fed into the cellar, it was dropped into the sighing vent of an incinerator which sat like evil Baal in a dark corner.

The dog ran upstairs, hysterically yelping to each door, at last realizing, as the house realized, that only silence was here.

It sniffed the air and scratched the kitchen door. Behind the door, the stove was making pancakes which filled the house with a rich baked odor and the scent of maple syrup.

The dog frothed at the mouth, lying at the door, sniffing, its eyes turned to fire. It ran wildly in circles, biting at its tail, spun in a frenzy, and died. It lay in the parlor for an hour.

Two o'clock, sang a voice.

Delicately sensing decay at last, the regiments of mice hummed out as softly as blown gray leaves in an electrical wind.

Two-fifteen.

The dog was gone.

In the cellar, the incinerator glowed suddenly and a whirl of sparks leaped up the chimney.

Two thirty-five.

Bridge tables sprouted from patio walls. Playing cards fluttered onto pads in a shower of pips. Martinis manifested on an oaken bench with egg-salad sandwiches. Music played.

But the tables were silent and the cards untouched.

At four o'clock the tables folded like great butterflies back through the paneled walls.

Four-thirty.

The nursery walls glowed.

Animals took shape: yellow giraffes, blue lions, pink antelopes, lilac panthers cavorting in crystal substance. The walls were glass. They looked out upon color and fantasy. Hidden films clocked through well-oiled sprockets, and the walls lived. The nursery floor was woven to resemble a crisp, cereal meadow. Over this ran aluminum roaches and iron crickets, and in the hot still air butterflies of delicate red tissue wavered among the sharp aroma of animal spoors! There was the sound like a great matted yellow hive of bees within a dark bellows, the lazy bumble of a purring lion. And there was the patter of okapi feet and the murmur of a fresh jungle rain, like other hoofs, falling upon the summer-starched grass. Now the walls dissolved into distances of parched weed, mile on mile, and warm endless sky. The animals drew away into thorn brakes and water holes.

It was the children's hour.

Five o'clock. The bath filled with clear hot water.

Six, seven, eight o'clock. The dinner dishes manipulated like magic tricks, and in the study a *click.* In the metal stand opposite the hearth where a fire now blazed up warmly, a cigar popped out, half an inch of soft gray ash on it, smoking, waiting.

Nine o'clock. The beds warmed their hidden circuits, for nights were cool here.

Nine-five. A voice spoke from the study ceiling:

"Mrs. McClellan, which poem would you like this evening?"

The house was silent.

The voice said at last, "Since you express no preference, I shall select a poem at random." Quiet music rose to back the voice. "Sara Teasdale. As I recall, your favorite. . . .

"There will come soft rains and the smell of the ground,
And swallows circling with their shimmering sound;

And frogs in the pools singing at night,
And wild plum trees in tremulous white;

Robins will wear their feathery fire,
Whistling their whims on a low fence-wire;

And not one will know of the war, not one
Will care at last when it is done.

Not one would mind, neither bird nor tree,
If mankind perished utterly;

And Spring herself, when she woke at dawn
Would scarcely know that we were gone."

The fire burned on the stone hearth and the cigar fell away into a mound of quiet ash on its tray. The empty chairs faced each other between the silent walls, and the music played.

At ten o'clock the house began to die.

The wind blew. A falling tree bough crashed through the kitchen window. Cleaning solvent, bottled, shattered over the stove. The room was ablaze in an instant!

"Fire!" screamed a voice. The house lights flashed, water pumps shot water from the ceilings. But the solvent spread on the linoleum, licking, eating, under the kitchen door, while the voices took it up in chorus: "Fire, fire, fire!"

The house tried to save itself. Doors sprang tightly shut, but the windows were broken by the heat and the wind blew and sucked upon the fire.

The house gave ground as the fire in ten billion angry sparks moved with flaming ease from room to room and then up the stairs. While scurrying water rats squeaked from the walls, pistoled their water, and ran for more. And the wall sprays let down showers of mechanical rain.

But too late. Somewhere, sighing, a pump shrugged to a stop. The quenching rain ceased. The reserve water supply which had filled baths and washed dishes for many quiet days was gone.

The fire crackled up the stairs. It fed upon Picassos and Matisses in the upper halls, like delicacies, baking off the oily flesh, tenderly crisping the canvases into black shavings.

Now the fire lay in beds, stood in windows, changed the colors of drapes!

And then, reinforcements.

From attic trapdoors, blind robot faces peered down with faucet mouths gushing green chemical.

The fire backed off, as even an elephant must at the sight of a dead snake. Now there were twenty snakes whipping over the floor, killing the fire with a clear cold venom of green froth.

But the fire was clever. It had sent flame outside the house, up through the attic to the pumps there. An explosion! The attic brain which directed the pumps was shattered into bronze shrapnel on the beams.

The fire rushed back into every closet and felt of the clothes hung there.

The house shuddered, oak bone on bone, its bared skeleton cringing from the heat, its wire, its nerves revealed as if a surgeon had torn the skin off to let the red veins and capillaries quiver in the scalded air. Help, help! Fire! Run, run! Heat snapped mirrors like the first brittle winter ice. And the voices wailed Fire, fire, run, run, like a tragic nursery rhyme, a dozen voices, high, low, like children dying in a forest, alone, alone. And the voices fading as the wires popped their sheathings like hot chestnuts. One, two, three, four, five voices died.

In the nursery the jungle burned. Blue lions roared, purple giraffes bounded off. The panthers ran in circles, changing color, and ten million animals, running before the fire, vanished off toward a distant steaming river. . . .

Ten more voices died. In the last instant under the fire avalanche, other choruses, oblivious, could be heard announcing the time, playing music, cutting the lawn by remote-control mower, or setting an umbrella frantically out and in the slamming and opening front door, a thousand things happening, like a clock shop when each clock strikes the hour insanely before or after the other, a scene of maniac confusion, yet unity; singing, screaming, a few last cleaning mice darting bravely out to carry the horrid ashes away! And one voice, with sublime disregard for the situation, read poetry aloud in the fiery study, until all the film spools burned, until all the wires withered and the circuits cracked.

The fire burst the house and let it slam flat down, puffing out skirts of spark and smoke.

In the kitchen, an instant before the rain of fire and timber, the stove could be seen making breakfasts at a psychopathic rate, ten dozen eggs, six loaves of toast, twenty dozen bacon strips, which, eaten by fire, started the stove working again, hysterically hissing!

The crash. The attic smashing into kitchen and parlor. The parlor into cellar, cellar into sub-cellar. Deep freeze, armchair, film tapes, circuits, beds, and all like skeletons thrown in a cluttered mound deep under.

Smoke and silence. A great quantity of smoke.

Dawn showed faintly in the east. Among the ruins, one wall stood alone. Within the wall, a last voice said, over and over again and again, even as the sun rose to shine upon the heaped rubble and steam:

"Today is August 5, 2026, today is August 5, 2026, today is . . ."

October 2026: THE MILLION-YEAR PICNIC

SOMEHOW THE idea was brought up by Mom that perhaps the whole family would enjoy a fishing trip. But they weren't Mom's words; Timothy knew that. They were Dad's words, and Mom used them for him somehow.

Dad shuffled his feet in a clutter of Martian pebbles and agreed. So immediately there was a tumult and a shouting, and very quickly the camp was tucked into capsules and containers, Mom slipped into traveling jumpers and blouse, Dad stuffed his pipe full with trembling hands, his eyes on the Martian sky, and the three boys piled yelling into the motorboat, none of them really keeping an eye on Mom and Dad, except Timothy.

Dad pushed a stud. The water boat sent a humming sound up into the sky. The water shook back and the boat nosed ahead, and the family cried, "Hurrah!"

Timothy sat in the back of the boat with Dad, his small fingers atop Dad's hairy ones, watching the canal twist, leaving the crumbled place behind where they had landed in their small family rocket all the way from Earth. He remembered the night before they left Earth, the hustling and hurrying, the rocket that Dad had found somewhere, somehow, and the talk of a vacation on Mars. A long way to go for a vacation, but Timothy said nothing because of his younger brothers. They came to Mars and now, first thing, or so they said, they were going fishing.

Dad had a funny look in his eyes as the boat went up-canal. A look that Timothy couldn't figure. It was made of strong light and maybe a sort of relief. It made the deep wrinkles laugh instead of worry or cry.

So there went the cooling rocket, around a bend, gone.

"How far are we going?" Robert splashed his hand. It looked like a small crab jumping in the violet water.

Dad exhaled. "A million years."

"Gee," said Robert.

"Look, kids." Mother pointed one soft long arm. "There's a dead city."

They looked with fervent anticipation, and the dead city lay dead for them alone, drowsing in a hot silence of summer made on Mars by a Martian weatherman.

And Dad looked as if he was pleased that it was dead.

It was a futile spread of pink rocks sleeping on a rise of sand, a few tumbled pillars, one lonely shrine, and then the sweep of sand again. Nothing else for miles. A white desert around the canal and a blue desert over it.

Just then a bird flew up. Like a stone thrown across a blue pond, hitting, falling deep, and vanishing.

Dad got a frightened look when he saw it. "I thought it was a rocket."

Timothy looked at the deep ocean sky, trying to see Earth and the war and the ruined cities and the men killing each other since the day he was born. But he saw nothing. The war was as removed and far off as two flies battling to the death in the arch of a great high and silent cathedral. And just as senseless.

William Thomas wiped his forehead and felt the touch of his son's hand on his arm, like a young tarantula, thrilled. He beamed at his son. "How goes it, Timmy?"

"Fine, Dad."

Timothy hadn't quite figured out what was ticking inside the vast adult mechanism beside him. The man with the immense hawk nose, sunburnt, peeling—and the hot blue eyes like agate marbles you play with after school in summer back on Earth, and the long thick columnar legs in the loose riding breeches.

"What are you looking at so hard, Dad?"

"I was looking for Earthian logic, common sense, good government, peace, and responsibility."

"All that up there?"

"No. I didn't find it. It's not there any more. Maybe it'll never be there again. Maybe we fooled ourselves that it was ever there."

"Huh?"

"See the fish," said Dad, pointing.

There rose a soprano clamor from all three boys as they rocked the boat in arching their tender necks to see. They *oohed* and *ahed.* A silver ring fish floated by them, undulating, and closing like an iris, instantly, around food particles, to assimilate them.

Dad looked at it. His voice was deep and quiet.

"Just like war. War swims along, sees food, contracts. A moment later—Earth is gone."

"William," said Mom.

"Sorry," said Dad.

They sat still and felt the canal water rush cool, swift, and glassy. The only sound was the motor hum, the glide of water, the sun expanding the air.

"When do we see the Martians?" cried Michael.

"Quite soon, perhaps," said Father. "Maybe tonight."

"Oh, but the Martians are a dead race now," said Mom.

"No, they're not. I'll show you some Martians, all right," Dad said presently.

Timothy scowled at that but said nothing. Everything was odd now. Vacations and fishing and looks between people.

The other boys were already engaged making shelves of their small hands and peering under them toward the seven-foot stone banks of the canal, watching for Martians.

"What do they look like?" demanded Michael.

"You'll know them when you see them." Dad sort of laughed, and Timothy saw a pulse beating time in his cheek.

Mother was slender and soft, with a woven plait of spun-gold hair over her head in a tiara, and eyes the color of the deep cool canal water where it ran in shadow, almost purple, with flecks of amber caught in it. You could see her thoughts swimming around in her eyes, like fish—some bright, some dark, some fast, quick, some slow and easy, and sometimes, like when she looked up where Earth was, being nothing but color and nothing else. She sat in the boat's prow, one hand resting on the side lip, the other on the lap of her dark blue breeches, and a line of sunburnt soft neck showing where her blouse opened like a white flower.

She kept looking ahead to see what was there, and, not being able to see it clearly enough, she looked backward toward her husband, and through his eyes, reflected then, she saw what was ahead; and since he added part of himself to this reflection, a determined firmness, her face relaxed and she accepted it and she turned back, knowing suddenly what to look for.

Timothy looked too. But all he saw was a straight pencil line of canal going violet through a wide shallow valley penned by low, eroded hills, and on until it fell over the sky's edge. And this canal went on and on, through cities that would have rattled like beetles in a dry skull if you shook them. A hundred or two hundred cities dreaming hot summer-day dreams and cool summer-night dreams . . .

They had come millions of miles for this outing—to fish. But there had been a gun on the rocket. This was a vacation. But why all the food, more than enough to last them years and years, left hidden back there near the rocket? Vacation. Just behind the veil of the vacation was not a soft face of laughter, but something hard and bony and perhaps terrifying. Timothy could not lift the veil, and the two other boys were busy being ten and eight years old, respectively.

"No Martians yet. Nuts." Robert put his V-shaped chin on his hands and glared at the canal.

Dad had brought an atomic radio along, strapped to his wrist. It functioned on an old-fashioned principle: you held it against the bones near your ear and it vibrated singing or talking to you. Dad listened to it now. His face looked like one of those fallen Martian cities, caved in, sucked dry, almost dead.

Then he gave it to Mom to listen. Her lips dropped open.

"What——" Timothy started to question, but never finished what he wished to say.

For at that moment there were two titanic, marrow-jolting explosions that grew upon themselves, followed by a half dozen minor concussions.

Jerking his head up, Dad notched the boat speed higher immediately. The boat leaped and jounced and spanked. This shook Robert out of his funk and elicited yelps of frightened but ecstatic joy from Michael, who clung to Mom's legs and watched the water pour by his nose in a wet torrent.

Dad swerved the boat, cut speed, and ducked the craft into a little branch canal and under an ancient, crumbling stone wharf that smelled of crab flesh. The boat rammed the wharf hard enough to throw them all forward, but no one was hurt, and Dad was already twisted to see if the ripples on the canal were enough to map their route into hiding. Water lines went across, lapped the stones, and rippled back to meet each other, settling, to be dappled by the sun. It all went away.

Dad listened. So did everybody.

Dad's breathing echoed like fists beating against the cold wet wharf stones. In the shadow, Mom's cat eyes just watched Father for some clue to what next.

Dad relaxed and blew out a breath, laughing at himself.

"The rocket, of course. I'm getting jumpy. The rocket."

Michael said, "What happened, Dad, what happened?"

"Oh, we just blew up our rocket, is all," said Timothy, trying to sound matter-of-fact. "I've heard rockets blown up before. Ours just blew."

"Why did we blow up our rocket?" asked Michael. "Huh, Dad?"

"It's part of the game, silly!" said Timothy.

"A game!" Michael and Robert loved the word.

"Dad fixed it so it would blow up and no one'd know where we landed or went! In case they ever came looking, see?"

"Oh boy, a secret!"

"Scared by my own rocket," admitted Dad to Mom. "I am nervous. It's silly to think there'll ever *be* any more rockets. Except *one*, perhaps, if Edwards and his wife get through with *their* ship."

He put his tiny radio to his ear again. After two minutes he dropped his hand as you would drop a rag.

"It's over at last," he said to Mom. "The radio just went off the atomic beam. Every other world station's gone. They dwindled down to a couple in the last few years. Now the air's completely silent. It'll probably remain silent."

"For how long?" asked Robert.

"Maybe—your great-grandchildren will hear it again," said Dad. He just sat there, and the children were caught in the center of his awe and defeat and resignation and acceptance.

Finally he put the boat out into the canal again, and they continued in the direction in which they had originally started.

It was getting late. Already the sun was down the sky, and a series of dead cities lay ahead of them.

Dad talked very quietly and gently to his sons. Many times in the past he had been brisk, distant, removed from them, but now he patted them on the head with just a word and they felt it.

"Mike, pick a city."

"What, Dad?"

"Pick a city, Son. Any one of these cities we pass."

"All right," said Michael. "How do I pick?"

"Pick the one you like the most. You, too, Robert and Tim. Pick the city you like best."

"I want a city with Martians in it," said Michael.

"You'll have that," said Dad. "I promise." His lips were for the children, but his eyes were for Mom.

They passed six cities in twenty minutes. Dad didn't say anything more about the explosions; he seemed much more interested in having fun with his sons, keeping them happy, than anything else.

Michael liked the first city they passed, but this was vetoed because everyone doubted quick first judgments. The second city nobody liked. It was an Earth Man's settlement, built of wood and already rotting into sawdust. Timothy liked the third city because it was large. The fourth and fifth were too small and the sixth brought acclaim from everyone, including Mother, who joined in the Gees, Goshes, and Look-at-thats!

There were fifty or sixty huge structures still standing, streets were dusty but paved, and you could see one or two old centrifugal fountains still pulsing wetly in the plazas. That was the only life—water leaping in the late sunlight.

"This is the city," said everybody.

Steering the boat to a wharf, Dad jumped out.

"Here we are. This is ours. This is where we live from now on!"

"From now on?" Michael was incredulous. He stood up, looking, and then turned to blink back at where the rocket used to be. "What about the rocket? What about Minnesota?"

"Here," said Dad.

He touched the small radio to Michael's blond head. "Listen."

Michael listened.

"Nothing," he said.

"That's right. Nothing. Nothing at all any more. No more Minneapolis, no more rockets, no more Earth."

Michael considered the lethal revelation and began to sob little dry sobs.

"Wait a moment," said Dad the next instant. "I'm giving you a lot more in exchange, Mike!"

"What?" Michael held off the tears, curious, but quite ready to continue in case Dad's further revelation was as disconcerting as the original.

"I'm giving you this city, Mike. It's yours."

"Mine?"

"For you and Robert and Timothy, all three of you, to own for yourselves."

Timothy bounded from the boat. "Look, guys, all for *us*! All of *that*!" He was playing the game with Dad, playing it large and playing it well. Later, after it was all over and things had settled, he could go off by himself and cry for ten minutes. But now it was still a game, still a family outing, and the other kids must be kept playing.

Mike jumped out with Robert. They helped Mom.

"Be careful of your sister," said Dad, and nobody knew what he meant until later.

They hurried into the great pink-stoned city, whispering among themselves, because dead cities have a way of making you want to whisper, to watch the sun go down.

"In about five days," said Dad quietly, "I'll go back down to where our rocket was and collect the food hidden in the ruins there and bring it here; and I'll hunt for Bert Edwards and his wife and daughters there."

"Daughters?" asked Timothy. "How many?"

"Four."

"I can see that'll cause trouble later." Mom nodded slowly.

"Girls." Michael made a face like an ancient Martian stone image. "Girls."

"Are they coming in a rocket too?"

"Yes. If they make it. Family rockets are made for travel to the Moon, not Mars. We were lucky we got through."

"Where did you get the rocket?" whispered Timothy, for the other boys were running ahead.

"I saved it. I saved it for twenty years, Tim. I had it hidden away, hoping I'd never have to use it. I suppose I should have given it to the government for the war, but I kept thinking about Mars. . . ."

"And a picnic!"

"Right. This is between you and me. When I saw everything was finishing on Earth, after I'd waited until the last moment, I packed us up. Bert Edwards had a ship hidden, too, but we decided it would be safer to take off separately, in case anyone tried to shoot us down."

"Why'd you blow up the rocket, Dad?"

"So we can't go back, ever. And so if any of those evil men ever come to Mars they won't know we're here."

"Is that why you look up all the time?"

"Yes, it's silly. They won't follow us, ever. They haven't anything to follow with. I'm being too careful, is all."

Michael came running back. "Is this really *our* city, Dad?"

"The whole darn planet belongs to us, kids. The whole darn planet."

They stood there, King of the Hill, Top of the Heap, Ruler of All They Surveyed, Unimpeachable Monarchs and Presidents, trying to understand what it meant to own a world and how big a world really was.

Night came quickly in the thin atmosphere, and Dad left them in the square by the pulsing fountain, went down to the boat, and came walking back carrying a stack of paper in his big hands.

He laid the papers in a clutter in an old courtyard and set them afire. To keep warm, they crouched around the blaze and laughed, and Timothy saw the little letters leap like frightened animals when the flames touched and engulfed them. The papers crinkled like an old man's skin, and the cremation surrounded innumerable words:

"GOVERNMENT BONDS; Business Graph, 1999; Religious Prejudice: An Essay; The Science of Logistics; Problems of the Pan-American Unity; Stock Report for July 3, 1998; The War Digest . . ."

Dad had insisted on bringing these papers for this purpose. He sat there and fed them into the fire, one by one, with satisfaction, and told his children what it all meant.

"It's time I told you a few things. I don't suppose it was fair, keeping so much from you. I don't know if you'll understand, but I have to talk, even if only part of it gets over to you."

He dropped a leaf in the fire.

"I'm burning a way of life, just like that way of life is being burned clean of Earth right now. Forgive me if I talk like a politician. I am, after all, a former state governor, and I was honest and they hated me for it. Life on Earth never settled down to doing anything very good. Science ran too far ahead of us too quickly, and the people got lost in a mechanical wilderness, like children making over pretty things, gadgets, helicopters, rockets; emphasizing the wrong items, emphasizing machines instead of how to run the machines. Wars got bigger and bigger and finally killed Earth. That's what the silent radio means. That's what we ran away from.

"We were lucky. There aren't any more rockets left. It's time you knew this isn't a fishing trip at all. I put off telling you. Earth is gone. Interplanetary travel won't be back for centuries, maybe never. But that way of life proved itself wrong and strangled itself with its own hands. You're young. I'll tell you this again every day until it sinks in."

He paused to feed more papers to the fire.

"Now we're alone. We and a handful of others who'll land in a few days. Enough to start over. Enough to turn away from all that back on Earth and strike out on a new line——"

The fire leaped up to emphasize his talking. And then all the papers were gone except one. All the laws and beliefs of Earth were burnt into small hot ashes which soon would be carried off in a wind.

Timothy looked at the last thing that Dad tossed in the fire. It was a map of the World, and it wrinkled and distorted itself hotly and went—flimpf—and was gone like a warm, black butterfly. Timothy turned away.

"Now I'm going to show you the Martians," said Dad. "Come on, all of you. Here, Alice." He took her hand.

Michael was crying loudly, and Dad picked him up and carried him, and they walked down through the ruins toward the canal.

The canal. Where tomorrow or the next day their future wives would come up in a boat, small laughing girls now, with their father and mother.

The night came down around them, and there were stars. But Timothy couldn't find Earth. It had already set. That was something to think about.

A night bird called among the ruins as they walked. Dad said, "Your mother and I will try to teach you. Perhaps we'll fail. I hope not. We've had a good lot to see and learn from. We planned this trip years ago, before you were born. Even if there hadn't been a war we would have come to Mars, I think, to live and form our own standard of living. It would have been another century before Mars would have been really poisoned by the Earth civilization. Now, of course——"

They reached the canal. It was long and straight and cool and wet and reflective in the night.

"I've always wanted to see a Martian," said Michael. "Where are they, Dad? You promised."

"There they are," said Dad, and he shifted Michael on his shoulder and pointed straight down.

The Martians were there. Timothy began to shiver.

The Martians were there—in the canal—reflected in the water. Timothy and Michael and Robert and Mom and Dad.

The Martians stared back up at them for a long, long silent time from the rippling water. . . .

FAHRENHEIT 451

FAHRENHEIT 451—
the temperature at which book-paper catches fire, and burns . . .

This one, with gratitude,
is for
DON CONGDON

Contents

If they give you ruled paper,
write the other way.

–Juan Ramón Jiménez

Illustration by Joe Mugnaini

Part One:
The Hearth and the Salamander

IT WAS A PLEASURE TO BURN.

It was a special pleasure to see things eaten, to see things blackened and *changed*. With the brass nozzle in his fists, with this great python spitting its venomous kerosene upon the world, the blood pounded in his head, and his hands were the hands of some amazing conductor playing all the symphonies of blazing and burning to bring down the tatters and charcoal ruins of history. With his symbolic helmet numbered 451 on his stolid head, and his eyes all orange flame with the thought of what came next, he flicked the igniter and the house jumped up in a gorging fire that burned the evening sky red and yellow and black. He strode in a swarm of fireflies. He wanted above all, like the old joke, to shove a marshmallow on a stick in the furnace, while the flapping pigeon-winged books died on the porch and lawn of the house. While the books went up in sparkling whirls and blew away on a wind turned dark with burning.

Montag grinned the fierce grin of all men singed and driven back by flame.

He knew that when he returned to the firehouse, he might wink at himself, a minstrel man, burnt-corked, in the mirror. Later, going to sleep, he would feel the fiery smile still gripped by his face muscles, in the dark. It never went away, that smile, it never ever went away, as long as he remembered.

He hung up his black beetle-colored helmet and shined it; he hung his flameproof jacket neatly; he showered luxuriously, and then, whistling, hands in pockets, walked across the upper floor of the fire station and fell down the hole. At the last moment, when disaster seemed positive, he pulled his hands from his pockets and broke his fall by grasping the golden pole. He slid to a squeaking halt, the heels one inch from the concrete floor downstairs.

He walked out of the fire station and along the midnight

street toward the subway where the silent air-propelled train slid soundlessly down its lubricated flue in the earth and let him out with a great puff of warm air onto the cream-tiled escalator rising to the suburb.

Whistling, he let the escalator waft him into the still night air. He walked toward the corner, thinking little at all about nothing in particular. Before he reached the corner, however, he slowed as if a wind had sprung up from nowhere, as if someone had called his name.

The last few nights he had had the most uncertain feelings about the sidewalk just around the corner here, moving in the starlight toward his house. He had felt that a moment prior to his making the turn, someone had been there. The air seemed charged with a special calm as if someone had waited there, quietly, and only a moment before he came, simply turned to a shadow and let him through. Perhaps his nose detected a faint perfume, perhaps the skin on the backs of his hands, on his face, felt the temperature rise at this one spot where a person's standing might raise the immediate atmosphere ten degrees for an instant. There was no understanding it. Each time he made the turn, he saw only the white, unused, buckling sidewalk, with perhaps, on one night, something vanishing swiftly across a lawn before he could focus his eyes or speak.

But now tonight, he slowed almost to a stop. His inner mind, reaching out to turn the corner for him, had heard the faintest whisper. Breathing? Or was the atmosphere compressed merely by someone standing very quietly there, waiting?

He turned the corner.

The autumn leaves blew over the moonlit pavement in such a way as to make the girl who was moving there seem fixed to a sliding walk, letting the motion of the wind and the leaves carry her forward. Her head was half bent to watch her shoes stir the circling leaves. Her face was slender and milk-white, and in it was a kind of gentle hunger that touched over everything with tireless curiosity. It was a look, almost, of pale surprise; the dark eyes were so fixed to the world that no move escaped them. Her dress was white and it whispered. He almost thought he heard the motion of her hands as she walked, and the infinitely small sound now, the white stir of her face turning when she discovered she was a moment away from a man who stood in the middle of the pavement waiting.

The trees overhead made a great sound of letting down their dry rain. The girl stopped and looked as if she might pull back in surprise, but instead stood regarding Montag with eyes so dark and shining and alive, that he felt he had said something quite wonderful. But he knew his mouth had only moved to say hello, and then when she seemed hypnotized by the salamander on his arm and the phoenix-disc on his chest, he spoke again.

"Of course," he said, "you're our new neighbor, aren't you?"

"And you must be—" She raised her eyes from his professional symbols, "—the fireman." Her voice trailed off.

"How oddly you say that."

"I'd—I'd have known it with my eyes shut," she said, slowly.

"What—the smell of kerosene? My wife always complains," he laughed. "You never wash it off completely."

"No, you don't," she said, in awe.

He felt she was walking in a circle about him, turning him end for end, shaking him quietly, and emptying his pockets, without once moving herself.

"Kerosene," he said, because the silence had lengthened, "is nothing but perfume to me."

"Does it seem like that, really?"

"Of course. Why not?"

She gave herself time to think of it. "I don't know." She turned to face the sidewalk going toward their homes. "Do you mind if I walk back with you? I'm Clarisse McClellan."

"Clarisse. Guy Montag. Come along. What are you doing out so late wandering around? How old are you?"

They walked in the warm-cool blowing night on the silvered pavement and there was the faintest breath of fresh apricots and strawberries in the air, and he looked around and realized this was quite impossible, so late in the year.

There was only the girl walking with him now, her face bright as snow in the moonlight, and he knew she was working his questions around, seeking the best answers she could possibly give.

"Well," she said, "I'm seventeen and I'm crazy. My uncle says the two always go together. When people ask your age, he said, always say seventeen and insane. Isn't this a nice time of night to walk? I like to smell things and look at things, and sometimes stay up all night, walking, and watch the sun rise."

They walked on again in silence and finally she said, thoughtfully, "You know, I'm not afraid of you at all."

He was surprised. "Why should you be?"

"So many people are. Afraid of firemen, I mean. But you're just a man, after all . . ."

He saw himself in her eyes, suspended in two shining drops of bright water, himself dark and tiny, in fine detail, the lines about his mouth, everything there, as if her eyes were two miraculous bits of violet amber that might capture and hold him intact. Her face, turned to him now, was fragile milk crystal with a soft and constant light in it. It was not the hysterical light of electricity but—what? But the strangely comfortable and rare and gently flattering light of the candle. One time, as a child, in a power failure, his mother had found and lit a last candle and there had been a brief hour of rediscovery, of such illumination that space lost its vast dimensions and drew comfortably around them, and they, mother and son, alone, transformed, hoping that the power might not come on again too soon. . . .

And then Clarisse McClellan said:

"Do you mind if I ask? How long've you worked at being a fireman?"

"Since I was twenty, ten years ago."

"Do you ever *read* any of the books you burn?"

He laughed. "That's against the law!"

"Oh. Of course."

"It's fine work. Monday burn Millay, Wednesday Whitman, Friday Faulkner, burn 'em to ashes, then burn the ashes. That's our official slogan."

They walked still further and the girl said, "Is it true that long ago firemen put fires *out* instead of going to start them?"

"No. Houses have *always* been fireproof, take my word for it."

"Strange. I heard once that a long time ago houses used to burn by accident and they needed firemen to *stop* the flames."

He laughed.

She glanced quickly over. "Why are you laughing?"

"I don't know." He started to laugh again and stopped. "Why?"

"You laugh when I haven't been funny and you answer right off. You never stop to think what I've asked you."

He stopped walking. "You *are* an odd one," he said, looking at her. "Haven't you any respect?"

"I don't mean to be insulting. It's just, I love to watch people too much, I guess."

"Well, doesn't this mean *anything* to you?" He tapped the numerals 451 stitched on his char-colored sleeve.

"Yes," she whispered. She increased her pace. "Have you ever watched the jet-cars racing on the boulevards down that way?"

"You're changing the subject!"

"I sometimes think drivers don't know what grass is, or flowers, because they never see them slowly," she said. "If you showed a driver a green blur, Oh yes! he'd say, that's grass! A pink blur? That's a rose-garden! White blurs are houses. Brown blurs are cows. My uncle drove slowly on a highway once. He drove forty miles an hour and they jailed him for two days. Isn't that funny, and sad, too?"

"You think too many things," said Montag, uneasily.

"I rarely watch the 'parlor walls' or go to races or Fun Parks. So I've lots of time for crazy thoughts, I guess. Have you seen the two hundred-foot-long billboards in the country beyond town? Did you know that once billboards were only twenty feet long? But cars started rushing by so quickly they had to stretch the advertising out so it would last."

"I didn't know that!" Montag laughed abruptly.

"Bet I know something else you don't. There's dew on the grass in the morning."

He suddenly couldn't remember if he had known this or not, and it made him quite irritable.

"And if you look—" she nodded at the sky, "there's a man in the moon."

He hadn't looked for a long time.

They walked the rest of the way in silence, hers thoughtful, his a kind of clenching and uncomfortable silence in which he shot her accusing glances. When they reached her house all its lights were blazing.

"What's going on?" Montag had rarely seen that many house lights.

"Oh, just my mother and father and uncle sitting around, talking. It's like being a pedestrian, only rarer. My uncle was arrested another time—did I tell you?—for being a pedestrian. Oh, we're *most* peculiar."

"But what do you *talk* about?"

She laughed at this. "Good night!" She started up her walk. Then she seemed to remember something and came back to look at him with wonder and curiosity. "Are you happy?" she said.

"Am I *what*?" he cried.

But she was gone—running in the moonlight. Her front door shut gently.

"Happy! Of all the nonsense."

He stopped laughing.

He put his hand into the glove-hole of his front door and let it know his touch. The front door slid open.

Of course I'm happy. What does she think? I'm *not*? he asked the quiet rooms. He stood looking up at the ventilator grille in the hall and suddenly remembered that something lay hidden behind the grille, something that seemed to peer down at him now. He moved his eyes quickly away.

What a strange meeting on a strange night. He remembered nothing like it save one afternoon a year ago when he had met an old man in the park and *they* had talked. . . .

Montag shook his head. He looked at a blank wall. The girl's face was there, really quite beautiful in memory: astonishing, in fact. She had a very thin face like the dial of a small clock seen faintly in a dark room in the middle of a night when you waken to see the time and see the clock telling you the hour and the minute and the second, with a white silence and a glowing, all certainty and knowing what it has to tell of the night passing swiftly on toward further darknesses, but moving also toward a new sun.

"*What?*" asked Montag of that other self, the subconscious idiot that ran babbling at times, quite independent of will, habit, and conscience.

He glanced back at the wall. How like a mirror, too, her face.

Impossible; for how many people did you know that refracted your own light to you? People were more often—he searched for a simile, found one in his work—torches, blazing away until they whiffed out. How rarely did other people's faces take of you and throw back to you your own expression, your own innermost trembling thought?

What incredible power of identification the girl had; she was like the eager watcher of a marionette show, anticipating each flicker of an eyelid, each gesture of his hand, each flick of a finger, the moment before it began. How long had they walked together? Three minutes? Five? Yet how large that time seemed now. How immense a figure she was on the stage before him; what a shadow she threw on the wall with her slender body! He felt that if his eye itched, she might blink. And if the muscles of his jaws stretched imperceptibly, she would yawn long before he would.

Why, he thought, now that I think of it, she almost seemed to be waiting for me there, in the street, so damned late at night . . .

He opened the bedroom door.

It was like coming into the cold marbled room of a mausoleum after the moon has set. Complete darkness, not a hint of the silver world outside, the windows tightly shut, the chamber a tomb-world where no sound from the great city could penetrate. The room was not empty.

He listened.

The little mosquito-delicate dancing hum in the air, the electrical murmur of a hidden wasp snug in its special pink warm nest. The music was almost loud enough so he could follow the tune.

He felt his smile slide away, melt, fold over and down on itself like a tallow skin, like the stuff of a fantastic candle burning too long and now collapsing and now blown out. Darkness. He was not happy. He was not happy. He said the words to himself. He recognized this as the true state of affairs. He wore his happiness like a mask and the girl had run off across the lawn with the mask and there was no way of going to knock on her door and ask for it back.

Without turning on the light he imagined how this room

would look. His wife stretched on the bed, uncovered and cold, like a body displayed on the lid of a tomb, her eyes fixed to the ceiling by invisible threads of steel, immovable. And in her ears the little Seashells, the thimble radios tamped tight, and an electronic ocean of sound, of music and talk and music and talk coming in, coming in on the shore of her unsleeping mind. The room was indeed empty. Every night the waves came in and bore her off on their great tides of sound, floating her, wide-eyed, toward morning. There had been no night in the last two years that Mildred had not swum that sea, had not gladly gone down in it for the third time.

The room was cold but nonetheless he felt he could not breathe. He did not wish to open the drapes and open the French windows, for he did not want the moon to come into the room. So, with the feeling of a man who will die in the next hour for lack of air, he felt his way toward his open, separate, and therefore cold bed.

An instant before his foot hit the object on the floor he knew he would hit such an object. It was not unlike the feeling he had experienced before turning the corner and almost knocking the girl down. His foot, sending vibrations ahead, received back echoes of the small barrier across its path even as the foot swung. His foot kicked. The object gave a dull clink and slid off in darkness.

He stood very straight and listened to the person on the dark bed in the completely featureless night. The breath coming out the nostrils was so faint it stirred only the furthest fringes of life, a small leaf, a black feather, a single fibre of hair.

He still did not want outside light. He pulled out his igniter, felt the salamander etched on its silver disc, gave it a flick. . . .

Two moonstones looked up at him in the light of his small hand-held fire; two pale moonstones buried in a creek of clear water over which the life of the world ran, not touching them.

"Mildred!"

Her face was like a snow-covered island upon which rain might fall, but it felt no rain; over which clouds might pass their moving shadows, but she felt no shadow. There was only the singing of the thimble-wasps in her tamped-shut ears, and her eyes all glass, and breath going in and out, softly, faintly, in and out her nostrils, and her not caring whether it came or went, went or came.

The object he had sent tumbling with his foot now glinted under the edge of his own bed. The small crystal bottle of sleeping tablets which earlier today had been filled with thirty capsules and which now lay uncapped and empty in the light of the tiny flare.

As he stood there the sky over the house screamed. There was a tremendous ripping sound as if two giant hands had torn ten thousand miles of black linen down the seam. Montag was cut in half. He felt his chest chopped down and split apart. The jet-bombers going over, going over, going over, one two, one two, one two, six of them, nine of them, twelve of them, one and one and one and another and another and another, did all the screaming for him. He opened his own mouth and let their shriek come down and out between his bared teeth. The house shook. The flare went out in his hand. The moonstones vanished. He felt his hand plunge toward the telephone.

The jets were gone. He felt his lips move, brushing the mouthpiece of the phone. "Emergency hospital." A terrible whisper.

He felt that the stars had been pulverized by the sound of the black jets and that in the morning the earth would be covered with their dust like a strange snow. That was his idiot thought as he stood shivering in the dark, and let his lips go on moving and moving.

They had this machine. They had two machines, really. One of them slid down into your stomach like a black cobra down an echoing well looking for all the old water and the old time gathered there. It drank up the green matter that flowed to the top in a slow boil. Did it drink of the darkness? Did it suck out all the poisons accumulated with the years? It fed in silence with an occasional sound of inner suffocation and blind searching. It had an Eye. The impersonal operator of the machine could, by wearing a special optical helmet, gaze into the soul of the person whom he was pumping out. What did the Eye see? He did not say. He saw but did not see what the Eye saw. The entire operation was not unlike the digging of a trench in one's yard. The woman on the bed was no more than a hard stratum of marble they had reached. Go on, anyway, shove the bore down, slush up the emptiness, if such a thing could be brought out in the throb of the suction snake. The operator stood smoking a cigarette. The other machine was working, too.

The other machine, operated by an equally impersonal fellow in nonstainable reddish-brown coveralls. This machine pumped all of the blood from the body and replaced it with fresh blood and serum.

"Got to clean 'em out both ways," said the operator, standing over the silent woman. "No use getting the stomach if you don't clean the blood. Leave that stuff in the blood and the blood hits the brain like a mallet, bang, a couple thousand times and the brain just gives up, just quits."

"Stop it!" said Montag.

"I was just sayin'," said the operator.

"Are you done?" said Montag.

They shut the machines up tight. "We're done." His anger did not even touch them. They stood with the cigarette smoke curling around their noses and into their eyes without making them blink or squint. "That's fifty bucks."

"First, why don't you tell me if she'll be all right?"

"Sure, she'll be okay. We got all the mean stuff right in our suitcase here, it can't get at her now. As I said, you take out the old and put in the new and you're okay."

"Neither of you is an M.D. Why didn't they send an M.D. from Emergency?"

"Hell!" The operator's cigarette moved on his lip. "We get these cases nine or ten a night. Got so many, starting a few years ago, we had the special machines built. With the optical lens, of course, that was new; the rest is ancient. You don't need an M.D., case like this; all you need is two handymen, clean up the problem in half an hour. Look—" he started for the door—"we gotta go. Just had another call on the old ear-thimble. Ten blocks from here. Someone else just jumped off the cap of a pillbox. Call if you need us again. Keep her quiet. We got a contra-sedative in her. She'll wake up hungry. So long."

And the men with the cigarettes in their straight-lined mouths, the men with the eyes of puff adders, took up their load of machine and tube, their case of liquid melancholy and the slow dark sludge of nameless stuff, and strolled out the door.

Montag sank down into a chair and looked at this woman. Her eyes were closed now, gently, and he put out his hand to feel the warmness of breath on his palm.

"Mildred," he said, at last.

There are too many of us, he thought. There are billions of us and that's too many. Nobody knows anyone. Strangers come and violate you. Strangers come and cut your heart out. Strangers come and take your blood. Good God, who *were* those men? I never saw them before in my *life*!

Half an hour passed.

The bloodstream in this woman was new and it seemed to have done a new thing to her. Her cheeks were very pink and her lips were very fresh and full of color and they looked soft and relaxed. Someone else's blood there. If only someone else's flesh and brain and memory. If only they could have taken her mind along to the dry-cleaner's and emptied the pockets and steamed and cleansed it and reblocked it and brought it back in the morning. If only . . .

He got up and put back the drapes and opened the windows wide to let the night air in. It was two o'clock in the morning. Was it only an hour ago, Clarisse McClellan in the street, and him coming in, and the dark room and his foot kicking the little crystal bottle? Only an hour, but the world had melted down and sprung up in a new and colorless form.

Laughter blew across the moon-colored lawn from the house of Clarisse and her father and mother and the uncle who smiled so quietly and so earnestly. Above all, their laughter was relaxed and hearty and not forced in any way, coming from the house that was so brightly lit this late at night while all the other houses were kept to themselves in darkness. Montag heard the voices talking, talking, talking, giving, talking, weaving, reweaving their hypnotic web.

Montag moved out through the French windows and crossed the lawn, without even thinking of it. He stood outside the talking house in the shadows, thinking he might even tap on their door and whisper, "Let me come in. I won't say anything. I just want to listen. What is it you're saying?"

But instead he stood there, very cold, his face a mask of ice, listening to a man's voice (the uncle?) moving along at an easy pace:

"Well, after all, this is the age of the disposable tissue. Blow your nose on a person, wad them, flush them away, reach for another, blow, wad, flush. Everyone using everyone else's coattails. How are you supposed to root for the home team when you don't even have a program or know the names? For that matter, what color jerseys are they wearing as they trot out on the field?"

Montag moved back to his own house, left the window wide, checked Mildred, tucked the covers about her carefully, and then lay down with the moonlight on his cheekbones and on the frowning ridges in his brow, with the moonlight distilled in each eye to form a silver cataract there.

One drop of rain. Clarisse. Another drop. Mildred. A third. The uncle. A fourth. The fire tonight. One, Clarisse. Two, Mildred. Three, uncle. Four, fire. One, Mildred, two, Clarisse. One, two, three, four, five, Clarisse, Mildred, uncle, fire, sleeping tablets, men, disposable tissue, coattails, blow, wad, flush, Clarisse, Mildred, uncle, fire, tablets, tissues, blow, wad, flush. One, two, three, one, two, three! Rain. The storm. The uncle laughing. Thunder falling downstairs. The whole world pouring down. The fire gushing up in a volcano. All rushing on down around in a spouting roar and rivering stream toward morning.

"I don't know anything any more," he said, and let a sleep-lozenge dissolve on his tongue.

At nine in the morning, Mildred's bed was empty.

Montag got up quickly, his heart pumping, and ran down the hall and stopped at the kitchen door.

Toast popped out of the silver toaster, was seized by a spidery metal hand that drenched it with melted butter.

Mildred watched the toast delivered to her plate. She had both ears plugged with electronic bees that were humming the hour away. She looked up suddenly, saw him and nodded.

"You all right?" he asked.

She was an expert at lip reading from ten years of apprenticeship at Seashell ear-thimbles. She nodded again. She set the toaster clicking away at another piece of bread.

Montag sat down.

His wife said, "I don't know *why* I should be so hungry."

"You——"

"I'm *hungry*."

"Last night," he began.

"Didn't sleep well. Feel terrible," she said. "God, I'm hungry. I can't figure it."

"Last night——" he said again.

She watched his lips casually. "What about last night?"

"Don't you remember?"

"What? Did we have a wild party or something? Feel like I've a hangover. God, I'm hungry. Who was here?"

"A few people," he said.

"That's what I thought." She chewed her toast. "Sore stomach, but I'm hungry as all get-out. Hope I didn't do anything foolish at the party."

"No," he said, quietly.

The toaster spidered out a piece of buttered bread for him. He held it in his hand, feeling obligated.

"You don't look so hot yourself," said his wife.

In the late afternoon it rained and the entire world was dark gray. He stood in the hall of his house, putting on his badge with the orange salamander burning across it. He stood looking up at the air-conditioning vent in the hall for a long time. His wife in the TV parlor paused long enough from reading her script to glance up. "Hey," she said. "The man's *thinking*!"

"Yes," he said. "I wanted to talk to you." He paused. "You took all the pills in your bottle last night."

"Oh, I wouldn't do that," she said, surprised.

"The bottle was empty."

"I wouldn't do a thing like that. Why would I do a thing like that?" she said.

"Maybe you took two pills and forgot and took two more, and forgot again and took two more, and were so dopey you kept right on until you had thirty or forty of them in you."

"Heck," she said, "what would I want to go and do a silly thing like that for?"

"I don't know," he said.

She was quite obviously waiting for him to go. "I didn't do that," she said. "Never in a billion years."

"All right if you say so," he said.

"That's what the lady said." She turned back to her script.

"What's on this afternoon?" he asked, tiredly.

She didn't look up from the script again. "Well, this is a play comes on the wall-to-wall circuit in ten minutes. They mailed me my part this morning. I sent in some box-tops. They write the script with one part missing. It's a new idea. The home-maker, that's me, is the missing part. When it comes time for the missing lines, they all look at me out of the three walls and I say the lines. Here, for instance, the man says, 'What do you think of this whole idea, Helen?' And he looks at me sitting here center stage, see? And I say, I say——" She paused and ran her finger under a line on the script. "'I think that's fine!' And then they go on with the play until he says, 'Do you agree to that, Helen?' and I say, 'I sure do!' Isn't that fun, Guy?"

He stood in the hall looking at her.

"It's sure fun," she said.

"What's the play about?"

"I just told you. There are these people named Bob and Ruth and Helen."

"Oh."

"It's really fun. It'll be even more fun when we can afford to have the fourth wall installed. How long you figure before we save up and get the fourth wall torn out and a fourth wall-TV put in? It's only two thousand dollars."

"That's one-third of my yearly pay."

"It's only two thousand dollars," she replied. "And I should think you'd consider me sometimes. If we had a fourth wall, why it'd be just like this room wasn't ours at all, but all kinds of exotic people's rooms. We could do without a few things."

"Were already doing without a few things to pay for the third wall. It was put in only two months ago, remember?"

"Is that all it was?" She sat looking at him for a long moment. "Well, good-by, dear."

"Good-by," he said. He stopped and turned around. "Does it have a happy ending?"

"I haven't read that far."

He walked over, read the last page, nodded, folded the script, and handed it back to her. He walked out of the house into the rain.

The rain was thinning away and the girl was walking in the center of the sidewalk with her head up and the few drops falling on her face. She smiled when she saw Montag.

"Hello!"

He said hello and then said, "What are you up to now?"

"I'm still crazy. The rain feels good. I love to walk in it."

"I don't think I'd like that," he said.

"You might if you tried."

"I never have."

She licked her lips. "Rain even tastes good."

"What do you do, go around trying everything once?" he asked.

"Sometimes twice." She looked at something in her hand.

"What've you got there?" he said.

"I guess it's the last of the dandelions this year. I didn't think I'd find one on the lawn this late. Have you ever heard of rubbing it under your chin? Look." She touched her chin with the flower, laughing.

"Why?"

"If it rubs off, it means I'm in love. Has it?"

He could hardly do anything else but look.

"Well?" she said.

"You're yellow under there."

"Fine! Let's try *you* now."

"It won't work for me."

"Here." Before he could move she had put the dandelion under his chin. He drew back and she laughed. "Hold still!"

She peered under his chin and frowned.

"Well?" he said.

"What a shame," she said. "You're not in love with anyone."

"Yes, I am!"

"It doesn't show."

"I am, very much in love!" He tried to conjure up a face to fit the words, but there was no face. "I am!"

"Oh, please don't look that way."

"It's that dandelion," he said. "You've used it all up on yourself. That's why it won't work for me."

"Of course, that must be it. Oh now I've upset you, I can see I have; I'm sorry, really I am." She touched his elbow.

"No, no," he said, quickly, "I'm all right."

"I've got to be going, so say you forgive me, I don't want you angry with me."

"I'm not angry. Upset, yes."

"I've got to go see my psychiatrist now. They *make* me go. I make up things to say. I don't know what he thinks of me. He says I'm a regular onion! I keep him busy peeling away the layers."

"I'm inclined to believe you need the psychiatrist," said Montag.

"You don't mean that."

He took a breath and let it out and at last said, "No, I don't mean that."

"The psychiatrist wants to know why I go out and hike around in the forests and watch the birds and collect butterflies. I'll show you my collection some day."

"Good."

"They want to know what I do with all my time. I tell them that sometimes I just sit and *think*. But I won't tell them what. I've got them running. And sometimes, I tell them, I like to put my head back, like this, and let the rain fall in my mouth. It tastes just like wine. Have you ever tried it?"

"No, I—"

"You *have* forgiven me, haven't you?"

"Yes." He thought about it. "Yes, I have. God knows why. You're peculiar, you're aggravating, yet you're easy to forgive. You say you're seventeen?"

"Well—next month."

"How odd. How strange. And my wife thirty and yet you seem so much older at times. I can't get over it."

"You're peculiar yourself, Mr. Montag. Sometimes I even forget you're a fireman. Now, may I make you angry again?"

"Go ahead."

"How did it start? How did you get into it? How did you pick your work and how did you happen to think to take the job you have? You're not like the others. I've seen a few; I *know*. When I talk, you look at me. When I said something about the moon, you looked at the moon, last night. The others would never do that. The others would walk off and leave me talking. Or threaten me. No one has time any more for anyone else. You're one of the few who put up with me. That's why I think it's so strange you're a fireman, it just doesn't seem right for you, somehow."

He felt his body divide itself into a hotness and a coldness, a softness and a hardness, a trembling and a not trembling, the two halves grinding one upon the other.

"You'd better run on to your appointment," he said.

And she ran off and left him standing there in the rain. Only after a long time did he move.

And then, very slowly, as he walked, he tilted his head back in the rain, for just a few moments, and opened his mouth. . . .

The Mechanical Hound slept but did not sleep, lived but did not live in its gently humming, gently vibrating, softly illuminated kennel back in a dark corner of the firehouse. The dim light of one in the morning, the moonlight from the open sky framed through the great window, touched here and there on the brass and the copper and the steel of the faintly trembling beast. Light flickered on bits of ruby glass and on sensitive capillary hairs in the Nylon-brushed nostrils of the creature that quivered gently, gently, its eight legs spidered under it on rubber-padded paws.

Montag slid down the brass pole. He went out to look at the city and the clouds had cleared away completely, and he lit a cigarette and came back to bend down and look at the Hound. It was like a great bee come home from some field where the honey is full of poison wildness, of insanity and nightmare, its body crammed with that over-rich nectar and now it was sleeping the evil out of itself.

"Hello," whispered Montag, fascinated as always with the dead beast, the living beast.

Nights when things got dull, which was every night, the men slid down the brass poles, and set the ticking combinations of the olfactory system of the Hound and let loose rats in the firehouse areaway, and sometimes chickens, and sometimes cats that would have to be drowned anyway, and there would be betting to see which of the cats or chickens or rats the Hound would seize first. The animals were turned loose. Three seconds later the game was done, the rat, cat, or chicken caught half across the areaway, gripped in gentling paws while a four-inch hollow steel needle plunged down from the proboscis of the Hound to inject massive jolts of morphine or procaine. The pawn was then tossed in the incinerator. A new game began.

Montag stayed upstairs most nights when this went on. There had been a time two years ago when he had bet with the best of them, and lost a week's salary and faced Mildred's insane anger, which showed itself in veins and blotches. But now nights he lay in his bunk, face turned to the wall, listening to the whoops of laughter below and the piano-string scurry of rat feet, the violin squeaking of mice, and the great shadowing, motioned silence of the Hound leaping out like a moth in the raw light, finding, holding its victim, inserting needle and going back to its kennel to die as if a switch had been turned.

Montag touched the muzzle.

The Hound growled.

Montag jumped back.

The Hound half rose in its kennel and looked at him with green-blue neon light flickering in its suddenly activated eyebulbs. It growled again, a strange rasping combination of electrical sizzle, a frying sound, a scraping of metal, a turning of cogs that seemed rusty and ancient with suspicion.

"No, no, boy," said Montag, his heart pounding.

He saw the silver needle extend upon the air an inch, pull back, extend, pull back. The growl simmered in the beast and it looked at him.

Montag backed up. The Hound took a step from its kennel. Montag grabbed the brass pole with one hand. The pole, reacting, slid upward, and took him through the ceiling, quietly. He stepped off in the half-lit deck of the upper level. He was trembling and his face was green-white. Below, the Hound had sunk back down upon its eight incredible insect legs and was humming to itself again, its multifaceted eyes at peace.

Montag stood, letting the fears pass, by the drop-hole. Behind him, four men at a card table under a green lidded light in the corner glanced briefly but said nothing. Only the man with the Captain's hat and the sign of the Phoenix on his hat, at last, curious, his playing cards in his thin hand, talked across the long room.

"Montag . . . ?"

"It doesn't *like* me," said Montag.

"What, the Hound?" The Captain studied his cards. "Come off it. It doesn't like or dislike. It just 'functions.' It's like a lesson in ballistics. It has a trajectory we decide on for it. It follows through. It targets itself, homes itself, and cuts off. It's only copper wire, storage batteries, and electricity."

Montag swallowed. "Its calculators can be set to any combination, so many amino acids, so much sulphur, so much butterfat and alkaline. Right?"

"We all know that."

"All of those chemical balances and percentages on all of us here in the House are recorded in the master file downstairs. It would be easy for someone to set up a partial combination on the Hound's 'memory,' a touch of amino acids, perhaps. That would account for what the animal did just now. Reacted toward me."

"Hell," said the Captain.

"Irritated, but not completely angry. Just enough 'memory' set up in it by someone so it growled when I touched it."

"Who would do a thing like that?" asked the Captain. "You haven't any enemies here, Guy."

"None that I know of."

"We'll have the Hound checked by our technicians tomorrow."

"This isn't the first time it's threatened me," said Montag. "Last month it happened twice."

"We'll fix it up. Don't worry."

But Montag did not move and only stood thinking of the ventilator grille in the hall at home and what lay hidden behind the grille. If someone here in the firehouse knew about the ventilator then mightn't they "tell" the Hound . . . ?

The Captain came over to the drop-hole and gave Montag a questioning glance.

"I was just figuring," said Montag, "what does the Hound think about down there nights? Is it coming alive on us, really? It makes me cold."

"It doesn't think anything we don't want it to think."

"That's sad," said Montag, quietly, "because all we put into it is hunting and finding and killing. What a shame if that's all it can ever know."

Beatty snorted, gently. "Hell! It's a fine bit of craftsmanship, a good rifle that can fetch its own target and guarantees the bulls-eye every time."

"That's why," said Montag, "I wouldn't want to be its next victim."

"Why? You got a guilty conscience about something?"

Montag glanced up swiftly.

Beatty stood there looking at him steadily with his eyes while his mouth opened and began to laugh, very softly.

One two three four five six seven days. And as many times he came out of the house and Clarisse was there somewhere in the world. Once he saw her shaking a walnut tree, once he saw her sitting on the lawn knitting a blue sweater, three or four times he found a bouquet of late flowers on his porch, or a handful of chestnuts in a little sack, or some autumn leaves neatly pinned to a sheet of white paper and thumbtacked to his door. Every day Clarisse walked him to the corner. One day it was raining, the next it was clear, the day after that the wind blew strong, and the day after that it was mild and calm, and the day after that calm day was a day like the furnace of summer and Clarisse with her face all sunburnt by late afternoon.

"Why is it," he said, one time, at the subway entrance, "I feel I've known you so many years?"

"Because I like you," she said, "and I don't want anything from you. And because we know each other."

"You make me feel very old and very much like a father."

"Now you explain," she said, "why you haven't any daughters like me, if you love children so much?"

"I don't know."

"You're joking!"

"I mean——" He stopped and shook his head. "Well, my wife, she . . . she just never wanted any children at all."

The girl stopped smiling. "I'm sorry. I really thought you were having fun at my expense. I'm a fool."

"No, no," he said. "It was a good question. It's been a long time since anyone cared enough to ask. A good question."

"Let's talk about something else. Have you ever smelled old leaves? Don't they smell like cinnamon? Here. Smell."

"Why, yes, it *is* like cinnamon in a way."

She looked at him with her clear dark eyes. "You always seem shocked."

"It's just I haven't had time——"

"Did you look at the stretched-out billboards like I told you?"

"I think so. Yes." He had to laugh.

"Your laugh sounds much nicer than it did."

"Does it?"

"Much more relaxed."

He felt at ease and comfortable. "Why aren't you in school? I see you every day wandering around."

"Oh, they don't miss me," she said. "I'm antisocial, they say. I don't mix. It's so strange. I'm very social indeed. It all depends on what you mean by social, doesn't it? Social to me means talking to you about things like this." She rattled some chestnuts that had fallen off the tree in the front yard. "Or talking about how strange the world is. Being with people is nice. But I don't think it's social to get a bunch of people together and then not let them talk, do you? An hour of TV class, an hour of basketball or baseball or running, another hour of transcription history or painting pictures, and more sports, but do you know, we never ask questions, or at least most don't; they just run the answers at you, bing, bing, bing, and us sitting there for four more hours of film-teacher. That's not social to me at all. It's a lot of funnels and a lot of water poured down the spout and out the bottom, and them telling us it's wine when it's not. They run us so ragged by the end of the day we can't do anything but go to bed or head for a Fun Park to bully people around, break windowpanes in the Window Smasher place or wreck cars in the Car Wrecker place with the big steel ball. Or go out in the cars and race on the streets, trying to see how close you can get to lampposts, playing 'chicken' and 'knock hubcaps.' I guess I'm everything they say I am, all right. I haven't any friends. That's supposed to prove I'm abnormal. But everyone I know is either shouting or dancing around like wild or beating up one another. Do you notice how people hurt each other nowadays?"

"You sound so very old."

"Sometimes I'm ancient. I'm afraid of children my own age. They kill each other. Did it always use to be that way? My uncle says no. Six of my friends have been shot in the last year alone. Ten of them died in car wrecks. I'm afraid of them and they don't like me because I'm afraid. My uncle says his grandfather remembered when children didn't kill each other. But that was a long time ago when they had things different. They believed in responsibility, my uncle says. Do you know, I'm responsible. I was spanked when I needed it, years ago. And I do all the shopping and housecleaning by hand.

"But most of all," she said, "I like to watch people. Sometimes I ride the subway all day and look at them and listen to them. I just want to figure out who they are and what they want and where they're going. Sometimes I even go to the Fun Parks and ride in the jet cars when they race on the edge of town at midnight and the police don't care as long as they're insured. As long as everyone has ten thousand insurance everyone's happy. Sometimes I sneak around and listen in subways. Or I listen at soda fountains, and do you know what?"

"What?"

"People don't talk about anything."

"Oh, they *must*!"

"No, not anything. They name a lot of cars or clothes or swimming pools mostly and say how swell! But they all say the same things and nobody says anything different from anyone else. And most of the time in the cafes they have the joke-boxes on and the same jokes most of the time, or the musical wall lit and all the colored patterns running up and down, but it's only color and all abstract. And at the museums, have you *ever* been? *All* abstract. That's all there is now. My uncle says it was different once. A long time back sometimes pictures said things or even showed *people*."

"Your uncle said, your uncle said. Your uncle must be a remarkable man."

"He is. He certainly is. Well, I got to be going. Good-by, Mr. Montag"

"Good-by."

"Good-by. . . ."

One two three four five six seven days: the firehouse.

"Montag, you shin that pole like a bird up a tree."

Third day.

"Montag, I see you came in the back door this time. The Hound bother you?"

"No, no."

Fourth day.

"Montag, a funny thing. Heard tell this morning. Fireman in Seattle, purposely set a Mechanical Hound to his own chemical complex and let it loose. What kind of suicide would you call *that*?"

Five, six, seven days.

And then, Clarisse was gone. He didn't know what there was about the afternoon, but it was not seeing her somewhere in the world. The lawn was empty, the trees empty, the street empty, and while at first he did not even know he missed her or was even looking for her, the fact was that by the time he reached the subway, there were vague stirrings of dis-ease in him. Something was the matter, his routine had been disturbed. A simple routine, true, established in a short few days, and yet . . . ? He almost turned back to make the walk again, to give her time to appear. He was certain if he tried the same route, everything would work out fine. But it was late, and the arrival of his train put a stop to his plan.

The flutter of cards, motion of hands, of eyelids, the drone of the time-voice in the firehouse ceiling ". . . one thirty-five, Thursday morning, November 4th, . . . one thirty-six . . . one thirty-seven A.M. . . ." The tick of the playing cards on the greasy table top, all the sounds came to Montag, behind his closed eyes, behind the barrier he had momentarily erected. He could feel the firehouse full of glitter and shine and silence, of brass colors, the colors of coins, of gold, of silver. The unseen men across the table were sighing on their cards, waiting. ". . . one forty-five . . ." The voice clock mourned out the cold hour of a cold morning of a still colder year.

"What's wrong, Montag?"

Montag opened his eyes.

A radio hummed somewhere. ". . . war may be declared any hour. This country stands ready to defend its . . ."

The firehouse trembled as a great flight of jet planes whistled a single note across the black morning sky.

Montag blinked. Beatty was looking at him as if he were a museum statue. At any moment, Beatty might rise and walk about him, touching, exploring his guilt and self-consciousness. Guilt? What guilt was that?

"Your play, Montag."

Montag looked at these men whose faces were sunburnt by a thousand real and ten thousand imaginary fires, whose work flushed their cheeks and fevered their eyes. These men who looked steadily into their platinum igniter flames as they lit their eternally burning black pipes. They and their charcoal hair and soot-colored brows and bluish-ash-smeared cheeks where they had shaven close; but their heritage showed. Montag started up, his mouth opened. Had he ever seen a fireman that *didn't* have black hair, black brows, a fiery face, and a blue-steel shaved but unshaved look? These men were all mirror images of himself! Were all firemen picked then for their looks as well as their proclivities? The color of cinders and ash about them, and the continual smell of burning from their pipes. Captain Beatty there, rising in thunderheads of tobacco smoke. Beatty opening a fresh tobacco packet, crumpling the cellophane into a sound of fire.

Montag looked at the cards in his own hands. "I—I've been thinking. About the fire last week. About the man whose library we fixed. What happened to him?"

"They took him screaming off to the asylum."

"He wasn't insane."

Beatty arranged his cards quietly. "Any man's insane who thinks he can fool the government and us."

"I've tried to imagine," said Montag, "just how it would feel. I mean, to have firemen burn *our* houses and *our* books."

"We haven't any books."

"But if we did have some."

"You *got* some?"

Beatty blinked slowly.

"No." Montag gazed beyond them to the wall with the typed lists of a million forbidden books. Their names leapt in fire, burning down the years under his ax and his hose which sprayed not water but kerosene. "No." But in his mind, a cool wind started up and blew out of the ventilator grille at home, softly, softly, chilling his face. And, again, he saw himself in a green park talking to an old man, a very old man, and the wind from the park was cold, too.

Montag hesitated. "Was—was it always like this? The firehouse, our work? I mean, well, once upon a time . . ."

"Once upon a time!" Beatty said. "What kind of talk is *that*?"

Fool, thought Montag to himself, you'll give it away. At the last fire, a book of fairy tales, he'd glanced at a single line. "I mean," he said, "in the old days, before homes were completely fireproofed——" Suddenly it seemed a much younger voice was speaking for him. He opened his mouth and it was Clarisse McClellan saying, "Didn't firemen *prevent* fires rather than stoke them up and get them going?"

"That's rich!" Stoneman and Black drew forth their rule books, which also contained brief histories of the Firemen of America, and laid them out where Montag, though long familiar with them, might read:

> "Established, 1790, to burn English-influenced books in the Colonies. First Fireman: Benjamin Franklin."
>
> RULE 1. Answer the alarm quickly.
> 2. Start the fire swiftly.
> 3. Burn everything.
> 4. Report back to firehouse immediately.
> 5. Stand alert for other Alarms.

Everyone watched Montag. He did not move.

The alarm sounded.

The bell in the ceiling kicked itself two hundred times. Suddenly there were four empty chairs. The cards fell in a flurry of snow. The brass pole shivered. The men were gone.

Montag sat in his chair. Below, the orange dragon coughed to life.

Montag slid down the pole like a man in a dream.

The Mechanical Hound leapt up in its kennel, its eyes all green flame.

"Montag, you forgot your helmet!"

He seized it off the wall behind him, ran, leapt, and they were off, the night wind hammering about their siren scream and their mighty metal thunder!

It was a flaking three-story house in the ancient part of the city, a century old if it was a day, but like all houses it had been given a thin fireproof plastic sheath many years ago, and this preservative shell seemed to be the only thing holding it in the sky.

"Here we are!"

The engine slammed to a stop. Beatty, Stoneman, and Black ran up the sidewalk, suddenly odious and fat in their plump fireproof slickers. Montag followed.

They crashed the front door and grabbed at a woman, though she was not running, she was not trying to escape. She was only standing, weaving from side to side, her eyes fixed upon a nothingness in the wall, as if they had struck her a terrible blow upon the head. Her tongue was moving in her mouth, and her eyes seemed to be trying to remember something and then they remembered and her tongue moved again:

"'Play the man, Master Ridley; we shall this day light such a candle, by God's grace, in England, as I trust shall never be put out.'"

"Enough of that!" said Beatty. "Where are they?"

He slapped her face with amazing objectivity and repeated the question. The old woman's eyes came to a focus upon Beatty. "You know where they are or you wouldn't be here," she said.

Stoneman held out the telephone alarm card with the complaint signed in telephone duplicate on the back:

"Have reason to suspect attic; 11 No. Elm, City.
E. B."

"That would be Mrs. Blake, my neighbor," said the woman, reading the initials.

"All right, men, let's get 'em!"

Next thing they were up in musty blackness swinging silver hatchets at doors that were, after all, unlocked, tumbling through like boys all rollick and shout. "Hey!" A fountain of books sprang down upon Montag as he climbed shuddering up the sheer stair well. How inconvenient! Always before it had been like snuffing a candle. The police went first and adhesive-taped the victim's mouth and bandaged him off into their glittering beetle cars, so when you arrived you found an empty house. You weren't hurting anyone, you were hurting only *things*! And since things really couldn't be hurt, since things felt nothing, and things don't scream or whimper, as this woman might begin to scream and cry out, there was nothing to tease your conscience later. You were simply cleaning up. Janitorial work, essentially. Everything to its proper place. Quick with the kerosene! Who's got a match!

But now, tonight, someone had slipped. This woman was spoiling the ritual. The men were making too much noise, laughing, joking, to cover her terrible accusing silence below. She made the empty rooms roar with accusation and shake down a fine dust of guilt that was sucked in their nostrils as they plunged about. It was neither cricket nor correct. Montag felt an immense irritation. She shouldn't be here, on top of everything!

Books bombarded his shoulders, his arms, his upturned face. A book lit, almost obediently, like a white pigeon, in his hands, wings fluttering. In the dim, wavering light, a page hung open and it was like a snowy feather, the words delicately painted thereon. In all the rush and fervor, Montag had only an instant to read a line, but it blazed in his mind for the next minute as if stamped there with fiery steel. "Time has fallen asleep in the afternoon sunshine." He dropped the book. Immediately, another fell into his arms.

"Montag, up here!"

Montag's hand closed like a mouth, crushed the book with

wild devotion, with an insanity of mindlessness to his chest. The men above were hurling shovelfuls of magazines into the dusty air. They fell like slaughtered birds and the woman stood below, like a small girl, among the bodies.

Montag had done nothing. His hand had done it all, his hand, with a brain of its own, with a conscience and a curiosity in each trembling finger, had turned thief. Now, it plunged the book back under his arm, pressed it tight to sweating armpit, rushed out empty, with a magician's flourish! Look here! Innocent! Look!

He gazed, shaken, at that white hand. He held it way out, as if he were farsighted. He held it close, as if he were blind.

"Montag!"

He jerked about.

"Don't stand there, idiot!"

The books lay like great mounds of fishes left to dry. The men danced and slipped and fell over them. Titles glittered their golden eyes, falling, gone.

"Kerosene!"

They pumped the cold fluid from the numeraled 451 tanks strapped to their shoulders. They coated each book, they pumped rooms full of it.

They hurried downstairs, Montag staggering after them in the kerosene fumes.

"Come on, woman!"

The woman knelt among the books, touching the drenched leather and cardboard, reading the gilt titles with her fingers while her eyes accused Montag.

"You can't ever have my books," she said.

"You know the law," said Beatty. "Where's your common sense? None of those books agree with each other. You've been locked up here for years with a regular damned Tower of Babel. Snap out of it! The people in those books never lived. Come on now!"

She shook her head.

"The whole house is going up," said Beatty.

The men walked clumsily to the door. They glanced back at Montag, who stood near the woman.

"You're not leaving her here?" he protested.

"She won't come."

"Force her, then!"

Beatty raised his hand in which was concealed the igniter, "We're due back at the House. Besides, these fanatics always try suicide; the pattern's familiar."

Montag placed his hand on the woman's elbow. "You can come with me."

"No," she said. "Thank you, anyway."

"I'm counting to ten," said Beatty. "One. Two."

"Please," said Montag.

"Go on," said the woman.

"Three. Four."

"Here." Montag pulled at the woman.

The woman replied quietly, "I want to stay here."

"Five. Six."

"You can stop counting," she said. She opened the fingers of one hand slightly and in the palm of the hand was a single slender object.

An ordinary kitchen match.

The sight of it rushed the men out and down away from the house. Captain Beatty, keeping his dignity, backed slowly through the front door, his pink face burnt and shiny from a thousand fires and night excitements. God, thought Montag, how true! Always at night the alarm comes. Never by day! Is it because fire is prettier by night? More spectacle, a better show? The pink face of Beatty now showed the faintest panic in the door. The woman's hand twitched on the single matchstick. The fumes of kerosene bloomed up about her. Montag felt the hidden book pound like a heart against his chest.

"Go on," said the woman, and Montag felt himself back away and away out the door, after Beatty, down the steps, across the lawn, where the path of kerosene lay like the track of some evil snail.

On the front porch where she had come to weigh them quietly with her eyes, her quietness a condemnation, the woman stood motionless.

Beatty flicked his fingers to spark the kerosene.

He was too late. Montag gasped.

The woman on the porch reached out with contempt to them all, and struck the kitchen match against the railing.

People ran out of houses all down the street.

They said nothing on their way back to the firehouse. Nobody looked at anyone else. Montag sat in the front seat with Beatty and Black. They did not even smoke their pipes. They sat there looking out the front of the great Salamander as they turned a corner and went silently on.

"Master Ridley," said Montag at last.

"What?" said Beatty.

"She said, 'Master Ridley.' She said some crazy thing when we came in the door. 'Play the man,' she said, 'Master Ridley.' Something, something, something."

"'We shall this day light such a candle, by God's grace, in England, as I trust shall never be put out,'" said Beatty. Stoneman glanced over at the Captain, as did Montag, startled.

Beatty rubbed his chin. "A man named Latimer said that to a man named Nicholas Ridley, as they were being burnt alive at Oxford, for heresy, on October 16, 1555."

Montag and Stoneman went back to looking at the street as it moved under the engine wheels.

"I'm full of bits and pieces," said Beatty. "Most fire captains have to be. Sometimes I surprise myself. *Watch* it, Stoneman!"

Stoneman braked the truck.

"Damn!" said Beatty. "You've gone right by the corner where we turn for the firehouse."

"Who is it?"

"Who would it be?" said Montag, leaning back against the closed door in the dark.

His wife said, at last, "Well, put on the light."

"I don't want the light."

"Come to bed."

He heard her roll impatiently; the bedsprings squealed.

"Are you drunk?" she said.

So it was the hand that started it all. He felt one hand and then the other work his coat free and let it slump to the floor. He held his pants out into an abyss and let them fall into darkness. His hands had been infected, and soon it would be his arms. He could feel the poison working up his wrists and into his elbows and his shoulders, and then the jump-over from shoulder blade to shoulder blade like a spark leaping a gap. His hands were ravenous. And his eyes were beginning to feel hunger, as if they must look at something, anything, everything.

His wife said, "What *are* you doing?"

He balanced in space with the book in his sweating cold fingers.

A minute later she said, "Well, just don't stand there in the middle of the floor."

He made a small sound.

"What?" she asked.

He made more soft sounds. He stumbled toward the bed and shoved the book clumsily under the cold pillow. He fell into bed and his wife cried out, startled. He lay far across the room from her, on a winter island separated by an empty sea. She talked to him for what seemed a long while and she talked about this and she talked about that and it was only words, like the words he had heard once in a nursery at a friend's house, a two-year-old child building word patterns, talking jargon, making pretty sounds in the air. But Montag said nothing and after a long while when he only made the small sounds, he felt her move in the room and come to his bed and stand over him and put her hand down to feel his cheek. He knew that when she pulled her hand away from his face it was wet.

Late in the night he looked over at Mildred. She was awake. There was a tiny dance of melody in the air, her Seashell was tamped in her ear again and she was listening to far people in far places, her eyes wide and staring at the fathoms of blackness above her in the ceiling.

Wasn't there an old joke about the wife who talked so much on the telephone that her desperate husband ran out to the nearest store and telephoned her to ask what was for dinner? Well, then, why didn't he buy himself an audio-Seashell broadcasting station and talk to his wife late at night, murmur, whisper, shout, scream, yell. But what would he whisper, what would he yell? What could he say?

And suddenly she was so strange he couldn't believe he knew

her at all. He was in someone else's house, like those other jokes people told of the gentleman, drunk, coming home late late at night, unlocking the wrong door, entering a wrong room, and bedding with a stranger and getting up early and going to work and neither of them the wiser.

"Millie . . . ?" he whispered.

"What?"

"I didn't mean to startle you. What I want to know is . . ."

"Well?"

"When did we meet? And *where*?"

"When did we meet for *what*?" she asked.

"I mean—originally."

He knew she must be frowning in the dark.

He clarified it. "The first time we ever met, where was it, and when?"

"Why, it was at——"

She stopped.

"I don't know," she said.

He was cold. "Can't you remember?"

"It's been so long."

"Only ten years, that's all, only ten!"

"Don't get excited, I'm trying to think." She laughed an odd little laugh that went up and up. "Funny, how funny, not to remember where or when you met your husband 'r wife."

He lay massaging his eyes, his brow, and the back of his neck, slowly. He held both hands over his eyes and applied a steady pressure there as if to crush memory into place. It was suddenly more important than any other thing in a lifetime that he know where he had met Mildred.

"It doesn't matter." She was up, in the bathroom now, and he heard the water running, and the swallowing sound she made.

"No, I guess not," he said.

He tried to count how many times she swallowed and he thought of the visit from the two zinc-oxide-faced men with the cigarettes in their straight-lined mouths and the Electronic-Eyed Snake winding down into the layer upon layer of night and stone and stagnant spring water, and he wanted to call out to her, how many have you taken *tonight*! the capsules! how many will you take later and not know? and so on, every hour!

or maybe not tonight, tomorrow night! And me not sleeping tonight or tomorrow night or any night for a long while, now that this has started. And he thought of her lying on the bed with the two technicians standing straight over her, not bent with concern, but only standing straight, arms folded. And he remembered thinking then that if she died, he was certain he wouldn't cry. For it would be the dying of an unknown, a street face, a newspaper image, and it was suddenly so very wrong that he had begun to cry, not at death but at the thought of *not crying* at death, a silly empty man near a silly empty woman, while the hungry snake made her still more empty.

How do you get so empty? he wondered. Who takes it out of you? And that awful flower the other day, the dandelion! It had summed up everything, hadn't it? "What a shame! You're not in love with anyone!" And why not?

Well, wasn't there a wall between him and Mildred, when you came down to it? Literally not just one wall but, so far, three! And expensive, too! And the uncles, the aunts, the cousins, the nieces, the nephews, that lived in those walls, the gibbering pack of tree-apes that said nothing, nothing, nothing and said it loud, loud, loud. He had taken to calling them relatives from the very first. "How's Uncle Louis today?" "Who?" "And Aunt Maude?" The most significant memory he had of Mildred, really, was of a little girl in a forest without trees (how odd!) or rather a little girl lost on a plateau where there used to be trees (you could feel the memory of their shapes all about) sitting in the center of the "living room." The living room; what a good job of labeling that was now. No matter when he came in, the walls were always talking to Mildred.

"Something must be done!"

"Yes, something must be *done*!"

"Well, let's not stand and talk!"

"Let's *do it*!"

"I'm so mad I could *spit*!"

What was it all about? Mildred couldn't say. Who was mad at whom? Mildred didn't quite know. What were they going to do? Well, said Mildred, wait around and see.

He had waited around to see.

A great thunderstorm of sound gushed from the walls. Music bombarded him at such an immense volume that his bones were almost shaken from their tendons; he felt his jaw vibrate, his eyes wobble in his head. He was a victim of concussion. When it was all over he felt like a man who had been thrown from a cliff, whirled in a centrifuge and spat out over a waterfall that fell and fell into emptiness and emptiness and never—quite—touched—bottom—never—never—quite—no not quite—touched—bottom . . . and you fell so fast you didn't touch the sides either . . . never . . . quite . . . touched . . . anything.

The thunder faded. The music died.

"There," said Mildred.

And it was indeed remarkable. Something had happened. Even though the people in the walls of the room had barely moved, and nothing had really been settled, you had the impression that someone had turned on a washing machine or sucked you up in a gigantic vacuum. You drowned in music and pure cacophony. He came out of the room sweating and on the point of collapse. Behind him, Mildred sat in her chair and the voices went on again:

"Well, everything will be all right now," said an "aunt."

"Oh, don't be too sure," said a "cousin."

"Now, don't get angry!"

"Who's angry?"

"*You* are!"

"*I* am?"

"You're mad!"

"Why would I be mad!"

"Because!"

"That's all very well," cried Montag, "but what are they mad about? Who *are* these people? Who's that man and who's that woman? Are they husband and wife, are they divorced, engaged, what? Good God, *nothing's* connected up."

"They——" said Mildred. "Well, they—they had this fight, you see. They certainly fight a lot. You should listen. I think they're married. Yes, they're married. Why?"

And if it was not the three walls soon to be four walls and the dream complete, then it was the open car and Mildred driving a hundred miles an hour across town, he shouting at her and she shouting back and both trying to hear what was said, but hearing only the scream of the car. "At least keep it down to the minimum!" he yelled. "What?" she cried. "Keep it down to fifty-five, the minimum!" he shouted. "The what?" she shrieked. "Speed!" he shouted. And she pushed it up to one hundred and five miles an hour and tore the breath from his mouth.

When they stepped out of the car, she had the Seashells stuffed in her ears.

Silence. Only the wind blowing softly.

"Mildred." He stirred in bed.

He reached over and pulled the tiny musical insect out of her ear. "Mildred. Mildred?"

"Yes." Her voice was faint.

He felt he was one of the creatures electronically inserted between the slots of the phono-color walls, speaking, but the speech not piercing the crystal barrier. He could only pantomime, hoping she would turn his way and see him. They could not touch through the glass.

"Mildred, do you know that girl I was telling you about?"

"What girl?" She was almost asleep.

"The girl next door."

"What girl next door?"

"You know, the high-school girl. Clarisse, her name is."

"Oh, yes," said his wife.

"I haven't seen her for a few days—four days to be exact. Have you seen her?"

"No."

"I've meant to talk to you about her. Strange."

"Oh, I know the one you mean."

"I thought you would."

"Her," said Mildred in the dark room.

"What about her?" asked Montag.

"I meant to tell you. Forgot. Forgot."

"Tell me now. What is it?"

"I think she's gone."

"Gone?"

"Whole family moved out somewhere. But she's gone for good. I think she's dead."

"We couldn't be talking about the same girl."

"No. The same girl. McClellan. McClellan. Run over by a car. Four days ago. I'm not sure. But I think she's dead.

The family moved out anyway. I don't know. But I think she's dead."

"You're not sure of it!"

"No, not sure. Pretty sure."

"Why didn't you tell me sooner?"

"Forgot."

"Four days ago!"

"I forgot all about it."

"Four days ago," he said, quietly, lying there.

They lay there in the dark room not moving, either of them. "Good night," she said.

He heard a faint rustle. Her hand moved. The electric thimble moved like a praying mantis on the pillow, touched by her hand. Now it was in her ear again, humming.

He listened and his wife was singing under her breath.

Outside the house, a shadow moved, an autumn wind rose up and faded away. But there was something else in the silence that he heard. It was like a breath exhaled upon the window. It was like a faint drift of greenish luminescent smoke, the motion of a single huge October leaf blowing across the lawn and away.

The Hound, he thought. It's out there tonight. It's out there now. If I opened the window . . .

He did not open the window.

He had chills and fever in the morning.

"You can't be sick," said Mildred.

He closed his eyes over the hotness. "Yes."

"But you were all right, last night."

"No, I wasn't all right." He heard the "relatives" shouting in the parlor.

Mildred stood over his bed, curiously. He felt her there, he saw her without opening his eyes, her hair burnt by chemicals to a brittle straw, her eyes with a kind of cataract unseen but suspect far behind the pupils, the reddened pouting lips, the body as thin as a praying mantis from dieting, and her flesh like white bacon. He could remember her no other way.

"Will you bring me aspirin and water?"

"You've got to get up," she said. "It's noon. You've slept five hours later than usual."

"Will you turn the parlor off?" he asked.

"That's my family."

"Will you turn it off for a sick man?"

"I'll turn it down."

She went out of the room and did nothing to the parlor and came back. "Is that better?"

"Thanks."

"That's my favorite program," she said.

"What about the aspirin?"

"You've never been sick before." She went away again.

"Well, I'm sick now. I'm not going to work tonight. Call Beatty for me."

"You acted funny last night." She returned, humming.

"Where's the aspirin?" He glanced at the water glass she handed him.

"Oh." She walked to the bath again. "Did something happen?"

"A fire, is all."

"I had a nice evening," she said, in the bathroom.

"What doing?"

"The parlor."

"What was on?"

"Programs."

"What programs?"

"Some of the best ever."

"Who?"

"Oh, you know, the bunch."

"Yes, the bunch, the bunch, the bunch." He pressed at the pain in his eyes and suddenly the odor of kerosene made him vomit.

Mildred came in, humming. She was surprised. "Why'd you do that?"

He looked with dismay at the floor. "We burned an old woman with her books."

"It's a good thing the rug's washable." She fetched a mop and worked on it. "I went to Helen's last night."

"Couldn't you get the shows in your own parlor?"

"Sure, but it's nice visiting."

She went out into the parlor. He heard her singing.

"Mildred?" he called.

She returned, singing, snapping her fingers softly.

"Aren't you going to ask me about last night?" he said.

"What about it?"

"We burned a thousand books. We burned a woman."

"Well?"

The parlor was exploding with sound.

"We burned copies of Dante and Swift and Marcus Aurelius."

"Wasn't he a European?"

"Something like that."

"Wasn't he a radical?"

"I never read him."

"He was a radical." Mildred fiddled with the telephone. "You don't expect me to call Captain Beatty, do you?"

"You must!"

"Don't shout!"

"I wasn't shouting." He was up in bed, suddenly, enraged and flushed, shaking. The parlor roared in the hot air. "I can't call him. I can't tell him I'm sick."

"Why?"

Because you're afraid, he thought. A child feigning illness, afraid to call because after a moment's discussion, the conversation would run so: "Yes, Captain, I feel better already. I'll be in at ten o'clock tonight."

"You're not sick," said Mildred.

Montag fell back in bed. He reached under his pillow. The hidden book was still there.

"Mildred, how would it be if, well, maybe I quit my job awhile?"

"You want to give up everything? After all these years of working, because, one night, some woman and her books——"

"You should have seen her, Millie!"

"She's nothing to me; she shouldn't have had books. It was her responsibility, she should've thought of that. I hate her. She's got you going and next thing you know we'll be out, no house, no job, nothing."

"You weren't there, you didn't *see*," he said. "There must be something in books, things we can't imagine, to make a woman stay in a burning house; there must be something there. You don't stay for nothing."

"She was simple-minded."

"She was as rational as you and I, more so perhaps, and we burned her."

"That's water under the bridge."

"No, not water; fire. You ever seen a burned house? It smolders for days. Well, this fire'll last me the rest of my life. God! I've been trying to put it out, in my mind, all night. I'm crazy with trying."

"You should've thought of that before becoming a fireman."

"Thought!" he said. "Was I given a choice? My grandfather and father were firemen. In my sleep, I ran after them."

The parlor was playing a dance tune.

"This is the day you go on the early shift," said Mildred. "You should've gone two hours ago. I just noticed."

"It's not just the woman that died," said Montag. "Last night I thought about all the kerosene I've used in the past ten years. And I thought about books. And for the first time I realized that a man was behind each one of the books. A man had to think them up. A man had to take a long time to put them down on paper. And I'd never even thought that thought before." He got out of bed.

"It took some man a lifetime maybe to put some of his thoughts down, looking around at the world and life and then I come along in two minutes and boom! it's all over."

"Let me alone," said Mildred. "I didn't do anything."

"Let you alone! That's all very well, but how can I leave myself alone? We need not to be let alone. We need to be really bothered once in a while. How long is it since you were *really* bothered? About something important, about something real?"

And then he shut up, for he remembered last week and the two white stones staring up at the ceiling and the pump-snake with the probing eye and the two soap-faced men with the cigarettes moving in their mouths when they talked. But that was another Mildred, that was a Mildred so deep inside this one, and so bothered, really bothered, that the two women had never met. He turned away.

Mildred said, "Well, now you've done it. Out front of the house. Look who's here."

"I don't care."

"There's a Phoenix car just drove up and a man in a black shirt with an orange snake stitched on his arm coming up the front walk."

"Captain Beatty?" he said.

"Captain Beatty."

Montag did not move, but stood looking into the cold whiteness of the wall immediately before him.

"Go let him in, will you? Tell him I'm sick."

"Tell him yourself!" She ran a few steps this way, a few steps that, and stopped, eyes wide, when the front door speaker called her name, softly, softly, Mrs. Montag, Mrs. Montag, someone here, someone here, Mrs. Montag, Mrs. Montag, someone's here. Fading.

Montag made sure the book was well hidden behind the pillow, climbed slowly back into bed, arranged the covers over his knees and across his chest, half-sitting, and after a while Mildred moved and went out of the room and Captain Beatty strolled in, his hands in his pockets.

"Shut the 'relatives' up," said Beatty, looking around at everything except Montag and his wife.

This time, Mildred ran. The yammering voices stopped yelling in the parlor.

Captain Beatty sat down in the most comfortable chair with a peaceful look on his ruddy face. He took time to prepare and light his brass pipe and puff out a great smoke cloud. "Just thought I'd come by and see how the sick man is."

"How'd you guess?"

Beatty smiled his smile which showed the candy pinkness of his gums and the tiny candy whiteness of his teeth. "I've seen it all. You were going to call for a night off."

Montag sat in bed.

"Well" said Beatty, "*take* the night off!" He examined his eternal matchbox, the lid of which said GUARANTEED: ONE MILLION LIGHTS IN THIS IGNITER, and began to strike the chemical match abstractedly, blow out, strike, blow out, strike, speak a few words, blow out. He looked at the flame. He blew, he looked at the smoke. "When will you be well?"

"Tomorrow. The next day maybe. First of the week."

Beatty puffed his pipe. "Every fireman, sooner or later, hits this. They only need understanding, to know how the wheels run. Need to know the history of our profession. They don't feed it to rookies like they used to. Damn shame." Puff. "Only fire chiefs remember it now." Puff. "I'll let you in on it."

Mildred fidgeted.

Beatty took a full minute to settle himself in and think back for what he wanted to say.

"When did it all start, you ask, this job of ours, how did it come about, where, when? Well, I'd say it really got started around about a thing called the Civil War. Even though our rule book claims it was founded earlier. The fact is we didn't get along well until photography came into its own. Then—motion pictures in the early Twentieth Century. Radio. Television. Things began to have *mass.*"

Montag sat in bed, not moving.

"And because they had mass, they became simpler," said Beatty. "Once, books appealed to a few people, here, there, everywhere. They could afford to be different. The world was roomy. But then the world got full of eyes and elbows and mouths. Double, triple, quadruple population. Films and radios, magazines, books leveled down to a sort of paste pudding norm, do you follow me?"

"I think so."

Beatty peered at the smoke pattern he had put out on the air. "Picture it. Nineteenth-century man with his horses, dogs, carts, slow motion. Then, in the Twentieth Century, speed up your camera. Books cut shorter. Condensations. Digests. Tabloids. Everything boils down to the gag, the snap ending."

"Snap ending." Mildred nodded.

"Classics cut to fit fifteen-minute radio shows, then cut again to fill a two-minute book column, winding up at last as a ten- or twelve-line dictionary resume. I exaggerate, of course. The dictionaries were for reference. But many were those whose sole knowledge of *Hamlet* (you know the title certainly, Montag; it is probably only a faint rumor of a title to you, Mrs. Montag) whose sole knowledge, as I say, of *Hamlet* was a one-page digest in a book that claimed: *now at last you can read all the classics; keep up with your neighbors.* Do you see? Out of the nursery into the college and back to the nursery; there's your intellectual pattern for the past five centuries or more."

Mildred arose and began to move around the room, picking

things up and putting them down. Beatty ignored her and continued:

"Speed up the film, Montag, quick. *Click, Pic, Look, Eye, Now, Flick, Here, There, Swift, Pace, Up, Down, In, Out, Why, How, Who, What, Where, Eh? Uh! Bang! Smack! Wallop, Bing, Bong, Boom!* Digest-digests, digest-digest-digests. Politics? One column, two sentences, a headline! Then, in mid-air, all vanishes! Whirl man's mind around about so fast under the pumping hands of publishers, exploiters, broadcasters that the centrifuge flings off all unnecessary, time-wasting thought!"

Mildred smoothed the bedclothes. Montag felt his heart jump and jump again as she patted his pillow. Right now she was pulling at his shoulder to try to get him to move so she could take the pillow out and fix it nicely and put it back. And perhaps cry out and stare or simply reach down her hand and say, "What's this?" and hold up the hidden book with touching innocence.

"School is shortened, discipline relaxed, philosophies, histories, languages dropped, English and spelling gradually gradually neglected, finally almost completely ignored. Life is immediate, the job counts, pleasure lies all about after work. Why learn anything save pressing buttons, pulling switches, fitting nuts and bolts?"

"Let me fix your pillow," said Mildred.

"No!" whispered Montag.

"The zipper displaces the button and a man lacks just that much time to think while dressing at dawn, a philosophical hour, and thus a melancholy hour."

Mildred said, "Here."

"Get away," said Montag.

"Life becomes one big pratfall, Montag; everything bang, boff, and wow!"

"Wow," said Mildred, yanking at the pillow.

"For God's sake, let me be!" cried Montag passionately.

Beatty opened his eyes wide.

Mildred's hand had frozen behind the pillow. Her fingers were tracing the book's outline and as the shape became familiar her face looked surprised and then stunned. Her mouth opened to ask a question . . .

"Empty the theaters save for clowns and furnish the rooms

with glass walls and pretty colors running up and down the walls like confetti or blood or sherry or sauterne. You like baseball, don't you, Montag?"

"Baseball's a fine game."

Now Beatty was almost invisible, a voice somewhere behind a screen of smoke.

"What's this?" asked Mildred, almost with delight. Montag heaved back against her arms. "What's this here?"

"Sit down!" Montag shouted. She jumped away, her hands empty. "We're talking!"

Beatty went on as if nothing had happened. "You like bowling, don't you, Montag?"

"Bowling, yes."

"And golf?"

"Golf is a fine game."

"Basketball?"

"A fine game."

"Billiards, pool? Football?"

"Fine games, all of them."

"More sports for everyone, group spirit, fun, and you don't have to think, eh? Organize and organize and super organize super-super sports. More cartoons in books. More pictures. The mind drinks less and less. Impatience. Highways full of crowds going somewhere, somewhere, somewhere, nowhere. The gasoline refugee. Towns turn into motels, people in nomadic surges from place to place, following the moon tides, living tonight in the room where you slept this noon and I the night before."

Mildred went out of the room and slammed the door. The parlor "aunts" began to laugh at the parlor "uncles."

"Now let's take up the minorities in our civilization, shall we? Bigger the population, the more minorities. Don't step on the toes of the dog-lovers, the cat-lovers, doctors, lawyers, merchants, chiefs, Mormons, Baptists, Unitarians, second-generation Chinese, Swedes, Italians, Germans, Texans, Brooklynites, Irishmen, people from Oregon or Mexico. The people in this book, this play, this TV serial are not meant to represent any actual painters, cartographers, mechanics anywhere. The bigger your market, Montag, the less you handle controversy, remember that! All the minor minor minorities with their navels to be kept clean. Authors, full of evil thoughts, lock up your typewriters. They *did*. Magazines became a nice blend of vanilla tapioca. Books, so the damned snobbish critics said, were dishwater. No *wonder* books stopped selling, the critics said. But the public, knowing what it wanted, spinning happily, let the comic-books survive. And the three-dimensional sex-magazines, of course. There you have it, Montag. It didn't come from the Government down. There was no dictum, no declaration, no censorship, to start with, no! Technology, mass exploitation, and minority pressure carried the trick, thank God. Today, thanks to them, you can stay happy all the time, you are allowed to read comics, the good old confessions, or trade-journals."

"Yes, but what about the firemen, then?" asked Montag.

"Ah." Beatty leaned forward in the faint mist of smoke from his pipe. "What more easily explained and natural? With school turning out more runners, jumpers, racers, tinkerers, grabbers, snatchers, fliers, and swimmers instead of examiners, critics, knowers, and imaginative creators, the word 'intellectual,' of course, became the swear word it deserved to be. You always dread the unfamiliar. Surely you remember the boy in your own school class who was exceptionally 'bright,' did most of the reciting and answering while the others sat like so many leaden idols, hating him. And wasn't it this bright boy you selected for beatings and tortures after hours? Of course it was. We must all be alike. Not everyone born free and equal, as the Constitution says, but everyone *made* equal. Each man the image of every other; then all are happy, for there are no mountains to make them cower, to judge themselves against. So! A book is a loaded gun in the house next door. Burn it. Take the shot from the weapon. Breach man's mind. Who knows who might be the target of the well-read man? Me? I won't stomach them for a minute. And so when houses were finally fireproofed completely, all over the world (you were correct in your assumption the other night) there was no longer need of firemen for the old purposes. They were given the new job, as custodians of our peace of mind, the focus of our understandable and rightful dread of being inferior; official censors, judges, and executors. That's you, Montag, and that's me."

The door to the parlor opened and Mildred stood there

looking in at them, looking at Beatty and then at Montag. Behind her the walls of the room were flooded with green and yellow and orange fireworks sizzling and bursting to some music composed almost completely of trap drums, tom-toms, and cymbals. Her mouth moved and she was saying something but the sound covered it.

Beatty knocked his pipe into the palm of his pink hand, studied the ashes as if they were a symbol to be diagnosed and searched for meaning.

"You must understand that our civilization is so vast that we can't have our minorities upset and stirred. Ask yourself, What do we want in this country, above all? People want to be happy, isn't that right? Haven't you heard it all your life? I want to be happy, people say. Well, aren't they? Don't we keep them moving, don't we give them fun? That's all we live for, isn't it? For pleasure, for titillation? And you must admit our culture provides plenty of these."

"Yes."

Montag could lip-read what Mildred was saying in the doorway. He tried not to look at her mouth, because then Beatty might turn and read what was there, too.

"Colored people don't like *Little Black Sambo*. Burn it. White people don't feel good about *Uncle Tom's Cabin*. Burn it. Someone's written a book on tobacco and cancer of the lungs? The cigarette people are weeping? Burn the book. Serenity, Montag. Peace, Montag. Take your fight outside. Better yet, into the incinerator. Funerals are unhappy and pagan? Eliminate them, too. Five minutes after a person is dead he's on his way to the Big Flue, the Incinerators serviced by helicopters all over the country. Ten minutes after death a man's a speck of black dust. Let's not quibble over individuals with memoriams. Forget them. Burn all, burn everything. Fire is bright and fire is clean."

The fireworks died in the parlor behind Mildred. She had stopped talking at the same time; a miraculous coincidence. Montag held his breath.

"There was a girl next door," he said, slowly. "She's gone now, I think, dead. I can't even remember her face. But she was different. How—how did she *happen*?"

Beatty smiled. "Here or there, that's bound to occur.

Clarisse McClellan? We've a record on her family. We've watched them carefully. Heredity and environment are funny things. You can't rid yourselves of all the odd ducks in just a few years. The home environment can undo a lot you try to do at school. That's why we've lowered the kindergarten age year after year until now we're almost snatching them from the cradle. We had some false alarms on the McClellans, when they lived in Chicago. Never found a book. Uncle had a mixed record; antisocial. The girl? She was a time bomb. The family had been feeding her subconscious, I'm sure, from what I saw of her school record. She didn't want to know *how* a thing was done, but *why*. That can be embarrassing. You ask Why to a lot of things and you wind up very unhappy indeed, if you keep at it. The poor girl's better off dead."

"Yes, dead."

"Luckily, queer ones like her don't happen often. We know how to nip most of them in the bud, early. You can't build a house without nails and wood. If you don't want a house built, hide the nails and wood. If you don't want a man unhappy politically, don't give him two sides to a question to worry him; give him one. Better yet, give him none. Let him forget there is such a thing as war. If the government is inefficient, top-heavy, and tax-mad, better it be all those than that people worry over it. Peace, Montag. Give the people contests they win by remembering the words to more popular songs or the names of state capitals or how much corn Iowa grew last year. Cram them full of noncombustible data, chock them so damned full of 'facts' they feel stuffed, but absolutely 'brilliant' with information. Then they'll feel they're thinking, they'll get a *sense* of motion without moving. And they'll be happy, because facts of that sort don't change. Don't give them any slippery stuff like philosophy or sociology to tie things up with. That way lies melancholy. Any man who can take a TV wall apart and put it back together again, and most men can, nowadays, is happier than any man who tries to slide-rule, measure, and equate the universe, which just won't be measured or equated without making man feel bestial and lonely. I know, I've tried it; to hell with it. So bring on your clubs and parties, your acrobats and magicians, your daredevils, jet cars, motorcycle helicopters, your sex and heroin, more of everything to do with automatic reflex. If the drama is bad, if the film says nothing, if the play is hollow, sting me with the theremin, loudly. I'll think I'm responding to the play, when it's only a tactile reaction to vibration. But I don't care. I just like solid entertainment."

Beatty got up. "I must be going. Lecture's over. I hope I've clarified things. The important thing for you to remember, Montag, is we're the Happiness Boys, the Dixie Duo, you and I and the others. We stand against the small tide of those who want to make everyone unhappy with conflicting theory and thought. We have our fingers in the dike. Hold steady. Don't let the torrent of melancholy and drear philosophy drown our world. We depend on you. I don't think you realize how important *you* are, *we* are, to our happy world as it stands now."

Beatty shook Montag's limp hand. Montag still sat, as if the house were collapsing about him and he could not move, in the bed. Mildred had vanished from the door.

"One last thing," said Beatty. "At least once in his career, every fireman gets an itch. What do the books *say*, he wonders. Oh, to *scratch* that itch, eh? Well, Montag, take my word for it, I've had to read a few in my time, to know what I was about, and the books say *nothing*! Nothing you can teach or believe. They're about nonexistent people, figments of imagination, if they're fiction. And if they're nonfiction, it's worse, one professor calling another an idiot, one philosopher screaming down another's gullet. All of them running about, putting out the stars and extinguishing the sun. You come away lost."

"Well, then, what if a fireman accidentally, really not intending anything, takes a book home with him?"

Montag twitched. The open door looked at him with its great vacant eye.

"A natural error. Curiosity alone," said Beatty. "We don't get overanxious or mad. We let the fireman keep the book twenty-four hours. If he hasn't burned it by then, we simply come burn it for him."

"Of course." Montag's mouth was dry.

"Well, Montag. Will you take another, later shift, today? Will we see you tonight perhaps?"

"I don't know," said Montag.

"What?" Beatty looked faintly surprised.

Montag shut his eyes. "I'll be in later. Maybe."

"We'd certainly miss you if you didn't show," said Beatty, putting his pipe in his pocket thoughtfully.

I'll never come in again, thought Montag.

"Get well and keep well," said Beatty.

He turned and went out through the open door.

Montag watched through the window as Beatty drove away in his gleaming yellow-flame-colored beetle with the black, char-colored tires.

Across the street and down the way the other houses stood with their flat fronts. What was it Clarisse had said one afternoon? "No front porches. My uncle says there used to be front porches. And people sat there sometimes at night, talking when they wanted to talk, rocking, and not talking when they didn't want to talk. Sometimes they just sat there and thought about things, turned things over. My uncle says the architects got rid of the front porches because they didn't look well. But my uncle says that was merely rationalizing it; the real reason, hidden underneath, might be they didn't want people sitting like that, doing nothing, rocking, talking; that was the wrong *kind* of social life. People talked too much. And they had time to think. So they ran off with the porches. And the gardens, too. Not many gardens anymore to sit around in. And look at the furniture. No rocking chairs anymore. They're too comfortable. Get people up and running around. My uncle says . . . and . . . my uncle . . . and . . . my uncle . . ." Her voice faded.

Montag turned and looked at his wife, who sat in the middle of the parlor talking to an announcer, who in turn was talking to her. "Mrs. Montag," he was saying. This, that, and the other. "Mrs. Montag——" Something else and still another. The converter attachment, which had cost them one hundred dollars, automatically supplied her name whenever the announcer addressed his anonymous audience, leaving a blank where the proper syllables could be filled in. A special spot-wavex-scrambler also caused his televised image, in the area immediately about his lips, to mouth the vowels and consonants beautifully. He was a friend, no doubt of it, a good friend. "Mrs. Montag—now look right here."

Her head turned. Though she quite obviously was not listening.

Montag said, "It's only a step from not going to work today to not working tomorrow, to not working at the firehouse ever again."

"You are going to work tonight, though, aren't you?" said Mildred.

"I haven't decided. Right now I've got an awful feeling I want to smash things and kill things."

"Go take the beetle."

"No, thanks."

"The keys to the beetle are on the night table. I always like to drive fast when I feel that way. You get it up around ninety-five and you feel wonderful. Sometimes I drive all night and come back and you don't know it. It's fun out in the country. You hit rabbits, sometimes you hit dogs. Go take the beetle."

"No, I don't want to, this time. I want to hold onto this funny thing. God, it's gotten big on me. I don't know what it is. I'm so damned unhappy, I'm so mad, and I don't know why. I feel like I'm putting on weight. I feel fat. I feel like I've been saving up a lot of things, and don't know what. I might even start reading books."

"They'd put you in jail, wouldn't they?" She looked at him as if he were behind the glass wall.

He began to put on his clothes, moving restlessly about the bedroom. "Yes, and it might be a good idea. Before I hurt someone. Did you hear Beatty? Did you listen to him? He knows all the answers. He's right. Happiness is important. Fun is everything. And yet I kept sitting there saying to myself, I'm not happy, I'm not happy."

"*I* am." Mildred's mouth beamed. "And proud of it."

"I'm going to do something," said Montag. "I don't even know what yet, but I'm going to do something big."

"I'm tired of listening to this junk," said Mildred, turning from him to the announcer again.

Montag touched the volume control in the wall and the announcer was speechless.

"Millie?" He paused. "This is your house as well as mine. I feel it's only fair that I tell you something now. I should have told you before, but I wasn't even admitting it to myself. I have something I want you to see, something I've put away and hid during the past year, now and again, once in a while, I didn't know why, but I did it and I never told you."

He took hold of a straight-backed chair and moved it slowly and steadily into the hall near the front door and climbed up on it and stood for a moment like a statue on a pedestal, his wife standing under him, waiting. Then he reached up and pulled back the grille of the air-conditioning system and reached far back inside to the right and moved still another sliding sheet of metal and took out a book. Without looking at it he dropped it to the floor. He put his hand back up and took out two books and moved his hand down and dropped the two books to the floor. He kept moving his hand and dropping books, small ones, fairly large ones, yellow, red, green ones. When he was done he looked down upon some twenty books lying at his wife's feet.

"I'm sorry," he said. "I didn't really think. But now it looks as if we're in this together."

Mildred backed away as if she were suddenly confronted by a pack of mice that had come up out of the floor. He could hear her breathing rapidly and her face was paled out and her eyes were fastened wide. She said his name over, twice, three times. Then, moaning, she ran forward, seized a book and ran toward the kitchen incinerator.

He caught her, shrieking. He held her and she tried to fight away from him, scratching.

"No, Millie, no! Wait! Stop it, will you? You don't know . . . stop it!" He slapped her face, he grabbed her again and shook her.

She said his name and began to cry.

"Millie!" he said. "Listen. Give me a second, will you? We can't do anything. We can't burn these. I want to look at them, at least look at them once. Then if what the Captain says is true, we'll burn them together, believe me, we'll burn them together. You must help me." He looked down into her face and took hold of her chin and held her firmly. He was looking not only at her, but for himself and what he must do, in her face. "Whether we like this or not, we're in it. I've never asked for much from you in all these years, but I ask it now, I plead for it. We've got to start somewhere here, figuring out why we're in such a mess, you and the medicine nights, and the car, and me and my work. We're heading right for the cliff, Millie. God, I don't want to go over. This isn't going to be easy. We haven't anything to go on, but maybe we can piece it out and figure it and help each other. I need you so much right now, I can't tell you. If you love me at all you'll put up with this, twenty-four, forty-eight hours, that's all I ask, then it'll be over, I promise, I swear! And if there is something here, just one little thing out of a whole mess of things, maybe we can pass it on to someone else."

She wasn't fighting any more, so he let her go. She sagged away from him and slid down the wall, and sat on the floor looking at the books. Her foot touched one and she saw this and pulled her foot away.

"That woman, the other night, Millie, you weren't there. You didn't see her face. And Clarisse. You never talked to her. I talked to her. And men like Beatty are afraid of her. I can't understand it. Why should they be so afraid of someone like her? But I kept putting her alongside the firemen in the House last night, and I suddenly realized I didn't like them at all, and I didn't like myself at all any more. And I thought maybe it would be best if the firemen themselves were burnt."

"Guy!"

The front door voice called softly:

"Mrs. Montag, Mrs. Montag, someone here, someone here, Mrs. Montag, Mrs. Montag, someone here."

Softly.

They turned to stare at the door and the books toppled everywhere, everywhere in heaps.

"Beatty!" said Mildred.

"It can't be him."

"He's come back!" she whispered.

The front door voice called again softly. "Someone here . . ."

"We won't answer." Montag lay back against the wall and then slowly sank to a crouching position and began to nudge the books, bewilderedly, with his thumb, his forefinger. He was shivering and he wanted above all to shove the books up through the ventilator again, but he knew he could not face Beatty again. He crouched and then he sat and the voice of the front door spoke again, more insistently. Montag picked a single small volume from the floor. "Where do we begin?" He opened the book halfway and peered at it. "We begin by beginning, I guess."

"He'll come in," said Mildred, "and burn us and the books!"

The front door voice faded at last. There was a silence. Montag felt the presence of someone beyond the door, waiting, listening. Then the footsteps going away down the walk and over the lawn.

"Let's see what this is," said Montag.

He spoke the words haltingly and with a terrible self-consciousness. He read a dozen pages here or there and came at last to this:

"'It is computed, that eleven thousand persons have at several times suffered death rather than submit to break their eggs at the smaller end.'"

Mildred sat across the hall from him. "What does it mean? It doesn't mean *anything*! The Captain was right!"

"Here now," said Montag. "We'll start over again, at the beginning."

Part Two:
The Sieve and the Sand

THEY READ the long afternoon through, while the cold November rain fell from the sky upon the quiet house. They sat in the hall because the parlor was so empty and gray-looking without its wall lit with orange and yellow confetti and skyrockets and women in goldmesh dresses and men in black velvet pulling one-hundred-pound rabbits from silver hats. The parlor was dead and Mildred kept peering in at it with a blank expression as Montag paced the floor and came back and squatted down and read a page as many as ten times, aloud.

"'We cannot tell the precise moment when friendship is formed. As in filling a vessel drop by drop, there is at last a drop which makes it run over; so in a series of kindnesses there is at last one which makes the heart run over.'"

Montag sat listening to the rain.

"Is that what it was in the girl next door? I've tried so hard to figure."

"She's dead. Let's talk about someone alive, for goodness' sake."

Montag did not look back at his wife as he went trembling along the hall to the kitchen, where he stood a long time watching the rain hit the windows before he came back down the hall in the gray light, waiting for the tremble to subside.

He opened another book.

"'That favourite subject, Myself.'"

He squinted at the wall. "'That favourite subject, Myself.'"

"I understand *that* one," said Mildred.

"But Clarisse's favorite subject wasn't herself. It was everyone else, and me. She was the first person in a good many years I've really liked. She was the first person I can remember who looked straight at me as if I counted." He lifted the two books. "These men have been dead a long time, but I know their words point, one way or another, to Clarisse."

Outside the front door, in the rain, a faint scratching.

Montag froze. He saw Mildred thrust herself back to the wall and gasp.

"Someone—the door—why doesn't the door-voice tell us—"

"I shut it off."

Under the doorsill, a slow, probing sniff, an exhalation of electric steam.

Mildred laughed. "It's only a dog, that's what! You want me to shoo him away?"

"Stay where you are!"

Silence. The cold rain falling. And the smell of blue electricity blowing under the locked door.

"Let's get back to work," said Montag quietly.

Mildred kicked at a book. "Books aren't people. You read and I look all around, but there isn't *anybody*!"

He stared at the parlor that was dead and gray as the waters of an ocean that might teem with life if they switched on the electronic sun.

"Now," said Mildred, "my 'family' is people. They tell me things; *I* laugh, *they* laugh! And the colors!"

"Yes, I know."

"And besides, if Captain Beatty knew about those books——" She thought about it. Her face grew amazed and then horrified. "He might come and burn the house and the 'family.' That's awful! Think of our investment. Why should I read? What *for*?"

"What for! Why!" said Montag. "I saw the damnedest snake in the world the other night. It was dead but it was alive. It could see but it couldn't see. You want to *see* that snake? It's at Emergency Hospital where they filed a report on all the junk the snake got out of you! Would you like to go and check their file? Maybe you'd look under Guy Montag or maybe under Fear or War. Would you like to go to that house that burnt last night? And rake ashes for the bones of the woman who set fire to her own house! What about Clarisse McClellan, where do we look for her? The morgue! Listen!"

The bombers crossed the sky and crossed the sky over the house, gasping, murmuring, whistling like an immense, invisible fan, circling in emptiness.

"Jesus God," said Montag. "Every hour so many damn things in the sky! How in hell did those bombers get up there every single second of our lives! Why doesn't someone want to talk about it! We've started and won two atomic wars since 1960! Is it because we're having so much fun at home we've forgotten the world? Is it because we're so rich and the rest of the world's so poor and we just don't care if they are? I've heard rumors; the world is starving, but we're well-fed. Is it true, the world works hard and we play? Is that why we're hated so much? I've heard the rumors about hate, too, once in a long while, over the years. Do *you* know why? *I* don't, that's *sure*! Maybe the books can get us half out of the cave. They just *might* stop us from making the same damn insane mistakes! I don't hear those idiot bastards in your parlor talking about it. God, Millie, don't you *see*? An hour a day, two hours, with these books, and maybe . . ."

The telephone rang. Mildred snatched the phone.

"Ann!" She laughed. "Yes, the White Clown's on tonight!"

Montag walked to the kitchen and threw the book down. "Montag," he said, "you're really stupid. Where do we go from here? Do we turn the books in, forget it?" He opened the book to read over Mildred's laughter.

Poor Millie, he thought. Poor Montag, it's mud to you, too. But where do you get help, where do you find a teacher this late?

Hold on. He shut his eyes. Yes, of course. Again he found himself thinking of the green park a year ago. The thought had been with him many times recently but now he remembered how it was that day in the city park when he had seen that old man in the black suit hide something, quickly, in his coat.

. . . The old man leapt up as if to run. And Montag said, "Wait!"

"I haven't done anything!" cried the old man, trembling.

"No one said you did."

They had sat in the green soft light without saying a word for a moment and then Montag talked about the weather and then the old man responded with a pale voice. It was a strange quiet meeting. The old man admitted to being a retired English Professor who had been thrown out upon the world forty years ago when the last liberal arts college shut for lack of students and patronage. His name was Faber, and when he finally lost his fear of Montag, he talked in a cadenced voice, looking at the sky and the trees and the green park, and when an hour had passed he said something to Montag and Montag sensed it was a rhymeless poem. Then the old man grew even more courageous and said something else and that was a poem, too. Faber held his hand over his left coat pocket and spoke these words gently, and Montag knew if he reached out, he might pull a book of poetry from the man's coat. But he did not reach out. His hands stayed on his knees, numbed and useless. "I don't talk *things*, sir," said Faber. "I talk the *meaning* of things. I sit here and *know* I'm alive."

That was all there was to it, really. An hour of monologue, a poem, a comment, and then without either acknowledging the fact that Montag was a fireman, Faber with a certain trembling, wrote his address on a slip of paper. "For your file," he said, "in case you decide to be angry with me."

"I'm not angry," Montag said, surprised.

Mildred shrieked with laughter in the hall.

Montag went to his bedroom closet and flipped through his file-wallet to the heading: FUTURE INVESTIGATIONS (?) Faber's name was there. He hadn't turned it in and he hadn't erased it.

He dialed the call on a secondary phone. The phone on the far end of the line called Faber's name a dozen times before the professor answered in a faint voice. Montag identified himself and was met with a lengthy silence. "Yes, Mr. Montag?"

"Professor Faber, I have a rather odd question to ask. How many copies of the Bible are left in this country?"

"I don't know what you're talking about!"

"I want to know if there are *any* copies left at all."

"This is some sort of trap! I can't talk to just *anyone* on the phone!"

"How many copies of Shakespeare and Plato?"

"None! You know as well as I do. None!"

Faber hung up.

Montag put down the phone. None. A thing he knew of course from the firehouse listings. But somehow he had wanted to hear it from Faber himself.

In the hall Mildred's face was suffused with excitement. "Well, the ladies are coming over!"

Montag showed her a book. "This is the Old and New Testament, and . . ."

"Don't start that again!"

"It might be the last copy in this part of the world."

"You've got to hand it back tonight, don't you? Captain Beatty *knows* you got it, doesn't he?"

"I don't think he knows *which* book I stole. But how do I choose a substitute? Do I turn in Mr. Jefferson? Mr. Thoreau? Which is least valuable? If I pick a substitute and Beatty does know which book I stole, he'll guess we've an entire library here!"

Mildred's mouth twitched. "See what you're *doing*? You'll ruin us! Who's more important, me or that Bible?" She was beginning to shriek now, sitting there like a wax doll melting in its own heat.

He could hear Beatty's voice. "Sit down, Montag. Watch. Delicately, like the petals of a flower. Light the first page, light the second page. Each becomes a black butterfly. Beautiful, eh? Light the third page from the second and so on, chain-smoking, chapter by chapter, all the silly things the words mean, all the false promises, all the second-hand notions and time-worn philosophies." There sat Beatty, perspiring gently, the floor littered with swarms of black moths that had died in a single storm.

Mildred stopped screaming as quickly as she started. Montag was not listening. "There's only one thing to do," he said. "Some time before tonight when I give the book to Beatty, I've got to have a duplicate made."

"You'll be here for the White Clown tonight, and the ladies coming over?" cried Mildred.

Montag stopped at the door, with his back turned. "Millie?"

A silence. "What?"

"Millie? Does the White Clown love you?"

No answer.

"Millie, does——" He licked his lips. "Does your 'family' love you, love you *very* much, love you with all their heart and soul, Millie?"

He felt her blinking slowly at the back of his neck. "Why'd you ask a silly question like that?"

He felt he wanted to cry, but nothing would happen to his eyes or his mouth.

"If you see that dog outside," said Mildred, "give him a kick for me."

He hesitated, listening at the door. He opened it and stepped out.

The rain had stopped and the sun was setting in the clear sky. The street and the lawn and the porch were empty. He let his breath go in a great sigh.

He slammed the door.

He was on the subway.

I'm numb, he thought. When did the numbness really begin in my face? In my body? The night I kicked the pill-bottle in the dark, like kicking a buried mine.

The numbness will go away, he thought. It'll take time, but I'll do it, or Faber will do it for me. Someone somewhere will give me back the old face and the old hands the way they were. Even the smile, he thought, the old burnt-in smile, that's gone. I'm lost without it.

The subway fled past him, cream-tile, jet-black, cream-tile, jet-black, numerals and darkness, more darkness and the total adding itself.

Once as a child he had sat upon a yellow dune by the sea in the middle of the blue and hot summer day, trying to fill a sieve with sand, because some cruel cousin had said, "Fill this sieve and you'll get a dime!" And the faster he poured, the faster it sifted through with a hot whispering. His hands were tired, the sand was boiling, the sieve was empty. Seated there in the midst of July, without a sound, he felt the tears move down his cheeks.

Now as the vacuum-underground rushed him through the dead cellars of town, jolting him, he remembered the terrible logic of that sieve, and he looked down and saw that he was carrying the Bible open. There were people in the suction train but he held the book in his hands and the silly thought came to him, if you read fast and read all, maybe some of the sand will stay in the sieve. But he read and the words fell through, and he thought, in a few hours, there will be Beatty, and here will be me handing this over, so no phrase must escape me, each line must be memorized. I will myself to do it.

He clenched the book in his fists.

Trumpets blared.

"Denham's Dentifrice."

Shut up, thought Montag. Consider the lilies of the field.

"Denham's Dentifrice."

They toil not——

"Denham's——"

Consider the lilies of the field, shut up, shut up.

"Dentifrice!"

He tore the book open and flicked the pages and felt of them as if he were blind, he picked at the shape of the individual letters, not blinking.

"Denham's. Spelled: D-E-N—"

They toil not, neither do they . . .

A fierce whisper of hot sand through empty sieve.

"*Denham's does it!*"

Consider the lilies, the lilies, the lilies . . .

"Denham's dental detergent."

"Shut up, shut up, shut up!" It was a plea, a cry so terrible that Montag found himself on his feet, the shocked inhabitants of the loud car staring, moving back from this man with the insane, gorged face, the gibbering, dry mouth, the flapping book in his fist. The people who had been sitting a moment before, tapping their feet to the rhythm of Denham's Dentifrice, Denham's Dandy Dental Detergent, Denham's Dentifrice Dentifrice Dentifrice, one two, one two three, one two, one two three. The people whose mouths had been faintly twitching the words Dentifrice Dentifrice Dentifrice. The train radio vomited upon Montag, in retaliation, a great tonload of music made of tin, copper, silver, chromium, and brass. The people were pounded into submission; they did not run, there was no place to run; the great air-train fell down its shaft in the earth.

"Lilies of the field."

"Denham's."

"*Lilies*, I said!"

The people stared.

"Call the guard."

"The man's off——"

"Knoll View!"

The train hissed to its stop.

"Knoll View!" A cry.

"Denham's." A whisper.

Montag's mouth barely moved. "Lilies . . ."

The train door whistled open. Montag stood. The door gasped, started shut. Only then did he leap past the other passengers, screaming in his mind, plunge through the slicing door only in time. He ran on the white tiles up through the tunnels, ignoring the escalators, because he wanted to feel his feet move, arms swing, lungs clench, unclench, feel his throat go raw with air. A voice drifted after him, "Denham's Denham's Denham's," the train hissed like a snake. The train vanished in its hole.

"Who is it?"

"Montag out here?"

"What do you want?"

"Let me in."

"I haven't done anything!"

"I'm alone, dammit!"

"You swear it?"

"I swear!"

The front door opened slowly. Faber peered out, looking very old in the light and very fragile and very much afraid. The old man looked as if he had not been out of the house in years. He and the white plaster walls inside were much the same. There was white in the flesh of his mouth and his cheeks and his hair was white and his eyes had faded, with white in the vague blueness there. Then his eyes touched on the book under Montag's arm and he did not look so old any more and not quite as fragile. Slowly, his fear went.

"I'm sorry. One has to be careful."

He looked at the book under Montag's arm and could not stop. "So it's true."

Montag stepped inside. The door shut.

"Sit down." Faber backed up, as if he feared the book might vanish if he took his eyes from it. Behind him, the door to a bedroom stood open, and in that room a litter of machinery and steel tools were strewn upon a desktop. Montag had only a glimpse, before Faber, seeing Montag's attention diverted, turned quickly and shut the bedroom door and stood holding the knob with a trembling hand. His gaze returned unsteadily to Montag, who was now seated with the book in his lap. "The book—where did you——?"

"I stole it."

Faber, for the first time, raised his eyes and looked directly into Montag's face. "You're brave."

"No," said Montag. "My wife's dying. A friend of mine's already dead. Someone who may have been a friend was burnt less than twenty-four hours ago. You're the only one I knew might help me. To see. To see . . ."

Faber's hands itched on his knees. "May I?"

"Sorry." Montag gave him the book.

"It's been a long time. I'm not a religious man. But it's been a long time." Faber turned the pages, stopping here and there to read. "It's as good as I remember. Lord, how they've changed it in our 'parlors' these days. Christ is one of the 'family' now. I often wonder if God recognizes His own son the way we've dressed him up, or is it dressed him down? He's a regular peppermint stick now, all sugar-crystal and saccharine when he isn't making veiled references to certain commercial products that every worshiper *absolutely* needs." Faber sniffed the book. "Do you know that books smell like nutmeg or some spice from a foreign land? I loved to smell them when I was a boy. Lord, there were a lot of lovely books once, before we let them go." Faber turned the pages. "Mr. Montag, you are looking at a coward. I saw the way things were going, a long time back. I said nothing. I'm one of the innocents who could have spoken up and out when no one would listen to the 'guilty,' but I did not speak and thus became guilty myself. And when finally they set the structure to burn the books, using the firemen, I grunted a few times and subsided, for there were no others grunting or yelling with me, by then. Now, it's too late." Faber closed the Bible. "Well—suppose you tell me why you came here?"

"Nobody listens any more. I can't talk to the walls because they're yelling at *me*. I can't talk to my wife; she listens to the *walls*. I just want someone to hear what I have to say. And maybe if I talk long enough, it'll make sense. And I want you to teach me to understand what I read."

Faber examined Montag's thin, blue-jowled face. "How

did you get shaken up? What knocked the torch out of your hands?"

"I don't know. We have everything we need to be happy, but we aren't happy. Something's missing. I looked around. The only thing I positively *knew* was gone was the books I'd burned in ten or twelve years. So I thought books might help."

"You're a hopeless romantic," said Faber. "It would be funny if it were not serious. It's not books you need, it's some of the things that once were in books. The same things *could* be in the 'parlor families' today. The same infinite detail and awareness could be projected through the radios and televisors, but are not. No, no, it's not books at all you're looking for! Take it where you can find it, in old phonograph records, old motion pictures, and in old friends; look for it in nature and look for it in yourself. Books were only one type of receptacle where we stored a lot of things we were afraid we might forget. There is nothing magical in them, at all. The magic is only in what books say, how they stitched the patches of the universe together into one garment for us. Of course you couldn't know this, of course you still can't understand what I mean when I say all this. You are intuitively right, that's what counts. Three things are missing.

"Number one: Do you know why books such as this are so important? Because they have quality. And what does the word quality mean? To me it means texture. This book has *pores.* It has features. This book can go under the microscope. You'd find life under the glass, streaming past in infinite profusion. The more pores, the more truthfully recorded details of life per square inch you can get on a sheet of paper, the more 'literary' you are. That's *my* definition, anyway. *Telling detail. Fresh* detail. The good writers touch life often. The mediocre ones run a quick hand over her. The bad ones rape her and leave her for the flies.

"So now do you see why books are hated and feared? They show the pores in the face of life. The comfortable people want only wax moon faces, poreless, hairless, expressionless. We are living in a time when flowers are trying to live on flowers, instead of growing on good rain and black loam. Even fireworks, for all their prettiness, come from the chemistry of the earth. Yet somehow we think we can grow, feeding on flowers and fireworks, without completing the cycle back to reality. Do you know the legend of Hercules and Antaeus, the giant wrestler, whose strength was incredible so long as he stood firmly on the earth. But when he was held, rootless, in midair, by Hercules, he perished easily. If there isn't something in that legend for us today, in this city, in our time, then I am completely insane. Well, there we have the first thing I said we needed. Quality, texture of information."

"And the second?"

"Leisure."

"Oh, but we've plenty of off-hours."

"Off-hours, yes. But time to think? If you're not driving a hundred miles an hour, at a clip where you can't think of anything else but the danger, then you're playing some game or sitting in some room where you can't argue with the four-wall televisor. Why? The televisor is 'real.' It is immediate, it has dimension. It tells you what to think and blasts it in. It *must* be right. It *seems* so right. It rushes you on so quickly to its own conclusions your mind hasn't time to protest, 'What nonsense!'"

"Only the 'family' is 'people.'"

"I beg pardon?"

"My wife says books aren't 'real.'"

"Thank God for that. You can shut them, say, 'Hold on a moment.' You play God to it. But who has ever torn himself from the claw that encloses you when you drop a seed in a TV parlor? It grows you any shape it wishes! It is an environment as real as the world. It *becomes* and *is* the truth. Books can be beaten down with reason. But with all my knowledge and skepticism, I have never been able to argue with a one hundred–piece symphony orchestra, full color, three dimensions, and being in and part of those incredible parlors. As you see, my parlor is nothing but four plaster walls. And here." He held out two small rubber plugs. "For my ears when I ride the subway-jets."

"Denham's Dentifrice; they toil not, neither do they spin," said Montag, eyes shut. "Where do we go from here? Would books help us?"

"Only if the third necessary thing could be given us. Number one, as I said, quality of information. Number two: leisure to digest it. And number three: the right to carry out actions based on what we learn from the interaction of the first two. And I hardly think a very old man and a fireman turned sour could *do* much this late in the game . . ."

"I can *get* books."

"You're running a risk."

"That's the good part of dying; when you've nothing to lose, you run any risk you want."

"There, you've said an interesting thing," laughed Faber, "without having read it!"

"Are things like *that* in books? But it came off the top of my mind!"

"All the better. You didn't fancy it up for me or anyone, even yourself."

Montag leaned forward. "This afternoon I thought that if it turned out that books *were* worthwhile, we might get a press and print some extra copies——"

"We?"

"You and I."

"Oh, no!" Faber sat up.

"But let me tell you my plan——"

"If you insist on telling me, I must ask you to leave."

"But aren't *you* interested?"

"Not if you start talking the sort of talk that might get me burnt for my trouble. The only way I could *possibly* listen to you would be if somehow the fireman structure itself could be burnt. Now if you suggest that we print extra books and arrange to have them hidden in firemen's houses all over the country, so that seeds of suspicion would be sown among these arsonists, bravo, I'd say!"

"Plant the books, turn in an alarm, and see the firemen's houses burn, is that what you mean?"

Faber raised his brows and looked at Montag as if he were seeing a new man. "I was joking."

"If you thought it would be a plan worth trying, I'd have to take your word it would help."

"You can't guarantee things like that! After all, when we *had* all the books we needed, we still insisted on finding the highest cliff to jump off. But we *do* need a breather. We *do* need knowledge. And perhaps in a thousand years we might pick smaller cliffs to jump off. The books are to remind us what asses and fools we are. They're Caesar's praetorian guard, whispering as the parade roars down the avenue, 'Remember, Caesar, thou art mortal.' Most of us can't rush around, talk to everyone, know all the cities of the world, we haven't time, money or that many friends. The things you're looking for, Montag, are in the world, but the only way the average chap will ever see ninety-nine per cent of them is in a book. Don't ask for guarantees. And don't look to be saved in any *one* thing, person, machine, or library. Do your own bit of saving, and if you drown, at least die knowing you were headed for shore."

Faber got up and began to pace the room.

"Well?" asked Montag.

"You're absolutely serious?"

"Absolutely."

"It's an insidious plan, if I do say so myself." Faber glanced nervously at his bedroom door. "To see the firehouses burn across the land, destroyed as hotbeds of treason. The salamander devours his tail! Ho, God!"

"I've a list of firemen's residences everywhere. With some sort of underground——"

"Can't trust people, that's the dirty part. You and I and who else will set the fires?"

"Aren't there professors like yourself, former writers, historians, linguists. . . ?"

"Dead or ancient."

"The older the better; they'll go unnoticed. You know dozens, admit it!"

"Oh, there are many actors alone who haven't acted Pirandello or Shaw or Shakespeare for years because their plays are too *aware* of the world. We could use their anger. And we could use the honest rage of those historians who haven't written a line for forty years. True, we might form classes in thinking and reading."

"Yes!"

"But that would just nibble the edges. The whole culture's shot through. The skeleton needs melting and reshaping. Good God, it isn't as simple as just picking up a book you laid down half a century ago. Remember, the firemen are rarely necessary. The public itself stopped reading of its own accord. You firemen provide a circus now and then at which buildings are set off and crowds gather for the pretty blaze, but it's a small sideshow indeed, and hardly necessary to keep things in line. So few want to be rebels anymore. And out of those few, most, like myself, scare easily. Can you dance faster than the White Clown, shout louder than 'Mr. Gimmick' and the parlor 'families'? If you can, you'll win your way, Montag. In any event, you're a fool. People are having *fun*."

"Committing suicide! Murdering!"

A bomber flight had been moving east all the time they talked, and only now did the two men stop and listen, feeling the great jet sound tremble inside themselves.

"Patience, Montag. Let the war turn off the 'families.' Our civilization is flinging itself to pieces. Stand back from the centrifuge."

"There has to be someone ready when it blows up."

"What? Men quoting Milton? Saying, I remember Sophocles? Reminding the survivors that man has his good side, too? They will only gather up their stones to hurl at each other. Montag, go home. Go to bed. Why waste your final hours racing about your cage denying you're a squirrel?"

"Then you don't care any more?"

"I care so much I'm sick."

"And you won't help me?"

"Good night, good night."

Montag's hands picked up the Bible. He saw what his hands had done and he looked surprised.

"Would you like to own this?"

Faber said, "I'd give my right arm."

Montag stood there and waited for the next thing to happen. His hands, by themselves, like two men working together, began to rip the pages from the book. The hands tore the flyleaf and then the first and then the second page.

"Idiot, what're you doing!" Faber sprang up, as if he had been struck. He fell against Montag. Montag warded him off and let his hands continue. Six more pages fell to the floor. He picked them up and wadded the paper under Faber's gaze.

"Don't, oh, don't!" said the old man.

"Who can stop me? I'm a fireman. I can burn you!"

The old man stood looking at him. "You wouldn't."

"I could!"

"The book. Don't tear it any more." Faber sank into a chair, his face very white, his mouth trembling. "Don't make me feel any more tired. What do you want?"

"I need you to teach me."

"All right, all right."

Montag put the book down. He began to unwad the crumpled paper and flatten it out as the old man watched tiredly.

Faber shook his head as if he were waking up.

"Montag, have you any money?"

"Some. Four, five hundred dollars. Why?"

"Bring it. I know a man who printed our college paper half a century ago. That was the year I came to class at the start of the new semester and found only one student to sign up for Drama from Aeschylus to O'Neill. You see? How like a beautiful statue of ice it was, melting in the sun. I remember the newspapers dying like huge moths. No one *wanted* them back. No one missed them. And then the Government, seeing how advantageous it was to have people reading only about passionate lips and the fist in the stomach, circled the situation with your fire-eaters. So, Montag, there's this unemployed printer. We might start a few books, and wait on the war to break the pattern and give us the push we need. A few bombs and the 'families' in the walls of all the houses, like harlequin rats, will shut up! In the silence, our stage-whisper might carry."

They both stood looking at the book on the table.

"I've tried to remember," said Montag. "But, hell, it's gone when I turn my head. God, how I want something to say to the Captain. He's read enough so he has all the answers, or seems to have. His voice is like butter. I'm afraid he'll talk me back the way I was. Only a week ago, pumping a kerosene hose, I thought: God, what fun!"

The old man nodded. "Those who don't build must burn. It's as old as history and juvenile delinquents."

"So that's what I am."

"There's some of it in all of us."

Montag moved toward the front door. "Can you help me in any way tonight, with the Fire Captain? I need an umbrella to keep off the rain. I'm so damned afraid I'll drown if he gets me again."

The old man said nothing, but glanced once more nervously, at his bedroom. Montag caught the glance. "Well?"

The old man took a deep breath, held it, and let it out. He took another, eyes closed, his mouth tight, and at last exhaled. "Montag . . ."

The old man turned at last and said, "Come along. I would actually have let you walk right out of my house. I *am* a cowardly old fool."

Faber opened the bedroom door and led Montag into a small chamber where stood a table upon which a number of metal tools lay among a welter of microscopic wire-hairs, tiny coils, bobbins and crystals.

"What's this?" asked Montag.

"Proof of my terrible cowardice. I've lived alone so many years, throwing images on walls with my imagination. Fiddling with electronics, radio-transmission, has been my hobby. My cowardice is of such a passion, complementing the revolutionary spirit that lives in its shadow, I was forced to design *this*."

He picked up a small green metal object no larger than a .22 bullet.

"I paid for all this—how? Playing the stock-market, of course, the last refuge in the world for the dangerous intellectual out of a job. Well, I played the market and built all this and I've waited. I've waited, trembling, half a lifetime for someone to speak to me. I dared speak to no one. That day in the park when we sat together, I knew that some day you might drop by, with fire or friendship, it was hard to guess. I've had this little item ready for months. But I almost let you go, I'm *that* afraid!"

"It looks like a Seashell Radio."

"And something more! It *listens*! If you put it in your ear, Montag, I can sit comfortably home, warming my frightened bones, and hear and analyze the firemen's world, find its weaknesses, without danger. I'm the Queen Bee, safe in the hive. You will be the drone, the traveling ear. Eventually, I could put out ears into all parts of the city, with various men, listening and evaluating. If the drones die, I'm still safe at home, tending my fright with a maximum of comfort and a minimum of chance. See how safe I play it, how contemptible I am?"

Montag placed the green bullet in his ear. The old man inserted a similar object in his own ear and moved his lips.

"Montag!"

The voice was in Montag's head.

"I *hear* you!"

The old man laughed. "You're coming over fine, too!" Faber whispered, but the voice in Montag's head was clear. "Go to the firehouse when it's time. I'll be with you. Let's listen to this Captain Beatty together. He could be one of us. God knows. I'll give you things to say. We'll give him a good show. Do you hate me for this electronic cowardice of mine? Here I am sending you out into the night, while I stay behind the lines with my damned ears listening for you to get your head chopped off."

"We all do what we do," said Montag. He put the Bible in the old man's hands. "Here. I'll chance turning in a substitute. Tomorrow——"

"I'll see the unemployed printer, yes; *that* much I can do."

"Good night, Professor."

"Not good night. I'll be with you the rest of the night, a vinegar gnat tickling your ear when you need me. But good night and good luck, anyway."

The door opened and shut. Montag was in the dark street again, looking at the world.

You could feel the war getting ready in the sky that night. The way the clouds moved aside and came back, and the way the stars looked, a million of them swimming between the clouds, like the enemy disks, and the feeling that the sky might fall upon the city and turn it to chalk dust, and the moon go up in red fire; that was how the night felt.

Montag walked from the subway with the money in his pocket (he had visited the bank which was open all night every night with robot tellers in attendance) and as he walked he was listening to the Seashell Radio in one ear. . . . "We have mobilized a million men. Quick victory is ours if the war comes. . . ." Music flooded over the voice quickly and it was gone.

"Ten million men mobilized," Faber's voice whispered in his other ear. "But *say* one million. It's happier."

"Faber?"

"Yes?"

"I'm not thinking. I'm just doing like I'm told, like always. You said get the money and I got it. I didn't really think of it myself. When do I start working things out on my own?"

"You've started already, by saying what you just said. You'll have to take me on faith."

"I took the others on faith!"

"Yes, and look where we're headed. You'll have to travel blind for awhile. Here's my arm to hold onto."

"I don't want to change sides and just be *told* what to do. There's no reason to change if I do that."

"You're wise already!"

Montag felt his feet moving him on the sidewalk toward his house. "Keep talking."

"Would you like me to read? I'll read so you can remember. I go to bed only five hours a night. Nothing to do. So if you like, I'll read you to sleep nights. They say you retain knowledge even when you're sleeping, if someone whispers it in your ear."

"Yes."

"Here." Far away across town in the night, the faintest whisper of a turned page. "The Book of Job."

The moon rose in the sky as Montag walked, his lips moving just a trifle.

He was eating a light supper at nine in the evening when the front door cried out in the hall and Mildred ran from the parlor like a native fleeing an eruption of Vesuvius. Mrs. Phelps and Mrs. Bowles came through the front door and vanished into the volcano's mouth with martinis in their hands. Montag stopped eating. They were like a monstrous crystal chandelier tinkling in a thousand chimes, he saw their Cheshire Cat smiles burning through the walls of the house, and now they were screaming at each other above the din.

Montag found himself at the parlor door with his food still in his mouth.

"Doesn't everyone look nice!"

"Nice."

"You look fine, Millie!"

"Fine."

"Everyone looks swell."

"Swell!"

Montag stood watching them.

"Patience," whispered Faber.

"I shouldn't be here," whispered Montag, almost to himself. "I should be on my way back to you with the money!"

"Tomorrow's time enough. Careful!"

"Isn't this show *wonderful*?" cried Mildred.

"Wonderful!"

On one wall a woman smiled and drank orange juice simultaneously. How does she do both at once, thought Montag, insanely. In the other walls an x-ray of the same woman revealed the contracting journey of the refreshing beverage on its way to her delighted stomach! Abruptly the room took off on a rocket flight into the clouds, it plunged into a lime-green sea where blue fish ate red and yellow fish. A minute later, Three White Cartoon Clowns chopped off each other's limbs to the accompaniment of immense incoming tides of laughter. Two minutes more and the room whipped out of town to the jet cars wildly circling an arena, bashing and backing up and bashing each other again. Montag saw a number of bodies in the air.

"Millie, did you *see* that!"

"I saw it, I *saw* it!"

Montag reached inside the parlor wall and pulled the main switch. The images drained away, as if the water had been let from a gigantic crystal bowl of hysterical fish.

The three women turned slowly and looked with unconcealed irritation and then dislike at Montag.

"When do you suppose the war will start?" he said. "I notice your husbands aren't here tonight?"

"Oh, they come and go, come and go," said Mrs. Phelps. "In again out again Finnegan, the Army called Pete yesterday. He'll be back next week. The Army said so. Quick war. Forty-eight hours they said, and everyone home. That's what the Army said. Quick war. Pete was called yesterday and they said he'd be back next week. Quick . . ."

The three women fidgeted and looked nervously at the empty mud-colored walls.

"I'm not worried," said Mrs. Phelps. "I'll let Pete do all the worrying." She giggled. "I'll let old Pete do all the worrying, Not me. I'm not worried."

"Yes," said Millie. "Let old Pete do the worrying."

"It's always someone else's husband dies, they say."

"I've heard that, too. I've never known any dead man killed in a war. Killed jumping off buildings, yes, like Gloria's husband last week, but from wars? No."

"Not from wars," said Mrs. Phelps. "Anyway, Pete and I always said, no tears, nothing like that. It's our third marriage each and we're independent. Be independent, we always said. He said, if I get killed off, you just go right ahead and don't cry, but get married again, and don't think of me."

"That reminds me," said Mildred. "Did you see that Clara Dove five-minute romance last night in your wall? Well, it was all about this woman who——"

Montag said nothing but stood looking at the women's faces as he had once looked at the faces of saints in a strange church he had entered when he was a child. The faces of those enameled creatures meant nothing to him, though he talked to them and stood in that church for a long time, trying to be of that religion, trying to know what that religion was, trying to get enough of the raw incense and special dust of the place into his lungs and thus into his blood to feel touched and concerned by the meaning of the colorful men and women with the porcelain eyes and the blood-ruby lips. But there was nothing, nothing; it was a stroll through another store, and his currency strange and unusable there, and his passion cold, even when he touched the wood and plaster and clay. So it was now, in his own parlor, with these women twisting in their chairs under his gaze, lighting cigarettes, blowing smoke, touching their sun-fired hair and examining their blazing fingernails as if they had caught fire from his look. Their faces grew haunted with silence. They leaned forward at the sound of Montag's swallowing his final bite of food. They listened to his feverish breathing. The three empty walls of the room were like the pale brows of sleeping giants now, empty of dreams. Montag felt that if you touched these three staring brows that you would feel a fine salt sweat on your fingertips. The perspiration gathered with the silence and the sub-audible trembling around and about and in the women who were burning with tension. Any moment they might hiss a long sputtering hiss and explode.

Montag moved his lips.

"Let's talk."

The women jerked and stared.

"How're your children, Mrs. Phelps?" he asked.

"You know I haven't any! No one in his right mind, the Good Lord knows, would have children!" said Mrs. Phelps, not quite sure why she was angry with this man.

"I wouldn't say that," said Mrs. Bowles. "I've had *two* children by Caesarian section. No use going through all that agony for a baby. The world must reproduce, you know, the race must go on. Besides, they sometimes look just like you, and that's nice. Two Caesarians turned the trick, yes, sir. Oh, my doctor said, Caesarians aren't necessary; you've got the hips for it, everything's normal, but I *insisted*."

"Caesarians or not, children are ruinous; you're out of your mind," said Mrs. Phelps.

"I plunk the children in school nine days out of ten. I put up with them when they come home three days a month; it's not bad at all. You heave them into the 'parlor' and turn the switch. It's like washing clothes; stuff laundry in and slam the lid." Mrs. Bowles tittered. "They'd just as soon kick as kiss me. Thank God, I can kick back!"

The women showed their tongues, laughing.

Mildred sat a moment and then, seeing that Montag was still in the doorway, clapped her hands. "Let's talk politics, to please Guy!"

"Sounds fine," said Mrs. Bowles. "I voted last election, same as everyone, and I laid it on the line for President Noble. I think he's one of the nicest looking men ever became president."

"Oh, but the man they ran against him!"

"He wasn't much, was he? Kind of small and homely and he didn't shave too close or comb his hair very well."

"What possessed the 'Outs' to run him? You just don't go running a little short man like that against a tall man. Besides—he mumbled. Half the time I couldn't hear a word he said. And the words I *did* hear I didn't understand!"

"Fat, too, and didn't dress to hide it. No wonder the landslide was for Winston Noble. Even their names helped. Compare

Winston Noble to Hubert Hoag for ten seconds and you can almost figure the results."

"Damn it!" cried Montag. "What do you know about Hoag and Noble!"

"Why, they were right in that parlor wall, not six months ago. One was always picking his nose; it drove me wild."

"Well, Mr. Montag," said Mrs. Phelps, "do you want us to vote for a man like that?"

Mildred beamed. "You just run away from the door, Guy, and don't make us nervous."

But Montag was gone and back in a moment with a book in his hand.

"Guy!"

"Damn it all, damn it all, damn it!"

"What've you got there; isn't that a book? I thought that all special training these days was done by film." Mrs. Phelps blinked. "You reading up on fireman theory?"

"Theory, hell," said Montag. "It's poetry."

"Montag." A whisper.

"Leave me alone!" Montag felt himself turning in a great circling roar and buzz and hum.

"Montag, hold on, don't . . ."

"Did you *hear* them, did you hear these monsters talking about monsters? Oh God, the way they jabber about people and their own children and themselves and the way they talk about their husbands and the way they talk about war, dammit, I stand here and I can't believe it!"

"I didn't say a single word about *any* war, I'll have you know," said Mrs. Phelps.

"As for poetry, I hate it," said Mrs. Bowles.

"Have you ever heard any?"

"Montag," Faber's voice scraped away at him. "You'll ruin everything. Shut up, you fool!"

All three women were on their feet.

"Sit down!"

They sat.

"I'm going home," quavered Mrs. Bowles.

"Montag, Montag, please, in the name of God, what're you up to?" pleaded Faber.

"Why don't you just read us one of those poems from your

little book." Mrs. Phelps nodded. "I think that'd be very interesting."

"That's not right," wailed Mrs. Bowles. "We can't do that!"

"Well, look at Mr. Montag, he wants to, I know he does. And if we listen nice, Mr. Montag will be happy and then maybe we can go on and do something else." She glanced nervously at the long emptiness of the walls enclosing them.

"Montag, go through with this and I'll cut off, I'll leave." The beetle jabbed his ear. "What good is this, what'll you prove!"

"Scare hell out of them, that's what, scare the living daylights out!"

Mildred looked at the empty air. "Now, Guy, just *who* are you talking to?"

A silver needle pierced his brain. "Montag, listen, only one way out, play it as a joke, cover up, pretend you aren't mad at all. Then—walk to your wall-incinerator, and throw the book in!"

Mildred had already anticipated this in a quavery voice. "Ladies, once a year, every fireman's allowed to bring one book home, from the old days, to show his family how silly it all was, how nervous that sort of thing can make you, how crazy. Guy's surprise tonight is to read you one sample to show how mixed-up things were, so none of us will ever have to bother our little old heads about that junk again, isn't that *right*, darling?"

He crushed the book in his fists.

"Say 'yes.'"

His mouth moved like Faber's:

"Yes."

Mildred snatched the book with a laugh. "Here! Read this one. No, I take it back. Here's that real funny one you read out loud today. Ladies, you won't understand a word. It goes umpty-tumpty-ump. Go ahead, Guy, that page, dear."

He looked at the opened page.

A fly stirred its wings softly in his ear. "Read."

"What's the title, dear?"

"*Dover Beach.*" His mouth was numb.

"Now read in a nice clear voice and go *slow*."

The room was blazing hot, he was all fire, he was all coldness; they sat in the middle of an empty desert with three chairs and him standing, swaying, and him waiting for Mrs. Phelps to stop straightening her dress hem and Mrs. Bowles to take her fingers away from her hair. Then he began to read in a low, stumbling voice that grew firmer as he progressed from line to line, and his voice went out across the desert, into the whiteness, and around the three sitting women there in the great hot emptiness.

"'The Sea of Faith
Was once, too, at the full, and round earth's shore
Lay like the folds of a bright girdle furled.
But now I only hear
Its melancholy, long, withdrawing roar,
Retreating, to the breath
Of the night-wind, down the vast edges drear
And naked shingles of the world.'"

The chairs creaked under the three women.

Montag finished it out:

"'Ah, love, let us be true
To one another! for the world, which seems
To lie before us like a land of dreams,
So various, so beautiful, so new,
Hath really neither joy, nor love, nor light,
Nor certitude, nor peace, nor help for pain;
And we are here as on a darkling plain
Swept with confused alarms of struggle and flight,
Where ignorant armies clash by night.'"

Mrs. Phelps was crying.

The others in the middle of the desert watched her crying grow very loud as her face squeezed itself out of shape. They sat, not touching her, bewildered with her display. She sobbed uncontrollably. Montag himself was stunned and shaken.

"Sh, sh," said Mildred. "You're all right, Clara, now, Clara, snap out of it! Clara, what's *wrong*?"

"I—I," sobbed Mrs. Phelps, "don't know, don't know, I just don't know, oh, oh . . ."

Mrs. Bowles stood up and glared at Montag. "You see? I

knew it, that's what I wanted to prove! I knew it would happen! I've always said, poetry and tears, poetry and suicide and crying and awful feelings, poetry and sickness; *all* that mush! Now I've had it proved to me. You're nasty, Mr. Montag, you're *nasty*!"

Faber said, "Now . . ."

Montag felt himself turn and walk to the wall-slot and drop the book in through the brass notch to the waiting flames.

"Silly words, silly words, silly awful hurting words," said Mrs. Bowles. "Why *do* people want to hurt people? Not enough hurt in the world, you got to tease people with stuff like that!"

"Clara, now, Clara," begged Mildred, pulling her arm. "Come on, let's be cheery, you turn the 'family' on, now. Go ahead. Let's laugh and be happy, now, stop crying, we'll have a party!"

"No," said Mrs. Bowles. "I'm trotting right straight home. You want to visit my house and my 'family,' well and good. But I won't come in this fireman's crazy house again in my lifetime!"

"Go home." Montag fixed his eyes upon her, quietly. "Go home and think of your first husband divorced and your second husband killed in a jet and your third husband blowing his brains out, go home and think of the dozen abortions you've had, go home and think of that and your damn Caesarian sections, too, and your children who hate your guts! Go home and think how it all happened and what did you ever do to stop it? Go home, go home!" he yelled. "Before I knock you down and kick you out the door!"

Doors slammed and the house was empty. Montag stood alone in the winter weather, with the parlor walls the color of dirty snow.

In the bathroom, water ran. He heard Mildred shake the sleeping tablets into her hand.

"Fool, Montag, fool, fool, oh God you silly fool . . ."

"Shut up!" He pulled the green bullet from his ear and jammed it into his pocket.

It sizzled faintly. ". . . fool . . . fool . . ."

He searched the house and found the books where Mildred had stacked them behind the refrigerator. Some were missing and he knew that she had started on her own slow process of dispersing the dynamite in her house, stick by stick. But he was not angry now, only exhausted and bewildered with himself. He carried the books into the backyard and hid them in the bushes near the alley fence. For tonight only, he thought, in case she decides to do any more burning.

He went back through the house. "Mildred?" He called at the door of the darkened bedroom. There was no sound.

Outside, crossing the lawn, on his way to work, he tried not to see how completely dark and deserted Clarisse McClellan's house was . . .

On the way downtown he was so completely alone with his terrible error that he felt the necessity for the strange warmness and goodness that came from a familiar and gentle voice speaking in the night. Already, in a few short hours, it seemed that he had known Faber a lifetime. Now, he knew that he was two people, that he was, above all, Montag who knew nothing, who did not even know himself a fool, but only suspected it. And he knew that he was also the old man who talked to him and talked to him as the train was sucked from one end of the night city to the other on one long sickening gasp of motion. In the days to follow, and in the nights when there was no moon and in the nights when there was a very bright moon shining on the earth, the old man would go on with this talking and this talking, drop by drop, stone by stone, flake by flake. His mind would well over at last and he would not be Montag any more, this the old man told him, assured him, promised him. He would be Montag-plus-Faber, fire plus water, and then, one day, after everything had mixed and simmered and worked away in silence, there would be neither fire nor water, but wine. Out of two separate and opposite things, a third. And one day he would look back upon the fool and know the fool. Even now he could feel the start of the long journey, the leave-taking, the going-away from the self he had been.

It was good listening to the beetle hum, the sleepy mosquito buzz and delicate filigree murmur of the old man's voice at first scolding him and then consoling him in the late hour of night as he emerged from the steaming subway toward the firehouse world.

"Pity, Montag, pity. Don't haggle and nag them; you were so recently *of* them yourself. They are so confident that they will run on forever. But they won't run on. They don't know that this is all one huge big blazing meteor that makes a pretty fire in space, but that some day it'll have to *hit.* They see only the blaze, the pretty fire, as you saw it.

"Montag, old men who stay at home, afraid, tending their peanut-brittle bones, have no right to criticize. Yet you almost killed things at the start. Watch it! I'm with you, remember that. I understand how it happened. I must admit that your blind raging invigorated me. God, how young I felt! But now—I want you to feel old, I want a little of my cowardice to be distilled in you tonight. The next few hours, when you see Captain Beatty, tiptoe 'round him, let *me* hear him for you, let *me* feel the situation out. Survival is our ticket. Forget the poor, silly women. . . ."

"I made them unhappier than they have been in years, I think," said Montag. "It shocked me to see Mrs. Phelps cry. Maybe they're right, maybe it's best not to face things, to run, have fun. I don't know. I feel guilty—"

"No, you mustn't! If there were no war, if there was peace in the world, I'd say fine, *have* fun! But, Montag you mustn't go back to being just a fireman. All *isn't* well with the world."

Montag perspired.

"Montag, you listening?"

"My feet," said Montag. "I can't move them. I feel so damn silly. My feet won't move!"

"Listen. Easy now," said the old man gently. "I know, I know. You're afraid of making mistakes. *Don't* be. Mistakes can be profited by. Man, when I was younger I *shoved* my ignorance in people's faces. They beat me with sticks. By the time I was forty my blunt instrument had been honed to a fine cutting point for me. If you hide your ignorance, no one will hit you and you'll never learn. Now, pick up your feet, into the firehouse with you! We're twins, we're not alone any more, we're not separated out in different parlors, with no contact between. If you need help when Beatty pries at you, I'll be sitting right here in your eardrum making notes!"

Montag felt his right foot, then his left foot, move.

"Old man," he said, "stay *with* me."

The Mechanical Hound was gone. Its kennel was empty and the firehouse stood all about in plaster silence and the orange

Salamander slept with its kerosene in its belly and the fire-throwers crossed upon its flanks and Montag came in through the silence and touched the brass pole and slid up in the dark air, looking back at the deserted kennel, his heart beating, pausing, beating. Faber was a gray moth asleep in his ear, for the moment.

Beatty stood near the drop-hole waiting, but with his back turned as if he were not waiting.

"Well," he said to the men playing cards, "here comes a very strange beast which in all tongues is called a fool."

He put his hand to one side, palm up, for a gift. Montag put the book in it. Without even glancing at the title, Beatty tossed the book in the trash-basket and lit a cigarette. "'Who are a little wise, the best fools be.' Welcome back, Montag. I hope you'll be staying with us, now that your fever is done and your sickness over. Sit in for a hand of poker?"

They sat and the cards were dealt. In Beatty's sight, Montag felt the guilt of his hands. His fingers were like ferrets that had done some evil and now never rested, always stirred and picked and hid in pockets, moving from under Beatty's alcohol-flame stare. If Beatty so much as breathed on them, Montag felt that his hands might wither, turn over on their sides, and never be shocked to life again; they would be buried the rest of his life in his coat-sleeves, forgotten. For these were the hands that had acted on their own, no part of him, here was where the conscience first manifested itself to snatch books, dart off with Job and Ruth and Willie Shakespeare, and now, in the firehouse, these hands seemed gloved with blood.

Twice in half an hour, Montag had to rise from the game and go to the latrine to wash his hands. When he came back he hid his hands under the table.

Beatty laughed. "Let's have your hands in sight, Montag. Not that we don't trust you, understand, but——"

They all laughed.

"Well," said Beatty, "the crisis is past and all is well, the sheep returns to the fold. We're all sheep who have strayed at times. Truth is truth, to the end of reckoning, we've cried. They are never alone that are accompanied with noble thoughts, we've shouted to ourselves. 'Sweet food of sweetly uttered knowledge,' Sir Philip Sidney said. But on the other hand: 'Words are like leaves and where they most abound, Much fruit of sense beneath is rarely found.' Alexander Pope. What do you think of that, Montag?"

"I don't know."

"Careful," whispered Faber, living in another world, far away.

"Or this? 'A little learning is a dangerous thing. Drink deep, or taste not the Pierian spring; There shallow draughts intoxicate the brain, and drinking largely sobers us again.' Pope. Same Essay. Where does that put you?"

Montag bit his lip.

"I'll tell you," said Beatty, smiling at his cards. "That made you for a little while a drunkard. Read a few lines and off you go over the cliff. Bang, you're ready to blow up the world, chop off heads, knock down women and children, destroy authority. I know, I've been through it all."

"I'm all right," said Montag, nervously.

"Stop blushing. I'm not needling, really I'm not. Do you know, I had a dream an hour ago. I lay down for a catnap and in this dream you and I, Montag, got into a furious debate on books. You towered with rage, yelled quotes at me. I calmly parried every thrust. *Power*, I said. And you, quoting Dr. Johnson, said 'Knowledge is more than equivalent to force!' And I said, 'Well, Dr. Johnson also said, dear boy, that "He is no wise man that will quit a certainty for an uncertainty."' Stick with the firemen, Montag. All else is dreary chaos!"

"Don't listen," whispered Faber. "He's trying to confuse. He's slippery. Watch out!"

Beatty chuckled. "And you said, quoting, 'Truth will come to light, murder will not be hid long!' And I cried in good humor, 'Oh God, he speaks only of his horse!' And 'The Devil can cite Scripture for his purpose.' And you yelled, 'This age thinks better of a gilded fool, than of a threadbare saint in wisdom's school!' And I whispered gently, 'The dignity of truth is lost with much protesting.' And you screamed, 'Carcasses bleed at the sight of the murderer!' And I said, patting your hand, 'What, do I give you trench mouth?' And you shrieked, 'Knowledge is power!' and 'A dwarf on a giant's shoulders sees the furthest of the two!' and I summed my side up with rare serenity in, 'The folly of mistaking a metaphor for a proof, a torrent of verbiage for a spring of capital truths, and oneself as an oracle, is inborn in us, Mr. Valery once said.'"

Montag's head whirled sickeningly. He felt beaten unmercifully on brow, eyes, nose, lips, chin, on shoulders, on upflailing arms. He wanted to yell, "No! shut up, you're confusing things, stop it!" Beatty's graceful fingers thrust out to seize his wrist.

"God, what a pulse! I've got you going, have I, Montag? Jesus God, your pulse sounds like the day after the war. Everything but sirens and bells! Shall I talk some more? I like your look of panic. Swahili, Indian, English Lit., I speak them all. A kind of excellent dumb discourse, Willie!"

"Montag, hold on!" The moth brushed Montag's ear. "He's muddying the waters!"

"Oh, you were scared silly," said Beatty, "for I was doing a terrible thing in using the very books you clung to, to rebut you on every hand, on every point! What traitors books can be! you think they're backing you up, and they turn on you. Others can use them, too, and there you are, lost in the middle of the moor, in a great welter of nouns and verbs and adjectives. And at the very end of my dream, along I came with the Salamander and said, Going my way? And you got in and we drove back to the firehouse in beatific silence, all dwindled away to peace." Beatty let Montag's wrist go, let the hand slump limply on the table. "All's well that is well in the end."

Silence. Montag sat like a carved white stone. The echo of the final hammer on his skull died slowly away into the black cavern where Faber waited for the echoes to subside. And then when the startled dust had settled down about Montag's mind, Faber began, softly, "All right, he's had his say. You must take it in. I'll say my say, too, in the next few hours. And you'll take it in. And you'll try to judge them and make your decision as to which way to jump, or fall. But I want it to be your decision, not mine, and not the Captain's. But remember that the Captain belongs to the most dangerous enemy to truth and freedom, the solid unmoving cattle of the majority. Oh, God, the terrible tyranny of the majority. We all have our harps to play. And it's up to you now to know with which ear you'll listen."

Montag opened his mouth to answer Faber and was saved this error in the presence of others when the station bell rang.

The alarm-voice in the ceiling chanted. There was a tacking-tacking sound as the alarm-report telephone typed out the address across the room. Captain Beatty, his poker cards in one pink hand, walked with exaggerated slowness to the phone and ripped out the address when the report was finished. He glanced perfunctorily at it, and shoved it in his pocket. He came back and sat down. The others looked at him.

"It can wait exactly forty seconds while I take all the money away from you," said Beatty, happily.

Montag put his cards down.

"Tired, Montag? Going out of this game?"

"Yes."

"Hold on. Well, come to think of it, we can finish this hand later. Just leave your cards face down and hustle the equipment. On the double now." And Beatty rose up again. "Montag, you don't look well? I'd hate to think you were coming down with another fever . . ."

"I'll be all right."

"You'll be fine. This is a special case. Come on, jump for it!"

They leaped into the air and clutched the brass pole as if it were the last vantage point above a tidal wave passing below, and then the brass pole, to their dismay, slid them down into darkness, into the blast and cough and suction of the gaseous dragon roaring to life!

"Hey!"

They rounded a corner in thunder and siren, with concussion of tires, with scream of rubber, with a shift of kerosene bulk in the glittery brass tank, like the food in the stomach of a giant, with Montag's fingers jolting off the silver rail, swinging into cold space, with the wind tearing his hair back from his head, with the wind whistling in his teeth, and him all the while thinking of the women, the chaff women in his parlor tonight, with the kernels blown out from under them by a neon wind, and his silly damned reading of a book to them. How like trying to put out fires with waterpistols, how senseless and insane. One rage turned in for another. One anger displacing another. When would he stop being entirely mad and be quiet, be very quiet indeed?

"Here we go!"

Montag looked up. Beatty never drove, but he was driving

tonight, slamming the Salamander around corners, leaning forward high on the driver's throne, his massive black slicker flapping out behind so that he seemed a great black bat flying above the engine, over the brass numbers, taking the full wind.

"Here we go to keep the world happy, Montag!"

Beatty's pink, phosphorescent cheeks glimmered in the high darkness, and he was smiling furiously.

"Here we are!"

The Salamander boomed to a halt, throwing men off in slips and clumsy hops. Montag stood fixing his raw eyes to the cold bright rail under his clenched fingers.

I can't do it, he thought. How can I go at this new assignment, how can I go on burning things? I can't go in this place.

Beatty, smelling of the wind through which he had rushed, was at Montag's elbow. "All right, Montag."

The men ran like cripples in their clumsy boots, as quietly as spiders.

At last Montag raised his eyes and turned.

Beatty was watching his face.

"Something the matter, Montag?"

"Why," said Montag slowly, "we've stopped in front of *my* house."

Part Three:
Burning Bright

LIGHTS FLICKED on and house doors opened all down the street, to watch the carnival set up. Montag and Beatty stared, one with dry satisfaction, the other with disbelief, at the house before them, this main ring in which torches would be juggled and fire eaten.

"Well," said Beatty, "now you *did* it. Old Montag wanted to fly near the sun and now that he's burnt his damn wings, he wonders why. Didn't I hint enough when I sent the Hound around your place?"

Montag's face was entirely numb and featureless; he felt his head turn like a stone carving to the dark place next door, set in its bright border of flowers.

Beatty snorted. "Oh, no! You weren't fooled by that little idiot's routine, now, were you? Flowers, butterflies, leaves, sunsets, oh, hell! It's all in her file. I'll be damned. I've hit the bullseye. Look at the sick look on your face. A few grass-blades and the quarters of the moon. What trash. What good did she ever *do* with all that?"

Montag sat on the cold fender of the Dragon, moving his head half an inch to the left, half an inch to the right, left, right, left, right, left . . .

"She saw everything. She didn't do anything to anyone. She just let them alone."

"Alone, hell! She chewed around you, didn't she? One of those damn do-gooders with their shocked, holier-than-thou silences, their one talent making others feel guilty. God damn, they rise like the midnight sun to sweat you in your bed!"

The front door opened; Mildred came down the steps, running, one suitcase held with a dream-like clenching rigidity in her fist, as a beetle-taxi hissed to the curb.

"Mildred!"

She ran past with her body stiff, her face floured with powder, her mouth gone, without lipstick.

"Mildred, you *didn't* put in the alarm!"

She shoved the valise in the waiting beetle, climbed in, and sat mumbling, "Poor family, poor family, oh everything gone, everything, everything gone now . . ."

Beatty grabbed Montag's shoulder as the beetle blasted away and hit seventy miles an hour, far down the street, gone.

There was a crash like the falling parts of a dream fashioned out of warped glass, mirrors, and crystal prisms. Montag drifted about as if still another incomprehensible storm had turned him, to see Stoneman and Black wielding axes, shattering window-panes to provide cross-veatilation.

The brush of a death's-head moth against a cold black screen. "Montag, this is Faber. Do you hear me? What's happening?"

"This is happening to *me*," said Montag.

"What a dreadful surprise." said Beatty. "For everyone nowadays knows, absolutely is *certain*, that nothing will ever happen to *me*. Others die, *I* go on. There are no consequences and no responsibilities. Except that there *are*. But let's not talk about them, eh? By the time the consequences catch up with you, it's too late, isn't it, Montag?"

"Montag, can you get away, run?" asked Faber.

Montag walked but did not feel his feet touch the cement and then the night grasses. Beatty flicked his igniter nearby and the small orange flame drew his fascinated gaze.

"What is there about fire that's so lovely? No matter what age we are, what draws us to it?" Beatty blew out the flame and lit it again. "It's perpetual motion; the thing man wanted to invent but never did. Or almost perpetual motion. If you let it go on, it'd burn our lifetimes out. What is fire? It's a mystery. Scientists give us gobbledegook about friction and molecules. But they don't really know. Its real beauty is that it destroys responsibility and consequences. A problem gets too burdensome, then into the furnace with it. Now, Montag, you're a burden. And fire will lift you off my shoulders, clean, quick, sure; nothing to rot later. Anti-biotic, aesthetic, practical."

Montag stood looking in now at this queer house, made strange by the hour of the night, by murmuring neighbor voices, by littered glass, and there on the floor, their covers torn off and spilled out like swan-feathers, the incredible books that looked so silly and really not worth bothering with, for these were nothing but black type and yellowed paper and raveled binding.

Mildred, of course. She must have watched him hide the books in the garden and brought them back in. Mildred. Mildred.

"I want you to do this job all by your lonesome, Montag. Not with kerosene and a match, but piecework, with a flame-thrower. Your house, your clean-up."

"Montag, can't you run, get away!"

"No!" cried Montag helplessly. "The Hound! Because of the Hound!"

Faber heard and Beatty, thinking it was meant for him, heard. "Yes, the Hound's somewhere about the neighborhood, so don't try anything. Ready?"

"Ready." Montag snapped the safety-catch on the flame-thrower.

"Fire!"

A great nuzzling gout of fire leapt out to lap at the books and knock them against the wall. He stepped into the bedroom and fired twice and the twinbeds went up in a great simmering whisper, with more heat and passion and light than he would have supposed them to contain. He burnt the bedroom walls and the cosmetics chest because he wanted to change everything, the chairs, the tables, and in the dining room the silverware and plastic dishes, everything that showed that he had lived here in this empty house with a strange woman who would forget him tomorrow, who had gone and quite forgotten him already, listening to her Seashell Radio pour in on her and in on her as she rode across town, alone. And as before, it was good to burn, he felt himself gush out in the fire, snatch, rend, rip in half with flame, and put away the senseless problem. If there was no solution, well then now there was no problem, either. Fire was best for everything!

"The books, Montag!"

The books leapt and danced like roasted birds, their wings ablaze with red and yellow feathers.

And then he came to the parlor where the great idiot monsters lay asleep with their white thoughts and their snowy dreams. And he shot a bolt at each of the three blank walls and the vacuum hissed out at him. The emptiness made an even emptier whistle, a senseless scream. He tried to think about the vacuum upon which the nothingnesses had performed, but he could not. He held his breath so the vacuum could not get into his lungs. He cut off its terrible emptiness, drew back, and gave the entire room a gift of one huge bright yellow flower of burning. The fire-proof plastic sheath on everything was cut wide and the house began to shudder with flame.

"When you're quite finished," said Beatty behind him. "You're under arrest."

The house fell in red-coals and black ash. It bedded itself down in sleepy pink-grey cinders and a smoke plume blew over it, rising and waving slowly back and forth in the sky. It was three-thirty in the morning. The crowd drew back into the houses; the great tents of the circus had slumped into charcoal and rubble and the show was well over.

Montag stood with the flame-thrower in his limp hands, great islands of perspiration drenching his armpits, his face smeared with soot. The other firemen waited behind him, in the darkness, their faces illumined faintly by the smouldering foundation.

Montag started to speak twice and then finally managed to put his thought together.

"Was it my wife turned in the alarm?"

Beatty nodded. "But her friends turned in an alarm earlier, that I let ride. One way or the other, you'd have got it. It was pretty silly, quoting poetry around free and easy like that. It was the act of a silly damn snob. Give a man a few lines of verse and he thinks he's the Lord of all Creation. You think you can walk on water with your books. Well, the world can get by just fine without them. Look where they got you, in slime up to your lip. If I stir the slime with my little finger, you'll drown!"

Montag could not move. A great earthquake had come with fire and leveled the house and Mildred was under there somewhere and his entire life under there and he could not move. The earthquake was still shaking and falling and shivering inside him and he stood there, his knees half bent under the great load of tiredness and bewilderment and outrage, letting Beatty hit him without raising a hand.

"Montag, you idiot, Montag, you damn fool; why did you *really* do it?"

Montag did not hear, he was far away, he was running with

his mind, he was gone, leaving this dead soot-covered body to sway in front of another raving fool.

"Montag, get out of there!" said Faber.

Montag listened.

Beatty struck him a blow on the head that sent him reeling back. The green bullet in which Faber's voice whispered and cried, fell to the sidewalk. Beatty snatched it up, grinning. He held it half in, half out of his ear.

Montag heard the distant voice calling, "Montag, you all right?"

Beatty switched the green bullet off and thrust it in his pocket. "Well—so there's more here than I thought. I saw you tilt your head, listening. First I thought you had a Seashell. But when you turned clever later, I wondered. We'll trace this and drop in on your friend."

"No!" said Montag.

He twitched the safety catch on the flame-thrower. Beatty glanced instantly at Montag's fingers and his eyes widened the faintest bit. Montag saw the surprise there and himself glanced to his hands to see what new thing they had done. Thinking back later he could never decide whether the hands or Beatty's reaction to the hands gave him the final push toward murder. The last rolling thunder of the avalanche stoned down about his ears, not touching him.

Beatty grinned his most charming grin. "Well, that's one way to get an audience. Hold a gun on a man and force him to listen to your speech. Speech away. What'll it be this time? Why don't you belch Shakespeare at me, you fumbling snob? 'There is *no* terror, Cassius, in your threats, for I am arm'd so strong in honesty that they pass by me as an idle wind, which I respect not!' How's that? Go ahead now, you second-hand literateur, pull the trigger." He took one step toward Montag.

Montag only said, "We never burned *right* . . ."

"Hand it over, Guy," said Beatty with a fixed smile.

And then he was a shrieking blaze, a jumping, sprawling gibbering mannikin, no longer human or known, all writhing flame on the lawn as Montag shot one continuous pulse of liquid fire on him. There was a hiss like a great mouthful of spittle banging a redhot stove, a bubbling and frothing as if salt had been poured over a monstrous black snail to cause a terrible liquefaction and a boiling over of yellow foam. Montag shut his eyes, shouted, shouted, and fought to get his hands at his ears to clamp and to cut away the sound. Beatty flopped over and over and over, and at last twisted in on himself like a charred wax doll and lay silent.

The other two firemen did not move.

Montag kept his sickness down long enough to aim the flame-thrower. "Turn around!"

They turned, their faces like blanched meat, streaming sweat; he beat their heads, knocking off their helmets and bringing them down on themselves. They fell and lay without moving.

The blowing of a single autumn leaf.

He turned and the Mechanical Hound was there.

It was half across the lawn, coming from the shadows, moving with such drifting ease that it was like a single solid cloud of black-grey smoke blown at him in silence.

It made a single last leap into the air coming down at Montag from a good three feet over his head, its spidered legs reaching, the procaine needle snapping out its single angry tooth. Montag caught it with a bloom of fire, a single wondrous blossom that curled in petals of yellow and blue and orange about the metal dog, clad it in a new covering as it slammed into Montag and threw him ten feet back against the bole of a tree, taking the flame-gun with him. He felt it scrabble and seize his leg and stab the needle in for a moment before the fire snapped the hound up in the air, burst its metal bones at the joints, and blew out its interior in a single flushing of red color like a skyrocket fastened to the street. Montag lay watching the dead-alive thing fiddle the air and die. Even now it seemed to want to get back at him and finish the injection which was now working through the flesh of his leg. He felt all of the mingled relief and horror at having pulled back only in time to have just his knee slammed by the fender of a car hurtling by at ninety miles an hour. He was afraid to get up, afraid he might not be able to gain his feet at all, with an anaesthetized leg. A numbness in a numbness hollowed into a numbness . . .

And now . . . ?

The street empty, the house burnt like an ancient bit of stage-scenery, the other homes dark, the Hound here, Beatty there, the three other firemen another place, and the Salamander . . . ? He gazed at the immense engine. That would have to go, too.

Well, he thought, let's see how badly off you are. On your feet now. Easy, easy . . . *there.*

He stood and he had only one leg. The other was like a chunk of burnt pinelog he was carrying along as a penance for some obscure sin. When he put his weight on it, a shower of silver needles gushed up the length of the calf and went off in the knee. He wept. Come on! Come on, you, you can't stay here!

A few house lights were going on again down the street, whether from the incidents just passed, or because of the abnormal silence following the fight, Montag did not know. He hobbled around the ruins, seizing at his bad leg when it lagged, talking and whimpering and shouting directions at it and cursing it and pleading with it to work for him now when it was vital. He heard a number of people crying out in the darkness and shouting. He reached the back yard and the alley. Beatty, he thought, you're not a problem now. You always said, don't face a problem, burn it. Well, now I've done both. Good-by, Captain.

And he stumbled along the alley in the dark.

* * * * *

A shotgun blast went off in his leg every time he put it down and he thought, you're a fool, a damn fool, an awful fool, an idiot, an awful idiot, a damn idiot, and a fool, a damn fool; look at the mess and where's the mop, look at the mess, and what do you do? Pride, damn it, and temper, and you've junked it all, at the very start you vomit on everyone and on yourself. But everything at once, but everything one on top of another, Beatty, the women, Mildred, Clarisse, everything. No excuse, though, no excuse. A fool, a damn fool, go give yourself up!

No, we'll save what we can, we'll do what there is left to do. If we have to burn, let's take a few more with us. Here!

He remembered the books and turned back. Just on the off chance.

He found a few books where he had left them, near the garden fence. Mildred, God bless her, had missed a few. Four books still lay hidden where he had put them. Voices were wailing in the night and flashbeams swirled about. Other Salamanders were roaring, their engines far away and police sirens were cutting their way across town with their sirens.

Montag took the four remaining books and hopped, jolted, hopped his way down the alley and suddenly fell as if his head had been cut off and only his body lay there. Something inside had jerked him to a halt and flopped him down. He lay where he had fallen and sobbed, his legs folded, his face pressed blindly to the gravel.

Beatty wanted to die.

In the middle of the crying Montag knew it for the truth. Beatty had wanted to die. He had just stood there, not really trying to save himself, just stood there, joking, needling, thought Montag, and the thought was enough to stifle his sobbing and let him pause for air. How strange, strange, to want to die so much that you let a man walk around armed and then instead of shutting up and staying alive, you go on yelling at people and making fun of them until you get them mad, and then . . .

At a distance, running feet.

Montag sat up. Let's get out of here. Come on, get up, get up, you just can't sit! But he was still crying and that had to be finished. It was going away now. He hadn't wanted to kill anyone, not even Beatty. His flesh gripped him and shrank as if it had been plunged in acid. He gagged. He saw Beatty, a torch, not moving, fluttering out on the grass. He bit at his knuckles. I'm sorry, I'm sorry, oh God, sorry . . .

He tried to piece it all together, to go back to the normal pattern of life a few short days ago before the sieve and the sand, Denham's Dentifrice, moth-voices, fireflies, the alarms and excursions, too much for a few short days, too much, indeed, for a lifetime.

Feet ran in the far end of the alley.

"Get up!" he told himself. "Damn it, get up!" he said to the leg, and stood. The pains were spikes driven in the kneecap and then only darning needles and then only common ordinary safety pins, and after he had shagged along fifty more hops and jumps, filling his hand with slivers from the board fence, the prickling was like someone blowing a spray of scalding water on that leg. And the leg was at last his own leg again. He had been afraid that running might break the loose ankle. Now, sucking all the night into his open mouth and blowing it out pale, with all the blackness left heavily inside himself, he set out in a steady jogging pace. He carried the books in his hands.

He thought of Faber.

Faber was back there in the steaming lump of tar that had no name or identity now. He had burnt Faber, too. He felt so suddenly shocked by this that he felt Faber was really dead, baked like a roach in that small green capsule shoved and lost in the pocket of a man who was now nothing but a frame skeleton strung with asphalt tendons.

You must remember, burn them or they'll burn you, he thought. Right now it's as simple as that.

He searched his pockets, the money was there, and in his other pocket he found the usual Seashell upon which the city was talking to itself in the cold black morning.

"Police Alert. Wanted: Fugitive in city. Has committed murder and crimes against the State. Name: Guy Montag. Occupation: Fireman. Last seen . . ."

He ran steadily for six blocks, in the alley and then the alley opened out onto a wide empty thoroughfare ten lanes wide. It seemed like a boatless river frozen there in the raw light of the high white arc-lamps; you could drown trying to cross it, he felt; it was too wide, it was too open. It was a vast stage without scenery, inviting him to run across, easily seen in the blazing illumination, easily caught, easily shot down.

The Seashell hummed in his ear.

". . . watch for a man running . . . watch for the running man . . . watch for a man alone, on foot . . . watch . . ."

Montag pulled back in the shadows. Directly ahead lay a gas station, a great chunk of porcelain snow shining there, and two silver beetles pulling in to fill up. Now he must be clean and presentable if he wished to walk, not run, stroll calmly across that wide boulevard. It would give him an extra margin of safety if he washed up and combed his hair before he went on his way to get *where* . . . ?

Yes, he thought, where *am* I running?

Nowhere. There was nowhere to go, no friend to turn to, really. Except Faber. And then he realized that he was, indeed, running toward Faber's house, instinctively. But Faber couldn't hide him; it would be suicide even to try. But he knew that he would go to see Faber anyway, for a few short minutes. Faber's would be the place where he might refuel his fast draining belief in his own ability to survive. He just wanted to know that there was a man like Faber in the world. He wanted to see the man alive and not burned back there like a body shelled in another body. And some of the money must be left with Faber, of course, to be spent after Montag ran on his way. Perhaps he could make the open country and live on or near the rivers and near the highways, in the fields and hills.

A great whirling whisper made him look to the sky.

The police helicopters were rising so far away that it seemed someone had blown the grey head off a dry dandelion flower. Two dozen of them flurried, wavering, indecisive, three miles off, like butterflies puzzled by autumn, and then they were plummeting down to land, one by one, here, there, softly kneading the streets where, turned back to beetles, they shrieked along the boulevards or, as suddenly, leapt back into the air, continuing their search.

And here was the gas station, its attendants busy now with customers. Approaching from the rear, Montag entered the men's wash room. Through the aluminum wall he heard a radio voice saying, "War has been declared." The gas was being pumped outside. The men in the beetles were talking and the attendants were talking about the engines, the gas, the money owed. Montag stood trying to make himself feel the shock of the quiet statement from the radio, but nothing would happen. The war would have to wait for him to come to it in his personal file, an hour, two hours from now.

He washed his hands and face and toweled himself dry, making little sound. He came out of the washroom and shut the door carefully and walked into the darkness and at last stood again on the edge of the empty boulevard.

There it lay, a game for him to win, a vast bowling alley in the cool morning. The boulevard was as clean as the surface of an arena two minutes before the appearance of certain unnamed victims and certain unknown killers. The air over and above the vast concrete river trembled with the warmth of Montag's body alone; it was incredible how he felt his temperature could cause the whole immediate world to vibrate. He was a phosphorescent target; he knew it, he felt it. And now he must begin his little walk.

Three blocks away a few headlights glared. Montag drew a deep breath. His lungs were like burning brooms in his chest. His mouth was sucked dry from running. His throat tasted of bloody iron and there was rusted steel in his feet.

What about those lights there? Once you started walking you'd have to gauge how fast those beetles could make it down here. Well, how far was it to the other curb? It seemed like a hundred yards. Probably not a hundred, but figure for that anyway, figure that with him going very slowly, at a nice stroll, it might take as much as thirty seconds, forty seconds to walk all that way. The beetles? Once started, they could leave three blocks behind them in about fifteen seconds. So, even if halfway across he started to run . . . ?

He put his right foot out and then his left foot and then his right. He walked on the empty avenue.

Even if the street were entirely empty, of course, you couldn't be sure of a safe crossing, for a car could appear suddenly over the rise four blocks further on and be on and past you before you had taken a dozen breaths.

He decided not to count his steps. He looked neither to left nor right. The light from the overhead lamps seemed as bright and revealing as the midday sun and just as hot.

He listened to the sound of the car picking up speed two blocks away on his right. Its movable headlights jerked back and forth suddenly, and caught at Montag.

Keep going.

Montag faltered, got a grip on the books, and forced himself not to freeze. Instinctively he took a few quick running steps then talked out loud to himself and pulled up to stroll again. He was now half across the street, but the roar from the beetle's engines whined higher as it put on speed.

The police, of course. They see me. But slow now slow, quiet, don't turn, don't look, don't seem concerned. Walk, that's it, walk, walk.

The beetle was rushing. The beetle was roaring. The beetle raised its speed. The beetle was whining. The beetle was in high thunder. The beetle came skimming. The beetle came in a single whistling trajectory, fired from an invisible rifle. It was up to 120 mph. It was up to 130 at least. Montag clamped his jaws. The heat of the racing headlights burnt his cheeks, it seemed, and jittered his eyelids and flushed the sour sweat out all over his body.

He began to shuffle idiotically and talk to himself and then he broke and just ran. He put out his legs as far as they would go and down and then far out again and down and back and out and down and back. God! God! He dropped a book, broke pace, almost turned, changed his mind, plunged on, yelling in concrete emptiness, the beetle scuttling after its running food, two hundred, one hundred feet away, ninety, eighty, seventy, Montag gasping, flailing his hands, legs up down out, up down out, closer, closer, hooting, calling, his eyes burnt white now as his head jerked about to confront the flashing glare, now the beetle was swallowed in its own light, now it was nothing but a torch hurtling upon him; all sound, all blare. Now—almost on top of him!

He stumbled and fell.

I'm done! It's over!

But the falling made a difference. An instant before reaching him the wild beetle cut and swerved out. It was gone. Montag lay flat, his head down. Wisps of laughter trailed back to him with the blue exhaust from the beetle.

His right hand was extended above him, flat. Across the extreme tip of his middle finger, he saw now as he lifted that hand, a faint sixteenth of an inch of black tread where the tire had touched in passing. He looked at that black line with disbelief, getting to his feet.

That wasn't the police, he thought.

He looked down the boulevard. It was clear now. A carful of children, all ages, God knew, from twelve to sixteen, out whistling, yelling, hurrahing, had seen a man, a very extraordinary sight, a man strolling, a rarity, and simply said, "Let's get him," not knowing he was the fugitive Mr. Montag, simply a number of children out for a long night of roaring five or six hundred miles in a few moonlit hours, their faces icy with wind, and coming home or not coming at dawn, alive or not alive, that made the adventure.

They would have killed me, thought Montag, swaying, the air still torn and stirring about him in dust, touching his bruised cheek. For no reason at all in the world they would have killed me.

He walked toward the far curb telling each foot to go and keep going. Somehow he had picked up the spilled books, he didn't remember bending or touching them. He kept moving them from hand to hand as if they were a poker hand he could not figure.

I wonder if they were the ones who killed Clarisse?

He stopped and his mind said it again, very loud.

I wonder if they were the ones who killed Clarisse!

He wanted to run after them yelling.

His eyes watered.

The thing that had saved him was falling flat. The driver of that car, seeing Montag down, instinctively considered the probability that running over a body at such a high speed might turn the car upside down and spill them out. If Montag had remained an *upright* target . . . ?

Montag gasped.

Far down the boulevard, four blocks away, the beetle had slowed, spun about on two wheels, and was now racing back, slanting over on the wrong side of the street, picking up speed.

But Montag was gone, hidden in the safety of the dark alley for which he had set out on a long journey, an hour, or was it a minute, ago? He stood shivering in the night, looking back out as the beetle ran by and skidded back to the center of the avenue, whirling laughter in the air all about it, gone.

Further on, as Montag moved in darkness, he could see the helicopters falling falling like the first flakes of snow in the long winter to come . . .

The house was silent.

Montag approached from the rear, creeping through a thick night-moistened scent of daffodils and roses and wet grass. He touched the screen door in back, found it open, slipped in, moved across the porch, listening.

Mrs. Black, are you asleep in there? he thought. This isn't good, but your husband did it to others and never asked and never wondered and never worried. And now since you're a fireman's wife, it's your house and your turn, for all the houses your husband burned and the people he hurt without thinking.

The house did not reply.

He hid the books in the kitchen and moved from the house again to the alley and looked back and the house was still dark and quiet, sleeping.

On his way across town, with the helicopters fluttering like torn bits of paper in the sky, he phoned the alarm at a lonely phone booth outside a store that was closed for the night. Then he stood in the cold night air, waiting and at a distance he heard the fire sirens start up and run, and the Salamanders coming, coming to burn Mr. Black's house while he was away at work, to make his wife stand shivering in the morning air while the roof let go and dropped in upon the fire. But now, she was still asleep.

Good night, Mrs. Black, he thought.

"Faber!"

Another rap, a whisper, and a long waiting. Then, after a minute, a small light flickered inside Faber's small house. After another pause, the back door opened.

They stood looking at each other in the half light, Faber and Montag, as if each did not believe in the other's existence. Then Faber moved and put out his hand and grabbed Montag and moved him in and sat him down and went back and stood in the door, listening. The sirens were wailing off in the morning distance. He came in and shut the door.

Montag said, "I've been a fool all down the line. I can't stay long. I'm on my way God knows where."

"At least you were a fool about the right things," said Faber. "I thought you were dead. The audio-capsule I gave you——"

"Burnt."

"I heard the captain talking to you and suddenly there was nothing. I almost came out looking for you."

"The captain's dead. He found the audio-capsule, he heard your voice, he was going to trace it. I killed him with the flame-thrower."

Faber sat down and did not speak for a time.

"My God, how did this happen?" said Montag. "It was only the other night everything was fine and the next thing I know

I'm drowning. How many times can a man go down and still be alive? I can't breathe. There's Beatty dead, and he was my friend once, and there's Millie gone, I thought she was my wife, but now I don't know. And the house all burnt. And my job gone and myself on the run, and I planted a book in a fireman's house on the way. Good Christ, the things I've done in a single week!"

"You did what you had to do. It was coming on for a long time."

"Yes, I believe that, if there's nothing else I believe. It saved itself up to happen. I could feel it for a long time, I was saving something up, I went around doing one thing and feeling another. God, it was all there. It's a wonder it didn't show on me, like fat. And now here I am, messing up your life, too. They might follow me here."

"I feel alive for the first time in years," said Faber. "I feel I'm doing what I should've done a lifetime ago. For a little while I'm not afraid. Maybe it's because I'm doing the right thing at last. Maybe it's because I've done a rash thing and don't want to look the coward to you. I suppose I'll have to do even more violent things, exposing myself so I won't fall down on the job and turn scared again. What are your plans?"

"To keep running."

"You know the war's on?"

"I heard."

"God, isn't it funny?" said the old man. "It seems so remote because we have our own troubles."

"I haven't had time to think." Montag drew out a hundred dollars. "I want this to stay with you, use it any way that'll help when I'm gone."

"But—"

"I might be dead by noon; use this."

Faber nodded. "You'd better head for the river if you can, follow along it, and if you can hit the old railroad lines going out into the country, follow them. Even though practically everything's airborne these days and most of the tracks are abandoned, the rails are still there, rusting. I've heard there are still hobo camps all across the country, here and there; walking camps they call them, and if you keep walking far enough and keep an eye peeled, they say there's lots of old

Harvard degrees on the tracks between here and Los Angeles. Most of them are wanted and hunted in the cities. They survive, I guess. There aren't many of them, and I guess the governments never considered them a great enough danger to go in and track them down. You might hole up with them for a time and get in touch with me in St. Louis, I'm leaving on the five A.M. bus this morning, to see a retired printer there, I'm getting out in the open myself, at last. This money will be put to good use. Thanks and God bless you. Do you want to sleep a few minutes?"

"I'd better run."

"Let's check."

He took Montag quickly into the bedroom and lifted a picture frame aside revealing a television screen the size of a postal card. "I always wanted something very small, something I could walk to, something I could blot out with the palm of my hand, if necessary, nothing that could shout me down, nothing monstrous big. So, you see." He snapped it on.

"Montag," the TV set said, and lit up. "M-O-N-T-A-G." The name was spelled out by a voice. "Guy Montag. Still running. Police helicopters are up. A new Mechanical Hound has been brought from another district—"

Montag and Faber looked at each other.

"—Mechanical Hound *never* fails. Never since its first use in tracking quarry has this incredible invention made a mistake. Tonight, this network is proud to have the opportunity to follow the Hound by camera helicopter as it starts on its way to the target——"

Faber poured two glasses of whiskey. "We'll need these."

They drank.

"—nose so sensitive the Mechanical Hound can remember and identify ten thousand odor indexes on ten thousand men without re-setting!"

Faber trembled the least bit and looked about at his house, at the walls, the door, the doorknob, and the chair where Montag now sat. Montag saw the look. They both looked quickly about the house and Montag felt his nostrils dilate and he knew that he was trying to track himself and his nose was suddenly good enough to sense the path he had made in the air of the room and the sweat of his hand hung from the doorknob, invisible but as numerous as the jewels of a small chandelier, he was everywhere, in and on and about everything, he was a luminous cloud, a ghost that made breathing once more impossible. He saw Faber stop up his own breath for fear of drawing that ghost into his own body, perhaps, being contaminated with the phantom exhalations and odors of a running man.

"The Mechanical Hound is now landing by helicopter at the site of the Burning!"

And there on the small screen was the burnt house, and the crowd and something with a sheet over it and out of the sky, fluttering, came the helicopter like a grotesque flower.

So they must have their game out, thought Montag. The circus must go on, even with war beginning within the hour . . .

He watched the scene, fascinated, not wanting to move. It seemed so remote and no part of him; it was a play apart and separate, wondrous to watch, not without its strange pleasure. That's all for me, you thought, that's all taking place just for *me*, by God.

If he wished, he could linger here, in comfort, and follow the entire hunt on through its swift phases, down alleys, across streets, over empty running avenues, crossing lots and playgrounds, with pauses here or there for the necessary commercials, up other alleys to the burning house of Mr. and Mrs. Black, and so on finally to this house with Faber and himself seated, drinking, while the Electric Hound snuffed down the last trail, silent as a drift of death itself, skidding to a halt outside that window there. Then, if he wished, Montag might rise, walk to the window, keep one eye on the TV screen, open the window, lean out, look back, and see himself dramatized, described, made over, standing there, limned in the bright small television screen from outside, a drama to be watched objectively, knowing that in other parlors he was large as life, in full color, dimensionally perfect! and if he kept his eye peeled quickly he would see himself, an instant before oblivion, being punctured for the benefit of how many civilian parlor-sitters who had been wakened from sleep a few minutes ago by the frantic sirening of their living room walls to come watch the big game, the hunt, the one-man carnival.

Would he have time for a speech? As the Hound seized him, in view of ten or twenty or thirty million people, mightn't he sum up his entire life in the last week in one single phrase or a word that would stay with them long after the Hound had turned, clenching him in its metal-plier jaws, and trotted off in darkness, while the camera remained stationary, watching the creature dwindle in the distance, a splendid fade-out! What could he say in a single word, a few words, that would sear all their faces and wake them up?

"There," whispered Faber.

Out of a helicopter glided something that was not machine, not animal, not dead, not alive, glowing with a pale green luminosity. It stood near the smoking ruins of Montag's house and the men brought his discarded flame-thrower to it and put it down under the muzzle of the Hound. There was a whirring, clicking, humming.

Montag shook his head and got up and drank the rest of his drink. "It's time. I'm sorry about this."

"About what? Me? My house? I deserve everything. Run, for God's sake. Perhaps I can delay them here——"

"Wait. There's no use you being discovered. When I leave, burn the spread of this bed, that I touched. Burn the chair in the living room, in your wall incinerator. Wipe down the furniture with alcohol, wipe the doorknobs. Burn the throw-rug in the parlor. Turn the air-conditioning on full in all the rooms and spray with moth spray if you have it. Then, turn on your lawn sprinklers as high as they'll go and hose off the sidewalks. With any luck at all, we can kill the trail *in* here, anyway."

Faber shook his hand. "I'll tend to it. Good luck. If we're both in good health, next week, the week after, get in touch, General Delivery, St. Louis. I'm sorry there's no way I can go with you this time, by ear-phone. That was good for both of us. But my equipment was limited. You see, I never thought I would use it. What a silly old man. No thought there. Stupid, stupid. So I haven't another green bullet, the right kind, to put in your head. Go now!"

"One last thing. Quick. A suitcase, get it, fill it with your dirtiest clothes, an old suit, the dirtier the better, a shirt, some old sneakers and socks . . ."

Faber was gone and back in a minute. They sealed the

cardboard valise with clear tape. "To keep the ancient odor of Mr. Faber in, of course," said Faber, sweating at the job.

Montag doused the exterior of the valise with whiskey. "I don't want that Hound picking up two odors at once. May I take this whiskey? I'll need it later. Christ, I hope this works!"

They shook hands again and going out the door glanced at the TV. The Hound was on its way, followed by hovering helicopter cameras, silently, silently, sniffing the great night wind. It was running down the first alley.

"Good-by!"

And Montag was out the back door lightly, running with the half-empty valise. Behind him he heard the lawn sprinkling system jump up, filling the dark air with rain that fell gently and then with a steady pour all about, washing on the sidewalks and draining into the alley. He carried a few drops of this rain with him on his face. He thought he heard the old man call good-by, but he wasn't certain.

He ran very fast away from the house, down toward the river.

* * * * *

Montag ran.

He could feel the Hound, like autumn, come cold and dry and swift, like a wind that didn't stir grass, that didn't jar windows or disturb leaf-shadows on the white sidewalks as it passed. The Hound did not touch the world. It carried its silence with it, so you could feel the silence building up a pressure behind you all across town. Montag felt the pressure rising, and ran.

He stopped for breath, on his way to the river, to peer through dimly lit windows of wakened houses, and saw the silhouettes of people inside watching their parlor walls and there on the walls the Mechanical Hound, a breath of neon vapor, spidered along, here and gone, here and gone! Now at Elm Terrace, Lincoln, Oak, Park, and up the alley toward Faber's house!

Go past, thought Montag, don't stop, go on, don't turn in!

On the parlor wall, Faber's house, with its sprinkler system pulsing in the night air.

The Hound paused, quivering.

No! Montag held to the window sill. This way! *Here!*

The procaine needle flicked out and in, out and in. A single clear drop of the stuff of dreams fell from the needle as it vanished in the Hound's muzzle.

Montag held his breath, like a doubled fist, in his chest.

The Mechanical Hound turned and plunged away from Faber's house down the alley again.

Montag snapped his gaze to the sky. The helicopters were closer, a great blowing of insects to a single light source.

With an effort, Montag reminded himself again that this was no fictional episode to be watched on his run to the river; it was in actuality his own chess game he was witnessing, move by move.

He shouted to give himself the necessary push away from this last house window, and the fascinating seance going on in there! *Hell!* and he was away and gone! The alley, a street, the alley, a street, and the smell of the river. Leg out, leg down, leg out and down. Twenty million Montags running, soon, if the cameras caught him. Twenty million Montags running, running like an ancient flickery Keystone Comedy, cops, robbers, chasers and the chased, hunters and hunted, he had seen it a thousand times. Behind him now twenty million silently baying Hounds, ricocheted across parlors, three-cushion shooting from right wall to center wall to left wall, gone, right wall, center wall, left wall, gone!

Montag jammed his Seashell to his ear:

"Police suggest entire population in the Elm Terrace area do as follows: Everyone in every house in every street open a front or rear door or look from the windows. The fugitive cannot escape if everyone in the next minute looks from his house. Ready!"

Of course! Why hadn't they done it before! Why, in all the years, hadn't this game been tried! Everyone up, everyone out! He couldn't be missed! The only man running alone in the night city, the only man proving his legs!

"At the count of ten now! *One! Two!*"

He felt the city rise.

"Three!"

He felt the city turn to its thousands of doors.

Faster! Leg up, leg down!

"Four!"

The people sleepwalking in their hallways.

"Five!"

He felt their hands on the doorknobs!

The smell of the river was cool and like a solid rain. His throat was burnt rust and his eyes were wept dry with running. He yelled as if this yell would jet him on, fling him the last hundred yards.

"Six, seven, eight!"

The doorknobs turned on five thousand doors.

"Nine!"

He ran out away from the last row of houses, on a slope leading down to a solid moving blackness.

"Ten!"

The doors opened.

He imagined thousands on thousands of faces peering into yards, into alleys, and into the sky, faces hid by curtains, pale, night-frightened faces, like gray animals peering from electric caves, faces with gray colorless eyes, gray tongues and gray thoughts looking out through the numb flesh of the face.

But he was at the river.

He touched it, just to be sure it was real. He waded in and stripped in darkness to the skin, splashed his body, arms, legs, and head with raw liquor; drank it and snuffed some up his nose. Then he dressed in Faber's old clothes and shoes. He tossed his own clothing into the river and watched it swept away. Then, holding the suitcase, he walked out in the river until there was no bottom and he was swept away in the dark.

He was three hundred yards downstream when the Hound reached the river. Overhead the great racketing fans of the helicopters hovered. A storm of light fell upon the river and Montag dived under the great illumination as if the sun had broken the clouds. He felt the river pull him further on its way, into darkness. Then the lights switched back to the land, the helicopters swerved over the city again, as if they had picked up another trail. They were gone. The Hound was gone. Now there was only the cold river and Montag floating in a sudden peacefulness, away from the city and the lights and the chase, away from everything.

He felt as if he had left a stage behind and many actors. He felt as if he had left the great seance and all the murmuring ghosts. He was moving from an unreality that was frightening into a reality that was unreal because it was new.

The black land slid by and he was going into the country among the hills. For the first time in a dozen years the stars were coming out above him, in great processions of wheeling fire. He saw a great juggernaut of stars form in the sky and threaten to roll over and crush him.

He floated on his back when the valise filled and sank; the river was mild and leisurely, going away from the people who ate shadows for breakfast and steam for lunch and vapors for supper. The river was very real; it held him comfortably and gave him the time at last, the leisure, to consider this month, this year, and a lifetime of years. He listened to his heart slow. His thoughts stopped rushing with his blood.

He saw the moon low in the sky now. The moon there, and the light of the moon caused by what? By the sun, of course. And what lights the sun? Its own fire. And the sun goes on, day after day, burning and burning. The sun and time. The sun and time and burning. Burning. The river bobbled him along gently. Burning. The sun and every clock on the earth. It all came together and became a single thing in his mind. After a long time of floating on the land and a short time of floating in the river he knew why he must never burn again in his life.

The sun burned every day. It burned Time. The world rushed in a circle and turned on its axis and time was busy burning the years and the people anyway, without any help from him. So if *he* burnt things with the firemen and the sun burnt Time, that meant that *everything* burned!

One of them had to stop burning. The sun wouldn't, certainly. So it looked as if it had to be Montag and the people he had worked with until a few short hours ago. Somewhere the saving and putting away had to begin again and someone had to do the saving and keeping, one way or another, in books, in records, in people's heads, any way at all so long as it was safe, free from moths, silver-fish, rust and dry-rot, and men with matches. The world was full of burning of all types and sizes. Now the guild of the asbestos-weaver must open shop very soon.

He felt his heel bump land, touch pebbles and rocks, scrape sand. The river had moved him toward shore.

He looked in at the great black creature without eyes or light, without shape, with only a size that went a thousand miles, without wanting to stop, with its grass hills and forests that were waiting for him.

He hesitated to leave the comforting flow of the water. He expected the Hound there. Suddenly the trees might blow under a great wind of helicopters.

But there was only the normal autumn wind high up, going by like another river. Why wasn't the Hound running? Why had the search veered inland? Montag *listened*. Nothing. Nothing.

Millie, he thought. All this country here. Listen to it! Nothing and nothing. So much silence, Millie, I wonder how you'd take it? Would you shout Shut up, shut up! Millie, Millie. And he was sad.

Millie was not here and the Hound was not here, but the dry smell of hay blowing from some distant field put Montag on the land. He remembered a farm he had visited when he was very young, one of the rare few times he discovered that somewhere behind the seven veils of unreality, beyond the walls of parlors and beyond the tin moat of the city, cows chewed grass and pigs sat in warm ponds at noon and dogs barked after white sheep on a hill.

Now, the dry smell of hay, the motion of the waters, made him think of sleeping in fresh hay in a lonely barn away from the loud highways, behind a quiet farmhouse, and under an ancient windmill that whirred like the sound of the passing years overhead. He lay in the high barn loft all night, listening to distant animals and insects and trees, the little motions and stirrings.

During the night, he thought, below the loft, he would hear a sound like feet moving, perhaps. He would tense and sit up. The sound would move away. He would lie back and look out the loft window, very late in the night and see the lights go out in the farmhouse itself, until a very young and beautiful woman would sit in an unlit window, braiding her hair. It would be hard to see her, but her face would be like the face of the girl so long ago in his past now, so very long ago, the girl who had known the weather and never been burned by the fireflies, the girl who had known what dandelions meant rubbed off on your chin. Then, she would be gone from the warm window and appear again upstairs in her moon-whitened room. And then, to the sound of death, the sound of the jets cutting the sky in two black pieces beyond the horizon, he would lie in the loft, hidden and safe, watching those strange new stars over the rim of the earth, fleeing from the soft color of dawn.

In the morning he would not have needed sleep, for all the warm odors and sights of a complete country night would have rested and slept him while his eyes were wide and his mouth, when he thought to test it, was half a smile.

And there at the bottom of the hayloft stair waiting for him, would be the incredible thing. He would step carefully down, in the pink light of early morning, so fully aware of the world that he would be afraid, and stand over the small miracle and at last bend to touch it.

A cool glass of fresh milk, and a few apples and pears laid at the foot of the steps.

This was all he wanted now. Some sign that the immense world would accept him and give him the long time he needed to think all the things that must be thought.

A glass of milk, an apple, a pear.

He stepped from the river.

The land rushed at him, a tidal wave. He was crushed by darkness and the look of the country and the million odors on a wind that iced his body. He fell back under the breaking curve of darkness and sound and smell, his ears roaring. He whirled. The stars poured over his sight like flaming meteors. He wanted to plunge in the river again and let it idle him safely on down somewhere. This dark land rising was like that day in his childhood, swimming, when from nowhere the largest wave in the history of remembering slammed him down in salt mud and green darkness, water burning mouth and nose, retching his stomach, screaming! Too much water!

Too much land.

Out of the black wall before him, a whisper. A shape. In the shape, two eyes. The night looking at him. The forest, seeing him.

The Hound!

After all the running and rushing and sweating it out and half-drowning, to come this far, work this hard, and think yourself safe and sigh with relief and come out on the land at last only to find . . .

The Hound!

Montag gave one last agonized shout as if this were too much for any man.

The shape exploded away. The eyes vanished. The leaf-piles flew up in a dry shower.

Montag was alone in the wilderness.

A deer. He smelled the heavy musk like perfume mingled with blood and the gummed exhalation of the animal's breath, all cardamom and moss and ragweed odor in this huge night where the trees ran at him, pulled away, ran, pulled away, to the pulse of the heart behind his eyes.

There must have been a billion leaves on the land; he waded in them, a dry river smelling of hot cloves and warm dust. And the other smells! There was a smell like a cut potato from all the land, raw and cold and white from having the moon on it most of the night. There was a smell like pickles from a bottle and a smell like parsley on the table at home. There was a faint yellow odor like mustard from a jar. There was a smell like carnations from the yard next door. He put down his hand and felt a weed rise up like a child brushing him. His fingers smelled of licorice.

He stood breathing, and the more he breathed the land in, the more he was filled up with all the details of the land. He was not empty. There was more than enough here to fill him. There would always be more than enough.

He walked in the shallow tide of leaves, stumbling.

And in the middle of the strangeness, a familiarity.

His foot hit something that rang dully.

He moved his hand on the ground, a yard this way, a yard that.

The railroad track.

The track that came out of the city and rusted across the land, through forests and woods, deserted now, by the river.

Here was the path to wherever he was going. Here was the single familiar thing, the magic charm he might need a little while, to touch, to feel beneath his feet, as he moved on into the bramble bushes and the lakes of smelling and feeling and touching, among the whispers and the blowing down of leaves.

He walked on the track.

And he was surprised to learn how certain he suddenly was of a single fact he could not prove.

Once, long ago, Clarisse had walked here, where he was walking now.

Half an hour later, cold, and moving carefully on the tracks, fully aware of his entire body, his face, his mouth, his eyes stuffed with blackness, his ears stuffed with sound, his legs prickled with burrs and nettles, he saw the fire ahead.

The fire was gone, then back again, like a winking eye. He stopped, afraid he might blow the fire out with a single breath. But the fire was there and he approached warily, from a long way off. It took the better part of fifteen minutes before he drew very close indeed to it, and then he stood looking at it from cover. That small motion, the white and red color, a strange fire because it meant a different thing to him.

It was not burning, it was *warming*.

He saw many hands held to its warmth, hands without arms, hidden in darkness. Above the hands, motionless faces that were only moved and tossed and flickered with firelight. He hadn't known fire could look this way. He had never thought in his life that it could give as well as take. Even its smell was different.

How long he stood he did not know, but there was a foolish and yet delicious sense of knowing himself as an animal come from the forest, drawn by the fire. He was a thing of brush and liquid eye, of fur and muzzle and hoof, he was a thing of horn and blood that would smell like autumn if you bled it out on the ground. He stood a long long time, listening to the warm crackle of the flames.

There was a silence gathered all about that fire and the silence was in the men's faces, and time was there, time enough to sit by this rusting track under the trees, and look at the world and turn it over with the eyes, as if it were held to the center of the bonfire, a piece of steel these men were all shaping. It was not only the fire that was different. It was the silence. Montag moved toward this special silence that was concerned with all of the world.

And then the voices began and they were talking, and he could hear nothing of what the voices said, but the sound rose and fell quietly and the voices were turning the world over and looking at it; the voices knew the land and the trees and the city which lay down the track by the river. The voices talked of everything, there was nothing they could not talk about, he knew, from the very cadence and motion and continual stir of curiosity and wonder in them.

And then one of the men looked up and saw him, for the first or perhaps the seventh time, and a voice called to Montag:

"All right, you can come out now!"

Montag stepped back in the shadows.

"It's all right," the voice said. "You're welcome here."

Montag walked slowly toward the fire and the five old men sitting there dressed in dark blue denim pants and jackets and dark blue shirts. He did not know what to say to them.

"Sit down," said the man who seemed to be the leader of the small group. "Have some coffee?"

He watched the dark steaming mixture pour into a collapsible tin cup, which was handed him straight off. He sipped it gingerly and felt them looking at him with curiosity. His lips were scalded, but that was good. The faces around him were bearded, but the beards were clean, neat and their hands were clean. They had stood up as if to welcome a guest, and now they sat down again. Montag sipped. "Thanks," he said. "Thanks very much."

"You're welcome, Montag. My name's Granger." He held out a small bottle of colorless fluid. "Drink this, too. It'll change the chemical index of your perspiration. Half an hour from now you'll smell like two other people. With the Hound after you, the best thing is Bottoms up."

Montag drank the bitter fluid.

"You'll stink like a bobcat, but that's all right," said Granger.

"You know my name," said Montag.

Granger nodded to a portable battery TV set by the fire. "We've watched the chase. Figured you'd wind up south along the river. When we heard you plunging around out in the forest like a drunken elk, we didn't hide as we usually do. We figured you were in the river, when the helicopter cameras swung back in over the city. Something funny there. The chase is still running. The other way, though."

"The other way?"

"Let's have a look."

Granger snapped the portable viewer on. The picture was a nightmare, condensed, easily passed from hand to hand, in the forest, all whirring color and flight. A voice cried:

"The chase continues north in the city! Police helicopters are converging on Avenue 87 and Elm Grove Park!"

Granger nodded. "They're faking. You threw them off at the river. They can't admit it. They know they can hold their audience only so long. The show's got to have a snap ending, quick! If they started searching the whole damn river it might take all night. So they're sniffing for a scapegoat to end things with a bang. Watch. They'll catch Montag in the next five minutes!"

"But how——"

"Watch."

The camera, hovering in the belly of a helicopter, now swung down at an empty street.

"See that?" whispered Granger. "It'll be you; right up at the end of that street is our victim. See how our camera is coming in? Building the scene. Suspense. Long shot. Right now, some poor fellow is out for a walk. A rarity. An odd one. Don't think the police don't know the habits of queer ducks like that, men who walk mornings for the hell of it, or for reasons of insomnia. Anyway, the police have had him charted for months, years. Never know when that sort of information might be handy. And today, it turns out, it's very usable indeed. It saves face. Oh, God, look there!"

The men at the fire bent forward.

On the screen, a man turned a corner. The Mechanical Hound rushed forward into the viewer, suddenly. The helicopter lights shot down a dozen brilliant pillars that built a cage all about the man.

A voice cried, "There's Montag! The search is *done*!"

The innocent man stood bewildered, a cigarette burning in his hand. He stared at the Hound, not knowing what it was. He probably never knew. He glanced up at the sky and the wailing sirens. The camera rushed down. The Hound leapt up into the air with a rhythm and a sense of timing that was incredibly beautiful. Its needle shot out. It was suspended for a moment in their gaze, as if to give the vast audience time to appreciate everything, the raw look of the victim's face, the empty street, the steel animal a bullet nosing the target.

"Montag, don't move!" said a voice from the sky.

The camera fell upon the victim, even as did the Hound. Both reached him simultaneously. The victim was seized by Hound and camera in a great spidering, clenching grip. He screamed. He screamed. He screamed!

Blackout.

Silence.

Darkness.

Montag cried out in the silence and turned away.

Silence.

And then, after a time of the men sitting around the fire, their faces expressionless, an announcer on the dark screen said, "The search is over, Montag is dead; a crime against society has been avenged."

Darkness.

"We now take you to the Sky Room of the Hotel Lux for a half hour of Just-Before-Dawn, a program of——"

Granger turned it off.

"They didn't show the man's face in focus. Did you notice? Even your best friends couldn't tell if it was you. They scrambled it just enough to let the imagination take over. Hell," he whispered. "Hell."

Montag said nothing but now, looking back, sat with his eyes fixed to the blank screen, trembling.

Granger touched Montag's arm. "Welcome back from the dead." Montag nodded. Granger went on. "You might as well know all of us, now. This is Fred Clement, former occupant of the Thomas Hardy chair at Cambridge in the years before it became an Atomic Engineering School. This other is Dr. Simmons from U.C.L.A., a specialist in Ortega y Gasset; Professor West here did quite a bit for ethics, an ancient study now, for Columbia University quite some years ago. Reverend Padover here gave a few lectures thirty years ago and lost his flock between one Sunday and the next for his views. He's been bumming with us some time now. Myself: I wrote a book called *The Fingers in the Glove; the Proper Relationship between the Individual and Society,* and here I *am*! Welcome, Montag!"

"I don't belong with you," said Montag, at last, slowly. "I've been an idiot all the way."

"We're used to that. We all made the *right* kind of mistakes, or we wouldn't be here. When we were separate individuals, all we had was rage. I struck a fireman when he came to burn my library years ago. I've been running ever since. You want to join us, Montag?"

"Yes."

"What have you to offer?"

"Nothing. I thought I had part of the Book of Ecclesiastes and maybe a little of Revelation, but I havent't even that now."

"The Book of Ecclesiastes would be fine. Where was it?"

"Here," Montag touched his head.

"Ah," Granger smiled and nodded.

"What's wrong? Isn't that all right?" said Montag.

"Better than all right; perfect!" Granger turned to the Reverend. "Do we have a Book of Ecclesiastes?"

"One. A man named Harris in Youngstown."

"Montag." Granger took Montag's shoulder firmly. "Walk carefully. Guard your health. If anything should happen to Harris, *you* are the Book of Ecclesiastes. See how important you've become in the last minute!"

"But I've forgotten!"

"No, nothing's ever lost. We have ways to shake down your clinkers for you."

"But I've tried to remember!"

"Don't try. It'll come when we need it. All of us have photographic memories, but spend a lifetime learning how to block off the things that are really *in* there. Simmons here has worked on it for twenty years and now we've got the method down to where we can recall anything that's been read once. Would you like, some day, Montag, to read Plato's *Republic*?"

"Of course!"

"*I* am Plato's *Republic.* Like to read Marcus Aurelius? Mr. Simmons is Marcus."

"How do you do?" said Mr. Simmons.

"Hello," said Montag.

"I want you to meet Jonathan Swift, the author of that evil political book, *Gulliver's Travels*! And this other fellow is Charles Darwin, and this one is Schopenhauer, and this one is Einstein, and this one here at my elbow is Mr. Albert Schweitzer, a very kind philosopher indeed. Here we all are, Montag. Aristophanes and Mahatma Gandhi and Gautama Buddha and Confucius and Thomas Love Peacock and Thomas Jefferson and Mr. Lincoln, if you please. We are also Matthew, Mark, Luke, and John."

Everyone laughed quietly.

"It can't *be*," said Montag.

"It *is*," replied Granger, smiling. "*We're* book-burners, too. We read the books and burnt them, afraid they'd be found. Micro-filming didn't pay off; we were always traveling, we didn't want to bury the film and come back later. Always the chance of discovery. Better to keep it in the old heads, where no one can see it or suspect it. We are all bits and pieces of history and literature and international law, Byron, Tom Paine, Machiavelli or Christ, it's here. And the hour's late. And the war's begun. And we are out here, and the city is there, all wrapped up in its own coat of a thousand colors. What do you think, Montag?"

"I think I was blind trying to go at things my way, planting books in firemen's houses and sending in alarms."

"You did what you had to do. Carried out on a national scale, it might have worked beautifully. But our way is simpler and, we think, better. All we want to do is keep the knowledge we think we will need, intact and safe. We're not out to incite or anger anyone yet. For if we are destroyed, the knowledge is dead, perhaps for good. We are model citizens, in our own special way; we walk the old tracks, we lie in the hills at night, and the city people let us be. We're stopped and searched occasionally, but there's nothing on our persons to incriminate us. The organization is flexible, very loose, and fragmentary. Some of us have had plastic surgery on our faces and fingerprints. Right now we have a horrible job; we're waiting for the war to begin and, as quickly, end. It's not pleasant, but then we're not in control, we're the odd minority crying in the wilderness. When the war's over, perhaps we can be of some use in the world."

"Do you really think they'll listen then?"

"If not, we'll just have to wait. We'll pass the books on to our children, by word of mouth, and let our children wait, in turn, on the other people. A lot will be lost that way, of course. But you can't *make* people listen. They have to come round in their own time, wondering what happened and why the world blew up under them. It can't last."

"How many of you are there?"

"Thousands on the roads, the abandoned railtracks, tonight, bums on the outside, libraries inside. It wasn't planned, at first. Each man had a book he wanted to remember, and did. Then, over a period of twenty years or so, we met each other, traveling, and got the loose network together and set out a plan. The most important single thing we had to pound into ourselves is that we were not important, we mustn't be pedants; we were not to feel superior to anyone else in the world. We're nothing more than dust-jackets for books, of no significance otherwise. Some of us live in small towns. Chapter One of Thoreau's *Walden* in Green River, Chapter Two in Willow Farm, Maine. Why, there's one town in Maryland, only twenty-seven people, no bomb'll ever touch that town, is the complete essays of a man named Bertrand Russell. Pick up that town, almost, and flip the pages, so many pages to a person. And when the war's over, some day, some year, the books can be written again, the people will be called in, one by one, to recite what they know and we'll set it up in type until another Dark Age, when we might have to do the whole damn thing over again. But that's the wonderful thing about man; he never gets so discouraged or disgusted that he gives up doing it all over again, because he knows very well it is important and *worth* the doing."

"What do we do tonight?" asked Montag.

"Wait," said Granger. "And move downstream a little ways, just in case."

He began throwing dust and dirt in the fire.

The other men helped, and Montag helped, and there, in the wilderness, the men all moved their hands, putting out the fire together.

They stood by the river in the starlight.

Montag saw the luminous dial of his waterproof. Five. Five

o'clock in the morning. Another year ticked by in a single hour, and dawn waiting beyond the far bank of the river.

"Why do you trust me?" said Montag.

A man moved in the darkness.

"The look of you's enough. You haven't seen yourself in a mirror lately. Beyond that, the city has never cared so much about us to bother with an elaborate chase like this to find us. A few crackpots with verses in their heads can't touch them, and they know it and we know it; everyone knows it. So long as the vast population doesn't wander about quoting the Magna Charta and the Constitution, it's all right. The firemen were enough to check that, now and then. No, the cities don't bother us. And *you* look like hell."

They moved along the bank of the river, going south. Montag tried to see the men's faces, the old faces he remembered from the firelight, lined and tired. He was looking for a brightness, a resolve, a triumph over tomorrow that hardly seemed to be there. Perhaps he had expected their faces to burn and glitter with the knowledge they carried, to glow as lanterns glow, with the light in them. But all the light had come from the campfire, and these men had seemed no different than any others who had run a long race, searched a long search, seen good things destroyed, and now, very late, were gathered to wait for the end of the party and the blowing out of the lamps. They weren't at all certain that the things they carried in their heads might make every future dawn glow with a purer light, they were sure of nothing save that the books were on file behind their quiet eyes, the books were waiting, with their pages uncut, for the customers who might come by in later years, some with clean and some with dirty fingers.

Montag squinted from one face to another as they walked.

"Don't judge a book by its cover," someone said.

And they all laughed quietly, moving downstream.

There was a shriek and the jets from the city were gone overhead long before the men looked up. Montag stared back at the city, far down the river, only a faint glow now.

"My wife's back there."

"I'm sorry to hear that. The cities won't do well in the next few days," said Granger.

"It's strange, I don't miss her, it's strange I don't feel much of anything," said Montag. "Even if she dies, I realized a moment ago, I don't think I'll feel sad. It isn't right. Something must be wrong with me."

"Listen," said Granger, taking his arm, and walking with him, holding aside the bushes to let him pass. "When I was a boy my grandfather died, and he was a sculptor. He was also a very kind man who had a lot of love to give the world, and he helped clean up the slum in our town; and he made toys for us and he did a million things in his lifetime; he was always busy with his hands. And when he died, I suddenly realized I wasn't crying for him at all, but for all the things he did. I cried because he would never do them again, he would never carve another piece of wood or help us raise doves and pigeons in the back yard or play the violin the way he did, or tell us jokes the way he did. He was part of us and when he died, all the actions stopped dead and there was no one to do them just the way he did. He was individual. He was an important man. I've never gotten over his death. Often I think, what wonderful carvings never came to birth because he died. How many jokes are missing from the world, and how many homing pigeons untouched by his hands. He shaped the world. He *did* things to the world. The world was bankrupted of ten million fine actions the night he passed on."

Montag walked in silence. "Millie, Millie," he whispered. "Millie."

"What?"

"My wife, my wife. Poor Millie, poor, poor Millie. I can't remember anything. I think of her hands but I don't see them doing anything at all. They just hang there at her sides or they lie there on her lap or there's a cigarette in them, but that's all."

Montag turned and glanced back.

What did you give to the city, Montag?

Ashes.

What did the others give to each other?

Nothingness.

Granger stood looking back with Montag. "Everyone must leave something behind when he dies, my grandfather said. A child or a book or a painting or a house or a wall built or a pair of shoes made. Or a garden planted. Something your hand touched some way so your soul has somewhere to go when you die, and when people look at that tree or that flower you planted, you're there. It doesn't matter what you do, he said, so long as you change something from the way it was before you touched it into something that's like you after you take your hands away. The difference between the man who just cuts lawns and a real gardener is in the touching, he said. The lawn-cutter might just as well not have been there at all; the gardener will be there a lifetime."

Granger moved his hand. "My grandfather showed me some V-2 rocket films once, fifty years ago. Have you ever seen the atom-bomb mushroom from two hundred miles up? It's a pinprick, it's nothing. With the wilderness all around it.

"My grandfather ran off the V-2 rocket film a dozen times and then hoped that some day our cities would open up more and let the green and the land and the wilderness in more, to remind people that we're allotted a little space on earth and that we survive in that wilderness that can take back what it has given, as easily as blowing its breath on us or sending the sea to tell us we are not so big. When we forget how close the wilderness is in the night, my grandpa said, some day it will come in and get us, for we will have forgotten how terrible and real it can be. You see?" Granger turned to Montag. "Grandfather's been dead for all these years, but if you lifted my skull, by God, in the convolutions of my brain you'd find the big ridges of his thumbprint. He touched me. As I said, earlier, he was a sculptor. 'I hate a Roman named Status Quo!' he said to me. 'Stuff your eyes with wonder,' he said, 'live as if you'd drop dead in ten seconds. See the world. It's more fantastic than any dream made or paid for in factories. Ask no guarantees, ask for no security, there never was such an animal. And if there were, it would be related to the great sloth which hangs upside down in a tree all day every day, sleeping its life away. To hell with that,' he said, 'shake the tree and knock the great sloth down on his ass.'"

"Look!" cried Montag.

And the war began and ended in that instant.

Later, the men around Montag could not say if they had

really seen anything. Perhaps the merest flourish of light and motion in the sky. Perhaps the bombs were there, and the jets, ten miles, five miles, one mile up, for the merest instant, like grain thrown over the heavens by a great sowing hand, and the bombs drifting with dreadful swiftness, yet sudden slowness, down upon the morning city they had left behind. The bombardment was to all intents and purposes finished, once the jets had sighted their target, alerted their bombardier at five thousand miles an hour; as quick as the whisper of a scythe the war was finished. Once the bomb-release was yanked, it was over. Now, a full three seconds, all of the time in history, before the bombs struck, the enemy ships themselves were gone half around the visible world, like bullets in which a savage islander might not believe because they were invisible; yet the heart is suddenly shattered, the body falls in separate motions and the blood is astonished to be freed on the air; the brain squanders its few precious memories and, puzzled, dies.

This was not to be believed. It was merely a gesture. Montag saw the flirt of a great metal fist over the far city and he knew the scream of the jets that would follow, would say, after the deed, *disintegrate, leave no stone on another, perish. Die.*

Montag held the bombs in the sky for a single moment, with his mind and his hands reaching helplessly up at them. "Run!" he cried to Faber. To Clarisse, "Run!" To Mildred, "Get out, get out of there!" But Clarisse, he remembered, was dead. And Faber *was* out; there in the deep valleys of the country somewhere the five A.M. bus was on its way from one desolation to another. Though the desolation had not yet arrived, was still in the air, it was certain as man could make it. Before the bus had run another fifty yards on the highway, its destination would be meaningless, and its point of departure changed from metropolis to junkyard.

And Mildred . . .

Get out, run!

He saw her in her hotel room somewhere now in the half second remaining with the bombs a yard, a foot, an inch from her building. He saw her leaning toward the great shimmering walls of color and motion where the family talked and talked and talked to her, where the family prattled and chatted and said her name and smiled at her and said nothing of the bomb that was an inch, now a half-inch, now a quarter-inch from the top of the hotel. Leaning into the wall as if all of the hunger of looking would find the secret of her sleepless unease there. Mildred, leaning anxiously nervously, as if to plunge, drop, fall into that swarming immensity of color to drown in its bright happiness.

The first bomb struck.

"Mildred!"

Perhaps, who would ever know? perhaps the great broadcasting stations with their beams of color and light and talk and chatter went first into oblivion.

Montag, falling flat, going down, saw or felt, or imagined he saw or felt the walls go dark in Millie's face, heard her screaming, because in the millionth part of time left, she saw her own face reflected there, in a mirror instead of a crystal ball, and it was such a wildly empty face, all by itself in the room, touching nothing, starved and eating of itself, that at last she recognized it as her own and looked quickly up at the ceiling as it and the entire structure of the hotel blasted down upon her, carrying her with a million pounds of brick, metal, plaster, and wood, to meet other people in the hives below, all on their quick way down to the cellar where the explosion rid itself of them in its own unreasonable way.

I remember. Montag clung to the earth. I remember. Chicago. Chicago a long time ago. Millie and I. *That's* where we met! I remember now. Chicago. A long time ago.

The concussion knocked the air across and down the river, turned the men over like dominos in a line, blew the water in lifting sprays, and blew the dust and made the trees above them mourn with a great wind passing away south. Montag crushed himself down, squeezing himself small, eyes tight. He blinked once. And in that instant saw the city, instead of the bombs, in the air. They had displaced each other. For another of those impossible instants the city stood, rebuilt and unrecognizable, taller than it had ever hoped or strived to be, taller than man had built it, erected at last in gouts of shattered concrete and sparkles of torn metal into a mural hung like a reversed avalanche, a million colors, a million oddities, a door where a window should be, a top for a bottom, a side for a back, and then the city rolled over and fell down dead.

The sound of its death came after.

Montag, lying there, eyes gritted shut with dust, a fine wet cement of dust in his now shut mouth, gasping and crying, now thought again, I remember, I remember, I remember something else. What is it? Yes, yes, part of Ecclesiastes. Part of Ecclesiastes and Revelation. Part of that book, part of it, quick now, quick, before it gets away, before the shock wears off, before the wind dies. Book of Ecclesiastes. Here. He said it over to himself silently, lying flat to the trembling earth, he said the words of it many times and they were perfect without trying and there was no Denham's Dentrifice anywhere, it was just the Preacher by himself, standing there in his mind, looking at him. . . .

"There," said a voice.

The men lay gasping like fish laid out on the grass. They held to the earth as children hold to familiar things no matter how cold or dead, no matter what has happened or will happen, their fingers were clawed into the dirt, and they were all shouting to keep their eardrums from bursting, to keep their sanity from bursting, mouths open, Montag shouting with them, a protest against the wind that ripped their faces and tore at their lips, making their noses bleed.

Montag watched the great dust settle and the great silence move down upon their world. And lying there it seemed that he saw every single grain of dust and every blade of grass and that he heard every cry and shout and whisper going up in the world now. Silence fell down in the sifting dust, and all the leisure they might need to look around, to gather the reality of this day into their senses.

Montag looked at the river. We'll go on the river. He looked at the old railroad tracks. Or we'll go that way. Or we'll walk on the highways now, and we'll have time to put things into ourselves. And some day, after it sets in us a long time, it'll come out our hands and our mouths. And a lot of it will be wrong, but just enough of it will be right. We'll just start walking today and see the world and the way the world walks around and talks, the way it really looks. I want to see everything now.

And while none of it will be me when it goes in, after awhile it'll all gather together inside and it'll be me. Look at the world out there, my God, my God, look at it out there, outside me, out there beyond my face and the only way to really touch it is to put it where it's finally me, where it's in the blood, where it pumps around a thousand times ten thousand a day. I get hold of it so it'll never run off. I'll hold onto the world tight some day. I've got one finger on it now; that's a beginning.

The wind died.

The other men lay awhile, on the dawn edge of sleep, not yet ready to rise up and begin the day's obligations, its fires and foods, its thousand details of putting foot after foot and hand after hand. They lay blinking their dusty eyelids. You could hear them breathing fast, then slower, then slow . . .

Montag sat up.

He did not move any farther, however. The other men did likewise. The sun was touching the black horizon with a faint red tip. The air was cold and smelled of a coming rain.

Silently, Granger arose, felt of his arms and legs, swearing, swearing incessantly under his breath, tears dripping from his face. He shuffled down to the river to look upstream.

"It's flat," he said, a long time later. "City looks like a heap of baking powder. It's gone." And a long time after that, "I wonder how many knew it was coming? I wonder how many were surprised?"

And across the world, thought Montag, how many other cities dead? And here in our country, how many? A hundred, a thousand?

Someone struck a match and touched it to a piece of dry paper taken from their pocket, and shoved this under a bit of grass and leaves, and after awhile added tiny twigs which were wet and sputtered but finally caught, and the fire grew larger in the early morning as the sun came up and the men slowly turned from looking up river and were drawn to the fire, awkwardly, with nothing to say, and the sun colored the back of their necks as they bent down.

Granger unfolded an oilskin with some bacon in it. "We'll have a bite. Then we'll turn around and walk upstream. They'll be needing us up that way."

Someone produced a small frying pan and the bacon went

into it and the frying pan was set on the fire. After a moment the bacon began to flutter and dance in the pan and the sputter of it filled the morning air with its aroma. The men watched this ritual silently.

Granger looked into the fire. "Phoenix."

"What?"

"There was a silly damn bird called a Phoenix back before Christ, every few hundred years he built a pyre and burned himself up. He must have been first cousin to Man. But every time he burnt himself up he sprang out of the ashes, he got himself born all over again. And it looks like we're doing the same thing, over and over, but we've got one damn thing the Phoenix never had. We know the damn silly thing we just did. We know all the damn silly things we've done for a thousand years and as long as we know that and always have it around where we can see it, some day we'll stop making the goddam funeral pyres and jumping in the middle of them. We pick up a few more people that remember, every generation."

He took the pan off the fire and let the bacon cool and they ate it, slowly, thoughtfully.

"Now, let's get on upstream," said Granger. "And hold onto one thought: You're not important. You're not anything. Some day the load we're carrying with us may help someone. But even when we had the books on hand, a long time ago, we didn't use what we got out of them. We went right on insulting the dead. We went right on spitting in the graves of all the poor ones who died before us. We're going to meet a lot of lonely people in the next week and the next month and the next year. And when they ask us what we're doing, you can say, We're remembering. That's where we'll win out in the long run. And some day we'll remember so much that we'll build the biggest goddam steamshovel in history and dig the biggest grave of all time and shove war in and cover it up. Come on now, we're going to go build a mirror-factory first and put out nothing but mirrors for the next year and take a long look in them."

They finished eating and put out the fire. The day was brightening all about them as if a pink lamp had been given more wick. In the trees, the birds that had flown away quickly now came back and settled down.

Montag began walking and after a moment found that the

others had fallen in behind him, going north. He was surprised, and moved aside to let Granger pass, but Granger looked at him and nodded him on. Montag went ahead. He looked at the river and the sky and the rusting track going back down to where the farms lay, where the barns stood full of hay, where a lot of people had walked by in the night on their way from the city. Later, in a month or six months, and certainly not more than a year, he would walk along here again, alone, and keep right on going until he caught up with the people.

But now there was a long morning's walk until noon, and if the men were silent it was because there was everything to think about and much to remember. Perhaps later in the morning, when the sun was up and had warmed them they would begin to talk, or just say the things they remembered, to be sure they were there, to be absolutely certain that things were safe in them. Montag felt the slow stir of words, the slow simmer. And when it came his turn, what could he say, what could he offer on a day like this, to make the trip a little easier? To everything there is a season. Yes. A time to break down, and a time to build up. Yes. A time to keep silence and a time to speak. Yes, all that. But what else. What else? Something, something . . .

And on either side of the river was there a tree of life, which bare twelve manner of fruits, and yielded her fruit every month; And the leaves of the tree were for the healing of the nations.

Yes, thought Montag, that's the one I'll save for noon. For noon . . .

When we reach the city.

DANDELION WINE

For Walter I. Bradbury
neither uncle nor cousin
but most decidedly
editor and friend.

IT WAS a quiet morning, the town covered over with darkness and at ease in bed. Summer gathered in the weather, the wind had the proper touch, the breathing of the world was long and warm and slow. You had only to rise, lean from your window, and know that this indeed was the first real time of freedom and living, this was the first morning of summer.

Douglas Spaulding, twelve, freshly wakened, let summer idle him on its early-morning stream. Lying in this third-story cupola bedroom, he felt the tall power it gave him, riding high in the June wind, the grandest tower in town. At night, when the trees washed together, he flashed his gaze like a beacon from this lighthouse in all directions over swarming seas of elm and oak and maple. Now . . .

"Boy," whispered Douglas.

A whole summer ahead to cross off the calendar, day by day. Like the goddess Siva in the travel books, he saw his hands jump everywhere, pluck sour apples, peaches, and midnight plums. He would be clothed in trees and bushes and rivers. He would freeze, gladly, in the hoarfrosted ice-house door. He would bake, happily, with ten thousand chickens, in Grandma's kitchen.

But now—a familiar task awaited him.

One night each week he was allowed to leave his father, his mother, and his younger brother Tom asleep in their small house next door and run here, up the dark spiral stairs to his grandparents' cupola, and in this sorcerer's tower sleep with thunders and visions, to wake before the crystal jingle of milk bottles and perform his ritual magic.

He stood at the open window in the dark, took a deep breath and exhaled.

The street lights, like candles on a black cake, went out. He exhaled again and again and the stars began to vanish.

Douglas smiled. He pointed a finger.

There, and there. Now over here, and here . . .

Yellow squares were cut in the dim morning earth as house

lights winked slowly on. A sprinkle of windows came suddenly alight miles off in dawn country.

"Everyone yawn. Everyone up."

The great house stirred below.

"Grandpa, get your teeth from the water glass!" He waited a decent interval. "Grandma and Great-grandma, fry hot cakes!"

The warm scent of fried batter rose in the drafty halls to stir the boarders, the aunts, the uncles, the visiting cousins, in their rooms.

"Street where all the Old People live, wake up! Miss Helen Loomis, Colonel Freeleigh, Miss Bentley! Cough, get up, take pills, move around! Mr. Jonas, hitch up your horse, get your junk wagon out and around!"

The bleak mansions across the town ravine opened baleful dragon eyes. Soon, in the morning avenues below, two old women would glide their electric Green Machine, waving at all the dogs. "Mr. Tridden, run to the carbarn!" Soon, scattering hot blue sparks above it, the town trolley would sail the rivering brick streets.

"Ready John Huff, Charlie Woodman?" whispered Douglas to the Street of Children. "Ready!" to baseballs sponged deep in wet lawns, to rope swings hung empty in trees.

"Mom, Dad, Tom, wake up."

Clock alarms tinkled faintly. The courthouse clock boomed. Birds leaped from trees like a net thrown by his hand, singing. Douglas, conducting an orchestra, pointed to the eastern sky.

The sun began to rise.

He folded his arms and smiled a magician's smile. Yes, sir, he thought, everyone jumps, everyone runs when I yell. It'll be a fine season.

He gave the town a last snap of his fingers.

Doors slammed open; people stepped out.

Summer 1928 began.

CROSSING THE lawn that morning, Douglas Spaulding broke a spider web with his face. A single invisible line on the air touched his brow and snapped without a sound.

So, with the subtlest of incidents, he knew that this day was going to be different. It would be different also, because, as his father explained, driving Douglas and his ten-year-old brother Tom out of town toward the country, there were some days compounded completely of odor, nothing but the world blowing in one nostril and out the other. And some days, he went on, were days of hearing every trump and trill of the universe. Some days were good for tasting and some for touching. And some days were good for all the senses at once. This day now, he nodded, smelled as if a great and nameless orchard had grown up overnight beyond the hills to fill the entire visible land with its warm freshness. The air felt like rain, but there were no clouds. Momentarily, a stranger might laugh off in the woods, but there was silence . . .

Douglas watched the traveling land. He smelled no orchards and sensed no rain, for without apple trees or clouds he knew neither could exist. And as for that stranger laughing deep in the woods . . . ?

Yet the fact remained—Douglas shivered—this, without reason, was a special day.

The car stopped at the very center of the quiet forest.

"All right, boys, behave."

They had been jostling elbows.

"Yes, sir."

They climbed out, carrying the blue tin pails away from the lonely dirt road into the smell of fallen rain.

"Look for bees," said Father. "Bees hang around grapes like boys around kitchens. Doug?"

Douglas looked up suddenly.

"You're off a million miles," said Father. "Look alive. Walk with us."

"Yes, sir."

And they walked through the forest, Father very tall, Douglas moving in his shadow, and Tom, very small, trotting in his brother's shade. They came to a little rise and looked ahead. Here, here, did they see? Father pointed. Here was where the big summer-quiet winds lived and passed in the green depths, like ghost whales, unseen.

Douglas looked quickly, saw nothing, and felt put upon by his father who, like Grandpa, lived on riddles. But . . . But, still . . . Douglas paused and listened.

Yes, something's going to happen, he thought, I know it!

"Here's maidenhair fern." Dad walked, the tin pail belling in his fist. "Feel this?" He scuffed the earth. "A million years of good rich leafmold laid down. Think of the autumns that got by to make this."

"Boy, I walk like an Indian," said Tom. "Not a sound."

Douglas felt but did not feel the deep loam, listening, watchful. We're surrounded! he thought. It'll happen! What? He stopped. Come out, wherever you are, whatever you are! he cried silently.

Tom and Dad strolled on the hushed earth ahead.

"Finest lace there is," said Dad quietly.

And he was gesturing up through the trees above to show them how it was woven across the sky or how the sky was woven into the trees, he wasn't sure which. But there it was, he smiled, and the weaving went on, green and blue, if you watched and saw the forest shift its humming loom. Dad stood comfortably saying this and that, the words easy in his mouth. He made it easier by laughing at his own declarations just so often. He liked to listen to the silence, he said, if silence could be listened to, for, he went on, in that silence you could hear wildflower pollen sifting down the bee-fried air, by God, the bee-fried air! Listen! the waterfall of birdsong beyond those trees!

Now, thought Douglas, here it comes! Running! I don't see it! Running! Almost on me!

"Fox grapes!" said Father. "We're in luck, look here!"

Don't! Douglas gasped.

But Tom and Dad bent down to shove their hands deep in rattling bush. The spell was shattered. The terrible prowler, the magnificent runner, the leaper, the shaker of souls, vanished.

Douglas, lost and empty, fell to his knees. He saw his fingers sink through green shadow and come forth stained with such color that it seemed he had somehow cut the forest and delved his hand in the open wound.

"Lunch time, boys!"

With buckets half burdened with fox grapes and wild strawberries, followed by bees which were, no more, no less, said Father, the world humming under its breath, they sat on a green-mossed log, chewing sandwiches and trying to listen to the forest the same way Father did. Douglas felt Dad watching him, quietly amused. Dad started to say something that had crossed his mind, but instead tried another bite of sandwich and mused over it.

"Sandwich outdoors isn't a sandwich any more. Tastes different than indoors, notice? Got more spice. Tastes like mint and pinesap. Does wonders for the appetite."

Douglas's tongue hesitated on the texture of bread and deviled ham. No . . . no . . . it was just a sandwich.

Tom chewed and nodded. "Know just what you mean, Dad!"

It almost happened, thought Douglas. Whatever it was it was Big, my gosh, it was Big! Something scared it off. Where is it now? Back of that bush! No, behind me! No, here . . . almost *here* . . . He kneaded his stomach secretly.

If I wait, it'll come back. It won't hurt; somehow I know it's not here to hurt me. What then? What? What?

"You know how many baseball games we played this year, last year, year before?" said Tom, apropos of nothing.

Douglas watched Tom's quickly moving lips.

"Wrote it down! One thousand five hundred sixty eight games! How many times I brushed my teeth in ten years? Six thousand! Washed my hands: fifteen thousand. Slept: four thousand some–odd times, not counting naps. Ate six hundred peaches, eight hundred apples. Pears: two hundred. I'm not hot for pears. Name a thing, I got the statistics! Runs to the billion millions, things I done, add 'em up, in ten years."

Now, thought Douglas, it's coming close again. Why? Tom talking? But why Tom? Tom chatting along, mouth crammed with sandwich, Dad there, alert as a mountain cat on the log, and Tom letting the words rise like quick soda bubbles in his mouth:

"Books I read: four hundred. Matinees I seen: forty Buck

Joneses, thirty Jack Hoxies, forty-five Tom Mixes, thirty-nine Hoot Gibsons, one hundred and ninety-two single and separate Felix-the-Cat cartoons, ten Douglas Fairbankses, eight repeats on Lon Chaney in *The Phantom of the Opera*, four Milton Sillses, and one Adolphe Menjou thing about love where I spent ninety hours in the theater toilet waiting for the mush to be over so I could see *The Cat and the Canary* or *The Bat*, where everybody held onto everybody else and screamed for two hours without letting go. During that time I figure four hundred lollipops, three hundred Tootsie Rolls, seven hundred ice-cream cones . . ."

Tom rolled quietly along his way for another five minutes and then Dad said, "How many berries you picked so far, Tom?"

"Two hundred fifty-six on the nose!" said Tom instantly.

Dad laughed and lunch was over and they moved again into the shadows to find fox grapes and the tiny wild strawberries, bent down, all three of them, hands coming and going, the pails getting heavy, and Douglas holding his breath, thinking, Yes, yes, it's near again! Breathing on my neck, almost! Don't look! Work. Just pick, fill up the pail. If you look you'll scare it off. Don't lose it this time! But how, how do you bring it around here where you can see it, stare it right in the eye? How? How?

"Got a snowflake in a matchbox," said Tom, smiling at the wine-glove on his hand.

Shut up! Douglas wanted to yell. But no, the yell would scare the echoes, and run the Thing away!

And, wait . . . the more Tom talked, the closer the great Thing came, it wasn't scared of Tom, Tom drew it with his breath, Tom was part of it!

"Last February," said Tom, and chuckled. "Held a matchbox up in a snowstorm, let one old snowflake fall in, shut it up, ran inside the house, stashed it in the icebox!"

Close, very close. Douglas stared at Tom's flickering lips. He wanted to jump around, for he felt a vast tidal wave lift up behind the forest. In an instant it would smash down, crush them forever . . .

"Yes, sir," mused Tom, picking grapes, "I'm the only guy in all Illinois who's got a snowflake in summer. Precious as diamonds, by gosh. Tomorrow I'll open it. Doug, you can look, too . . ."

Any other day Douglas might have snorted, struck out, denied it all. But now, with the great Thing rushing near, falling down in the clear air above him, he could only nod, eyes shut.

Tom, puzzled, stopped picking berries and turned to stare over at his brother.

Douglas, hunched over, was an ideal target. Tom leaped, yelling, landed. They fell, thrashed, and rolled.

No! Douglas squeezed his mind shut. No! But suddenly . . . Yes, it's all right! Yes! The tangle, the contact of bodies, the falling tumble had not scared off the tidal sea that crashed now, flooding and washing them along the shore of grass deep through the forest. Knuckles struck his mouth. He tasted rusty warm blood, grabbed Tom hard, held him tight, and so in silence they lay, hearts churning, nostrils hissing. And at last, slowly, afraid he would find nothing, Douglas opened one eye.

And everything, absolutely everything, was there.

The world, like a great iris of an even more gigantic eye, which has also just opened and stretched out to encompass everything, stared back at him.

And he knew what it was that had leaped upon him to stay and would not run away now.

I'm alive, he thought.

His fingers trembled, bright with blood, like the bits of a strange flag now found and before unseen, and him wondering what country and what allegiance he owed to it. Holding Tom, but not knowing him there, he touched his free hand to that blood as if it could be peeled away, held up, turned over. Then he let go of Tom and lay on his back with his hand up in the sky and he was a head from which his eyes peered like sentinels through the portcullis of a strange castle out along a bridge, his arm, to those fingers where the bright pennant of blood quivered in the light.

"You all right, Doug?" asked Tom.

His voice was at the bottom of a green moss well somewhere underwater, secret, removed.

The grass whispered under his body. He put his arm down,

feeling the sheath of fuzz on it, and, far away, below, his toes creaking in his shoes. The wind sighed over his shelled ears. The world slipped bright over the glassy round of his eyeballs like images sparked in a crystal sphere. Flowers were sun and fiery spots of sky strewn through the woodland. Birds flickered like skipped stones across the vast inverted pond of heaven. His breath raked over his teeth, going in ice, coming out fire. Insects shocked the air with electric clearness. Ten thousand individual hairs grew a millionth of an inch on his head. He heard the twin hearts beating in each ear, the third heart beating in his throat, the two hearts throbbing his wrists, the real heart pounding his chest. The million pores on his body opened.

I'm *really* alive! he thought. I never knew it before, or if I did I don't remember!

He yelled it loud but silent, a dozen times! Think of it, think of it! Twelve years old and only now! Now discovering this rare timepiece, this clock gold-bright and guaranteed to run threescore and ten, left under a tree and found while wrestling.

"Doug, you okay?"

Douglas yelled, grabbed Tom, and rolled.

"Doug, you're crazy!"

"Crazy!"

They spilled downhill, the sun in their mouths, in their eyes like shattered lemon glass, gasping like trout thrown out on a bank, laughing till they cried.

"Doug, you're not mad?"

"No, no, no, no, no!"

Douglas, eyes shut, saw spotted leopards pad in the dark.

"Tom!" Then quieter. "Tom . . . does everyone in the world . . . know he's alive?"

"Sure. Heck, yes!"

The leopards trotted soundlessly off through darker lands where eyeballs could not turn to follow.

"I hope they do," whispered Douglas. "Oh, I sure hope they know."

Douglas opened his eyes. Dad was standing high above him there in the green-leaved sky, laughing, hands on hips. Their eyes met. Douglas quickened. Dad knows, he thought. It was all planned. He brought us here on purpose, so this could happen to me! He's in on it, he knows it all. And now he knows that I know.

A hand came down and seized him through the air. Swayed on his feet with Tom and Dad, still bruised and rumpled, puzzled and awed, Douglas held his strange-boned elbows tenderly and licked the fine cut lip with satisfaction. Then he looked at Dad and Tom.

"I'll carry all the pails," he said. "This once, let me haul everything."

They handed over the pails with quizzical smiles.

He stood swaying slightly, the forest collected, full-weighted and heavy with syrup, clenched hard in his down-slung hands. I want to feel all there is to feel, he thought. Let me feel tired, now, let me feel tired. I mustn't forget, I'm alive, I know I'm alive, I mustn't forget it tonight or tomorrow or the day after that.

The bees followed and the smell of fox grapes and yellow summer followed as he walked heavy-laden and half drunk, his fingers wondrously callused, arms numb, feet stumbling so his father caught his shoulder.

"No," mumbled Douglas, "I'm all right. I'm fine . . ."

It took half an hour for the sense of the grass, the roots, the stones, the bark of the mossy log, to fade from where they had patterned his arms and legs and back. While he pondered this, let it slip, slide, dissolve away, his brother and his quiet father followed behind, allowing him to pathfind the forest alone out toward that incredible highway which would take them back to the town. . . .

THE TOWN, then, later in the day.

And yet another harvest.

Grandfather stood on the wide front porch like a captain surveying the vast unmotioned calms of a season dead ahead. He questioned the wind and the untouchable sky and the lawn on which stood Douglas and Tom to question only him.

"Grandpa, are they ready? Now?"

Grandfather pinched his chin. "Five hundred, a thousand, two thousand easy. Yes, yes, a good supply. Pick 'em easy, pick 'em all. A dime for every sack delivered to the press!"

"Hey!"

The boys bent, smiling. They picked the golden flowers. The flowers that flooded the world, dripped off lawns onto brick streets, tapped softly at crystal cellar windows and agitated themselves so that on all sides lay the dazzle and glitter of molten sun.

"Every year," said Grandfather. "They run amuck; I let them. Pride of lions in the yard. Stare, and they burn a hole in your retina. A common flower, a weed that no one sees, yes. But for us, a noble thing, the dandelion."

So, plucked carefully, in sacks, the dandelions were carried below. The cellar dark glowed with their arrival. The wine press stood open, cold. A rush of flowers warmed it. The press, replaced, its screw rotated, twirled by Grandfather, squeezed gently on the crop.

"There . . . so . . ."

The golden tide, the essence of this fine fair month ran, then gushed from the spout below, to be crocked, skimmed of ferment, and bottled in clean ketchup shakers, then ranked in sparkling rows in cellar gloom.

Dandelion wine.

The words were summer on the tongue. The wine was summer caught and stoppered. And now that Douglas knew, he really knew he was alive, and moved turning through the world to touch and see it all, it was only right and proper that some of his new knowledge, some of this special vintage day would be sealed away for opening on a January day with snow falling fast and the sun unseen for weeks or months and perhaps some of the miracle by then forgotten and in need of renewal. Since this was going to be a summer of unguessed wonders, he wanted it all salvaged and labeled so that any time he wished, he might tiptoe down in this dank twilight and reach up his finger tips.

And there, row upon row, with the soft gleam of flowers opened at morning, with the light of this June sun glowing through a faint skin of dust, would stand the dandelion wine. Peer through it at the wintry day—the snow melted to grass, the trees were reinhabited with bird, leaf, and blossoms like a continent of butterflies breathing on the wind. And peering through, color sky from iron to blue.

Hold summer in your hand, pour summer in a glass, a tiny glass of course, the smallest tingling sip for children; change the season in your veins by raising glass to lip and tilting summer in.

"Ready, now, the rain barrel!"

Nothing else in the world would do but the pure waters which had been summoned from the lakes far away and the sweet fields of grassy dew on early morning, lifted to the open sky, carried in laundered clusters nine hundred miles, brushed with wind, electrified with high voltage, and condensed upon cool air. This water, falling, raining, gathered yet more of the heavens in its crystals. Taking something of the east wind and the west wind and the north wind and the south, the water made rain and the rain, within this hour of rituals, would be well on its way to wine.

Douglas ran with the dipper. He plunged it deep in the rain barrel. "Here we go!"

The water was silk in the cup; clear, faintly blue silk. It softened the lip and the throat and the heart, if drunk. This water must be carried in dipper and bucket to the cellar, there to be leavened in freshets, in mountain streams, upon the dandelion harvest.

Even Grandma, when snow was whirling fast, dizzying the world, blinding windows, stealing breath from gasping mouths, even Grandma, one day in February, would vanish to the cellar.

Above, in the vast house, there would be coughings, sneezings, wheezings, and groans, childish fevers, throats raw as butcher's meat, noses like bottled cherries, the stealthy microbe everywhere.

Then, rising from the cellar like a June goddess, Grandma would come, something hidden but obvious under her knitted shawl. This, carried to every miserable room upstairs-and-down would be dispensed with aroma and clarity into neat glasses, to be swigged neatly. The medicines of another time, the balm of sun and idle August afternoons, the faintly heard sounds of ice wagons passing on brick avenues, the rush of silver sky-rockets and the fountaining of lawn mowers moving through ant countries, all these, all these in a glass.

Yes, even Grandma, drawn to the cellar of winter for a June adventure, might stand alone and quietly, in secret conclave with her own soul and spirit, as did Grandfather and Father and Uncle Bert, or some of the boarders, communing with a last touch of a calendar long departed, with the picnics and the warm rains and the smell of fields of wheat and new popcorn and bending hay. Even Grandma, repeating and repeating the fine and golden words, even as they were said now in this moment when the flowers were dropped into the press, as they would be repeated every winter for all the white winters in time. Saying them over and over on the lips, like a smile, like a sudden patch of sunlight in the dark.

Dandelion wine. Dandelion wine. Dandelion wine.

YOU DID not hear them coming. You hardly heard them go. The grass bent down, sprang up again. They passed like cloud shadows downhill . . . the boys of summer, running.

Douglas, left behind, was lost. Panting, he stopped by the rim of the ravine, at the edge of the softly blowing abyss. Here, ears pricked like a deer, he snuffed a danger that was old a billion years ago. Here the town, divided, fell away in halves. Here civilization ceased. Here was only growing earth and a million deaths and rebirths every hour.

And here the paths, made or yet unmade, that told of the need of boys traveling, always traveling, to be men.

Douglas turned. This path led in a great dusty snake to the ice house where winter lived on the yellow days. This path raced for the blast-furnace sands of the lake shore in July. This to trees where boys might grow like sour and still-green crab apples, hid among leaves. This to peach orchard, grape arbor, watermelons lying like tortoise-shell cats slumbered by sun. That path, abandoned, but wildly swiveling, to school! This, straight as an arrow, to Saturday cowboy matinees. And this, by the creek waters, to wilderness beyond town. . . .

Douglas squinted.

Who could say where town or wilderness began? Who could say which owned what and what owned which? There was always and forever that indefinable place where the two struggled and one of them won for a season to possess a certain avenue, a dell, a glen, a tree, a bush. The thin lapping of the great continental sea of grass and flower, starting far out in lonely farm country, moved inward with the thrust of seasons. Each night the wilderness, the meadows, the far country flowed down-creek through ravine and welled up in town with a smell of grass and water, and the town was disinhabited and dead and gone back to earth. And each morning a little more of the ravine edged up into town, threatening to swamp garages like leaking rowboats, devour ancient cars which had been left to the flaking mercies of rain and therefore rust.

"Hey! Hey!" John Huff and Charlie Woodman ran through the mystery of ravine and town and time. "Hey!"

Douglas moved slowly down the path. The ravine was indeed the place where you came to look at the two things of life, the ways of man and the ways of the natural world. The town was, after all, only a large ship filled with constantly moving survivors, bailing out the grass, chipping away the rust. Now and again a lifeboat, a shanty, kin to the mother ship, lost out to the quiet storm of seasons, sank down in silent waves of termite and ant into swallowing ravine to feel the flicker of grasshoppers rattling like dry paper in hot weeds, become soundproofed with spider dust and finally, in avalanche of shingle and tar, collapse like kindling shrines into a bonfire, which thunderstorms ignited with blue lightning, while flash-photographing the triumph of the wilderness.

It was this then, the mystery of man seizing from the land and the land seizing back, year after year, that drew Douglas, knowing the towns never really won, they merely existed in calm peril, fully accoutered with lawn mower, bug spray and hedge shears, swimming steadily as long as civilization said to swim, but each house ready to sink in green tides, buried forever, when the last man ceased and his trowels and mowers shattered to cereal flakes of rust.

The town. The wilderness. The houses. The ravine. Douglas blinked back and forth. But how to relate the two, make sense of the interchange when . . .

His eyes moved down to the ground.

The first rite of summer, the dandelion picking, the starting of the wine, was over. Now the second rite waited for him to make the motions, but he stood very still.

"Doug . . . come on . . . Doug . . . !" The running boys faded.

"I'm alive," said Douglas. "But what's the use? They're more alive than me. How come? How come?"

And standing alone, he knew the answer, staring down at his motionless feet. . . .

LATE THAT night, going home from the show with his mother and father and his brother Tom, Douglas saw the tennis shoes in the bright store window. He glanced quickly away, but his ankles were seized, his feet suspended, then rushed. The earth spun; the shop awnings slammed their canvas wings overhead with the thrust of his body running. His mother and father and brother walked quietly on both sides of him. Douglas walked backward, watching the tennis shoes in the midnight window left behind.

"It was a nice movie," said Mother.

Douglas murmured, "It was . . ."

It was June and long past time for buying the special shoes that were quiet as a summer rain falling on the walks. June and the earth full of raw power and everything everywhere in motion. The grass was still pouring in from the country, surrounding the sidewalks, stranding the houses. Any moment the town would capsize, go down and leave not a stir in the clover and weeds. And here Douglas stood, trapped on the dead cement and the red-brick streets, hardly able to move.

"Dad!" He blurted it out. "Back there in that window, those Cream-Sponge Para Litefoot Shoes . . ."

His father didn't even turn. "Suppose you tell me why you need a new pair of sneakers. Can you do that?"

"Well . . ."

It was because they felt the way it feels every summer when you take off your shoes for the first time and run in the grass. They felt like it feels sticking your feet out of the hot covers in wintertime to let the cold wind from the open window blow on them suddenly and you let them stay out a long time until you pull them back in under the covers again to feel them, like packed snow. The tennis shoes felt like it always feels the first time every year wading in the slow waters of the creek and seeing your feet below, half an inch further downstream, with refraction, than the real part of you above water.

"Dad," said Douglas, "it's hard to explain."

Somehow the people who made tennis shoes knew what boys

needed and wanted. They put marshmallows and coiled springs in the soles and they wove the rest out of grasses bleached and fired in the wilderness. Somewhere deep in the soft loam of the shoes the thin hard sinews of the buck deer were hidden. The people that made the shoes must have watched a lot of winds blow the trees and a lot of rivers going down to the lakes. Whatever it was, it was in the shoes, and it was summer.

Douglas tried to get all this in words.

"Yes," said Father, "but what's wrong with last year's sneakers? Why can't you dig *them* out of the closet?"

Well, he felt sorry for boys who lived in California where they wore tennis shoes all year and never knew what it was to get winter off your feet, peel off the iron leather shoes all full of snow and rain and run barefoot for a day and then lace on the first new tennis shoes of the season, which was better than barefoot. The magic was always in the new pair of shoes. The magic might die by the first of September, but now in late June there was still plenty of magic, and shoes like these could jump you over trees and rivers and houses. And if you wanted, they could jump you over fences and sidewalks and dogs.

"Don't you see?" said Douglas. "I just *can't* use last year's pair."

For last year's pair were dead inside. They had been fine when he started them out, last year. But by the end of summer, every year, you always found out, you always knew, you couldn't really jump over rivers and trees and houses in them, and they were dead. But this was a new year, and he felt that this time, with this new pair of shoes, he could do anything, anything at all.

They walked up on the steps to their house. "Save your money," said Dad. "In five or six weeks——"

"Summer'll be over!"

Lights out, with Tom asleep, Douglas lay watching his feet, far away down there at the end of the bed in the moonlight, free of the heavy iron shoes, the big chunks of winter fallen away from them.

"Reasons. I've got to think of reasons for the shoes."

Well, as anyone knew, the hills around town were wild with friends putting cows to riot, playing barometer to the atmospheric changes, taking sun, peeling like calendars each day to take more sun. To catch those friends, you must run much faster than foxes or squirrels. As for the town, it steamed with enemies grown irritable with heat, so remembering every winter argument and insult. *Find friends, ditch enemies!* That was the Cream-Sponge Para Litefoot motto. *Does the world run too fast? Want to catch up? Want to be alert, stay alert? Litefoot, then! Litefoot!*

He held his coin bank up and heard the faint small tinkling, the airy weight of money there.

Whatever you want, he thought, you got to make your own way. During the night now, let's find that path through the forest. . . .

Downtown, the store lights went out, one by one. A wind blew in the window. It was like a river going downstream and his feet wanting to go with it.

In his dreams he heard a rabbit running running running in the deep warm grass.

Old Mr. Sanderson moved through his shoe store as the proprietor of a pet shop must move through his shop where are kenneled animals from everywhere in the world, touching each one briefly along the way. Mr. Sanderson brushed his hands over the shoes in the window, and some of them were like cats to him and some were like dogs; he touched each pair with concern, adjusting laces, fixing tongues. Then he stood in the exact center of the carpet and looked around, nodding.

There was a sound of growing thunder.

One moment, the door to Sanderson's Shoe Emporium was empty. The next, Douglas Spaulding stood clumsily there, staring down at his leather shoes as if these heavy things could not be pulled up out of the cement. The thunder had stopped when his shoes stopped. Now, with painful slowness, daring to look only at the money in his cupped hand, Douglas moved out of the bright sunlight of Saturday noon. He made careful stacks of nickels, dimes, and quarters on the counter, like someone playing chess and worried if the next move carried him out into sun or deep into shadow.

"Don't say a word!" said Mr. Sanderson.

Douglas froze.

"First, I know just what you want to buy," said Mr.

Sanderson. "Second, I see you every afternoon at my window; you think I don't see? You're wrong. Third, to give it its full name, you want the Royal Crown Cream-Sponge Para Litefoot Tennis Shoes: 'LIKE MENTHOL ON YOUR FEET!' Fourth, you want credit."

"No!" cried Douglas, breathing hard, as if he'd run all night in his dreams. "I got something better than credit to offer!" he gasped. "Before I tell, Mr. Sanderson, you got to do me one small favor. Can you remember when was the last time you yourself wore a pair of Litefoot sneakers, sir?"

Mr. Sanderson's face darkened. "Oh, ten, twenty, say, thirty years ago. Why . . . ?"

"Mr. Sanderson, don't you think you owe it to your customers, sir, to at least try the tennis shoes you sell, for just one minute, so you know how they feel? People forget if they don't keep testing things. United Cigar Store man smokes cigars, don't he? Candy-store man samples his own stuff, I should think. So . . ."

"You may have noticed," said the old man, "I'm wearing shoes."

"But not sneakers, sir! How you going to sell sneakers unless you can rave about them and how you going to rave about them unless you know them?"

Mr. Sanderson backed off a little distance from the boy's fever, one hand to his chin. "Well . . ."

"Mr. Sanderson," said Douglas, "you sell me something and I'll sell you something just as valuable."

"Is it absolutely necessary to the sale that I put on a pair of the sneakers, boy?" said the old man.

"I sure wish you could, sir!"

The old man sighed. A minute later, seated panting quietly, he laced the tennis shoes to his long narrow feet. They looked detached and alien down there next to the dark cuffs of his business suit. Mr. Sanderson stood up.

"How do they *feel*?" asked the boy.

"How do they feel, he asks; they feel fine." He started to sit down.

"Please!" Douglas held out his hand. "Mr. Sanderson, now could you kind of rock back and forth a little, sponge around, bounce kind of, while I tell you the rest? It's this: I give you my money, you give me the shoes, I owe you a dollar. But, Mr. Sanderson, *but*—soon as I get those shoes on, you know what *happens*?"

"What?"

"Bang! I deliver your packages, pick up packages, bring you coffee, burn your trash, run to the post office, telegraph office, library! You'll see twelve of me in and out, in and out, every minute. Feel those shoes, Mr. Sanderson, *feel* how fast they'd take me? All those springs inside? Feel all the running inside? Feel how they kind of grab hold and can't let you alone and don't like you just *standing* there? Feel how quick I'd be doing the things you'd rather not bother with? You stay in the nice cool store while I'm jumping all around town! But it's not me really, it's the shoes. They're going like mad down alleys, cutting corners, and back! There they go!"

Mr. Sanderson stood amazed with the rush of words. When the words got going the flow carried him; he began to sink deep in the shoes, to flex his toes, limber his arches, test his ankles. He rocked softly, secretly, back and forth in a small breeze from the open door. The tennis shoes silently hushed themselves deep in the carpet, sank as in a jungle grass, in loam and resilient clay. He gave one solemn bounce of his heels in the yeasty dough, in the yielding and welcoming earth. Emotions hurried over his face as if many colored lights had been switched on and off. His mouth hung slightly open. Slowly he gentled and rocked himself to a halt, and the boy's voice faded and they stood there looking at each other in a tremendous and natural silence.

A few people drifted by on the sidewalk outside, in the hot sun.

Still the man and boy stood there, the boy glowing, the man with revelation in his face.

"Boy," said the old man at last, "in five years, how would you like a job selling shoes in this emporium?"

"Gosh, thanks, Mr. Sanderson, but I don't know what I'm going to be yet."

"Anything you want to be, son," said the old man, "you'll be. No one will ever stop you."

The old man walked lightly across the store to the wall of ten thousand boxes, came back with some shoes for the boy, and wrote up a list on some paper while the boy was lacing the shoes on his feet and then standing there, waiting.

The old man held out his list. "A dozen things you got to do for me this afternoon. Finish them, we're even Stephen, and you're fired."

"Thanks, Mr. Sanderson!" Douglas bounded away.

"Stop!" cried the old man.

Douglas pulled up and turned.

Mr. Sanderson leaned forward. "How do they *feel*?"

The boy looked down at his feet deep in the rivers, in the fields of wheat, in the wind that already was rushing him out of the town. He looked up at the old man, his eyes burning, his mouth moving, but no sound came out.

"Antelopes?" said the old man, looking from the boy's face to his shoes. "Gazelles?"

The boy thought about it, hesitated, and nodded a quick nod. Almost immediately he vanished. He just spun about with a whisper and went off. The door stood empty. The sound of the tennis shoes faded in the jungle heat.

Mr. Sanderson stood in the sun-blazed door, listening. From a long time ago, when he dreamed as a boy, he remembered the sound. Beautiful creatures leaping under the sky, gone through brush, under trees, away, and only the soft echo their running left behind.

"Antelopes," said Mr. Sanderson. "Gazelles."

He bent to pick up the boy's abandoned winter shoes, heavy with forgotten rains and long-melted snows. Moving out of the blazing sun, walking softly, lightly, slowly, he headed back toward civilization. . . .

HE BROUGHT out a yellow nickel tablet. He brought out a yellow Ticonderoga pencil. He opened the tablet. He licked the pencil.

"Tom," he said, "you and your statistics gave me an idea. I'm going to do the same, keep track of things. For instance: you realize that every summer we do things over and over we did the whole darn summer before?"

"Like what, Doug?"

"Like making dandelion wine, like buying these new tennis shoes, like shooting off the first firecracker of the year, like making lemonade, like getting slivers in our feet, like picking wild fox grapes. Every year the same things, same way, no change, no difference. That's one half of summer, Tom."

"What's the other half?"

"Things we do for the first time ever."

"Like eating olives?"

"Bigger than that. Like finding out maybe that Grandpa or Dad don't know everything in the world."

"They know every darn thing there is to know, and don't you forget it!"

"Tom, don't argue, I already got it written down under Discoveries and Revelations. They don't know everything. But it's no crime. That I discovered, too."

"What other new crazy stuff you got in there?"

"I'm alive."

"Heck, that's old!"

"*Thinking* about it, *noticing* it, is new. You do things and don't watch. Then all of a sudden you look and see what you're doing and it's the first time, really. I'm going to divide the summer up in two parts. First part of this tablet is titled: RITES AND CEREMONIES. The first root beer pop of the year. The first time running barefoot in the grass of the year. First time almost drowning in the lake of the year. First watermelon. First mosquito. First harvest of dandelions. Those are the things we do over and over and over and never think. Now here in back, like I said, is DISCOVERIES AND REVELATIONS or maybe ILLUMINATIONS, that's a swell word, or INTUITIONS, okay? In other words you do an old familiar thing, like bottling dandelion wine, and you put that under RITES AND CEREMONIES. And then you think about it, and what you think, crazy or not, you put under DISCOVERIES AND REVELATIONS. Here's what I got on the wine: *Every time you bottle it, you got a whole chunk of 1928 put away, safe.* How you like that, Tom?"

"I got lost a mile back somewhere."

"Let me show you another. Up front under CEREMONIES I got: *First argument and licking of Summer 1928 by Dad, morning of June 24th.* In back under REVELATIONS I got: *The reason why grownups and kids fight is because they belong to separate races. Look at them, different from us. Look at us, different from them. Separate races, and 'never the twain shall meet.'* Put that in your pipe and smoke it, Tom!"

"Doug, you hit it, you hit it! That's right! That's exactly why we don't get along with Mom or Dad. Trouble, trouble, from sunrise to supper! Boy, you're a genius!"

"Any time this next three months you see something done over and over, tell me. Think about it, and tell me *that.* Come Labor Day, we'll add up the summer and see what we got!"

"I got a statistic for you right now. Grab your pencil, Doug. There are five billion trees in the world. I looked it up. Under every tree is a shadow, right? So, then, what makes night? I'll tell you: shadows crawling out from under five billion trees! Think of it! Shadows running around in the air, muddying the waters you might say. If only we could figure a way to keep those darn five billion shadows under those trees, we could stay up half the night, Doug, because there'd be no night! There you are; something old, something new."

"That's old and new, all right." Douglas licked the yellow Ticonderoga pencil, whose name he dearly loved. "Say it again."

"*Shadows are under five billion trees . . .*"

YES, SUMMER was rituals, each with its natural time and place. The ritual of lemonade or ice-tea making, the ritual of wine, shoes, or no shoes, and at last, swiftly following the others, with quiet dignity, the ritual of the front-porch swing.

On the third day of summer in the late afternoon Grandfather reappeared from the front door to gaze serenely at the two empty eye rings in the ceiling of the porch. Moving to the geranium-pot-lined rail like Ahab surveying the mild mild day and the mild-looking sky, he wet his finger to test the wind, and shucked his coat to see how shirt sleeves felt in the westering hours. He acknowledged the salutes of other captains on yet other flowered porches, out themselves to discern the gentle ground swell of weather, oblivious to their wives chirping or snapping like fuzzball hand dogs hidden behind black porch screens.

"All right, Douglas, let's set it up."

In the garage they found, dusted, and carried forth the howdah, as it were, for the quiet summer-night festivals, the swing chair which Grandpa chained to the porch-ceiling eyelets.

Douglas, being lighter, was first to sit in the swing. Then, after a moment, Grandfather gingerly settled his pontifical weight beside the boy. Thus they sat, smiling at each other, nodding, as they swung silently back and forth, back and forth.

Ten minutes later Grandma appeared with water buckets and brooms to wash down and sweep off the porch. Other chairs, rockers and straight-backs, were summoned from the house.

"Always like to start sitting early in the season," said Grandpa, "before the mosquitoes thicken."

About seven o'clock you could hear the chairs scraping back from the tables, someone experimenting with a yellow-toothed piano, if you stood outside the dining-room window and listened. Matches being struck, the first dishes bubbling in the suds and tinkling on the wall racks, somewhere, faintly, a phonograph playing. And then as the evening changed the hour, at house after house on the twilight streets, under the immense oaks and elms, on shady porches, people would begin to appear, like those figures who tell good or bad weather in rain-or-shine clocks.

Uncle Bert, perhaps Grandfather, then Father, and some of the cousins; the men all coming out first into the syrupy evening, blowing smoke, leaving the women's voices behind in the cooling-warm kitchen to set their universe aright. Then the first male voices under the porch brim, the feet up, the boys fringed on the worn steps or wooden rails where sometime during the evening something, a boy or a geranium pot, would fall off.

At last, like ghosts hovering momentarily behind the door screen, Grandma, Great-grandma, and Mother would appear, and the men would shift, move, and offer seats. The women carried varieties of fans with them, folded newspapers, bamboo whisks, or perfumed kerchiefs, to start the air moving about their faces as they talked.

What they talked of all evening long, no one remembered next day. It wasn't important to anyone what the adults talked about; it was only important that the sounds came and went over the delicate ferns that bordered the porch on three sides; it was only important that the darkness filled the town like black water being poured over the houses, and that the cigars glowed and that the conversations went on, and on. The female gossip moved out, disturbing the first mosquitoes so they danced in frenzies on the air. The male voices invaded the old house timbers; if you closed your eyes and put your head down against the floor boards you could hear the men's voices rumbling like a distant, political earthquake, constant, unceasing, rising or falling a pitch.

Douglas sprawled back on the dry porch planks, completely contented and reassured by these voices, which would speak on through eternity, flow in a stream of murmurings over his body, over his closed eyelids, into his drowsy ears, for all time. The rocking chairs sounded like crickets, the crickets sounded like rocking chairs, and the moss-covered rain barrel by the dining-room window produced another generation of mosquitoes to provide a topic of conversation through endless summers ahead.

Sitting on the summer-night porch was so good, so easy

and so reassuring that it could never be done away with. These were rituals that were right and lasting; the lighting of pipes, the pale hands that moved knitting needles in the dimness, the eating of foil-wrapped, chill Eskimo Pies, the coming and going of all the people. For at some time or other during the evening, everyone visited here; the neighbors down the way, the people across the street; Miss Fern and Miss Roberta humming by in their electric runabout, giving Tom or Douglas a ride around the block and then coming up to sit down and fan away the fever in their cheeks; or Mr. Jonas, the junkman, having left his horse and wagon hidden in the alley, and ripe to bursting with words, would come up the steps looking as fresh as if his talk had never been said before, and somehow it never had. And last of all, the children, who had been off squinting their way through a last hide-and-seek or kick-the-can, panting, glowing, would sickle quietly back like boomerangs along the soundless lawn, to sink beneath the talking talking talking of the porch voices which would weigh and gentle them down. . . .

Oh, the luxury of lying in the fern night and the grass night and the night of susurrant, slumbrous voices weaving the dark together. The grownups had forgotten he was there, so still, so quiet Douglas lay, noting the plans they were making for his and their own futures. And the voices chanted, drifted, in moonlit clouds of cigarette smoke while the moths, like late appleblossoms come alive, tapped faintly about the far street lights, and the voices moved on into the coming years. . . .

IN FRONT of the United Cigar Store this evening the men were gathered to burn dirigibles, sink battleships, blow up dynamite works and, all in all, savor the very bacteria in their porcelain mouths that would some day stop them cold. Clouds of annihilation loomed and blew away in their cigar smoke about a nervous figure who could be seen dimly listening to the sound of shovels and spades and the intonations of "ashes to ashes, dust to dust." This figure was that of Leo Auffmann, the town jeweler, who, widening his large liquid-dark eyes, at last threw up his childlike hands and cried out in dismay.

"Stop! In God's name, get out of that graveyard!"

"Leo, how right you are," said Grandfather Spaulding, passing on his nightly stroll with his grandsons Douglas and Tom. "But, Leo, only you can shut these doom-talkers up. Invent something that will make the future brighter, well rounded, infinitely joyous. You've invented bicycles, fixed the penny-arcade contraptions, been our town movie projectionist, haven't you?"

"Sure," said Douglas. "Invent us a happiness machine!"

The men laughed.

"Don't," said Leo Auffmann. "How have we used machines so far, to make people cry? Yes! Every time man and the machine look like they will get on all right—boom! Someone adds a cog, airplanes drop bombs on us, cars run us off cliffs. So is the boy wrong to ask? No! No . . ."

His voice faded as Leo Auffmann moved to the curb to touch his bicycle as if it were an animal.

"What can I lose?" he murmured. "A little skin off my fingers, a few pounds of metal, some sleep? I'll do it, so help me!"

"Leo," said Grandfather, "we didn't mean——"

But Leo Auffmann was gone, pedaling off through the warm summer evening, his voice drifting back. ". . . I'll do it . . ."

"You know," said Tom, in awe, "I bet he *will*."

WATCHING HIM cycle the brick streets of evening, you could see that Leo Auffmann was a man who coasted along, enjoying the way the thistles ticked in the hot grass when the wind blew like a furnace, or the way the electric power lines sizzled on the rain-wet poles. He was a man who did not suffer but pleasured in sleepless nights of brooding on the great clock of the universe running down or winding itself up, who could tell? But many nights, listening, he decided first one way and then the other . . .

The shocks of life, he thought, biking along, what were they? Getting born, growing up, growing old, dying. Not much to do about the first. But—the other three?

The wheels of his Happiness Machine spun whirling golden light spokes along the ceiling of his head. A machine, now, to help boys change from peach fuzz to briar bramble, girls from toadstool to nectarine. And in the years when your shadow leaned clear across the land as you lay abed nights with your heartbeat mounting to the billions, his invention must let a man drowse easy in the falling leaves like the boys in autumn who, comfortably strewn in the dry stacks, are content to be a part of the death of the world. . . .

"Papa!"

His six children, Saul, Marshall, Joseph, Rebecca, Ruth, Naomi, all ages from five to fifteen, came rushing across the lawn to take his bike, each touching him at once.

"We waited. We got ice cream!"

Moving toward the porch, he could feel his wife's smile there in the dark.

Five minutes passed in comfortable eating silence, then, holding a spoonful of moon-colored ice cream up as if it were the whole secret of the universe to be tasted carefully he said, "Lena? What would you think if I tried to invent a happiness machine?"

"Something's wrong?" she asked quickly.

GRANDFATHER WALKED Douglas and Tom home. Halfway there, Charlie Woodman and John Huff and some other boys rushed by like a swarm of meteors, their gravity so huge they pulled Douglas away from Grandfather and Tom and swept him off toward the ravine.

"Don't get lost, son!"

"I won't . . . . I won't . . ."

The boys plunged into darkness.

Tom and Grandfather walked the rest of the way in silence, except when they turned in at home and Tom said, "Boy, a Happiness Machine—hot diggety!"

"Don't hold your breath," said Grandpa.

The courthouse clock struck eight.

The courthouse clock struck nine and it was getting late and it was really night on this small street in a small town in a big state on a large continent on a planet earth hurtling down the pit of space toward nowhere or somewhere and Tom feeling every mile of the long drop. He sat by the front-door screen looking out at that rushing blackness that looked very innocent, as if it was holding still. Only when you closed your eyes and lay down could you feel the world spinning under your bed and hollowing your ears with a black sea that came in and broke on cliffs that weren't there.

There was a smell of rain. Mother was ironing and sprinkling water from a corked ketchup bottle over the crackling dry clothes behind Tom.

One store was still open about a block away—Mrs. Singer's.

Finally, just before it was time for Mrs. Singer to close her store, Mother relented and told Tom, "Run get a pint of ice cream and be sure she packs it tight."

He asked if he could get a scoop of chocolate on top, because he didn't like vanilla, and Mother agreed. He clutched the money and ran barefooted over the warm evening cement sidewalk, under the apple and oak trees, toward the store. The town was so quiet and far off you could hear only the crickets sounding in the spaces beyond the hot indigo trees that hold back the stars.

His bare feet slapped the pavement. He crossed the street and found Mrs. Singer moving ponderously about her store, singing Yiddish melodies.

"Pint ice cream?" she said. "Chocolate on top? Yes!"

He watched her fumble the metal top off the ice-cream freezer and manipulate the scoop, packing the cardboard pint chock-full with "chocolate on top, yes!" He gave the money, received the chill, icy pack, and rubbing it across his brow and cheek, laughing, thumped barefootedly homeward. Behind him the lights of the lonely little store blinked out and there was only a street light shimmering on the corner, and the whole city seemed to be going to sleep.

Opening the screen door, he found Mom still ironing. She looked hot and irritated but she smiled just the same.

"When will Dad be home from lodge meeting?" he asked.

"About eleven or eleven-thirty," Mother replied. She took the ice cream to the kitchen, divided it. Giving him his special portion of chocolate, she dished out some for herself and the rest was put away, "for Douglas and your father when they come."

They sat enjoying the ice cream, wrapped at the core of the deep quiet summer night. His mother and himself and the night all around their small house on the small street. He licked each spoonful of ice cream thoroughly before digging for another, and Mom put her ironing board away and the hot iron in its open case cooling, and she sat in the armchair by the phonograph, eating her dessert and saying, "My land, it was a hot day today. Earth soaks up all the heat and lets it out at night. It'll be soggy sleeping."

They both sat listening to the night, pressed down by every window and door and complete silence because the radio needed a new battery, and they had played all the Knickerbocker Quartet records and Al Jolson and Two Black Crows records to exhaustion; so Tom just sat on the hardwood floor and looked out into the dark dark dark, pressing his nose against the screen until the flesh of its tip was molded into small dark squares.

"I wonder where Doug is? It's almost nine-thirty."

"He'll be here," Tom said, knowing very well that Douglas would be.

He followed Mom out to wash the dishes. Each sound, each rattle of spoon or dish was amplified in the baked evening. Silently they went to the living room, removed the couch cushions and, together, yanked it open and extended it down into the double bed it secretly was. Mother made the bed, punching pillows neatly to flump them up for their heads. Then, as he was unbuttoning his shirt, she said, "Wait awhile, Tom."

"Why?"

"Because I say so."

"You look funny, Mom."

Mom sat down a moment, then stood up, went to the door and called. He listened to her calling and calling, "Douglas, Douglas, oh Doug! Douglasssssss!" over and over. Her calling floated out into the summer warm dark and never came back. The echoes paid no attention.

Douglas. Douglas. Douglas.

Douglas!

And as he sat on the floor, a coldness that was not ice cream and not winter, and not part of summer's heat, went through Tom. He noticed Mom's eyes sliding, blinking; the way she stood undecided and was nervous. All of these things.

She opened the screen door. Stepping out into the night, she walked down the steps and down the front sidewalk under the lilac bush. He listened to her moving feet.

She called again.

Silence.

She called twice more. Tom sat in the room. Any moment now, Douglas would answer from down the long long narrow street, "All right, Mom! All right, Mother! Hey!"

But he didn't answer. And for two minutes Tom sat looking at the made-up bed, the silent radio, the silent phonograph, at the chandelier with the crystal bobbins gleaming quietly, at the rug with the scarlet and purple curlicues on it. He stubbed his toe on the bed purposely to see if it hurt. It did.

Whining, the screen door opened and Mother said, "Come on, Tom. We'll take a walk."

"Where to?"

"Just down the block. Come on."

He took her hand. Together they walked down St. James Street. Underfoot the concrete was still warm, and the crickets were sounding louder against the darkening dark. They reached a corner, turned, and walked toward the West Ravine.

Off somewhere a car floated by, flashing its lights in the distance. There was such a complete lack of life, light, and activity. Here and there, back off from where they were walking, faint squares of light glowed where people were still up. But most of the houses, darkened, were sleeping already, and there were a few lightless places where the occupants of a dwelling sat talking low night talk on their front porches. You heard a porch swing squeaking as you walked by.

"I wish your father was home," said Mother. Her large hand squeezed around his small one. "Just wait'll I get that boy. The Lonely One's around again. Killing people. No one's safe any more. You never know when The Lonely One'll turn up or where. So help me, when Doug gets home I'll spank him within an inch of his life."

Now they had walked another block and were standing by the holy black silhouette of the German Baptist Church at the corner of Chapel Street and Glen Rock. In back of the church, a hundred yards away, the ravine began. He could smell it. It had a dark-sewer, rotten-foliage, thick-green odor. It was a wide ravine that cut and twisted across town—a jungle by day, a place to let alone at night, Mother often declared.

He should have felt encouraged by the nearness of the German Baptist Church but he was not, because the building was not illumined, was cold and useless as a pile of ruins on the ravine edge.

He was only ten years old. He knew little of death, fear, or dread. Death was the waxen effigy in the coffin when he was six and Great-grandfather passed away, looking like a great fallen vulture in his casket, silent, withdrawn, no more to tell him how to be a good boy, no more to comment succinctly on politics. Death was his little sister one morning when he awoke at the age of seven, looked into her crib, and saw her staring up at him with a blind, blue, fixed and frozen stare until the men came with a small wicker basket to take her away. Death was when he stood by her high chair four weeks later and suddenly realized she'd never be in it again, laughing and crying and making him jealous of her because she was born. That was death. And Death was The Lonely One, unseen, walking and standing behind trees, waiting in the country to come in, once or twice a year, to this town, to these streets, to these many places where there was little light, to kill one, two, three women in the past three years. That was Death. . . .

But this was more than Death. This summer night deep down under the stars was all things you would ever feel or see or hear in your life, drowning you all at once.

Leaving the sidewalk, they walked along a trodden, pebbled, weed-fringed path while the crickets rose in a loud full drumming chorus. He followed obediently behind brave, fine, tall Mother—defender of the universe. Together, then, they approached, reached, and paused at the very end of civilization.

The Ravine.

Here and now, down in that pit of jungled blackness were suddenly all the things he would never know or understand; all the things without names lived in the huddled tree shadow, in the odor of decay.

He realized he and his mother were alone.

Her hand *trembled*.

He felt the tremble. . . . Why? But she was bigger, stronger, more intelligent than himself, wasn't she? Did she, too, feel that intangible menace, that groping out of darkness, that crouching malignancy down below? Was there, then, no strength in growing up? No solace in being an adult? No sanctuary in life? No fleshly citadel strong enough to withstand the scrabbling assault of midnights? Doubts flushed him. Ice cream lived again in his throat, stomach, spine and limbs; he was instantly cold as a wind out of December gone.

He realized that all men were like this; that each person was to himself one alone. One oneness, a unit in a society, but always afraid. Like here, standing. If he should scream, if he should holler for help, would it matter?

Blackness could come swiftly, swallowing; in one titanically freezing moment all would be concluded. Long before dawn, long before police with flashlights might probe the dark, disturbed pathway, long before men with trembling brains could rustle down the pebbles to his help. Even if they were within five hundred yards of him now, and help *certainly* was, in three seconds a dark tide could rise to take all ten years from him and——

The essential impact of life's loneliness crushed his beginning-to-tremble body. Mother was alone, too. She could not look to the sanctity of marriage, the protection of her family's love, she could not look to the United States Constitution or the City Police, she could not look anywhere, in this very instant, save into her heart, and there she would find nothing but uncontrollable repugnance and a will to fear. In this instant it was an individual problem seeking an individual solution. He must accept being alone and work on from there.

He swallowed hard, clung to her. *Oh, Lord, don't let her die, please,* he thought. *Don't do anything to us. Father will be coming home from lodge meeting in an hour and if the house is empty——*

Mother advanced down the path into the primeval jungle. His voice trembled. "Mom, Doug's all right. Doug's all right. He's all right. Doug's all right!"

Mother's voice was strained, high. "He always comes through here. I tell him not to, but those darned kids, they come through here anyway. Some night he'll come through and never come out again——"

Never come out again. That could mean anything. Tramps. Criminals. Darkness. Accident. Most of all—death!

Alone in the universe.

There were a million small towns like this all over the world. Each as dark, as lonely, each as removed, as full of shuddering and wonder. The reedy playing of minor-key violins was the small towns' music, with no lights, but many shadows. Oh, the vast swelling loneliness of them. The secret damp ravines of them. Life was a horror lived in them at night, when at all sides sanity, marriage, children, happiness, were threatened by an ogre called Death.

Mother raised her voice into the dark. "Doug! Douglas!"

Suddenly both of them realized something was wrong.

The crickets had stopped chirping.

Silence was complete.

Never in his life a silence like this one. One so utterly complete. Why should the crickets cease? Why? What reason? They'd never stopped ever before. Not ever.

Unless. Unless—

Something was going to happen.

It was as if the whole ravine was tensing, bunching together its black fibers, drawing in power from sleeping countrysides all about, for miles and miles. From dew-sodden forest and dells and rolling hills where dogs tilted heads to moons, from all around the great silence was sucked into one center, and they were the core of it. In ten seconds now, something would happen, something would happen. The crickets kept their truce, the stars were so low he could almost brush the tinsel. There were swarms of them, hot and sharp.

Growing, growing, the silence. Growing, growing, the tenseness. Oh, it was so dark, so far away from everything. Oh, God!

And then, way way off across the ravine:

"Okay, Mom! Coming, Mother!"

And again: "Hi, Mom! Coming, Mom!"

And then the quick scuttering of tennis shoes padding down through the pit of the ravine as three kids came dashing, giggling. His brother Douglas, Chuck Woodman, and John Huff. Running, giggling . . .

The stars sucked up like the stung antennae of ten million snails.

The crickets sang!

The darkness pulled back, startled, shocked, angry. Pulled back, losing its appetite at being so rudely interrupted as it prepared to feed. As the dark retreated like a wave on the shore, three children piled out of it, laughing.

"Hi, Mom! Hi, Tom! Hey!"

It smelled like Douglas, all right. Sweat and grass and the odor of trees and branches and the creek about him.

"Young man, you're going to get a licking," declared Mother. She put away her fear instantly. Tom knew she would never tell anyone of it, ever. It would be in her heart, though, for all time, as it was in his heart for all time.

They walked home to bed in the late summer night. He was glad Douglas was alive. Very glad. For a moment there he had thought——

* * *

Far off in the dim moonlit country, over a viaduct and down a valley, a train rushed along whistling like a lost metal thing, nameless and running. Tom went to bed shivering, beside his brother, listening to that train whistle, and thinking of a cousin who lived way out in the country where that train ran now; a cousin who died of pneumonia late at night years and years ago——

He smelled the sweat of Doug beside him. It was magic. Tom stopped trembling.

"Only two things I know for sure, Doug," he whispered.

"What?"

"Nighttime's awful dark—is one."

"What's the other?"

"The ravine at night don't belong in Mr. Auffmann's Happiness Machine, if he ever builds it."

Douglas considered this awhile. "You can say that again."

They stopped talking. Listening, suddenly they heard footsteps coming down the street, under the trees, outside the house now, on the sidewalk. From her bed Mother called quietly,

"That's your father."

It was.

LATE AT night, on the front porch, Leo Auffmann wrote a list he could not see in the dark, exclaiming, "Ah!" or, "That's another!" when he hit upon a fine component. Then the front-door screen made a moth sound, tapping.

"Lena?" he whispered.

She sat down next to him on the swing, in her nightgown, not slim the way girls get when they are not loved at seventeen, not fat the way women get when they are not loved at fifty, but absolutely right, a roundness, a firmness, the way women are at any age, he thought, when there is no question.

She was miraculous. Her body, like his, was always thinking for her, but in a different way, shaping the children, or moving ahead of him into any room to change the atmosphere there to fit any particular mood he was in. There seemed no long periods of thought for her; thinking and doing moved from her head to her hand and back in a natural and gentle circuiting he could not and cared not to blueprint.

"That machine," she said at last, ". . . we don't need it."

"No," he said, "but sometimes you got to build for others. I been figuring, what to put in. Motion pictures? Radios? Stereoscopic viewers? All those in one place so any man can run his hand over it and smile and say, 'Yes, sir, that's happiness.'"

Yes, he thought, to make a contraption that in spite of wet feet, sinus trouble, rumpled beds, and those three-in-the-morning hours when monsters ate your soul, would manufacture happiness, like that magic salt mill that, thrown in the ocean, made salt forever and turned the sea to brine. Who wouldn't sweat his soul out through his pores to invent a machine like that? he asked the world, he asked the town, he asked his wife!

In the porch swing beside him, Lena's uneasy silence was an opinion.

Silent now, too, head back, he listened to the elm leaves above hissing in the wind.

Don't forget, he told himself, that sound, too, must be in the machine.

A minute later the porch swing, the porch, stood empty in the dark.

GRANDFATHER SMILED in his sleep.

Feeling the smile and wondering why it was there, he awoke. He lay quietly listening, and the smile was explained.

For he heard a sound which was far more important than birds or the rustle of new leaves. Once each year he woke this way and lay waiting for the sound which meant that summer had officially begun. And it began on a morning such as this when a boarder, a nephew, a cousin, a son or a grandson came out on the lawn below and moved in consecutively smaller quadrangles north and east and south and west with a clatter of rotating metal through the sweet summer grass. Clover blossoms, the few unharvested dandelion fires, ants, sticks, pebbles, remnants of last year's July Fourth squibs and punks, but predominantly clear green, a fount leaped up from the chattering mower. A cool soft fount; Grandfather imagined it tickling his legs, spraying his warm face, filling his nostrils with the timeless scent of a new season begun, with the promise that, yes, we'll *all* live another twelve months.

God bless the lawn mower, he thought. Who was the fool who made January first New Year's Day? No, they should set a man to watch the grasses across a million Illinois, Ohio, and Iowa lawns, and on that morning when it was long enough for cutting, instead of rachets and horns and yelling, there should be a great swelling symphony of lawn mowers reaping fresh grass upon the prairie lands. Instead of confetti and serpentine, people should throw grass spray at each other on the one day each year that really represents the Beginning!

He snorted at his own lengthy discussion of the affair, went to the window and leaned out into the mellow sunshine, and sure enough, there was a boarder, a young newspaperman named Forrester, just finishing a row.

"Morning, Mr. Spaulding!"

"Give 'em hell, Bill!" cried Grandpa heartily, and was soon downstairs eating Grandma's breakfast, with the bay window open so the rattling buzz of the lawn mower lolled about his eating.

"It gives you confidence," Grandpa said. "That lawn mower. *Listen* to it!"

"Won't be using the lawn mower much longer." Grandma set down a stack of wheat cakes. "They got a new kind of grass Bill Forrester's putting in this morning, never needs cutting. Don't know what they call it, but it just grows so long and no longer."

Grandpa stared at the woman. "You're finding a poor way to joke with me."

"Go look for yourself. Land's sake," said Grandma, "it was Bill Forrester's idea. The new grass is waiting in little flats by the side of the house. You just dig small holes here and there and put the new grass in spots. By the end of the year the new grass kills off the old, and you sell your lawn mower."

Grandpa was up from his chair, through the hall, and out the front door in ten seconds.

Bill Forrester left his machine and came over, smiling, squinting in the sun. "That's right," he said. "Bought the grass yesterday. Thought, while I'm on vacation I'd just plant it for you."

"Why wasn't I consulted about this? It's *my* lawn!" cried Grandfather.

"Thought you'd appreciate it, Mr. Spaulding."

"Well, I don't think I do appreciate it. Let's see this confounded grass of yours."

They stood by the little square pads of new grass. Grandpa toed at it with the end of his shoe suspiciously. "Looks like plain old grass to me. You sure some horse trader didn't catch you early in the morning when you weren't fully awake?"

"I've seen the stuff growing in California. Only so high and no higher. If it survives our climate it'll save us getting out here next year, once a week, to keep the darned stuff trimmed."

"That's the trouble with your generation," said Grandpa. "Bill, I'm ashamed of you, you a newspaperman. All the things in life that were put here to savor, you eliminate. Save time, save work, you say." He nudged the grass trays disrespectfully. "Bill, when you're my age, you'll find out it's the little savors and little things that count more than big ones. A walk on a spring morning is better than an eighty-mile ride in a hopped-up car, you know why? Because it's full of flavors, full of a lot of things growing. You've time to seek and find. I know—you're after the broad effect now, and I suppose that's fit and proper. But for a young man working on a newspaper, you got to look for grapes as well as watermelons. You greatly admire skeletons and I like fingerprints; well and good. Right now such things are bothersome to you, and I wonder if it isn't because you've never learned to use them. If you had your way you'd pass a law to abolish all the little jobs, the little things. But then you'd leave yourselves nothing to do between the big jobs and you'd have a devil of a time thinking up things to do so you wouldn't go crazy. Instead of that, why not let nature show you a few things? Cutting grass and pulling weeds can be a way of life, son."

Bill Forrester was smiling quietly at him.

"I know," said Grandpa, "I talk too much."

"There's no one I'd rather hear."

"Lecture continued, then. Lilacs on a bush are better than orchids. And dandelions and devil grass are better! Why? Because they bend you over and turn you away from all the people and the town for a little while and sweat you and get you down where you remember you got a nose again. And when you're all to yourself that way, you're really yourself for a little while; you get to thinking things through, alone. Gardening is the handiest excuse for being a philosopher. Nobody guesses, nobody accuses, nobody knows, but there you are, Plato in the peonies, Socrates force-growing his own hemlock. A man toting a sack of blood manure across his lawn is kin to Atlas letting the world spin easy on his shoulder. As Samuel Spaulding, Esquire, once said, 'Dig in the earth, delve in the soul.' Spin those mower blades, Bill, and walk in the spray of the Fountain of Youth. End of lecture. Besides, a mess of dandelion greens is good eating once in a while."

"How many years since you had dandelion greens for supper, sir?"

"We won't go into that!"

Bill kicked one of the grass flats slightly and nodded. "About this grass now. I didn't finish telling. It grows so close it's guaranteed to kill off clover and dandelions——"

"Great God in heaven! That means no dandelion wine next

year! That means no bees crossing our lot! You're out of your mind, son! Look here, how much did all this cost you?"

"A dollar a flat. I bought ten flats as a surprise."

Grandpa reached into his pocket, took out the old deep-mouthed purse, unclasped the silver clasp, and removed from it three five-dollar bills. "Bill, you've just made a great profit of five dollars on this transaction. I want you to deliver this load of unromantic grass into the ravine, the garbage dump—anywhere—but I ask you in a civil and humble voice not to plant it in my yard. Your motives are above reproach, but my motives, I feel, because I'm approaching my tenderest years, must be considered first."

"Yes, sir." Bill pocketed the bills reluctantly.

"Bill, you just plant this new grass some other year. The day after I die, Bill, you're free to tear up the whole damn lawn. Think you can wait another five years or so for an old orator to kick off?"

"I know darn well I can wait," Bill said.

"There's a thing about the lawn mower I can't even tell you, but to me it's the most beautiful sound in the world, the freshest sound of the season, the sound of summer, and I'd miss it fearfully if it wasn't there, and I'd miss the smell of cut grass."

Bill bent to pick up a flat. "Here I go to the ravine."

"You're a good, understanding young man, and will make a brilliant and sensitive reporter," said Grandfather, helping him. "This I predict!"

The morning passed, noon came on, Grandpa retired after lunch, read a little Whittier, and slept well on through the day. When he awoke at three the sun was streaming through the windows, bright and fresh. He lay in bed and was startled to hear the old, the familiar, the memorable sound.

"Why," he said, "someone's using the lawn mower! But the lawn was cut just this morning!"

He listened again. And yes, there it was, the endless droning chatter up and down, up and down.

He leaned out the window and gaped. "Why, it's Bill. Bill Forrester, you there! Has the sun got you? You're cutting the lawn *again*!"

Bill looked up, smiled a white smile, and waved. "I know! I think I missed a few spots!"

And while Grandpa lay in bed for the next five minutes, smiling and at ease, Bill Forrester cut the lawn north, then west, then south, and finally, in a great green spraying fountain, toward the east.

ON SUNDAY morning Leo Auffmann moved slowly through his garage, expecting some wood, a curl of wire, a hammer or wrench to leap up crying, "Start here!" But nothing leaped, nothing cried for a beginning.

Should a Happiness Machine, he wondered, be something you can carry in your pocket?

Or, he went on, should it be something that carries you in *its* pocket?

"One thing I absolutely *know*," he said aloud. "It should be *bright*!"

He set a can of orange paint in the center of the workbench, picked up a dictionary, and wandered into the house.

"Lena?" He glanced at the dictionary. "Are you 'pleased, contented, joyful, delighted'? Do you feel 'Lucky, fortunate'? Are things 'clever and fitting,' 'successful and suitable' for you?"

Lena stopped slicing vegetables and closed her eyes. "Read me the list again, please," she said.

He shut the book.

"What have I done, you got to stop and think an hour before you can tell me. All I ask is a simple yes or no! You're *not* contented, delighted, joyful?"

"Cows are contented, babies and old people in second childhood are delighted, God help them," she said. "As for 'joyful,' Leo? Look how I laugh scrubbing out the sink . . ."

He peered closely at her and his face relaxed. "Lena, it's true. A man doesn't appreciate. Next month, maybe, we'll get away."

"*I'm* not complaining!" she cried. "*I'm* not the one comes in with a list saying, 'Stick out your tongue.' Leo, do you ask what makes your heart beat all night? No! Next will you ask, What's marriage? Who knows, Leo? Don't ask. A man who thinks like that, how it runs, how things work, falls off the trapeze in the circus, chokes wondering how the muscles work in the throat. Eat, sleep, breathe, Leo, and stop staring at me like I'm something new in the house!"

Lena Auffmann froze. She sniffed the air.

"Oh, my God, look what you done!"

She yanked the oven door open. A great cloud of smoke poured through the kitchen.

"Happiness!" she wailed. "And for the first time in six months we have a fight! Happiness, and for the first time in twenty years it's not bread, it's charcoal for supper!"

When the smoke cleared, Leo Auffmann was gone.

The fearful clangor, the collision of man and inspiration, the flinging about of metal, lumber, hammer, nails, T square, screw driver, continued for many days. On occasion, defeated, Leo Auffmann loitered out through the streets, nervous, apprehensive, jerking his head at the slightest sound of distant laughter, listened to children's jokes, watching what made them smile. At night he sat on neighbors' crowded porches, listening to the old folks weigh and balance life, and at each explosion of merriment Leo Auffmann quickened like a general who has seen the forces of darkness routed and whose strategy has been reaffirmed. On his way home he felt triumphant until he was in his garage with the dead tools and the inanimate lumber. Then his bright face fell away in a pale funk, and to cover his sense of failure he banged and crashed the parts of his machine about as if they really did make sense. At last it began to shape itself and at the end of the ten days and nights, trembling with fatigue, self-dedicated, half starved, fumbling and looking as if he had been riven by lightning, Leo Auffmann wandered into his house.

The children, who had been screaming horribly at each other, fell silent, as if the Red Death had entered at the chiming of the clock.

"The Happiness Machine," husked Leo Auffmann, "is ready."

"Leo Auffmann," said his wife, "has lost fifteen pounds. He hasn't talked to his children in two weeks, they are nervous, they fight, listen! His wife is nervous, she's gained ten pounds, she'll need new clothes, look! Sure—the machine is ready. But happy? Who can say? Leo, leave off with the clock you're building. You'll never find a cuckoo big enough to go in it! Man was not made to tamper with such things. It's not against God, no, but it sure looks like it's against Leo Auffmann. Another week of this and we'll bury him in his machine!"

But Leo Auffmann was too busy noticing that the room was falling swiftly up.

How interesting, he thought, lying on the floor.

Darkness closed in a great wink on him as someone screamed something about that Happiness Machine, three times.

The first thing he noticed the next morning was dozens of birds fluttering around in the air stirring up ripples like colored stones thrown into an incredibly clear stream, gonging the tin roof of the garage softly.

A pack of multibred dogs pawfooted one by one into the yard to peer and whine gently through the garage door; four boys, two girls, and some men hesitated in the driveway and then edged along under the cherry trees.

Leo Auffmann, listening, knew what it was that had reached out and called them all into the yard.

The sound of the Happiness Machine.

It was the sort of sound that might be heard coming from a giant's kitchen on a summer day. There were all kinds of hummings, low and high, steady and then changing. Incredible foods were being baked there by a host of whirring golden bees as big as teacups. The giantess herself, humming contentedly under her breath, might glide to the door, as vast as all summer, her face a huge peach-colored moon gazing calmly out upon smiling dogs, corn-haired boys and flour-haired old men.

"Wait," said Leo Auffmann out loud. "I didn't turn the machine on this morning! Saul!"

Saul, standing in the yard below, looked up.

"Saul, did you turn it on?"

"You told me to warm it up half an hour ago!"

"All right, Saul. I forgot. I'm not awake." He fell back in bed.

His wife, bringing his breakfast up, paused by the window, looking down at the garage.

"Tell me," she said quietly. "If that machine is like you say, has it got an answer to making babies in it somewhere? Can that machine make seventy-year-old people twenty? Also, how does death look when you hide in there with all that happiness?"

"Hide!"

"If you died from overwork, what should I do today, climb in that big box down there and be happy? Also tell me, Leo, how is our life? You know how our house is. Seven in the morning, breakfast, the kids; all of you gone by eight-thirty and it's just me and washing and me and cooking and socks to be darned, weeds to be dug, or I run to the store or polish silver. Who's complaining? I'm just reminding you how the house is put together, Leo, what's in it! So now answer: How do you get all those things I said in one machine?"

"That's not how it's built!"

"I'm sorry. I got no time to look, then."

And she kissed his cheek and went from the room and he lay smelling the wind that blew from the hidden machine below, rich with the odor of those roasted chestnuts that sold in the autumn streets of a Paris he had never known. . . .

A cat moved unseen among the hypnotized dogs and boys to purr against the garage door, in the sound of snow-waves crumbling down a faraway and rhythmically breathing shore.

Tomorrow, thought Leo Auffmann, we'll try the machine, all of us, together.

Late that night he awoke and knew something had wakened him. Far away in another room he heard someone crying.

"Saul?" he whispered, getting out of bed.

In his room Saul wept, his head buried in his pillow. "No . . . no . . ." he sobbed. "Over . . . over . . ."

"Saul, you had a nightmare? Tell me about it, son."

But the boy only wept.

And sitting there on the boy's bed, Leo Auffmann suddenly thought to look out the window. Below, the garage doors stood open.

He felt the hairs rise along the back of his neck.

When Saul slept again, uneasily, whimpering, his father went downstairs and out to the garage where, not breathing, he put his hand out.

In the cool night the Happiness Machine's metal was too hot to touch.

So, he thought, Saul was here tonight.

Why? Was Saul unhappy, in need of the machine? No, happy,

but wanting to hold onto happiness always. Could you blame a boy wise enough to know his position who tried to keep it that way? No! And yet . . .

Above, quite suddenly, something white was exhaled from Saul's window. Leo Auffmann's heart thundered. Then he realized the window curtain had blown out into the open night. But it had seemed as intimate and shimmering a thing as a boy's soul escaping his room. And Leo Auffmann had flung up his hands as if to thwart it, push it back into the sleeping house.

Cold, shivering, he moved back into the house and up to Saul's room where he seized the blowing curtain in and locked the window tight so the pale thing could not escape again. Then he sat on the bed and put his hand on Saul's back.

"*A Tale of Two Cities*? Mine. *The Old Curiosity Shop*? Ha, that's Leo Auffmann's all right! *Great Expectations*? That *used* to be mine. But let *Great Expectations* be his, now!"

"What's this?" asked Leo Auffmann, entering.

"This," said his wife, "is sorting out the community property! When a father scares his son at night it's time to chop everything in half! Out of the way, Mr. Bleak House, Old Curiosity Shop. In all these books, no mad scientist lives like Leo Auffmann, none!"

"You're leaving, and you haven't even tried the machine!" he protested. "Try it once, you'll unpack, you'll stay!"

"*Tom Swift and His Electric Annihilator*—whose is that?" she asked. "Must I *guess*?"

Snorting, she gave *Tom Swift* to Leo Auffmann.

Very late in the day all the books, dishes, clothes, linens had been stacked one here, one there, four here, four there, ten here, ten there. Lena Auffmann, dizzy with counting, had to sit down. "All right," she gasped. "Before I go, Leo, prove you don't give nightmares to innocent sons!"

Silently Leo Auffmann led his wife into the twilight. She stood before the eight-foot-tall, orange-colored box.

"That's *happiness*?" she said. "Which button do I press to be overjoyed, grateful, contented, and much-obliged?"

The children had gathered now.

"Mama," said Saul, "don't!"

"I got to know what I'm yelling about, Saul." She got in the machine, sat down, and looked out at her husband, shaking her head. "It's not me needs this, it's you, a nervous wreck, shouting."

"Please," he said, "you'll see!"

He shut the door.

"Press the button!" he shouted in at his unseen wife.

There was a click. The machine shivered quietly, like a huge dog dreaming in its sleep.

"Papa!" said Saul, worried.

"Listen!" said Leo Auffmann.

At first there was nothing but the tremor of the machine's own secretly moving cogs and wheels.

"Is Mama all right?" asked Naomi.

"All right, she's fine! There, now . . . there!"

And inside the machine Lena Auffmann could be heard saying, "Oh!" and then again, "Ah!" in a startled voice. "Look at that!" said his hidden wife. "Paris!" and later, "London! There goes Rome! The Pyramids! The Sphinx!"

"The Sphinx, you hear, children?" Leo Auffmann whispered and laughed.

"Perfume!" cried Lena Auffmann, surprised.

Somewhere a phonograph played "The Blue Danube" faintly.

"Music! I'm dancing!"

"Only *thinks* she's dancing," the father confided to the world.

"Amazing!" said the unseen woman.

Leo Auffmann blushed. "What an understanding wife."

And then inside the Happiness Machine, Lena Auffmann began to weep.

The inventor's smile faded.

"She's crying," said Naomi.

"She can't be!"

"She is," said Saul.

"She simply can't be crying!" Leo Auffmann, blinking, pressed his ear to the machine. "But . . . yes . . . like a baby . . ."

He could only open the door.

"Wait." There his wife sat, tears rolling down her cheeks. "Let me finish." She cried some more.

Leo Auffmann turned off the machine, stunned.

"Oh, it's the saddest thing in the world!" she wailed. "I feel awful, terrible." She climbed out through the door. "First, there was Paris . . ."

"What's wrong with Paris?"

"I never even *thought* of being in Paris in my life. But now you got me thinking: Paris! So suddenly I want to be in Paris and I know I'm not!"

"It's almost as good, this machine."

"No. Sitting in there, I knew. I thought, it's not real!"

"Stop crying, Mama."

She looked at him with great dark wet eyes. "You had me dancing. We haven't danced in twenty years."

"I'll take you dancing tomorrow night!"

"No, no! It's not important, it *shouldn't* be important. But your machine says it's important! So I believe! It'll be all right, Leo, after I cry some more."

"What else?"

"What else? The machine says, 'You're young?' I'm not. It lies, that Sadness Machine!"

"Sad in what way?"

His wife was quieter now. "Leo, the mistake you made is you forgot some hour, some day, we all got to climb out of that thing and go back to dirty dishes and the beds not made. While you're in that thing, sure, a sunset lasts forever almost, the air smells good, the temperature is fine. All the things you want to last, last. But outside, the children wait on lunch, the clothes need buttons. And then, let's be frank, Leo, how long can you *look* at a sunset? Who *wants* a sunset to last? Who wants perfect temperature? Who wants air smelling good always? So after a while, who would notice? Better, for a minute or two, a sunset. After that, let's have something else. People are like that, Leo. How could you forget?"

"Did I?"

"Sunsets we always liked because they only happen once and go away."

"But, Lena, that's sad."

"No, if the sunset stayed and we got bored, that would be a real sadness. So two things you did you should never have. You made quick things go slow and stay around. You brought things faraway to our backyard where they don't belong, where they just tell you, 'No, you'll never travel, Lena Auffmann,

Paris you'll never see! Rome you'll *never* visit.' But I *always* knew that, so why tell me? Better to forget and make do, Leo, make do, eh?"

Leo Auffmann leaned against the machine for support. He snatched his burned hand away, surprised.

"So now what, Lena?" he said.

"It's not for me to say. I know only so long as this thing is here I'll want to come out, or Saul will want to come out like he did last night, and against our judgment sit in it and look at all those places so far away and every time we will cry and be no fit family for you."

"I don't understand," he said, "how I could be so wrong. Just let me check to see what you say is true." He sat down inside the machine. "You won't go away?"

His wife nodded. "We'll wait, Leo."

He shut the door. In the warm darkness he hesitated, pressed the button, and was just relaxing back in color and music, when he heard someone screaming.

"Fire, Papa! The machine's on fire!"

Someone hammered the door. He leaped up, bumped his head, and fell as the door gave way and the boys dragged him out. Behind him he heard a muffled explosion. The entire family was running now. Leo Auffmann turned and gasped, "Saul, call the fire department!"

Lena Auffmann caught Saul as he ran. "Saul," she said. "Wait."

There was a gush of flame, another muffled explosion. When the machine was burning very well indeed, Lena Auffmann nodded.

"All right, Saul," she said. "Run call the fire department."

Everybody who was anybody came to the fire. There was Grandpa Spaulding and Douglas and Tom and most of the boarders and some of the old men from across the ravine and all the children from six blocks around. And Leo Auffmann's children stood out front, proud of how fine the flames looked jumping from the garage roof.

Grandfather Spaulding studied the smoke ball in the sky and said, quietly, "Leo, was that it? Your Happiness Machine?"

"Some year," said Leo Auffmann, "I'll figure it and tell you."

Lena Auffmann, standing in the dark now, watched as the firemen ran in and out of the yard; the garage, roaring, settled upon itself.

"Leo," she said, "it won't take a year to figure. Look around. Think. Keep quiet a little bit. Then come tell me. I'll be in the house, putting books back on shelves, and clothes back in closets, fixing supper, supper's late, look how dark. Come, children, help Mama."

When the firemen and the neighbors were gone, Leo Auffmann was left with Grandfather Spaulding and Douglas and Tom, brooding over the smoldering ruin. He stirred his foot in the wet ashes and slowly said what he had to say.

"The first thing you learn in life is you're a fool. The last thing you learn in life is you're the same fool. In one hour, I've done a lot of thinking. I thought, Leo Auffmann is blind! . . . You want to see the *real* Happiness Machine? The one they patented a couple thousand years ago, it still runs, not good all the time, no! but it runs. It's been here all along."

"But the fire——" said Douglas.

"Sure, the fire, the garage! But like Lena said, it don't take a year to figure; what burned in the garage don't count!"

They followed him up the front-porch steps.

"Here," whispered Leo Auffmann, "the front window. Quiet, and you'll see it."

Hesitantly, Grandfather, Douglas, and Tom peered through the large windowpane.

And there, in small warm pools of lamplight, you could see what Leo Auffmann wanted you to see. There sat Saul and Marshall, playing chess on the coffee table. In the dining room Rebecca was laying out the silver. Naomi was cutting paper-doll dresses. Ruth was painting water colors. Joseph was running his electric train. Through the kitchen door, Lena Auffmann was sliding a pot roast from the steaming oven. Every hand, every head, every mouth made a big or little motion. You could hear their faraway voices under glass. You could hear someone singing in a high sweet voice. You could smell bread baking, too, and you knew it was real bread that would soon be covered with real butter. Everything was there and it was working.

Grandfather, Douglas, and Tom turned to look at Leo

Auffmann, who gazed serenely through the window, the pink light on his cheeks.

"Sure," he murmured. "There it is." And he watched with now-gentle sorrow and now-quick delight, and at last quiet acceptance as all the bits and pieces of this house mixed, stirred, settled, poised, and ran steadily again. "The Happiness Machine," he said. "The Happiness Machine."

A moment later he was gone.

Inside, Grandfather, Douglas, and Tom saw him tinkering, make a minor adjustment here, eliminate friction there, busy among all those warm, wonderful, infinitely delicate, forever mysterious, and ever-moving parts.

Then, smiling, they went down the steps into the fresh summer night.

TWICE A year they brought the big flapping rugs out into the yard and laid them where they looked out of place and uninhabited, on the lawn. Then Grandma and Mother came from the house with what looked to be the back rungs of those beautiful looped wire chairs downtown in the soda-fountain place. These great wire wands were handed around so they stood, Douglas, Tom, Grandma, Great-grandma, and Mother poised like a collection of witches and familiars over the dusty patterns of old Armenia. Then at a signal from Great-grandma, a blink of the eyes or a gumming of the lips, the flails were raised, the harping wires banged down again and again upon the rugs.

"Take that! And that!" said Great-grandma. "Get the flies, boys, kill the cooties!"

"Oh, you!" said Grandma to her mother.

They all laughed. The dust storm puffed up about them. Their laughing became choked.

Showers of lint, tides of sand, golden flakes of pipe tobacco fluttered, shivered on the exploded and re-exploded air. Pausing, the boys saw the tread of their shoes and the older people's shoes pressed a billion times in the warp and woof of this rug, now to be smoothed clean as the tide of their beating swept again and again along the oriental shore.

"There's where your husband spilled that coffee!" Grandma gave the rug a blow.

"Here's where you dropped the cream!" Great-grandma whacked up a great twister of dust.

"Look at the scuff marks. Boys, boys!"

"Double-Grandma, here's the ink from your pen!"

"Pshaw! Mine was purple ink. That's common blue!"

Bang!

"Look at the path worn from the hall door here to the kitchen door. Food. That's what brings the lions to the water hole. Let's shift it, put it back the other way around."

"Better yet, lock the men out of the house."

"Make them leave their shoes outside the door."

Bang, bang!

They hung the rugs on the wash line now, to finish the job. Tom looked at the intricate scrolls and loops, the flowers, the mysterious figures, the shuttling patterns.

"Tom, don't stand there. Strike, boy!"

"It's fun, seeing things," said Tom.

Douglas glanced up suspiciously. "What do you see?"

"The whole darn town, people, houses, here's our house!" Bang! "Our street!" Bang! "That black part there's the ravine!" Bang! "There's school!" Bang! "This funny cartoon here's you, Doug!" Bang! "Here's Great-grandma, Grandma, Mom." Bang! "How many years this rug been down?"

"Fifteen."

"Fifteen years of people stomping across it; I see every shoe print," gasped Tom.

"Land, boy, you got a tongue," said Great-grandma.

"I see all the things happened in that house in all those years right here!" Bang! "All the past, sure, but I can see the future, too. Just squinch up my eyes and peek around at the patterns, there, to see where we'll be walking, running around, tomorrow."

Douglas stopped swinging the beater. "What else you see in the rug?"

"Threads mostly," said Great-grandma. "Not much left but the underskin. See how the manufacturer wove the thing."

"Right!" said Tom mysteriously. "Threads one way, threads another. I see it all. Dire fiends. Deadly sinners. There's bad weather, there's good. Picnics. Banquets. Strawberry festivals." He tapped the beater from place to place portentously.

"That's some boardinghouse you got me running," said Grandma, glowing with exertion.

"It's all there, fuzzy-like. Hold your head on one side, Doug, get one eye almost shut. It's better at night, of course, inside, the rug on the floor, lamplight and all. Then you get shadows all shapes, light and dark, and watch the threads running off, feel the nap, run your hand around on the fur. Smells just like a desert, I bet. All hot and sandy, like inside a mummy case, maybe. Look, that red spot, that's the Happiness Machine burning up!"

"Catsup from somebody's sandwich, no doubt," said Mom.

"No, Happiness Machine," said Douglas, and was sad to see it burning there. He had been counting on Leo Auffmann to keep things in order, keep everybody smiling, keep the small gyroscope he often felt inside himself tilting toward the sun every time the earth tilted toward outer space and darkness. But no, there was Auffmann's folly, ashes and cinders. Bang! Bang! Douglas struck.

"Look, there's the green electric runabout! Miss Fern! Miss Roberta!" said Tom. "Honk, Honk!" Bang!

They all laughed.

"There's your life-strings, Doug, running along in knots. Too many sour apples. Pickles at bedtime!"

"Which one, where?" cried Douglas, peering.

"This one, one year from now, this one, two years from now, and this one, three, four, five years from now!"

Bang! The wire beater hissed like a snake in the blind sky.

"And one to grow on!" said Tom.

He hit the rug so hard all the dust of five thousand centuries jumped from the shocked texture, paused on the air a terrible moment, and even as Douglas stood, eyes squinted to see the warp, the woof, the shivering pattern, the Armenian avalanche of dust roared soundless upon, over, down and around, burying him forever before their eyes. . . .

HOW IT began with the children, old Mrs. Bentley never knew. She often saw them, like moths and monkeys, at the grocer's, among the cabbages and hung bananas, and she smiled at them and they smiled back. Mrs. Bentley watched them making footprints in winter snow, filling their lungs with autumn smoke, shaking down blizzards of spring apple-blossoms, but felt no fear of them. As for herself, her house was in extreme good order, everything set to its station, the floors briskly swept, the foods neatly tinned, the hatpins thrust through cushions, and the drawers of her bedroom bureaus crisply filled with the paraphernalia of years.

Mrs. Bentley was a saver. She saved tickets, old theater programs, bits of lace, scarves, rail transfers; all the tags and tokens of existence.

"I've a stack of records," she often said. "Here's Caruso. That was in 1916, in New York; I was sixty and John was still alive. Here's June Moon, 1924, I think, right after John died."

That was the huge regret of her life, in a way. The one thing she had most enjoyed touching and listening to and looking at she hadn't saved. John was far out in the meadow country, dated and boxed and hidden under grasses, and nothing remained of him but his high silk hat and his cane and his good suit in the closet. So much of the rest of him had been devoured by moths.

But what she could keep she had kept. Her pink-flowered dresses crushed among moth balls in vast black trunks, and cut-glass dishes from her childhood—she had brought them all when she moved to this town five years ago. Her husband had owned rental property in a number of towns, and, like a yellow ivory chess piece, she had moved and sold one after another, until now she was here in a strange town, left with only the trunks and furniture, dark and ugly, crouched about her like the creatures of a primordial zoo.

The thing about the children happened in the middle of summer. Mrs. Bentley, coming out to water the ivy upon her front porch, saw two cool-colored sprawling girls and a small boy lying on her lawn, enjoying the immense prickling of the grass.

At the very moment Mrs. Bentley was smiling down upon them with her yellow mask face, around a corner like an elfin band came an ice-cream wagon. It jingled out icy melodies, as crisp and rimmed as crystal wineglasses tapped by an expert, summoning all. The children sat up, turning their heads, like sunflowers after the sun.

Mrs. Bentley called, "Would you like some? Here!" The ice-cream wagon stopped and she exchanged money for pieces of the original Ice Age. The children thanked her with snow in their mouths, their eyes darting from her buttoned-up shoes to her white hair.

"Don't you want a bite?" said the boy.

"No, child. I'm old enough and cold enough; the hottest day won't thaw me," laughed Mrs. Bentley.

They carried the miniature glaciers up and sat, three in a row, on the shady porch glider.

"I'm Alice, she's Jane, and that's Tom Spaulding."

"How nice. And I'm Mrs. Bentley. They called me Helen."

They stared at her.

"Don't you believe they called me Helen?" said the old lady.

"I didn't know old ladies had first names," said Tom, blinking.

Mrs. Bentley laughed dryly.

"You never hear them used, he means," said Jane.

"My dear, when you are as old as I, they won't call you Jane, either. Old age is dreadfully formal. It's always 'Mrs.' Young people don't like to call you 'Helen.' It seems much too flip."

"How old *are* you?" asked Alice.

"I remember the pterodactyl." Mrs. Bentley smiled.

"No, but how old?"

"Seventy-two."

They gave their cold sweets an extra long suck, deliberating.

"That's *old*," said Tom.

"I don't feel any different now than when I was your age," said the old lady.

"*Our* age?"

"Yes. Once I was a pretty little girl just like you, Jane, and you, Alice."

They did not speak.

"What's the matter?"

"Nothing." Jane got up.

"Oh, you don't have to go so soon, I hope. You haven't finished eating . . . Is something the matter?"

"My mother says it isn't nice to fib," said Jane.

"Of course it isn't. It's very bad," agreed Mrs. Bentley.

"And not to *listen* to fibs."

"Who was fibbing to you, Jane?"

Jane looked at her and then glanced nervously away. "You were."

"I?" Mrs. Bentley laughed and put her withered claw to her small bosom. "About what?"

"About your age. About being a little girl."

Mrs. Bentley stiffened. "But I *was*, many years ago, a little girl just like you."

"Come on, Alice, Tom."

"Just a moment," said Mrs. Bentley. "Don't you believe me?"

"I don't know," said Jane. "No."

"But how ridiculous! It's perfectly obvious. Everyone was young once!"

"Not you," whispered Jane, eyes down, almost to herself. Her empty ice stick had fallen in a vanilla puddle on the porch floor.

"But of course I was eight, nine, ten years old, like all of you."

The two girls gave a short, quickly-sealed-up laugh.

Mrs. Bentley's eyes glittered. "Well, I can't waste a morning arguing with ten-year-olds. Needless to say, I was ten myself once and just as silly."

The two girls laughed. Tom looked uneasy.

"You're joking with us," giggled Jane. "You weren't really ten ever, were you, Mrs. Bentley?"

"You run on home!" the woman cried suddenly, for she could not stand their eyes. "I won't have you laughing."

"And your name's not really Helen?"

"Of course it's Helen!"

"Good-by," said the two girls, giggling away across the lawn under the seas of shade, Tom following them slowly. "Thanks for the ice cream!"

"Once I played *hopscotch*!" Mrs. Bentley cried after them, but they were gone.

Mrs. Bentley spent the rest of the day slamming teakettles about, loudly preparing a meager lunch, and from time to time going to the front door, hoping to catch those insolent fiends on their laughing excursions through the late day. But if they had appeared, what could she say to them, why should she worry about them?

"The idea!" said Mrs. Bentley to her dainty, rose-clustered teacup. "No one ever doubted I was a girl before. What a silly, horrible thing to do. I don't mind being old—not really—but I do resent having my childhood taken away from me."

She could see the children racing off under the cavernous trees with her youth in their frosty fingers, invisible as air.

After supper, for no reason at all, with a senseless certainty of motion, she watched her own hands, like a pair of ghostly gloves at a séance, gather together certain items in a perfumed kerchief. Then she went to her front porch and stood there stiffly for half an hour.

As suddenly as night birds the children flew by, and Mrs. Bentley's voice brought them to a fluttering rest.

"Yes, *Mrs.* Bentley?"

"Come up on this porch!" she commanded them, and the girls climbed the steps, Tom trailing after.

"Yes, Mrs. Bentley?" They thumped the "Mrs." like a bass piano chord, extra heavily, as if that were her first name.

"I've some treasures to show you." She opened the perfumed kerchief and peered into it as if she herself might be surprised. She drew forth a hair comb, very small and delicate, its rim twinkling with rhinestones.

"I wore this when I was nine," she said.

Jane turned it in her hand and said, "How nice."

"Let's see!" cried Alice.

"And here is a tiny ring I wore when I was eight," said Mrs. Bentley. "It doesn't fit my finger now. You look through it and see the Tower of Pisa ready to fall."

"Let's see it lean!" The girls passed it back and forth between them until Jane fitted it to her hand. "Why, it's just *my* size!" she exclaimed.

"And the comb fits *my* head!" gasped Alice.

Mrs. Bentley produced some jackstones. "Here," she said. "I once played with these."

She threw them. They made a constellation on the porch.

"And here!" In triumph she flashed her trump card, a postal picture of herself when she was seven years old, in a dress like a yellow butterfly, with her golden curls and blown blue-glass eyes and angelic pouting lips.

"Who's this little girl?" asked Jane.

"It's *me*!"

The two girls held onto it.

"But it doesn't look like you," said Jane simply. "Anybody could get a picture like this, somewhere."

They looked at her for a long moment.

"Any more pictures, Mrs. Bentley?" asked Alice. "Of you, later? You got a picture of you at fifteen, and one at twenty, and one at forty and fifty?"

The girls chortled.

"I don't have to show you anything!" said Mrs. Bentley.

"Then we don't have to believe you," replied Jane.

"But this picture proves I was young!"

"That's some other little girl, like us. You borrowed it."

"I was married!"

"Where's *Mr.* Bentley?"

"He's been gone a long time. If he were here, he'd tell you how young and pretty I was when I was twenty-two."

"But he's not here and he can't tell, so what does that prove?"

"I have a marriage certificate."

"You could have borrowed that, too. Only way I'll believe you were ever young"—Jane shut her eyes to emphasize how sure she was of herself—"is if you have someone say they saw you when you were ten."

"Thousands of people saw me but they're dead, you little fool—or ill, in other towns. I don't know a soul here, just moved here a few years ago, so no one saw me young."

"Well, there you *are*!" Jane blinked at her companions. "Nobody *saw* her!"

"Listen!" Mrs. Bentley seized the girl's wrist. "You must take these things on faith. Someday you'll be as old as I. People will say the same. 'Oh, no,' they'll say, 'Those vultures were never hummingbirds, those owls were never orioles, those parrots were never bluebirds!' One day you'll be like me!"

"No, we won't!" said the girls. "Will we?" they asked one another.

"Wait and see!" said Mrs. Bentley.

And to herself she thought, Oh, God, children are children, old women are old women, and nothing in between. They can't imagine a change they can't see.

"Your mother," she said to Jane. "Haven't you noticed, over the years, the change?"

"No," said Jane. "She's always the same."

And that was true. You lived with people every day and they never altered a degree. It was only when people had been off on a long trip, for years, that they shocked you. And she felt like a woman who has been on a roaring black train for seventy-two years, landing at last upon the rail platform and everyone crying: "Helen Bentley, is that *you*?"

"I guess we better go home," said Jane. "Thanks for the ring. It just fits me."

"Thanks for the comb. It's fine."

"Thanks for the picture of the little girl."

"Come back—you can't have those!" Mrs. Bentley shouted as they raced down the steps. "They're *mine*!"

"Don't!" said Tom, following the girls. "Give them back!"

"No, she stole them! They belonged to some other little girl. She stole them. Thanks!" cried Alice.

So no matter how she called after them, the girls were gone, like moths through darkness.

"I'm sorry," said Tom, on the lawn, looking up at Mrs. Bentley. He went away.

They took my ring and my comb and my picture, thought Mrs. Bentley, trembling there on the steps. Oh, I'm empty, empty; it's part of my life.

She lay awake for many hours into the night, among her trunks and trinkets. She glanced over at the neat stacks of materials and toys and opera plumes and said, aloud, "Does it really belong to me?"

Or was it the elaborate trick of an old lady convincing herself that she had a past? After all, once a time was over, it was done.

You were always in the present. She may have been a girl once, but was not now. Her childhood was gone and nothing could fetch it back.

A night wind blew in the room. The white curtain fluttered against a dark cane, which had leaned against that wall near the other bric-a-brac for many years. The cane trembled and fell out into a patch of moonlight, with a soft thud. Its gold ferule glittered. It was her husband's opera cane. It seemed as if he were pointing it at her, as he often had, using his soft, sad, reasonable voice when they, upon rare occasions, disagreed.

"Those children are right," he would have said. "They stole nothing from you, my dear. These things don't belong to you *here*, you *now*. They belonged to her, that other you, so long ago."

Oh, thought Mrs. Bentley. And then, as though an ancient phonograph record had been set hissing under a steel needle, she remembered a conversation she had once had with Mr. Bentley—Mr. Bentley, so prim, a pink carnation in his whisk-broomed lapel, saying, "My dear, you never will understand time, will you? You're always trying to be the things you were, instead of the person you are tonight. Why do you save those ticket stubs and theater programs? They'll only hurt you later. Throw them away, my dear."

But Mrs. Bentley had stubbornly kept them.

"It won't work," Mr. Bentley continued, sipping his tea. "No matter how hard you try to be what you once were, you can only be what you are here and now. Time hypnotizes. When you're nine, you think you've always been nine years old and will always be. When you're thirty, it seems you've always been balanced there on that bright rim of middle life. And then when you turn seventy, you are always and forever seventy. You're in the present, you're trapped in a young now or an old now, but there is no other now to be seen."

It had been one of the few, but gentle, disputes of their quiet marriage. He had never approved of her bric-a-brackery. "Be what you are, bury what you are not," he had said. "Ticket stubs are trickery. Saving things is a magic trick, with mirrors."

If he were alive tonight, what would he say?

"You're saving cocoons." That's what he'd say. "Corsets, in a way, you can never fit again. So why save them? You can't really

"YOU GOT the nickel tablet ready, Doug?"

"Sure." Doug licked his pencil good.

"What you got in there so far?"

"All the ceremonies."

"July Fourth and all that, dandelion-wine making and junk like bringing out the porch swing, huh?"

"Says here, I ate the first Eskimo Pie of the summer season June first, 1928."

"That wasn't summer, that was still spring."

"It was a 'first' anyway, so I put it down. Bought those new tennis shoes June twenty-fifth. Went barefoot in the grass June twenty-sixth. Busy, busy, busy, heck! Well, what you got to report this time, Tom? A new first, a fancy ceremony of some sort to do with vacation like creek-crab catching or water-strider-spider grabbing?"

"Nobody ever grabbed a water-strider spider in his life. You ever *know* anybody grabbed a water-strider spider? Go ahead, think!"

"I'm thinking."

"Well?"

"You're right. Nobody ever did. Nobody ever will, I guess. They're just too fast."

"It's not that they're fast. They just don't exist," said Tom. He thought about it and nodded. "That's right, they just never did exist at all. Well, what I got to report is this."

He leaned over and whispered in his brother's ear.

Douglas wrote it.

They both looked at it.

"I'll be darned!" said Douglas. "I never thought of that. That's brilliant! It's true. Old people never *were* children!"

"And it's kind of sad," said Tom, sitting still. "There's nothing we can do to help them."

"SEEMS LIKE the town is full of machines," said Douglas, running. "Mr. Auffmann and his Happiness Machine, Miss Fern and Miss Roberta and their Green Machine. Now, Charlie, what you handing me?"

"A Time Machine!" panted Charlie Woodman, pacing him. "Mother's, scout's, Injun's honor!"

"Travels in the past and future?" John Huff asked, easily circling them.

"Only in the past, but you can't have everything. Here we are."

Charlie Woodman pulled up at a hedge.

Douglas peered in at the old house. "Heck, that's Colonel Freeleigh's place. Can't be no Time Machine in there. He's no inventor, and if he was, we'd known about an important thing like a Time Machine years ago."

Charlie and John tiptoed up the front-porch steps. Douglas snorted and shook his head, staying at the bottom of the steps.

"Okay, Douglas," said Charlie. "Be a knucklehead. Sure, Colonel Freeleigh didn't *invent* this Time Machine. But he's got a proprietary interest in it, and it's been here all the time. We were too darned dumb to notice! So long, Douglas Spaulding, to you!"

Charlie took John's elbow as though he was escorting a lady, opened the front-porch screen and went in. The screen door did not slam.

Douglas had caught the screen and was following silently.

Charlie walked across the enclosed porch, knocked, and opened the inside door. They all peered down a long dark hall toward a room that was lit like an undersea grotto, soft green, dim, and watery.

"Colonel Freeleigh?"

Silence.

"He don't hear so good," whispered Charlie. "But he told me to just come on in and yell. *Colonel!*"

The only answer was the dust sifting down and around the

spiral stair well from above. Then there was a faint stir in that undersea chamber at the far end of the hall.

They moved carefully along and peered into a room which contained but two pieces of furniture—an old man and a chair. They resembled each other, both so thin you could see just how they had been put together, ball and socket, sinew and joint. The rest of the room was raw floor boards, naked walls and ceiling, and vast quantities of silent air.

"He looks dead," whispered Douglas.

"No, he's just thinking up new places to travel to," said Charlie, very proud and quiet. "Colonel?"

One of the pieces of brown furniture moved and it was the colonel, blinking around, focusing, and smiling a wild and toothless smile. "Charlie!"

"Colonel, Doug and John here came to——"

"Welcome, boys; sit down, sit down!"

The boys sat, uneasily, on the floor.

"But where's the——" said Douglas. Charlie jabbed his ribs quickly.

"Where's the what?" asked Colonel Freeleigh.

"Where's the point in *us* talking, he means." Charlie grimaced at Douglas, then smiled at the old man. "We got nothing to say. Colonel, *you* say something."

"Beware, Charlie, old men only lie in wait for people to ask them to talk. Then they rattle on like a rusty elevator wheezing up a shaft."

"Ching Ling Soo," suggested Charlie casually.

"Eh?" said the colonel.

"Boston," Charlie prompted, "1910."

"Boston, 1910 . . ." The colonel frowned. "Why, Ching Ling Soo, of course!"

"Yes, sir, Colonel."

"Let me see, now . . ." The colonel's voice murmured, it drifted away on serene lake waters. "Let me see . . ."

The boys waited.

Colonel Freeleigh closed his eyes.

"October first, 1910, a calm cool fine autumn night, the Boston Variety Theatre, yes, there it *is*. Full house, all waiting. Orchestra, fanfare, curtain! Ching Ling Soo, the great

Oriental Magician! There he is, on stage! And there I am, front row center! 'The Bullet Trick!' he cries. 'Volunteers!' The man next to me goes up. 'Examine the rifle!' says Ching. 'Mark the bullet!' says he. 'Now, fire this marked bullet from this rifle, using my face for a target, and,' says Ching, 'at the far end of the stage I will catch the bullet in my *teeth*!'"

Colonel Freeleigh took a deep breath and paused.

Douglas was staring at him, half puzzled, half in awe. John Huff and Charlie were completely lost. Now the old man went on, his head and body frozen, only his lips moving.

"'Ready, aim, fire!' cries Ching Ling Soo. Bang! The rifle cracks. Bang! Ching Ling Soo shrieks, he staggers, he falls, his face all red. Pandemonium. Audience on its feet. Something wrong with the rifle. 'Dead,' someone says. And they're right. Dead. Horrible, horrible . . . I'll always remember . . . his face a mask of red, the curtain coming down fast and the women weeping . . . 1910 . . . Boston . . . Variety Theatre . . . poor man . . . poor man . . ."

Colonel Freeleigh slowly opened his eyes.

"Boy, Colonel," said Charlie, "that was fine. Now how about Pawnee Bill?"

"Pawnee Bill . . . ?"

"And the time you was on the prairie way back in '75."

"Pawnee Bill . . ." The colonel moved into darkness. "Eighteen seventy-five . . . yes, me and Pawnee Bill on a little rise in the middle of that prairie, waiting. 'Sh!' says Pawnee Bill. 'Listen.' The prairie like a big stage all set for the storm to come. Thunder. Soft. Thunder again. Not so soft. And across that prairie as far as the eye could see this big ominous yellow-dark cloud full of black lightning, somehow sunk to earth, fifty miles wide, fifty miles long, a mile high, and no more than an inch off the ground. 'Lord!' I cried, 'Lord!'—from up on my hill—'Lord!' The earth pounded like a mad heart, boys, a heart gone to panic. My bones shook fit to break. The earth shook: rat-a-tat rat-a-tat, boom! Rumble. That's a rare word: rumble. Oh, how that mighty storm rumbled along down, up, and over the rises, and all you could see was the cloud and nothing inside. 'That's them!' cried Pawnee Bill. And the cloud was dust! Not vapors or rain, no, but prairie dust flung up from the tinder-dry grass like fine corn meal, like pollen all blazed with sunlight now, for the sun had come out. I shouted again! Why? Because in all that hell-fire filtering dust now a veil moved aside and I saw them, I swear it! The grand army of the ancient prairie: the bison, the buffalo!"

The colonel let the silence build, then broke it again.

"Heads like giant Negroes' fists, bodies like locomotives! Twenty, fifty, two hundred thousand iron missiles shot out of the west, gone off the track and flailing cinders, their eyes like blazing coals, rumbling toward oblivion!

"I saw that the dust rose up and for a little while showed me that sea of humps, of dolloping manes, black shaggy waves rising, falling . . . 'Shoot!' says Pawnee Bill. 'Shoot!' And I cock and aim. 'Shoot!' he says. And I stand there feeling like God's right hand, looking at that great vision of strength and violence going by, going by, midnight at noon, like a glinty funeral train all black and long and sad and forever and you don't fire at a funeral train, now do you, boys? *do* you? All I wanted then was for the dust to sink again and cover the black shapes of doom which pummeled and jostled on in great burdensome commotions. And, boys, the dust came down. The cloud hid the million feet that were drumming up the thunder and dusting out the storm. I heard Pawnee Bill curse and hit my arm. But I was glad I hadn't touched that cloud or the power within that cloud with so much as a pellet of lead. I just wanted to stand watching time bundle by in great trundlings all hid by the storm the bison made and carried with them toward eternity.

"An hour, three hours, six, it took for the storm to pass on away over the horizon toward less kind men than me. Pawnee Bill was gone, I stood alone, stone deaf. I walked all numb through a town a hundred miles south and heard not the voices of men and was satisfied not to hear. For a little while I wanted to remember the thunder. I hear it still, on summer afternoons like this when the rain shapes over the lake; a fearsome, wondrous sound . . . one I wish you might have heard. . . ."

The dim light filtered through Colonel Freeleigh's nose which was large and like white porcelain which cupped a very thin and tepid orange tea indeed.

"Is he asleep?" asked Douglas at last.

"No," said Charlie. "Just recharging his batteries."

Colonel Freeleigh breathed swiftly, softly, as if he'd run a long way. At last he opened his eyes.

"Yes, *sir*!" said Charlie, in admiration.

"Hello, Charlie." The colonel smiled at the boys puzzledly.

"That's Doug and that's John," said Charlie.

"How-de-do, boys."

The boys said hello.

"But——" said Douglas. "Where is the——?"

"My gosh, you're dumb!" Charlie jabbed Douglas in the arm. He turned to the colonel. "You were saying, sir?"

"*Was* I?" murmured the old man.

"The Civil War," suggested John Huff quietly. "Does he remember that?"

"Do I remember?" said the colonel. "Oh, I do, I do!" His voice trembled as he shut up his eyes again. "Everything! Except . . . which side I fought on. . . ."

"The *color* of your uniform——" Charlie began.

"Colors begin to run on you," whispered the colonel. "It's gotten hazy. I see soldiers with me, but a long time ago I stopped seeing color in their coats or caps. I was born in Illinois, raised in Virginia, married in New York, built a house in Tennessee and now, very late, here I am, good Lord, back in Green Town. So you see why the colors run and blend. . . ."

"But you remember which side of hills you fought on?" Charlie did not raise his voice. "Did the sun rise on your left or right? Did you march toward Canada or Mexico?"

"Seems some mornings the sun rose on my good right hand, some mornings over my left shoulder. We marched all directions. It's most seventy years since. You forget suns and mornings that long past."

"You remember winning, don't you? A battle won, somewhere?"

"No," said the old man, deep under. "I don't remember anyone winning anywhere any time. War's never a winning thing, Charlie. You just lose all the time, and the one who loses last asks for terms. All I remember is a lot of losing and sadness and nothing good but the end of it. The end of it, Charles, that was a winning all to itself, having nothing to do with guns. But I don't suppose that's the kind of victory you boys mean for me to talk on."

"Antietam," said John Huff. "Ask about Antietam."

"I was there."

The boys' eyes grew bright. "Bull Run, ask him Bull Run . . ."

"I was there." Softly.

"What about Shiloh?"

"There's never been a year in my life I haven't thought, what a lovely name and what a shame to see it only on battle records."

"Shiloh, then. Fort Sumter?"

"I saw the first puffs of powder smoke." A dreaming voice. "So many things come back, oh, so many things. I remember songs. 'All's quiet along the Potomac tonight, where the soldiers lie peacefully dreaming; their tents in the rays of the clear autumn moon, or the light of the watchfire, are gleaming.' Remember, remember . . . 'All quiet along the Potomac tonight; no sound save the rush of the river; while soft falls the dew on the face of the dead—the picket's off duty forever!' . . . After the surrender, Mr. Lincoln, on the White House balcony asked the band to play, 'Look away, look away, look away, Dixie land . . .' And then there was the Boston lady who one night wrote a song will last a thousand years: 'Mine eyes have seen the glory of the coming of the Lord; He is trampling out the vintage where the grapes of wrath are stored.' Late nights I feel my mouth move singing back in another time. 'Ye Cavaliers of Dixie! Who guard the Southern shores . . .' 'When the boys come home in triumph, brother, with the laurels they shall gain . . .' So many songs, sung on both sides, blowing north, blowing south on the night winds. 'We are coming, Father Abraham, three hundred thousand more . . .' 'Tenting tonight, tenting tonight, tenting on the old camp ground.' 'Hurrah, hurrah, we bring the Jubilee, hurrah, hurrah, the flag that makes us free . . .'"

The old man's voice faded.

The boys sat for a long while without moving. Then Charlie turned and looked at Douglas and said, "Well, is he or isn't he?"

Douglas breathed twice and said, "He sure *is*."

The colonel opened his eyes.

"I sure am *what*?" he asked.

"A Time Machine," murmured Douglas. "A Time Machine."

The colonel looked at the boys for a full five seconds. Now it was his voice that was full of awe.

"Is that what you boys call me?"

"Yes, sir, Colonel."

"Yes, sir."

The colonel sat slowly back in his chair and looked at the boys and looked at his hands and then looked at the blank wall beyond them steadily.

Charlie arose. "Well, I guess we better go. So long and thanks, Colonel."

"What? Oh, so long, boys."

Douglas and John and Charlie went on tiptoe out the door.

Colonel Freeleigh, though they crossed his line of vision, did not see them go.

In the street, the boys were startled when someone shouted from a first-floor window above, "Hey!"

They looked up.

"Yes, sir, Colonel?"

The colonel leaned out, waving one arm.

"I thought about what you said, boys!"

"Yes, sir?"

"And—you're right! Why didn't I *think* of it before! A Time Machine, by God, a Time Machine!"

"Yes, sir."

"So long, boys. Come aboard any time!"

At the end of the street they turned again and the colonel was still waving. They waved back, feeling warm and good, then went on.

"Chug-a-chug," said John. "I can travel twelve years into the past. Wham-chug-ding!"

"Yeah," said Charlie, looking back at that quiet house, "but you can't go a hundred years."

"No," mused John, "I can't go a hundred years. That's really traveling. That's really some machine."

They walked for a full minute in silence, looking at their feet. They came to a fence.

"Last one over this fence," said Douglas, "is a girl."

All the way home they called Douglas "Dora."

LONG AFTER midnight Tom woke to find Douglas scribbling rapidly in the nickel tablet, by flashlight.

"Doug, what's up?"

"Up? Everything's up! I'm counting my blessings, Tom! Look here; the Happiness Machine didn't work out, did it? But, who cares! I got the whole year lined up, anyway. Need to run anywhere on the main streets, I got the Green Town Trolley to look around and spy on the world from. Need to run anywhere *off* the main streets, I knock on Miss Fern and Miss Roberta's door and they charge up the batteries on their electric runabout and we go sailing down the sidewalks. Need to run down alleys and over fences, to see that part of Green Town you only see around back and behind and creep up on, and I got my brand-new sneakers. Sneakers, runabout, trolley! I'm set! But even better, Tom, even better, listen! If I want to go where no one else can go because they're not smart enough to even think of it, if I want to charge back to 1890 and then transfer to 1875 and transfer again crosstown to 1860 I just hop on the old Colonel Freeleigh Express! I'm writing it down here this way: 'Maybe old people were never children, like we claim with Mrs. Bentley, but, big or little, some of them were standing around at Appomattox the summer of 1865.' They got Indian vision and can sight back further than you and me will ever sight ahead."

"That sounds swell, Doug; what does it mean?"

Douglas went on writing. "It means you and me ain't got half the chance to be far-travelers they have. If we're lucky we'll hit forty, forty-five, fifty. That's just a jog around the block to them. It's when you hit ninety, ninety-five, a hundred, that you're far-traveling like heck."

The flashlight went out.

They lay there in the moonlight.

"Tom," whispered Douglas. "I got to travel all those ways. See what I can see. But most of all I got to visit Colonel Freeleigh once, twice, three times a week. He's better than all the other machines. He talks, you listen. And the more he talks the more he gets you to peering around and noticing things. He tells you you're riding on a very special train, by gosh, and sure enough, it's true. He's been down the track, and knows. And now here we come, you and me, along the same track, but further on, and so much looking and snuffing and handling things to do, you need old Colonel Freeleigh to shove and say look alive so you remember every second! Every darn thing there is to remember! So when kids come around when you're real old, you can do for them what the colonel once did for you. That's the way it is, Tom, I got to spend a lot of time visiting him and listening so I can go far-traveling with him as often as he can."

Tom was silent a moment. Then he looked over at Douglas there in the dark.

"Far-traveling. You make that up?"

"Maybe yes and maybe no."

"Far-traveling," whispered Tom.

"Only one thing I'm sure of," said Douglas, closing his eyes. "It sure sounds lonely."

BANG!

A door slammed. In an attic dust jumped off bureaus and bookcases. Two old women collapsed against the attic door, each scrabbling to lock it tight, tight. A thousand pigeons seemed to have leaped off the roof right over their heads. They bent as if burdened, ducked under the drum of beating wings. Then they stopped, their mouths surprised. What they heard was only the pure sound of panic, their hearts in their chests . . . Above the uproar, they tried to make themselves heard.

"What've we done! Poor Mister Quartermain!"

"We must've killed him. And someone must've seen and followed us. Look . . ."

Miss Fern and Miss Roberta peered from the cobwebbed attic window. Below, as if no great tragedy had occurred, the oaks and elms continued to grow in fresh sunlight. A boy strolled by on the sidewalk, turned, strolled by again, looking up.

In the attic the old women peered at each other as if trying to see their faces in a running stream.

"The police!"

But no one hammered the downstairs door and cried, "In the name of the law!"

"Who's that boy down there?"

"Douglas, Douglas Spaulding! Lord, he's come to ask for a ride in our Green Machine. He doesn't know. Our pride has ruined us. Pride and that electrical contraption!"

"That terrible salesman from Gumport Falls. It's his fault, him and his talking."

Talking, talking, like soft rain on a summer roof.

Suddenly it was another day, another noon. They sat with white fans and dishes of cool, trembling lime Jell-O on their arbored porch.

Out of the blinding glare, out of the yellow sun, glittering, splendid as a prince's coach . . .

THE GREEN MACHINE!

It glided. It whispered, an ocean breeze. Delicate as maple leaves, fresher than creek water, it purred with the majesty of cats prowling the noontide. In the machine, his Panama hat afloat in Vaseline above his ears, the salesman from Gumport Falls! The machine, with a rubber tread, soft, shrewd, whipped up their scalded white sidewalk, whirred to the lowest porch step, twirled, stopped. The salesman leaped out, blocked off the sun with his Panama. In this small shadow, his smile flashed.

"The name is William Tara! And this—" He pinched a bulb. A seal barked. "—is the horn!" He lifted black satin cushions. "Storage batteries!" A smell of lightning blew on the hot air. "Steering lever! Foot rest! Overhead parasol! Here, *in toto*, is The Green Machine!"

In the dark attic the ladies shuddered, remembering, eyes shut.

"Why didn't we stab him with our darning needles!"

"Shh! Listen."

Someone knocked on the front door downstairs. After a time the knocking stopped. They saw a woman cross the yard and enter the house next door.

"Only Lavinia Nebbs, come with an empty cup, to borrow sugar, I guess."

"Hold me, I'm afraid."

They shut their eyes. The memory-play began again. An old straw hat on an iron trunk was suddenly flourished, it seemed, by the man from Gumport Falls.

"Thanks, I *will* have some iced tea." You could hear the cool liquid shock his stomach, in the silence. Then he turned his gaze upon the old ladies like a doctor with a small light, looking into their eyes and nostrils and mouths. "Ladies, I know you're both vigorous. You *look* it. Eighty years"—he snapped his fingers—"mean nothing to you! But there are times, mind, when you're so busy, busy, you need a friend indeed, a friend in need, and *that* is the two-seater Green Machine."

He fixed his bright, stuffed-fox, green-glass-eyed gaze upon that wonderful merchandise. It stood, smelling new, in the hot sunlight, waiting for them, a parlor chair comfortably put to wheels.

"Quiet as a swan's feather." They felt him breathe softly in their faces. "Listen." They listened. "The storage batteries are fully charged and ready now! Listen! Not a tremor, not a sound. Electric, ladies. You recharge it every night in your garage!"

"It couldn't—that is——" The younger sister gulped some iced tea. "It couldn't electrocute us accidentally?"

"Perish the thought!"

He vaulted to the machine again, his teeth like those you saw in dental windows, alone, grimacing at you, as you passed by late at night.

"Tea parties!" He waltzed the runabout in a circle. "Bridge clubs. *Soirées.* Galas. Luncheons. Birthday gatherings! D.A.R. breakfasts." He purred away as if running off forever. He returned in a rubber-tired hush. "Gold Star Mother suppers." He sat primly, corseted by his supple characterization of a woman. "Easy steering. Silent, elegant arrivals and departures. No license needed. On hot days—take the breeze. Ah . . ." He glided by the porch, head back, eyes closed deliciously, hair tousling in the wind thus cleanly sliced through.

He trudged reverently up the porch stairs, hat in hand, turning to gaze at the trial model as at the altar of a familiar church. "Ladies," he said softly, "twenty-five dollars down. Ten dollars a month, for two years."

Fern was first down the steps onto the double seat. She sat apprehensively. Her hand itched. She raised it. She dared tweak the rubber bulb horn.

A seal barked.

Roberta, on the porch, screamed hilariously and leaned over the railing.

The salesman joined their hilarity. He escorted the older sister down the steps, roaring, at the same time taking out his pen and searching in his straw hat for some piece of paper or other.

"And so we bought it!" remembered Miss Roberta, in the attic, horrified at their nerve. "We should've been warned! Always *did* think it looked like a little car off the carnival roller coaster!"

"Well," said Fern defensively, "my hip's bothered me for years, and you always get tired walking. It seemed so refined, so regal. Like in the old days when women wore hoop skirts. They *sailed*! The Green Machine sailed *so* quietly."

Like an excursion boat, wonderfully easy to steer, a baton handle you twitched with your hand, so.

Oh, that glorious and enchanted first week—the magical afternoons of golden light, humming through the shady town on a dreaming, timeless river, seated stiffly, smiling at passing acquaintances, sedately putting out their wrinkled claws at every turn, squeezing a hoarse cry from the black rubber horn at intersections, sometimes letting Douglas or Tom Spaulding or any of the other boys who trotted, chatting, alongside, hitch a little ride. Fifteen slow and pleasurable miles an hour top speed. They came and went through the summer sunlight and shadow, their faces freckled and stained by passing trees, going and coming like an ancient, wheeled vision.

"And then," whispered Fern, "this afternoon! Oh, this afternoon!"

"It was an accident."

"But we ran away, and that's criminal!"

This noon. The smell of the leather cushions under their bodies, the gray perfume smell of their own sachets trailing back as they moved in their silent Green Machine through the small, languorous town.

It happened quickly. Rolling soft onto the sidewalk at noon, because the streets were blistering and fiery, and the only shade was under the lawn trees, they had glided to a blind corner, bulbing their throaty horn. Suddenly, like a jack-in-the-box, Mister Quartermain had tottered from nowhere!

"Look out!" screamed Miss Fern.

"Look out!" screamed Miss Roberta.

"Look out!" cried Mister Quartermain.

The two women grabbed each other instead of the steering stick.

There was a terrible thud. The Green Machine sailed on in the hot daylight, under the shady chestnut trees, past the ripening apple trees. Looking back only once, the two old ladies' eyes filled with faded horror.

The old man lay on the sidewalk, silent.

"And here we are," mourned Miss Fern in the darkening attic. "Oh, why didn't we stop! Why did we run away?"

"Shh!" They both listened.

The rapping downstairs came again.

When it stopped they saw a boy cross the lawn in the dim light. "Just Douglas Spaulding come for a ride again." They both sighed.

The hours passed; the sun was going down.

"We've been up here all afternoon," said Roberta tiredly. "We can't stay in the attic three weeks hiding till everybody forgets."

"We'd starve."

"What'll we do, then? Do you think anyone saw and followed us?" They looked at each other.

"No. Nobody saw."

The town was silent, all the tiny houses putting on lights. There was a smell of watered grass and cooking suppers from below.

"Time to put on the meat," said Miss Fern. "Frank'll be coming home in ten minutes."

"Do we dare go down?"

"Frank'd call the police if he found the house empty. That'd make things worse."

The sun went swiftly. Now they were only two moving things in the musty blackness. "Do you," wondered Miss Fern, "think he's dead?"

"Mister Quartermain?"

A pause. "Yes."

Roberta hesitated. "We'll check the evening paper."

They opened the attic door and looked carefully at the steps leading down. "Oh, if Frank hears about this, he'll take our Green Machine away from us, and it's *so* lovely and nice riding and getting the cool wind and seeing the town."

"We won't tell him."

"Won't we?"

They helped each other down the creaking stairs to the second floor, stopping to listen. . . . In the kitchen they peered at the pantry, peeked out windows with frightened eyes, and finally set to work frying hamburger on the stove. After five minutes of working silence Fern looked sadly over at Roberta and said, "I've been thinking. We're old and feeble and don't like to admit it. We're dangerous. We owe a debt to society for running off——"

"And——?" A kind of silence fell on the frying in the kitchen as the two sisters faced each other, nothing in their hands.

"I think that"—Fern stared at the wall for a long time—"we shouldn't drive the Green Machine ever again."

Roberta picked up a plate and held it in her thin hand. "Not—ever?" she said.

"No."

"But," said Roberta, "we don't have to—to get rid of it, do we? We *can* keep it, can't we?"

Fern considered this. "Yes, I guess we can keep it."

"At least that'll be something. I'll go out now and disconnect the batteries."

Roberta was leaving just as Frank, their younger brother, only fifty-six years, entered.

"Hi, sisters!" he cried.

Roberta brushed past him without a word and walked out into the summer dusk. Frank was carrying a newspaper which Fern immediately snatched from him. Trembling, she looked it through and through, and, sighing, gave it back to him.

"Saw Doug Spaulding outside just now. Said he had a message for you. Said for you not to worry—he saw everything and everything's all right. What did he mean by that?"

"I'm sure I wouldn't know." Fern turned her back and searched for her handkerchief.

"Oh well, these kids." Frank looked at his sister's back for a long moment, then shrugged.

"Supper almost ready?" he asked pleasantly.

"Yes." Fern set the kitchen table.

There was a bulbing cry from outside. Once, twice, three times—far away.

"What's that?" Frank peered through the kitchen window into the dusk. "What's Roberta up to? Look at her out there, sitting in the Green Machine, poking the rubber horn!"

Once, twice more, in the dusk, softly, like some kind of mournful animal, the bulbing sound was pinched out.

"What's got into *her*?" demanded Frank.

"You just leave her alone!" screamed Fern.

Frank looked surprised.

A moment later Roberta entered quietly, without looking at anyone, and they all sat down to supper.

THE FIRST light on the roof outside; very early morning. The leaves on all the trees tremble with a soft awakening to any breeze the dawn may offer. And then, far off, around a curve of silver track, comes the trolley, balanced on four small steel-blue wheels, and it is painted the color of tangerines. Epaulets of shimmery brass cover it, and pipings of gold; and its chrome bell bings if the ancient motorman taps it with a wrinkled shoe. The numerals on the trolley's front and sides are bright as lemons. Within, its seats prickle with cool green moss. Something like a buggy whip flings up from its roof to brush the spider thread high in the passing trees from which it takes its juice. From every window blows an incense, the all-pervasive blue and secret smell of summer storms and lightning.

Down the long elm-shadowed streets the trolley moves along, the motorman's gray-gloved hand touched gently, timelessly, to the levered controls.

At noon the motorman stopped his car in the middle of the block and leaned out. "Hey!"

And Douglas and Charlie and Tom and all the boys and girls on the block saw the gray glove waving, and dropped from trees and left skip ropes in white snakes on lawns, to run and sit in the green plush seats, and there was no charge. Mr. Tridden, the conductor, kept his glove over the mouth of the money box as he moved the trolley on down the shady block, calling.

"Hey!" said Charlie. "Where we going?"

"Last ride," said Mr. Tridden, eyes on the high electric wire ahead. "No more trolley. Bus starts to run tomorrow. Going to retire me with a pension, they are. So—a free ride for everyone! Watch out!"

He ricocheted the brass handle, the trolley groaned and swung round an endless green curve, and all the time in the world held still, as if only the children and Mr. Tridden and his miraculous machine were riding an endless river, away.

"Last day?" asked Douglas, stunned. "They can't *do* that! It's bad enough the Green Machine is gone, locked up in the garage, and no arguments. And bad enough my new tennis shoes are getting old and slowing down! How'll I get around? But . . . But . . . They *can't* take off the trolley! Why," said Douglas, "no matter how you look at it, a bus ain't a trolley. Don't make the same kind of noise. Don't have tracks or wires, don't throw sparks, don't pour sand on the tracks, don't have the same colors, don't have a bell, don't let down a step like a trolley does!"

"Hey, that's right," said Charlie. "I always get a kick watching a trolley let down the step, like an accordion."

"Sure," said Douglas.

And then they were at the end of the line, the silver tracks, abandoned for eighteen years, ran on into rolling country. In 1910 people took the trolley out to Chessman's Park with vast picnic hampers. The track, never ripped up, still lay rusting among the hills.

"Here's where we turn around," said Charlie.

"Here's where you're wrong!" Mr. Tridden snapped the emergency generator switch. "Now!"

The trolley, with a bump and a sailing glide, swept past the city limits, turned off the street, and swooped downhill through intervals of odorous sunlight and vast acreages of shadow that smelled of toadstools. Here and there creek waters flushed the tracks and sun filtered through trees like green glass. They slid whispering on meadows washed with wild sunflowers past abandoned way stations empty of all save transfer-punched confetti, to follow a forest stream into a summer country, while Douglas talked.

"Why, just the *smell* of a trolley, that's different. I been on Chicago busses; they smell funny."

"Trolleys are too slow," said Mr. Tridden. "Going to put busses on. Busses for people and busses for school."

The trolley whined to a stop. From overhead Mr. Tridden reached down huge picnic hampers. Yelling, the children helped him carry the baskets out by a creek that emptied into a silent lake where an ancient bandstand stood crumbling into termite dust.

They sat eating ham sandwiches and fresh strawberries and waxy oranges and Mr. Tridden told them how it had been twenty years ago, the band playing on that ornate stand at night, the men pumping air into their brass horns, the plump conductor flinging perspiration from his baton, the children and fireflies running in the deep grass, the ladies with long dresses and high pompadours treading the wooden xylophone walks with men in choking collars. There was the walk now, all softened into a fiber mush by the years. The lake was silent and blue and serene, and fish peacefully threaded the bright reeds, and the motorman murmured on and on, and the children felt it was some other year, with Mr. Tridden looking wonderfully young, his eyes lighted like small bulbs, blue and electric. It was a drifting, easy day, nobody rushing, and the forest all about, the sun held in one position, as Mr. Tridden's voice rose and fell, and a darning needle sewed along the air, stitching, restitching designs both golden and invisible. A bee settled into a flower, humming and humming. The trolley stood like an enchanted calliope, simmering where the sun fell on it. The trolley was on their hands, a brass smell, as they ate ripe cherries. The bright odor of the trolley blew from their clothes on the summer wind.

A loon flew over the sky, crying.

Somebody shivered.

Mr. Tridden worked on his gloves. "Well, time to go. Parents'll think I stole you all for good."

The trolley was silent and cool dark, like the inside of an ice-cream drugstore. With a soft green rustling of velvet buff, the seats were turned by the quiet children so they sat with their backs to the silent lake, the deserted bandstand and the wooden planks that made a kind of music if you walked down the shore on them into other lands.

Bing! went the soft bell under Mr. Tridden's foot and they soared back over sun-abandoned, withered flower meadows, through woods, toward a town that seemed to crush the sides of the trolley with bricks and asphalt and wood when Mr. Tridden stopped to let the children out in shady streets.

Charlie and Douglas were the last to stand near the opened tongue of the trolley, the folding step, breathing electricity, watching Mr. Tridden's gloves on the brass controls.

Douglas ran his fingers on the green creek moss, looked at the silver, the brass, the wine color of the ceiling.

"Well . . . So long again, Mr. Tridden."

"Good-by, boys."

"See you around, Mr. Tridden."

"See you around."

There was a soft sigh of air; the door collapsed gently shut, tucking up its corrugated tongue. The trolley sailed slowly down the late afternoon, brighter than the sun, all tangerine, all flashing gold and lemon, turned a far corner, wheeling, and vanished, gone away.

"School busses!" Charlie walked to the curb. "Won't even give us a chance to be late to school. Come get you at your front door. Never be late again in all our lives. Think of that nightmare, Doug, just think it all over."

But Douglas, standing on the lawn, was seeing how it would be tomorrow, when the men would pour hot tar over the silver tracks so you would never know a trolley had ever run this way. He knew it would take as many years as he could think of now to forget the tracks, no matter how deeply buried. Some morning in autumn, spring, or winter he knew he'd wake and, if he didn't go near the window, if he just lay deep and snug and warm in his bed, he would hear it, faint and far away.

And around the bend of the morning street, up the avenue, between the even rows of sycamore, elm and maple, in the quietness before the start of living, past his house he would hear the familiar sounds. Like the ticking of a clock, the rumble of a dozen metal barrels rolling, the hum of a single immense dragonfly at dawn. Like a merry-go-round, like a small electrical storm, the color of blue lightning, coming, here, and gone. The trolley's chime! The hiss like a soda-fountain spigot as it let down and took up its step, and the starting of the dream again, as on it sailed along its way, traveling a hidden and buried track to some hidden and buried destination. . . .

"Kick-the-can after supper?" asked Charlie.

"Sure," said Douglas. "Kick-the-can."

THE FACTS about John Huff, aged twelve, are simple and soon stated. He could pathfind more trails than any Choctaw or Cherokee since time began, could leap from the sky like a chimpanzee from a vine, could live underwater two minutes and slide fifty yards downstream from where you last saw him. The baseballs you pitched him he hit in the apple trees, knocking down harvests. He could jump six-foot orchard walls, swing up branches faster and come down, fat with peaches, quicker than anyone else in the gang. He ran laughing. He sat easy. He was not a bully. He was kind. His hair was dark and curly and his teeth were white as cream. He remembered the words to all the cowboy songs and would teach you if you asked. He knew the names of all the wild flowers and when the moon would rise and set and when the tides came in or out. He was, in fact, the only god living in the whole of Green Town, Illinois, during the twentieth century that Douglas Spaulding knew of.

And right now he and Douglas were hiking out beyond town on another warm and marble-round day, the sky blue blown-glass reaching high, the creeks bright with mirror waters fanning over white stones. It was a day as perfect as the flame of a candle.

Douglas walked through it thinking it would go on this way forever. The perfection, the roundness, the grass smell traveled on out ahead as far and fast as the speed of light. The sound of a good friend whistling like an oriole, pegging the softball, as you horse-danced, key-jingled the dusty paths, all of it was complete, everything could be touched; things stayed near, things were at hand and would remain.

It was such a fine day and then suddenly a cloud crossed the sky, covered the sun, and did not move again.

John Huff had been speaking quietly for several minutes. Now Douglas stopped on the path and looked over at him.

"John, say that again."

"You heard me the first time, Doug."

"Did you say you were—going away?"

"Got my train ticket here in my pocket. Whoo-whoo, clang! Shush-shush-shush-shush. Whoooooooo . . ."

His voice faded.

John took the yellow and green train ticket solemnly from his pocket and they both looked at it.

"Tonight!" said Douglas. "My gosh! Tonight we were going to play Red Light, Green Light and Statues! How come, all of a sudden? You been here in Green Town all my life. You just don't pick up and leave!"

"It's my father," said John. "He's got a job in Milwaukee. We weren't sure until today . . ."

"My gosh, here it is with the Baptist picnic next week and the big carnival Labor Day and Halloween—can't your dad wait till then?"

John shook his head.

"Good grief!" said Douglas. "Let me sit down!"

They sat under an old oak tree on the side of the hill looking back at town, and the sun made large trembling shadows around them; it was cool as a cave in under the tree. Out beyond, in sunlight, the town was painted with heat, the windows all gaping. Douglas wanted to run back in there where the town, by its very weight, its houses, their bulk, might enclose and prevent John's ever getting up and running off.

"But we're friends," Douglas said helplessly.

"We always will be," said John.

"You'll come back to visit every *week* or so, won't you?"

"Dad says only once or twice a year. It's eighty miles."

"Eighty miles ain't far!" shouted Douglas.

"No, it's not far at all," said John.

"My grandma's got a phone. I'll call you. Or maybe we'll all visit up your way, too. That'd be great!"

John said nothing for a long while.

"Well," said Douglas, "let's talk about something."

"What?"

"My gosh, if you're going away, we got a million things to talk about! All the things we would've talked about next month, the month after! Praying mantises, zeppelins, acrobats, sword swallowers! Go on like you was back there, grasshoppers spitting tobacco!"

"Funny thing is I don't feel like talking about grasshoppers."

"You always did!"

"Sure." John looked steadily at the town. "But I guess this just ain't the time."

"John, what's wrong? You look funny . . ."

John had closed his eyes and screwed up his face. "Doug, the Terle house, upstairs, you know?"

"Sure."

"The colored windowpanes on the little round windows, have they *always* been there?"

"Sure."

"You *positive*?"

"Darned old windows been there since before we were born. Why?"

"I never saw them before today," said John. "On the way walking through town I looked up and there they were. Doug, what was I *doing* all these years I didn't see them?"

"You had other things to do."

"Did I?" John turned and looked in a kind of panic at Douglas. "Gosh, Doug, why should those darn windows scare me? I mean, that's nothing to be scared of, is it? It's just . . ." He floundered. "It's just, if I didn't see those windows until today, what *else* did I miss? And what about all the things I *did* see here in town? Will I be able to remember them when I go away?"

"Anything you want to remember, you remember. I went to camp two summers ago. Up *there* I remembered."

"No, you didn't! You told me. You woke nights and couldn't remember your mother's face."

"*No!*"

"Some nights it happens to me in my own house; scares heck out of me. I got to go in my folks' room and look at their faces while they sleep, to be sure! And I go back to my room and lose it again. Gosh, Doug, oh gosh!" He held onto his knees tight. "Promise me just one thing, Doug. Promise you'll remember me, promise you'll remember my face and everything. Will you promise?"

"Easy as pie. Got a motion-picture machine in my head. Lying in bed nights I can just turn on a light in my head and out it comes on the wall, clear as heck, and there you'll be, yelling and waving at me."

"Shut your eyes, Doug. Now, tell me, what color eyes I got? Don't peek. What color eyes I got?"

Douglas began to sweat. His eyelids twitched nervously. "Aw heck, John, that's not fair."

"Tell me!"

"Brown!"

John turned away. "No, sir."

"What you mean, no?"

"You're not even close!" John closed his eyes.

"Turn around here," said Douglas. "Open up, let me see."

"It's no use," said John. "You forgot already. Just the way I said."

"Turn around here!" Douglas grabbed him by the hair and turned him slowly.

"Okay, Doug."

John opened his eyes.

"Green." Douglas, dismayed, let his hand drop. "Your eyes are green . . . Well, that's close to brown. Almost hazel!"

"Doug, don't lie to me."

"All right," said Doug quietly. "I won't."

They sat there listening to the other boys running up the hill, shrieking and yelling at them.

They raced along the railroad tracks, opened their lunch in brown-paper sacks, and sniffed deeply of the wax-wrapped deviled-ham sandwiches and green-sea pickles and colored peppermints. They ran and ran again and Douglas bent to scorch his ear on the hot steel rails, hearing trains so far away they were unseen voyagings in other lands, sending Morse-code messages to him here under the killing sun. Douglas stood up, stunned.

"John!"

For John was running, and this was terrible. Because if you ran, time ran. You yelled and screamed and raced and rolled and tumbled and all of a sudden the sun was gone and the whistle was blowing and you were on your long way home to supper. When you weren't looking, the sun got around behind you! The only way to keep things slow was to watch everything and do nothing! You could stretch a day to three days, sure, just by watching!

"John!"

There was no way to get him to help now, save by a trick.

"John, ditch, ditch the others!"

Yelling, Douglas and John sprinted off, kiting the wind downhill, letting gravity work for them, over meadows, around barns until at last the sound of the pursuers faded.

John and Douglas climbed into a haystack which was like a great bonfire crisping under them.

"Let's not do anything," said John.

"Just what I was going to say," said Douglas.

They sat quietly, getting their breath.

There was a small sound like an insect in the hay.

They both heard it, but they didn't look at the sound. When Douglas moved his wrist the sound ticked in another part of the haystack. When he brought his arm around on his lap the sound ticked in his lap. He let his eyes fall in a brief flicker. The watch said three o'clock.

Douglas moved his right hand stealthily to the ticking, pulled out the watch stem. He set the hands back.

Now they had all the time they would ever need to look long and close at the world, feel the sun move like a fiery wind over the sky.

But at last John must have felt the bodiless weight of their shadows shift and lean, and he spoke.

"Doug, what time is it?"

"Two-thirty."

John looked at the sky.

Don't! thought Douglas.

"Looks more like three-thirty, four," said John. "Boy scout. You learn them things."

Douglas sighed and slowly turned the watch ahead.

John watched him do this, silently. Douglas looked up. John punched him, not hard at all, in the arm.

With a swift stroke, a plunge, a train came and went so quickly the boys all leaped aside, yelling, shaking their fists after it, Douglas and John with them. The train roared down the track, two hundred people in it, gone. The dust followed it a little way toward the south, then settled in the golden silence among the blue rails.

The boys were walking home.

"I'm going to Cincinnati when I'm seventeen and be a railroad fireman," said Charlie Woodman.

"I got an uncle in New York," said Jim. "I'll go there and be a printer."

Doug did not ask the others. Already the trains were chanting and he saw their faces drifting off on back observation platforms, or pressed to windows. One by one they slid away. And then the empty track and the summer sky and himself on another train run in another direction.

Douglas felt the earth move under his feet and saw their shadows move off the grass and color the air.

He swallowed hard, then gave a screaming yell, pulled back his fist, shot the indoor ball whistling in the sky. "Last one home's a rhino's behind!"

They pounded down the tracks, laughing, flailing the air. There went John Huff, not touching the ground at all. And here came Douglas, touching it all the time.

It was seven o'clock, supper over, and the boys gathering one by one from the sound of their house doors slammed and their parents crying to them not to slam the doors. Douglas and Tom and Charlie and John stood among half a dozen others and it was time for hide-and-seek and Statues.

"Just one game," said John. "Then I got to go home. The train leaves at nine. Who's going to be 'it'?"

"Me," said Douglas.

"That's the first time I ever heard of anybody volunteering to be 'it,'" said Tom.

Douglas looked at John for a long moment. "Start running," he said.

The boys scattered, yelling. John backed away, then turned and began to lope. Douglas counted slowly. He let them run far, spread out, separate each to his own small world. When they had got their momentum up and were almost out of sight he took a deep breath.

"Statues!"

Everyone froze.

Very quietly Douglas moved across the lawn to where John Huff stood like an iron deer in the twilight.

Far away, the other boys stood hands up, faces grimaced, eyes bright as stuffed squirrels.

But here was John, alone and motionless and no one rushing or making a great outcry to spoil this moment.

Douglas walked around the statue one way, walked around the statue the other way. The statue did not move. It did not speak. It looked at the horizon, its mouth half smiling.

It was like that time years ago in Chicago when they had visited a big place where the carved marble figures were, and his walking around among them in the silence. So here was John Huff with grass stains on his knees and the seat of his pants, and cuts on his fingers and scabs on his elbows. Here was John Huff with the quiet tennis shoes, his feet sheathed in silence. There was the mouth that had chewed many an apricot pie come summer, and said many a quiet thing or two about life and the lay of the land. And there were the eyes, not blind like statues' eyes, but filled with molten green-gold. And there the dark hair blowing now north now south or any direction in the little breeze there was. And there the hands with all the town on them, dirt from roads and bark-slivers from trees, the fingers that smelled of hemp and vine and green apple, old coins or pickle-green frogs. There were the ears with the sunlight shining through them like bright warm peach wax and here, invisible, his spearmint-breath upon the air.

"John, now," said Douglas, "don't you move so much as an eyelash. I absolutely command you to stay here and not move at all for the next three hours!"

"Doug . . ."

John's lips moved.

"Freeze!" said Douglas.

John went back to looking at the sky, but he was not smiling now.

"I got to go," he whispered.

"Not a muscle, it's the game!"

"I just got to get home now," said John.

Now the statue moved, took its hands down out of the air and turned its head to look at Douglas. They stood looking at each other. The other kids were putting their arms down, too.

"We'll play one more round," said John, "except this time, I'm 'it.' Run!"

The boys ran.

"Freeze!"

The boys froze, Douglas with them.

"Not a muscle!" shouted John. "Not a hair!"

He came and stood by Douglas.

"Boy, this is the only way to do it," he said.

Douglas looked off at the twilight sky.

"Frozen statues, every single one of you, the next three minutes!" said John.

Douglas felt John walking around him even as he had walked around John a moment ago. He felt John sock him on the arm once, not too hard. "So long," he said.

Then there was a rushing sound and he knew without looking that there was nobody behind him now.

Far away, a train whistle sounded.

Douglas stood that way for a full minute, waiting for the sound of the running to fade, but it did not stop. He's still running away, but he doesn't sound any further off, thought Douglas. Why doesn't he stop running?

And then he realized it was only the sound of his heart in his body.

Stop! He jerked his hand to his chest. Stop running! I don't *like* that sound!

And then he felt himself walking across the lawns among all the other statues now, and whether they, too, were coming to life he did not know. They did not seem to be moving at all. For that matter he himself was only moving from the knees down. The rest of him was cold stone, and very heavy.

Going up the front porch of his house, he turned suddenly to look at the lawns behind him.

The lawns were empty.

A series of rifle shots. Screen doors banged one after the other, a sunset volley, along the street.

Statues are best, he thought. They're the only things you can keep on your lawn. Don't ever let them move. Once you do, you can't do a thing with them.

Suddenly his fist shot out like a piston from his side and it shook itself hard at the lawns and the street and the gathering dusk. His face was choked with blood, his eyes were blazing.

"John!" he cried. "You, John! John, you're my enemy, you hear? You're no friend of mine! Don't come back now, ever! Get away, you! Enemy, you hear? That's what you are! It's all off between us, you're dirt, that's all, dirt! John, you hear me, John!"

As if a wick had been turned a little lower in a great clear lamp beyond the town, the sky darkened still more. He stood on the porch, his mouth gasping and working. His fist still thrust straight out at that house across the street and down the way. He looked at the fist and it dissolved, the world dissolved beyond it.

Going upstairs, in the dark, where he could only feel his face but see nothing of himself, not even his fists, he told himself over and over, I'm mad, I'm angry, I hate him, I'm mad, I'm angry, I hate him!

Ten minutes later, slowly he reached the top of the stairs, in the dark . . .

"TOM," SAID Douglas, "just promise me one thing, okay?"

"It's a promise. What?"

"You may be my brother and maybe I hate you sometimes, but stick around, all right?"

"You mean you'll let me follow you and the older guys when you go on hikes?"

"Well . . . sure . . . even that. What I mean is, don't go away, huh? Don't let any cars run over you or fall off a cliff."

"I should say not! Whatta you think I *am*, anyway?"

"'Cause if worst comes to worst, and both of us are real old—say forty or forty-five some day—we can own a gold mine out West and sit there smoking corn silk and growing beards."

"Growing beards! Boy!"

"Like I say, you stick around and don't let nothing happen."

"You can depend on me," said Tom.

"It's not you I worry about," said Douglas. "It's the way God runs the world."

Tom thought about this for a moment.

"He's all right, Doug," said Tom. "He *tries*."

SHE CAME out of the bathroom putting iodine on her finger where she had almost lopped it off cutting herself a chunk of cocoanut cake. Just then the mailman came up the porch steps, opened the door, and walked in. The door slammed. Elmira Brown jumped a foot.

"Sam!" she cried. She waved her iodined finger on the air to cool it. "I'm still not used to my husband being a postman. Every time you just walk in, scares the life out of me!"

Sam Brown stood there with the mail pouch half empty, scratching his head. He looked back out the door as if a fog had suddenly rolled in on a calm sweet summer morn.

"Sam, you're home early," she said.

"Can't stay," he said in a puzzled voice.

"Spit it out, what's wrong?" She came over and looked into his face.

"Maybe nothing, maybe lots. I just delivered some mail to Clara Goodwater up the street. . . ."

"Clara Goodwater!"

"Now don't get your dander up. Books it was, from the Johnson-Smith Company, Racine, Wisconsin. Title of one book . . . let's see now." He screwed up his face, then unscrewed it. *"Albertus Magnus*—that's it. *Being the approved, verified, sympathetic and natural EGYPTIAN SECRETS or . . ."* He peered at the ceiling to summon the lettering. *"White and Black Art for Man and Beast, Revealing the Forbidden Knowledge and Mysteries of Ancient Philosophers!"*

"Clara Goodwater's, you say?"

"Walking along, I had a good chance to peek at the front pages, no harm in that. 'Hidden Secrets of Life Unveiled by that celebrated Student, Philosopher, Chemist, Naturalist, Psychomist, Astrologer, Alchemist, Metallurgist, Sorcerer, Explanator of the Mysteries of Wizards and Witchcraft, together with recondite views of numerous Arts and Sciences—Obscure, Plain, Practical, etc.' There! By God, I got a head like a box Brownie. Got the words, even if I haven't got the sense."

Elmira stood looking at her iodined finger as if it were pointed at her by a stranger.

"Clara Goodwater," she murmured.

"Looked me right in the eye as I handed it over, said, 'Going to be a witch, first-class, no doubt. Get my diploma in no time. Set up business. Hex crowds and individuals, old and young, big and small.' Then she kinda laughed, put her nose in that book, and went in."

Elmira stared at a bruise on her arm, carefully tongued a loose tooth in her jaw.

A door slammed. Tom Spaulding, kneeling on Elmira Brown's front lawn, looked up. He had been wandering about the neighborhood, seeing how the ants were doing here or there, and had found a particularly good hill with a big hole in which all kinds of fiery bright pismires were tumbling about scissoring the air and wildly carrying little packets of dead grasshopper and infinitesimal bird down into the earth. Now here was something else: Mrs. Brown, swaying on the edge of her porch as if she'd just found out the world was falling through space at sixty trillion miles a second. Behind her was Mr. Brown, who didn't know the miles per second and probably wouldn't care if he did know.

"You, Tom!" said Mrs. Brown. "I need moral support and the equivalent of the blood of the Lamb with me. Come along!"

And off she rushed, squashing ants and kicking tops off dandelions and trotting big spiky holes in flower beds as she cut across yards.

Tom knelt a moment longer studying Mrs. Brown's shoulder blades and spine as she toppled down the street. He read the bones and they were eloquent of melodrama and adventure, a thing he did not ordinarily connect with ladies, even though Mrs. Brown had the remnants of a pirate's mustache. A moment later he was in tandem with her.

"Mrs. Brown, you sure look mad!"

"You don't know what mad *is*, boy!"

"Watch out!" cried Tom.

Mrs. Elmira Brown fell right over an iron dog lying asleep there on the green grass.

"Mrs. Brown!"

"You see?" Mrs. Brown sat there. "Clara Goodwater did this to me! Magic!"

"Magic?"

"Never mind, boy. Here's the steps. You go first and kick any invisible strings out of the way. Ring that doorbell, but pull your finger off quick, the juice'll burn you to a cinder!"

Tom did not touch the bell.

"Clara Goodwater!" Mrs. Brown flicked the bell button with her iodined finger.

Far away in the cool dim empty rooms of the big old house, a silver bell tinkled and faded.

Tom listened. Still farther away there was a stir of mouse-like running. A shadow, perhaps a blowing curtain, moved in a distant parlor.

"Hello," said a quiet voice.

And quite suddenly Mrs. Goodwater was there, fresh as a stick of peppermint, behind the screen.

"Why, hello there, Tom, Elmira. What——"

"Don't rush me! We came over about your practicing to be a full-fledged witch!"

Mrs. Goodwater smiled. "Your husband's not only a mailman, but a guardian of the law. Got a nose out to *here*!"

"He didn't look at no mail."

"He's ten minutes between houses laughing at post cards and tryin' on mail-order shoes."

"It ain't what he seen; it's what you yourself told him about the books you got."

"Just a joke. Goin' to be a witch! I said, and bang! Off gallops Sam, like I'd flung lightning at him. I declare there can't be one wrinkle in that man's brain."

"You talked about your magic other places yesterday——"

"You must mean the Sandwich Club . . ."

"To which I pointedly was *not* invited."

"Why, lady, we thought that was your regular day with your grandma."

"I can always have another Grandma day, if people'd only ask me places."

"All there was to it at the Sandwich Club was me sitting there with a ham and pickle sandwich, and I said right out loud, "At last I'm going to get my witch's diploma. Been studying for years!"

"That's what come back to me over the phone!"

"Ain't modern inventions wonderful!" said Mrs. Goodwater.

"Considering you been president of the Honeysuckle Ladies Lodge since the Civil War, it seems, I'll put it to you bang on the nose, have you used witchcraft all these years to spell the ladies and win the ayes-have-it?"

"Do you doubt it for a moment, lady?" said Mrs. Goodwater.

"Election's tomorrow again, and all I want to know is, you runnin' for another term—and ain't you ashamed?"

"Yes to the first question and no to the second. Lady, look here, I bought those books for my boy cousin, Raoul. He's just ten and goes around looking in hats for rabbits. I told him there's about as much chance finding rabbits in hats as brains in heads of certain people I could name, but look he does and so I got these gifts for him."

"Wouldn't believe you on a stack of Bibles."

"God's truth, anyway. I love to fun about the witch thing. The ladies all yodeled when I explained about my dark powers. Wish you'd been there."

"I'll be there tomorrow to fight you with a cross of gold and all the powers of good I can organize behind me," said Elmira. "Right now, tell me how much other magic junk you got in your house."

Mrs. Goodwater pointed to a side table inside the door.

"I been buyin' all kinds of magic herbs. Smell funny and make Raoul happy. That little sack of stuff, that's called Thisis rue, and this is Sabisse root and that there's Ebon herbs; here's black sulphur, and this they claim is bone dust."

"Bone dust!" "Bone dust!" Elmira skipped back and kicked Tom's ankle. Tom yelped.

"And here's wormwood and fern leaves so you can freeze shotguns and fly like a bat in your dreams, it says in Chapter X of the little book here. I think it's fine for growing boys' heads to think about things like this. Now, from the look on your face you don't believe Raoul exists. Well, I'll give you his Springfield address."

"Yes," said Elmira, "and the day I write him you'll take the

Springfield bus and go to General Delivery and get my letter and write back to me in a boy's hand. I know you!"

"Mrs. Brown, speak up—you want to be president of the Honeysuckle Ladies Lodge, right? You run every year now for ten years. You nominate yourself. And always wind up gettin' *one* vote. Yours. Elmira, if the ladies wanted you they'd landslide you in. But from where I stand looking up the mountain, ain't so much as one pebble come rattlin' down save yours. Tell you what, I'll nominate and vote for you myself come noon tomorrow, how's that?"

"Damned for sure, then," said Elmira. "Last year I got a deathly cold right at election time; couldn't get out and campaign back-fence-to-back-fence. Year before that, broke my leg. Mighty strange." She squinted darkly at the lady behind the screen. "That's not all. Last month I cut my fingers six times, bruised my knee ten times, fell off my back porch twice, you hear—twice! I broke a window, dropped four dishes, one vase worth a dollar forty-nine at Bixby's, and I'm billin' you for every dropped dish from now on in my house and environs!"

"I'll be poor by Christmas," said Mrs. Goodwater. She opened the screen door and came out suddenly and let the door slam. "Elmira Brown, how old are you?"

"You probably got it written in one of your black books. Thirty-five!"

"Well, when I think of thirty-five years of your life . . ." Mrs. Goodwater pursed her lips and blinked her eyes, counting. "That's about twelve thousand seven hundred and seventy-five days, or counting three of them per day, twelve thousand–odd commotions, twelve thousand much-ados and twelve thousand calamities. It's a full rich life you lead, Elmira Brown. Shake hands!"

"Get away!" Elmira fended her off.

"Why, lady, you're only the second most clumsy woman in Green Town, Illinois. You can't sit down without playing the chair like an accordion. You can't stand up but what you kick the cat. You can't trot across an open meadow without falling into a well. Your life has been one long decline, Elmira Alice Brown, so why not admit it?"

"It wasn't clumsiness that caused my calamities, but you

being within a mile of me at those times when I dropped a pot of beans or juiced my finger in the electric socket at home."

"Lady, in a town this size, *everybody's* within a mile of some-one at one time or other in the day."

"You admit being around then?"

"I admit being born here, yes, but I'd give anything right now to have been born in Kenosha or Zion. Elmira, go to your dentist and see what he can do about that serpent's tongue in there."

"Oh!" said Elmira. "Oh, oh, oh!"

"You've pushed me too far. I wasn't interested in witchcraft, but I think I'll just look into this business. Listen here! You're invisible right now. While you stood there I put a spell on you. You're clean out of sight."

"You didn't!"

"Course," admitted the witch, "I never *could* see you, lady."

Elmira pulled out her pocket minor. "There I am!" She peered closer and gasped. She reached up like someone tuning a harp and plucked a single thread. She held it up, Exhibit A. "I never had a gray hair in my life till this second!"

The witch smiled charmingly. "Put it in a jar of still water, be an angleworm come morning. Oh, Elmira, look at yourself at last, won't you? All these years, blaming others for your own mallet feet and floaty ways! You ever read Shakespeare? There's little stage directions in there: ALARUMS AND EXCUR-SIONS. That's you, Elmira. Alarums and Excursions! Now get home before I feel the bumps on your head and predict gas all night for you! Shoo!"

She waved her hands in the air as if Elmira were a cloud of things. "My, the flies are thick this summer!" she said.

She went inside and hooked the door.

"The line is drawn, Mrs. Goodwater," Elmira said, folding her arms. "I'll give you one last chance. Withdraw from the candidacy of the Honeysuckle Lodge or face me face-to-face tomorrow when I run for office and wrest it from you in a fair fight. I'll bring Tom here with me. An innocent good boy. And innocence and good will win the day."

"I wouldn't count on me being innocent, Mrs. Brown," said the boy. "My mother says——"

"Shut up, Tom, good's good! You'll be there on my right hand, boy."

"Yes'm," said Tom.

"If, that is," said Elmira, "I can live through the night with this lady making wax dummies of me—shoving rusty needles through the very heart and soul of them. If you find a great big fig in my bed all shriveled up come sunrise, Tom, you'll know who picked the fruit in the vineyard. And look to see Mrs. Goodwater president till she's a hundred and ninety-five years old."

"Why, lady," said Mrs. Goodwater, "I'm three hundred and five *now.* Used to call me SHE in the old days." She poked her fingers at the street. "Abracadabra-zimmity-ZAM! How's *that?*"

Elmira ran down off the porch.

"Tomorrow!" she cried.

"Till then, lady!" said Mrs. Goodwater.

Tom followed Elmira, shrugging and kicking ants off the sidewalk as he went.

Running across a driveway, Elmira screamed.

"Mrs. Brown!" cried Tom.

A car backing out of a garage ran right over Elmira's right big toe.

Mrs. Elmira Brown's foot hurt her in the middle of the night, so she got up and went down to the kitchen and ate some cold chicken and made a neat, painfully accurate list of things. First, illnesses in the past year. Three colds, four mild attacks of indigestion, one seizure of bloat, arthritis, lumbago, what she imagined to be gout, a severe bronchial cough, incipient asthma, and spots on her arms, plus an abscessed semicircular canal which made her reel like a drunken moth some days, backache, head pains, and nausea. Cost of medicine: *ninety-eight dollars and seventy-eight cents.*

Secondly, things broken in the house during the twelve months just past: two lamps, six vases, ten dishes, one soup tureen, two windows, one chair, one sofa cushion, six glasses, and one crystal chandelier prism. Total cost: *twelve dollars and ten cents.*

Thirdly, her pains this very night. Her toe hurt from being run over. Her stomach was upset. Her back was stiff, her legs were pulsing with agony. Her eyeballs felt like wads of blazing cotton. Her tongue tasted like a dust mop. Her ears were belling and ringing away. Cost? She debated, going back to bed.

Ten thousand dollars in personal suffering.

"Try to settle this out of court!" she said half aloud.

"Eh?" said her husband, awake.

She lay down in bed. "I simply refuse to die."

"Beg pardon?" he said.

"I won't die!" she said, staring at the ceiling.

"That's what I always claimed," said her husband, and turned over to snore.

In the morning Mrs. Elmira Brown was up early and down to the library and then to the drugstore and back to the house where she was busy mixing all kinds of chemicals when her husband, Sam, came home with an empty mail pouch at noon.

"Lunch's in the icebox." Elmira stirred a green-looking porridge in a large glass.

"Good Lord, what's that?" asked her husband. "Looks like a milk shake been left out in the sun for forty years. Got kind of a fungus on it."

"Fight magic with magic."

"You goin' to *drink that*?"

"Just before I go up into the Honeysuckle Ladies Lodge for the big doings."

Samuel Brown sniffed the concoction. "Take my advice. Get up those steps first, *then* drink it. What's in it?"

"Snow from angels' wings, well, really menthol, to cool hell's fires that burn you, it says in this book I got at the library. The juice of a fresh grape off the vine, for thinking clear sweet thoughts in the face of dark visions, it says. Also red rhubarb, cream of tartar, white sugar, white of eggs, spring water and clover buds with the strength of the good earth in them. Oh, I could go on all day. It's here in the list, good against bad, white against black. I can't lose!"

"Oh, you'll win, all right," said her husband. "But will you *know* it?"

"Think good thoughts. I'm on my way to get Tom for my charm."

"Poor boy," said her husband. "Innocent, like you say, and about to be torn limb from limb, bargain-basement day at the Honeysuckle Lodge."

"Tom'll survive," said Elmira, and, taking the bubbling concoction with her, hid inside a Quaker Oats box with the lid on, went out the door without catching her dress or snagging her new ninety-eight-cent stockings. Realizing this, she was smug all the way to Tom's house where he waited for her in his white summer suit as she had instructed.

"Phew!" said Tom. "What you got in that box?"

"Destiny," said Elmira.

"I sure hope so," said Tom, walking about two paces ahead of her.

The Honeysuckle Ladies Lodge was full of ladies looking in each other's mirrors and tugging at their skirts and asking to be sure their slips weren't showing.

At one o'clock Mrs. Elmira Brown came up the steps with a boy in white clothes. He was holding his nose and screwing up one eye so he could only half see where he was going. Mrs. Brown looked at the crowd and then at the Quaker Oats box and opened the top and looked in and gasped, and put the top back on without drinking any of that stuff in there. She moved inside the hall and with her moved a rustling as of taffeta, all the ladies whispering in a tide after her.

She sat down in back with Tom, and Tom looked more miserable than ever. The one eye he had open looked at the crowd of ladies and shut up for good. Sitting there, Elmira got the potion out and drank it slowly down.

At one-thirty, the president, Mrs. Goodwater, banged the gavel and all but two dozen of the ladies quit talking.

"Ladies," she called out over the summer sea of silks and laces, capped here and there with white or gray, "it's election time. But before we start, I believe Mrs. Elmira Brown, wife of our eminent graphologist——"

A titter ran through the room.

"What's graphologist?" Elmira elbowed Tom twice.

"I don't know," whispered Tom fiercely, eyes shut, feeling that elbow come out of darkness at him.

"—wife, as I say, of our eminent handwriting expert, Samuel Brown . . . (more laughter) . . . of the U.S. Postal Service," continued Mrs. Goodwater. "Mrs. Brown wants to give us some opinions. Mrs. Brown?"

Elmira stood up. Her chair fell over backward and snapped shut like a bear trap on itself. She jumped an inch off the floor and teetered on her heels, which gave off cracking sounds like they would fall to dust any moment. "I got plenty to say," she said, holding the empty Quaker Oats box in one hand with a a Bible. She grabbed Tom with the other and plowed forward, hitting several people's elbows and muttering to them, "Watch what you're doing! Careful, you!" to reach the platform, turn, and knock a glass of water dripping over the table. She gave Mrs. Goodwater another bristly scowl when this happened and let her mop it up with a tiny handkerchief. Then with a secret look of triumph, Elmira drew forth the empty philter glass and held it up, displaying it for Mrs. Goodwater and whispering, "You know what was in this? It's inside me, now, lady. The charmed circle surrounds me. No knife can cleave, no hatchet break through."

The ladies, all talking, did not hear.

Mrs. Goodwater nodded, held up her hands, and there was silence.

Elmira held tight to Tom's hand. Tom kept his eyes shut, wincing.

"Ladies," Elmira said, "I sympathize with you. I know what you've been through these last ten years. I know why you voted for Mrs. Goodwater here. You've got boys, girls, and men to feed. You've got budgets to follow. You couldn't afford to have your milk sour, your bread fall, or your cakes as flat as wheels. You didn't want mumps, chicken pox and whooping cough in your house all in three weeks. You didn't want your husband crashing his car or electrocuting himself on the high-tension wires outside town. But now all of that's over. You can come out in the open now. No more heartburns or backaches, because I've brought the good word and we're going to exorcise this witch we've got here!"

Everybody looked around but didn't see any witch.

"I mean your *president*!" cried Elmira.

"*Me!*" Mrs. Goodwater waved at everyone.

"Today," breathed Elmira, holding onto the desk for support, "I went to the library. I looked up counteractions. How to get rid of people who take advantage of others, how to make witches leave off and go. And I found a way to fight for all our rights. I can feel the power growing. I got the magic of all kinds of good roots and chemicals in me. I got . . ." She paused and swayed. She blinked once. "I got cream of tartar and . . . I got . . . white hawkweed and milk soured in the light of the moon and . . ." She stopped and thought for a moment. She shut her mouth and a tiny sound came from deep inside her and worked up through to come out the corners of her lips. She closed her eyes for a moment to see where the strength was.

"Mrs. Brown, you feelin' all right?" asked Mrs. Goodwater.

"Feelin' fine!" said Mrs. Brown slowly. "I put in some pulverized carrots and parsley root, cut fine; juniper berry . . ."

Again she paused as if a voice had said STOP to her and she looked out across all those faces.

The room, she noticed, was beginning to turn slowly, first from left to right, then right to left.

"Rosemary roots and crowfoot flower . . ." she said rather dimly. She let go of Tom's hand. Tom opened one eye and looked at her.

"Bay leaves, nasturtium petals . . ." she said.

"Maybe you better sit down," said Mrs. Goodwater.

One lady at the side went and opened a window.

"Dry betel nuts, lavender and crab-apple seed," said Mrs. Brown and stopped. "Quick now, let's have the election. Got to have the votes. I'll tabulate."

"No hurry, Elmira," said Mrs. Goodwater.

"Yes, there is." Elmira took a deep trembling breath. "Remember, ladies, no more fear. Do like you always wanted to do. Vote for me, and . . ." The room was moving again, up and down. "Honesty in government. All those in favor of Mrs. Goodwater for president say 'Aye.'"

"Aye," said the whole room.

"All those in favor of Mrs. Elmira Brown?" said Elmira in a faint voice.

She swallowed.

After a moment she spoke, alone.

"Aye," she said.

She stood stunned on the rostrum.

A silence filled the room from wall to wall. In that silence Mrs. Elmira Brown made a croaking sound. She put her hand on her throat. She turned and looked dimly at Mrs. Goodwater, who now very casually drew forth from her purse a small wax doll in which were a number of rusted thumbtacks.

"Tom," said Elmira, "show me the way to the ladies' room."

"Yes'm."

They began to walk and then hurry and then run. Elmira ran on ahead, through the crowd, down the aisle . . . She reached the door and started left.

"No, Elmira, right, right!" cried Mrs. Goodwater.

Elmira turned left and vanished.

There was a noise like coal down a chute.

"Elmira!"

The ladies ran around like a girls' basketball team, colliding with each other.

Only Mrs. Goodwater made a straight line.

She found Tom looking down the stair well, his hands clenched to the banister.

"Forty steps!" he moaned. "Forty steps to the ground!"

Later on and for months and years after it was told how like an inebriate Elmira Brown negotiated those steps touching every one on her long way down. It was claimed that when she began the fall she was sick to unconsciousness and that this made her skeleton rubber, so she kind of rolled rather than ricocheted. She landed at the bottom, blinking and feeling better, having left whatever it was that had made her uneasy all along the way. True, she was so badly bruised she looked like a tattooed lady. But, no, not a wrist was sprained or an ankle twisted. She held her head funny for three days, kind of peering out of the sides of her eyeballs instead of turning to look. But the important thing was Mrs. Goodwater at the bottom of the steps, pillowing Elmira's head on her lap and dropping tears on her as the ladies gathered hysterically.

"Elmira, I promise, Elmira, I swear, if you just live, if you don't die, you hear me, Elmira, listen! I'll use my magic for nothing but good from now on. No more black, nothing but white magic. The rest of your life, if I have my way, no more falling over iron dogs, tripping on sills, cutting fingers, or dropping downstairs for you! Elysium, Elmira, Elysium, I promise! If you just live! Look, I'm pulling the tacks out of the doll! Elmira, speak to me! Speak now and sit up! And come upstairs for another vote. President, I promise, president of the Honeysuckle Ladies Lodge, by acclamation, won't we, ladies?"

At this all the ladies cried so hard they had to lean on each other.

Tom, upstairs, thought this meant death down there.

He was halfway down when he met the ladies coming back up, looking like they had just wandered out of a dynamite explosion.

"Get out of the way, boy!"

First came Mrs. Goodwater, laughing and crying.

Next came Mrs. Elmira Brown, doing the same.

And after the two of them came all the one hundred twenty-three members of the lodge, not knowing if they'd just returned from a funeral or were on their way to a ball.

He watched them pass and shook his head.

"Don't need me no more," he said. "No more at all."

So he tiptoed down the stairs before they missed him, holding tight to the rail all the way.

"FOR WHAT it's worth," said Tom, "there's the whole thing in a nutshell. The ladies carrying on like crazy. Everybody standing around blowing their noses. Elmira Brown sitting there at the bottom of the steps, nothing broke, her bones made out of Jell-O, I suspect, and the witch sobbin' on her shoulder, and then all of them goin' upstairs suddenly laughing. Cry-*yi*, you figure it out. I got out of there fast!"

Tom loosened his shirt and took off his tie.

"Magic, you say?" asked Douglas.

"Magic six ways from Sunday."

"You believe it?"

"Yes I do and no I don't."

"Boy, this town is full of stuff!" Douglas peered off at the horizon where clouds filled the sky with immense shapes of old gods and warriors. "Spells and wax dolls and needles and elixirs, you said?"

"Wasn't much as an elixir, but awful fine as an upchuck. Blap! Wowie!" Tom clutched his stomach and stuck out his tongue.

"Witches . . ." said Douglas. He squinted his eyes mysteriously.

AND THEN there is that day when all around, all around you hear the dropping of the apples, one by one, from the trees. At first it is one here and one there, and then it is three and then it is four and then nine and twenty, until the apples plummet like rain, fall like horse hoofs in the soft, darkening grass, and you are the last apple on the tree; and you wait for the wind to work you slowly free from your hold upon the sky, and drop you down and down. Long before you hit the grass you will have forgotten there ever was a tree, or other apples, or a summer, or green grass below. You will fall in darkness . . .

"No!"

Colonel Freeleigh opened his eyes quickly, sat erect in his wheel chair. He jerked his cold hand out to find the telephone. It was still there! He crushed it against his chest for a moment, blinking.

"I don't like that dream," he said to his empty room.

At last, his fingers trembling, he lifted the receiver and called the long-distance operator and gave her a number and waited, watching the bedroom door as if at any moment a plague of sons, daughters, grandsons, nurses, doctors, might swarm in to seize away this last vital luxury he permitted his failing senses. Many days, or was it years, ago, when his heart had thrust like a dagger through his ribs and flesh, he had heard the boys below . . . their names, what were they? Charles, Charlie, Chuck, yes! And Douglas! And Tom! He remembered! Calling his name far down the hall, but the door being locked in their faces, the boys turned away. You can't be excited, the doctor said. No visitors, no visitors, no visitors. And he heard the boys moving across the street, he saw them, he waved. And they waved back. "Colonel . . . Colonel . . ." And now he sat alone with the little gray toad of a heart flopping weakly here or there in his chest from time to time.

"Colonel Freeleigh," said the operator. "Here's your call. Mexico City. Erickson 3899."

And now the far away but infinitely clear voice:

"Bueno."

"Jorge!" cried the old man.

"Señor Freeleigh! Again? This costs money."

"Let it cost! You know what to do."

"*Si.* The window?"

"The window, Jorge, if you please."

"A moment," said the voice.

And, thousands of miles away, in a southern land, in an office in a building in that land, there was the sound of footsteps retreating from the phone. The old man leaned forward, gripping the receiver tight to his wrinkled ear that ached with waiting for the next sound.

The raising of a window.

Ah, sighed the old man.

The sounds of Mexico City on a hot yellow noon rose through the open window into the waiting phone. He could see Jorge standing there holding the mouthpiece out, out into the bright day.

"Señor . . ."

"No, no, please. Let me *listen.*"

He listened to the hooting of many metal horns, the squealing of brakes, the calls of vendors selling red-purple bananas and jungle oranges in their stalls. Colonel Freeleigh's feet began to move, hanging from the edge of his wheel chair, making the motions of a man walking. His eyes squeezed tight. He gave a series of immense sniffs, as if to gain the odors of meats hung on iron hooks in sunshine, cloaked with flies like a mantle of raisins; the smell of stone alleys wet with morning rain. He could feel the sun burn his spiny-bearded cheek, and he was twenty-five years old again, walking, walking, looking, smiling, happy to be alive, very much alert, drinking in colors and smells.

A rap on the door. Quickly he hid the phone under his lap robe.

The nurse entered. "Hello," she said. "Have you been good?"

"Yes," The old man's voice was mechanical. He could hardly see. The shock of a simple rap on a door was such that part of him was still in another city, far removed. He waited for his mind to rush home—it must be here to answer questions, act sane, be polite.

"I've come to check your pulse."

"Not now!" said the old man.

"You're not going anywhere, are you?" She smiled.

He looked at the nurse steadily. He hadn't been anywhere in ten years.

"Give me your wrist."

Her fingers, hard and precise, searched for the sickness in his pulse like a pair of calipers.

"What've you been doing to *excite* yourself?" she demanded.

"Nothing."

Her gaze shifted and stopped on the empty phone table. At that instant a horn sounded faintly, two thousand miles away.

She took the receiver from under the lap robe and held it before his face. "Why do you do this to yourself? You promised you wouldn't. That's how you hurt yourself in the first place, isn't it? Getting excited, talking too much. Those boys up here jumping around——"

"They sat quietly and listened," said the colonel. "And I told them things they'd never heard. The buffalo, I told them, the bison. It was worth it. I don't care. I was in a pure fever and I was alive. It doesn't matter if being so alive kills a man; it's better to have the quick fever every time. Now give me that phone. If you won't let the boys come up and sit politely I can at least talk to someone outside the room."

"I'm sorry, Colonel. Your grandson will have to know about this. I prevented his having the phone taken out last week. Now it looks like I'll let him go ahead."

"This is *my* house, my phone. I pay your salary!" he said.

"To make you well, not get you excited." She wheeled his chair across the room. "To bed with you now, young man!"

From bed he looked back at the phone and kept looking at it.

"I'm going to the store for a few minutes," the nurse said. "Just to be sure you don't use the phone again, I'm hiding your wheel chair in the hall."

She wheeled the empty chair out the door. In the downstairs entry, he heard her pause and dial the extension phone.

Was she phoning Mexico City? he wondered. She wouldn't dare!

The front door shut.

He thought of the last week here, alone, in his room, and the secret, narcotic calls across continents, an isthmus, whole jungle countries of rain forest, blue-orchid plateaus, lakes and hills . . . talking . . . talking . . . to Buenos Aires . . . and . . . Lima . . . Rio de Janeiro . . .

He lifted himself in the cool bed. Tomorrow the telephone gone! What a greedy fool he had been! He slipped his brittle ivory legs down from the bed, marveling at their desiccation. They seemed to be things which had been fastened to his body while he slept one night, while his younger legs were taken off and burned in the cellar furnace. Over the years, they had destroyed all of him, removing hands, arms, and legs and leaving him with substitutes as delicate and useless as chess pieces. And now they were tampering with something more intangible—the memory; they were trying to cut the wires which led back into another year.

He was across the room in a stumbling run. Grasping the phone, he took it with him as he slid down the wall to sit upon the floor. He got the long-distance operator, his heart exploding within him, faster and faster, a blackness in his eyes. "Hurry, hurry!"

He waited.

"Bueno?"

"Jorge, we were cut off."

"You must not phone again, Señor," said the faraway voice. "Your nurse called me. She says you are very ill. I must hang up."

"No, Jorge! Please!" the old man pleaded. "One last time, listen to me. They're taking the phone out tomorrow. I can never call you again."

Jorge said nothing.

The old man went on. "For the love of God, Jorge! For friendship, then, for the old days! You don't know what it means. You're my age, but you can *move*! I haven't moved anywhere in ten years."

He dropped the phone and had trouble picking it up, his chest was so thick with pain. "Jorge! You *are* still there, aren't you?"

"This will be the last time?" said Jorge.

"I promise!"

The phone was laid on a desk thousands of miles away. Once

more, with that clear familiarity, the footsteps, the pause, and, at last, the raising of the window.

"*Listen*," whispered the old man to himself.

And he heard a thousand people in another sunlight, and the faint, tinkling music of an organ grinder playing "La Marimba"—oh, a lovely, dancing tune.

With eyes tight, the old man put up his hand as if to click pictures of an old cathedral, and his body was heavier with flesh, younger, and he felt the hot pavement underfoot.

He wanted to say, "You're still there, aren't you? All of you people in that city in the time of the early siesta, the shops closing, the little boys crying *lotería nacional para hoy!* to sell lottery tickets. You are all there, the people in the city. I can't believe I was ever among you. When you are away from a city it becomes a fantasy. Any town, New York, Chicago, with its people, becomes improbable with distance. Just as I am improbable here, in Illinois, in a small town by a quiet lake. All of us improbable to one another because we are not present to one another. And so it is good to hear the sounds, and know that Mexico City is still there and the people moving and living . . ."

He sat with the receiver tightly pressed to his ear.

And at last, the clearest, most improbable sound of all—the sound of a green trolley car going around a corner—a trolley burdened with brown and alien and beautiful people, and the sound of other people running and calling out with triumph as they leaped up and swung aboard and vanished around a corner on the shrieking rails and were borne away in the sun-blazed distance to leave only the sound of *tortillas* frying on the market stoves, or was it merely the ever rising and falling hum and burn of static quivering along two thousand miles of copper wire . . .

The old man sat on the floor.

Time passed.

A downstairs door opened slowly. Light footsteps came in, hesitated, then ventured up the stairs. Voices murmured.

"We shouldn't be here!"

"He phoned me, I tell you. He needs visitors bad. We can't let him down."

"He's sick!"

"Sure! But he said to come when the nurse's out. We'll only stay a second, say hello, and . . ."

The door to the bedroom moved wide. The three boys stood looking in at the old man seated there on the floor.

"Colonel Freeleigh?" said Douglas softly.

There was something in his silence that made them all shut up their mouths.

They approached, almost on tiptoe.

Douglas, bent down, disengaged the phone from the old man's now quite cold fingers. Douglas lifted the receiver to his own ear, listened. Above the static he heard a strange, a far, a final sound.

Two thousand miles away, the closing of a window.

"BOOM!" SAID Tom. "Boom. Boom. Boom."

He sat on the Civil War cannon in the courthouse square.

Douglas, in front of the cannon, clutched his heart and fell down on the grass. But he did not get up; he just lay there, his face thoughtful.

"You look like you're going to get out the old pencil any second now," said Tom.

"Let me think!" said Douglas, looking at the cannon. He rolled over and gazed at the sky and the trees above him. "Tom, it just hit me."

"What?"

"Yesterday Ching Ling Soo died. Yesterday the Civil War ended right here in this town forever. Yesterday Mr. Lincoln died right here and so did General Lee and General Grant and a hundred thousand others facing north and south. And yesterday afternoon, at Colonel Freeleigh's house, a herd of buffalo-bison as big as all Green Town, Illinois, went off the cliff into nothing at all. Yesterday a whole lot of dust settled for good. And I didn't even appreciate it at the time. It's awful, Tom, it's awful! What we going to do without all those buffalo . . . what we going to do without all those soldiers and Generals Lee and Grant and Honest Abe; what we going to do without Ching Ling Soo? I never dreamed so many people could die so fast, Tom. But they did. They sure did!"

Tom sat astride the cannon, looking down at his brother as his voice trailed away.

"You got your tablet with you?"

Douglas shook his head.

"Better get home and put all that down before you forget it. It ain't every day you got half the population of the world keeling over on you."

Douglas sat up and then stood up. He walked across the courthouse lawn slowly, chewing his lower lip.

"Boom," said Tom quietly. "Boom. Boom!"

Then he raised his voice:

"Doug! I killed you three times, crossing the grass! Doug, you hear me? Hey, Doug! Okay. All right for you." He lay down on the cannon and sighted along the crusted barrel. He squinted one eye. "Boom!" he whispered at that dwindling figure. "Boom!"

"THERE!"

"Twenty-nine!"

"There!"

"Thirty!"

"There!"

"Thirty-one!"

The lever plunged. The tin caps, crushed atop the filled bottles, flickered bright yellow. Grandfather handed the last bottle to Douglas.

"Second harvest of the summer. June's on the shelf. Here's July. Now, just August up ahead."

Douglas raised the bottle of warm dandelion wine but did not set it on the shelf. He saw the other numbered bottles waiting there, one like another, in no way different, all bright, all regular, all self-contained.

There's the day I found I was alive, he thought, and why isn't it brighter than the others?

There's the day John Huff fell off the edge of the world, gone; why isn't it darker than the others?

Where, where all the summer dogs leaping like dolphins in the wind-braided and unbraided tides of wheat? Where lightning smell of Green Machine or trolley? Did the wine remember? It did not! Or seemed not, anyway.

Somewhere, a book said once, all the talk ever talked, all the songs ever sung, still lived, had vibrated way out in space and if you could travel to Far Centauri you could hear George Washington talking in his sleep or Caesar surprised at the knife in his back. So much for sounds. What about light then? All things, once seen, they didn't just die, that *couldn't* be. It must be then that somewhere, searching the world, perhaps in the dripping multiboxed honeycombs where light was an amber sap stored by pollen-fired bees, or in the thirty thousand lenses of the noon dragonfly's gemmed skull you might find all the colors and sights of the world in any one year. Or pour one single drop of this dandelion wine beneath a microscope and perhaps the entire world of July Fourth would firework out in Vesuvius showers. This he would have to believe.

And yet . . . looking here at this bottle which by its number signalized the day when Colonel Freeleigh had stumbled and fallen six feet into the earth, Douglas could not find so much as a gram of dark sediment, not a speck of the great flouring buffalo dust, not a flake of sulphur from the guns at Shiloh . . .

"August up ahead," said Douglas. "Sure. But the way things are going, there'll be no machines, no friends, and darn few dandelions for the last harvest."

"Doom. Doom. You sound like a funeral bell tolling," said Grandfather. "Talk like that is worse than swearing. I won't wash out your mouth with soap, however. A thimbleful of dandelion wine is indicated. Here, now, swig it down. What's it taste like?"

"I'm a fire-eater! Whoosh!"

"Now upstairs, run three times around the block, do five somersets, six pushups, climb two trees, and you'll be concertmaster instead of chief mourner. Get!"

On his way, running, Douglas thought, *Four* pushups, *one* tree, and *two* somersets will *do* it!

AND OUT there in the middle of the first day of August, just getting into his car, was Bill Forrester, who shouted he was going downtown for some extraordinary ice cream or other and would anyone join him? So, not five minutes later, jiggled and steamed into a better mood, Douglas found himself stepping in off the fiery pavements and moving through the grotto of soda-scented air, of vanilla freshness at the drugstore, to sit at the snow-marble fountain with Bill Forrester. They then asked for a recital of the most unusual ices and when the fountain man said, "Old fashioned lime-vanilla ice . . ."

"That's it!" said Bill Forrester.

"Yes, sir!" said Douglas.

And, while waiting, they turned slowly on their rotating stools. The silver spigots, the gleaming mirrors, the hushed whirl-around ceiling fans, the green shades over the small windows, the harp-wire chairs, passed under their moving gaze. They stopped turning. Their eyes had touched upon the face and form of Miss Helen Loomis, ninety-five years old, ice-cream spoon in hand, ice cream in mouth.

"Young man," she said to Bill Forrester, "you are a person of taste and imagination. Also, you have the will power of ten men; otherwise you would not dare veer away from the common flavors listed on the menu and order, straight out, without quibble or reservation, such an unheard-of thing as lime-vanilla ice."

He bowed his head solemnly to her.

"Come sit with me, both of you," she said. "We'll talk of strange ice creams and such things as we seem to have a bent for. Don't be afraid; I'll foot the bill."

Smiling, they carried their dishes to her table and sat.

"You look like a Spaulding," she said to the boy. "You've got your grandfather's head. And you, you're William Forrester. You write for the *Chronicle*, a good enough column. I've heard more about you than I'd care to tell."

"I know you," said Bill Forrester. "You're Helen Loomis."

He hesitated, then continued. "I was in love with you once," he said.

"Now that's the way I like a conversation to open." She dug quietly at her ice cream. "That's grounds for another meeting. No—don't tell me where or when or how you were in love with me. We'll save that for next time. You've taken away my appetite with your talk. Look there now! Well, I must get home anyway. Since you're a reporter, come for tea tomorrow between three and four; it's just possible I can sketch out the history of this town, since it was a trading post, for you. And, so we'll both have something for our curiosity to chew on, Mr. Forrester, you remind me of a gentleman I went with seventy, yes, seventy years ago."

She sat across from them and it was like talking with a gray and lost and quivering moth. The voice came from far away inside the grayness and the oldness, wrapped in the powders of pressed flowers and ancient butterflies.

"Well." She arose. "Will you come tomorrow?"

"I most certainly will," said Bill Forrester.

And she went off into the town on business, leaving the young boy and the young man there, looking after her, slowly finishing their ice cream.

William Forrester spent the next morning checking some local news items for the paper, had time after lunch for some fishing in the river outside town, caught only some small fish which he threw back happily, and, without thinking about it, or at least not noticing that he had thought about it, at three o'clock he found his car taking him down a certain street. He watched with interest as his hands turned the steering wheel and motored him up a vast circular drive where he stopped under an ivy-covered entry. Letting himself out, he was conscious of the fact that his car was like his pipe—old, chewed-on, unkempt in this huge green garden by this freshly painted, three-story Victorian house. He saw a faint ghostlike movement at the far end of the garden, heard a whispery cry, and saw that Miss Loomis was there, removed across time and distance, seated alone, the tea service glittering its soft silver surfaces, waiting for him.

"This is the first time a woman has ever been ready and waiting," he said, walking up. "It is also," he admitted, "the first time in my life I have been on time for an appointment."

"Why is that?" she asked, propped back in her wicker chair.

"I don't know," he admitted.

"Well." She started pouring tea. "To start things off, what do you think of the world?"

"I don't know anything."

"The beginning of wisdom, as they say. When you're seventeen you know everything. When you're *twenty*-seven if you *still* know everything you're still seventeen."

"You seem to have learned quite a lot over the years."

"It is the privilege of old people to seem to know everything. But it's an act and a mask, like every other act and mask. Between ourselves, we old ones wink at each other and smile, saying, How do you like *my* mask, *my* act, *my* certainty? Isn't life a play? Don't I play it well?"

They both laughed quietly. He sat back and let the laughter come naturally from his mouth for the first time in many months. When they quieted she held her teacup in her two hands and looked into it. "Do you know, it's lucky we met so late. I wouldn't have wanted you to meet me when I was twenty-one and full of foolishness."

"They have special laws for pretty girls twenty-one."

"So you think I was pretty?"

He nodded good-humoredly.

"But how can you tell?" she asked. "When you meet a dragon that has eaten a swan, do you guess by the few feathers left around the mouth? That's what it is—a body like this is a dragon, all scales and folds. So the dragon ate the white swan, I haven't seen her for years. I can't even remember what she looks like. I *feel* her, though. She's safe inside, still alive; the essential swan hasn't changed a feather. Do you know, there are some mornings in spring or fall, when I wake and think, I'll run across the fields into the woods and pick wild strawberries! Or I'll swim in the lake, or I'll dance all night tonight until dawn! And then, in a rage, discover I'm in this old and ruined dragon. I'm the princess in the crumbled tower, no way out, waiting for her Prince Charming."

"You should have written books."

"My dear boy, I *have* written. What else was there for an old maid? I was a crazy creature with a headful of carnival spangles until I was thirty, and then the only man I ever really cared for stopped waiting and married someone else. So in spite, in anger at myself, I told myself I deserved my fate for not having married when the best chance was at hand. I started traveling. My luggage was snowed under blizzards of travel stickers. I have been alone in Paris, alone in Vienna, alone in London, and, all in all, it is very much like being alone in Green Town, Illinois. It is, in essence, being alone. Oh, you have plenty of time to think, improve your manners, sharpen your conversations. But I sometimes think I could easily trade a verb tense or a curtsy for some company that would stay over for a thirty-year weekend."

They drank their tea.

"Oh, such a rush of self-pity," she said good-naturedly. "About yourself, now. You're thirty-one and still not married?"

"Let me put it this way," he said. "Women who act and think and talk like you are rare."

"My," she said seriously, "you mustn't expect young women to talk like me. That comes later. They're much too young, first of all. And secondly, the average man runs helter-skelter the moment he finds anything like a brain in a lady. You've probably met quite a few brainy ones who hid it most successfully from you. You'll have to pry around a bit to find the odd beetle. Lift a few boards."

They were laughing again.

"I shall probably be a meticulous old bachelor," he said.

"No, no, you mustn't do that. It wouldn't be right. You shouldn't even be here this afternoon. This is a street which ends only in an Egyptian pyramid. Pyramids are all very nice, but mummies are hardly fit companions. Where would you like to go, what would you really like to do with your life?"

"See Istanbul, Port Said, Nairobi, Budapest. Write a book. Smoke too many cigarettes. Fall off a cliff, but get caught in a tree halfway down. Get shot at a few times in a dark alley on a Moroccan midnight. Love a beautiful woman."

"Well, I don't think I can provide them all," she said. "But I've traveled and I can tell you about many of those places. And if you'd care to run across my front lawn tonight about eleven and if I'm still awake, I'll fire off a Civil War musket at you. Will that satisfy your masculine urge for adventure?"

"That would be just fine."

"Where would you like to go first? I can take you there, you know. I can weave a spell. Just name it. London? Cairo? Cairo makes your face turn on like a light. So let's go to Cairo. Just relax now. Put some of that nice tobacco in that pipe of yours and sit back."

He sat back, lit his pipe, half smiling, relaxing, and listened, and she began to talk. "Cairo . . ." she said.

The hour passed in jewels and alleys and winds from the Egyptian desert. The sun was golden and the Nile was muddy where it lapped down to the deltas, and there was someone very young and very quick at the top of the pyramid, laughing, calling to him to come on up the shadowy side into the sun, and he was climbing, she putting her hand down to help him up the last step, and then they were laughing on camel back, loping toward the great stretched bulk of the Sphinx, and late at night, in the native quarter, there was the tinkle of small hammers on bronze and silver, and music from some stringed instruments fading away and away and away. . . .

William Forrester opened his eyes. Miss Helen Loomis had finished the adventure and they were home again, very familiar to each other, on the best of terms, in the garden, the tea cold in the silver pourer, the biscuits dried in the latened sun. He sighed and stretched and sighed again.

"I've never been so comfortable in my life."

"Nor I."

"I've kept you late. I should have gone an hour ago."

"You know I love every minute of it. But what you should see in an old silly woman . . . "

He lay back in his chair and half closed his eyes and looked at her. He squinted his eyes so the merest filament of light came through. He tilted his head ever so little this way, then that.

"What are you doing?" she asked uncomfortably.

He said nothing, but continued looking.

"If you do this just right," he murmured, "you can adjust,

make allowances . . ." To himself he was thinking, You can erase lines, adjust the time factor, turn back the years.

Suddenly he started.

"What's wrong?" she asked.

But then it was gone. He opened his eyes to catch it. That was a mistake. He should have stayed back, idling, erasing, his eyes gently half closed.

"For just a moment," he said, "I saw it."

"Saw what?"

"The swan, of course," he thought. His mouth must have pantomimed the words.

The next instant she was sitting very straight in her chair. Her hands were in her lap, rigid. Her eyes were fixed upon him and as he watched, feeling helpless, each of her eyes cupped and brimmed itself full.

"I'm sorry," he said, "terribly sorry."

"No, don't be." She held herself rigid and did not touch her face or her eyes; her hands remained, one atop the other, holding on. "You'd better go now. Yes, you may come tomorrow, but go now, please, and don't say any more."

He walked off through the garden, leaving her by her table in the shade. He could not bring himself to look back.

Four days, eight days, twelve days passed, and he was invited to teas, to suppers, to lunches. They sat talking through the long green afternoons—they talked of art, of literature, of life, of society and politics. They ate ice creams and squabs and drank good wines.

"I don't care what anyone says," she said. "And people are saying things, aren't they?"

He shifted uneasily.

"I knew it. A woman's never safe, even when ninety-five, from gossip."

"I could stop visiting."

"Oh no," she cried, and recovered. In a quieter voice she said, "You know you can't do that. You know you don't care what they think, do you? So long as we know it's all right?"

"I don't care," he said.

"Now"—she settled back—"let's play our game. Where shall it be this time? Paris? I think Paris."

"Paris," he said, nodding quietly.

"Well," she began, "it's the year 1885 and we're boarding the ship in New York harbor. There's our luggage, here are our tickets, there goes the sky line. Now we're at sea. Now we're coming into Marseilles . . . ."

Here she was on a bridge looking into the clear waters of the Seine, and here he was, suddenly, a moment later, beside her, looking down at the tides of summer flowing past. Here she was with an apéritif in her talcum-white fingers, and here he was, with amazing quickness, bending toward her to tap her wineglass with his. His face appeared in mirrored halls at Versailles, over steaming *smörgasbörds* in Stockholm, and they counted the barber poles in the Venice canals. The things she had done alone, they were now doing together.

In the middle of August they sat staring at one another one late afternoon.

"Do you realize," he said, "I've seen you nearly every day for two and a half weeks?"

"Impossible!"

"I've enjoyed it immensely."

"Yes, but there are so many young girls . . ."

"You're everything they are not—kind, intelligent, witty."

"Nonsense. Kindness and intelligence are the preoccupations of age. Being cruel and thoughtless is far more fascinating when you're twenty." She paused and drew a breath. "Now, I'm going to embarrass you. Do you recall that first afternoon we met in the soda fountain, you said that you had had some degree of—shall we say affection for me at one time? You've purposely put me off on this by never mentioning it again. Now I'm forced to ask you to explain the whole uncomfortable thing."

He didn't seem to know what to say. "That's embarrassing," he protested.

"Spit it out!"

"I saw your picture once, years ago."

"I never let my picture be taken."

"This was an old one, taken when you were twenty."

"Oh, that. It's quite a joke. Each time I give to a charity or attend a ball they dust that picture off and print it. Everyone in town laughs; even *I*."

"It's cruel of the paper."

"No. I told them, If you want a picture of me, use the one taken back in 1853. Let them remember me that way. Keep the lid down, in the name of the good Lord, during the service."

"I'll tell you all about it." He folded his hands and looked at them and paused a moment. He was remembering the picture now and it was very clear in his mind. There was time, here in the garden to think of every aspect of the photograph and of Helen Loomis, very young, posing for her picture the first time, alone and beautiful. He thought of her quiet, shyly smiling face.

It was the face of spring, it was the face of summer, it was the warmness of clover breath. Pomegranate glowed in her lips, and the noon sky in her eyes. To touch her face was that always new experience of opening your window one December morning, early, and putting out your hand to the first white cool powdering of snow that had come, silently, with no announcement, in the night. And all of this, this breath-warmness and plum-tenderness was held forever in one miracle of photographic chemistry which no clock winds could blow upon to change one hour or one second; this fine first cool white snow would never melt, but live a thousand summers.

That was the photograph; that was the way he knew her. Now he was talking again, after the remembering and the thinking over and the holding of the picture in his mind. "When I first saw that picture—it was a simple, straightforward picture with a simple hairdo—I didn't know it had been taken that long ago. The item in the paper said something about Helen Loomis marshaling the Town Ball that night. I tore the picture from the paper. I carried it with me all that day. I intended going to the ball. Then, late in the afternoon, someone saw me looking at the picture, and told me about it. How the picture of the beautiful girl had been taken so long ago and used every year since by the paper. And they said I shouldn't go to the Town Ball that night, carrying that picture and looking for you."

They sat in the garden for a long minute. He glanced over at her face. She was looking at the farthest garden wall and the pink roses climbing there. There was no way to tell what she was thinking. Her face showed nothing. She rocked for a little while in her chair and then said softly, "Shall we have some more tea? There you are."

They sat sipping the tea. Then she reached over and patted his arm. "Thank you."

"For what?"

"For wanting to come to find me at the dance, for clipping out my picture, for everything. Thank you so very much."

They walked about the garden on the paths.

"And now," she said, "it's my turn. Do you remember, I mentioned a certain young man who once attended me, seventy years ago? Oh, he's been dead fifty years now, at least, but when he was very young and very handsome he rode a fast horse off for days, or on summer nights over the meadows around town. He had a healthy, wild face, always sunburned, his hands were always cut and he fumed like a stovepipe and walked as if he were going to fly apart; wouldn't keep a job, quit those he had when he felt like it, and one day he sort of rode off away from me because I was even wilder than he and wouldn't settle down, and that was that. I never thought the day would come when I would see him alive again. But you're pretty much alive, you spill ashes around like he did, you're clumsy and graceful combined, I know everything you're going to do before you do it, but after you've done it I'm always surprised. Reincarnation's a lot of milk-mush to me, but the other day I felt, What if I called Robert, Robert, to you on the street, would William Forrester turn around?"

"I don't know," he said.

"Neither do I. That's what makes life interesting."

August was almost over. The first cool touch of autumn moved slowly through the town and there was a softening and the first gradual burning fever of color in every tree, a faint flush and coloring in the hills, and the color of lions in the wheat fields. Now the pattern of days was familiar and repeated like a penman beautifully inscribing again and again, in practice, a series of *l*'s and *w*'s and *m*'s, day after day the line repeated in delicate rills.

William Forrester walked across the garden one early September afternoon to find Helen Loomis writing with great care at the tea table.

She put aside her pen and ink.

"I've been writing you a letter," she said.

"Well, my being here saves you the trouble."

"No, this is a special letter. Look at it." She showed him the blue envelope, which she now sealed and pressed flat. "Remember how it looks. When you receive this in the mail, you'll know I'm dead."

"That's no way to talk, is it?"

"Sit down and listen to me."

He sat.

"My dear William," she said, under the parasol shade. "In a few days I will be dead. No," She put up her hand. "I don't want you to say a thing. I'm not afraid. When you live as long as I've lived you lose that, too. I never liked lobster in my life, and mainly because I'd never tried it. On my eightieth birthday I tried it. I can't say I'm greatly excited over lobster still, but I have no doubt as to its taste now, and I don't fear it. I dare say death will be a lobster, too, and I can come to terms with it." She motioned with her hands. "But enough of that. The important thing is that I shan't be seeing you again. There will be no services. I believe that a woman who has passed through that particular door has as much right to privacy as a woman who has retired for the night."

"You can't predict death," he said at last.

"For fifty years I've watched the grandfather clock in the hall, William. After it is wound I can predict to the hour when it will stop. Old people are no different. They can feel the machinery slow down and the last weights shift. Oh, please don't look that way—please don't."

"I can't help it," he said.

"We've had a nice time, haven't we? It has been very special here, talking every day. It was that much-overburdened and worn phrase referred to as a 'meeting of the minds.'" She turned the blue envelope in her hands. "I've always known that the quality of love was the mind, even though the body sometimes refuses this knowledge. The body lives for itself. It lives only to feed and wait for the night. It's essentially nocturnal. But what of the mind which is born of the sun, William, and must spend thousands of hours of a lifetime awake and aware? Can you balance off the body, that pitiful, selfish thing of night against a whole lifetime of sun and intellect? I don't know. I only know there has been your mind here and my mind here, and the afternoons have been like none I can remember. There is still so much to talk about, but we must save it for another time."

"We don't seem to have much time now."

"No, but perhaps there *will* be another time. Time is so strange and life is twice as strange. The cogs miss, the wheels turn, and lives interlace too early or too late. I lived too long, that much is certain. And you were born either too early or too late. It was a terrible bit of timing. But perhaps I am being punished for being a silly girl. Anyway, the next spin around, wheels might function right again. Meantime you must find a nice girl and be married and be happy. But you must promise me one thing."

"Anything."

"You must promise me not to live to be too old, William. If it is at all convenient, die before you're fifty. It may take a bit of doing. But I advise this simply because there is no telling when another Helen Loomis might be born. It would be dreadful, wouldn't it, if you lived on to be very, very old and some afternoon in 1999 walked down Main Street and saw me standing there, aged twenty-one, and the whole thing out of balance again? I don't think we could go through any more afternoons like these we've had, no matter how pleasant, do you? A thousand gallons of tea and five hundred biscuits is enough for one friendship. So you must have an attack of pneumonia some time in about twenty years. For I don't know how long they let you linger on the other side. Perhaps they send you back immediately. But I shall do my best, William, really I shall. And everything put right and in balance, do you know what might happen?"

"You tell me."

"Some afternoon in 1985 or 1990 a young man named Tom Smith or John Green or a name like that, will be walking downtown and will stop in the drugstore and order, appropriately, a dish of some unusual ice cream. A young girl the same age will be sitting there and when she hears the name of that ice cream, something will happen. I can't say what or how. *She* won't know why or how, assuredly. Nor will the young man. It will simply be that the name of that ice cream will be a very good thing to both of them. They'll talk. And later, when they know each other's names, they'll walk from the drugstore together."

She smiled at him.

"This is all very neat, but forgive an old lady for tying things in neat packets. It's a silly trifle to leave you. Now, let's talk of something else. What shall we talk about? Is there any place in the world we haven't traveled to yet? Have we been to Stockholm?"

"Yes, it's a fine town."

"Glasgow? Yes? Where then?"

"Why not Green Town, Illinois?" he said. "Here. We haven't really visited our own town together at all."

She settled back, as did he, and she said, "I'll tell you how it was, then, when I was only nineteen, in this town, a long time ago . . ."

It was a night in winter and she was skating lightly over a pond of white moon ice, her image gliding and whispering under her. It was a night in summer in this town of fire in the air, in the cheeks, in the heart, your eyes full of the glowing and shutting-off color of fireflies. It was a rustling night in October, and there she stood, pulling taffy from a hook in the kitchen, singing, and there she was, running on the moss by the river, and swimming in the granite pit beyond town on a spring night, in the soft deep warm waters, and now it was the Fourth of July with rockets slamming the sky and every porch full of now red-fire, now blue-fire, now white-fire faces, hers dazzling bright among them as the last rocket died.

"Can you see all these things?" asked Helen Loomis. "Can you see me doing them and being with them?"

"Yes," said William Forrester, eyes closed. "I can see you."

"And then," she said, "and then . . ."

Her voice moved on and on as the afternoon grew late and the twilight deepened quickly, but her voice moved in the garden and anyone passing on the road, at a far distance, could have heard its moth sound, faintly, faintly . . .

Two days later William Forrester was at his desk in his room when the letter came. Douglas brought it upstairs and handed it to Bill and looked as if he knew what was in it.

William Forrester recognized the blue envelope, but did not open it. He simply put it in his shirt pocket, looked at the boy for a moment, and said, "Come on, Doug; my treat."

They walked downtown, saying very little, Douglas preserving the silence he sensed was necessary. Autumn, which had threatened for a time, was gone. Summer was back full, boiling the clouds and scouring the metal sky. They turned in at the drugstore and sat at the marble fountain. William Forrester took the letter out and laid it before him and still did not open it.

He looked out at the yellow sunlight on the concrete and on the green awnings and shining on the gold letters of the window signs across the street, and he looked at the calendar on the wall, August 27, 1928. He looked at his wrist watch and felt his heart beat slowly, saw the second hand of the watch moving moving with no speed at all, saw the calendar frozen there with its one day seeming forever, the sun nailed to the sky with no motion toward sunset whatever. The warm air spread under the sighing fans over his head. A number of women laughed by the open door and were gone through his vision, which was focused beyond them at the town itself and the high courthouse clock. He opened the letter and began to read.

He turned slowly on the revolving chair. He tried the words again and again, silently, on his tongue, and at last spoke them aloud and repeated them.

"A dish of lime-vanilla ice," he said. "A dish of lime-vanilla ice."

DOUGLAS AND Tom and Charlie came panting along the unshaded street.

"Tom, answer me true, now."

"Answer what true?"

"What ever happened to happy endings?"

"They got them on shows at Saturday matinees."

"Sure, but what about life?"

"All I know is I feel good going to bed nights, Doug. That's a happy ending once a day. Next morning I'm up and maybe things go bad. But all I got to do is remember that I'm going to bed that night and just lying there a while makes everything okay."

"I'm talking about Mr. Forrester and old Miss Loomis."

"Nothing we can do; she's dead."

"I know! But don't you figure someone slipped up there?"

"You mean about him thinking she was the same age as her picture and her a trillion years old all the time? No, sir, I think it's swell!"

"Swell, for gosh sakes?"

"The last few days when Mr. Forrester told me a little here or a little there and I finally put it all together—boy, did I bawl my head off, I don't even know why. I wouldn't change one bit of it. If you changed it, what would we have to talk about? Nothing! And besides, I like to cry. After I cry hard it's like it's morning again and I'm starting the day over."

"I heard everything now."

"You just won't admit you like crying, too. You cry just so long and everything's fine. And there's your happy ending. And you're ready to go back out and walk around with folks again. And it's the *start* of gosh-knows-what-all! Any time now, Mr. Forrester will think it over and see it's just the only way and have a good cry and then look around and see it's morning again, even though it's five in the afternoon."

"That don't sound like no happy ending to me."

"A good night's sleep, or a ten-minute bawl, or a pint of

chocolate ice cream, or all three together, is good medicine, Doug. You listen to Tom Spaulding, M.D."

"Shut up, you guys," said Charlie. "We're almost there!"

They turned a corner.

Deep in winter they had looked for bits and pieces of summer and found it in furnace cellars or in bonfires on the edge of frozen skating ponds at night. Now, in summer, they went searching for some little bit, some piece of the forgotten winter.

Rounding the corner, they felt a continual light rain spray down from a vast brick building to refresh them as they read the sign they knew by heart, the sign which showed them what they'd come searching for:

SUMMER'S ICE HOUSE.

Summer's Ice House on a summer day! They said the words, laughing, and moved to peer into that tremendous cavern where in fifty, one-hundred, and two-hundred-pound chunks, the glaciers, the icebergs, the fallen but not forgotten snows of January slept in ammoniac steams and crystal drippings.

"Feel that," sighed Charlie Woodman. "What more could you ask?"

For the winter breath was exhaled again and again about them as they stood in the glary day, smelling the wet wood platform with the perpetual mist shimmering in rainbows down from the ice machinery above.

They chewed icicles that froze their fingers so they had to grip the ice in handkerchiefs and suck the linen.

"All that steam, all that fog," whispered Tom. "The Snow Queen. Remember that story? Nobody believes in that stuff, Snow Queens, now. So don't be surprised if this is where she came to hide out because nobody believes in her any more."

They looked and saw the vapors rise and drift in long swathes of cool smoke.

"No," said Charlie. "You know who lives here? Only one guy. A guy who gives you goose-pimples just to think of him." Charlie dropped his voice very low. "The Lonely One."

"The Lonely One?"

"Born, raised, and *lives* here! All that winter, Tom, all that cold, Doug! Where else would he come from to make us shiver the hottest nights of the year? Don't it *smell* like him? You know darn well it does. The Lonely One . . . The Lonely One . . ."

The mists and vapors curled in darkness.

Tom screamed.

"It's O.K., Doug." Charlie grinned. "I just dropped a little bitty hunk of ice down Tom's back, is all."

THE COURTHOUSE clock chimed seven times. The echoes of the chimes faded.

Warm summer twilight here in upper Illinois country in this little town deep far away from everything, kept to itself by a river and a forest and a meadow and a lake. The sidewalks still scorched. The stores closing and the streets shadowed. And there were two moons; the clock moon with four faces in four night directions above the solemn black courthouse, and the real moon rising in vanilla whiteness from the dark east.

In the drugstore fans whispered in the high ceiling. In the rococo shade of porches, a few invisible people sat. Cigars glowed pink, on occasion. Screen doors whined their springs and slammed. On the purple bricks of the summer-night streets, Douglas Spaulding ran; dogs and boys followed after.

"Hi, Miss Lavinia!"

The boys loped away. Waving after them quietly, Lavinia Nebbs sat all alone with a tall cool lemonade in her white fingers, tapping it to her lips, sipping, waiting.

"Here I am, Lavinia."

She turned and there was Francine, all in snow white, at the bottom steps of the porch, in the smell of zinnias and hibiscus.

Lavinia Nebbs locked her front door and, leaving her lemonade glass half empty on the porch, said, "It's a fine night for the movie."

They walked down the street.

"Where you going, girls?" cried Miss Fern and Miss Roberta from their porch over the way.

Lavinia called back through the soft ocean of darkness: "To the Elite Theater to see CHARLIE CHAPLIN!"

"Won't catch us out on no night like this," wailed Miss Fern. "Not with the Lonely One strangling women. Lock ourselves up in our closet with a gun."

"Oh, bosh!" Lavinia heard the old women's door bang and lock, and she drifted on, feeling the warm breath of summer night shimmering off the oven-baked sidewalks. It was like walking on a hard crust of freshly warmed bread. The heat pulsed under your dress, along your legs, with a stealthy and not unpleasant sense of invasion.

"Lavinia, you don't believe all that about the Lonely One, do you?"

"Those women like to see their tongues dance."

"Just the same, Hattie McDollis was killed two months ago, Roberta Ferry the month before, and now Elizabeth Ramsell's disappeared . . ."

"Hattie McDollis was a silly girl, walked off with a traveling man, I bet."

"But the others, all of them, strangled, their tongues sticking out their mouths, they say."

They stood upon the edge of the ravine that cut the town half in two. Behind them were the lit houses and music, ahead was deepness, moistness, fireflies and dark.

"Maybe we shouldn't go to the show tonight," said Francine. "The Lonely One might follow and kill us. I don't like that ravine. Look at it, will you!"

Lavinia looked and the ravine was a dynamo that never stopped running, night or day; there was a great moving hum, a bumbling and murmuring of creature, insect, or plant life. It smelled like a greenhouse, of secret vapors and ancient, washed shales and quicksands. And always the black dynamo humming, with sparkles like great electricity where fireflies moved on the air.

"It won't be *me* coming back through this old ravine tonight late, so darned late; it'll be you, Lavinia, you down the steps and over the bridge and maybe the Lonely One there."

"Bosh!" said Lavinia Nebbs.

"It'll be you alone on the path, listening to your shoes, not me. You all alone on the way back to your house. Lavinia, don't you get lonely living in that house?"

"Old maids love to live alone." Lavinia pointed at the hot shadowy path leading down into the dark. "Let's take the short cut."

"I'm afraid!"

"It's early. Lonely One won't be out till late." Lavinia took the other's arm and led her down and down the crooked path into the cricket warmth and frog sound and mosquito-delicate silence. They brushed through summer-scorched grass, burrs prickling at their bare ankles.

"Let's run!" gasped Francine.

"No!"

They turned a curve in the path—and there it was.

In the singing deep night, in the shade of warm trees, as if she had laid herself out to enjoy the soft stars and the easy wind, her hands at either side of her like the oars of a delicate craft, lay Elizabeth Ramsell!

Francine screamed.

"Don't scream!" Lavinia put out her hands to hold onto Francine, who was whimpering and choking. "Don't! Don't!"

The woman lay as if she had floated there, her face moonlit, her eyes wide and like flint, her tongue sticking from her mouth.

"She's dead!" said Francine. "Oh, she's dead, dead! She's dead!"

Lavinia stood in the middle of a thousand warm shadows with the crickets screaming and the frogs loud.

"We'd better get the police," she said at last.

"Hold me, Lavinia, hold me, I'm cold, oh, I've never been so cold in all my life!"

Lavinia held Francine and the policemen were brushing through the crackling grass, flashlights ducked about, voices mingled, and the night grew toward eight-thirty.

"It's like December. I need a sweater," said Francine, eyes shut, against Lavinia.

The policeman said, "I guess you can go now, ladies. You might drop by the station tomorrow for a little more questioning."

Lavinia and Francine walked away from the police and the sheet over the delicate thing upon the ravine grass.

Lavinia felt her heart going loudly in her and she was cold, too, with a February cold; there were bits of sudden snow all over her flesh, and the moon washed her brittle fingers whiter, and she remembered doing all the talking while Francine just sobbed against her.

A voice called from far off, "You want an escort, ladies?"

"No, we'll make it," said Lavinia to nobody, and they walked on. They walked through the nuzzling, whispering ravine, the ravine of whispers and clicks, the little world of investigation growing small behind them with its lights and voices.

"I've never seen a dead person before," said Francine.

Lavinia examined her watch as if it was a thousand miles away on an arm and wrist grown impossibly distant. "It's only eight-thirty. We'll pick up Helen and get on to the show."

"The show!" Francine jerked.

"It's what we need. We've got to forget this. It's not good to remember. If we went home now we'd remember. We'll go to the show as if nothing happened."

"Lavinia, you don't *mean* it!"

"I never meant anything more in my life. We need to laugh now and forget."

"But Elizabeth's back there—your friend, my friend——"

"We can't help her; we can only help ourselves. Come on."

They started up the ravine side, on the stony path, in the dark. And suddenly there, barring their way, standing very still in one spot, not seeing them, but looking on down at the moving lights and the body and listening to the official voices, was Douglas Spaulding.

He stood there, white as a mushroom, with his hands at his sides, staring down into the ravine.

"Get home!" cried Francine.

He did not hear.

"You!" shrieked Francine. "Get home, get out of this place, you hear? Get home, get home, get *home*!"

Douglas jerked his head, stared at them as if they were not there. His mouth moved. He gave a bleating sound. Then, silently, he whirled about and ran. He ran silently up the distant hills into the warm darkness.

Francine sobbed and cried again and, doing this, walked on with Lavinia Nebbs.

"There you are! I thought you ladies'd never come!" Helen Greer stood tapping her foot atop her porch steps. "You're only an hour late, that's all. What happened?"

"We——" started Francine.

Lavinia clutched her arm tight. "There was a commotion. Somebody found Elizabeth Ramsell in the ravine."

"Dead? Was she—dead?"

Lavinia nodded. Helen gasped and put her hand to her throat. "Who found her?"

Lavinia held Francine's wrist firmly. "We don't know."

The three young women stood in the summer night looking at each other. "I've got a notion to go in the house and lock the doors," said Helen at last.

But finally she went to get a sweater, for though it was still warm, she, too, complained of the sudden winter night. While she was gone Francine whispered frantically, "Why didn't you *tell* her?"

"Why upset her?" said Lavinia. "Tomorrow. Tomorrow's plenty of time."

The three women moved along the street under the black trees, past suddenly locked houses. How soon the news had spread outward from the ravine, from house to house, porch to porch, telephone to telephone. Now, passing, the three women felt eyes looking out at them from curtained windows as locks rattled into place. How strange the popsicle, the vanilla night, the night of close-packed ice cream, of mosquito-lotioned wrists, the night of running children suddenly veered from their games and put away behind glass, behind wood, the popsicles in melting puddles of lime and strawberry where they fell when the children were scooped indoors. Strange the hot rooms with the sweating people pressed tightly back into them behind the bronze knobs and knockers. Baseball bats and balls lay upon the unfootprinted lawns. A half-drawn, white-chalk game of hopscotch lay on the broiled, steamed sidewalk. It was as if someone had predicted freezing weather a moment ago.

"We're crazy being out on a night like this," said Helen.

"Lonely One won't kill three ladies," said Lavinia. "There's safety in numbers. And besides, it's too soon. The killings always come a month separated."

A shadow fell across their terrified faces. A figure loomed behind a tree. As if someone had struck an organ a terrible blow with his fist, the three women gave off a scream, in three different shrill notes.

"Got you!" roared a voice. The man plunged at them. He came into the light, laughing. He leaned against a tree, pointing at the ladies weakly, laughing again.

"Hey! I'm the Lonely One!" said Frank Dillon.

"Frank Dillon!"

"Frank!"

"Frank," said Lavinia, "if you ever do a childish thing like that again, may someone riddle you with bullets!"

"What a thing to do!"

Francine began to cry hysterically.

Frank Dillon stopped smiling, "Say. I'm sorry."

"Go away!" said Lavinia. "Haven't you heard about Elizabeth Ramsell—found dead in the ravine? You running around scaring women! Don't speak to us again!"

"Aw, now——"

They moved. He moved to follow.

"Stay right there, Mr. Lonely One, and scare yourself. Go take a look at Elizabeth Ramsell's face and see if it's funny. Good night!" Lavinia took the other two on along the street of trees and stars, Francine holding a kerchief to her face.

"Francine, it was only a joke." Helen turned to Lavinia. "Why's she crying so hard?"

"We'll tell you when we get downtown. We're going to the show no matter what! Enough's enough. Come on now, get your money ready, we're almost there!"

The drugstore was a small pool of sluggish air which the great wooden fans stirred in tides of arnica and tonic and soda-smell out onto the brick streets.

"I need a nickel's worth of green peppermint chews," said Lavinia to the druggist. His face was set and pale, like all the faces they had seen on the half-empty streets. "For eating in the show," said Lavinia as the druggist weighed out a nickel's worth of the green candy with a silver shovel.

"You sure look pretty tonight, ladies. You looked cool this afternoon, Miss Lavinia, when you was in for a chocolate soda. So cool and nice that someone asked after you."

"Oh?"

"Man sitting at the counter—watched you walk out. Said to me, 'Say, who's that?' Why, that's Lavinia Nebbs, prettiest maiden lady in town, I said. 'She's beautiful,' he said. 'Where does she live?'" Here the druggist paused uncomfortably.

"You didn't!" said Francine. "You didn't give him her address, I hope? You didn't!"

"I guess I didn't think. I said, 'Oh, over on Park Street, you know, near the ravine.' A casual remark. But now, tonight, them finding the body, I heard a minute ago, I thought, My God, what've I done!" He handed over the package, much too full.

"You fool!" cried Francine, and tears were in her eyes.

"I'm sorry. Course, maybe it was nothing."

Lavinia stood with the three people looking at her, staring at her. She felt nothing. Except, perhaps, the slightest prickle of excitement in her throat. She held out her money automatically.

"There's no charge on those peppermints," said the druggist, turning to shuffle some papers.

"Well, I know what I'm going to do right now!" Helen stalked out of the drugshop. "I'm calling a taxi to take us all home. I'll be no part of a hunting party for you, Lavinia. That man was up to no good. Asking about you. You want to be dead in the ravine next?"

"It was just a man," said Lavinia, turning in a slow circle to look at the town.

"So is Frank Dillon a man, but maybe he's the Lonely One."

Francine hadn't come out with them, they noticed, and turning, they found her arriving. "I made him give me a description—the druggist. I made him tell what the man looked like. A stranger," she said, "in a dark suit. Sort of pale and thin."

"We're all overwrought," said Lavinia. "I simply won't take a taxi if you get one. If I'm the next victim, let me *be* the next. There's all too little excitement in life, especially for a maiden lady thirty-three years old, so don't you mind if I enjoy it. Anyway, it's silly; I'm not beautiful."

"Oh, but you are, Lavinia; you're the loveliest lady in town, now that Elizabeth is——" Francine stopped. "You keep men off at a distance. If you'd only relax, you'd been married years ago!"

"Stop sniveling, Francine! Here's the theater box office. I'm paying forty-one cents to see Charlie Chaplin. If you two want a taxi, go on. I'll sit alone and go home alone."

"Lavinia, you're crazy; we can't let you do that——"

They entered the theater.

The first showing was over, intermission was on, and the dim auditorium was sparsely populated. The three ladies sat halfway down front, in the smell of ancient brass polish, and watched the manager step through the worn red velvet curtains to make an announcement.

"The police have asked us to close early tonight so everyone can be out at a decent hour. Therefore we are cutting our short subjects and running our feature again immediately. The show will be over at eleven. Everyone is advised to go straight home. Don't linger on the streets."

"That means us, Lavinia!" whispered Francine.

The lights went out. The screen leaped to life.

"Lavinia," whispered Helen.

"What?"

"As we came in, a man in a dark suit, across the street, crossed over. He just walked down the aisle and is sitting in the row behind us."

"Oh, Helen!"

"Right behind us?"

One by one the three women turned to look.

They saw a white face there, flickering with unholy light from the silver screen. It seemed to be all men's faces hovering there in the dark.

"I'm going to get the manager!" Helen was gone up the aisle. "Stop the film! Lights!"

"Helen, come back!" cried Lavinia, rising.

They tapped their empty soda glasses down, each with a vanilla mustache on their upper lip, which they found with their tongues, laughing.

"You see how silly?" said Lavinia. "All that riot for nothing. How embarrassing!"

"I'm sorry," said Helen faintly.

The clock said eleven-thirty now. They had come out of the dark theater, away from the fluttering rush of men and women hurrying everywhere, nowhere, on the street while laughing at Helen. Helen was trying to laugh at herself.

"Helen, when you ran up that aisle crying, 'Lights!' I thought I'd *die*! That *poor* man!"

"The theater manager's brother from Racine!"

"I apologized," said Helen, looking up at the great fan still whirling, whirling the warm late night air, stirring, restirring the smells of vanilla, raspberry, peppermint and Lysol.

"We shouldn't have stopped for these sodas. The police warned——"

"Oh, bosh the police," laughed Lavinia. "I'm not afraid of anything. The Lonely One is a million miles away now. He won't be back for weeks and the police'll get him then, just wait. Wasn't the film wonderful?"

"Closing up, ladies." The druggist switched off the lights in the cool white-tiled silence.

Outside, the streets were swept clean and empty of cars or trucks or people. Bright lights still burned in the small store windows where the warm wax dummies lifted pink wax hands fired with blue-white diamond rings, or flourished orange wax legs to reveal hosiery. The hot blue-glass eyes of the mannequins watched as the ladies drifted down the empty river bottom street, their images shimmering in windows like blossoms seen under darkly moving waters.

"Do you suppose if we screamed they'd do anything?"

"Who?"

"The dummies, the window people."

"Oh, Fran*cine*."

"Well . . ."

There were a thousand people in the windows, stiff and silent, and three people on the street, the echoes following like gunshots from store fronts across the way when they tapped their heels on the baked pavement.

A red neon sign flickered dimly, buzzed like a dying insect, as they passed.

Baked and white, the long avenues lay ahead. Blowing and tall in a wind that touched only their leafy summits, the trees stood on either side of the three small women. Seen from the courthouse peak, they appeared like three thistles far away.

"First, we'll walk you home, Francine."

"No, I'll walk *you* home."

"Don't be silly. You live way out at Electric Park. If you walked me home you'd have to come back across the ravine alone, yourself. And if so much as a leaf fell on you, you'd drop dead."

Francine said, "I can stay the night at your house. You're the *pretty* one!"

And so they walked, they drifted like three prim clothes forms over a moonlit sea of lawn and concrete, Lavinia watching the black trees flit by each side of her, listening to the voices of her friends murmuring, trying to laugh; and the night seemed to quicken, they seemed to run while walking slowly, everything seemed fast and the color of hot snow.

"Let's sing," said Lavinia.

They sang, "Shine On, Shine On, Harvest Moon . . ."

They sang sweetly and quietly, arm in arm, not looking back. They felt the hot sidewalk cooling underfoot, moving, moving.

"Listen!" said Lavinia.

They listened to the summer night. The summer-night crickets and the far-off tone of the courthouse clock making it eleven forty-five.

"*Listen!*"

Lavinia listened. A porch swing creaked in the dark and there was Mr. Terle, not saying anything to anybody, alone on his swing, having a last cigar. They saw the pink ash swinging gently to and fro.

Now the lights were going, going, gone. The little house lights and big house lights and yellow lights and green hurricane lights, the candles and oil lamps and porch lights, and everything felt locked up in brass and iron and steel, everything, thought Lavinia, is boxed and locked and wrapped and shaded. She imagined the people in their moonlit beds. And their breathing in the summer-night rooms, safe and together. And here we are, thought Lavinia, our footsteps on along the baked summer evening sidewalk. And above us the lonely street lights shining down, making a drunken shadow.

"Here's your house, Francine. Good night."

"Lavinia, Helen, stay here tonight. It's late, almost midnight now. You can sleep in the parlor. I'll make hot chocolate—it'll be such fun!" Francine was holding them both now, close to her.

"No, thanks," said Lavinia.

And Francine began to cry.

"Oh, not again, Francine," said Lavinia.

"I don't want you dead," sobbed Francine, the tears running straight down her cheeks. "You're so fine and nice, I want you alive. Please, oh, please!"

"Francine, I didn't know how much this has done to you. I promise I'll phone when I get home."

"Oh, will you?"

"And tell you I'm safe, yes. And tomorrow we'll have a picnic lunch at Electric Park. With ham sandwiches I'll make myself, how's that? You'll see, I'll live forever!"

"You'll phone, then?"

"I promised, didn't I?"

"Good night, good night!" Rushing upstairs, Francine whisked behind a door, which slammed to be snap-bolted tight on the instant.

"Now," said Lavinia to Helen, "I'll walk *you* home."

The courthouse clock struck the hour. The sounds blew across a town that was empty, emptier than it had ever been. Over empty streets and empty lots and empty lawns the sound faded.

"Nine, ten, eleven, twelve," counted Lavinia, with Helen on her arm.

"Don't you feel funny?" asked Helen.

"How do you mean?"

"When you think of us being out here on the sidewalks, under the trees, and all those people safe behind locked doors, lying in their beds. We're practically the only walking people out in the open in a thousand miles, I bet."

The sound of the deep warm dark ravine came near.

In a minute they stood before Helen's house, looking at each other for a long time. The wind blew the odor of cut grass between them. The moon was sinking in a sky that was beginning to cloud. "I don't suppose it's any use asking you to stay, Lavinia?"

"I'll be going on."

"Sometimes——"

"Sometimes what?"

"Sometimes I think people *want* to die. You've acted odd all evening."

"I'm just not afraid," said Lavinia. "And I'm curious, I suppose. And I'm using my head. Logically, the Lonely One can't be around. The police and all."

"The police are home with their covers up over their ears."

"Let's just say I'm enjoying myself, precariously, but safely. If there was any real chance of anything happening to me, I'd stay here with you, you can be sure of that."

"Maybe part of you doesn't want to live any more."

"You and Francine. Honestly!"

"I feel so guilty. I'll be drinking some hot cocoa just as you reach the ravine bottom and walk on the bridge."

"Drink a cup for me. Good night."

Lavinia Nebbs walked alone down the midnight street, down the late summer-night silence. She saw houses with the dark windows and far away she heard a dog barking. In five minutes, she thought, I'll be safe at home. In five minutes I'll be phoning silly little Francine. I'll——

She heard the man's voice.

A man's voice singing far away among the trees.

"Oh, give me a June night, the moonlight and you . . ."

She walked a little faster.

The voice sang, "In my arms . . . with all your charms . . ."

Down the street in the dim moonlight a man walked slowly and casually along.

I can run knock on one of these doors, thought Lavinia, if I must.

"Oh, give me a June night," sang the man, and he carried a long club in his hand. "The moonlight and you. Well, look who's *here*! What a time of night for you to be out, Miss Nebbs!"

"Officer Kennedy!"

And that's who it was, of course.

"I'd better see you home!"

"Thanks, I'll make it."

"But you live across the ravine . . ."

Yes, she thought, but I won't walk through the ravine with any man, not even an officer. How do I know who the Lonely One is? "No," she said, "I'll hurry."

"I'll wait right here," he said. "If you need any help, give a yell. Voices carry good here. I'll come running."

"Thank you."

She went on, leaving him under a light, humming to himself, alone.

Here I am, she thought.

The ravine.

She stood on the edge of the one hundred and thirteen steps that went down the steep hill and then across the bridge seventy yards and up the hills leading to Park Street. And only one lantern to see by. Three minutes from now, she thought, I'll be putting my key in my house door. Nothing can happen in just one hundred eighty seconds.

She started down the long dark-green steps into the deep ravine.

"One, two, three, four, five, six, seven, eight, nine, ten steps," she counted in a whisper.

She felt she was running, but she was not running.

"Fifteen, sixteen, seventeen, eighteen, nineteen, twenty steps," she breathed.

"One fifth of the way!" she announced to herself.

The ravine was deep, black and black, black! And the world was gone behind, the world of safe people in bed, the locked doors, the town, the drugstore, the theater, the lights, everything was gone. Only the ravine existed and lived, black and huge, about her.

"Nothing's happened, has it? No one around, is there? Twenty-four, twenty-five steps. Remember that old ghost story you told each other when you were children?"

She listened to her shoes on the steps.

"The story about the dark man coming in your house and you upstairs in bed. And now he's at the first step coming up to your room. And now he's at the second step. And now he's at the third step and the fourth step and the fifth! Oh, how you used to laugh and scream at that story! And now the horrid dark man's at the twelfth step and now he's opening the door of your room and now he's standing by your bed. 'I GOT YOU!'"

She screamed. It was like nothing she'd ever heard, that scream. She had never screamed that loud in her life. She stopped, she froze, she clung to the wooden banister. Her heart exploded in her. The sound of the terrified beating filled the universe.

"There, *there*!" she screamed to herself. "At the bottom of the steps. A man, under the light! No, now he's gone! He was *waiting* there!"

She listened.

Silence.

The bridge was empty.

Nothing, she thought, holding her heart. Nothing. Fool! That story I told myself. How silly. What shall I do?

Her heartbeats faded.

Shall I call the officer—did he hear me scream?

She listened. Nothing. Nothing.

I'll go the rest of the way. That silly story.

She began again, counting the steps.

"Thirty-five, thirty-six, careful, don't fall. Oh, I am a fool. Thirty-seven steps, thirty-eight, nine and forty, and two makes forty-two—almost halfway."

She froze again.

Wait, she told herself.

She took a step. There was an echo.

She took another step.

Another echo. Another step, just a fraction of a moment later.

"Someone's following me," she whispered to the ravine, to the black crickets and dark-green hidden frogs and the black stream. "Someone's on the steps behind me. I don't dare turn around."

Another step, another echo.

"Every time I take a step, they take one."

A step and an echo.

Weakly she asked of the ravine, "Officer Kennedy, is that *you*?"

The crickets were still.

The crickets were *listening*. The night was listening to *her*. For a change, all of the far summer-night meadows and close summer-night trees were suspending motion; leaf, shrub, star, and meadow grass ceased their particular tremors and were listening to Lavinia Nebbs' heart. And perhaps a thousand miles away, across locomotive-lonely country, in an empty way station, a single traveler reading a dim newspaper under a solitary naked light bulb, might raise up his head, listen, and think, What's that? and decide, Only a woodchuck, surely, beating on a hollow log. But it was Lavinia Nebbs, it was most surely the heart of Lavinia Nebbs.

Silence. A summer-night silence which lay for a thousand miles, which covered the earth like a white and shadowy sea.

Faster, faster! She went down the steps.

Run!

She heard music. In a mad way, in a silly way, she heard the great surge of music that pounded at her, and she realized as she ran, as she ran in panic and terror, that some part of her mind was dramatizing, borrowing from the turbulent musical score of some private drama, and the music was rushing and pushing her now, higher and higher, faster, faster, plummeting and scurrying, down, and down into the pit of the ravine.

Only a little way, she prayed. One hundred eight, nine, one hundred ten steps! The bottom! Now, run! Across the bridge!

She told her legs what to do, her arms, her body, her terror; she advised all parts of herself in this white and terrible moment, over the roaring creek waters, on the hollow, thudding, swaying, almost alive, resilient bridge planks she ran, followed by the wild footsteps behind, behind, with the music following, too, the music shrieking and babbling.

He's following, don't turn, don't look, if you see him, you'll not be able to move, you'll be so frightened. Just run, run!

She ran across the bridge.

Oh God, God, please, please let me get up the hill! Now up, the path, now between the hills, oh God, it's dark, and everything so far away. If I screamed now it wouldn't help; I can't scream anyway. Here's the top of the path, here's the street, oh, God, please let me be safe, if I get home safe I'll never go out alone; I was a fool, let me admit it, I was a fool, I didn't know what terror was, but if you let me get home from this I'll never go without Helen or Francine again! Here's the street. Across the street!

She crossed the street and rushed up the sidewalk.

Oh God, the porch! My house! Oh God, please give me time to get inside and lock the door and I'll be safe!

And there—silly thing to notice—why did she notice, instantly, no time, no time—but there it was anyway, flashing by—there on the porch rail, the half-filled glass of lemonade she had abandoned a long time, a year, half an evening ago! The lemonade glass sitting calmly, imperturbably there on the rail . . . and . . .

She heard her clumsy feet on the porch and listened and felt her hands scrabbling and ripping at the lock with the key. She heard her heart. She heard her inner voice screaming.

The key fit.

Unlock the door, quick, quick!

The door opened.

Now, inside. Slam it!

She slammed the door.

"Now lock it, bar it, lock it!" she gasped wretchedly.

"Lock it, tight, *tight*!"

The door was locked and bolted tight.

The music stopped. She listened to her heart again and the sound of it diminishing into silence.

Home! Oh God, safe at home! Safe, safe and safe at home! She slumped against the door. Safe, safe. Listen. Not a sound. Safe, safe, oh thank God, safe at home. I'll never go out at night again. I'll stay home. I won't go over that ravine again ever. Safe, oh safe, safe home, so good, so good, safe! Safe inside, the door locked. Wait.

Look out the window.

She looked.

Why, there's no one there at all! Nobody. There was nobody following me at all. Nobody running after me. She got her breath and almost laughed at herself. It stands to *reason*. If a man *had* been following me, he'd have *caught* me! I'm not a fast runner . . . There's no one on the porch or in the yard. How silly of me. I wasn't running from anything. That ravine's as safe as anyplace. Just the same, it's nice to be home. Home's the really good warm place, the only place to be.

She put her hand out to the light switch and stopped.

"What?" she asked. "What? *What*?"

Behind her in the living room, someone cleared his throat.

"GOOD GRIEF, they ruin everything!"

"Don't take it so hard, Charlie."

"Well, what're we going to talk about now? It's no use talking the Lonely One if he ain't even alive! It's not scary any more!"

"Don't know about you, Charlie," said Tom. "I'm going back to Summer's Ice House and sit in the door and pretend he's alive and get cold all up and down my spine."

"That's cheating."

"You got to take your chills where you can find them, Charlie."

Douglas did not listen to Tom and Charlie. He looked at Lavinia Nebbs' house and spoke, almost to himself.

"I was there last night in the ravine. I saw it. I saw everything. On my way home I cut across here. I saw that lemonade glass right on the porch rail, half empty. Thought I'd like to drink it. Like to drink it, I thought. I was in the ravine and I was here, right in the middle of it all."

Tom and Charlie, in turn, ignored Douglas.

"For that matter," said Tom, "I don't really think the Lonely One is dead."

"You were here this morning when the ambulance came to bring that man out on the stretcher, weren't you?"

"Sure," said Tom.

"Well, *that* was the Lonely One, dumb! Read the papers! After ten long years escaping, old Lavinia Nebbs up and stabbed him with a handy pair of sewing scissors. I wish she'd minded her own business."

"You want she'd laid down and let him squeeze her windpipe?"

"No, but the least she could've done is gallop out of the house and down the street screaming 'Lonely One! Lonely One!' long enough to give him a chance to beat it. This town used to have some good stuff in it up until about twelve o'clock last night. From here on, we're vanilla junket."

"Let me say it for the last time, Charlie; I figure the Lonely

One ain't dead. I saw his face, you saw his face, Doug saw his face, didn't you, Doug?"

"What? Yes. I think so. Yes."

"Everybody saw his face. Answer me this, then: Did it *look* like the Lonely One to you?"

"I . . ." said Douglas, and stopped.

The sun buzzed in the sky for about five seconds.

"My gosh . . ." whispered Charlie at last.

Tom waited, smiling.

"It didn't look like the Lonely One at all," gasped Charlie. "It looked like a *man*."

"Right, yes, sir, a plain everyday man, who wouldn't pull the wings off even so much as a fly, Charlie, a fly! The least the Lonely One would do if he was the Lonely One is look like the Lonely One, right? Well, he looked like the candy butcher down front the Elite Theater nights."

"What you think he was, a tramp coming through town, got in what he thought was an empty house, and got killed by Miss Nebbs?"

"Sure!"

"Hold on, though. None of us know what the Lonely One should look like. There're no pictures. Only people ever saw him wound up dead."

"You know and Doug knows and I know what he looks like. He's got to be tall, don't he?"

"Sure . . ."

"And he's got to be pale, don't he?"

"Pale, that's right."

"And skinny like a skeleton and have long dark hair, don't he?"

"That's what I always said."

"And big eyes bulging out, green eyes like a cat?"

"That's him to the t."

"Well, then." Tom snorted. "You saw that poor guy they lugged out of the Nebbs' place a couple hours ago. What was he?"

"Little and red-faced and kind of fat and not much hair and what there was was sandy. Tom, you hit on it! Come on! Call the guys! You go tell them like you told me! The Lonely One ain't dead. He'll still be out lurkin' around tonight."

"Yeah," said Tom, and stopped, suddenly thoughtful.

"Tom, you're a pal, you got a real brain. None of us would've saved the day this way. The summer was sure going bad up to this very minute. You got your thumb in the dike just in time. August won't be a *total* loss. Hey, kids!"

And Charlie was off, waving his arms, yelling.

Tom stood on the sidewalk in front of Lavinia Nebbs' house, his face pale.

"My gosh!" he whispered. "What've I gone and done *now*!"

He turned to Douglas.

"I say, Doug, what've I gone and done now?"

Douglas was staring at the house. His lips moved.

"I was there, last night, in the ravine. I saw Elizabeth Ramsell. I came by here last night on the way home. I saw the lemonade glass there on the rail. Just last night it was. I could drink that, I thought . . . I could drink that . . ."

SHE WAS a woman with a broom or a dustpan or a washrag or a mixing spoon in her hand. You saw her cutting piecrust in the morning, humming to it, or you saw her setting out the baked pies at noon or taking them in, cool, at dusk. She rang porcelain cups like a Swiss bell ringer, to their place. She glided through the halls as steadily as a vacuum machine, seeking, finding, and setting to rights. She made mirrors of every window, to catch the sun. She strolled but twice through any garden, trowel in hand, and the flowers raised their quivering fires upon the warm air in her wake. She slept quietly and turned no more than three times in a night, as relaxed as a white glove to which, at dawn, a brisk hand will return. Waking, she touched people like pictures, to set their frames straight.

But, now . . . ?

"Grandma," said everyone. "Great-grandma."

Now it was as if a huge sum in arithmetic were finally drawing to an end. She had stuffed turkeys, chickens, squabs, gentlemen, and boys. She had washed ceilings, walls, invalids, and children. She had laid linoleum, repaired bicycles, wound clocks, stoked furnaces, swabbed iodine on ten thousand grievous wounds. Her hands had flown all around about and down, gentling this, holding that, throwing baseballs, swinging bright croquet mallets, seeding black earth, or fixing covers over dumplings, ragouts, and children wildly strewn by slumber. She had pulled down shades, pinched out candles, turned switches, and—grown old. Looking back on thirty billions of things started, carried, finished and done, it all summed up, totaled out; the last decimal was placed, the final zero swung slowly into line. Now, chalk in hand, she stood back from life a silent hour before reaching for the eraser.

"Let me see now," said Great-grandma. "Let me see . . ."

With no fuss or further ado, she traveled the house in an ever-circling inventory, reached the stairs at last, and, making no special announcement, she took herself up three flights to her room where, silently, she laid herself out like a fossil imprint under the snowing cool sheets of her bed and began to die.

Again the voices:

"Grandma! Great-grandma!"

The rumor of what she was doing dropped down the stair well, hit, and spread ripples through the rooms, out doors and windows and along the street of elms to the edge of the green ravine.

"Here now, here!"

The family surrounded her bed.

"Just let me lie," she whispered.

Her ailment could not be seen in any microscope; it was a mild but ever-deepening tiredness, a dim weighting of her sparrow body; sleepy, sleepier, sleepiest.

As for her children and her children's children—it seemed impossible that with such a simple act, the most leisurely act in the world, she could cause such apprehension.

"Great-grandma, now listen—what you're doing is no better than breaking a lease. This house will fall down without you. You must give us at least a year's notice!"

Great-grandma opened one eye. Ninety years gazed calmly out at her physicians like a dust-ghost from a high cupola window in a fast-emptying house. "Tom . . . ?"

The boy was sent, alone, to her whispering bed.

"Tom," she said, faintly, far away, "in the Southern Seas there's a day in each man's life when he knows it's time to shake hands with all his friends and say good-by and sail away, and he does, and it's natural—it's just his time. That's how it is today. I'm so like you sometimes, sitting through Saturday matinees until nine at night when we send your dad to bring you home. Tom, when the time comes that the same cowboys are shooting the same Indians on the same mountaintop, then it's best to fold back the seat and head for the door, with no regrets and no walking backward up the aisle. So, I'm leaving while I'm still happy and still entertained."

Douglas was summoned next to her side.

"Grandma, who'll shingle the roof next spring?"

Every April for as far back as there were calendars, you thought you heard woodpeckers tapping the housetop. But no, it was Great-grandma somehow transported, singing, pounding nails, replacing shingles, high in the sky!

"Douglas," she whispered, "don't ever let anyone do the shingles unless it's fun for them."

"Yes'm."

"Look around come April, and say, 'Who'd like to fix the roof?' And whichever face lights up is the face you want, Douglas. Because up there on that roof you can see the whole town going toward the country and the country going toward the edge of the earth and the river shining, and the morning lake, and birds on the trees down under you, and the best of the wind all around above. Any one of those should be enough to make a person climb a weather vane some spring sunrise. It's a powerful hour, if you give it half a chance. . . ."

Her voice sank to a soft flutter.

Douglas was crying.

She roused herself again. "Now, why are you doing that?"

"Because," he said, "you won't be here tomorrow."

She turned a small hand mirror from herself to the boy. He looked at her face and himself in the mirror and then at her face again as she said, "Tomorrow morning I'll get up at seven and wash behind my ears; I'll run to church with Charlie Woodman; I'll picnic at Electric Park; I'll swim, run barefoot, fall out of trees, chew spearmint gum . . . Douglas, Douglas, for shame! You cut your fingernails, don't you?"

"Yes'm."

"And you don't yell when your body makes itself over every seven years or so, old cells dead and new ones added to your fingers and your heart. You don't mind that, do you?"

"No'm."

"Well, consider then, boy. Any man saves fingernail clippings is a fool. You ever see a snake bother to keep his peeled skin? That's about all you got here today in this bed is fingernails and snake skin. One good breath would send me up in flakes. Important thing is not the me that's lying here, but the me that's sitting on the edge of the bed looking back at me, and the me that's downstairs cooking supper, or out in the garage under the car, or in the library reading. All the new parts, they count. I'm not really dying today. No person ever died that had a family. I'll be around a long time. A thousand years from now a whole township of my offspring will be biting sour apples in the gumwood shade. That's my answer to anyone asks big questions! Quick now, send in the rest!"

At last the entire family stood, like people seeing someone off at the rail station, waiting in the room.

"Well," said Great-grandma, "there I am. I'm not humble, so it's nice seeing you standing around my bed. Now next week there's late gardening and closet-cleaning and clothes-buying for the children to do. And since that part of me which is called, for convenience, Great-grandma, won't be here to step it along, those other parts of me called Uncle Bert and Leo and Tom and Douglas, and all the other names, will have to take over, each to his own."

"Yes, Grandma."

"I don't want any Halloween parties here tomorrow. Don't want anyone saying anything sweet about me; I said it all in my time and my pride. I've tasted every victual and danced every dance; now there's one last tart I haven't bit on, one tune I haven't whistled. But I'm not afraid. I'm truly curious. Death won't get a crumb by my mouth I won't keep and savor. So don't you worry over me. Now, all of you go, and let me find my sleep . . ."

Somewhere a door closed quietly.

"That's better." Alone, she snuggled luxuriously down through the warm snowbank of linen and wool, sheet and cover, and the colors of the patchwork quilt were bright as the circus banners of old time. Lying there, she felt as small and secret as on those mornings eighty-some-odd years ago when, wakening, she comforted her tender bones in bed.

A long time back, she thought, I dreamed a dream, and was enjoying it so much when someone wakened me, and that was the day when I was born. And now? Now, let me see . . . She cast her mind back. Where was I? she thought. Ninety years . . . how to take up the thread and the pattern of that lost dream again? She put out a small hand. *There* . . . Yes, that was it. She smiled. Deeper in the warm snow hill she turned her head upon her pillow. That was better. Now, yes, now she saw it shaping in her mind quietly, and with a serenity like a sea moving along an endless and self-refreshing shore. Now she let the old dream touch and lift her from the snow and drift her above the scarce-remembered bed.

Downstairs, she thought, they are polishing the silver, and rummaging the cellar, and dusting in the halls. She could hear them living all through the house.

"It's all right," whispered Great-grandma, as the dream floated her. "Like everything else in this life, it's fitting."

And the sea moved her back down the shore.

"A GHOST!" cried Tom.

"No," said a voice. "Just me."

The ghastly light flowed into the dark apple-scented bedroom. A quart-size Mason jar, seemingly suspended upon space, flickered many twilight-colored flakes of light on and off. In this pallid illumination Douglas's eyes shone pale and solemn. He was so tan his face and hands were dissolved in darkness and his nightgown seemed a disembodied spirit.

"My gosh!" hissed Tom. "Two dozen, three dozen fireflies!"

"Sh, for cri-yi!"

"What you got 'em for?"

"We got caught reading nights with flashlights under our sheets, right? So, nobody'll suspect an old jar of fireflies; folks'll think it's just a night museum."

"Doug, you're a genius!"

But Douglas did not answer. Very gravely he placed the intermittently signaling light source upon the night table and picked up his pencil and began to write large and long on his tablet. With the fireflies burning, dying, burning, dying, and his eyes glinting with three dozen fugitive bits of pale green color, he block printed for ten and then twenty minutes, aligning and realigning, writing and rewriting the facts that he had gathered all too swiftly during the season. Tom watched, hypnotized by the small bonfire of insects leaping and furling within the jar, until he froze, sleeping, raised on elbow, while Douglas wrote on. He summed it all up on a final page:

YOU CAN'T DEPEND ON *THINGS* BECAUSE . . .

. . . like machines, for instance, they fall apart or rust or rot, or maybe never get finished at all . . . or wind up in garages . . .

. . . like tennis shoes, you can only run so far, so fast, and then the earth's got you again . . .

. . . like trolleys. Trolleys, big as they are, always come to the end of the line . . .

YOU CAN'T DEPEND ON *PEOPLE* BECAUSE . . .
. . . they go away.
. . . strangers die.
. . . people you know fairly well die.
. . . friends die.
. . . people murder *people, like in books.*
. . . your own folks can die.

So . . . !

He held onto a double fistful of breath, let it hiss out slow, grabbed more breath, and let it whisper through his tight-gritted teeth.

SO. He finished in huge heavily blocked capitals.

SO IF TROLLEYS AND RUNABOUTS AND FRIENDS AND NEAR FRIENDS CAN GO AWAY FOR A WHILE OR GO AWAY FOR EVER, OR RUST, OR FALL APART OR DIE, AND IF PEOPLE CAN BE MURDERED, AND IF SOMEONE LIKE GREAT-GRANDMA, WHO WAS GOING TO LIVE FOREVER, CAN DIE . . . IF ALL OF THIS IS TRUE . . . THEN . . . I, DOUGLAS SPAULDING, SOME DAY . . . MUST . . .

But the fireflies, as if extinguished by his somber thoughts, had softly turned themselves off.

I can't write any more, anyway, thought Douglas. I won't write any more. I won't, I won't finish it tonight.

He looked over at Tom asleep on his upraised elbow and hand. He touched Tom's wrist and Tom collapsed into a sighing ruin, back upon the bed.

Douglas picked up the Mason jar with the cold dark lumps in it and the cool lights flicked on again, as if given life by his hand. He lifted the Mason jar to where it shone fitfully on his summing-up. The final words waited to be written. But he went instead to the window and pushed the screen frame out. He unscrewed the top of the jar and tilted the fireflies in a pale shower of sparks down the windless night. They found their wings and flew away.

Douglas watched them go. They departed like the pale fragments of a final twilight in the history of a dying world. They went like the few remaining shreds of warm hope from his hand. They left his face and his body and the space inside his body to darkness. They left him empty as the Mason jar which now, without knowing that he did so, he took back into bed with him, when he tried to sleep . . .

THERE SHE sat in her glass coffin, night after night, her body melted by the carnival blaze of summer, frozen in the ghost winds of winter, waiting with her sickle smile and carved, hooked, and wax-pored nose hovering above her pale pink and wrinkled wax hands poised forever above the ancient fanned-out deck of cards. The Tarot Witch. A delicious name. The Tarot Witch. You thrust a penny in the silver slot and far away below, behind, inside, machinery groaned and cogged, levers stroked, wheels spun. And in her case the witch raised up her glittery face to blind you with a single needle stare. Her implacable left hand moved down to stroke and fritter enigmatic tarot-card skulls, devils, hanging men, hermits, cardinals and clowns, while her head hung close to delve your misery or murder, hope or health, your rebirths each morning and death's renewals by night. Then she spidered a calligrapher's pen across the back of a single card and let it titter down the chute into your hands. Whereupon the witch, with a last veiled glimmer of her eyes, froze back in her eternal caul for weeks, months, years, awaiting the next copper penny to revive her from oblivion. Now, waxen dead, she suffered the two boys' approach.

Douglas fingerprinted the glass.

"There she is."

"It's a wax dummy," said Tom. "Why do you want me to see her?"

"All the time asking why!" yelled Douglas. "Because, *that's* why, because!"

Because . . . the arcade lights dimmed . . . because . . .

One day you discover you are alive.

Explosion! Concussion! Illumination! Delight!

You laugh, you dance around, you shout.

But, not long after, the sun goes out. Snow falls, but no one sees it, on an August noon.

At the cowboy matinee last Saturday a man had dropped down dead on the white-hot screen. Douglas had cried out. For years he had seen billions of cowboys shot, hung, burned, destroyed. But now, this one particular man . . .

He'll never walk, run, sit, laugh, cry, won't do anything ever, thought Douglas. Now he's turning cold. Douglas's teeth chattered, his heart pumped sludge in his chest. He shut his eyes and let the convulsion shake him.

He had to get away from these other boys because they weren't thinking about death, they just laughed and yelled at the dead man as if he still lived. Douglas and the dead man were on a boat pulling away, with all the others left behind on the bright shore, running, jumping, hilarious with motion, not knowing that the boat, the dead man and Douglas were going, going, and now gone into darkness. Weeping, Douglas ran to the lemon-smelling men's room where, sick, it seemed a fire hydrant churned three times from his throat.

And waiting for the sickness to pass he thought: All the people I know who died this summer! Colonel Freeleigh, dead! I didn't know it before; why? Great-grandma, dead, too. Really-truly. Not only that but . . . He paused. Me! No, they can't kill me! Yes, said a voice, yes, any time they want to they can, no matter how you kick or scream, they just put a big hand over you and you're still . . . I don't want to die! Douglas screamed, without a sound. You'll have to anyway, said the voice, you'll have to anyway. . . .

The sunlight outside the theater blazed down upon unreal street, unreal buildings, and people moving slowly, as if under a bright and heavy ocean of pure burning gas and him thinking that now, now at last he must go home and finish out the final line in his nickel tablet: SOME DAY, I, DOUGLAS SPAULDING, MUST DIE . . .

It had taken him ten minutes to get up enough courage to cross the street, his heart slowing, and there was the arcade and he saw the strange wax witch back where she had always hidden in cool dusty shadow with the Fates and Furies tucked under her fingernails. A car passing flashed an explosion of light through the arcade, jumping the shadows, making it seem that the wax woman nodded swiftly for him to enter.

And he had gone in at the witch's summoning and come forth five minutes later, certain of survival. Now, he must show Tom . . .

"She looks almost alive," said Tom.

"She *is* alive. I'll show you."

He shoved a penny in the slot.

Nothing happened.

Douglas yelled across the arcade at Mr. Black, the proprietor, seated on an upended soda-pop crate uncorking and taking a swig from a three-quarters empty bottle of brown-yellow liquid.

"Hey, something's wrong with the witch!"

Mr. Black shuffled over, his eyes half closed, his breath sharp and strong. "Something's wrong with the pinball, wrong with the peep show, wrong with the ELECTROCUTE YOURSELF FOR A PENNY machine." He struck the case. "Hey, in there! Come alive!" The witch sat unperturbed. "Costs me more to fix her each month than she earns." Mr. Black reached behind the case and hung a sign "OUT OF ORDER" over her face. "She ain't the only thing's out of order. Me, you, this town, this country, the whole world! To hell with it!" He shook his fist at the woman. "The junk heap for you, you hear me, the junk heap!" He walked off and plunged himself down on the soda-pop crate to feel the coins in his money apron again, like it was his stomach giving him pain.

"She just can't—oh, she can't be out of order," said Douglas, stricken.

"She's old," said Tom. "Grandpa says she was here when he was a boy and before. So it's bound to be some day she'd konk out and . . ."

"Come on now," whispered Douglas. "Oh, please, please, write so Tom can see!"

He shoved another coin stealthily into the machine. "Please . . ."

The boys pressed the glass, their breath made cumulus clouds on the pane.

Then, deep inside the box, a whisper, a whir.

And slowly, the witch's head rose up and looked at the boys and there was something in her eyes that froze them as her hand began to scrabble almost frantically back and forth upon the tarots, to pause, hurry on, return. Her head bent down, one hand came to rest and a shuddering shook the machine as the other hand wrote, paused, wrote, and stopped at last with a paroxysm so violent the glass in the case chimed. The witch's face bent in a rigid mechanical misery, almost fisted into a ball.

Then the machinery gasped and a single cog slipped and a tiny tarot card tickled down the flue into Douglas's cupped hands.

"She's alive! She's working again!"

"What's the card say, Doug?"

"It's the same one she wrote for me last Saturday! Listen . . ."

And Douglas read:

> *"Hey, nonny no!*
> *Men are fools that wish to die!*
> *Is't not fine to dance and sing*
> *When the bells of death do ring?*
> *Is't not fine to swim in wine,*
> *And turn upon the toe,*
> *And sing Hey, nonny no!*
> *When the winds blow and the seas flow?*
> *Hey, nonny no!"*

"Is that *all* it says?" said Tom.

"At the bottom is a message: 'PREDICTION: A long life and a lively one.'"

"That's more like it! Now how about one for me?"

Tom put his coin in. The witch shuddered. A card fell into his hand.

"Last one off the premises is the witch's behind," said Tom calmly.

They ran out so fast, the proprietor gasped and clutched forty-five copper pennies in one fist, thirty-six in the other.

Outside in the glare of the uneasy street lights Douglas and Tom made a terrible discovery.

The tarot card was empty, there was no message.

"That can't be!"

"Don't get excited, Doug. It's just a plain old card; we only lost a penny."

"It's not a plain old card, it's more than a penny, it's life and death."

Under the fluttering moth light in the street Douglas's face was milky as he stared at the card and turned it, rustling, trying somehow to put words on it.

"She ran out of ink."

"She *never* runs out of ink!"

He looked at Mr. Black sitting there finishing off his bottle and cursing, not knowing how lucky he was, living in the arcade. Please, he thought, don't let the arcade fall apart, too. Bad enough that friends disappeared, people were killed and buried in the real world, but let the arcade run along the way it was, please, please. . . .

Now Douglas knew why the arcade had drawn him so steadily this week and drew him still tonight. For there was a world completely set in place, predictable, certain, sure, with its bright silver slots, its terrible gorilla behind glass forever stabbed by waxen hero to save still more waxen heroine, and then the flipping waterfalling chitter of Keystone Kops on eternal photographic spindles set spiraling in darkness by Indian-head pennies under naked bulb light. The Kops, forever in collision or near-collision with train, truck, streetcar, forever gone off piers in oceans which did not drown, because there they rushed to collide again with train, truck, streetcar, dive off old and beautifully familiar piers. Worlds within worlds, the penny peek shows which you cranked to repeat old rites and formulas. There, when you wished, the Wright Brothers sailed sandy winds at Kittyhawk, Teddy Roosevelt exposed his dazzling teeth, San Francisco was built and burned, burned and built, as long as sweaty coins fed self-satisfied machines.

Douglas looked around at this night town, where anything at all might happen now, a minute from now. Here, by night or day, how few the slots to shove your money in, how few the cards delivered to your hand for reading, and, if read, how few made sense. Here in the world of people you might give time, money, and prayer with little or no return.

But there in the arcade you could hold lightning with the CAN YOU TAKE IT? electrical machine when you pried its chromed handles apart as the power wasp-stung, sizzled, sewed your vibrant fingers. You punched a bag and saw how many hundred pounds of sinew were available in your arm to strike the world if it need be struck. There grip a robot's hand to Indian-wrestle out your fury and light the bulbs half up a numbered chart where fireworks at the summit proved your violence supreme.

In the arcade, then, you did this and this, and that and that occurred. You came forth in peace as from a church unknown before.

And now? Now?

The witch moving but silent, and perhaps soon dead in her crystal coffin. He looked at Mr. Black droning there, defying all worlds, even his own. Someday the fine machinery would rust from lack of loving care, the Keystone Kops freeze forever half in, half out the lake, half caught, half struck by locomotive; the Wright Brothers never get their kite machine off the ground. . . .

"Tom," Douglas said, "we got to sit in the library and figure this thing out."

They moved on down the street, the white unwritten card passing between them.

They sat inside the library in the lidded green light and then they sat outside on the carved stone lion, dangling their feet over its back, frowning.

"Old man Black, all the time screaming at her, threatening to kill her."

"You can't kill what's never lived, Doug."

"He treats the witch like she's alive or was once alive, or something. Screaming at her, so maybe she's finally given up. Or maybe she hasn't given up at all, but's taken a secret way to warn us her life's in danger. Invisible ink. Lemon juice, maybe! There's a message here she didn't want Mr. Black to see, in case he looked while we were in his arcade. Hold on! I got some matches."

"Why would she write us, Doug?"

"Hold the card. Here!" Douglas struck a match and ran it under the card.

"Ouch! The words ain't on my fingers, Doug, so keep the match away."

"There!" cried Douglas. And there it was, a faint spidery scrawl which began to shape itself in a spiral of incredible corkscrew calligrapher's letters, dark on light . . . a word, two words, three . . .

"The card, it's on fire!"

Tom yelled and let it drop.

"Stomp on it!"

But by the time they had jumped up to smash their feet on the stony spine of the ancient lion, the card was a black ruin.

"Doug! Now we'll never know what it said!"

Douglas held the flaking warm ashes in the palm of his hand. "No, I saw. I remember the words."

The ashes blew about in his fingers, whispering.

"You remember in that Charlie Chase Comedy last spring where the Frenchman was drowning and kept yelling something in French which Charlie Chase couldn't figure. *Secours, Secours!* And someone told Charlie what it meant and he jumped in and saved the man. Well, on this card, with my own eyes, I saw it. *Secours!*"

"Why would she write in French?"

"So Mr. Black wouldn't know, dumb!"

"Doug, it was just an old watermark coming out when you scorched the card . . ." Tom saw Douglas's face and stopped. "Okay, don't look mad. It was 'sucker' or whatever. But there were other words . . ."

"Mme. Tarot, it said, Tom, I got it now! Mme. Tarot's real, lived a long time ago, told fortunes. I saw her picture once in the encyclopedia. People came from all over Europe to see her. Well, don't you figure it now yourself? Think, Tom, think!"

Tom sat back down on the lion's back, looking along the street to where the arcade lights flickered.

"That's not the *real* Mrs. Tarot?"

"Inside that glass box, under all that red and blue silk and all that old half-melted wax, sure! Maybe a long time ago someone got jealous or hated her and poured wax over her and kept her prisoner forever and she's passed down the line from villain to villain and wound up here, centuries later, in Green Town, Illinois—working for Indian-head pennies instead of the crown heads of Europe!"

"Villains? Mr. Black?"

"Name's Black, shirt's black, pants're black, tie's black. Movie villains wear black, don't they?"

"But why didn't she yell last year, the year before?"

"Who knows, every night for a hundred years she's been

writing messages in lemon juice on cards, but everybody read her regular message, nobody thought, like us, to run a match over the back to bring out the *real* message. Lucky I know what *secours* means."

"Okay, she said 'Help!' Now what?"

"We save her, of course."

"Steal her out from under Mr. Black's nose, huh? And wind up witches ourselves in glass boxes with wax poured on our faces the next ten thousand years."

"Tom, the library's here. We'll arm ourselves with spells and magic philters to fight Mr. Black."

"There's only one magic philter will fix Mr. Black," said Tom. "Soon's he gets enough pennies any one evening, he—well, let's see." Tom drew some coins from his pocket. "This just might do it. Doug, you go read the books. I'll run back and look at the Keystone Kops fifteen times; I never get tired. By the time you meet me at the arcade, it might be the old philter will be working for us."

"Tom, I hope you know what you're doing."

"Doug, you want to rescue this princess or not?"

Douglas whirled and plunged.

Tom watched the library doors wham shut and settle. Then he leaped over the lion's back and down into the night. On the library steps, the ashes of the tarot card fluttered, blew away.

The arcade was dark; inside, the pinball machines lay dim and enigmatic as dust scribblings in a giant's cave. The peep shows stood with Teddy Roosevelt and the Wright Brothers faintly smirking or just cranking up a wooden propeller. The witch sat in her case, her waxen eyes cauled. Then, suddenly, one eye glittered. A flashlight bobbed outside through the dusty arcade windows. A heavy figure lurched against the locked door, a key scrabbled into the lock. The door slammed open, stayed open. There was a sound of thick breathing.

"It's only me, old girl," said Mr. Black, swaying.

Outside on the street, coming along with his nose in a book, Douglas found Tom hiding in a door nearby.

"Shh!" said Tom. "It worked. The Keystone Kops, fifteen times; and when Mr. Black heard me drop all that money in, his eyes popped, he opened the machine, took out the pennies, threw me out and went across to the speak-easy for the magic philter."

Douglas crept up and peered into the shadowy arcade and saw the two gorilla figures there, one not moving at all, the wax heroine in his arms, the other one standing stunned in the middle of the room, weaving slightly from side to side.

"Oh, Tom," whispered Douglas, "you're a genius. He's just *full* of magic philter, ain't he?"

"You can say *that* again. What did *you* find out?"

Douglas tapped the book and talked in a low voice. "Mme. Tarot, like I said, told all about death and destiny and stuff in rich folks' parlors, but she made one mistake. She predicted Napoleon's defeat and death to his *face*! So . . ."

Douglas's voice faded as he looked again through the dusty window at that distant figure seated quietly in her crystal case.

"*Secours*," murmured Douglas. "Old Napoleon just called in Mme. Tussaud's waxworks and had them drop the Tarot Witch alive in boiling wax, and now . . . now . . ."

"Watch out, Doug, Mr. Black, in there! He's got a club or something!"

This was true. Inside, cursing horribly, the huge figure of Mr. Black lurched. In his hand a camping knife seethed on the air six inches from the witch's face.

"He's picking on her because she's the only human-looking thing in the whole darn joint," said Tom. "He won't do her no harm. He'll fall over any second and sleep it off."

"No, sir," said Douglas. "He knows she warned us and we're coming to rescue her. He doesn't want us revealing his guilty secret, so maybe tonight he's going to destroy her once and for all."

"How could he know she warned us? We didn't even know ourselves till we got away from here."

"He made her tell, put coins in the machine; that's one thing she can't lie on, the cards, all them tarot skulls and bones. She just can't help telling the truth and she gave him a card, sure, with two little knights on it, no bigger than kids, you see? That's us, clubs in our hands, coming down the street."

"One last time!" cried Mr. Black from the cave inside. "I'm puttin' the coin in. One last time now, dammit, tell me! Is this damn arcade ever goin' to make money or do I declare bankruptcy? Like all women; sit there, cold fish, while a man starves! Gimme the card. There! Now, let me see." He held the card up to the light.

"Oh, my gosh!" whispered Douglas. "Get ready."

"No!" cried Mr. Black. "Liar! Liar! Take that!" He smashed his fist through the case. Glass exploded in a great shower of starlight, it seemed, and fell away in darkness. The witch sat naked, in the open air, reserved and calm, waiting for the second blow.

"No!" Douglas plunged through the door. "Mr. Black!"

"Doug!" cried Tom.

Mr. Black wheeled at Tom's shout. He raised the knife blindly in the air as if to strike. Douglas froze. Then, eyes wide, lids blinking once, Mr. Black turned perfectly so he fell with his back toward the floor and took what seemed a thousand years to strike, his flashlight flung from his right hand, the knife scuttling away like a silverfish from the left.

Tom moved slowly in to look at the long-strewn figure in the dark. "Doug, is he dead?"

"No, just the shock of Mme. Tarot's predictions. Boy, he's got a scalded look. Horrible, that's what the cards must have been."

The man slept noisily on the floor.

Douglas picked up the strewn tarot cards, put them, trembling, in his pocket. "Come on, Tom, let's get her out of here before it's too late."

"Kidnap her? You're crazy!"

"You wanna be guilty of aiding and abetting an even worse crime? Murder, for instance?"

"For gosh sakes, you can't kill a darn old dummy!"

But Doug was not listening. He had reached through the open case and now, as if she had waited for too many years, the wax Tarot Witch with a rustling sigh, leaned forward and fell slowly slowly down into his arms.

The town clock struck nine forty-five. The moon was high and filled all the sky with a warm but wintry light. The sidewalk was solid silver on which black shadows moved. Douglas moved with the thing of velvet and fairy wax in his arms, stopping to hide in pools of shadow under trembling trees, alone. He listened, looking back. A sound of running mice. Tom burst around the corner and pulled up beside him.

"Doug, I stayed behind. I was afraid Mr. Black was, well . . . then he began to come alive . . . swearing . . . Oh, Doug, if he catches you with his dummy! What will our folks think? Stealing!"

"Quiet!"

They listened to the moonlit river of street behind them. "Now, Tom, you can come help me rescue her, but you can't if you say 'dummy' or talk loud or drag along as so much dead weight."

"I'll help!" Tom assumed half the weight. "My gosh, she's light!"

"She was real young when Napoleon . . ." Douglas stopped. "Old people are heavy. That's how you tell."

"But why? Tell me why all this running around for her, Doug. Why?"

Why? Douglas blinked and stopped. Things had gone so fast, he had run so far and his blood was so high, he had long since forgotten why. Only now, as they moved again along the sidewalk, shadows like black butterflies on their eyelids, the thick smell of dusty wax on their hands, did he have time to reason why, and, slowly, speak of it, his voice as strange as moonlight.

"Tom, a couple weeks ago, I found out I was alive. Boy, did I hop around. And then, just last week in the movies, I found out I'd have to die someday. I never thought of that, really. And all of a sudden it was like knowing the Y.M.C.A. was going to be shut up forever—or school, which isn't so bad as we like to think, being over for good, and all the peach trees outside town shriveling up and the ravine being filled in and no place to play ever again and me sick in bed for as long as I could think and everything dark, and I got scared. So, I don't know; what I want to do is this: help Mme. Tarot. I'll hide her a few weeks or months while I look up in the black-magic books at the library how to undo spells and get her out of the wax to run around in the world again after all this time. And she'll be so grateful, she'll lay out the cards with all those devils and cups and swords and bones on them and tell me what sump holes to walk around and when to stay in bed on certain Thursday afternoons. I'll live forever, or next thing to it."

"You don't believe that."

"Yes, I do, or most of it. Watch it now, here's the ravine. We'll cut down through by the dump heap, and . . ."

Tom stopped. Douglas had stopped him. The boys did not turn, but they heard the heavy clubbing blows of feet behind them, each one like a shotgun set off in the bed of a dry lake not far away. Someone was shouting and cursing.

"Tom, you let him follow you!"

As they ran a giant hand lifted and tossed them aside, and Mr. Black was there laying to left and right and the boys, crying out, on the grass, saw the raving man, spittle showering the air from his biting teeth and widened lips. He held the witch by her neck and one arm and glared with fiery eyes down on the boys.

"This is mine! To do with like I want! What you mean, taking her? Caused all my trouble—money, business, every thing. Here's what I think of her!"

"No!" shouted Douglas.

But like a great iron catapult, the huge arms hoisted the figure up against the moon and flourished and wheeled the fragile body upon the stars and let it fly out with a curse and a rustling wind down the air into the ravine to tumble and take avalanches of junk with her into white dust and cinders.

"No!" said Douglas, sitting there, looking down. "NO!"

The big man toppled on the rim of the hill, gasping. "You just thank God it wasn't you I did that to!" He moved unsteadily away, falling once, getting up, talking to himself, laughing, swearing, then gone.

Douglas sat on the edge of the ravine and wept. After a long while he blew his nose. He looked at Tom.

"Tom, it's late. Dad'll be out walking, looking for us. We should've been home an hour ago. Run back along Washington Street, get Dad and bring him here."

"You're not going down in that ravine?"

"She's city property now, on the trash dump, and nobody cares what happens, not even Mr. Black. Tell Dad what he's coming here for and he don't have to be seen coming home with me and her. I'll take her the back way around and nobody'll ever know."

"She won't be no good to you now, her machinery all busted."

"We can't leave her out in the rain, don't you see, Tom?"

"Sure."

Tom moved slowly off.

Douglas let himself down the hill, walking in piles of cinder and old paper and tin cans. Halfway down he stopped and listened. He peered at the multicolored dimness, the great landslide below. "Mme. Tarot?" he almost whispered. "Mme. Tarot?"

At the bottom of the hill in the moonlight he thought he saw her white wax hand move. It was a piece of white paper blowing. But he went toward it anyway. . . .

The town clock struck midnight. The house lights around were mostly turned out. In the workshop garage the two boys and the man stood back from the witch, who now sat, rearranged and at peace, in an old wicker chair before an oilcloth-covered card table, upon which were spread, in fantastic fans of popes and clowns and cardinals and deaths and suns and comets, the tarot cards upon which one wax hand touched.

Father was speaking.

". . . know how it is. When I was a boy, when the circus left town I ran around collecting a million posters. Later it was breeding rabbits, and magic. I built illusions in the attic and couldn't get them out." He nodded to the witch. "Oh, I remember she told my fortune once, thirty years ago. Well, clean her up good, then come in to bed. We'll build her a special case Saturday." He moved out the garage door but stopped when Douglas spoke softly.

"Dad. Thanks. Thanks for the walk home. Thanks."

"Heck," said Father, and was gone.

The two boys left alone with the witch looked at each other. "Gosh, right down the main street we go, all four of us, you, me, Dad, the witch! Dad's one in a million!"

"Tomorrow," said Douglas, "I go down and buy the rest of

the machine from Mr. Black, for ten bucks, or he'll throw it out."

"Sure." Tom looked at the old woman there in the wicker chair. "Boy, she sure looks alive. I wonder what's inside."

"Little tiny bird bones. All that's left of Mme. Tarot after Napoleon——"

"No machinery at all? Why don't we just cut her open and see?"

"Plenty of time for that, Tom."

"When?"

"Well, in a year, two years, when I'm fourteen or fifteen, then's the time to do it. Right now I don't want to know nothing except she's here. And tomorrow I get to work on the spells to let her escape forever. Some night you'll hear that a strange, beautiful Italian girl was seen downtown in a summer dress, buying a ticket for the East and everyone saw her at the station and saw her on the train as it pulled out and everyone said she was the prettiest girl they ever saw, and when you hear that, Tom—and believe me, the news will get around fast! nobody knowing *where* she came from or *where* she went—then you'll know I worked the spell and set her free. And then, as I said, a year, two years from now, on that night when that train pulls out, it'll be the time when we can cut through the wax. With her gone, you're liable to find nothing but little cogs and wheels and stuff inside her. That's how it is."

Douglas picked up the witch's hand and moved it over the dance of life, the frolic of bone-white death, the dates and dooms, the fates and follies, tapping, touching, whispering her worn-down fingernails. Her face tilted with some secret equilibrium and looked at the boys and the eyes flashed bright in the raw bulb light, unblinking.

"Tell your fortune, Tom?" asked Douglas quietly.

"Sure."

A card fell from the witch's voluminous sleeve.

"Tom, you see that? A card, hidden away, and now she throws it out at us!" Douglas held the card to the light. "It's blank. I'll put it in a matchbox full of chemicals during the night. Tomorrow we'll open the box and there the message'll be!"

"What'll it say?"

Douglas closed his eyes the better to see the words.

"It'll say, 'Thanks from your humble servant and grateful friend, Mme. Floristan Mariani Tarot, the Chiromancer, Soul Healer, and Deep-Down Diviner of Fates and Furies.'"

Tom laughed and shook his brother's arm.

"Go on, Doug, what else, what else?"

"Let me see . . . And it'll say, 'Hey nonny no! . . . is't not fine to dance and sing? . . . when the bells of death do ring . . . and turn upon the toe . . . and sing Hey nonny no!' And it'll say, 'Tom and Douglas Spaulding, everything you wish for, all your life through, you'll get . . .' And it'll say that we'll live forever, you and me, Tom, we'll live forever . . ."

"All that on just this one card?"

"All that, every single bit of it, Tom."

In the light of the electric bulb they bent, the two boys' heads down, the witch's head down, staring and staring at the beautiful blank but promising white card, their bright eyes sensing each and every incredibly hidden word that would soon rise up from pale oblivion.

"Hey," said Tom in the softest of voices.

And Douglas repeated in a glorious whisper, "Hey . . ."

FAINTLY, THE voice chanted under the fiery green trees at noon.

". . . nine, ten, eleven, twelve . . ."

Douglas moved slowly across the lawn. "Tom, what you counting?"

". . . thirteen, fourteen, shut up, sixteen, seventeen, cicadas, eighteen, nineteen . . . !"

"Cicadas?"

"Oh hell!" Tom unsqueezed his eyes. "Hell, hell, hell!"

"Better not let people hear you swearing."

"Hell, hell, hell is a place!" Tom cried. "Now I got to start all over. I was counting the times the cicadas buzz every fifteen seconds." He held up his two dollar watch. "You time it, then add thirty-nine and you get the temperature at that very moment." He looked at the watch, one eye shut, tilted his head and whispered again, "One, two, three . . . !"

Douglas turned his head slowly, listening. Somewhere in the burning bone-colored sky a great copper wire was strummed and shaken. Again and again the piercing metallic vibrations, like charges of raw electricity, fell in paralyzing shocks from the stunned trees.

"Seven!" counted Tom. "Eight."

Douglas walked slowly up the porch steps. Painfully he peered into the hall. He stayed there a moment, then slowly he stepped back out on the porch and called weakly to Tom. "It's exactly eighty-seven degrees Fahrenheit."

"—twenty-seven, twenty-eight—"

"Hey, Tom, you hear me?"

"I hear you—thirty, thirty-one! Get away! Two, three, thirty-four!"

"You can stop counting now, right inside on that old thermometer it's eighty-seven and going up, without the help of no katydids."

"Cicadas! Thirty-nine, forty! Not katydids! Forty-two!"

"Eighty-seven degrees, I thought you'd like to know."

"Forty-five, that's inside, not outside! Forty-nine, fifty,

fifty-one! Fifty-two, fifty-three! Fifty-three plus thirty-nine is—ninety-two degrees!"

"Who says?"

"I say! Not eighty-seven degrees Fahrenheit! But ninety-two degrees Spaulding!"

"You and who else?"

Tom jumped up and stood red-faced, staring at the sun. "Me and the cicadas, that's who! Me and the cicadas! You're outnumbered! Ninety-two, ninety-two, ninety-two degrees Spaulding, by gosh!"

They both stood looking at the merciless unclouded sky like a camera that has broken and stares, shutter wide, at a motionless and stricken town dying in a fiery sweat.

Douglas shut his eyes and saw two idiot suns dancing on the reverse side of the pinkly translucent lids.

"One . . . two . . . three . . ."

Douglas felt his lips move.

". . . four . . . five . . . six . . ."

This time the cicadas sang even faster.

FROM NOONTIME to sundown, from midnight to sunrise, one man, one horse, and one wagon were known to all twenty-six thousand three hundred forty-nine inhabitants of Green Town, Illinois.

In the middle of the day, for no reason quickly apparent, children would stop still and say:

"Here comes Mr. Jonas!"

"Here comes Ned!"

"Here comes the wagon!"

Older folks might peer north or south, east or west and see no sign of the man named Jonas, the horse named Ned, or the wagon which was a Conestoga of the kind that bucked the prairie tides to beach on the wilderness.

But then if you borrowed the ear of a dog and tuned it high and stretched it taut you could hear, miles and miles across the town a singing like a rabbi in the lost lands, a Moslem in a tower. Always, Mr. Jonas' voice went clear before him so people had a half an hour, an hour, to prepare for his arrival. And by the time his wagon appeared, the curbs were lined by children, as for a parade.

So here came the wagon and on its high board seat under a persimmon-colored umbrella, the reins like a stream of water in his gentle hands, was Mr. Jonas, singing.

"Junk! Junk!
No, sir, not Junk!
Junk! Junk!
No, ma'am, not Junk!
Bricabracs, brickbats!
Knitting needles, knick-knacks!
Kickshaws! Curios!
Camisoles! Cameos!
But . . . Junk!
Junk!
No, sir, not . . . Junk!"

* * *

As anyone could tell who had heard the songs Mr. Jonas made up as he passed, he was no ordinary junkman. To all appearances, yes, the way he dressed in tatters of moss-corduroy and the felt cap on his head, covered with old presidential campaign buttons going back before Manila Bay. But he was unusual in this way: not only did he tread the sunlight, but often you could see him and his horse swimming along the moonlit streets, circling and recircling by night the islands, the blocks where all the people lived he had known all of his life. And in that wagon he carried things he had picked up here and there and carried for a day or a week or a year until someone wanted and needed them. Then all they had to say was, "I want that clock," or "How about the mattress?" And Jonas would hand it over, take no money, and drive away, considering the words for another tune.

So it happened that often he was the only man alive in all Green Town at three in the morning and often people with headaches, seeing him amble by with his moon-shimmered horse, would run out to see if by any chance he had aspirin, which he did. More than once he had delivered babies at four in the morning and only then had people noticed how incredibly clean his hands and fingernails were—the hands of a rich man who had another life somewhere they could not guess. Sometimes he would drive people to work downtown, or sometimes, when men could not sleep, go up on their porch and bring cigars and sit with them and smoke and talk until dawn.

Whoever he was or whatever he was and no matter how different and crazy he seemed, he was not crazy. As he himself had often explained gently, he had tired of business in Chicago many years before and looked around for a way to spend the rest of his life. Couldn't stand churches, though he appreciated their ideas, and having a tendency toward preaching and decanting knowledge, he bought the horse and wagon and set out to spend the rest of his life seeing to it that one part of town had a chance to pick over what the other part of town had cast off. He looked upon himself as a kind of process, like osmosis, that made various cultures within the city limits available one to another. He could not stand waste, for he knew that one man's junk is another man's luxury.

So adults, and especially children, clambered up to peer over into the vast treasure hoard in the back of the wagon.

"Now, remember," said Mr. Jonas, "you can have what you want if you really want it. The test is, ask yourself, Do I want it with all my heart? Could I live through the day without it? If you figure to be dead by sundown, grab the darned thing and run. I'll be happy to let you have whatever it is."

And the children searched the vast heaps of parchments and brocades and bolts of wallpaper and marble ash trays and vests and roller skates and great fat overstuffed chairs and end tables and crystal chandeliers. For a while you just heard whispering and rattling and tinkling. Mr. Jonas watched, comfortably puffing on his pipe, and the children knew he watched. Sometimes their hands reached out for a game of checkers or a string of beads or an old chair, and just as they touched it they looked up and there were Mr. Jonas's eyes gently questioning them. And they pulled their hand away and looked further on. Until at last each of them put their hand on a single item and left it there. Their faces came up and this time their faces were so bright Mr. Jonas had to laugh. He put up his hand as if to fend off the brightness of their faces from his eyes. He covered his eyes a moment. When he did this, the children yelled their thanks, grabbed their roller skates or clay tiles or bumbershoots and, dropping off, ran.

And the children came back in a moment with something of their own in their hands, a doll or a game they had grown tired of, something the fun had gone out of, like flavor from gum, and now it was time for it to pass on to some other part of town where, seen for the first time, it would be revivified and would revivify others. These tokens of exchange were shyly dropped over the rim of the wagon down into unseen riches and then the wagon was trundling on, flickering light on its great spindling sunflower wheels and Mr. Jonas singing again . . .

"Junk! Junk!
No, sir, not Junk!
No, ma'am, not junk!"

until he was out of sight and only the dogs, in the shadow pools under trees, heard the rabbi in the wilderness, and twitched their tails . . .

"... junk . . ."

Fading.

"... junk . . ."

A whisper.

"... *junk* . . ." Gone.

And the dogs asleep.

THE SIDEWALKS were haunted by dust ghosts all night as the furnace wind summoned them up, swung them about, and gentled them down in a warm spice on the lawns. Trees, shaken by the footsteps of late-night strollers, sifted avalanches of dust. From midnight on, it seemed a volcano beyond the town was showering red-hot ashes everywhere, crusting slumberless night watchmen and irritable dogs. Each house was a yellow attic smoldering with spontaneous combustion at three in the morning.

Dawn, then, was a time where things changed element for element. Air ran like hot spring waters nowhere, with no sound. The lake was a quantity of steam very still and deep over valleys of fish and sand held baking under its serene vapors. Tar was poured licorice in the streets, red bricks were brass and gold, roof tops were paved with bronze. The high-tension wires were lightning held forever, blazing, a threat above the unslept houses.

The cicadas sang louder and yet louder.

The sun did not rise, it overflowed.

In his room, his face a bubbled mass of perspiration, Douglas melted on his bed.

"Wow," said Tom, entering. "Come on, Doug. We'll drown in the river all day."

Douglas breathed out. Douglas breathed in. Sweat trickled down his neck.

"Doug, you awake?"

The slightest nod of the head.

"You don't feel good, huh? Boy, this house'll burn down today." He put his hand on Douglas's brow. It was like touching a blazing stove lid. He pulled his fingers away, startled. He turned and went downstairs.

"Mom," he said, "Doug's really sick."

His mother, taking eggs out of the icebox, stopped, let a quick look of concern cross her face, put the eggs back, and followed Tom upstairs.

Douglas had not moved so much as a finger.

The cicadas were screaming now.

At noon, running as if the sun were after him to smash him to the ground, the doctor pulled up on the front porch, gasping, his eyes weary already, and gave his bag to Tom.

At one o'clock the doctor came out of the house, shaking his head. Tom and his mother stood behind the screen door, as the doctor talked in a low voice, saying over and over again he didn't know, he didn't know. He put his Panama hat on his head, gazed at the sunlight blistering and shriveling the trees overhead, hesitated like a man plunging into the outer rim of hell, and ran again for his car. The exhaust of the car left a great pall of blue smoke in the pulsing air for five minutes after he was gone.

Tom took the ice pick in the kitchen and chipped a pound of ice into prisms which he carried upstairs. Mother was sitting on the bed and the only sound in the room was Douglas breathing in steam and breathing out fire. They put the ice in handkerchiefs on his face and along his body. They drew the shades and made the room like a cave. They sat there until two o'clock, bringing up more ice. Then they touched Douglas's brow again and it was like a lamp that had burned all night. After touching him you looked at your fingers to make sure they weren't seared to the bone.

Mother opened her mouth to say something, but the cicadas were so loud now they shook dust down from the ceiling.

Inside redness, inside blindness, Douglas lay listening to the dim piston of his heart and the muddy ebb and flow of the blood in his arms and legs.

His lips were heavy and would not move. His thoughts were heavy and barely ticked like seed pellets falling in an hourglass slow one by falling one. Tick.

Around a bright steel corner of rail a trolley swung, throwing a crumbling wave of sizzling sparks, its clamorous bell knocking ten thousand times until it blended with the cicadas. Mr. Tridden waved. The trolley stormed around a corner like a cannonade and dissolved. Mr. Tridden!

Tick. A pellet fell. *Tick.*

"Chug-a-chug-ding! Woo-woooo!"

On the roof top a boy locomoted, pulling an invisible whistle string, then froze into a statue. "John! John Huff, you! Hate you, John! John, we're pals! Don't hate you, no."

John fell down the elm-tree corridor like someone falling down an endless summer well, dwindling away.

Tick. John Huff. Tick. Sand pellet dropping. Tick. John . . .

Douglas moved his head flat over, crashing on the white white terribly white pillow.

The ladies in the Green Machine sailed by in a sound of black seal barking, lifting hands as white as doves. They sank into the lawn's deep waters, their gloves still waving to him as the grass closed over . . .

Miss Fern! Miss Roberta!

Tick . . . Tick . . .

And quickly then from a window across the way Colonel Freeleigh leaned out with the face of a clock, and buffalo dust sprang up in the street. Colonel Freeleigh spanged and rattled, his jaw fell open, a mainspring shot out and dangled on the air instead of his tongue. He collapsed like a puppet on the sill, one arm still waving . . .

Mr. Auffmann rode by in something that was bright and something like the trolley and the green electric runabout; and it trailed glorious clouds and it put out your eyes like the sun. "Mr. Auffmann, did you invent it?" he cried. "Did you finally build the Happiness Machine?"

But then he saw there was no bottom to the machine. Mr. Auffmann ran along on the ground, carrying the whole incredible frame from his shoulders.

"Happiness, Doug, here goes happiness!" And he went the way of the trolley, John Huff, and the dove-fingered ladies.

Above on the roof a tapping sound. Tap-rap-bang. Pause. Tap-rap-bang. Nail and hammer. Hammer and nail. A bird choir. And an old woman singing in a frail but hearty voice.

"Yes, we'll gather at the river . . . river . . . river . . .
Yes, we'll gather at the river . . .
That flows by the throne of God . . ."

"Grandma! Great-grandma!"

Tap, softly, tap. Tap, softly, tap.

". . . river . . . river . . ."

And now it was only the birds picking up their tiny feet and putting them down again on the roof. Rattle-rattle. Scratch. Peep. Peep. Soft. Soft.

". . . river . . ."

Douglas took one breath and let it all out at once, wailing.

He did not hear his mother run into the room.

A fly, like the burning ash of a cigarette, fell upon his senseless hand, sizzled, and flew away.

Four o'clock in the afternoon. Flies dead on the pavement. Dogs wet mops in their kennels. Shadows herded under trees. Downtown stores shut up and locked. The lake shore empty. The lake full of thousands of people up to their necks in the warm but soothing water.

Four-fifteen. Along the brick streets of town the junk wagon moved, with Mr. Jonas singing on it.

Tom, driven out of the house by the scorched look on Douglas's face, walked slowly down to the curb as the wagon stopped.

"Hi, Mr. Jonas."

"Hello, Tom."

Tom and Mr. Jonas were alone on the street with all that beautiful junk in the wagon to look at and neither of them looking at it. Mr. Jonas didn't say anything right away. He lit his pipe and puffed it, nodding his head as if he knew before he asked, that something was wrong.

"Tom?" he said.

"It's my brother," said Tom. "It's Doug."

Mr. Jonas looked up at the house.

"He's sick," said Tom. "He's dying!"

"Oh, now, that can't be so," said Mr. Jonas, scowling around at the very real world where nothing that vaguely looked like death could be found on this quiet day.

"He's dying," said Tom. "And the doctor doesn't know what's wrong. The heat, he said, nothing but the heat. Can that be, Mr. Jonas? Can the heat kill people, even in a dark room?"

"Well," said Mr. Jonas and stopped.

For Tom was crying now.

"I always thought I hated him . . . that's what I thought . . .

we fight half the time . . . I guess I did hate him . . . sometimes . . . but now . . . now. Oh, Mr. Jonas, if only . . ."

"If only what, boy?"

"If only you had something in this wagon would help. Something I could pick and take upstairs and make him okay."

Tom cried again.

Mr. Jonas took out his red bandanna handkerchief and handed it to Tom. Tom wiped his nose and eyes with the handkerchief.

"It's been a tough summer," Tom said. "Lots of things have happened to Doug."

"Tell me about them," said the junkman.

"Well," said Tom, gasping for breath, not quite done crying yet, "he lost his best aggie for one, a real beaut. And on top of that somebody stole his catcher's mitt, it cost a dollar ninety-five. Then there was the bad trade he made of his fossil stones and shell collection with Charlie Woodman for a Tarzan clay statue you got by saving up macaroni box tops. Dropped the Tarzan statue on the sidewalk second day he had it."

"That's a shame," said the junkman and really saw all the pieces on the cement.

"Then he didn't get the book of magic tricks he wanted for his birthday, got a pair of pants and a shirt instead. That's enough to ruin the summer right there."

"Parents sometimes forget how it is," said Mr. Jonas.

"Sure," Tom continued in a low voice, "then Doug's genuine set of Tower-of-London manacles left out all night and rusted. And worst of all, I grew one inch taller, catching up with him almost."

"Is that all?" asked the junkman quietly.

"I could think of ten dozen other things, all as bad or worse. Some summers you get a run of luck like that. It's been silverfish getting in his comics collection or mildew in his new tennis shoes ever since Doug got out of school."

"I remember years like that," said the junkman.

He looked off at the sky and there were all the years.

"So there you are, Mr, Jonas. That's it. That's why he's dying . . ."

Tom stopped and looked away.

"Let me think," said Mr. Jonas.

"Can you help, Mr. Jonas? *Can* you?"

Mr. Jonas looked deep in the big old wagon and shook his head. Now, in the sunlight, his face looked tired and he was beginning to perspire. Then he peered into the mounds of vases and peeling lamp shades and marble nymphs and satyrs made of greening copper. He sighed. He turned and picked up the reins and gave them a gentle shake. "Tom," he said, looking at the horse's back, "I'll see you later. I got to plan. I got to look around and come again after supper. Even then, who knows? Until then . . ." He reached down and picked up a little set of Japanese wind-crystals. "Hang these in his upstairs window. They make a nice cool music!"

Tom stood with the wind-crystals in his hands as the wagon rolled away. He held them up and there was no wind, they did not move. They could not make a sound.

Seven o'clock. The town resembled a vast hearth over which the shudderings of heat moved again and again from the west. Charcoal-colored shadows quivered outward from every house, every tree. A red-haired man moved along below. Tom, seeing him illumined by the dying but ferocious sun, saw a torch proudly carrying itself, saw a fiery fox, saw the devil marching in his own country.

At seven-thirty Mrs. Spaulding came out of the back door of the house to empty some watermelon rinds into the garbage pail and saw Mr. Jonas standing there.

"How is the boy?" said Mr. Jonas.

Mrs. Spaulding stood there for a moment, a response trembling on her lips.

"May I see him, please?" said Mr. Jonas.

Still she could say nothing.

"I know the boy well," he said. "Seen him most every day of his life since he was out and around. I've something for him in the wagon."

"He's not——" She was going to say "conscious," but she said, "awake. He's not awake, Mr. Jonas. The doctor said he's not to be disturbed. Oh, we don't know *what's* wrong!"

"Even if he's not 'awake,'" said Mr. Jonas, "I'd like to talk to him. Sometimes the things you hear in your sleep are more important, you listen better, it gets through."

"I'm sorry, Mr. Jonas, I just can't take the chance." Mrs. Spaulding caught hold of the screen-door handle and held fast to it. "Thanks. Thank you, anyway, for coming by."

"Yes, ma'am," said Mr. Jonas.

He did not move. He stood looking up at the window above. Mrs. Spaulding went in the house and shut the screen door.

Upstairs, on his bed, Douglas breathed.

It was a sound like a sharp knife going in and out, in and out, of a sheath.

At eight o'clock the doctor came and went again shaking his head, his coat off, his tie untied, looking as if he had lost thirty pounds that day. At nine o'clock Tom and Mother and Father carried a cot outside and brought Douglas down to sleep in the yard under the apple tree where, if there might be a wind, it would find him sooner than in the terrible rooms above. Then they went back and forth until eleven o'clock, when they set the alarm clock to wake them at three and chip more ice to refill the packs.

The house was dark and still at last, and they slept.

At twelve thirty-five, Douglas's eyes flinched.

The moon had begun to rise.

And far away a voice began to sing.

It was a high sad voice rising and falling. It was a clear voice and it was in tune. You could not make out the words.

The moon came over the edge of the lake and looked upon Green Town, Illinois, and saw it all and showed it all, every house, every tree, every prehistoric-remembering dog twitching in his simple dreams.

And it seemed that the higher the moon the nearer and louder and clearer the voice that was singing.

And Douglas turned in his fever and sighed.

Perhaps it was an hour before the moon spilled all its light upon the world, perhaps less. But the voice was nearer now and a sound like the beating of a heart which was really the motion of a horse's hoofs on the brick streets muffled by the hot thick foliage of the trees.

And there was another sound like a door slowly opening or closing, squeaking, squealing softly from time to time. The sound of a wagon.

And down the street in the light of the risen moon came the horse pulling the wagon and the wagon riding the lean body of Mr. Jonas easy and casual on the high seat. He wore his hat as if he were still out under the summer sun and he moved his hands on occasion to ripple the reins like a flow of water on the air above the horse's back. Very slowly the wagon moved down the street with Mr. Jonas singing, and in his sleep Douglas seemed for a moment to stop breathing and listen.

"Air, air . . . who will buy this air . . . Air like water and air like ice . . . buy it once and you'll buy it twice . . . here's the April air . . . here's an autumn breeze . . . here's papaya wind from the Antilles . . . Air, air, sweet pickled air . . . fair . . . rare . . . from everywhere . . . bottled and capped and scented with thyme, all that you want of air for a dime!"

At the end of this the wagon was at the curb. And someone stood in the yard, treading his shadow, carrying two beetle-green bottles which glittered like cats' eyes. Mr. Jonas looked at the cot there and called the boy's name once, twice, three times, softly. Mr. Jonas swayed in indecision, looked at the bottles he carried, made his decision, and moved forward stealthily to sit on the grass and look at this boy crushed down by the great weight of summer.

"Doug," he said, "you just lie quiet. You don't have to say anything or open your eyes. You don't even have to pretend to listen. But inside there, I know you hear me, and it's old Jonas, your friend. Your friend," he repeated and nodded.

He reached up and picked an apple off the tree, turned it round, took a bite, chewed, and continued.

"Some people turn sad awfully young," he said. "No special reason, it seems, but they seem almost to be born that way. They bruise easier, tire faster, cry quicker, remember longer and, as I say, get sadder younger than anyone else in the world. I know, for I'm one of them."

He took another bite of the apple and chewed it.

"Well, now, where are we?" he asked.

"A hot night, not a breath stirring, in August," he answered himself. "Killing hot. And a long summer it's been and too much happening, eh? Too much. And it's getting on toward one o'clock and no sign of a wind or rain. And in a moment now I'm going to get up and go. But when I go, and remember this clearly, I will leave these two bottles here upon your bed. And when I've gone I want you to wait a little while and then slowly open your eyes and sit up and reach over and drink the contents of these bottles. Not with your mouth, no. Drink with your nose. Tilt the bottles, uncork them, and let what is in them go right down into your head. Read the labels first, of course. But here, let me read them for you."

He lifted one bottle into the light.

"'GREEN DUSK FOR DREAMING BRAND PURE NORTHERN AIR,'" he read. "'Derived from the atmosphere of the white Arctic in the spring of 1900, and mixed with the wind from the upper Hudson Valley in the month of April, 1910, and containing particles of dust seen shining in the sunset of one day in the meadows around Grinnell, Iowa, when a cool air rose to be captured from a lake and a little creek and a natural spring.'

"Now the small print," he said. He squinted. "'Also containing molecules of vapor from menthol, lime, papaya and watermelon and all other water-smelling, cool-savored fruits and trees like camphor and herbs like wintergreen and the breath of a rising wind from the Des Plaines River itself. Guaranteed most refreshing and cool. To be taken on summer nights when the heat passes ninety.'"

He picked up the other bottle.

"This one the same, save I've collected a wind from the Aran Isles and one from off Dublin Bay with salt on it and a strip of flannel fog from the coast of Iceland."

He put the two bottles on the bed.

"One last direction." He stood by the cot and leaned over and spoke quietly. "When you're drinking these, remember: It was bottled by a friend. The S. J. Jonas Bottling Company, Green Town, Illinois—August, 1928. A vintage year, boy . . . a vintage year."

A moment later there was the sound of reins slapping the back of the horse in the moonlight, and the rumble of the wagon down the street and away.

After a moment Douglas's eyes twitched and, very slowly, opened.

"Mother!" whispered Tom. "Dad! Doug, it's Doug! He's going to be well. I just went down to check and—come *on*!"

Tom ran out of the house. His parents followed.

Douglas was asleep as they approached. Tom motioned to his parents, smiling wildly. They bent over the cot.

A single exhalation, a pause, a single exhalation, a pause, as the three bent there.

Douglas's mouth was slightly open and from his lips and from the thin vents of his nostrils, gently there rose a scent of cool night and cool water and cool white snow and cool green moss, and cool moonlight on silver pebbles lying at the bottom of a quiet river and cool clear water at the bottom of a small white stone well.

It was like holding their heads down for a brief moment to the pulse of an apple-scented fountain flowing cool up into the air and washing their faces.

They could not move for a long time.

THE NEXT morning was a morning of no caterpillars.

The world that had been full to bursting with tiny bundles of black and brown fur trundling on their way to green leaf and tremulous grass blade, was suddenly empty. The sound that was no sound, the billion footfalls of the caterpillars stomping through their own universe, died. Tom, who said he could hear that sound, precious as it was, looked with wonder at a town where not a single bird's mouthful stirred. Too, the cicadas had ceased.

Then, in the silence, a great sighing rustle began and they knew then why the absence of caterpillar and abrupt silence of cicada.

Summer rain.

The rain began light, a touch. The rain increased and fell heavily. It played the sidewalks and roofs like great pianos.

And upstairs, Douglas, inside again, like a fall of snow in his bed, turned his head and opened his eyes to see the freshly falling sky and slowly slowly twitch his fingers toward his yellow nickel pad and yellow Ticonderoga pencil. . . .

THERE WAS a great flurry of arrival. Somewhere trumpets were shouting. Somewhere rooms were teeming with boarders and neighbors having afternoon tea. An aunt had arrived and her name was Rose and you could hear her voice clarion clear above the others, and you could imagine her warm and huge as a hothouse rose, exactly like her name, filling any room she sat in. But right now, to Douglas, the voice, the commotion, were nothing at all. He had come from his own house, and now stood outside Grandma's kitchen door just as Grandma, having excused herself from the chicken squabble in the parlor, whisked into her own domain and set about making supper. She saw him standing there, opened the screen door for him, kissed his brow, brushed his pale hair back from his eyes, looked him straight on in the face to see if the fever had fallen to ashes and, seeing that it had, went on, singing, to her work.

Grandma, he had often wanted to say, Is this where the world began? For surely it had begun in no other than a place like this. The kitchen, without doubt, was the center of creation, all things revolved about it; it was the pediment that sustained the temple.

Eyes shut to let his nose wander, he snuffed deeply. He moved in the hell-fire steams and sudden baking-powder flurries of snow in this miraculous climate where Grandma, with the look of the Indies in her eyes and the flesh of two firm warm hens in her bodice, Grandma of the thousand arms, shook, basted, whipped, beat, minced, diced, peeled, wrapped, salted, stirred.

Blind, he touched his way to the pantry door. A squeal of laughter rang from the parlor, teacups tinkled. But he moved on into the cool underwater green and wild-persimmon country where the slung and hanging odor of creamy bananas ripened silently and bumped his head. Gnats fizzed angrily about vinegar cruets and his ears.

He opened his eyes. He saw bread waiting to be cut into slices of warm summer cloud, doughnuts strewn like clown hoops from some edible game. The faucets turned on and off in his cheeks. Here on the plum-shadowed side of the house with maple leaves making a creek-water running in the hot wind at the window he read spice-cabinet names.

How do I thank Mr. Jonas, he wondered, for what he's done? How do I thank him, how pay him back? No way, no way at all. You just can't pay. What then? What? Pass it on somehow, he thought, pass it on to someone else. Keep the chain moving. Look around, find someone, and pass it on. That was the only way . . .

"Cayenne, marjoram, cinnamon."

The names of lost and fabulous cities through which storms of spice bloomed up and dusted away.

He tossed the cloves that had traveled from some dark continent where once they had spilled on milk marble, jackstones for children with licorice hands.

And looking at one single label on a jar, he felt himself gone round the calendar to that private day this summer when he had looked at the circling world and found himself at its center.

The word on the jar was RELISH.

And he was glad he had decided to live.

RELISH! What a special name for the minced pickle sweetly crushed in its white-capped jar. The man who had named it, what a man he must have been. Roaring, stamping around, he must have tromped the joys of the world and jammed them in this jar and writ in a big hand, shouting, RELISH! For its very sound meant rolling in sweet fields with roistering chestnut mares, mouths bearded with grass, plunging your head fathoms deep in trough water so the sea poured cavernously through your head. RELISH!

He put out his hand. And here was—SAVORY.

"What's Grandma cooking for dinner tonight?" said Aunt Rose's voice from the real world of afternoon in the parlor.

"No one knows what Grandma cooks," said Grandfather, home from the office early to tend this immense flower, "until we sit at table. There's always mystery, always suspense."

"Well, I always like to know what I'm going to eat," cried Cousin Rose, and laughed. The chandelier prisms in the dining room rang with pain.

Douglas moved deeper into pantry darkness.

"Savory . . . that's a swell word. And Basil and Betel. Capsicum. Curry. All great. But Relish, now, Relish with a capital R. No argument, that's the best."

Trailing veils of steam, Grandma came and went and came again with covered dishes from kitchen to table while the assembled company waited in silence. No one lifted the lids to peer in at the hidden victuals. At last Grandma sat down, Grandpa said grace, and immediately thereafter the silverware flew up like a plague of locusts on the air.

When everyone's mouths were absolutely crammed full of miracles, Grandmother sat back and said, "Well, how do you like it?"

And the relatives, including Aunt Rose, and the boarders, their teeth deliciously mortared together at this moment, faced a terrible dilemma. Speak and break the spell, or continue allowing this honey-syrup food of the gods to dissolve and melt away to glory in their mouths? They looked as if they might laugh or cry at the cruel dilemma. They looked as if they might sit there forever, untouched by fire or earthquake, a shooting in the street, a massacre of innocents in the yard, overwhelmed with effluviums and promises of immortality. All villains were innocent in this moment of tender herbs, sweet celeries, luscious roots. The eye sped over a snow field where lay fricassees, salmagundis, gumbos, freshly invented succotashes, chowders, ragouts. The only sound was a primeval bubbling from the kitchen and the clocklike chiming of fork-on-plate announcing the seconds instead of the hours.

And then Aunt Rose gathered her indomitable pinkness and health and strength into herself with one deep breath and, fork poised on air, looking at the mystery there impaled, spoke in much too loud a voice.

"Oh, it's beautiful food all right. But what *is* this thing we're eating?"

The lemonade stopped tinkling in the frosty glasses, the forks ceased flashing on the air and came to rest on the table.

Douglas gave Aunt Rose that look which a shot deer gives the hunter before it falls dead. Wounded surprise appeared in each face down the line. The food was self-explanatory, wasn't it? It was its own philosophy, it asked and answered its own questions. Wasn't it enough that your blood and your body asked no more than this moment of ritual and rare incense?

"I really don't believe," said Aunt Rose, "that anyone heard my question."

At last Grandma let her lips open a trifle to allow the answer out.

"I call this our Thursday Special. We have it regularly."

This was a lie.

In all the years not one single dish resembled another. Was this one from the deep green sea? Had that one been shot from blue summer air? Was it a swimming food or a flying food, had it pumped blood or chlorophyll, had it walked or leaned after the sun? No one knew. No one asked. No one cared.

The most people did was stand in the kitchen door and peer at the baking-powder explosions, enjoy the clangs and rattles and bangs like a factory gone wild where Grandma stared half blindly about, letting her fingers find their way among canisters and bowls.

Was she conscious of her talent? Hardly. If asked about her cooking, Grandma would look down at her hands which some glorious instinct sent on journeys to be gloved in flour, or to plumb disencumbered turkeys, wrist-deep in search for their animal souls. Her gray eyes blinked from spectacles warped by forty years of oven blasts and blinded with strewings of pepper and sage, so she sometimes flung corn starch over steaks, amazingly tender, succulent steaks! And sometimes dropped apricots into meat loaves, cross-pollinated meats, herbs, fruits, vegetables with no prejudice, no tolerance for recipe or formula, save that at the final moment of delivery, mouths watered, blood thundered in response. Her hands then, like the hands of Great-grandma before her, were Grandma's mystery, delight, and life. She looked at them in astonishment, but let them live their life the way they must absolutely lead it.

But now for the first time in endless years, here was an upstart, a questioner, a laboratory scientist almost, speaking out where silence could have been a virtue.

"Yes, yes, but what did you put *in* this Thursday Special?"

"Why," said Grandma evasively, "what does it *taste* like to you?"

Aunt Rose sniffed the morsel on the fork.

"Beef, or is it lamb? Ginger, or is it cinnamon? Ham sauce? Bilberries? Some biscuit thrown in? Chives? Almonds?"

"That's it *exactly*." said Grandma. "Second helpings, everyone?"

A great uproar ensued, a clashing of plates, a swarming of arms, a rush of voices which hoped to drown blasphemous inquiry forever, Douglas talking louder and making more motions than the rest. But in their faces you could see their world tottering, their happiness in danger. For they were the privileged members of a household which rushed from work or play when the first dinner bell was so much as clapped once in the hall. Their arrival in the dining room had been for countless years a sort of frantic musical chairs, as they shook out napkins in a white fluttering and seized up utensils as if recently starved in solitary confinement, waiting for the summons to fall downstairs in a mass of twitching elbows and overflow themselves at table. Now they clamored nervously, made obvious jokes, darting glances at Aunt Rose as if she concealed a bomb in that ample bosom that was ticking steadily on toward their doom.

Aunt Rose, sensing that silence was indeed a blessing, devoted herself to three helpings of whatever it was on the plate and went upstairs to unlace her corset.

"Grandma," said Aunt Rose, down again. "Oh, what a kitchen you keep. It's really a mess, now, you must admit. Bottles and dishes and boxes all over, the labels off most everything, so how do you tell what you're using? I'd feel guilty if you didn't let me help you set things to rights while I'm visiting here. Let me roll up my sleeves."

"No, thank you very much," said Grandma.

Douglas heard them through the library walls and his heart thumped.

"It's like a Turkish bath in here," said Aunt Rose. "Let's have some windows open, roll up those shades so we can see what we're doing."

"Light hurts my eyes," said Grandma.

"I got the broom. I'll wash the dishes and stack them away neat. I got to help, now don't say a word."

"Go sit down," said Grandma.

"Why, Grandma, think how it'd help your cooking. You're a wonderful cook, it's true, but if you're this good in all this chaos—pure chaos—why, think how fine you'd be, once things were put where you could lay hands on them."

"I never thought of that . . ." said Grandma.

"Think on it, then. Say, for instance, modern kitchen methods helped you improve your cooking just ten or fifteen per cent. Your menfolk are already pure animal at the table. This time next week they'll be dying like flies from overeating. Food so pretty and fine they won't be able to stop the knife and fork."

"You really think so?" said Grandma, beginning to be interested.

"Grandma, don't give in!" whispered Douglas to the library wall.

But to his horror he heard them sweeping and dusting, throwing out half-empty sacks, pasting new labels on cans, putting dishes and pots and pans in drawers that had stood empty for years. Even the knives, which had lain like a catch of silvery fish on the kitchen tables, were dumped into boxes.

Grandfather had been listening behind Douglas for a full five minutes. Somewhat uneasily he scratched his chin. "Now that I think of it, that kitchen's been a mess right on down the line. Things need a little arrangement, no doubt. And if what Aunt Rose claims is true, Doug boy, it'll be a rare experience at supper tomorrow night."

"Yes, sir," said Douglas. "A rare experience."

"What's that?" asked Grandma.

Aunt Rose took a wrapped gift from behind her back.

Grandma opened it.

"A cookbook!" she cried. She let it drop on the table. "I don't need one of those! A handful of this, a pinch of that, a thimbleful of something else is all I ever use——"

"I'll help you market," said Aunt Rose. "And while we're at it, I been noticing your glasses, Grandma. You mean to say you been going around all these years peering through spectacles like those, with chipped lenses, all kind of bent? How do you see your way around without falling flat in the flour bin? We're taking you right down for new glasses."

And off they marched, Grandma bewildered, on Rose's elbow, into the summer afternoon.

They returned with groceries, new glasses, and a hairdo for Grandma. Grandma looked as if she had been chased around town. She gasped as Rose helped her into the house.

"There you are, Grandma. Now you got everything where you can find it. Now you can *see*!"

"Come on, Doug," said Grandfather. "Let's take a walk around the block and work up an appetite. This is going to be a night in history. One of the best darned suppers ever served, or I'll eat my vest."

Suppertime.

Smiling people stopped smiling. Douglas chewed one bite of food for three minutes, and then, pretending to wipe his mouth, lumped it in his napkin. He saw Tom and Dad do the same. People swashed the food together, making roads and patterns, drawing pictures in the gravy, forming castles of the potatoes, secretly passing meat chunks to the dog.

Grandfather excused himself early. "I'm full," he said.

All the boarders were pale and silent.

Grandma poked her own plate nervously.

"Isn't it a *fine* meal?" Aunt Rose asked everyone. "Got it on the table half an hour early, too!"

But the others were thinking that Monday followed Sunday, and Tuesday followed Monday, and so on for an entire week of sad breakfasts, melancholy lunches, and funereal dinners. In a few minutes the dining room was empty. Upstairs the boarders brooded in their rooms.

Grandma moved slowly, stunned, into her kitchen.

"This," said Grandfather, "has gone far enough!" He went to the foot of the stairs and called up into the dusty sunlight: "Come on down, everyone!"

The boarders murmured, all of them, locked in the dim, comfortable library. Grandfather quietly passed a derby hat. "For the kitty," he said. Then he put his hand heavily on Douglas's shoulder. "Douglas, we have a great mission for you, son. Now listen . . ." And he whispered his warm, friendly breath into the boy's ear.

* * *

Douglas found Aunt Rose, alone, cutting flowers in the garden the next afternoon.

"Aunt Rose," he said gravely, "why don't we go for a walk right now? I'll show you the butterfly ravine just down *that* way."

They walked together all around town. Douglas talked swiftly, nervously, not looking at her, listening only to the courthouse clock strike the afternoon hours.

Strolling back under the warm summer elms toward the house, Aunt Rose suddenly gasped and put her hand to her throat.

There, on the bottom of the porch step, was her luggage, neatly packed. On top of one suitcase, fluttering in the summer breeze, was a pink railroad ticket.

The boarders, all ten of them, were seated on the porch stiffly. Grandfather, like a train conductor, a mayor, a good friend, came down the steps solemnly.

"Rose," he said to her, taking her hand and shaking it up and down, "I have something to say to you."

"What is it?" said Aunt Rose.

"Aunt Rose," he said. "Good-by."

They heard the train chant away into the late afternoon hours. The porch was empty, the luggage gone, Aunt Rose's room unoccupied. Grandfather in the library, groped behind E.A. Poe for a small medicine bottle, smiling.

Grandma came home from a solitary shopping expedition to town.

"Where's Aunt Rose?"

"We said good-by to her at the station," said Grandfather. "We all wept. She hated to go, but she sent her best love to you and said she would return again in twelve years." Grandfather took out his solid gold watch. "And now I suggest we all repair to the library for a glass of sherry while waiting for Grandma to fix one of her amazing banquets."

Grandma walked off to the back of the house.

Everyone talked and laughed and listened—the boarders,

Grandfather, and Douglas, and they heard the quiet sounds in the kitchen. When Grandma rang the bell they herded to the dining room, elbowing their way.

Everyone took a huge bite.

Grandma watched the faces of her boarders. Silently they stared at their plates, their hands in their laps, the food cooling, unchewed, in their cheeks.

"I've lost it!" Grandma said. "I've lost my touch . . ."

And she began to cry.

She got up and wandered out into her neatly-ordered, labeled kitchen, her hands moving futilely before her. The boarders went to bed hungry.

Douglas heard the courthouse clock chime ten-thirty, eleven, then midnight, heard the boarders stirring in their beds, like a tide moving under the moonlit roof of the vast house. He knew they were all awake, thinking, and sad. After a long time, he sat up in bed. He began to smile at the wall and the mirror. He saw himself grinning as he opened the door and crept downstairs. The parlor was dark and smelled old and alone. He held his breath.

He fumbled into the kitchen and stood waiting a moment.

Then he began to move.

He took the baking powder out of its fine new tin and put it in an old flour sack the way it had always been. He dusted the white flour into an old cookie crock. He removed the sugar from the metal bin marked sugar and sifted it into a familiar series of smaller bins marked spices, cutlery, string. He put the cloves where they had lain for years, littering the bottom of half a dozen drawers. He brought the dishes and the knives and forks and spoons back out on top of the tables.

He found Grandma's new eyeglasses on the parlor mantel and hid them in the cellar. He kindled a great fire in the old wood-burning stove, using pages from the new cookbook. By one o'clock in the still morning a huge husking roar shot up in the black stovepipe, such a wild roar that the house, if it had ever slept at all, awoke. He heard the rustle of Grandma's slippers down the hall stairs. She stood in the kitchen, blinking at the chaos. Douglas was hidden behind the pantry door.

At one-thirty in the deep dark summer morning, the cooking

AND THEN, quite suddenly, summer was over.

He knew it first when walking downtown. Tom grabbed his arm and pointed gasping, at the dime-store window. They stood there unable to move because of the things from another world displayed so neatly, so innocently, so frighteningly, there.

"Pencils, Doug, ten thousand pencils!"

"Oh, my gosh!"

"Nickel tablets, dime tablets, notebooks, erasers, water colors, rulers, compasses, a hundred thousand of them!"

"Don't look. Maybe it's just a mirage."

"No," moaned Tom in despair. "School. School straight on ahead! Why, why do dime stores show things like that in windows before summer's even over! Ruin half the vacation!"

They walked on home and found Grandfather alone on the sere, bald-spotted lawn, plucking the last few dandelions. They worked with him silently for a time and then Douglas, bent in his own shadow, said:

"Tom, if this year's gone like this, what will next year be, better or worse?"

"Don't ask me." Tom blew a tune on a dandelion stem. "I didn't make the world." He thought about it. "Though some days I *feel* like I did." He spat happily.

"I got a hunch," said Douglas.

"What?"

"Next year's going to be even bigger, days will be brighter, nights longer and darker, more people dying, more babies born, and me in the middle of it all."

"You and two zillion other people, Doug, remember."

"Day like today," murmured Douglas, "I feel it'll be . . . just me!"

"Need any help," said Tom, "just yell."

"What could a ten-year-old brother do?"

"A ten-year-old brother'll be eleven next summer. I'll unwind the world like the rubber hand on a golf ball's insides every morning, put it back together every night. Show you how, if you ask."

"Crazy."

"Always was." Tom crossed his eyes, stuck out his tongue. "Always will be."

Douglas laughed. They went down in the cellar with Grandpa and while he decapitated the flowers they looked at all the summer shelved and glimmering there in the motionless streams, the bottles of dandelion wine. Numbered from one to ninety-odd, there the ketchup bottles, most of them full now, stood burning in the cellar twilight, one for every living summer day.

"Boy," said Tom, "what a swell way to save June, July, and August. Real practical."

Grandfather looked up, considered this, and smiled.

"Better than putting things in the attic you never use again. This way, you get to live the summer over for a minute or two here or there along the way through the winter, and when the bottles are empty the summer's gone for good and no regrets and no sentimental trash lying about for you to stumble over forty years from now. Clean, smokeless, efficient, that's dandelion wine."

The two boys pointed along the rows of bottles.

"There's the first day of summer."

"There's the new tennis shoes day."

"Sure! And there's the Green Machine!"

"Buffalo dust and Ching Ling Soo!"

"The Tarot Witch! The Lonely One!"

"It's not really over," said Tom. "It'll never be over. I'll remember what happened on every day of this year, forever."

"It was over before it began," said Grandpa, unwinding the wine press. "I don't remember a thing that happened except some new type of grass that wouldn't need cutting."

"You're joking!"

"No, sir, Doug, Tom, you'll find as you get older the days kind of blur . . . can't tell one from the other . . ."

"But, heck," said Tom. "On Monday this week I roller-skated at Electric Park, Tuesday I ate chocolate cake, Wednesday I fell in the crick, Thursday fell off a swinging vine, the week's been *full* of things! And today, I'll remember today because the leaves outside are beginning to get all red and yellow. Won't be long they'll be all over the lawn and we'll jump in piles of them and burn them. I'll never forget today! I'll always remember, I know!"

Grandfather looked up through the cellar window at the late-summer trees stirring in a colder wind. "Of course you will, Tom," he said. "Of course you will."

And they left the mellow light of the dandelion wine and went upstairs to carry out the last few rituals of summer, for they felt that now the final day, the final night had come. As the day grew late they realized that for two or three nights now, porches had emptied early of their inhabitants. The air had a different, drier smell and Grandma was talking of hot coffee instead of iced tea; the open, white-flutter-curtained windows were closing in the great bays; cold cuts were giving way to steamed beef. The mosquitos were gone from the porch, and surely when they abandoned the conflict the war with Time was really done, there was nothing for it but that humans also forsake the battleground.

Now Tom and Douglas and Grandfather stood, as they had stood three months, or was it three long centuries ago, on this front porch which creaked like a ship slumbering at night in growing swells, and they sniffed the air. Inside, the boys' bones felt like chalk and ivory instead of green mint sticks and licorice whips as earlier in the year. But the new cold touched Grandfather's skeleton first, like a raw hand chording the yellow bass piano keys in the dining room.

As the compass turns, so turned Grandfather, north.

"I guess," he said, deliberating, "we won't be coming out here any more."

And the three of them clanked the chains shaken down from the porch-ceiling eyelets and carried the swing like a weathered bier around to the garage, followed by a blowing of the first dried leaves. Inside, they heard Grandma poking up a fire in the library. The windows shook with a sudden gust of wind.

Douglas, spending a last night in the cupola tower above Grandma and Grandpa, wrote in his tablet:

"Everything runs backward now. Like matinee films sometimes, where people jump out of water onto diving boards. Come September you push down the windows you pushed up, take off the sneakers you put on, pull on the hard shoes you threw away last June. People run in the house now like birds jumping back inside clocks. One minute, porches loaded, everyone gabbing thirty to a dozen. Next minute, doors slam, talk stops, and leaves fall off trees like crazy."

He looked from the high window at the land where the crickets were strewn like dried figs in the creek beds, at a sky where birds would wheel south now through the cry of autumn loons and where trees would go up in a great fine burning of color on the steely clouds. Way out in the country tonight he could smell the pumpkins ripening toward the knife and the triangle eye and the singeing candle. Here in town the first few scarves of smoke unwound from chimneys and the faint faraway quaking of iron was the rush of black hard rivers of coal down chutes, building high dark mounds in cellar bins.

But it was late and getting later.

Douglas in the high cupola above the town, moved his hand.

"Everyone, clothes off!"

He waited. The wind blew, icing the windowpane.

"Brush teeth."

He waited again.

"Now," he said at last, "out with the lights!"

He blinked. And the town winked out its lights, sleepily, here, there, as the courthouse clock struck ten, ten-thirty, eleven, and drowsy midnight.

"The last ones now . . . there . . . there . . ."

He lay in his bed and the town slept around him and the ravine was dark and the lake was moving quietly on its shore and everyone, his family, his friends, the old people and the young, slept on one street or another, in one house or another, or slept in the far country churchyards.

He shut his eyes.

June dawns, July noons, August evenings over, finished, done, and gone forever with only the sense of it all left here in his head. Now, a whole autumn, a white winter, a cool and greening spring to figure sums and totals of summer past. And if he should forget, the dandelion wine stood in the cellar, numbered huge for each and every day. He would go there often, stare straight into the sun until he could stare no more, then close his eyes and consider the burned spots, the fleeting scars left dancing on his warm eyelids; arranging, rearranging each fire and reflection until the pattern was clear. . . .

So thinking, he slept.

And, sleeping, put an end to Summer, 1928.

SOMETHING WICKED THIS WAY COMES

With gratitude to
JENNET JOHNSON, who taught
me how to write the short story,
and to SNOW LONGLEY HOUSH,
who taught me poetry
at Los Angeles High School
a long time ago,
and to
JACK GUSS,
who helped with this novel
not so long ago

Contents

Man is in love, and loves what vanishes.

—W. B. Yeats

They sleep not, except they have done mischief;
And their sleep is taken away, unless they cause some to fall.
For they eat the bread of wickedness,
And drink the wine of violence.

—Proverbs 4:16–17

I know not all that may be coming, but be it what it will, I'll go to it laughing.

—Stubb in *Moby-Dick*

Prologue

FIRST OF all, it was October, a rare month for boys. Not that all months aren't rare. But there be bad and good, as the pirates say. Take September, a bad month: school begins. Consider August, a good month: school hasn't begun yet. July, well, July's really fine: there's no chance in the world for school. June, no doubting it, June's best of all, for the school doors spring wide and September's a billion years away.

But you take October, now. School's been on a month and you're riding easier in the reins, jogging along. You got time to think of the garbage you'll dump on old man Prickett's porch, or the hairy-ape costume you'll wear to the YMCA the last night of the month. And if it's around October twentieth and everything smoky-smelling and the sky orange and ash gray at twilight, it seems Halloween will never come in a fall of broomsticks and a soft flap of bedsheets around corners.

But one strange wild dark long year, Halloween came early.

One year Halloween came on October 24, three hours after midnight.

At that time, James Nightshade of 97 Oak Street was thirteen years, eleven months, twenty-three days old. Next door, William Halloway was thirteen years, eleven months and twenty-*four* days old. Both touched toward fourteen; it almost trembled in their hands.

And that was the October week when they grew up overnight, and were never so young any more. . . .

I. ARRIVALS

Chapter One

THE SELLER of lightning rods arrived just ahead of the storm. He came along the street of Green Town, Illinois, in the late cloudy October day, sneaking glances over his shoulder. Somewhere not so far back, vast lightnings stomped the earth. Somewhere, a storm like a great beast with terrible teeth could not be denied.

So the salesman jangled and clanged his huge leather kit in which oversized puzzles of ironmongery lay unseen but which his tongue conjured from door to door until he came at last to a lawn which was cut all wrong.

No, not the grass. The salesman lifted his gaze. But two boys, far up the gentle slope, lying *on* the grass. Of a like size and general shape, the boys sat carving twig whistles, talking of olden or future times, content with having left their fingerprints on every movable object in Green Town during summer past and their footprints on every open path between here and the lake and there and the river since school began.

"Howdy, boys!" called the man all dressed in storm-colored clothes. "Folks home?"

The boys shook their heads.

"Got any money, yourselves?"

The boys shook their heads.

"Well—" The salesman walked about three feet, stopped and hunched his shoulders. Suddenly he seemed aware of house windows or the cold sky staring at his neck. He turned slowly, sniffing the air. Wind rattled the empty trees. Sunlight, breaking through a small rift in the clouds, minted a last few oak leaves all gold. But the sun vanished, the coins were spent, the air blew gray; the salesman shook himself from the spell.

The salesman edged slowly up the lawn.

"Boy," he said. "What's your name?"

And the first boy, with hair as blond-white as milk thistle, shut up one eye, tilted his head, and looked at the salesman with a single eye as open, bright and clear as a drop of summer rain.

"Will," he said. "William Halloway."

The storm gentleman turned. "And *you*?"

The second boy did not move, but lay stomach down on the autumn grass, debating as if he might make up a name. His hair was wild, thick, and the glossy color of waxed chestnuts. His eyes, fixed to some distant point within himself, were mint rock-crystal green. At last he put a blade of dry grass in his casual mouth.

"Jim Nightshade," he said.

The storm salesman nodded as if he had known it all along. "Nightshade. That's quite a name."

"And only fitting," said Will Halloway. "I was born one minute *before* midnight, October thirtieth. Jim was born one minute *after* midnight, which makes it October thirty-first."

"Halloween," said Jim.

By their voices, the boys had told the tale all their lives, proud of their mothers, living house next to house, running for the hospital together, bringing sons into the world seconds apart; one light, one dark. There was a history of mutual celebration behind them. Each year Will lit the candles on a single cake at one minute to midnight. Jim, at one minute after, with the last day of the month begun, blew them out.

So much Will said, excitedly. So much Jim agreed to, silently. So much the salesman, running before the storm, but poised here uncertainly, heard looking from face to face.

"Halloway. Nightshade. No money, you say?"

The man, grieved by his own conscientiousness, rummaged in his leathery bag and seized forth an iron contraption.

"Take this, free! Why? One of those houses will be struck by lightning! Without this rod, bang! Fire and ash, roast pork and cinders! Grab!"

The salesman released the rod. Jim did not move. But Will caught the iron and gasped.

"Boy, it's heavy! And funny-looking. Never seen a lightning rod like this. Look, Jim!"

And Jim, at last, stretched like a cat, and turned his head. His green eyes got big and then very narrow.

The metal thing was hammered and shaped half-crescent, half-cross. Around the rim of the main rod little curlicues and doohingies had been soldered on, later. The entire surface of the rod was finely scratched and etched with strange languages, names that could tie the tongue or break the jaw, numerals that added to incomprehensible sums, pictographs of insect-animals all bristle, chaff, and claw.

"That's Egyptian." Jim pointed his nose at a bug soldered to the iron. "Scarab beetle."

"So it is, boy!"

Jim squinted. "And those there—Phoenician hen tracks."

"Right!"

"Why?" asked Jim.

"Why?" said the man. "Why the Egyptian, Arabic, Abyssinian, Choctaw? Well, what tongue does the wind talk? What nationality is a storm? What country do rains come from? What color is lightning? Where does thunder go when it dies? Boys, you got to be ready in every dialect with every shape and form to hex the St. Elmo's fires, the balls of blue light that prowl the earth like sizzling cats. I got the only lightning rods in the world that hear, feel, know, and sass back any storm, no matter what tongue, voice, or sign. No foreign thunder so loud this rod can't soft-talk it!"

But Will was staring beyond the man now.

"Which," he said. "Which house will it strike?"

"Which? Hold on. Wait." The salesman searched deep in their faces. "Some folks draw lightning, suck it like cats suck babies' breath. Some folks' polarities are negative, some positive. Some glow in the dark. Some snuff out. You now, the two of you . . . I—"

"What makes you so sure lightning will strike anywhere around here?" said Jim suddenly, his eyes bright.

The salesman almost flinched. "Why, I got a nose, an eye, an ear. Both those houses, their timbers! Listen!"

They listened. Maybe their houses leaned under the cool afternoon wind. Maybe not.

"Lightning needs channels, like rivers, to run in. One of those attics is a dry river bottom, itching to let lightning pour through! Tonight!"

"Tonight?" Jim sat up, happily.

"No ordinary storm!" said the salesman. "Tom Fury tells you. Fury, ain't that a fine name for one who sells lightning rods? Did I *take* the name? No! Did the name fire *me* to my occupations? Yes! Grown up, I saw cloudy fires jumping the world, making men hop and hide. Thought: I'll chart hurricanes, map storms, then run ahead shaking my iron cudgels, my miraculous defenders, in my fists! I've shielded and made snug-safe one hundred thousand, count'em, God-fearing homes. So when I tell you, boys, you're in dire need, listen! Climb that roof, nail this rod high, ground it in the good earth before nightfall!"

"But which house, which!" asked Will.

The salesman reared off, blew his nose in a great kerchief, then walked slowly across the lawn as if approaching a huge time bomb that ticked silently there.

He touched Will's front porch newels, ran his hand over a post, a floorboard, then shut his eyes and leaned against the house to let its bones speak to him.

Then, hesitant, he made his cautious way to Jim's house next door.

Jim stood up to watch.

The salesman put his hand out to touch, to stroke, to quiver his fingertips on the old paint.

"This," he said at last, "is the one."

Jim looked proud.

Without looking back, the salesman said, "Jim Nightshade, this your place?"

"Mine," said Jim.

"I should've known," said the man.

"Hey, what about *me*?" said Will.

The salesman snuffed again at Will's house. "No, no. Oh, a few sparks'll jump on your rainspouts. But the real show's next door here, at the Nightshades'! Well!"

The salesman hurried back across the lawn to seize his huge leather bag.

"I'm on my way. Storm's coming. Don't wait, Jim boy. Otherwise—bamm! You'll be found, your nickels, dimes and Indian-heads fused by electroplating. Abe Lincolns melted into Miss Columbias, eagles plucked raw on the backs of quarters, all run to quicksilver in your jeans. More! Any boy hit by lightning, lift his lid and there on his eyeball, pretty as the Lord's Prayer on a pin, find the last scene the boy ever saw! A box-Brownie photo, by God, of that fire climbing down the sky to blow you like a penny whistle, suck your soul back up along the bright stair! Git, boy! Hammer it high or you're dead come dawn!"

And jangling his case full of iron rods, the salesman wheeled about and charged down the walk, blinking wildly at the sky, the roof, the trees, at last closing his eyes, moving, sniffing, muttering. "Yes, bad, here it comes, feel it, way off now, but running fast. . . ."

And the man in the storm-dark clothes was gone, his cloud-colored hat pulled down over his eyes, and the trees rustled and the sky seemed very old suddenly and Jim and Will stood testing the wind to see if they could smell electricity, the lightning rod fallen between them.

"Jim," said Will. "Don't stand there. *Your* house, he said. You going to nail up the rod or ain't you?"

"No," smiled Jim. "Why spoil the fun?"

"Fun! You *crazy*? I'll get the ladder! You the hammer, some nails and wire!"

But Jim did not move. Will broke and ran. He came back with the ladder.

"Jim. Think of your mom. You want *her* burnt?"

Will climbed the side of the house, alone, and looked down. Slowly, Jim moved to the ladder below and started up.

Thunder sounded far off in the cloud-shadowed hills.

The air smelled fresh and raw, on top of Jim Nightshade's roof.

Even Jim admitted that.

Chapter Two

THERE'S NOTHING in the living world like books on water cures, deaths-of-a-thousand-slices, or pouring white-hot lava off castle walls on drolls and mountebanks.

So said Jim Nightshade, that's all he read. If it wasn't how to burgle the First National, it was how to build catapults, or shape black bumbershoots into lurking bat costumes for Cabbage Night.

Jim breathed it out all fine.

And Will, he breathed it in.

With the lightning rod nailed to Jim's roof, Will proud, and Jim ashamed of what he considered mutual cowardice, it was late in the day. Supper over, it was time for their weekly jog to the library.

Like all boys, they never walked anywhere, but named a goal and lit for it, scissors and elbows. Nobody won. Nobody wanted to win. It was in their friendship they just wanted to run forever, shadow and shadow. Their hands slapped library door handles together, their chests broke track tapes together, their tennis shoes beat parallel pony tracks over lawns, trimmed bushes, squirreled trees, no one losing, both winning, thus saving their friendship for other times of loss.

So it was on this night that blew warm, then cool, as they let the wind take them downtown at eight o'clock. They felt the wings on their fingers and elbows flying, then, suddenly plunged in new sweeps of air, the clear autumn river flung them headlong where they must go.

Up steps, three, six, nine, twelve! Slap! Their palms hit the library door.

Jim and Will grinned at each other. It was all so good, these blowing quiet October nights and the library waiting inside now with its green-shaded lamps and papyrus dust.

Jim listened. "What's *that*?"

"What, the wind?"

"Like music . . ." Jim squinted at the horizon.

"Don't hear no music."

Jim shook his head. "Gone. Or it wasn't even there. Come on!"

They opened the door and stepped in.

They stopped.

The library deeps lay waiting for them.

Out in the world, not much happened. But here in the special night, a land bricked with paper and leather, anything might happen, always did. Listen! and you heard ten thousand people screaming so high only dogs feathered their ears. A million folk ran toting cannons, sharpening guillotines; Chinese, four abreast, marched on forever. Invisible, silent, yes, but Jim and Will had the gift of ears and noses as well as the gift of tongues. This was a factory of spices from far countries. Here alien deserts slumbered. Up front was the desk where the nice old lady, Miss Watriss, purple-stamped your books, but down off away were Tibet and Antarctica, the Congo. There went Miss Wills, the other librarian, through Outer Mongolia, calmly toting fragments of Peiping and Yokohama and the Celebes. Way down the third book corridor, an oldish man whispered his broom along in the dark, mounding the fallen spices. . . .

Will stared.

It was always a surprise—that old man, his work, his name.

That's Charles William Halloway, thought Will, not grandfather, not far-wandering, ancient uncle, as some might think, but . . . *my father.*

So, looking back down the corridor, was Dad shocked to see he owned a son who visited this separate 20,000-fathoms-deep world? Dad always seemed stunned when Will rose up before him, as if they had met a lifetime ago and one had grown old while the other stayed young, and this fact stood between. . . .

Far off, the old man smiled.

They approached each other, carefully.

"Is that you, Will? Grown an inch since this morning." Charles Halloway shifted his gaze. "Jim? Eyes darker, cheeks paler; you burn yourself at both ends, Jim?"

"Heck," said Jim.

"No such place as Heck. But hell's right here under 'A' for Alighieri."

"Allegory's beyond me," said Jim.

"How stupid of me," Dad laughed. "I mean Dante. Look at this. Pictures by Mister Doré, showing all the aspects. Hell never looked better. Here's souls sunk to their gills in slime. There's someone upside down, wrong-side out."

"Boy howdy!" Jim eyed the pages two different ways and thumbed on. "Got any dinosaur pictures?"

Dad shook his head. "That's over in the next aisle." He strolled them around and reached out. "Here we are: *Pterodactyl, Kite of Destruction*! Or what about *Drums of Doom: The Saga of the Thunder Lizards*! Pep you up, Jim?"

"I'm pepped!"

Dad winked at Will. Will winked back. They stood now, a boy with corn-colored hair and a man with moon-white hair, a boy with a summer-apple, a man with a winter-apple face. Dad, Dad, thought Will, why, why, he looks . . . like *me* in a smashed mirror!

And suddenly Will remembered nights rising at two in the morning to go to the bathroom and spying across town to see that one single light in the high library window and know Dad had lingered on late murmuring and reading alone under these green jungle lamps. It made Will sad and funny to see that light, to know the old man—he stopped to change the word—his father, was here in all this shadow.

"Will," said the old man who was also a janitor who happened to be his father, "what about you?"

"Huh?" Will shook himself.

"You need a white-hat or a black-hat book?"

"Hats?" said Will.

"Well, Jim—" they perambulated, Dad running his fingers along the book spines—"he wears the black ten-gallon hats and reads books to fit. Middle name's Moriarty, right, Jim? Any day now he'll move up from Fu Manchu to Machiavelli here—medium-size dark fedora. Or over along to Dr. Faustus—extra large black Stetson. That leaves the white-hat boys to you, Will. Here's Gandhi. Next door is St. Thomas. And on the next level, well . . . Buddha."

"You don't mind," said Will, "I'll settle for *The Mysterious Island*."

"What," asked Jim, scowling, "is all this talk about white and black hats?"

"Why—" Dad handed Jules Verne to Will—"it's just, a long time ago, I had to decide, myself, which color I'd wear."

"So," said Jim, "which *did* you pick?"

Dad looked surprised. Then he laughed, uneasily.

"Since you need to ask, Jim, you make me wonder. Will, tell Mom I'll be home soon. Get out of here, both of you. Miss Watriss!" he called softly to the librarian at the desk. "Dinosaurs and mysterious islands, coming up!"

The door slammed.

Outside, a weather of stars ran clear in an ocean sky.

"Heck." Jim sniffed north, Jim sniffed south. "Where's the storm? That darn salesman promised. I just *got* to watch that lightning fizz down my drainpipes!"

Will let the wind ruffle and refit his clothes, his skin, his hair. Then he said, faintly, "It'll be here. By morning."

"Who says?"

"The huckleberries all down my arms. *They* say."

"Great!"

The wind flew Jim away.

A similar kite, Will swooped to follow.

Chapter Three

WATCHING THE boys vanish away, Charles Halloway suppressed a sudden urge to run with them, make the pack. He knew what the wind was doing to them, where it was taking them, to all the secret places that were never so secret again in life. Somewhere in him, a shadow turned mournfully over. You had to run with a night like this, so the sadness could not hurt.

Look! he thought. Will runs because running is its own excuse. Jim runs because something's up ahead of him.

Yet, strangely, they *do* run together.

What's the answer, he wondered, walking through the library, putting out the lights, putting out the lights, putting out the lights, is it all in the whorls on our thumbs and fingers? Why are some people all grasshopper fiddlings, scrapings, all antennae shivering, one big ganglion eternally knotting, slip-knotting, square-knotting themselves? They stoke a furnace all their lives, sweat their lips, shine their eyes and start it all in the crib. Caesar's lean and hungry friends. They eat the dark, who only stand and breathe.

That's Jim, all bramblehair and itchweed.

And Will? Why, he's the last peach, high on a summer tree. Some boys walk by and you cry, seeing them. They feel good, they look good, they are good. Oh, they're not above peeing off a bridge, or stealing an occasional dime-store pencil sharpener; it's not that. It's just, you know, seeing them pass, that's how they'll be all their life; they'll get hit, hurt, cut, bruised, and always wonder why, why does it happen? how can it happen to *them*?

But Jim, now, he knows it happens, he watches for it happening, he sees it start, he sees it finish, he licks the wound he expected, and never asks why: he *knows.* He *always* knew. Someone knew before him, a long time ago, someone who had wolves for pets and lions for night conversants. Hell, Jim doesn't know with his mind. But his body knows. And while Will's putting a bandage on his latest scratch, Jim's ducking, weaving, bouncing away from the knockout blow which must inevitably come.

So there they go, Jim running slower to stay with Will, Will running faster to stay with Jim, Jim breaking two windows in a haunted house because Will's along, Will breaking one window instead of none, because Jim's watching. God, how we get our fingers in each other's clay. That's friendship, each playing the potter to see what shapes we can make of the other.

Jim, Will, he thought, strangers. Go on. I'll catch up, some day. . . .

The library door gasped open, slammed.

Five minutes later, he turned into the corner saloon for his nightly one-and-only drink, in time to hear a man say:

". . . I read when alcohol was invented, the Italians thought it was the big thing they'd been looking for for centuries. The Elixir of Life! Did you know that?"

"No." The bartender's back was turned.

"Sure," the man went on. "Distilled wine. Ninth, tenth century. Looked like water. But it burnt. I mean, it not only burnt the mouth and stomach, but you could set it on fire. So they thought they'd mixed water and fire. Fire-water, the Elixir Vitae, By God. Maybe they weren't so far wrong thinking it was the Cure-all, the thing that worked miracles. Have a drink!?"

"I don't need it," said Halloway. "But someone inside me does."

"Who?"

The boy I once was, thought Halloway, who runs like the leaves down the sidewalk autumn nights.

But he couldn't say that.

So he drank, eyes shut, listening to hear if that thing inside turned over again, rustling in the deep bons that were stacked for burning but never burned.

Chapter Four

WILL STOPPED. Will looked at the Friday night town.

It seemed when the first stroke of nine banged from the big courthouse clock all the lights were on and business humming in the shops. But by the time the last stroke of nine shook everyone's fillings in his teeth, the barbers had yanked off the sheets, powdered the customers, trotted them forth; the druggist's fount had stopped fizzing like a nest of snakes, the insect neons everywhere had ceased buzzing, and the vast glittering acreage of the dime store with its ten billion metal, glass and paper oddments waiting to be fished over, suddenly blacked out. Shades slithered, doors boomed, keys rattled their bones in locks, people fled with hordes of torn newspaper mice nibbling their heels.

Bang! they were gone!

"Boy!" yelled Will. "Folks run like they thought the storm was here!"

"It is!" shouted Jim. "*Us!*"

They stomp-pound-thundered over iron grates, steel trapdoors, past a dozen unlit shops, a dozen half-lit, a dozen dying dark. The city was dead as they rounded the United Cigar Store corner to see a wooden Cherokee glide in darkness, by himself.

"Hey!"

Mr. Tetley, the proprietor, peered over the Indian's shoulder.

"Scare you, boys?"

"Naw!"

But Will shivered, feeling cold tidal waves of strange rain moving down the prairie as on a deserted shore. When the lightning nailed the town, he wanted to be layered under sixteen blankets and a pillow.

"Mr. Tetley?" said Will, quietly.

For now there were two wooden Indians upright in ripe tobacco darkness. Mr. Tetley, amidst his jest, had frozen, mouth open, listening.

"Mr. Tetley?"

He heard something far away on the wind, but couldn't say what it was.

The boys backed off.

He did not see them. He did not move. He only listened.

They left him. They ran.

In the fourth empty block from the library, the boys came upon a third wooden Indian.

Mr. Crosetti, in front of his barber shop, his door key in his trembling fingers, did not see them stop.

What had stopped them?

A teardrop.

It moved shining down Mr. Crosetti's left cheek. He breathed heavily.

"Crosetti, you fool! *Something* happens, *nothing* happens, you cry like a baby!"

Mr. Crosetti took a trembling breath, snuffing. "Don't you *smell* it?"

Jim and Will sniffed.

"Licorice!"

"Heck, no. Cotton candy!"

"I haven't smelled that in years," said Mr. Crosetti.

Jim snorted. "It's around."

"Yes, but who notices? When? Now, my nose tells me, breathe! And I'm crying. Why? Because I remember how a long time ago, boys ate that stuff. Why haven't I stopped to think and smell the last thirty years?"

"You're busy, Mr. Crosetti," Will said. "You haven't got time."

"Time, time." Mr. Crosetti wiped his eyes. "Where does that smell come from? There's no place in town sells cotton candy. Only circuses."

"Hey," said Will. "That's right!"

"Well, Crosetti is done crying." The barber blew his nose and turned to lock his shop door. As he did this, Will watched the barber pole whirl its red serpentine up out of nothing, leading his gaze around, rising to vanish into more nothing. On countless noons Will had stood here trying to unravel that ribbon, watch it come, go, end without ending.

Mr. Crosetti put his hand to the light switch under the spinning pole.

"Don't," said Will. Then, murmuring, "Don't turn it off."

Mr. Crosetti looked at the pole, as if freshly aware of its

miraculous properties. He nodded, gently, his eyes soft. "Where does it come from, where does it go, eh? Who knows? Not you, not him, not me. Oh, the mysteries, by God. So. We'll leave it on!"

It's good to know, thought Will, it'll be running until dawn, winding up from nothing, winding away to nothing, while we sleep.

"Good night!"

"Good night."

And they left him behind in a wind that very faintly smelled of licorice and cotton candy.

Chapter Five

CHARLES HALLOWAY put his hand to the saloon's double swing doors, hesitant, as if the gray hairs on the back of his hand, like antennae, had felt something beyond slide by in the October night. Perhaps great fires burned somewhere and their furnace blasts warned him not to step forth. Or another Ice Age had loomed across the land, its freezing bulk might already have laid waste a billion people in the hour. Perhaps Time itself was draining off down an immense glass, with powdered darkness falling after to bury all.

Or maybe it was only that man in a dark suit, seen through the saloon window, across the street. Great paper rolls under one arm, a brush and bucket in his free hand, the man was whistling a tune, very far away.

It was a tune from another season, one that never ceased making Charles Halloway sad when he heard it. The song was incongruous for October, but immensely moving, overwhelming, no matter what day or what month it was sung:

I heard the bells on Christmas Day
Their old, familiar carols play,
  And wild and sweet
  Their words repeat
Of peace on earth, good will to men!

Charles Halloway shivered. Suddenly there was the old sense of terrified elation, of wanting to laugh and cry together when he saw the innocents of the earth wandering the snowy streets the day before Christmas among all the tired men and women whose faces were dirty with guilt, unwashed of sin, and smashed like small windows by life that hit without warning, ran, hid, came back and hit again.

Then pealed the bells more loud and deep:
"God is not dead, nor doth He sleep!
  The Wrong shall fail,
  The Right prevail.
With peace on earth, good will to men!"

The whistling died.

Charles Halloway stepped out. Far up ahead, the man who had whistled the tune was motioning his arms by a telegraph pole, silently working. Now he vanished into the open door of a shop.

Charles Halloway, not knowing why, crossed the street to watch the man pasting up one of the posters inside the unrented and empty store.

Now the man stepped out the door with his brush, his paste bucket, his rolled papers. His eyes, a fierce and lustful shine, fixed on Charles Halloway. Smiling, he gestured an open hand.

Halloway stared.

The palm of that hand was covered with fine black silken hair. It looked like—

The hand clenched, tight. It waved. The man swept around the corner. Charles Halloway, stunned, flushed with sudden summer heat, swayed, then turned to gaze into the empty shop.

Two sawhorses stood parallel to each other under a single spotlight.

Placed over these two sawhorses like a funeral of snow and crystal was a block of ice six feet long. It shone dimly with its own effulgence, and its color was light green-blue. It was a great cool gem resting there in the dark.

On a little white placard at one side near the window the following calligraphic message could be read by lamplight:

Cooger & Dark's Pandemonium Shadow Show—
Fantoccini, Marionette Circus, and Your
Plain Meadow Carnival. Arriving
Immediately! Here on Display, one of
our many attractions:

THE MOST BEAUTIFUL WOMAN IN THE WORLD!

Halloway's eyes leaped to the poster on the inside of the window.

THE MOST BEAUTIFUL WOMAN IN THE WORLD!

And back to the cold long block of ice.

It was such a block of ice as he remembered from traveling

magician's shows when he was a boy, when the local ice company contributed a chunk of winter in which, for 12 hours on end, frost maidens lay embedded, on display while people watched and comedies toppled down the raw white screen and coming attractions came and went and at last the pale ladies slid forth all rimed, chipped free by perspiring sorcerers to be led off smiling into the dark behind the curtains.

THE MOST BEAUTIFUL WOMAN IN THE WORLD!

And yet this vast chunk of wintry glass held nothing but frozen river water.

No. Not quite empty.

Halloway felt his heart pound one special time.

Within the huge winter gem was there not a special vacuum? a voluptuous hollow, a prolonged emptiness which undulated from tip to toe of the ice? and wasn't this vacuum, this emptiness waiting to be filled with summer flesh, was it not shaped somewhat like a . . . woman?

Yes.

The ice. And the lovely hollows, the horizontal flow of emptiness within the ice. The lovely nothingness. The exquisite flow of an invisible mermaid daring the ice to capture it.

The ice was cold.

The emptiness within the ice was warm.

He wanted to go away from here.

But Charles Halloway stood in the strange night for a long time looking in at the empty shop and the two sawhorses and the cold waiting arctic coffin set there like a vast Star of India in the dark. . . .

Chapter Six

JIM NIGHTSHADE stopped at the corner of Hickory and Main, breathing easily, his eyes fixed tenderly on the leafy darkness of Hickory Street.

"Will . . . ?"

"No!" Will stopped, surprised at his own violence.

"It's just there. The fifth house. Just *one* minute, Will," Jim pleaded, softly.

"Minute . . . ?" Will glanced down the street.

Which was the street of the Theater.

Until this summer it had been an ordinary street where they stole peaches, plums and apricots, each in its day. But late in August, while they were monkey-climbing for the sourest apples, the "thing" happened which changed the houses, the taste of the fruit, and the very air within the gossiping trees.

"Will! It's waiting. Maybe something's *happening*!" hissed Jim.

Maybe something is. Will swallowed hard, and felt Jim's hand pinch his arm.

For it was no longer the street of the apples or plums or apricots, it was the one house with a window at the side and this window, Jim said, was a stage, with a curtain—the shade, that is—up. And in that room, on that strange stage, were the actors, who spoke mysteries, mouthed wild things, laughed, sighed, murmured so much; so *much* of it was whispers Will did not understand.

"Just one last time, Will."

"You know it won't be last!"

Jim's face was flushed, his cheeks blazing, his eyes green-glass fire. He thought of that night, them picking the apples, Jim suddenly crying softly, "Oh, there!"

And Will, hanging to the limbs of the tree, tight-pressed, terribly excited, staring in at the Theater, that peculiar stage where people, all unknowing, flourished shirts above their heads, let fall clothes to the rug, stood raw and animal-crazy, naked, like shivering horses, hands out to touch each other.

What're they *doing*! thought Will. Why are they laughing? What's wrong with them, what's *wrong*!?

He wished the light would go out.

But he hung tight to the suddenly slippery tree and watched the bright window Theater, heard the laughing, and numb at last let go, slid, fell, lay dazed, then stood in dark gazing up at Jim, who still clung to his high limb. Jim's face, hearth-flushed, cheeks fire-fuzzed, lips parted, stared in. "Jim, Jim, come down!" But Jim did not hear. "Jim!" And when Jim looked down at last he saw Will as a stranger below with some silly request to give off living and come down to earth. So Will ran off, alone, thinking too much, thinking nothing at all, not knowing what to think.

"Will, please . . ."

Will looked at Jim now, with the library books in his hands.

"We been to the library. Ain't that enough?"

Jim shook his head. "Carry these for me."

He handed Will his books and trotted softly off under the hissing whispering trees. Three houses down he called back: "Will? Know what you *are*? A darn old dimwit Episcopal Baptist!"

Then Jim was gone.

Will seized the books tight to his chest. They were wet from his hands.

Don't look back! he thought.

I won't! I won't!

And looking only toward home, he walked that way. Quickly.

Chapter Seven

HALFWAY HOME, Will felt a shadow breathing hard behind him.

"Theater closed?" said Will, not looking back.

Jim walked in silence beside him for a long while and then said, "Nobody home."

"Swell!"

Jim spat. "Darn Baptist preacher, you!"

And around the corner a tumbleweed slithered, a great cotton ball of pale paper which bounced, then clung shivering to Jim's legs.

Will grabbed the paper, laughing, pulled it off, let it fly! He stopped laughing.

The boys, watching the pale throwaway rattle and flit through the trees, were suddenly cold.

"Wait a minute . . ." said Jim, slowly.

All of a sudden they were yelling, running, leaping. "Don't tear it! Careful!"

The paper fluttered like a snare drum in their hands.

"COMING, OCTOBER TWENTY-FOURTH!"

Their lips moved, shadowing the words set in rococo type.

"Cooger and Dark's . . ."

"Carnival!"

"October twenty-fourth! That's tomorrow!"

"It can't be," said Will. "All carnivals stop after Labor Day—"

"Who cares? A thousand and one wonders! See! MEPHISTOPHELE, THE LAVA DRINKER! MR. ELECTRICO! THE MONSTER MONTGOLFIER?"

"Balloon," said Will. "A Montgolfier is a balloon."

"MADEMOISELLE TAROT!" read Jim. "THE DANGLING MAN. THE DEMON GUILLOTINE! THE ILLUSTRATED MAN! Hey!"

"That's just an old guy with tattoos."

"No." Jim breathed warm on the paper. "He's *illustrated*. Special. See! Covered with monsters! A menagerie!" Jim's eyes jumped. "SEE! THE SKELETON! Ain't that fine, Will? Not Thin

Man, no, but SKELETON! SEE! THE DUST WITCH! What's a Dust Witch, Will?"

"Dirty old Gypsy—"

"No." Jim squinted off, seeing things. "A Gypsy that was born in the Dust, raised in the Dust, and some day winds up *back* in the Dust. Here's more: EGYPTIAN MIRROR MAZE! SEE YOURSELF TEN THOUSAND TIMES! SAINT ANTHONY'S TEMPLE OF TEMPTATION!"

"THE MOST BEAUTIFUL—" read Will.

"—WOMAN IN THE WORLD," finished Jim.

They looked at each other.

"*Can* a carnival have the Most Beautiful Woman on Earth in its side show, Will?"

"You ever *seen* carnival ladies, Jim?"

"Grizzly bears. But how come this handbill claims—"

"Oh, shut up!"

"You mad at me, Will?"

"No, it's just—get it!"

The wind had torn the paper from their hands.

The handbill blew over the trees and away in an idiot caper, gone.

"It's not true, anyway," Will gasped. "Carnivals don't come this late in the year. Silly darn-sounding thing. Who'd go to it?"

"Me." Jim stood quiet in the dark.

Me, thought Will, seeing the guillotine flash, the Egyptian mirrors unfold accordions of light, and the sulphur-skinned devil-man sipping lava, like gunpowder tea.

"That music . . ." Jim murmured. "Calliope. Must be coming *tonight*!"

"Carnivals come at sunrise."

"Yeah, but what about the licorice and cotton candy we smelled, close?"

And Will thought of the smells and the sounds flowing on the river of wind from beyond the darkening houses, Mr. Tetley listening by his wooden Indian friend, Mr. Crosetti with the single tear shining down his cheek, and the barber pole sliding its red tongue up and around forever out of nowhere and away to eternity.

Will's teeth chattered.

"Let's go home."

"We *are* home!" cried Jim, surprised.

For, not knowing it, they had reached their separate houses and now moved up separate walks.

On his porch, Jim leaned over and called softly.

"Will. You're not mad?"

"Heck, no."

"We won't go by that street, that house, the Theater, again for a month. A *year*! I swear."

"Sure, Jim, sure."

They stood with their hands on the doorknobs of their houses, and Will looked up at Jim's roof where the lightning rod glittered against the cold stars.

The storm was coming. The storm *wasn't* coming.

No matter which, he was glad Jim had that grand contraption up there.

"Night!"

"Night."

Their separate doors slammed.

Chapter Eight

WILL OPENED the door and shut it again. Quietly, this time.

"That's better," said his mother's voice.

Framed through the hall door Will saw the only theater he cared for now, the familiar stage where sat his father (home already! he and Jim *must* have run the long way round!) holding a book but reading the empty spaces. In a chair by the fire mother knitted and hummed like a teakettle.

He wanted to be near and not near them, he saw them close, he saw them far. Suddenly they were awfully small in too large a room in too big a town and much too huge a world. In this unlocked place they seemed at the mercy of anything that might break in from the night.

Including me, Will thought. Including me.

Suddenly he loved them more for their smallness than he ever had when they seemed tall.

His mother's fingers twitched, her mouth counted, the happiest woman he had ever seen. He remembered a greenhouse on a winter day, pushing aside thick jungle leaves to find a creamy pink hothouse rose poised alone in the wilderness. That was mother, smelling like fresh milk, happy, to herself, in this room.

Happy? But how and why? Here, a few feet off, was the janitor, the library man, the stranger, his uniform gone, but his face still the face of a man happier at night alone in the deep marble vaults, whispering his broom in the drafty corridors.

Will watched, wondering why this woman was so happy and this man so sad.

His father stared deep in the fire, one hand relaxed. Half cupped in that hand lay a crumpled paper ball.

Will blinked.

He remembered the wind blowing the pale handbill skittering in the trees. Now the same color paper lay crushed, its rococo type hidden, in his father's fingers.

"Hey!"

Will stepped into the parlor.

Immediately Mom opened a smile that was like lighting a second fire.

Dad, stricken, looked dismayed, as if caught in a criminal act.

Will wanted to say, "Hey, what'd you think of the handbill . . . ?"

But Dad was cramming the handbill deep in the chair upholstery.

And mother was leafing the library books.

"Oh, these are fine, Willy!"

So Will just stood with Cooger and Dark on his tongue and said:

"Boy, the wind really *flew* us home. Streets full of *paper* blowing."

Dad did not flinch at this.

"Anything new, Dad?"

Dad's hand still lay tucked in the side of the chair. He lifted a gray, slightly worried, very tired gaze to his son:

"Stone lion blew off the library steps. Prowling the town now, looking for Christians. Won't find any. Got the only one in captivity here, and she's a good cook."

"Bosh," said Mom.

Walking upstairs, Will heard what he half expected to hear.

A soft fluming sigh as something fresh was tossed on the fire. In his mind, he saw Dad standing at the hearth looking down as the paper crinkled to ash:

". . . COOGER . . . DARK . . . CARNIVAL . . . WITCH . . . WONDERS . . ."

He wanted to go back down and stand with Dad, hands out, to be warmed by the fire.

Instead he went slowly up to shut the door of his room.

Some nights, abed, Will put his ear to the wall to listen, and if his folks talked things that were right, he stayed, and if not right he turned away. If it was about time and passing years or himself or town or just the general inconclusive way God ran the world, he listened warmly, comfortably, secretly, for it was usually Dad talking. He could not often speak with Dad anywhere in the world, inside or out, but this was different. There was a thing in Dad's voice, up, over, down, easy as a hand winging soft in the air like a white bird describing flight patterns, made the ear want to follow and the mind's eye to see.

And the odd thing in Dad's voice was the sound truth makes being said. The sound of truth, in a wild roving land of city or plain country lies, will spell any boy. Many nights Will drowsed this way, his senses like stopped clocks long before that half-singing voice was still. Dad's voice was a midnight school, teaching deep fathom hours, and the subject was life.

So it was this night, Will's eyes shut, head leaned to the cool plaster. At first Dad's voice, a Congo drum, boomed softly, horizons away. Mother's voice, she used her water-bright soprano in the Baptist choir, did not sing, yet sang back replies. Will imagined Dad sprawled talking to the empty ceiling:

". . . Will . . . makes me feel so *old* . . . a man should play baseball with his son. . . ."

"Not necessary," said the woman's voice, kindly. "You're a good man."

"—in a bad season. Hell, I was forty when he was *born*! And *you*. Who's your *daughter*? people say. God, when you lie down your thoughts turn to mush. Hell!"

Will heard the shift of weight as Dad sat up in the dark. A match was being struck, a pipe was being smoked. The wind rattled the windows.

". . . man with posters under his arm . . ."

". . . carnival . . ." said his mother's voice, ". . . *this* late in the year??"

Will wanted to turn away, but couldn't.

". . . most beautiful . . . woman . . . in the world," Dad's voice murmured.

Mother laughed softly. "You know I'm not."

No! thought Will, that's from the handbill! Why doesn't Dad *tell*!!?

Because, Will answered himself. Something's going on. Oh, something *is* going on!

Will saw that paper frolicked in the trees, its words THE MOST BEAUTIFUL WOMAN, and fever prickled his cheeks. He thought: Jim, the street of the Theater, the naked people in the stage of that Theater window, crazy as Chinese opera, darn odd crazy as old Chinese opera, judo, jujitsu, Indian puzzles, and now his father's voice, dreaming off, sad, sadder, saddest, much too much to understand. And suddenly he was scared because Dad wouldn't talk about the handbill he had secretly burned. Will gazed out the window. There! Like a milkweed plume! White paper danced in the air.

"No," he whispered, "no carnival's coming *this* late. It can't!" He hid under the covers, switched on his flashlight, opened a book. The first picture he saw was a prehistoric reptile trap-drumming a night sky a million years lost.

Heck, he thought, in the rush I got Jim's book, he's got one of mine.

But it was a pretty fine reptile.

And flying toward sleep, he thought he heard his father, restless, below. The front door shut. His father was going back to work late, for no reason, with brooms, or books, downtown, away . . . away. . . .

And mother asleep, content, not knowing he had gone.

Chapter Nine

NO ONE else in the world had a name came so well off the tongue.

"Jim Nightshade. That's me."

Jim stood tall and now lay long in bed, strung together by marsh-grass, his bones easy in his flesh, his flesh easy on his bones. The library books lay unopened by his relaxed right hand.

Waiting, his eyes were dark as twilight, with shadows under the eyes from the time, his mother said, he had almost died when he was three and still remembered. His hair was dark autumn chestnut and the veins in his temples and brow and in his neck and ticking in his wrists and on the backs of his slender hands, all these were dark blue. He was marbled with dark, was Jim Nightshade, a boy who talked less and smiled less as the years increased.

The trouble with Jim was he looked at the world and could not look away. And when you never look away all your life, by the time you are thirteen you have done *twenty* years taking in the laundry of the world.

Will Halloway, it was in him young to always look just beyond, over or to one side. So at thirteen he had saved up only six years of staring.

Jim knew every centimeter of his shadow, could have cut it out of tar paper, furled it, and run it up a flagpole—his banner.

Will, he was occasionally surprised to see his shadow following him somewhere, but that was that.

"Jim? You awake?"

"Hi, Mom."

A door opened and now shut. He felt her weight on the bed.

"Why, Jim, your hands are ice. You shouldn't have the window so high. Mind your health."

"Sure."

"Don't say 'sure' that way. You don't know until you've had three children and lost all but one."

"Never going to have any," said Jim.

"You just say that."

"I *know* it. I know everything."

She waited a moment. "What do you know?"

"No use making more people. People die."

His voice was very calm and quiet and almost sad.

"That's everything."

"Almost everything. *You're* here, Jim. If you weren't, I'd given up long ago."

"Mom." A long silence. "Can you remember Dad's face? Do I look like him?"

"The day you go away is the day he leaves forever."

"Who's going away?"

"Why, just lying there, Jim, you run so fast. I never saw anyone move so much, just sleeping. Promise me, Jim. Wherever you go and come back, bring lots of kids. Let them run wild. Let me spoil them, some day."

"I'm never going to own anything can hurt me."

"You going to collect rocks, Jim? No, some day, you've got to be hurt."

"No, I don't."

He looked at her. Her face had been hit a long time ago. The bruises had never gone from around her eyes.

"You'll live and get hurt," she said, in the dark. "But when it's time, tell me. Say goodbye. Otherwise, I might not let you go. Wouldn't that be terrible, to just grab ahold?"

She rose up suddenly and went to put the window down.

"Why do boys want their windows open wide?"

"Warm blood."

"Warm blood." She stood alone. "That's the story of all our sorrows. And don't ask why."

The door shut.

Jim, alone, raised the window, and leaned into the absolutely clear night.

Storm, he thought, you *there*?

Yes.

Feel . . . away to the west . . . a real humdinger, rushing along!

The shadow of the lightning rod lay on the drive below.

He sucked in cold air, gave out a vast exhilaration of heat.

Why, he thought, why don't I climb up, knock that lightning rod loose, throw it away?

And then see what happens?
Yes.
And *then* see what happens!

Chapter Ten

JUST AFTER midnight.

Shuffling footsteps.

Along the empty street came the lightning-rod salesman, his leather valise swung almost empty in his baseball-mitt hand, his face at ease. He turned a corner and stopped.

Paper-soft white moths tapped at an empty store window, looking in.

And in the window, like a great coffin boat of star-colored glass, beached on two sawhorses lay a chunk of Alaska Snow Company ice chopped to a size great enough to flash in a giant's ring.

And sealed in this ice was the most beautiful woman in the world.

The lightning-rod salesman's smile faded.

In the dreaming coldness of ice like someone fallen and slept in snow avalanches a thousand years, forever young, was this woman.

She was as fair as this morning and fresh as tomorrow's flowers and lovely as any maid when a man shuts up his eyes and traps her, in cameo perfection, on the shell of his eyelids.

The lightning-rod salesman remembered to breathe.

Once, long ago, traveling among the marbles of Rome and Florence, he had seen women like this, kept in stone instead of ice. Once, wandering in the Louvre, he had found women like this, washed in summer color and kept in paint. Once, as a boy, sneaking the cool grottos behind a motion picture theater screen, on his way to a free seat, he had glanced up and there towering and flooding the haunted dark seen a woman's face as he had never seen it since, of such size and beauty built of milk-bone and moon-flesh as to freeze him there alone behind the stage, shadowed by the motion of her lips, the bird-wing flicker of her eyes, the snow-pale-death-shimmering illumination from her cheeks.

So from other years there jumped forth images which flowed and found new substance here within the ice.

What color was her hair? It was blond to whiteness and might take any color, once set free of cold.

How tall was she?

The prism of the ice might well multiply her size or diminish her as you moved this way or that before the empty store, the window, the night-soft rap-tapping ever-fingering, gently probing moths.

Not important.

For above all—the lightning-rod salesman shivered—he knew the most extraordinary thing.

If by some miracle her eyelids should open within that sapphire and she should look at him, he knew what color her eyes would be.

He knew what color her eyes would be.

If one were to enter this lonely night shop—

If one were to put forth one's hand, the warmth of that hand would . . . what?

Melt the ice.

The lightning-rod salesman stood there for a long moment, his eyes quickened shut.

He let his breath out.

It was warm as summer on his teeth.

His hand touched the shop door. It swung open. Cold arctic air blew out around him. He stepped in.

The door shut.

The white snowflake moths tapped at the window.

Chapter Eleven

MIDNIGHT THEN and the town clocks chiming on toward one and two and then three in the deep morning and the peals of the great clocks shaking dust off old toys in high attics and shedding silver off old mirrors in yet higher attics and stirring up dreams about clocks in all the beds where children slept.

Will heard it.

Muffled away in the prairie lands, the chuffing of an engine, the slow-following dragon-glide of a train.

Will sat up in bed.

Across the way, like a mirror image, Jim sat up, too.

A calliope began to play oh so softly, grieving to itself, a million miles away.

In one single motion, Will leaned from his window, as did Jim. Without a word they gazed over the trembling surf of trees.

Their rooms were high, as boys' rooms should be. From these gaunt windows they could rifle-fire their gaze artillery distances past library, city hall, depot, cow barns, farmlands to empty prairie!

There, on the world's rim, the lovely snail-gleam of the railway tracks ran, flinging wild gesticulations of lemon or cherry-colored semaphore to the stars.

There, on the precipice of earth, a small steam feather uprose like the first of a storm cloud yet to come.

The train itself appeared, link by link, engine, coal-car, and numerous and numbered all-asleep-and-slumbering-dreamfilled cars that followed the firefly-sparked churn, chant, drowsy autumn hearthfire roar. Hellfires flushed the stunned hills. Even at this remote view, one imagined men with buffalo-haunched arms shoveling black meteor falls of coal into the open boilers of the engine.

The engine!

Both boys vanished, came back to lift binoculars.

"The engine!"

"Civil War! No other stack like that since 1900!"

"The rest of the train, *all* of it's old!"

"The flags! The cages! It's the carnival!"

They listened. At first Will thought he heard the air whistling fast in his nostrils. But no—it was the train, and the calliope sighing, weeping, on that train.

"Sounds like church music!"

"Hell. Why would a carnival play church music?"

"Don't say hell," hissed Will.

"Hell." Jim ferociously leaned out. "I've saved up all day. Everyone's asleep so—hell!"

The music drifted by their windows. Goose pimples rose big as boils on Will's arms.

"That *is* church music. Changed."

"For cri-yi, I'm froze, let's go watch them set up!"

"At three A.M.?"

"At three A.M.!"

Jim vanished.

For a moment, Will watched Jim dance around over there, shirt uplifted, pants going on, while off in night country, panting, churning was this funeral train all black plumed cars, licorice-colored cages, and a sooty calliope clamoring, banging three different hymns mixed and lost, maybe not there at all.

"Here goes nothing!"

Jim slid down the drainpipe on his house, toward the sleeping lawns.

"Jim! Wait!"

Will thrashed into his clothes.

"Jim, don't go *alone*!"

And followed after.

Chapter Twelve

SOMETIMES YOU see a kite so high, so wise it almost knows the wind. It travels, then chooses to land in one spot and no other and no matter how you yank, run this way or that, it will simply break its cord, seek its resting place and bring you, blood-mouthed, running.

"Jim! Wait for me!"

So now Jim was the kite, the wild twine cut, and whatever wisdom was his taking him away from Will who could only run, earthbound, after one so high and dark silent and suddenly strange.

"Jim, here I come!"

And running, Will thought, Boy, it's the same old thing. I talk. Jim runs. I tilt stones, Jim grabs the cold junk under the stones and—lickety-split! I climb hills. Jim yells off church steeples. I got a bank account. Jim's got the hair on his head, the yell in his mouth, the shirt on his back and the tennis shoes on his feet. How come I think *he's* richer? Because, Will thought, I sit on a rock in the sun and old Jim, he prickles his arm-hairs by moonlight and dances with hoptoads. I tend cows. Jim tames Gila monsters. Fool! I yell at Jim. Coward! he yells back. And here we—*go*!

And they ran from town, across fields and both froze under a rail bridge with the moon ready beyond the hills and the meadows trembling with a fur of dew.

WHAM!

The carnival train thundered the bridge. The calliope wailed.

"There's no one playing it!" Jim stared up.

"Jim, no jokes!"

"Mother's honor, look!"

Going away, away, the calliope pipes shimmered with star explosions, but no one sat at the high keyboard. The wind, sluicing ice-water air in the pipes, made the music.

The boys ran. The train curved away, gonging its undersea funeral bell, sunk, rusted, green-mossed, tolling, tolling. Then the engine whistle blew a great steam whiff and Will broke out in pearls of ice.

Way late at night Will had heard—how often?—train whistles jetting steam along the rim of sleep, forlorn, alone and far, no matter how near they came. Sometimes he woke to find tears on his cheek, asked why, lay back, listened and thought, Yes! *they* make me cry, going east, going west, the trains so far gone in country deeps they drown in tides of sleep that escape the towns.

Those trains and their grieving sounds were lost forever between stations, not remembering where they had been, not guessing where they might go, exhaling their last pale breaths over the horizon, gone. So it was with all trains, ever.

Yet *this* train's whistle!

The wails of a lifetime were gathered in it from other nights in other slumbering years; the howl of moon-dreamed dogs, the seep of river-cold winds through January porch screens which stopped the blood, a thousand fire sirens weeping, or worse! the outgone shreds of breath, the protests of a billion people dead or dying, not wanting to be dead, their groans, their sighs, burst over the earth!

Tears jumped to Will's eyes. He lurched. He knelt. He pretended to lace one shoe.

But then he saw Jim's hands clap *his* ears, his eyes wet, too. The whistle screamed. Jim screamed against the scream. The whistle shrieked. Will shrieked against the shriek.

Then the billion voices ceased, instantly, as if the train had plunged in a fire storm off the earth.

The train skimmed on softly, slithering, black pennants fluttering, black confetti lost on its own sick-sweet candy wind, down the hill, with the boys pursuing, the air so cold they ate ice cream with each breath.

They climbed a last rise to look down.

"Boy," whispered Jim.

The train had pulled off into Rolfe's moon meadow, so-called because town couples came out to see the moon rise here over a land so wide, so long, it was like an inland sea, filled with grass in spring, or hay in late summer or snow in winter, it was fine walking here along its crisp shore with the moon coming up to tremble in its tides.

Well, the carnival train was crouched there now in the autumn grass on the old rail spur near the woods, and the boys crept and lay down under a bush, waiting.

"It's so quiet," whispered Will.

The train just stood in the middle of the dry autumn field, no one in the locomotive, no one in the tender, no one in any of the cars behind, all black under the moon, and just the small sounds of its metal cooling, ticking on the rails.

"Ssst," said Jim. "I *feel* them *moving* in there."

Will felt the cat fuzz on his body bramble up by the thousands.

"You think they *mind* us watching?"

"Maybe," said Jim, happily.

"Then why the noisy calliope?"

"When I figure that," Jim smiled, "I'll tell you. Look!"

Whisper.

As if exhaling itself straight down from the sky, a vast moss-green balloon touched at the moon.

It hovered two hundred yards above and away, quietly riding the wind.

"The basket under the balloon, someone *in* it!"

But then a tall man stepped down from the train caboose platform like a captain assaying the tidal weathers of this inland sea. All dark suit, shadow-faced, he waded to the center of the meadow, his shirt as black as the gloved hands he now stretched to the sky.

He gestured, once.

And the train came to life.

At first a head lifted in one window, then an arm, then another head like a puppet in a marionette theater. Suddenly two men in black were carrying a dark tent pole out across the hissing grass.

It was the silence that made Will pull back, even as Jim leaned forward, eyes moon-bright.

A carnival should be all growls, roars like timberlands stacked, bundled, rolled and crashed, great explosions of lion dust, men ablaze with working anger, pop bottles jangling, horse buckles shivering, engines and elephants in full stampede through rains of sweat while zebras neighed and trembled like cage trapped in cage.

But this was like old movies, the silent theater haunted with black-and-white ghosts, silvery mouths opening to let moonlight smoke out, gestures made in silence so hushed you could hear the wind fizz the hair on your cheeks.

More shadows rustled from the train, passing the animal cages where darkness prowled with unlit eyes and the calliope stood mute save for the faintest idiot tune the breeze piped wandering up the flues.

The ringmaster stood in the middle of the land. The balloon like a vast moldy green cheese stood fixed to the sky. Then—darkness came.

The last thing Will saw was the balloon swooping down, as clouds covered the moon.

In the night he felt the men rush to unseen tasks. He sensed the balloon, like a great fat spider, fiddling with the lines and poles, rearing a tapestry in the sky.

The clouds arose. The balloon sifted up.

In the meadow stood the skeleton main poles and wires of the main tent, waiting for its canvas skin.

More clouds poured over the white moon. Shadowed, Will shivered. He heard Jim crawling forward, seized his ankle, felt him stiffen.

"Wait!" said Will. "They're bringing out the canvas!"

"No," said Jim. "Oh, no . . ."

For somehow instead, they both knew, the wires high-flung on the poles were catching swift clouds, ripping them free from the wind in streamers which, stitched and sewn by some great monster shadow, made canvas and more canvas as the tent took shape. At last there was the clearwater sound of vast flags blowing.

The motion stopped. The darkness within darkness was still.

Will lay, eyes shut, hearing the beat of great oil-black wings as if a huge, ancient bird had drummed down to live, to breathe, to survive in the night meadow.

The clouds blew away.

The balloon was gone.

The men were gone.

The tents rippled like black rain on their poles.

Suddenly it seemed a long way to town.

Instinctively, Will glanced behind himself.

Nothing but grass and whispers.

Slowly he looked back at the silent, dark, seemingly empty tents.

"I don't like it," he said.

Jim could not tear his eyes away.

"Yeah," he whispered. "Yeah."

Will stood up. Jim lay on the earth.

"Jim!" said Will.

Jim jerked his head as if slapped. He was on his knees, he swayed up. His body turned, but his eyes were fastened to those black flags, the great side-show signs swarming with unguessed wings, horns, and demon smiles.

A bird screamed.

Jim jumped. Jim gasped.

Cloud shadows panicked them over the hills to the edge of town.

From there, the two boys ran alone.

Chapter Thirteen

THE AIR was cold blowing in through the wide-open library window.

Charles Halloway had stood there for a long time.

Now, he quickened.

Along the street below fled two shadows, two boys above them matching shadow stride for stride. They softly printed the night air with treads.

"Jim!" cried the old man. "Will!"

But not aloud.

The boys went away toward home.

Charles Halloway looked out into the country.

Wandering alone in the library, letting his broom tell him things no one else could hear, he had heard the whistle and the disjointed calliope hymns.

"Three," he now said, half-aloud. "Three in the morning . . ."

In the meadow, the tents, the carnival waited. Waited for someone, anyone to wade along the grassy surf. The great tents filled like bellows. They softly issued forth exhalations of air that smelled like ancient yellow beasts.

But only the moon looked in at the hollow dark, the deep caverns. Outside, night beasts hung in midgallop on a carousel. Beyond lay fathoms of Mirror Maze which housed a multifold series of empty vanities one wave on another, still, serene, silvered with age, white with time. Any shadow, at the entrance, might stir reverberations the color of fright, unravel deep-buried moons.

If a man stood here would he see himself unfolded away a billion times to eternity? Would a billion images look back, each face and the face after and the face after that old, older, oldest? Would he find himself lost in a fine dust away off deep down there, not fifty but sixty, not sixty but seventy, not seventy but eighty, ninety, ninety-nine years old?

The maze did not ask.

The maze did not tell.

It simply stood and waited like a great arctic floe.

"Three o'clock . . ."

Charles Halloway was cold. His skin was suddenly a lizard's skin. His stomach filled with blood turned to rust. His mouth tasted of night damps.

Yet he could not turn from the library window.

Far off, something glittered in the meadow.

It was moonlight, flashing on a great glass.

Perhaps the light said something, perhaps it spoke in code.

I'll *go* there, thought Charles Halloway, I *won't* go there.

I *like* it, he thought, I *don't* like it.

A moment later the library door slammed.

Going home, he passed the empty store window.

Inside stood two abandoned sawhorses.

Between lay a pool of water. In the water floated a few shards of ice. In the ice were a few long strands of hair.

Charles Halloway saw but chose not to see. He turned and was gone. The street was soon as empty as the hardware-store window.

Far away, in the meadow, shadows flickered in the Mirror Maze, as if parts of someone's life, yet unborn, were trapped there, waiting to be lived.

So the maze waited, its cold gaze ready, for so much as a bird to come look, see, and fly away shrieking.

But no bird came.

Chapter Fourteen

"THREE," A voice said.

Will listened, cold but warming, glad to be in with a roof above, floor below, wall and door between too much exposure, too much freedom, too much night.

"Three . . ."

Dad's voice, home now, moving down the hall, speaking to itself.

"Three . . ."

Why, thought Will, that's when the train came. Had Dad seen, heard, followed?

No, he *mustn't*! Will hunched himself. Why not? He trembled. What did he fear?

The carnival rushing in like a black stampede of storm waves on the shore out beyond? Of him and Jim and Dad knowing, of the town asleep, not knowing, was *that* it?

Yes. Will buried himself, deep. Yes . . .

"Three . . ."

Three in the morning, thought Charles Halloway, seated on the edge of his bed. Why did the train come at that hour?

For, he thought, it's a special hour. Women never wake then, do they? They sleep the sleep of babes and children. But men in middle age? They know that hour well. Oh God, midnight's not bad, you wake and go back to sleep, one or two's not bad, you toss but sleep again. Five or six in the morning, there's hope, for dawn's just under the horizon. But three, now, Christ, three A.M.! Doctors say the body's at low tide then. The soul is out. The blood moves slow. You're the nearest to dead you'll ever be save dying. Sleep is a patch of death, but three in the morn, full wide-eyed staring, is living death! You dream with your eyes open. God, if you had strength to rouse up, you'd slaughter your half-dreams with buckshot! But no, you lie pinned to a deep well-bottom that's burned dry. The moon rolls by to look at you down there, with its idiot face. It's a long way back to sunset, a far way on to dawn, so you summon all the fool things of your life, the stupid lovely things done with people known so very well who are now so very dead— And wasn't it true, had he read it somewhere, more people in hospitals die at 3 A.M. than at any other time . . . ?

Stop! he cried silently.

"Charlie?" his wife said in her sleep.

Slowly, he took off the other shoe.

His wife smiled in her sleep.

Why?

She's immortal. She has a son.

Your son, too!

But what father ever really believes it? He carries no burden, he feels no pain. What man, like woman, lies down in darkness and gets up with child? The gentle, smiling ones own the good secret. Oh, what strange wonderful clocks women are. They nest in Time. They make the flesh that holds fast and binds eternity. They live inside the gift, know power, accept, and need not mention it. Why speak of Time when you *are* Time, and shape the universal moments, as they pass, into warmth and action? How men envy and often hate these warm clocks, these wives, who know they will live forever. So what do we do? We men turn terribly mean, because we can't hold to the world or ourselves or anything. We are blind to continuity, all breaks down, falls, melts, stops, rots, or runs away. So, since we cannot shape Time, where does that leave men? Sleepless. Staring.

Three A.M. That's our reward. Three in the morn. The soul's midnight. The tide goes out, the soul ebbs. And a train arrives at an hour of despair. . . . *Why?*

"Charlie . . . ?"

His wife's hand moved to his.

"You . . . *all right* . . . Charlie?"

She drowsed.

He did not answer.

He could not tell her how he was.

Chapter Fifteen

THE SUN rose yellow as a lemon.

The sky was round and blue.

The birds looped clear water songs in the air.

Will and Jim leaned from their windows.

Nothing had changed.

Except the look in Jim's eyes.

"Last night . . ." said Will. "Did or didn't it happen?"

They both gazed toward the far meadows.

The air was sweet as syrup. They could find no shadows, anywhere, even under trees.

"Six minutes!" cried Jim.

"Five!"

Four minutes later, corn flakes lurching in their stomachs, they frisked the leaves to a fine red dust going out of town.

With a wild flutter of breath, they raised their eyes from the earth they had been treading.

And the carnival was there.

"Hey . . ."

For the tents were lemon like the sun, brass like wheat fields a few weeks ago. Flags and banners bright as bluebirds snapped above lion-colored canvas. From booths painted cotton-candy colors, fine Saturday smells of bacon and eggs, hot dogs and pancakes swam the wind. Everywhere ran boys. Everywhere, sleepy fathers followed.

"It's just a plain old carnival," said Will.

"Like heck," said Jim. "We weren't blind last night. Come on!"

They marched one hundred yards straight on and deep into the midway. And the deeper they went, the more obvious it became they would find no night men cat-treading balloon shadow while strange tents plumed like thunder clouds. Instead, close up, the carnival was mildewed rope, moth-eaten canvas, rain-worn, sun-bleached tinsel. The side show paintings, hung like sad albatrosses on their poles, flapped and let fall flakes of ancient paint, shivering and at the same time revealing the unwondrous wonders of a thin man, fat man, needle-head, tattooed man, hula dancer. . . .

They prowled on but found no mysterious midnight spheres of evil gas tied by mysterious Oriental knots to daggers plunged in dark earth, no maniac ticket takers bent on terrible revenges. The calliope by the ticket booth neither screamed deaths nor hummed idiot songs to itself. The train? Pulled off on a spur in the warming grass, it was old, yes, and welded tight with rust, but it looked like a titanic magnet that had collected to itself, from locomotive boneyards across three continents, drive shafts, flywheels, smoke stacks, and hand-me-down second-rate nightmares. It did not cut a black and mortuary silhouette. It asked permission but to lie dead in autumn strewings, so much tired steam and iron gunpowder blowing away.

"Jim! Will!"

Here came Miss Foley, their seventh-grade schoolteacher, along the midway, all smiles.

"Boys," she said, "what's wrong? You look as if you lost something."

"Well," said Will, "last night, did you hear that calliope—"

"Calliope? No—"

"Then why're you out here so early, Miss Foley?" asked Jim.

"I love carnivals," said Miss Foley, a little woman lost somewhere in her gray fifties, beaming around. "I'll buy hot dogs and you eat while I look for my fool nephew. You *seen* him?"

"Nephew?"

"Robert. Staying with me a few weeks. Father's dead, mother's sick in Wisconsin. I took him in. He ran out here early today. Said he'd meet me. But you know boys! My, you look glum." She shoved food at them. "Eat! Cheer up! Rides'll open in ten minutes. Meantime, I think I'll spy through that Mirror Maze and—"

"No," said Will.

"No what?" asked Miss Foley.

"No Mirror Maze." Will swallowed. He stared at fathoms of reflections. You could never strike bottom there. It was like winter standing tall, waiting to kill you with a glance. "Miss Foley," he said at last, and wondered to hear his mouth say it, "don't go in there."

"Why not?"

Jim peered, fascinated, into Will's face. "Yeah, tell us. Why not?"

"People get lost," said Will, lamely.

"All the more reason. Robert might be wandering, loose, and not find his way out if I don't grab his ear—"

"Never can tell—" Will could not take his eyes off the millions of miles of blind glass—"what might be swimming around in there. . . ."

"Swimming!" Miss Foley laughed. "What a lovely mind you have, Willy. Well, yes, but I'm an old fish. So . . ."

"Miss Foley!"

Miss Foley waved, poised, took a step, and vanished into the mirror ocean. They watched as she settled, wandered, sank deep, deep, and was finally dissolved, gray among silver.

Jim grabbed Will. "What was all *that*?"

"Gosh, Jim, it's the mirrors! They're the only things I don't like, I mean, they're the only things *like* last night."

"Boy, boy, you been out in the sun," snorted Jim. "That maze there is . . ." His voice trailed off. He sniffed the cold air blowing out as from an ice house between the tall reflections.

"Jim? You were saying?"

But Jim said nothing. After a long time he clapped his hand to the back of his neck. "It really *does*!" he cried, in soft amaze.

"What does?"

"Hair! I read it all my life. In scary stories, it stands on end! Mine's doing it—now!"

"Gosh, Jim. So's mine!"

They stood entranced with the delicious cold bumps on their necks and the suddenly stiffened small hairs quilled up over their scalps.

There was a flourish of light and shadow.

Bumping out through the Mirror Maze they saw two, four, a dozen Miss Foleys.

They didn't know which one was real, so they waved to all of them.

But none of the Miss Foleys saw or waved back. Blind, she walked. Blind, she tacked her nails to cold glass.

"Miss Foley!"

Her eyes, flexed wide as from blasts of photographic powder, were skinned white like a statue's. Deep under the glass, she spoke. She murmured. She whimpered. Now she cried. Now she shouted. Now she yelled. She knocked glass with her head, her elbows, tilted drunken as a light-blind moth, raised her hands in claws. "Oh God! Help!" she wailed. "Help, oh God!"

Jim and Will saw their own faces, pale, their own eyes, wide, in the mirrors as they plunged.

"Miss Foley, here!" Jim cracked his brow.

"*This* way!" But Will found only cold glass.

A hand flew from empty space. An old woman's hand, sinking for the last time. It seized anything to save itself. The anything was Will. She pulled him under.

"Will!"

"Jim! Jim!"

And Jim held him and he held her and pulled her free of the silently rushing mirrors coming in coming in from the desolate seas.

They stepped into sunlight.

Miss Foley, one hand to her bruised cheek, bleated, muttered, then laughed quickly, then gasped, and wiped her eyes.

"Thank you, Will, Jim, oh thank you, I'd of drowned! I mean . . . oh, Will you were *right*! My God, did you *see* her, she's lost, drowned in there, poor girl, oh the poor lost sweet . . . save her, oh, we must *save* her!"

"Miss Foley, boy, you're hurting." Will firmly removed her fists from clenching the flesh of his arm. "There's no one in there."

"I saw her! Please! Look! Save her!"

Will jumped to the maze entrance and stopped. The ticket taker gave him an idle glance of contempt. Will backed away to Miss Foley.

"I swear, no one went in ahead or after you, ma'am. It's my fault, I joked about the water, you must've got mixed up, lost, and scared. . . ."

But if she heard, she went on biting the back of her hand, her voice the voice of someone come out of the sea after no air, a long dread time deep, no hope of life and now set free.

"Gone? She's at the bottom! Poor girl. I knew her. 'I *know* you!' I said when I first saw her a minute ago. I waved, she waved. 'Hello!' I ran!—bang! I fell. *She* fell. A dozen, a thousand of her fell. 'Wait!' I said. Oh, she looked so fine, so lovely, so young. But it scared me. 'What're you doing *here*?' I said. 'Why,' I think she said, '*I'm* real. You're *not*!' she laughed, way under water. She ran off in the maze. We *must* find her! before—"

Miss Foley, Will's arm around her, took a last trembling breath and grew strangely quiet.

Jim was staring deep into those cold mirrors, looking for sharks that could not be seen.

"Miss Foley," he said, "what did *she* look like?"

Miss Foley's voice was pale but calm.

"The fact is . . . she looked like myself, many, many years ago.

"I'll go home now," she said.

"Miss Foley, we'll—"

"No. Stay. I'm just fine. Have fun, boys. Enjoy."

And she walked slowly away, alone, down the midway.

Somewhere a vast animal made water. Ammonia made the wind turn ancient as it passed.

"I'm leaving!" said Will.

"Will," said Jim. "We're staying until sundown, boy, dark sundown, and figure it *all*. You chicken?"

"No," murmured Will. "But . . . anybody want to dive back in that maze?"

Jim gazed fiercely deep into the bottomless sea, where now only the pure light glanced back at itself, held up emptiness upon emptiness beyond emptiness before their eyes.

"Nobody." Jim let his heart beat twice. ". . . I guess."

Chapter Sixteen

A BAD thing happened at sunset.

Jim vanished.

Through noon and after noon, they had screamed up half the rides, knocked over dirty milk-bottles, smashed kewpie-doll winning plates, smelling, listening, looking their way through the autumn crowd trampling the leafy sawdust.

And then quite suddenly Jim was gone.

And Will, not asking anyone but himself, absolutely silent certain-sure, walked steadily through the late crowd as the sky was turning plum colored until he came to the maze and paid his dime and stepped up inside and called softly just one time:

". . . Jim . . . ?"

And Jim was there, half in, half out of the cold glass tides like someone abandoned on a seashore when a close friend has gone far out, and there is wonder if he will ever come back. Jim stood as if he had not moved so much as an eyelash in five minutes, staring, his mouth half-open, waiting for the next wave to come in and show him more.

"Jim! Get outa there!"

"Will . . ." Jim sighed faintly. "Let me be."

"Like heck!" With one leap, Will grabbed Jim's belt and hauled. Shuffling backward, Jim did not seem to know he was being dragged from the maze, for he kept protesting in awe at some unseen wonder: "Oh, Will, oh, Willy, Will, oh, Willy . . ."

"Jim, you nut, I'm taking you home!"

"What? What? What?"

They were in the cold air. The sky was darker than plums now, with a few clouds burning late sun-fire above. The sun-fire flamed on Jim's feverish cheeks, his open lips, his wide and terribly rich green shining eyes.

"Jim, what'd you see in there? The same as Miss Foley?"

"What, what?"

"I'm gonna bust your nose! Come on!" He hustled, pulled, shoved, half carried this fever, this elation, this unstruggling friend.

"Can't tell you, Will, wouldn't believe, can't tell you, in there, oh, in there, in there . . ."

"Shut up!" Will socked his arm. "Scare heck outa me, just like *she* scared us. Bugs! It's almost suppertime. Folks'll think we're dead and buried!"

They were striding now, slashing the autumn grass with their shoes, beyond the tents in the hay-smelling, leaf-mold fields, Will glaring at town, Jim staring back at the high now-darkening banners as the last of the sun hid under the earth.

"Will, we got to come back. Tonight—"

"Okay, come back alone."

Jim stopped.

"You wouldn't let me come alone. You're always going to be around, aren't you, Will? To protect me?"

"Look who needs protection." Will laughed and then did not laugh again, for Jim was looking at him, the last wild light dying in his mouth and caught in the thin hollows of his nostrils and in his suddenly deep-set eyes.

"You'll always be with me, huh, Will?"

Jim simply breathed warm upon him and his blood stirred with the old, the familiar answers: yes, yes, you know it, yes, yes.

And turning together, they stumbled over a clanking dark mound of leather bag.

Chapter Seventeen

THEY STOOD for a long moment over the huge leather bag. Almost secretively, Will kicked it. It made a sound of iron indigestion.

"Why," said Will, "that belongs to the lightning-rod salesman!"

Jim slipped his hand through the leather mouth and hefted forth a metal shaft clustered with chimeras, Chinese dragons all fang, eyeball and moss-green armor, all cross and crescent; every symbol around the world that made men safe, or seemed to, clung here, greaving the boys' hands with odd weight and meaning.

"Storm never came. But he *went*."

"*Where?* And why did he leave his bag?"

They both looked to the carnival where dusk colored the canvas billows. Shadows ran coolly out to engulf them. People in cars honked home in tired commotions. Boys on skeleton bikes whistled dogs after. Soon night would own the midway, while shadows rode the ferris wheel up to cloud the stars.

"People," said Jim, "don't leave their whole life lying around. This is everything that old man owned. Something important—" Jim breathed soft fire—"made him forget. So he just walked off and left this here."

"What? What's so important you forget *everything*?"

"Why—" Jim examined his friend, curiously, twilight in his face—"no one can tell you. You find out yourself. Mysteries and mysteries. Storm salesman. Storm salesman's bag. If we don't look now, we might never know."

"Jim, in ten minutes—"

"Sure! Midway'll be dark. Everyone home for dinner. Just us alone. But won't it feel great? Just *us*! And here we go, back in!"

Passing the Mirror Maze, they saw two armies—a billion Jims, a billion Wills—collide, melt, vanish. And like those armies, so vanished the real army of people.

The boys stood alone among the encampments of dusk thinking of all the boys in town sitting down to warm food in bright rooms.

Chapter Eighteen

THE RED-lettered sign said: OUT OF ORDER! KEEP OFF!

"Sign's been up all day. I don't believe signs," said Jim.

They peered in at the merry-go-round which lay under a dry rattle and roar of wind-tumbled oak trees. Its horses, goats, antelopes, zebras, speared through their spines with brass javelins, hung contorted as in a death rictus, asking mercy with their fright-colored eyes, seeking revenge with their panic-colored teeth.

"Don't look broke to me."

Jim ambled across the clanking chain, leaped to a turntable surface vast as the moon, among the frantic but forever spelled beasts.

"Jim!"

"Will, this is the only ride we haven't *looked* at. So . . ."

Jim swayed. The lunatic carousel world stirred atilt with his lean bulk. He strolled through brass forests amidst animal rousts. He swung astride a plum-dusk stallion.

"Ho, boy, *git*!"

A man rose from machinery darkness.

"Jim!"

Reaching out from the shadows among the calliope tubes and moon-skinned drums the man hoisted Jim yelling out on the air.

"Help, Will, help!"

Will leaped through the animals.

The man smiled easily, welcomed him handily, swung him high beside Jim. They stared down at bright flame-red hair, bright flame-blue eyes, and rippling biceps.

"Out of order," said the man. "Can't you read?"

"Put them down," said a gentle voice.

Hung high, Jim and Will glanced over at a second man standing tall beyond the chains.

"Down," he said again.

And they were carried through the brass forest of wild but uncomplaining brutes and set in the dust.

"We were—" said Will.

"Curious?" This second man was tall as a lamp post. His pale face, lunar pockmarks denting it, cast light on those who stood below. His vest was the color of fresh blood. His eyebrows, his hair, his suit were licorice black, and the sun-yellow gem which stared from the tie pin thrust in his cravat was the same unblinking shade and bright crystal as his eyes. But in this instant, swiftly, and with utter clearness, it was the suit which fascinated Will. For it seemed woven of boar-bramble, clock-spring hair, bristle, and a sort of ever-trembling, ever-glistening dark hemp. The suit caught light and stirred like a bed of black tweed-thorns, interminably itching, covering the man's long body with motion so it seemed he should excruciate, cry out, and tear the clothes free. Yet here he stood, moon-calm, inhabiting his itch-weed suit and watching Jim's mouth with his yellow eyes. He never looked once at Will.

"The name is Dark."

He flourished a white calling card. It turned blue.

Whisper. Red.

Whisk. A green man dangled from a tree stamped on the card.

Flit. Shh.

"Dark. And my friend with the red hair there is Mr. Cooger. Of Cooger and Dark's . . ."

Flip-flick-shhh.

Names appeared, disappeared on the white square:

". . . Combined Shadow Shows . . ."

Tick-wash.

A mushroom-witch stirred moldering herb pots.

". . . and cross-continental Pandemonium Theater Company . . ."

He handed the card to Jim. It now read:

> *Our specialty: to examine, oil,*
> *polish, and repair Death-Watch*
> *Beetles.*

Calmly, Jim read it. Calmly, Jim put a fist into his copious and richly treasured pockets, rummaged, and held out his hand.

On his palm lay a dead brown insect.

"Here," Jim said. "Fix *this*."

Mr. Dark exploded his laugh. "Superb! I will!" He extended his hand. His shirt sleeve pulled up.

Bright purple, black, green and lightning-blue eels, worms, and Latin scrolls slid to view on his wrist.

"Boy!" cried Will. "You must be the Tattooed Man!"

"No." Jim studied the stranger. "The Illustrated Man. There's a difference."

Mr. Dark nodded, pleased. "What's your name, boy?"

Don't tell him! thought Will, and stopped. Why not? he wondered, why?

Jim's lips hardly twitched.

"Simon," he said.

He smiled to show it was a lie.

Mr. Dark smiled to show he knew it.

"Want to see more, 'Simon'?"

Jim would not give him the satisfaction of a nod.

Slowly, with great mouth-working pleasure, Mr. Dark pushed his sleeve high to his elbow.

Jim stared. The arm was like a cobra weaving, bobbing, swaying to strike. Mr. Dark clenched his fist, wriggled his fingers. The muscles danced.

Will wanted to run around and see, but could only watch, thinking Jim, oh, Jim!

For there stood Jim and there was this tall man, each examining the other as if he were a reflection in a shop window late at night. The tall man's brambled suit, shadowed out now to color Jim's cheeks and storm over his wide and drinking eyes with a look of rain instead of the sharp cat-green they always were. Jim stood like a runner who has come a long way, fever in his mouth, hands open to receive any gift. And right now it was a gift of pictures twitched in pantomime, as Mr. Dark made his illustrations jerk cold-skinned over his warm-pulsed wrist as the stars came out above and Jim stared and Will could not see and a long way off the last of the town people went away toward town in their warm cars, and Jim said, faintly, "Gosh . . ." and Mr. Dark rolled down his sleeve.

"Show's over. Suppertime. Carnival's shut up until seven. Everyone out. Come back, 'Simon,' and ride the merry-go-round, when it's fixed. Take this card. Free ride."

Jim stared at the hidden wrist and put the card in his pocket.

"So long!"

Jim ran. Will ran.

Jim whirled, glanced back, leaped, and for the second time in the hour, vanished.

Will looked up into the tree where Jim squirmed on a limb, hidden. He looked back. Mr. Dark and Mr. Cooger were turned away, busy with the merry-go-round.

"Quick, Will!"

"Jim . . . ?"

"They'll *see* you. Jump!"

Will jumped. Jim hauled him up. The great tree shook. A wind roared by in the sky. Jim helped him cling, gasping, among the branches.

"Jim, we don't belong here!"

"Shut up! Look!" whispered Jim.

Somewhere in the carousel machinery there were taps and brass knockings, a faint squeal and whistle of calliope steam.

"What was on his arm, Jim?"

"A picture."

"Yeah, but what kind?"

"It was—" Jim shut his eyes. "It was—a picture of a . . . snake . . . that's it . . . snake." But when he opened his eyes, he would not look at Will.

"Okay, if you don't want to tell me."

"I told you, Will, a snake. I'll get him to show it to you, later, you want that?"

No, thought Will, I don't want that.

He looked down at the billion footprints left in the sawdust on the empty midway and suddenly it was a lot closer to midnight than to noon.

"I'm going home. . . ."

"Sure, Will, go on. Mirror mazes, old teacher-ladies, lost lightning-rod bags, lightning-rod salesmen disappear, snake pictures dancing, unbroken merry-go-rounds, and you want to go home!? Sure, old friend Will, so long."

"I . . ." Will started down the tree, and froze.

"All clear?" cried a voice below.

"Clear!" someone shouted at the far end of the midway.

Mr. Dark moved, not fifty feet away, to a red control box

near the merry-go-round ticket booth. He glared in all directions. He glared into the tree.

Will hugged, Jim hugged the limb, tightened into smallness.

"Start up!"

With a pop, a bang, a jangle of reins, a lift and downfall, a rise and descent of brass, the carousel moved.

But, thought Will, it's broke, out of order!

He flicked a glance at Jim, who pointed wildly down.

The merry-go-round was running, yes, but . . .

It was running *backward.*

The small calliope inside the carousel machinery rattle-snapped its nervous-stallion shivering drums, clashed its harvest-moon cymbals, toothed its castanets, and throatily choked and sobbed its reeds, whistles, and baroque flutes.

The music, Will thought, it's backwards, *too*!

Mr. Dark jerked about, glanced up, as if he had heard Will's thought. A wind shook the trees in black tumults. Mr. Dark shrugged and looked away.

The carousel wheeled faster, shrieking, plunging, going roundabout-back!

Now Mr. Cooger, with his flaming red hair and fire-blue eyes, was pacing the midway, making a last check. He stood under their tree. Will could have let spit down on him. Then the calliope gave a particularly violent cry of foul murder which made dogs howl in far counties, and Mr. Cooger, spinning, ran and leaped on the backwhirling universe of animals who, tail first, head last, pursued an endless circling night toward unfound and never to be discovered destinations. Hand-slapping brass poles, he flung himself into a seat where with his bristly red hair, pink face, and incredible sharp blue eyes he sat silent, going back around, back around, the music squealing swift back with him like insucked breath.

The music, thought Will, what is it? And how do I know it's backside first? He hugged the limb, tried to catch the tune, then hum it forward in his head. But the brass bells, the drums, hammered his chest, revved his heart so he felt his pulse reverse, his blood turn back in perverse thrusts through all his flesh, so he was nearly shaken free to fall, so all he did was clutch, hang pale, and drink the sight of the backward-turning machine and Mr. Dark, alert at the controls, on the sidelines.

It was Jim who first noticed the new thing happening, for he kicked Will, once, Will looked over, and Jim nodded frantically at the man in the machine as he came around the next time.

Mr. Cooger's face was melting like pink wax.

His hands were becoming doll's hands.

His bones sank away beneath his clothes; his clothes then shrank down to fit his dwindling frame.

His face flickered going, and each time around he melted more.

Will saw Jim's head shift, circling.

The carousel wheeled, a great back-drifting lunar dream, the horses thrusting, the music in-gasped after, while Mr. Cooger, as simple as shadows, as simple as light, as simple as time, got younger. And younger. And younger.

Each time he wheeled to view he sat alone with his bones, which shaped like warm candles burning away to tender years. He gazed serenely at the fiery constellations, the children-inhabited trees, which went away from him as he removed himself from them and his nose diminished and his sweet wax ears reshaped themselves to small pink roses.

Now no longer forty where he had begun his back-spiraled journey, Mr. Cooger was nineteen.

Around went the reverse parade of horse, pole, music, man become young man, young man fast rendered down to boy. . . .

Mr. Cooger was seventeen, sixteen. . . .

Another and another time around under the sky and trees and Will whispering, Jim counting the times around, around, while the night air warmed to summer heat by friction of sun-metal brass, the passionate backturned flight of beasts, wore the wax doll down and down and washed him clean with still stranger musics until all ceased, all died away to stillness, the calliope shut up its brassworks, the ironmongery machines hissed off, and with a last faint whine like desert sands blown back up Arabian hourglasses, the carousel rocked on seaweed waters and stood still.

The figure seated in the carved white wooden sleigh chair was very small.

Mr. Cooger was twelve years old.

No. Will's mouth shaped the word. No. Jim's did the same.

The small shape stepped down from the silent world, its face in shadow, but its hands, newborn wrinkled pink, held out in raw carnival lamplight.

The strange man-boy shot his gaze up, down, smelling fright somewhere, terror and awe in the vicinity. Will balled himself tight and shut his eyes. He felt the terrible gaze shoot through the leaves like blown needle-darts, pass on. Then, rabbit-running, the small shape lit off down the empty midway.

Jim was first to stir the leaves aside.

Mr. Dark was gone, too, in the evening hush.

It seemed to take Jim forever to fall down to earth. Will fell after and they both stood, clamorous with alarms, shaken by concussions of silent pantomime, blasted by events all the more numbing because they ran off into night and unknown. And it was Jim who spoke from their mutual confusion and trembling as each held to the other's arm, seeing the small shadow rush, luring them across the meadow.

"Oh, Will, I wish we could go home, I wish we could eat. But it's too late, we saw! We got to see more! *Don't* we?"

"Lord," said Will, miserably. "I guess we do."

And they ran together, following they didn't know what on out and away to who could possibly guess where.

Chapter Nineteen

OUT ON the highway the last faint water colors of the sun were gone beyond the hills and whatever they were chasing was so far ahead as to be only a swift fleck now shown in lamplight now set free, running, into dark.

"Twenty-eight!" gasped Jim. "Twenty-eight times!"

"The merry-go-round, sure!" Will jerked his head. "Twenty-eight times I counted, it went around back!"

Up ahead, the small shape stopped and looked back.

Jim and Will ducked in by a tree and let it move on.

"It," thought Will. Why do I think "it"? He's a boy, he's a man . . . no . . . *it* is something that has changed, that's what *it* is.

They reached and passed the city limits, and swiftly jogging, Will said, "Jim, there must've been *two* people on that ride, Mr. Cooger *and* this boy and—"

"No. I never took my eyes off him!"

They ran by the barber shop. Will saw but did not see a sign in the window. He read but did not read. He remembered, he forgot. He plunged on.

"Hey! He's turned on Culpepper Street! Quick!"

They rounded a corner.

"He's gone!"

The street lay long and empty in the lamplight.

Leaves blew on the hopscotch-chalked sidewalks.

"Will, Miss Foley lives on this street."

"Sure, fourth house, but—"

Jim strolled, casually whistling, hands in pockets, Will with him. At Miss Foley's house, they glanced up.

In one of the softly lit front windows, someone stood looking out.

A boy, no more and no less than twelve years old.

"Will!" cried Jim, softly. "That boy—"

"Her nephew . . . ?"

"Nephew, heck! Keep your head away. Maybe he can read lips. Walk slow. To the corner and back. You see his face? The eyes, Will! That's one part of people don't change, young, old, six or sixty! Boy's face, sure, but the eyes were the eyes of Mr. Cooger!"

"No!"

"Yes!"

They both stopped to enjoy the swift pound of each other's heart.

"Keep moving." They moved. Jim held Will's arm tight, leading him. "You did see Mr. Cooger's eyes, huh? When he held us up fit to crack our heads together? You did see the boy, just off the ride? He looked right up near me, hid in the tree, and boy! it was like opening the door of a furnace! I'll never forget those eyes! And there they are now, in the window. Turn around. Now, let's walk back easy and nice and slow. . . . We got to warn Miss Foley what's hiding in her house, don't we?"

"Jim, look, you don't give a darn about Miss Foley or what's in her house!"

Jim said nothing. Walking arm in arm with Will he just looked over at his friend and blinked once, let the lids come down over his shiny green eyes and go up.

And again Will had the feeling about Jim that he had always had about an old almost forgotten dog. Some time every year that dog, good for many months, just ran on out into the world and didn't come back for days and finally did limp back all burred and scrawny and odorous of swamps and dumps; he had rolled in the dirty mangers and foul dropping places of the world, simply to turn home with a funny little smile pinned to his muzzle. Dad had named the dog Plato, the wilderness philosopher, for you saw by his eyes there was nothing he didn't know. Returned, the dog would live in innocence again, tread patterns of grace, for months, then vanish, and the whole thing start over. Now, walking here he thought he heard Jim whimper under his breath. He could feel the bristles stiffen all over Jim. He felt Jim's ears flatten, saw him sniff the new dark. Jim smelled smells that no one knew, heard ticks from clocks that told another time. Even his tongue was strange now, moving along his lower, and now his upper lip as they stopped in front of Miss Foley's house again.

The front window was empty.

"Going to walk up and ring the bell," said Jim.

"What, meet him face to face?!"

"My aunt's eyebrows, Will. We got to check, don't we? Shake his paw, stare him in his good eye or some such, and if it *is* him—"

"We don't warn Miss Foley right in front of him, *do* we?"

"We'll phone her, later, dumb. Up we go!"

Will sighed and let himself be walked up the steps wanting but not wanting to know if the boy in this house had Mr. Cooger hid but showing like a firefly between his eyelashes.

Jim rang the bell.

"What if *he* answers?" Will demanded. "Boy, I'm so scared I could sprinkle dust. Jim, why aren't you scared, why?"

Jim examined both of his untrembled hands. "I'll be darned," he gasped. "You're right! I'm *not*!"

The door swung wide.

Miss Foley beamed out at them.

"Jim! Will! How nice."

"Miss Foley," blurted Will. "You *okay*?"

Jim glared at him. Miss Foley laughed.

"Why shouldn't I be?"

Will flushed. "All those darn carnival mirrors—"

"Nonsense, I've forgotten all about it. Well, boys, are you coming in?"

She held the door wide.

Will shuffled a foot and stopped.

Beyond Miss Foley, a beaded curtain hung like a dark blue thunder shower across the parlor entry.

Where the colored rain touched the floor, a pair of dusty small shoes poked out. Just beyond the downpour the evil boy loitered.

Evil? Will blinked. Why evil? Because. "Because" was reason enough. A boy, yes, and evil.

"Robert?" Miss Foley turned, calling through the dark blue always-falling beads of rain. She took Will's hand and gently pulled him inside. "Come meet two of my students."

The rain poured aside. A fresh candy-pink hand broke through, all by itself, as if testing the weather in the hall.

Good grief, thought Will, he'll look me in the eye! see the merry-go-round and himself on it moving back, back. I *know* it's printed on my eyeball like I been struck by lightning!

"Miss Foley!" said Will.

Now a pink face stuck out through the dim frozen necklaces of storm.

"We got to tell you a terrible thing."

Jim struck Will's elbow, hard, to shut him.

Now the body came out through the dark watery flow of beads. The rain shushed behind the small boy.

Miss Foley leaned toward him, expectant. Jim gripped his elbow, fiercely. He stammered, flushed, then spat it out:

"Mr. Crosetti!"

Quite suddenly, clearly, he saw the sign in the barber's window. The sign seen but not seen as they ran by:

CLOSED ON ACCOUNT OF ILLNESS.

"Mr. Crosetti!" he repeated, and added, swiftly, "He's . . . dead!"

"What . . . the barber?"

"The barber?" echoed Jim.

"See this haircut?" Will turned, trembling, his hand to his head. "He did it. And we just walked by there and the sign was up and people told us—"

"What a shame." Miss Foley was reaching out to fetch the strange boy forward. "I'm so sorry. Boys, this is Robert, my nephew from Wisconsin."

Jim stuck out his hand. Robert the Nephew examined it, curiously. "What are you *looking* at?" he asked.

"You look familiar," said Jim.

Jim! Will yelled to himself.

"Like an uncle of mine," said Jim, all sweet and calm.

The nephew flicked his eyes to Will, who looked only at the floor, afraid the boy would see his eyeballs whirl with the remembered carousel. Crazily, he wanted to hum the backward music.

Now, he thought, face him!

He looked up straight at the boy.

And it was wild and crazy and the floor sank away beneath for there was the pink shiny Halloween mask of a small pretty boy's face, but almost as if holes were cut where the eyes of Mr. Cooger shone out, old, old, eyes as bright as sharp blue stars and the light from those stars taking a million years to get here. And through the little nostrils cut in the shiny wax mask, Mr. Cooger's breath went in steam came out ice. And the Valentine candy tongue moved small behind those trim white candy-kernel teeth.

Mr. Cooger, somewhere behind the eye slits, went *blink-click* with his insect-Kodak pupils. The lenses exploded like suns, then burnt chilly and serene again.

He swiveled his glance to Jim. *Blink-click.* He had Jim flexed, focussed, shot, developed, dried, filed away in dark. *Blink-click.*

Yet this was only a boy standing in a hall with two other boys and a woman. . . .

And all the while Jim gazed steadily back, feathers unruffled, taking his own pictures of Robert.

"Have you boys had supper?" asked Miss Foley. "We're just sitting down—"

"We got to go!"

Everyone looked at Will as if amazed he didn't want to stick here forever.

"Jim—" he stammered. "Your mom's home alone—"

"Oh, sure," Jim said, reluctantly.

"I know what." The nephew paused for their attention. When their faces turned, Mr. Cooger inside the nephew went silently *blink-click*, *blink-click*, listening through the toy ears, watching through the toy-charm eyes, whetting the doll's mouth with a Pekingese tongue. "Join us later for dessert, huh?"

"Dessert?"

"I'm taking Aunt Willa to the carnival." The boy stroked Miss Foley's arm until she laughed nervously.

"Carnival?" cried Will, and lowered his voice. "Miss Foley, you said—"

"I said I was foolish and scared myself," said Miss Foley. "It's Saturday night, the best night for tent shows and showing my nephew the sights."

"Join us?" asked Robert, holding Miss Foley's hand. "Later?"

"Great!" said Jim.

"Jim," said Will. "We been out all day. Your mom's sick."

"I forgot." Jim flashed him a look filled with purest snake poison.

Flick. The nephew made an X-ray of both, showing them,

no doubt, as cold bones trembling in warm flesh. He stuck out his hand.

"Tomorrow, then. Meet you by the side shows."

"Swell!" Jim grabbed the small hand.

"So long!" Will jumped out the door, then turned with a last agonized appeal to the teacher.

"Miss Foley . . . ?"

"Yes, Will?"

Don't go with that boy, he thought. Don't go near the shows. Stay home, oh, please! But then he said:

"Mr. Crosetti's dead."

She nodded, touched, waiting for his tears. And while she waited, he dragged Jim outside and the door swung shut on Miss Foley and the pink small face with the lenses in it going *blink-click*, snapshotting two incoherent boys, and them fumbling down the steps in October dark, while the merry-go-round started again in Will's head, rushing while the leaves in the trees above cracked and fried with wind. Aside, Will spluttered, "Jim, you shook hands with him! Mr. Cooger! You're not going to *meet* him!?"

"It's Mr. Cooger, all right. Boy, those eyes. If I met him tonight, we'd solve the whole shooting match. What's eating you, Will?"

"Eating *me*!" At the bottom of the steps now, they tussled in fierce and frantic whispers, glancing up at the empty windows where, now and again, a shadow passed. Will stopped. The music turned in his head. Stunned, he squinched his eyes. "Jim, the music that the calliope played when Mr. Cooger got younger—"

"Yeah?"

"It was the 'Funeral March'! Played *backwards*!"

"*Which* 'Funeral March'?"

"Which! Jim, Chopin only wrote one tune! *The* 'Funeral March'!"

"But why played backward?"

"Mr. Cooger was marching *away* from the grave, not toward it, wasn't he, getting younger, smaller, instead of older and dropping dead?"

"Willy, you're terrific!"

"Sure, but—" Will stiffened. "He's there. The window,

again. Wave at him. So long! Now, walk and whistle something. *Not* Chopin, for gosh sakes—"

Jim waved. Will waved. Both whistled, "Oh, Susanna."

The shadow gestured small in the high window.

The boys hurried off down the street.

Chapter Twenty

TWO SUPPERS were waiting in two houses.

One parent yelled at Jim, two parents yelled at Will.

Both were sent hungry upstairs.

It started at seven o'clock. It was done by seven-three.

Doors slammed. Locks clacked.

Clocks ticked.

Will stood by the door. The telephone was locked away outside. And even if he called, Miss Foley wouldn't answer. By now she'd be gone beyond town . . . good grief! Anyway, what could he say? Miss Foley, that nephew's no nephew? That boy's no boy? Wouldn't she laugh? She would. For the nephew was a nephew, the boy was a boy, or seemed such.

He turned to the window. Jim, across the way, stood facing the same dilemma, in his room. Both struggled. It was too early to raise the windows and stage-whisper to each other. Parents below were busy growing crystal-radio peach fuzz in their ears, alert.

The boys threw themselves on their separate beds in their separate houses, probed mattresses for chocolate chunks put away against the lean years, and ate moodily.

Clocks ticked.

Nine. Nine-thirty. Ten.

The knob rattled, softly, as Dad unlocked the door.

Dad! thought Will. Come in! We got to talk!

But Dad chewed his breath in the hall. Only his confusion, his always puzzled, half-bewildered face could be felt beyond the door.

He won't come in, thought Will. Walk around, talk around, back off from a thing, yes. But come sit, listen? When had he, when *would* he, ever?

"Will . . . ?"

Will quickened.

"Will . . ." said Dad, ". . . be careful."

"Careful?" cried mother, coming along the hall. "Is *that* all you're going to say?"

"What else?" Dad was going downstairs now. "He jumps,

I creep. How can you get two people together like that? He's too young, I'm too old. God, sometimes I wish we'd never . . ."

The door shut. Dad was walking away on the sidewalk.

Will wanted to fling up the window and call. Suddenly, Dad was so lost in the night. Not me, don't worry about me, Dad, he thought, you, Dad, stay in! It's not safe! Don't go!

But he didn't shout. And when he softly raised the window at last, the street was empty, and he knew it would be just a matter of time before that light went on in the library across town. When rivers flooded, when fire fell from the sky, what a fine place the library was, the many rooms, the books. With luck, no one found you. How could they!—when you were off to Tanganyika in '98, Cairo in 1812, Florence in 1492!?

". . . careful . . ."

What did Dad mean? Did he smell the panic, had he heard the music, had he prowled near the tents? No. Not Dad ever.

Will tossed a marble over at Jim's window.

Tap. Silence.

He imagined Jim seated alone in the dark, his breath like phosphorus on the air, ticking away to himself.

Tap. Silence.

This wasn't like Jim. Always before, the window slid up, Jim's head popped out, ripe with yells, secret hissings, giggles, riots and rebel charges.

"Jim, I know you're there!"

Tap.

Silence.

Dad's out in the town. Miss Foley's with you-know-who! he thought. Good gosh, Jim, we got to do something! Tonight!

He threw a last small marble.

. . . *tap* . . .

It fell to the hushed grass below.

Jim did not come to the window.

Tonight, thought Will. He bit his knuckles. He lay back cold straight stiff on his bed.

Chapter Twenty-One

IN THE alley behind the house was a huge old-fashioned pine-plank boardwalk. It had been there ever since Will remembered, since civilization unthinkingly poured forth the dull hard unresisting cement sidewalks. His grandfather, a man of strong sentiment and wild impulse, who let nothing go without a roar, had flexed his muscles in favor of this vanishing landmark, and with a dozen handymen had toted a good forty feet of the walk into the alley where it had lain like the skeleton of some indefinable monster through the years, baked by sun, lushly rotted by rains.

The town clock struck ten.

Lying abed, Will realized he had been thinking about Grandfather's vast gift from another time. He was waiting to hear the boardwalk speak. In what language? Well . . .

Boys have never been known to go straight up to houses to ring bells to summon forth friends. They prefer to chunk dirt at clapboards, hurl acorns down roof shingles, or leave mysterious notes flapping from kites stranded on attic window sills.

So it was with Jim and Will.

Late nights, if there were gravestones to be leapfrogged or dead cats to be hurled down sour people's chimneys, one or the other of the boys would prowl out under the moon and xylophone-dance on that old hollow-echoing musical boardwalk.

Over the years, they had *tuned* the walk, prying up an *A* board and nailing it here, lifting up an *F* board and pounding it back down there until the walk was as near onto being melodious as weather and two entrepreneurs could fashion it.

By the tune treaded out, you could tell the night's venture. If Will heard Jim tromping hard on seven or eight notes of "Way Down Upon the Swanee River," he scrambled out knowing it was moon-trail time on the creek leading to the river caves. If Jim heard Will out leaping about like a scalded airedale on the timbers and the tune remotely suggested "Marching Through Georgia," it meant plums, peaches, or apples were ripe enough to get sick on out beyond town.

So this night Will held his breath waiting for some tune to call him forth.

What kind of tune would Jim play to represent the carnival, Miss Foley, Mr. Cooger, and/or the evil nephew?

Ten-fifteen. Ten-thirty.

No music.

Will did not like Jim sitting in his room thinking *what*? Of the Mirror Maze? What *had* he seen there? And, seeing, what did he plan?

Will stirred, restively.

Especially he did not like to think of Jim with no father between him and the tent shows and all that lay dark in the meadows. And a mother who wanted him around so very much, he just *had* to get away, get out, breathe free night air, know free night waters running toward bigger freer seas.

Jim! he thought. Let's have the music!

And at ten-thirty-five, it came.

He heard, or thought he heard, Jim out in the starlight leaping way up and coming flat down like a spring tomcat on the vast xylophone. And the tune! Was or wasn't it like the funeral dirge played backwards by the old carousel calliope?!!

Will started to raise his window to be sure. But suddenly, Jim's window slid quietly up.

He hadn't been down on the boards! It was just Will's wild wish that made the tune! Will started to whisper, but stopped.

For Jim, without a word, scuttled down the drainpipe.

Jim! Will thought.

Jim, on the lawn, stiffened as if hearing his name.

You're not going without me, Jim?

Jim glanced swiftly up.

If he saw Will, he made no sign.

Jim, Will thought, we're still pals, smell things nobody else smells, hear things no one else hears, got the same blood, run the same way. Now, this first time ever, you're sneaking out! Ditching me!

But the driveway was empty.

A salamander flicking the hedge, there went Jim.

Will was out the window, down the trellis, and over the hedge, before he thought: *I'm* alone. If I lose Jim, it's the first ever I'll be out alone at night, too. And where am I going? Wherever Jim goes.

Lord, let me keep up!

Jim skimmed like a dark owl after a mouse. Will loped like a weaponless hunter after the owl. They sailed their shadows over October lawns.

And when they stopped . . .

There was Miss Foley's house.

Chapter Twenty-Two

JIM GLANCED back.

Will became a bush behind a bush, a shadow among shadows, with two starlight rounds of glass, his eyes, holding the image of Jim calling up in a whisper toward the second-floor windows.

"Hey there . . . hey . . ."

Good grief, thought Will, he wants to be slit and stuffed with broken Mirror Maze glass.

"Hey!" called Jim, softly. "You . . . !"

A shadow uprose on a dim-lit shade, above. A small shadow. The nephew had brought Miss Foley home, they were in their separate rooms or— Oh Lord, thought Will, I *hope* she's safe home. Maybe, like the lightning-rod salesman, she—

"Hey . . . !"

Jim gazed up with that funny warm look of breathless anticipation he often had nights in summer at the shadow-show window Theater in that house a few streets over. Looking up with love, with devotion, like a cat Jim waited for some special dark mouse to run forth. Crouched, now slowly he seemed to grow taller, as if his bones were pulled by the thing in the window above, which now suddenly vanished.

Will ground his teeth.

He felt the shadow sift down through the house like a cold breath. He could wait no longer. He leaped forth.

"Jim!"

He seized Jim's arm.

"Will, what *you* doing here?!"

"Jim, don't talk to *him*! Get out of here. My gosh, he'll chew and spit out your bones!"

Jim writhed himself free.

"Will, go home! You'll spoil everything!"

"He scares me, Jim, what you *want* from him!? This afternoon . . . in the maze, did you *see* something!!?"

". . . Yes . . ."

"For gosh sakes, *what*!"

Will grabbed Jim's shirt front, felt his heart bang under the chest bones. "Jim—"

"Let go." Jim was terribly quiet. "If he knows you're here, he won't come out. Willy, if you don't let go, I'll remember when—"

"When *what*!"

"When I'm older, darn it, *older*!"

Jim spat.

As if he was struck by lightning, Will jumped back.

He looked at his empty hands and put one up to wipe the spittle off his cheek.

"Oh, Jim," he mourned.

And he heard the merry-go-round motioning, gliding on black night waters around, around, and Jim on a black stallion riding off and about, circling in tree-shadow and he wanted to cry out, Look! the merry-go-round! you want it to go forward, don't you, Jim? forward instead of back! and you on it, around once and you're fifteen, circling and you're sixteen, three times more and nineteen! music! and you're twenty and off, standing tall! not Jim any more, still thirteen, almost fourteen on the empty midway, with me small, me young, me scared!

Will hauled off and hit Jim, hard, on the nose.

Then he jumped Jim, wrapped him tight, and toppled him rolling down, yelling, in the bushes. He slapped Jim's mouth, stuffed it, mashed it full of fingers to snap and bite at, suffocating the angry grunts and yells.

The front door opened.

Will crushed the air out of Jim, lay heavy on him, fisting his mouth tight.

Something stood on the porch. A tiny shadow scanned the town, searching for but not finding Jim.

But it was just the boy Robert, the friendly nephew, come almost casually forth, hands in pockets, whistling under his breath, to breathe the night air as boys do, curious for adventures that they themselves must make, that rarely happen by. Threshed tight, mortally locked and bound to Jim, staring up, Will was all the more shaken to see the normal boy, the airy glance, the unassuming poise, the small, the easy self in which no man at all was revealed by street light.

At any moment, Robert, in full cry, might leap to play with them, tangle legs, lock arms, bark-snap like pups in May, the whole thing end with them strewn in laughing tears on the lawn, the terror spent, the fear melted off in dew, a dream of nothings quickly gone as such dreams go when the eye snaps wide. For there indeed stood the nephew, his face round fresh, and cream-smooth as a peach.

And he was smiling down at the two boys he now saw locked limb in limb on the grass.

Then, swiftly, he darted in. He must have run upstairs, scrabbled about, and hurtled down again, for suddenly as the two boys outthrashed, outgripped, outraged each other, there was a rain of tinkling, rattling glitter on the lawn.

The nephew leaped the porch rail and landed panther-soft, imbedded in his shadow, on the grass. His hands were delicious with stars. These he liberally sprinkled. They thudded, slithered, winked at Jim's side. Both boys lay stricken by the rain of gold and diamond fire that pelted them.

"Help, police!" cried Robert.

Will was so shocked he let go Jim.

Jim was so shocked he let go Will.

Both reached at the same time for the cold strewn ice.

"Good grief, a bracelet!"

"A ring! A necklace!"

Robert kicked. Two trash cans at the curb fell thundering.

A bedroom light, above, flicked on.

"Police!" Robert threw one last spray of glitter at their feet, shut up his fresh-peach smile like locking an explosion away in a box, and shot away down the street.

"Wait!" Jim jumped. "We won't hurt you!"

Will tripped him, Jim fell.

The window upstairs opened. Miss Foley leaned out. Jim, on his knees, held a woman's wrist watch. Will blinked at a necklace in his hands.

"Who's there!" she cried. "Jim? Will? What's *that* you got?!"

But Jim was running. Will stopped only long enough to see the window empty itself with a wail as Miss Foley pulled in to see her room. When he heard her full scream, he knew she had discovered the burglary.

Running, Will knew he was doing just what the nephew

wanted. He should turn back, pick up the jewels, tell Miss Foley what happened. But he must save Jim!

Far back, he heard Miss Foley's new cries turn on more lights! Will Halloway! Jim Nightshade! Night runners! Thieves! That's us, thought Will, oh my Lord! That's us! No one'll believe *anything* we say from now on! Not about carnivals, not about carousels, not about mirrors or evil nephews, not about nothing!

And so they ran, three animals in starlight. A black otter. A tomcat. A rabbit.

Me, thought Will, I'm the rabbit.

And he was white, and much afraid.

Chapter Twenty-Three

THEY HIT the carnival grounds at a good twenty miles an hour, give or take a mile, the nephew in the lead, Jim close behind, and Will further back, gasping, shotgun blasts of fatigue in his feet, his head, his heart.

The nephew, running scared, looked back, not smiling.

Fooled him, thought Will, he figured I wouldn't follow, figured I'll call the police, get stuck, not be believed, or run hide. Now he's scared I'll beat the tar out of him, and wants to jump on that ride and run around getting older and bigger than me. Oh, Jim, Jim, we got to stop him, keep him young, tear his skin off!

But he knew from Jim's running there'd be no help from Jim. Jim wasn't running after nephews. He was running toward free rides.

The nephew vanished around a tent far ahead. Jim followed. By the time Will reached the midway, the merry-go-round was popping to life. In the pulse, the din, the squeal-around of music the small fresh-faced nephew rode the great platform in a swirl of midnight dust.

Jim, ten feet back, watched the horses leap, his eyes striking fire from the high-jumped stallion's eyes.

The merry-go-round was going *forward*!

Jim *leaned* at it.

"Jim!" cried Will.

The nephew swept from sight borne around by the machine. Drifted back again he stretched out pink fingers urging softly: ". . . Jim . . . ?"

Jim twitched one foot forward.

"No!" Will plunged.

He knocked, seized, held Jim; they toppled; they fell in a heap.

The nephew, surprised, whisked on in darkness, one year older. One year older, thought Will, on the earth, one year taller, bigger, meaner!

"Oh God, Jim, quick!" He jumped up, ran to the control box, the complex mysteries of brass switch and porcelain covering and sizzling wires. He struck the switch. But Jim, behind, babbling, tore at Will's hands.

"Will, you'll spoil it! No!"

Jim knocked the switch full back.

Will spun and slapped his face. Each clenched the other's elbows, rocked, flailed. They fell against the control box.

Will saw the evil boy, a year older still, glide around into night. Five or six more times around and he'd be bigger than the two of them!

"Jim, he'll kill us!"

"Not me, no!"

Will felt a sting of electricity. He yelled, pulled back, hit the switch handle. The control box spat. Lightning jumped to the sky. Jim and Will, flung by the blast, lay watching the merry-go-round run wild.

The evil boy whistled by, clenched to a brass tree. He cursed. He spat. He wrestled with wind, with centrifuge. He was trying to clutch his way through the horses, the poles, to the outer rim of the carousel. His face came, went, came, went. He clawed. He brayed. The control box erupted blue showers. The carousel jumped and bucked. The nephew slipped. He fell. A black stallion's steel hoof kicked him. Blood printed his brow.

Jim hissed, rolled, thrashed, Will riding him hard, pressing him to grass, trading yell for yell, both fright-pale, heart ramming heart. Electric bolts from the switch flushed up in white stars a gush of fireworks. The carousel spun thirty, spun forty—"Will, let me up!"—spun fifty times. The calliope howled, boiled steam, ran ancient dry, then played nothing, its keys gibbering as only chitterings boiled up through the vents. Lightning unraveled itself over the sweated outflung boys, delivered flame to the silent horse stampede to light their way around, around with the figure lying on the platform no longer a boy but a man no longer a man but more than a man and even more and even more, much more than that, around, around.

"He's, he's, oh he's, oh look, Will, he's—" gasped Jim, and began to sob, because it was the only thing to do, locked down, nailed tight. "Oh God, Will, get up! We *got* to make it run backward!"

Lights flashed on in the tents.

But no one came out.

Why not? Will thought crazily. The explosions? The electric storm? Do the freaks think the whole world's jumping through the midway? Where's Mr. Dark? In town? Up to no good? What, where, why?

He thought he heard the agonized figure sprawled on the carousel platform drum his heart superfast, then slow, fast, slow, very fast, very slow, incredibly fast, then as slow as the moon going down the sky on a white night in winter.

Someone, something, on the carousel wailed faintly.

Thank God it's dark, thought Will. Thank God, I can't see. There goes someone. Here comes something. There, whatever it is, goes again. There . . . there . . .

A bleak shadow on the shuddering machine tried to stagger up, but it was late, late, later still, very late, latest of all, oh, very late. The shadow crumbled. The carousel, like the earth spinning, whipped away air, sunlight, sense and sensibility, leaving only dark, cold, and age.

In a final vomit, the switch box blew itself completely apart.

All the carnival lights blinked out.

The carousel slowed itself through the cold night wind.

Will let Jim go.

How many times, thought Will, did it go around? Sixty, eighty . . . ninety . . . ?

How many times? said Jim's face, all nightmare, watching the dead carousel shiver and halt in the dead grass, a stopped world now which nothing, not their hearts, hands or heads, could send back anywhere.

They walked slowly to the merry-go-round, their shoes whispering.

The shadowy figure lay on the near side, on the plank floor, its face turned away.

One hand hung off the platform.

It did not belong to a boy.

It seemed a huge wax hand shriveled by fire.

The man's hair was long, spidery, white. It blew like milkweed in the breathing dark.

They bent to see the face.

The eyes were mummified shut. The nose was collapsed upon gristle. The mouth was a ruined white flower, the petals twisted into a thin wax sheath over the clenched teeth through which faint bubblings sighed. The man was small inside his clothes, small as a child, but tall, strung out, and old, so old, very old, not ninety, not one hundred, no, not one hundred ten, but one hundred twenty or one hundred thirty impossible years old.

Will touched.

The man was cold as an albino frog.

He smelled of moon swamps and old Egyptian bandages. He was something found in museums, wrapped in nicotine linens, sealed in glass.

But he was alive, puling like a babe, and shriveling unto death, fast, very fast, before their eyes.

Will was sick over the side of the carousel.

Then, falling against each other, Jim and Will sledgehammered the insane leaves, the unbelievable grass, the insubstantial earth with their numbed shoes, fleeing off down the midway. . . .

Chapter Twenty-Four

MOTHS TICKED off the high tin-shaded arc light which swung abandoned above the crossroads. Below, in a deserted gas station in the midst of country wilderness there was another ticking. In a coffin-sized phone booth speaking to people lost somewhere across night hills, two white-faced boys were crammed, holding to each other at every flit of bat, each sliding of cloud across the stars.

Will hung up the phone. The police and an ambulance were coming.

At first he and Jim had shout-whispered-wheezed at each other, pumping along, stumbling: they should go home, sleep, forget—no! they should take a freight train west!—no! for Mr. Cooger, if he survived what they'd done to him, that old man, that old old old man, would follow them over the world until he found and tore them apart! Arguing, shivering, they ended up in a phone booth, and now saw the police car bouncing along the road, its siren moaning, with the ambulance behind. All the men looked out at the two boys whose teeth chattered in the moth-flicked light.

Three minutes later they all advanced down the dark midway, Jim leading the way, talking, gibbering.

"He's alive. He's *got* to be alive. We didn't mean to do it! We're sorry!" He stared at the black tents. "You hear? We're sorry!"

"Take it easy, boy," said one of the policemen. "Go on."

The two policemen in midnight blue, the two internes like ghosts, the two boys, made the last turn past the ferris wheel and reached the merry-go-round.

Jim groaned.

The horses trampled the night air, in midplunge. Starlight glittered on the brass poles. That was all.

"He's *gone*. . . ."

"He was here, we swear!" said Jim. "One hundred fifty, two hundred years old, and *dying* of it!"

"Jim," said Will.

The four men stirred uneasily.

"They must've taken him in a tent." Will started off. A policeman took his elbow.

"Did you say one hundred fifty years old?" he asked Jim. "Why not *three* hundred?"

"Maybe he was! Oh God." Jim turned, yelling. "Mr. Cooger! We brought *help*!"

Lights blinked on in the Freak Tent. The huge banners out front rumbled and lashed as arc lights flushed over them. The police glanced up. MR. SKELETON, THE DUST WITCH, THE CRUSHER, VESUVIO THE LAVA SIPPER! danced soft, big, painted each on its separate flag.

Jim paused by the rustling freak show entry.

"Mr. Cooger?" he pleaded. "You . . . *there*?"

The tent flaps mouthed out a warm lion air.

"What?" asked a policeman.

Jim read the moving flaps.

"They said 'Yes.' They said, 'Come in.'"

Jim stepped through. The others followed.

Inside they squinted through crisscrossed tent pole shadows to the high freak platforms and all the world-wandered aliens, crippled of face, of bone, of mind, waiting there.

At a rickety card table nearby four men sat playing orange, lime-green, sun-yellow cards printed with moon beasts and winged sun-symboled men. Here the akimbo Skeleton one might play like a piccolo; here the Blimp who could be punctured every night, pumped up at dawn; here the midget known as The Wart who could be mailed parcel post dirt-cheap; and next to him an even littler accident of cell and time, a Dwarf so small and perched in such a way you could not see his face behind the cards clenched before him in arthritic and tremulous oak-gnarled fingers.

The Dwarf! Will started. Something about those hands! Familiar, familiar. Where? Who? What? But his eyes snapped on.

There stood Monsieur Guillotine, black tights, black long stockings, black hood over head, arms crossed over his chest, stiff straight by his chopping machine, the blade high in the tent sky, a hungry knife all flashes and meteor shine, much desiring to cleave space. Below, in the head cradle, a dummy sprawled waiting quick doom.

There stood the Crusher, all ropes and tendons, all steel and iron, all bone-monger, jaw-cruncher, horseshoe-taffy-puller.

And there the Lava Sipper, Vesuvio of the chafed tongue, of the scalded teeth, who spun scores of fireballs up, hissing in a ferris of flame which streaked shadows along the tent roof.

Nearby, in booths, another thirty freaks watched the fires fly until the Lava Sipper glanced, saw intruders, and let his universe fall. The suns drowned in a water tub.

Steam billowed. All froze in a tableau.

An insect stopped buzzing.

Will glanced swiftly.

There, on the biggest stage, a tattoo needle poised like a blowgun dart in his rose-crusted hand, stood Mr. Dark, the Illustrated Man.

His picture crowds flooded raw upon his flesh. Stripped bare to the navel, he had been stinging himself, adding a picture to his left palm with this dragonfly contraption. Now with the insect droned dead in his hand, he wheeled. But Will, staring beyond him, cried:

"There he is! There's Mr. Cooger!"

The police, the internes, quickened.

Behind Mr. Dark sat the Electric Chair.

In this chair sat a ruined man, last seen strewn wheezing in a collapse of bones and albino wax on the broken carousel. Now he was erected, propped, strapped in this device full of lightning power.

"That's him! He was . . . *dying*."

The Blimp *ascended* to his feet.

The Skeleton spun about, tall.

The Wart flea-hopped to the sawdust.

The Dwarf let fall his cards and flirted his now mad, now idiot eyes ahead, around, over.

I *know* him, thought Will. Oh, God, what they've *done* to him!

The lightning-rod salesman!

That's who it was. Squeezed tight, smashed small, convulsed by some terrible nature into a clenched fist of humanity . . .

The seller of lightning rods.

But now two things happened with beautiful promptitude.

Monsieur Guillotine cleared his throat.

And the blade, above, in the canvas sky, like a homing hawk scythed down. Whisper-whisk-slither-thunder-rush—wham!

The dummy head, chop-cut, fell.

And falling, looked like Will's own head, own face, destroyed.

He wanted, he did not want, to run lift the head, turn it to see if it held his own profile. But how could you ever dare do that? Never, never in a billion years, could one empty that wicker basket.

The second thing happened.

A mechanic, working at the back of an upright glass-fronted coffin booth, released a trip wire. This made a last cog click within the machinery under the sign, MLLE TAROT, THE DUST WITCH. The wax woman's figure within the glass box nodded her head and fixed the boys with her pointing nose as the boys passed, leading the men. Her cold wax hand brushed the Dust of Destiny on a ledge within the coffin. Her eyes did not see; they were sewn shut with laced black-widow web, dark threads. A waxworks fright, good and proper, she was, and the policemen beamed, viewing her, and strolled on, and beamed at Monsieur Guillotine for his act, too, and moving, the police were relaxing now, and seemed not to mind being called late on a jolly venture into a rehearsing world of acrobats and seedy magicians.

"Gentlemen!" Mr. Dark and his mob of illustrations surged forward on the pine platform, a jungle beneath each arm, an Egyptian viper scrolled on each bicep. "Welcome! You're just in time! We're rehearsing all our new acts!" Mr. Dark waved, and strange monsters gaped their fangs from his chest, a Cyclops with a navel for a squinted moron eye twitched on his stomach as he strode.

Lord, thought Will, is he bringing that crowd with him or is the crowd pulling him along by his skin?

From all the creaked platforms, from the muffled sawdust, Will felt the freaks wheel and fix their eyes, enchanted, as were internes and police, by this illustrated throng of humanity that in one agglomerative move dominated and filled the immediate air and tent sky with silent shoutings for attention.

Now part of the wasp-needle tattooed population spoke. It was Mr. Dark's mouth over and above this calligraphic explosion, this railroad accident of monsters in tumult upon his sweating skin. Mr. Dark chanted forth the organ tones from his chest. His personal electric blue-green populations trembled, even as the real freaks on the sawdust tent floor trembled, even as, hearing in their most secret marrow, Jim and Will trembled and felt more freak than the freaks themselves.

"Gentlemen! Boys! We've just perfected the new act! You'll be the first to see!" cried Mr. Dark.

The first policeman, his hand casually nestled to his pistol holster, squinted up at that vast corral of beasts and beings. "This boy said—"

"*Said*?!" The Illustrated Man barked a laugh. The freaks leaped in a frolic of shock, then calmed as the carnival owner continued with great ease, patting and soothing his own illustrations, which somehow patted and soothed the freaks. "Said? But what did he *see*? Boys always scare themselves at side shows, eh? Run like rabbits when the freaks pop out. But tonight, especially tonight!"

The policemen glanced beyond to the Erector-set-papier-mâché relic constricted in the Electric Chair.

"Who's he?"

"Him?" Will saw fire lick up through Mr. Dark's smoke-clouded eyes, saw him just as quickly snuff it out. "The new act. Mr. Electrico."

"No! Look at the old man! Look!" Will yelled. The police turned to appraise his demon cry.

"Don't you see!" said Will. "He's dead! Only thing holds him up is the straps!"

The internes gazed up at the great flake of winter flung into and held by the black chair.

Oh gosh, thought Will, we thought it would all be simple. The old man, Mr. Cooger, dying, so we bring doctors to save him, so he forgives us, maybe, maybe the carnival doesn't hurt us, lets us go. But now this, what's next? He's dead! It's too late! Everyone hates us!

And Will stood among the others feeling the cold air waft down from the unearthed mummy, from the cold mouth and cold eyes locked up in frozen eyelids. Inside the frozen nostrils not a white hair stirred. Mr. Cooger's ribs under his collapsed shirt were stone-rigid and his teeth under his clay lips were dry-ice cold. Put him out at noon and fog would steam off him.

The internes glanced at each other. They nodded.

The policemen, at this, took one step forward.

"Gentlemen!"

Mr. Dark scuttled a tarantula hand up an electric brass switchboard.

"One hundred thousand volts will now burn Mr. Electrico's body!"

"No, don't let him!" Will cried.

The policemen took another step. The internes opened their mouths to speak. Mr. Dark flicked a swift demanding glance at Jim. Jim cried:

"No! It's all right!"

"Jim!"

"Will, yes, it's okay!"

"Stand back!" The spider clutched the switch handle. "This man is in a trance! As part of our new act. I have hypnotized him! He could suffer injury if you shocked him from his spell!"

The internes shut their mouths. The police stopped moving.

"One hundred thousand volts! Yet he will come forth alive, whole in sound mind and body!"

"No!"

A policeman grabbed Will.

The Illustrated Man and all the men and beasts asprawl in frenzies on him now snatched and banged the switch.

The tent lights snuffed out.

Policemen, internes, boys jumped up their flesh in cobbles and boils.

But now in the swift midnight shuttering, the Electric Chair was a hearth and on it the old man blazed like a blue autumn tree.

The police flinched back, the internes leaned ahead, as did the freaks, blue fire in their eyes.

The Illustrated Man, hand glued to switch, looked upon the old old old man.

The old man was flintrock dead, yes, but electricity alive sheathed over him. It swarmed on his cold shell ears, it flickered in his deep-as-an-abandoned-stone-well nostrils. It crept blue eels of power on his praying-mantis fingers and his grasshopper knees.

The Illustrated Man's lips thrust wide, perhaps he yelled,

but no one heard against the immense fry, blast, the slam and sizzle of power which prowled in around over under about man and prisoning chair. Come alive! cried the hum! Come alive! cried the storming color and light. Come alive! yelled Mr. Dark's mouth, which no one heard but Jim, reading lips, read thunderous loud in his mind, and Will the same, Come alive! willing the old man to live, start up, tick, hum, work juice, summon spit, ungum spirit, melt wax soul. . . .

"He's dead!" But no one heard Will, either, no matter how he pushed against the lightning clamor.

Alive! Mr. Dark's lips licked and savored. Alive. Come alive. He ratcheted the switch to the last notch. Live, live! Somewhere, dynamos protested, skirled, shrilled, moaned a bestial energy. The light turned bottle-green. Dead, dead, thought Will. But live alive! cried machines, cried flame and fire, cried mouths of crowds of livid beasts on illustrated flesh.

So the old man's hair stood up in prickling fumes. Sparks, bled from his fingernails, dripped seething spatters on pine planks. Green simmerings wove shuttles through dead eyelids.

The Illustrated Man bent violently above the old old dead dead thing, his prides of beasts drowned deep in sweat, his right hand thrust in hammering demand upon the air: Live, live.

And the old man came alive.

Will yelled himself hoarse.

And no one heard.

For now, very slowly, as if roused by thunder, as if the electric fire were new dawn, one dead eyelid peeled itself slowly open.

The freaks gaped.

A long way off in the storm, Jim was yelling, too, for Will had his elbow tight and felt the yell pouring out through the bones, as the old man's lips fell apart and frightful sizzles zigzagged between lips and threaded teeth.

The Illustrated Man cut the power to a whine. Then, turning, he fell to his knees, and put out his hand.

Away off up there on the platform, there was the faintest stir as of an autumn leaf beneath the old man's shirt.

The freaks exhaled.

The old old man sighed.

Yes, Will thought, they're breathing for him, helping him, making him to live.

Inhale, exhale, inhale, exhale—yet it looked like an act. What could he say, or do?

". . . lungs so . . . so . . . so . . ." someone whispered.

The Dust Witch, back in her glass box?

Inhale. The freaks breathed. Exhale. Their shoulders slumped.

The old old man's lips trembled.

". . . heart beat . . . one . . . two . . . so . . . so . . ."

The Witch again? Will feared to look.

A vein ticked a small watch in the old man's throat.

Very slowly now that right eye of the old man opened full wide, fixed, stared like a broken camera. It was like looking through a hole in space, with no bottom forever. He grew warmer.

The boys, below, grew colder.

Now the old and terribly-wise-with-nightmare eye was so wide and so deep and so alive all to itself in that smashed porcelain face that there at the bottom of the eye somewhere the evil nephew peered along and out at the freaks, internes, police, and . . .

Will.

Will saw himself, saw Jim, two little pictures posed in reflection on that single eye. If the old man blinked, the two images would be *crushed* by his lid!

The Illustrated Man, on his knees, turned at last and gentled all with his smile.

"Gentlemen, boys, here *indeed* is the man who lives with lightning!"

The second policeman laughed; this motion shook his hand off his holster.

Will shuffled to the right.

The old spittle-eye followed, sucking at him with its emptiness.

Will squirmed left.

As did the phlegm that was the old man's gaze, while his chill lips peeled wide to shape, reshape an echoed gasp, a flutter. From deep below the old man bounced his voice ricocheting off the dank stone walls of his body until it fell out his mouth:

"... welcome ... mmmmmm ..."

The word fell back in.

"well ... cummm ... mmmm ..."

The policemen nudged each other with identical smiles.

"No!" cried Will, suddenly. "That's no act! He was dead! He'd die again if you cut the power—!"

Will slapped his own hand to his mouth.

Oh Lord, he thought, what am I doing? I want him alive, so he'll forgive us, let us be! But, oh Lord, even more I want him dead, I want them all dead, they scare me so much I got hairballs big as cats in my stomach!

"I'm sorry ..." he whispered.

"Don't be!" cried Mr. Dark.

The freaks made a commotion of blinks and glares. What next from the statue in the cold sizzling chair? The old old man's one eye gummed itself. The mouth collapsed, a bubble of yellow mud in a sulphur bath.

The Illustrated Man banged the switch a notch, grinning wildly at no one. He thrust a steel sword in the old man's empty glove-like hand.

A drench of electricity prickled from the sere music-box tines of the ancient stubbled cheeks. That deep eye showed swift as a bullet hole. Hungry for Will, it found and ate of his image. The lips steamed:

"I ... sssaw ... the ... boysssssss ... ssssneak into ... thee ... tent ... tttttt. ..."

The desiccated bellows refilled, then pin-punctured the swamp air out in faint wails:

"... We ... rehearsing ... sssso I thought ... play ... thissss trick ... pretend to be ... dead."

Again the pause to drink oxygen like ale, electricity like wine.

"... let myself fall ... like ... I ... wasssss ... dying. ... The ... boyssssssssss ... ssscreaming ... *ran*!"

The old man husked out syllable on syllable.

"Ha." Pause. "Ha." Pause. "Ha."

Electricity hemstitched the whistling lips.

The Illustrated Man coughed gently. "This act, it *tires* Mr. Electrico. . . ."

"Oh, sure." One of the policemen started. "Sorry." He touched his cap. "Fine show."

"Fine," said one of the internes.

Will glanced swiftly to see the interne's mouth, what it looked like saying this, but Jim stood in the way.

"Boys! A dozen free passes!" Mr. Dark held them out. "Here!"

Jim and Will didn't move.

"Well?" said one policeman.

Sheepishly, Will reached up for the flame-colored tickets, but stopped as Mr. Dark said, "Your names?"

The officers winked at each other.

"Tell him, boys."

Silence. The freaks watched.

"Simon," said Jim. "Simon Smith."

Mr. Dark's hand, holding the tickets, constricted.

"Oliver," said Will. "Oliver Brown."

The Illustrated Man sucked in a mighty breath. The freaks *inhaled*! The vast ingasped sigh might have, seemed to, stir Mr. Electrico. His sword twitched. Its tip leaped to spark-sting Will's shoulder, then sizzle over in blue-green explosions at Jim. Lightning shot Jim's shoulder.

The policemen laughed.

The old old man's one wide eye blazed.

"I dub thee . . . asses and foolssssss . . . I dub . . . thee . . . Mr. Sickly . . . and . . . Mr. Pale . . . !"

Mr. Electrico finished. The sword tapped them.

"A . . . sssshort . . . sad life . . . for you both!"

Then his mouth slit shut, his raw eye glued over. Containing his cellar breath, he let the simple sparks swarm his blood like dark champagne.

"The tickets," murmured Mr. Dark. "Free rides. Free rides. Come any time. Come back. Come back."

Jim grabbed, Will grabbed the tickets.

They jumped, they bolted from the tent.

The police, smiling and waving all around, followed at their leisure.

The internes, not smiling, like ghosts in their white suits, came after.

They found the boys huddled in the back of the police car.

They looked as though they wanted to go home.

II. PURSUITS

Chapter Twenty-Five

SHE COULD feel the mirrors waiting for her in each room much the same as you felt, without opening your eyes, that the first snow of winter has just fallen outside your window.

Miss Foley had first noticed, some years ago, that her house was crowded with bright shadows of herself. Best, then, to ignore the cold sheets of December ice in the hall, above the bureaus, in the bath. Best skate the thin ice, lightly. Paused, the weight of your attention might crack the shell. Plunged through the crust, you might drown in depths so cold, so remote, that all the Past lay carved in tombstone marbles there. Ice water would syringe your veins. Transfixed at the mirror sill, you would stand forever, unable to lift your gaze from the proofs of Time.

Yet tonight, with the echo of the running feet of the three boys dying away, she kept feeling snow fall in the mirrors of her house. She wanted to thrust through the frames to test their weather. But she was afraid that doing this might cause all the mirrors to somehow assemble in billionfold multiplications of self, an army of women marching away to become girls and girls marching to become infinitely small children. So many people, crammed in one house, would provoke suffocation.

So what must she do about mirrors, Will Halloway, Jim Nightshade, and . . . the nephew?

Strange. Why not say *my* nephew?

Because, she thought, from the first when he came in the door, he didn't belong, his proof was not proof, she kept waiting for . . . what?

Tonight. The carnival. Music, the nephew said, that *must* be heard, rides that *must* be ridden. Stay away from the maze where winter slept. Swim around with the carousel where summer, sweet as clover, honey-grass, and wild mint, kept its lovely time.

She looked out at the night lawn from which she had not yet retrieved the scattered jewels. Somehow she guessed this was a way the nephew had of getting rid of the two boys who might stop her using this ticket she took from the mantel:

CAROUSEL. ADMIT ONE.

She had waited for the nephew to come back. With time passing, she must act on her own. Something must be done not to hurt, no, but slow down interference from such as Jim and Will. No one must stand between her and nephew, her and carousel, her and lovely gliding ride-around summer.

The nephew had said as much, by saying nothing, by just holding her hands, and breathing baked-apple-pie scent from his small pink mouth upon her face.

She lifted the telephone.

Across town she saw the light in the stone library building, as all the town had seen it, over the years. She dialed. A quiet voice answered. She said:

"Library? Mr. Halloway? This is Miss Foley. Will's teacher. In ten minutes, please, meet me in the police station. . . . Mr. Halloway?"

A pause.

"Are you still *there* . . . ?"

Chapter Twenty-Six

"I'D HAVE sworn," said one interne. "When we first got there . . . that old man was dead."

The ambulance and the police car had pulled up at the same moment at the crossroads, going back into town. One of the internes had called over. Now one of the policemen called back:

"You're joking!"

The internes sat in their ambulance. They shrugged.

"Yeah. Sure. Joking."

They drove on ahead, their faces as quiet and white as their uniforms.

The police followed, with Jim and Will huddled in back, trying to say more, but the police started talking and laughing, retelling everything that happened to one another, so Will and Jim wound up lying, giving wrong names again, saying they lived around the corner from the police station.

They let the police drop them at two dark houses near the station and they ran up on those porches and grabbed the doorknobs and waited for the prowl car to swing off around the corner into the station, and then they came down and followed and stood looking at the yellow lights of the station all sun-colored at midnight and Will glanced over and saw the whole evening come and go in Jim's face and Jim watching the police station windows as if at any moment darkness might fill every room and put the lights out forever.

On my way back into town, thought Will, I threw away my tickets. But—look . . .

Jim still has his, in his hand.

Will trembled.

What did Jim think, want, plan, now that dead men lived and only lived through the fire of white-hot electric chair machines? Did he still very much love carnivals? Will searched. Faint echoes, yes, they came, they went in Jim's eyes, for Jim, after all, was Jim, even standing here with the calm light of Justice falling on his cheekbones.

"The Chief of Police," Will said. "He'd listen to us—"

"Yeah," said Jim. "He'd wake just long enough to send

for the butterfly net. Hell, William, hell, even *I* don't believe what's happened the last twenty-four hours."

"But we got to find someone higher up, keep trying, now we know what the score is."

"Okay, what's the score? What's the carnival done is so bad? Scared a woman with a mirror maze? So, she scared herself, the police'd say. Burgled a house? Okay, where's the burglar? Hiding inside an old man's skin? Who'd believe that? Who'd believe an old old man was ever a boy twelve? What else is the score? Did a lightning-rod salesman disappear? Sure, and left his bag. But he could've left town—"

"That dwarf in the side show—"

"I saw him, you saw him, looks kinda like the lightning-rod man, sure, but again, can you prove he was ever big? No, just like you can't prove Cooger was ever small, so that leaves us right here, Will, on the sidewalk, no proof except what we saw, and us just kids, the carnival's word against ours, and the police had a fine time anyway there. Oh gosh, it's a mess. If only, if only there was *still* some way to apologize to Mr. Cooger—"

"Apologize?" Will yelled. "To a man-eating crocodile? Jehoshaphat! You still don't see we can't do business with those ulmers and goffs!"

"Ulmers? Goffs?" Jim gazed upon him thoughtfully, for that was how the boys talked of the creatures who dragged and swayed and slumped through their dreams. In the bad dreams of William, the "ulmers" moaned and gibbered and had no faces. In the equally bad dreams of Jim, the "goffs," his peculiar name for them, grew like monster meringue-paste mushrooms, which fed on rats which fed on spiders which fed, in turn, because they were large enough, on cats.

"Ulmers! Goffs!" said Will. "You need a ten-ton safe to fall on you? Look what happened to two folks already, Mr. Electrico, and that terrible crazy dwarf! All kinds of things can go wrong with people on that darn machine. We know, we seen it. Maybe they squashed the lightning-rod man down that way on purpose, or maybe something went wrong. Fact is, he wound up in a wine press anyway, got run over by a steam-roller carousel and's so crazy now he doesn't even *know* us! Ain't that enough to scare the Jesus out of you, Jim? Why, maybe even Mr. Crosetti—"

"Mr. Crosetti's on vacation."

"Maybe yes, maybe no. There's his shop. There's the sign: CLOSED ON ACCOUNT OF ILLNESS. What *kind* of illness, Jim? He eat too much candy out at the show? He get seasick on everybody's favorite ride?"

"Cut it, Will."

"No, sir, I won't cut it. Sure, sure, the merry-go-round sounds keen. You think *I* like being thirteen all the time? Not me! But for cri-yi, Jim, face it, you don't *really* want to be twenty!"

"What *else* we talked about all summer?"

"Talk, sure. But throwing yourself head first in that taffy machine and getting your bones pulled long, Jim, you wouldn't know what to do with your bones then!"

"I'd know," said Jim, in the night. "I'd know."

"Sure. You'd just go away and leave me here, Jim."

"Why," protested the other, "I wouldn't leave you, Will. We'd be together."

"Together? You two feet taller and going around feeling your leg-and-arm-bones? You looking down at me, Jim, and what'd we talk about, me with my pockets full of kite-string and marbles and frog-eyes, and you with clean nice and empty pockets and making fun, is that what we'd talk, and you able to run faster and ditch me—"

"I'd never ditch you, Will—"

"Ditch me in a minute. Well, go on, Jim, just go on leave me because I got my pocket knife and there's nothing wrong with me sitting under a tree playing mumblety-peg while you get yourself plain crazy with the heat of all those horses racing around, but thank God they're not racing any more—"

"And it's your fault!" cried Jim. He stopped.

Will stiffened and made fists. "You mean I should've let young mean-and-terrible get old mean-and-terrible enough to chew our heads off? Just let him ride around and hock his spit in our eye? and maybe you with him, waving goodbye, going around again, waving so long! and all I got to do is wave back, Jim, that what you mean?"

"Sh," said Jim. "Like you say, it's too late. The carousel's broke—"

"And when it's fixed, they ride old horrible Cooger back,

make him young enough so he can speak and remember our names, and then they come like cannibals after us, or just me, if you want to get in good with them and go tell them my name and where I live—"

"I wouldn't do that, Will." Jim touched him.

"Oh, Jim, Jim, you *do* see, don't you? Everything in its time, like the preacher said only last month, everything one by one, not two by two, will you remember?"

"Everything," said Jim, "in its time . . ."

And then they heard voices from the police station. In one of the rooms to the right of the entrance, a woman was talking now, and men were talking.

Will nodded to Jim and they ran quietly over to pick their way through bushes and look into the room.

There sat Miss Foley. There sat Will's father.

"I don't understand," said Miss Foley. "To think Will and Jim would break in my house, steal, run off—"

"You saw their faces?" asked Mr. Halloway.

"When I screamed, they looked back under the light."

She's not mentioning the nephew, thought Will. And she won't, of course.

You see, Jim, he wanted to shout, it was a trap! The nephew *waited* for us to come prowling. He wanted to get us in so much trouble, no matter what we said to anybody, police, parents, that nobody'd listen to us about carnivals, late hours, merry-go-rounds, because our word'd be no good!

"I don't want to prosecute," said Miss Foley. "But if they are innocent, where are the boys?"

"Here!" someone cried.

"Will!" said Jim.

Too late.

For Will had jumped high and was scrambling through the window.

"Here," he said, simply, as he touched the floor.

Chapter Twenty-Seven

THEY WALKED home quietly on the moon-colored sidewalks, Mr. Halloway between the boys. When they reached home, Will's father sighed.

"Jim, I don't see any reason to tear your mother to bits at this hour. If you promise to tell her this whole thing at breakfast, I'll let you off. Can you get in without waking her up?"

"Sure. Look what we got."

"We?"

Jim nodded and took them over to fumble among the clusters of thick moss and leaves on the side of the house until they found the iron rungs they had secretly nailed and placed to make a hidden ladder up to Jim's room. Mr. Halloway laughed, once, almost with pain, and a strange wild sadness shook his head.

"How long has this gone on? No, don't tell. I did it, too, your age." He looked up the ivy toward Jim's window. "Fun being out late, free as all hell." He caught himself. "You don't stay out too long—?"

"This week was the very first time after midnight."

Dad pondered a moment. "Having permission would spoil everything, I suppose? It's sneaking out to the lake, the graveyard, the rail tracks, the peach orchards summer nights that counts. . . ."

"Gosh, Mr. Halloway, did you once—"

"Yes. But don't let the women know I told you. Up." He motioned. "And don't come out again *any* night for the next month."

"Yes, sir!"

Jim swung monkeywise to the stars, flashed through his window, shut it, drew the shade.

Dad looked up at the hidden rungs coming down out of the starlight to the running-free world of sidewalks that invited the one-thousand-yard dash, and the high hurdles of the dark bushes, and the pole-vault cemetery trellises and walls. . . .

"You know what I hate most of all, Will? Not being able to run any more, like you."

"Yes, sir," said his son.

"Let's have it clear now," said Dad. "Tomorrow, go apologize to Miss Foley again. Check her lawn. We may have missed some of the—stolen property—with matches and flashlights. Then go to the Police Chief to report. You're lucky you turned yourself in. You're lucky Miss Foley won't press charges."

"Yes, sir."

They walked back to the side of their own house. Dad raked his hand in the ivy.

"Our place, too?"

His hand found a rung Will had nailed away among the leaves.

"Our place, too."

He took out his tobacco pouch, filled his pipe as they stood by the ivy, the hidden rungs leading up to warm beds, safe rooms, then lit his pipe and said, "I know you. You're not *acting* guilty. You didn't steal anything."

"No."

"Then why did you say you did, to the police?"

"Because. Miss Foley—who knows why?—*wants* us guilty. If she says we are, we are. You saw how surprised she was to see us come in through the window? She never figured we'd confess. Well, we did. We got enough enemies without the law on us, too. I figured if we made a clean breast, they'd go easy. They did. At the same time, boy, Miss Foley's won, too, because now we're criminals. Nobody'll believe what we say."

"I'll believe."

"Will you?" Will searched the shadows on his father's face, saw whiteness of skin, eyeball, and hair.

"Dad, the other night, at three o'clock in the morning—"

"Three in the morning—"

He saw Dad flinch as from a cold wind, as if he smelled and knew the whole thing and simply could not move, reach out, touch and pat Will.

And he knew he could not say it. Tomorrow, yes, some other day, yes, for perhaps with the sun coming up, the tents would be gone, the freaks off over the world, leaving them alone, knowing they were scared enough not to push it, say anything, just keep their mouths shut. Maybe it would all blow over, maybe . . . maybe. . . .

"Yes, Will?" said his father, with difficulty, the pipe in his hand going dead. "Go on."

No, thought Will, let Jim and me be cannibalized, but no one else. Anyone that knows gets hurt. So no one else must know. Aloud he said:

"In a couple days, Dad, I'll tell you everything. I swear. Mom's honor."

"Mom's honor," said Dad, at last, "is good enough for me."

Chapter Twenty-Eight

THE NIGHT was sweet with the dust of autumn leaves that smelled as if the fine sands of ancient Egypt were drifting to dunes beyond the town. How come, thought Will, at a time like this, I can even think of four thousand years of dust of ancient people sliding around the world, and me sad because no one notices except me and Dad here maybe, and even us not telling each other.

It was indeed a time between, one second their thoughts all brambled airedale, the next all silken slumbering cat. It was a time to go to bed, yet still they lingered reluctant as boys to give over and wander in wide circles to pillow and night thoughts. It was a time to say much but not all. It was a time after first discoveries but not last ones. It was wanting to know everything and wanting to know nothing. It was the new sweetness of men starting to talk as they must talk. It was the possible bitterness of revelation.

So while they should have gone upstairs, they could not depart this moment that promised others on not so distant nights when man and boy-becoming-man might almost sing. So Will at last said, carefully:

"Dad? Am I a good person?"

"I think so. I *know* so, yes."

"Will—will that help when things get really rough?"

"It'll help."

"Will it save me if I need saving? I mean, if I'm around bad people and there's no one else good around for miles, what then?"

"It'll help."

"That's not good enough, Dad!"

"Good is no guarantee for your body. It's mainly for peace of mind—"

"But sometimes, Dad, aren't you so scared that even—"

"—the mind isn't peaceful?" His father nodded, his face uneasy.

"Dad," said Will, his voice very faint. "Are *you* a good person?"

"To you and your mother, yes, I try. But no man's a hero to himself. I've lived with me a lifetime, Will. I know everything worth knowing about myself—"

"And, adding it all up . . . ?"

"The sum? As they come and go, and I mostly sit very still and tight, yes, I'm all right."

"Then, Dad," asked Will, "why aren't you happy?"

"The front lawn at . . . let's see . . . one-thirty in the morning . . . is no place to start a philosophical . . ."

"I just wanted to know is all."

There was a long moment of silence. Dad sighed.

Dad took his arm, walked him over and sat him down on the porch steps, relit his pipe. Puffing, he said, "All right. Your mother's asleep. She doesn't know we're out here with our tomcat talk. We can go on. Now, look, since when did you think being good meant being happy?"

"Since always."

"Since now learn otherwise. Sometimes the man who looks happiest in town, with the biggest smile, is the one carrying the biggest load of sin. There are smiles and smiles; learn to tell the dark variety from the light. The seal-barker, the laugh-shouter, half the time he's covering up. He's had his fun and he's guilty. And men *do* love sin, Will, oh how they love it, never doubt, in all shapes, sizes, colors, and smells. Times come when troughs, not tables, suit our appetites. Hear a man too loudly praising others, and look to wonder if he didn't just get up from the sty. On the other hand, that unhappy, pale, put-upon man walking by, who looks all guilt and sin, why, often that's your good man with a capital G, Will. For being good *is* a fearful occupation; men strain at it and sometimes break in two. I've known a few. You work twice as hard to be a farmer as to be his hog. I suppose it's thinking about trying to be good makes the crack run up the wall one night. A man with high standards, too, the least hair falls on him sometimes wilts his spine. He can't let himself alone, won't lift himself off the hook if he falls just a breath from grace.

"Oh, it would be lovely if you could just *be* fine, *act* fine, not think of it all the time. But it's hard, right? with the last piece of lemon cake waiting in the icebox, middle of the night, not yours, but you lie awake in a hot sweat for it, eh? do I need tell you? Or, a hot spring day, noon, and there you are chained to your school desk and away off there goes the river, cool and fresh over the rock-fall. Boys can hear clear water like that miles away. So, minute by minute, hour by hour, a lifetime, it never ends, never stops, you got the choice this second, now this next, and the next after that, be good, be bad, that's what the clock ticks, that's what it says in the ticks. Run swim, or stay hot, run eat or lie hungry. So you stay, but once stayed, Will, you know the secret, don't you? don't think of the river again. Or the cake. Because if you do, you'll go crazy. Add up all the rivers never swum in, cakes never eaten, and by the time you get my age, Will, it's a lot missed out on. But then you console yourself, thinking, the more times in, the more times possibly drowned, or choked on lemon frosting. But then, through plain dumb cowardice, I guess, maybe you hold off from too much, wait, play it safe.

"Look at me: married at thirty-nine, Will, thirty-nine! But I was so busy wrestling myself two falls out of three, I figured I couldn't marry until I had licked myself good and forever. Too late, I found you can't wait to become perfect, you got to go out and fall down and get up with everybody else. So at last I looked up from my great self-wrestling match one night when your mother came to the library for a book, and got me, instead. And I saw then and there you take a man half-bad and a woman half-bad and put their two good halves together and you got one human all good to share between. That's you, Will, for my money. And the strange thing is, son, and sad, too, though you're always racing out there on the rim of the lawn, and me on the roof using books for shingles, comparing life to libraries, I soon saw you were wiser, sooner and better, than I will ever be. . . ."

Dad's pipe was dead. He paused to tap it out and reload it.

"No, sir," Will said.

"Yes," said his father, "I'd be a fool not to know I'm a fool. My one wisdom is: you're wise."

"Funny," Will said, after a long pause. "You've told me more, tonight, than I've told you. I'll think some more. Maybe I'll tell you everything, at breakfast. Okay?"

"I'll be ready, if you are."

"Because . . . I want you to be happy, Dad."

He hated the tears that sprang to his eyes.

"I'll be all right, Will."

"Anything I could say or do to make you happy, I would."

"Willy, William." Dad lit his pipe again and watched the smoke blow away in sweet dissolvings. "Just tell me I'll live forever. That would do nicely."

His voice, Will thought, I never noticed. It's the same color as his hair.

"Pa," he said, "don't sound so sad."

"Me? I'm the original sad man. I read a book and it makes me sad. See a film: sad. Plays? they really work me over."

"Is there anything," said Will, "*doesn't* make you sad?"

"One thing. Death,"

"Boy!" Will started. "I should think *that* would!"

"No," said the man with the voice to match his hair. "Death makes everything else sad. But death itself only scares. If there wasn't death, all the other things wouldn't get tainted."

And, Will thought, here comes the carnival, Death like a rattle in one hand, Life like candy in the other; shake one to scare you, offer one to make your mouth water. Here comes the side show, both hands *full*!

He jumped to his feet.

"Dad, oh, listen! You'll live forever! Believe me, or you're sunk! Sure, you were sick a few years ago—but that's over. Sure, you're fifty-four, but that's young! And another thing—"

"Yes, Willy?"

His father waited for him. He swayed. He bit his lips, then blurted out:

"Don't go near the carnival."

"Strange," his father said, "that's what I was going to tell you."

"I wouldn't go back to that place for a billion dollars!"

But, Will thought, that won't stop the carnival searching through town to visit *me*.

"Promise, Dad?"

"Why don't you want me to go there, Will?"

"That's one of the things I'll tell tomorrow or next week or next year. You just got to trust me, Dad."

"I do, son." Dad took his hand. "It's a promise."

As if at a signal, both turned to the house. The time was up, the hour was late, enough had been said, they properly sensed they must go.

"The way you came out," said Dad, "is the way you go in."

Will walked silently to touch the iron rungs hidden under the rustling ivy.

"Dad. You won't pull these *off* . . . ?"

Dad probed one with his fingers.

"Some day, when you're tired of them, you'll take them off yourself."

"I'll never be tired of them."

"Is that how it seems? Yes, to someone your age, you figure you'll never get tired of anything. All right, son, up you go."

He saw how his father looked up along the ivy and the hidden path.

"You want to come up this way, too?"

"No, no," his father said, quickly.

"Because," said Will, "you're welcome."

"That's all right. Go on."

But still he looked at the ivy stirring in the dark morning light.

Will sprang up, grabbed the first, the second, the third rungs and looked down.

From just this distance, Dad looked as if he were shrinking, there on the ground. Somehow he didn't want to leave him behind, there in the night, like someone ditched by someone else, one hand up to move, but not moving.

"Dad!" he whispered. "You ain't got the *stuff*!"

Who says!? cried Dad's mouth, silently.

And he jumped.

And laughing without sound, the boy, the man swung up the side of the house, unceasingly, hand over hand, foot after foot.

He heard Dad slip, scrabble, grab.

Hold tight! he thought.

"Ah . . . !"

The man breathed hard.

Eyes tight, Will prayed: hold . . . *there* . . . now . . . !!

The old man gusted out, sucked in, swore in a fierce whisper, then climbed again.

Will opened his eyes and climbed and the rest was smooth,

high, higher, fine, sweet, wondrous, done! They swung in and sat upon the sill, same size, same weight, colored same by the stars, and sat embraced once more with grand fine exhaustion, gasping on huge ingulped laughs which swept their bones together, and for fear of waking God, country, wife, Mom, and hell, they snug-clapped hands to each other's mouths, felt the vibrant warm hilarity fountained there, and sat one instant longer, eyes bright with each other and wet with love.

Then, with a last strong clasp, Dad was gone, the bedroom door shut.

Drunk on the long night's doings, lolled away from fear toward better, grander things found in Dad, Will slung off limp-falling clothes with tipsy arms and delightfully aching legs, and like a fall of timber chopped himself to bed. . . .

Chapter Twenty-Nine

HE SLEPT for exactly one hour.

And then, as if remembering something he had only half seen, he woke, sat up, and peered out at Jim's rooftop.

"The lightning rod!" he yelped. "It's *gone*!"

Which indeed it was.

Stolen? No. Jim take it down? Yes! Why? For the shucks of it. Smiling, he had climbed to scuttle the iron, dare any storm to strike *his* house! Afraid? No. Fear was a new electric-power suit Jim must try for size.

Jim! Will wanted to smash his confounded window. Go nail the rod back! Before morn, Jim, the blasted carnival'll send someone to find where we live, don't know how they'll come or what they'll look like, but, Lord, your roof's so *empty*! the clouds are moving fast, that storm's rushing at us and . . .

Will stopped.

What sort of noise does a balloon make, adrift?

None.

No, not quite. It noises itself, it soughs, like the wind billowing your curtains all white as breaths of foam. Or it makes a sound like the stars turning over in your sleep. Or it announces itself like moonrise and moonset. That last is best: like the moon sailing the universal deeps, so rides a balloon.

How do you hear it, how are you warned? The ear, does it hear? No. But the hairs on the back of your neck, and the peach-fuzz in your ears, *they* do, and the hair along your arms sings like grasshopper legs frictioned and trembling with strange music. So you know, you feel, you are sure, lying abed, that a balloon is submerging the ocean sky.

Will sensed a stir in Jim's house; Jim, too, with his fine dark antennae, must have felt the waters part high over town to let a Leviathan pass.

Both boys felt a shadow bulk the drive between houses, both flung up their windows, both poked their heads out, both dropped their jaws in surprise at this friendly, this always exquisite timing, this delightful pantomime of intuition, of apprehension, their tandem teamwork over the years. Then, silver-faced, for the moon was rising, both glanced up.

As a balloon wafted over and vanished.

"Holy cow, what's a balloon doing *here*!?" Jim asked, but wished no answer.

For, peering, they both knew the balloon was searching the best search ever; no car-motor racket, no tires whining asphalt, no footstepped street, just the wind clearing a great amazon through the clouds for a solemn voyage of wicker basket and storm sail riding over.

Neither Jim nor Will crashed his window or pulled his shade, they simply *had* to stay motionless waiting, for they *heard* the noise again like a murmur in someone else's dream. . . .

The temperature dropped forty degrees.

Because now the storm-bleached balloon whisper-purled, plummet-sank softly down, its elephant shadow cooling gemmed lawns and sundials as they flaunted their swift gaze high through that shadow.

And what they saw was something akimbo and arustle in the down-hung wicker carriage. Was that head and shoulders? Yes, with the moon like a silver cloak thrown up behind. Mr. Dark! thought Will. The Crusher! thought Jim. The Wart! thought Will. The Skeleton! The Lava Sipper! The Hanging Man! Monsieur Guillotine!

No.

The Dust Witch.

The Witch who might draw skulls and bones in the dust, then sneeze it away.

Jim looked to Will and Will to Jim; both read their lips: *the Witch!*

But why a wax crone flung out in a night balloon to search? thought Will, why none of the others, with their lizard-venom, wolf-fire, snake-spit eyes? Why send a crumbled statue with blind-newt lashes sewn tight with black-widow thread?

And then, looking up, they knew.

For the Witch, though peculiar wax, was peculiarly alive. Blind, yes, but she thrust down rust-splotched fingers which petted, stroked the sluices of air, which cut and splayed the wind, peeled layers of space, blinded stars, which hovered and danced, then fixed and pointed as did her nose.

And the boys knew even more.

They knew that she was blind, but special blind. She could dip down her hands to feel the bumps of the world, touch house roofs, probe attic bins, reap dust, examine draughts that blew through halls and souls that blew through people, draughts vented from bellows to thump-wrist, to pound-temples, to pulse-throat, and back to bellows again. Just as they felt that balloon sift down like an autumn rain, so she could feel their souls disinhabit, reinhabit their tremulous nostrils. Each soul, a vast warm fingerprint, *felt* different, she could roil it in her hand like clay; smelled different, Will could hear her snuffing his life away; *tasted* different, she savored them with her raw-gummed mouth, her puff-adder tongue; *sounded* different, she stuffed their souls in one ear, tissued them out the other!

Her hands played down the air, one for Will, one for Jim.

The balloon shadow washed them with panic, rinsed them with terror.

The Witch exhaled.

The balloon, freed of this small sour ballast, uprose. The shadow passed.

"Oh God!" said Jim. "Now they know where we live!"

Both gasped. Some monstrous baggage brushed and dragged across the shingles of Jim's house.

"Will! She's *got* me!"

"No! I think—"

The drag, brush, rustle scurried from bottom to top of Jim's roof. Then Will saw the balloon whirl up, fly off toward the hills.

"She's gone, there she goes! Jim, she *did* something to your roof. Shove the monkey pole over!"

Jim slid the long slender clothesline pole over, Will fixed it on his sill, then swung out, hand over hand, swung until Jim pulled him through his window and they barefooted it into Jim's clothes closet and boosted and hoisted each other up inside the attic that smelled like lumber mills, old, dark, and too silent. Perched out on the high roof, shivering, Will cried: "Jim, there it *is*."

And there it was, in the moonlight.

It was a track like a snail paints on a sidewalk. It glistered. It was silver-slick. But this was a path left by a *gigantic* snail that, if it existed at all, weighed a hundred pounds. The silver ribbon was a yard across. Starting down at the leaf-filled rain trough, the silver track shimmered to the rooftop, then tremored down the other side.

"Why?" gasped Jim. "Why?"

"Easier than looking for house numbers or street names. She marked your roof so you can see it for miles around, night *or* day!"

"Ohmigosh." Jim bent to touch the track. A faint evil-smelling glue covered his finger. "Will, what'll we do?"

"I got a hunch," the other whispered, "they won't be back till morning. They can't just start a rumpus. They got some plan. Right now—*there's* what we do!"

Coiled across the lawn below like a vast boa constrictor, waiting for them, was the garden hose.

Will was gone, down, fast, and didn't knock anything over or wake anyone up. Jim, on the roof, was surprised, in no time at all, when Will came scuttling up all panting teeth, the water-fizzing hose in his fist.

"Will, you're a genius!"

"Sure! Quick!"

They dragged the hose to drench the shingles, to wash the silver, flood the evil mercury paint away.

Working, Will glanced off at the pure color of night turning toward morn and saw the balloon trying to make decisions on the wind. Did it sense, would it come back? Would she mark the roof again, and they have to wash it off, and she mark it, and they wash it, until dawn? Yes, if need be.

If only, thought Will, I could stop the Witch for good. They don't know our names or where we live, Mr. Cooger's too near dead to remember or tell. The Dwarf—if he *is* the lightning-rod man—is mad—and, God willing, won't recollect! And they won't dare bother Miss Foley until morning. So, grinding their teeth way out in the meadows, they've sent the Dust Witch to search. . . .

"I'm a fool," grieved Jim, quietly, rinsing the roof where the lightning rod had been. "Why didn't I leave it *up*?"

"Lightning hasn't struck yet," Will said. "And if we jump lively, it won't. Now—over here!"

They showered the roof.

Below, someone put down a window.

"Mom," Jim laughed, bleakly. "She thinks it's raining."

Chapter Thirty

THE RAIN ceased.

The roof was clean.

They let the hose snake away to thump on the night grass a thousand miles below.

Beyond town, the balloon still paused between unpromising midnight and promised and hoped-for sun.

"Why's she waiting?"

"Maybe she *smells* what we're up to."

They went back down through the attic and soon were in separate rooms and beds after many fevers and chills of talk and now lay quietly separate listening to hearts and clocks beat too quickly toward dawn.

Whatever they do, thought Will, we *must* do it first. He wished the balloon might fly back, the Witch might guess they had washed her mark off and soar down to trace the roof again. Why?

Because.

He found himself staring at his Boy Scout archery set, the big beautiful bow and quiver of arrows arranged on the east wall of his room.

Sorry, Dad, he thought, and sat up, smiling. This time it's me out, alone. I don't want *her* going back to report on us for hours, maybe days.

He grabbed the bow and quiver from the wall, hesitated, thinking, then stealthily ran the window up and leaned out. No need to holler loud and long, no. But just think real hard. *They* can't read thoughts, I know, that's sure, or they wouldn't send her, and *she* can't read thoughts, but she *can* feel body heat and special temperatures and special smells and excitements, and if I jump up and down and let her know just by my feeling good about having tricked her, maybe, maybe . . .

Four o'clock in the morning, said a drowsy clock chime, off in another land.

Witch, he thought, *come back*.

Witch, he thought louder and let his blood pound, the roof's clean, hear!? We made our own rain! You got to come back and re-mark it! Witch . . . ?

And the Witch moved.

He felt the earth turn under the balloon.

Okay, Witch, come on, there's just me, the no-name boy, you can't read my mind, but here's me spitting on you! and here's me yelling we tricked you, and the general idea gets through, so come on, come on! dare! double-dare you!

Miles away, there was a gasp of assent rising, coming near.

Holy cow, he thought suddenly, I don't want her back to *this* house! Come on! He thrashed into his clothes.

Clutching his weapons, he aped down the hidden ivy rungs and dogged the wet grass.

Witch! Here! He ran leaving patterns, ran feeling crazy fine, wild as a hare who has chewed some secret, delicious, sweetly poisonous root that now gallops him berserk. Knees striking his chin, shoes crushing wet leaves, he soared over a hedge, his hands full of bristly porcupine weapons, fear and joy a tumble of mixed marbles in his mouth.

He looked back. The balloon swung near! It inhaled, exhaled itself along from tree to tree, from cloud to cloud.

Where am I *going*? he thought. Wait! The Redman house! Not lived in in years! Two blocks more!

There was the swift shush of his feet in the leaves and the big shush of the creature in the sky, while moonlight snowed everything and stars glittered.

He pulled up in front of the Redman house, a torch in each lung, tasting blood, crying out silently: here! this is *my* house!

He felt a great river change its bed in the sky.

Good! he thought.

His hand turned the doorknob of the old house. Oh God, he thought, what if *they* are inside, waiting for me?

He opened a door on darkness.

Dust came and went in that dark, and a harpstring gesticulation of spiders. Nothing else.

Will jumped two at a time up the crumbling stairs, around and out on the roof where he stashed his weapons behind the chimney and stood tall.

The balloon, green as slime, printed with titan pictures of

winged scorpions, ancient phoenixes, smokes, fires, clouded weathers, swung its wicker basket wheezing, down.

Witch, he thought, *here*!

The dank shadow struck him like a batwing.

Will toppled. He flung up his hands. The shadow was almost black flesh, striking.

He fell. He clutched the chimney.

The shadow draped him, hushing down.

It was cold as a sea cave in that cloud-dark.

But suddenly the wind, of itself, veered.

The Witch hissed in frustration. The balloon swam a washing circle up around.

The wind! thought the boy wildly, it's on *my* side!

No, don't go! he thought. Come back.

For he feared she had smelled his plan.

She had. She itched for his scheme. She snuffed, she gasped at it. He saw the way her nails filed and scraped the air as if running over grooved wax to seek patterns. She turned her palms out and down as if he were a small stove burning softly somewhere in a nether world and she came to warm her hands at him. As the basket swung in an upglided pendulum he saw her squinched blind-sewn eyes, the ears with moss in them, the pale wrinkled apricot mouth mummifying the air it drew in, trying to taste what was wrong with his act, his thought. He was too good, too rare, too fine, too available to be true! surely she knew that!

And knowing it, she held her breath.

Which made the balloon suspend itself, half between inhale and exhale.

Now, tremulously, experimentally, daring to test, the Witch inhaled. The balloon, so weighted, sank. Exhaled—so freed of vapor—the craft ascended!

Now, now, the waiting, the holding of dank sour breath in the wry tissues of her childlike body.

Will waggled his fingers, thumb to nose.

She sucked air. The weight of this one breath skimmed the balloon down.

Closer! he thought.

But, careful, she circled her craft, scenting the sharp

adrenalin wafted from his pores. He wheeled, following as the balloon spun, and him reeling. You! he thought, you want me sick! Spin me, will you? Make me dizzy?

There was one last thing to try.

He stood very still with his back to the balloon.

Witch, he thought, you can't resist.

He felt the sound of the green slime cloud, the kept bag of sour air, the squeal and stir of mouse-wicker on wicker as the shadow cooled his legs, his spine, his neck.

Close!

The Witch took air, weight, night burden, star-and-cold-wind ballast.

Closer!

Elephant shadow stroked his ears.

He nudged his weapons.

The shadow engulfed him.

A spider flicked his hair—her *hand*?

Choking a scream, he spun.

The Witch, leaned out, was a mere foot away.

He bent. He snatched.

The Witch tried to scream out breath when she smelled, felt, knew what he held tight.

But, in reaction, horrified, she seized a breath, sucked weight, burdened the balloon. It dragged the roof.

Will pulled the bowstring back, freighted with single destruction.

The bow broke in two pieces. He stared at the unshot arrow in his hands.

The Witch let out her breath in one great sigh of relief and triumph.

The balloon swung up. It struck him with its dry rattle-chuckling heavy-laden basket.

The Witch shouted again with insane happiness.

Clutched to the basket rim, Will with one free hand drew back and with all his strength threw the arrowhead flint up at the balloon flesh.

The Witch gagged. She tore at his face.

Then the arrow, a long hour it seemed in flight, razored a small vent in the balloon. Rapidly the shaft sank as if cutting a vast green cheese. The surface slit itself further in a wide ripping smile across the entire surface of the gigantic pear, as the blind Witch gabbled, moaned, blistered her lips, shrieked in protest, and Will hung fast, hands gripped to wicker, kicking legs, as the balloon wailed, whiffled, guzzled, mourned its own swift gaseous death, as dungeon air raved out, as dragon breath gushed forth and the bag, thus driven, retreated up.

Will let go. Space whistled about him. He turned, hit shingles, fell skidding down the inclined ancient roof, over down to rim, to rainspout where, feet first, he spilled into further emptiness, yelling, clawed at the rain gutter, held, felt it groan, give way, as he swept the sky to see the balloon whistling, wrinkling, flying up like a wounded beast to evacuate its terrified exhalations in the clouds; a gunshot mammoth, not wanting to expire, yet in terrible flux coughing out its stinking winds.

All this in a flash. Then Will flailed into space, with no time to be glad for a tree beneath when it netted him, cut him, but broke his fall with mattress twig, branch and limb. Like a kite he was held face up to the moon where, at his exhausted leisure, he might hear the last Witch lamentations for a wake in progress as the balloon spiraled her away from house, street, town with inhuman mourns.

The balloon smile, the balloon rip was all-encompassing now as it wandered in deliriums to die in the meadows from which it had come, sinking down now beyond all the sleeping, ignorant and unknowing houses.

For a long while Will could not move. Buoyed in the tree branches, afraid he might slip through and kill himself on the black earth below, he waited for the sledge hammer to subside in his head.

The blows of his heart might jar him loose, crash him down, but he was glad to hear them, know himself alive.

But then at last, gone calm, he gathered his limbs, most carefully searched for a prayer, and climbed himself down through the tree.

Chapter Thirty-One

NOTHING MUCH else happened, all the rest of that night.

Chapter Thirty-Two

AT DAWN, a juggernaut of thunder wheeled over the stony heavens in a spark-throwing tumult. Rain fell softly on town cupolas, chuckled from rainspouts, and spoke in strange subterranean tongues beneath the windows where Jim and Will knew fitful dreams, slipping out of one, trying another for size, but finding all cut from the same dark, mouldered cloth.

In the rustling drumbeat, a second thing occurred:

From the sodden carnival grounds, the carousel suddenly spasmed to life. Its calliope fluted up malodorous steams of music.

Perhaps only one person in town heard and guessed that the carousel was working again.

The door to Miss Foley's house opened and shut; her footsteps hurried away along the street.

Then the rain fell hard as lightning did a crippled dance down the now-totally-revealed, now-vanishing-forever land.

In Jim's house, in Will's house, as the rain nuzzled the breakfast windows, there was a lot of quiet talk, some shouting, and more quiet talk again.

At nine-fifteen, Jim shuffled out into the Sunday weather, wearing his raincoat, cap, and rubbers.

He stood gazing at his roof where the giant snail track was washed away. Then he stared at Will's door to make it open. It did. Will emerged. His father's voice followed: "Want me to come along?" Will shook his head, firmly.

The boys walked solemnly, the sky washing them, toward the police station where they would talk, to Miss Foley's where they would apologize again, but right now they only walked, hands in pockets, thinking of yesterday's fearful puzzles. At last, Jim broke the silence:

"Last night, after we washed off the roof, and I finally got to sleep, I dreamed a funeral. It came right down Main Street, like a visit."

"Or . . . a parade?"

"That's it! A thousand people, all dressed in black coats, black hats, black shoes, and a coffin *forty feet long*!"

"Criminently!"

"Right! What's forty feet long needs to be buried?! I thought. And in the dream I ran up and looked in. Don't laugh."

"I don't feel funny, Jim."

"In the long coffin was a big long wrinkled thing like a prune or a big grape lying in the sun. Like a big skin or a giant's head, drying."

"The *balloon*!"

"Hey." Jim stopped. "You must've had the same dream! But . . . balloons can't die, can they?"

Will was silent.

"And you don't have funerals for them, *do* you?"

"Jim, I . . ."

"Darn balloon laid out like a hippo someone leaked the wind out of—"

"Jim, last night . . ."

"Black plumes waving, band banging on black velvet-muffled drums with black ivory bones, boy, boy! Then on top of it, have to get up this morning and tell Mom, not everything, but enough so she cried and yelled and cried some more, women sure like to cry, don't they? and called me her criminal son but—we *didn't* do anything bad, did we, Will?"

"Someone *almost* took a ride on a merry-go-round."

Jim walked along in the rain. "I don't think I want any more of that."

"You don't *think*!? After all *this*!? Good grief, let me *tell* you! The Witch, Jim, the balloon! Last night, all alone, I—"

But there was no time to tell it.

No time to tell his stabbing the balloon so it gusted away to die in the lonely country sinking the blind woman with it.

No time because walking in the cold rain now, they heard a sad sound.

They were passing an empty lot, deep within which stood a vast oak tree. Under it were rainy shadows, and the sound.

"Jim," said Will, "someone's—*crying*."

"No." Jim moved on.

"There's a little girl in there."

"No." Jim would not look. "What would a girl be doing out under a tree in the rain? Come on."

"Jim! You *hear* her!"

"No! I don't, I don't!"

But then the crying came stronger across the dead grass, flew like a sad bird through the rain, and Jim had to turn, for there was Will marching across the rubble.

"Jim—that voice—I know it!"

"Will, don't go there!"

And Jim did not move, but Will stumbled and walked until he entered the shade of the raining tree where the sky fell and was lost in autumn leaves and crept down at last in shining rivers along the branches and trunk and there was the little girl, crouched, face buried in her hands, weeping as if the town were gone and the people in it and herself lost in terrible woods.

And at last Jim came edging up and stood at the edge of the shadow and said, "Who is it?"

"I don't know." But Will felt tears start to his eyes, as if some part of him guessed.

"It's not Jenny Holdridge, is it . . . ?"

"No."

"Jane Franklin?"

"No." His mouth felt full of novocaine, his tongue merely stirred in his numb lips. ". . . no . . ."

The little girl wept, feeling them near, but not looking up yet.

". . . me . . . me . . . help me . . . nobody'll help me . . . me . . . me . . . I don't *like* this . . ."

Then when she had strength enough and was quieter she turned her face, her eyes almost swollen shut with weeping. She was shocked to see anyone near, then surprised.

"Jim! Will! Oh God, it's you!"

She seized Jim's hand. He writhed back, yelling. "No! I don't know you, let go!"

"Will, help me, Jim, oh don't go, don't leave!" she gasped, brokenly, new tears bursting from her eyes.

"No, no, don't!" screamed Jim, he thrashed, he broke free, fell, leaped to his feet, one fist raised to strike. He stopped, trembling, held it to his side. "Oh, Will, Will, let's get out of here, I'm sorry, oh God, God."

The little girl in the shadow of the tree, flung back, widened her eyes to fix the two in wetness, moaned, clutched herself and rocked back and forth, her own child-baby, comforting her elbows . . . soon she might sing to herself and sing that way, alone beneath the dark tree, forever, no one able to join or stop the song.

". . . someone must help me . . . someone must help *her* . . ." she mourned as for one dead, "someone must help her . . . nobody will . . . nobody has . . . help her if not me . . . terrible . . . terrible . . ."

"She knows us!" said Will, hopelessly, half bent down to her, half turned to Jim. "I can't leave her!"

"Lies!" said Jim, wildly. "Lies! She don't know us! Never saw her before!"

"She's gone, bring her back, she's gone, bring her back," mourned the girl, eyes shut.

"Find who?" Will got down on one knee, dared to touch her hand. She grabbed him. Almost immediately she knew this was wrong for he tried to tear free, so she let him go, and wept, while he waited near and Jim, far out in the dead grass, called in for them to go, he didn't like it, they must, they must go.

"Oh, she's lost," sobbed the little girl. "She ran off in that place and never came back. Will you find her, please, please . . . ?"

Shivering, Will touched her cheek. "Hey now," he whispered. "You'll be okay. I'll find help," he said, gently. She opened her eyes. "This is Will Halloway, okay? Cross my heart, we'll be back. Ten minutes. But you mustn't go away." She shook her head. "You'll wait here under the tree for us?" She nodded, mutely. He stood up. This simple motion frightened her and she flinched. So he waited and looked at her and said, "I know who you are." He saw the great familiar eyes open gray in the small wounded face. He saw the long rain-washed black hair and the pale cheeks. "I know who you are. But I got to check."

"Who'll believe?" she wailed.

"*I* believe," Will said.

And she lay back against the tree, her hands in her lap, trembling, very thin, very white, very lost, very small.

"Can I go now?" he said.

She nodded.

And he walked away.

At the edge of the lot, Jim stomped his feet in disbelief, almost hysterical with outrage and declamation.

"It can't be!"

"It *is*," said Will. "The eyes. That's how you tell. Like it was with Mr. Cooger and the evil boy— There's one way to be sure. Come on!"

And he took Jim through the town and they stopped at last in front of Miss Foley's house and looked at the unlit windows in the morning gloom and walked up the steps and rang the bell, once, twice, three times.

Silence.

Very slowly, the front door moved whining back on its hinges.

"Miss Foley?" Jim called, softly.

Somewhere off in the house, shadows of rain moved on far windowpanes.

"Miss Foley . . . ?"

They stood in the hall by the bead-rain in the entry door, listening to the great attic beams ashift and astir in the downpour.

"Miss Foley!" Louder.

But only the mice in the walls, warmly nested, made sgraffito sounds in answer.

"She's gone out to shop," said Jim.

"No," said Will. "We know where she is."

"Miss Foley, I know you're here!" shouted Jim suddenly, savagely, dashing upstairs. "Come on out, you!"

Will waited for him to search and drag slowly back down. As Jim reached the bottom of the steps, they both heard the music blowing through the front door with the smell of fresh rain and ancient grass.

The carousel calliope, among the hills, piping the "Funeral March" backwards.

Jim opened the door wider and stood in the music, as one stands in the rain.

"The merry-go-round. They fixed it!"

Will nodded. "She must've heard the music, gone out at sunrise. Something went wrong. Maybe the carousel wasn't fixed right. Maybe accidents happen all the time. Like to the lightning-rod man, him inside-out and crazy. Maybe the carnival *likes* accidents, gets a kick out of them. Or maybe they did something to her on purpose. Maybe they wanted to know more about us, our names, where we live, or wanted her to help them hurt us. Who knows *what*? Maybe she got suspicious or scared. Then they just gave her *more* than she ever wanted or asked for."

"I don't understand—"

But now, in the doorway, in the cold rain, there was time to think of Miss Foley afraid of mirror mazes, Miss Foley alone not so long ago at the carnival, and maybe screaming when they did what they finally did to her, around and around, around and around, too many years, more years than she had ever dreamed of shucked away, rubbing her raw, leaving her naked small, alone, and bewildered because unknown-even-to-herself, around and around, until all the years were gone and the carousel rocked to a halt like a roulette wheel, and nothing gained and all lost and nowhere for her to go, no way to tell the strangeness, and nothing to do but . . . weep under a tree, alone, in the autumn rain. . . .

Will thought this. Jim thought it, and said:

"Oh, the poor . . . the poor . . ."

"We got to help her, Jim. Who else would believe? If she tells anyone, 'I'm Miss Foley!' 'Get away!' they'd say, 'Miss Foley's left town, disappeared!' 'Go on, little girl!' Oh, Jim, I bet she'd pounded a dozen doors this morning, wanting help, scared people with her screaming and yelling, then run off, gave up, and hid under that tree. Police are probably looking for her now, but so what? it's just a wild girl crying and they'll lock her away and she'll go crazy. That carnival, boy, do they know how to punish so you can't hit back. They just shake you up and change you so no one ever knows you again and let you run free, it's okay, go ahead, talk, 'cause folks are too scared of you to listen. Only *we* hear, Jim, only you and me, and right now I feel like I just ate a cold snail raw."

They looked back a last time at the shadows of rain crying on the windows inside the parlor where a teacher had often served them cookies and hot chocolate and waved to them from the window and moved tall through the town. Then they stepped out and shut the door and ran back toward the empty lot.

"We got to hide her, until we can help—"

"Help?" panted Jim. "We can't help *ourselves*!"

"There's got to be weapons, right in front of us, we're just too blind—"

They stopped.

Beyond the thump of their own hearts, a greater heart thumped. Brass trumpets wailed. Trombones blared. A herd of tubas made an elephant charge, alarmed for unknown reasons.

"The carnival!" gasped Jim. "We never thought! It can come *right into town.* A parade! Or that funeral I dreamt about, for the balloon?"

"Not a funeral and only what *looks* like a parade but's a search for us, Jim, for us, or Miss Foley, if they want her back! They can march down any old street, fine and dandy, and spy as they go, drum and bugle! Jim, we got to get her before they—"

And breaking off, they flung themselves down an alley, but stopped suddenly, and leaped to hide in some bushes.

At the far end of the alley, the carnival band, animal wagons, clowns, freaks and all, banged and crashed between them and the empty lot and the great oak tree.

It must have taken five minutes for the parade to pass. The rain seemed to move on away, the clouds moving with them. The rain ceased. The strut of drums faded. The boys loped down the alley, across the street, and stopped by the empty lot.

There was no little girl under the tree.

They circled it, looked up in it, not daring to call a name.

Then, very much afraid, they ran to hide themselves somewhere in the town.

Chapter Thirty-Three

THE PHONE rang.

Mr. Halloway picked it up.

"Dad, this is Willy, we can't go to the police station, we may not be home today, tell Mom, tell Jim's mom."

"Willy, where are you?"

"We got to hide. *They're* looking for us."

"*Who*, for God's sake?"

"I don't want you in it, Dad. You got to believe, we'll just hide one day, two, until they go away. If we came home they'd follow and hurt you or Ma or Jim's mom. I got to go."

"Willy, don't!"

"Oh, Dad," said Will. "Wish me luck."

Click.

Mr. Halloway looked out at the trees, the houses, the streets, hearing a faraway music.

"Willy," he said to the dead phone. "Luck."

And he put on his coat and hat and went out into the strange bright rainy sunshine that filled the cold air.

Chapter Thirty-Four

IN FRONT of the United Cigar Store on this before-noon Sunday with the bells of all churches ringing across here, colliding with each other there, showering sound from the sky now that the rain was spent, in front of the cigar store the Cherokee wooden Indian stood, his carved plumes pearled with water, oblivious to Catholic or Baptist bells, oblivious to the steadily approaching sun-bright cymbals, the thumping pagan heart of the carnival band. The flourished drums, the old-womanish shriek of calliope, the shadow drift of creatures far stranger than he, did not witch the Indian's yellow hawk-fierce gaze. Still, the drums did tilt churches and plummet forth mobs of boys curious and eager for any change mild or wild, so, as the church bells stopped up their silver and iron rain, pew-stiffened crowds became relaxed parade crowds as the carnival, a promotion of brass, a flush of velvet, all lion-pacing, mammoth-shuffling, flag-fluttered by.

The shadow of the Indian's wooden tomahawk lay on an iron grille imbedded in the sidewalk in front of the cigar store. Over this grille, with faint metallic reverberations, year after year, people passed, dropping tonnages of mint-gum wrapper, gold cigar band, matchstub, cigarette butt or copper penny which vanished below forever.

Now, with the parade, hundreds of feet rang and, clustered on the grille as the carnival strode by on stilts, roared by in tiger and volcano sounds and colors.

Under the grille, two shapes trembled.

Above, like a great baroque peacock striding the bricks and asphalt, the freaks' eyes opened out, to stare, to search office roofs, church spires, read dentists' and opticians' signs, check dime and dry goods stores as drums shocked plate glass windows and wax dummies quaked in facsimiles of fear. A multitude of hot and incredibly bright fierce eyes, the parade moved, desiring, but not quenching its desire.

For the things it most wanted were hidden in dark.

Jim and Will, under the cigar store sidewalk grille.

Crouch-pressed knee to knee, heads up, eyes alert, they

sucked their breaths like iron Popsicles. Above, women's dresses flowered in a cold breeze. Above, men tilted on the sky. The band, in a collision of cymbals, knocked children against their mothers' knees with concussion.

"There!" exclaimed Jim. "The parade! It's right out front the cigar store! What're we *doing* here, Will? Let's go!"

"No!" cried Will, hoarsely, clenching Jim's knee. "It's the most *obvious* place, in front of everybody! They'll never think to check here! Shut up!"

Thrrrummmmm . . .

The grille, above, rang with the touch of a man's shoe, and the worn nails in that shoe.

Dad! Will almost cried.

He rose, sank back, biting his lips.

Jim saw the man above wheel this way, wheel that, searching, so near, yet so far, three feet away.

I could just reach up . . . thought Will.

But Dad, pale, nervous, hurried on.

And Will felt his soul fall over cold and white-jelly quivering inside.

Bang!

The boys jerked.

A chewed lump of pink bubble gum, falling, had hit a pile of old paper near Jim's foot.

A five-year-old boy, above, crouched on the grille, peered down with dismay after his vanished sweet.

Get! thought Will.

The boy knelt, hands to the grille.

Go on! thought Will.

He had a crazy wish to grab the gum and stuff it back up into the little boy's mouth.

A parade-drum thumped one huge time, then—silence.

Jim and Will glanced at each other.

The parade, both thought, it's *halted*!

The small boy stuck one hand half through the grille.

Above, in the street, Mr. Dark, the Illustrated Man, glanced back over his river of freaks, cages, at the sunburst tubas and python brass horns. He nodded.

The parade fell apart.

The freaks hurried half to one sidewalk, half to the other,

mingling with the crowd, passing out handbills, eyes fire-crystal, quick, striking like snakes.

The small boy's shadow cooled Will's cheek.

The parade's over, he thought, now the search begins.

"Look, Ma!" The small boy pointed down through the grille. "*There!*"

Chapter Thirty-Five

IN NED'S Night Spot, half a block from the cigar store, Charles Halloway, exhausted from no sleep, too much thinking, far too much walking, finished his second coffee and was about to pay when the sharp silence from the street outside made him uneasy. He sensed rather than saw the mild intermingled disturbance as the parade melted among the sidewalk crowds. Not knowing why, Charles Halloway put his money away.

"Warm it up again, Ned?"

Ned was pouring coffee when the door swung wide, someone entered, and splayed his right hand lightly on the counter.

Charles Halloway stared.

The hand stared back at him.

There was a single eye tattooed on the back of each finger.

"Mom! Down there! Look!"

The boy cried, pointing through the grille.

More shadows passed and lingered.

Including—the Skeleton.

Tall as a dead tree in winter, all skull, all scarecrow-stilted bones, the thin man, the Skeleton, Mr. Skull played his xylophone shadow upon hidden things, cold paper rubbish, warm flinching boys, below.

Go! thought Will. Go!

The plump fingers of the child gesticulated through the grille.

Go.

Mr. Skull walked away.

Thank God, thought Will, then gasped, "Oh, *no*!"

For the Dwarf as suddenly appeared, waddling along, a fringe of bells on his dirty shirt jingling softly, his toad-shadow tucked under him, his eyes like broken splinters of brown marble now bright-on-the-surface mad, now deeply mournfully forever-lost-and-gone-buried-away mad, looking for something could not be found, a lost self somewhere, lost boys for an instant, then the lost self again, two parts of the little squashed man fought to jerk his flashing eyes here, there, around, up, down, one seeking the past, one the immediate present.

"Mama!" said the child.

The Dwarf stopped and looked at the boy no bigger than himself. Their eyes met.

Will flung himself back, tried to gum his body into the concrete. He felt Jim do the same, not moving but moving his mind, his soul, thrusting it into darkness to hide from the little drama above.

"Come on, Junior!" A woman's voice.

The boy was pulled up and away.

Too late.

For the Dwarf was looking down.

And in his eyes were the lost bits and fitful pieces of a man named Fury who had sold lightning rods how many days how many years ago in the long, the easy, the safe and wondrous time before this fright was born.

Oh, Mr. Fury, thought Will, what they've done to you. Threw you under a pile driver, squashed you in a steel press, squeezed the tears and screams out of you, trapped you in a jack-in-a-box all pressed down until there's nothing left of you, Mr. Fury . . . nothing left but this . . .

Dwarf. And the Dwarf's face was less human, more machine now; in fact, a camera.

The shuttering eyes flexed, sightless, opening upon darkness. Tick. Two lenses expanded—contracted with liquid swiftness: a picture-snap of the grille.

A snap, also, of what lay beneath?

Is he staring at the metal, thought Will, or the spaces between the metal?

For a long moment, the ruined-squashed clay doll Dwarf squatted while standing tall. His flash-camera eyes were bulbed wide, perhaps still taking pictures?

Will, Jim, were not seen really at all, only their shape, their color and size were borrowed by these dwarf camera eyes. They were clapped away in the box-Brownie skull. Later—how much later?—the picture would be developed by the wild, the tiny, the forgetful, the wandering and lost lightning-rod mind. What lay under the grille would then be really seen. And after that? Revelation! Revenge! Destruction!

Click-snap-tick.

Children ran laughing by.

The Dwarf-child, drawn by their running joy, was swept along with them. Madly, he skipped off, remembered himself, and went looking for something, he knew not what.

The cloudy sun poured light through all the sky.

The two boys, boxed in light-slotted pit, hisstled their breath softly out through gritted teeth.

Jim squeezed Will's hand, tight, tight.

Both waited for more eyes to stride along and rake the steel grille.

The blue-red-green tattooed eyes, all five of them, fell away from the counter top.

Charles Halloway, sipping his third coffee, turned slightly on the revolving stool.

The Illustrated Man was watching him.

Charles Halloway nodded.

The Illustrated Man did not nod or blink, but stared until the janitor wanted to turn away, but did not, and simply *gazed* as calmly as possible at the impertinent intruder.

"What'll it be?" asked the cafe proprietor.

"Nothing." Mr. Dark watched Will's father. "I'm looking for two boys."

Who *isn't*? Charles Halloway rose, paid, walked off. "Thanks, Ned." In passing, he saw the man with the tattoos hold his hands out, palms up toward Ned.

"Boys?" said Ned. "How old?"

The door slammed.

Mr. Dark watched Charles Halloway walk off outside the window.

Ned talked.

But the Illustrated Man did not hear.

Outside, Will's father moved toward the library, stopped, moved toward the courthouse, stopped, waited for some better sense to direct him, felt his pocket, missed his smokes, and turned toward the United Cigar Store.

Jim looked up, saw familiar feet, pale face, salt and pepper hair. "Will! Your dad! Call to him. He'll help us!"

Will could not speak.

"*I'll* call to him!"

Will hit Jim's arm, shook his head, violently, No!

Why not? mouthed Jim.

Because, said Will's lips.

Because . . . he gazed up . . . Dad looked even smaller up there than he had last night, seen from the side of the house. It would be like calling to one more boy passing. They didn't need one more boy, they needed a general, no, a major general! He tried to see Dad's face at the cigar counter window, and discover whether it looked really older, firmer, stronger, than it did last night washed with all the milk colors of the moon. But all he saw was Dad's fingers twitching nervously, his mouth working, as if he didn't dare ask his needs from Mr. Tetley. . . .

"One . . . that is . . . one twenty-five cent cigar."

"My God," said Mr. Tetley, above. "The man's rich!"

Charles Halloway took his time removing the cellophane, waiting for some hint, some move on the part of the universe to show him where he was going, why he had come back this way for a cigar he did not really want. He thought he heard himself called, twice, glanced swiftly at the crowds, saw clowns passing with handbills, then lit the cigar he did not want from the eternal blue-gas flame that burned in a small silver jet pipe on the counter, and, puffing smoke, dropped the cigar band with his free hand, saw the band bounce on the metal grille, and vanish, his eyes following it farther down to where . . .

It lit at the feet of Will Halloway, his son.

Charles Halloway choked on cigar smoke.

Two shadows there, yes! And the eyes, terror gazing up out of the dark well under the street. He almost bent to seize the grate, yelling.

Instead, incredulous, he only blurted softly, with the crowd around, and the weather clearing:

"Jim? Will! What the hell's going on?"

At which moment, one hundred feet away, the Illustrated Man came out of Ned's Night Spot.

"Mr. Halloway—" said Jim.

"Come up out of there," said Charles Halloway.

The Illustrated Man, a crowd among crowds, pivoted slowly, then walked toward the cigar store.

"Dad, we can't! Don't look at us down here!"

The Illustrated Man was some eighty feet away.

"Boys," said Charles Halloway. "The police—"

"Mr. Halloway," said Jim, hoarsely, "we're dead if you don't look up! The Illustrated Man, if he—"

"The *what*?" asked Mr. Halloway.

"The man with the tattoos!"

From the café counter, five electric blue-inked eyes fixed Mr. Halloway's memory.

"Dad, look over at the courthouse clock, while we tell you what happened—"

Mr. Halloway straightened up.

And the Illustrated Man arrived.

He stood studying Charles Halloway.

"Sir," said the Illustrated Man.

"Eleven-fifteen." Charles Halloway judged the courthouse clock, adjusted his wrist watch, cigar in mouth. "One minute slow."

"Sir," said the Illustrated Man.

Will held Jim, Jim held Will fast in the gum-wrapper, tobacco-littered pit, as the four shoes rocked, shuffled, tilted above.

"Sir," said the man named Dark, probing Charles Halloway's face for the bones there to compare to other bones in other half-similar people, "the Cooger-Dark Combined Shows have picked two local boys, two! to be our special guests during our celebratory visit!"

"Well, I—" Will's father tried not to glance at the sidewalk.

"These two boys—"

Will watched the tooth-sharp shoe nails of the Illustrated Man flash, sparking the grille.

"—these boys will ride all rides, see each show, shake hands with every performer, go home with magic kits, baseball bats—"

"Who," interrupted Mr. Halloway, "are these lucky boys?"

"Two selected from photos snapped on our midway yesterday. Identify them, sir, and you will share their fortune. *There* are the boys!"

He *sees* us down here! thought Will. Oh, God!

The Illustrated Man thrust out his hands.

Will's father lurched.

Tattooed in bright blue ink, Will's face gazed up at him from the palm of the right hand.

Ink-sewn to the left palm, Jim's face was indelible and natural as life.

"You know them?" The Illustrated Man saw Mr. Halloway's throat clench, his eyelids squinch, his bones struck vibrant as from a sledge-hammer blow. "Their names?"

Dad, careful! Will thought.

"I don't—" said Will's father.

"You know them."

The Illustrated Man's hands shook, held out to view, asking for the gift of names, making Jim's face on the flesh, Will's face on the flesh, Jim's face hidden beneath the street, Will's face hidden beneath the street, tremble, writhe, pinch.

"Sir, you wouldn't want them to lose out . . . ?"

"No, but—"

"But, but, but?" Mr. Dark loomed closer, magnificent in his picture-gallery flesh, his eyes, the eyes of all his beasts and hapless creatures cutting through his shirt, coat, trousers, fastening the old man tight, biting him with fire, fixing him with thousandfold attentions. Mr. Dark shoved his two palms near. "*But?*"

Mr. Halloway needing something to excruciate, bit his cigar. "I thought for a moment—"

"Thought what?" Grand delight from Mr. Dark.

"One of them looked like—"

"Like *who*?"

Too eager, thought Will. You see that, Dad, don't you?

"Mister," said Will's father. "Why are you so jumpy about two boys?"

"Jumpy . . . ?"

Mr. Dark's smile melted like cotton candy.

Jim scootched himself down into a dwarf, Will crammed himself down into a midget, both looking up, waiting.

"Sir," said Mr. Dark, "is my enthusiasm *that* to you? *Jumpy*?"

Will's father noted the muscles cord along the arms, roping and unroping themselves with a writhe like the puff adders and sidewinders doubtless inked and venomous there.

"One of those pictures," drawled Mr. Halloway, "looks like Milton Blumquist."

Mr. Dark clenched a fist.

A blinding ache struck Jim's head.

"The other," Will's father was almost bland, "looks like Avery Johnson."

Oh, Dad, thought Will, you're great!

The Illustrated Man clenched his other fist.

Will, his head in a vise, almost screamed.

"Both boys," finished Mr. Halloway, "moved to Milwaukee some weeks ago."

"You," said Mr. Dark, coldly, "lie."

Will's father was truly shocked.

"Me? And spoil the prizewinners' fun?"

"Fact is," said Mr. Dark, "we found the names of the boys ten minutes ago. Just want to double-check."

"So?" said Will's father, disbelieving.

"Jim," said Mr. Dark. "Will."

Jim writhed in the dark. Will sank his head deep in his shoulder blades, eyes tight.

Will's father's face was a pond into which the two dark stone names sank without a ripple.

"First names? Jim? Will? Lots of Jims and Wills, couple hundred, town like this."

Will, crouched and squirming, thought, who told? Miss Foley? But she was gone, her house empty and full of rain shadows. Only one other person . . .

The little girl who looked like Miss Foley weeping under the tree? The little girl who frightened us so bad? he wondered. In the last half hour the parade, going by, found her, and her crying for hours, afraid, and ready to do anything, say anything, if only with music, horses plunging, world racing, they would grow her old again, grow her around again, lift her, shut up her crying, stop up the awful thing and make her as she was. Did the carnival promise, lie to her, when they found her under the tree and ran her off? The little girl crying, but not telling all, because—

"Jim. Will," said Will's father. "First names. What about the last?"

Mr. Dark did not know the last names.

His universe of monsters sweated phosphorus on his hide,

soured his armpits, reeked, slammed between his iron-sinewed legs.

"Now," said Will's father, with a strange, and to him almost-delightful-because-new, calm, "I think you're lying. You don't know the last names. Now, why should you, a carnival stranger, lie to me here on a street in some town on the backside of nowhere?"

The Illustrated Man clenched his two calligraphic fists very hard.

Will's father, his face pale, considered these mean, constricted fingers, knuckles, digging nails, inside which two boys' faces, crushed hard in dark vise, tight, very tight in prison flesh, were kept in fury.

Two shadows, below, thrashed in agony.

The Illustrated Man erased his face to serenity.

But a bright drop fell from his right fist.

A bright drop fell from his left fist.

The drops vanished through the steel sidewalk grille.

Will gasped. Wetness had struck his face. He clapped his hand to it, then looked at his palm.

The wetness that had hit his cheek was bright red.

He glanced from it to Jim, who lay still now also, for the scarification, real or imagined, seemed over and both flicked their eyes up to where the Illustrated Man's shoes flint-sparked the grille, grinding steel on steel.

Will's father saw the blood ooze from the clenched fists, but forced himself to look only at the Illustrated Man's face, as he said:

"Sorry I can't be more help."

Beyond the Illustrated Man, rounding the corner, hands weaving the air, dressed in harlequin Gypsy colors, face waxen, eyes hid behind plum-dark glasses, the Fortune Teller, the Dust Witch came mumbling.

A moment later, looking up, Will saw her. Not dead! he thought. Carried off, bruised, fallen, yes, but now back, and mad! Lord, yes, mad, looking *especially* for *me*!

Will's father saw her. His blood slowed, by instinct alone, to a pudding in his chest.

The crowd opened happily, laughing and commenting on

her bright if tattered costume, trying to remember what she rhymed, so as to tell it later. She moved, fingers feeling the town as if it were an immensely complicated and lush tapestry. And she sang:

"Tell you your husbands. Tell you your wives. Tell you your fortunes. Tell you your lives. See me, I know. See me at the show. Tell you the color of his eyes. Tell you the color of her lies. Tell you the color of his goal. Tell you the color of her soul. Come now, don't go. See me, see me at the show."

Children appalled, children impressed, parents delighted, parents in high good humor, and still the Gypsy from the dusts of living sang. Time walked in her murmuring. She made and broke microscopic webs between her fingers wherewith to feel soot fly up, breath fly out. She touched the wings of flies, the souls of invisible bacteria, all specks, mites, and mica-snowings of sunlight filtrated with motion and much more hidden emotion.

Will and Jim cracked their bones, cowered down, hearing:

"Blind, yes, blind. But I see what I see, I see where I be," said the Witch, softly. "There's a man with a straw hat in autumn. Hello. And—why there's Mr. Dark, and . . . an old man . . . an *old* man."

He's not that old! cried Will to himself, blinking up at the three, as the Witch stopped, her shadow falling moist-frog cool on the hidden boys.

". . . old man . . ."

Mr. Halloway was jolted as by a series of cold knives thrust in his stomach.

". . . old man . . . old man . . ." said the Witch.

She stopped this. "Ah . . ." The hairs in her nostrils bristled. She gaped her mouth to savor air. "Ah . . ."

The Illustrated Man quickened.

"Wait . . . !" sighed the Gypsy.

Her fingernails scraped down an unseen blackboard of air.

Will felt himself yip, bark, whimper like an aggravated hound.

Slowly her fingers climbed down, feeling the spectrums, weighing the light. In another moment, a forefinger might thrust to the sidewalk grille, implying: there! there!

Dad! thought Will. *Do* something!

The Illustrated Man, gone sweetly patient now that his blind but immensely aware dust lady was here, watched her with love.

"Now . . ." The Witch's fingers itched.

"Now!" said Will's father, loud.

The Witch flinched.

"Now, *this* is a fine cigar!" yelled Will's father, turning with great pomp back to the counter.

"Quiet . . ." said the Illustrated Man.

The boys looked up.

"Now—" The Witch sniffed the wind.

"Got to light it again!" Mr. Halloway stuck the cigar in the eternal blue flame.

"Silence . . ." suggested Mr. Dark.

"Ever smoke, yourself?" asked Dad.

The Witch, from the concussion of his fiercely erupted and overly jovial words, dropped one wounded hand to her side, wiped sweat from it, as one wipes an antenna for better reception, and drifted it up again, her nostrils flared with wind.

"Ah!" Will's father blew a dense cloud of cigar smoke. It made a fine thick cumulus surrounding the woman.

"Gah!" she choked.

"Fool!" The Illustrated Man barked, but whether at man or woman, the boys below could not tell.

"Here, let's buy you one!" Mr. Halloway blew more smoke, handing Mr. Dark a cigar.

The Witch exploded a sneeze, recoiled, staggered away. The Illustrated Man snatched Dad's arm, saw that he had gone too far, let go, and could only follow his Gypsy woman off, in some clumsy and totally unexpected defeat. But then, in going, he heard Will's father say, "A *fine* day to you, sir!"

No, Dad! thought Will.

The Illustrated Man came back.

"Your name, sir?" he asked, directly.

Don't tell him! thought Will.

Will's father debated a moment, took the cigar from his mouth, tapped ash and said, quietly:

"Halloway. Work in the library. Drop by some time."

"You can be sure, Mr. Halloway. I will."

The Witch was waiting near the corner.

Mr. Halloway whetted his forefinger, tested the wind, and sent a cumulus her way.

She flailed back, gone.

The Illustrated Man went rigid, spun about, and strode off, the ink portraits of Jim and Will crushed hard iron tight in his fists.

Silence.

It was so quiet under the grille, Mr. Halloway thought the two boys had died of fright.

And Will, below, gazing up, eyes wet, mouth wide, thought, Oh my gosh, why didn't I see it before?

Dad's tall. Dad's very tall indeed.

Still Charles Halloway did not look down at the grille but only at the small comets of splashed red color left on the sidewalk, trailed around the corner, dropped from the clenched hands of the vanished Mr. Dark. He was also gazing with surprise at himself, accepting the surprise, the new purpose, which was half despair, half serenity, now that the incredible deed was done. Let no one ask why he had given his true name; even he could not assay and give its real weight. Now he could only read the numerals on the courthouse clock and speak to it, while the boys below, listened.

"Oh, Jim, Will, something *is* going on. Can you hide, keep out from under, the rest of the day? We got to have time. With things like this, where do you begin? No law's been broken, none on the books, anyway. But I feel dead and buried a month. My flesh ripples. Hide, Jim, Will, hide. I'll tell your mothers you've got jobs at the carnival, good excuse for you not coming home. Stay hid until dark, then come to the library at seven. Meantime, I'll check police records on carnivals, newspaper files at the library, books, old folios, everything that might fit. God willing, by the time you show up, after dark, I'll have a plan. Walk easy until then. Bless you, Jim. Bless you, Will."

The small father who was very tall now walked slowly away.

His cigar, unnoticed, fell from his hand, dropped in a spark shower through the grate.

It lay in the square pit glowing its single fiery pink eye at Jim and Will, who looked back and at last snatched to blind and put it out.

Chapter Thirty-Six

THE DWARF, bearing his demented and wildly lighted eyes, made his way south on Main Street.

Stopping suddenly, he developed a film strip in his head, scanned it, bleated, and blundered back through the forest of legs to reach for and pull the Illustrated Man down where a whisper was as good as a shout. Mr. Dark listened, then fled, leaving the Dwarf far behind.

Reaching the cigar store Indian, the Illustrated Man sank to his knees. Clutching the steel lattice-grille, he peered down in the pit.

Below lay yellow newspapers, wilted candy wrappers, burnt cigars, and gum.

Mr. Dark's cry was muffled fury.

"*Lose* something?"

Mr. Tetley blinked over his counter.

The Illustrated Man clenched the grate, nodding once.

"I clean under the grate once a month for the money," said Mr. Tetley. "How much you lose? Dime? Quarter? Half dollar?"

Bing!

The Illustrated Man glared up.

In the cash-register window a small fire-red sign jumped high:

NO SALE.

Chapter Thirty-Seven

THE TOWN clock struck seven.

The echoes of the great chime wandered in the unlit halls of the library.

An autumn leaf, very crisp, fell somewhere in the dark.

But it was only the page of a book, turning.

Off in one of the catacombs, bent to a table under a grass-green-shaded lamp, lips pursed, eyes narrowed, sat Charles Halloway, his hands trembling the pages, lifting, rearranging the books. Now and then he hurried off to peer into the autumn night, watchful of the streets. Then again he came back to paper-clip pages, to insert papers, to scribble out quotations, whispering to himself. His voice brought forth quick echoes from the library vaults:

"Look here!"

". . . here . . . !" said the night passages.

"This picture . . . !"

". . . picture . . . !" said the halls.

"And *this*!"

". . . this . . ." The dust settled.

It had been the longest day of all the days he could remember in his life. He had mingled with strange and not-so-strange crowds, he had searched after the searchers, in the wake of the wide-scattering parade. He had resisted telling Jim's mother, Will's mother, more than they needed to know for a happy Sunday, and meantime crossed shadows with Dwarf, traded nods with Pinhead and Fire-eater, kept free of shadowed alleys, and controlled his panic when, doubling back, he saw the basement pit empty under the cigar store grille and knew that the boys were at hide-and-seek somewhere nearby or somewhere, praise God, very far away.

Then, in the crowds, he moved to the carnival ground, stayed out of tents, stayed free of rides, observed, watched the sun go down, and just at twilight, surveyed the cold glass waters of the Mirror Maze and saw just enough on the shore to pull him back before he drowned. Wet all over, cold to the bone, before night caught him he let the crowd protect, warm, and bear him away up into town, to the library, and to most important books . . . which he arranged in a great literary clock on a table, like someone learning to tell a new time. So he paced round and round the huge clock squinting at the yellowed pages as if they were mothwings pinned dead to the wood.

Here lay a portrait of the Prince of Darkness. Next a series of fantastic sketches of the Temptations of St. Anthony. Next some etchings from the *Bizarie* by Giovanbatista Bracelli, depicting a set of curious toys, humanlike robots engaged in various alchemical rites. At five minutes to twelve stood a copy of *Dr. Faustus*, at two lay an *Occult Iconography*; at six, under Mr. Halloway's trailed fingers now, a history of circuses, carnivals, shadow shows, puppet menageries inhabited by mountebanks, minstrels, stilt-walking sorcerers and their fantoccini. More: *A Manual of the Air Kingdoms* (Things That Fly Down History). At nine sharp: *By Demons Possessed*, lying atop *Egyptian Philtres*, lying atop the *Torments of the Damned*, which in turn crushed flat *The Spell of Mirrors.* Very late up the literary clock one named *Locomotives and Trains, The Mystery of Sleep, Between Midnight and Dawn, The Witches' Sabbath*, and *Pacts With Demons.* It was all laid out. He could see the face.

But there were no hands on this clock.

He could not tell what hour of the night of life it was for himself, the boys, or the unknowing town.

For, in sum, what had he to go by?

A three-o'clock-in-the-morning arrival, a grotesque looking-glass maze, a Sunday parade, a tall man with a swarm of electric-blue pictures itching on his sweaty hide, a few drops of blood falling down through a pavement grille, two frightened boys staring up out of the earth, and himself, alone in mausoleum quiet, nudging the puzzle together.

What was there about the boys that made him believe the simplest word they whispered up through the grille? Fear itself was proof here, and he had seen enough fear in his life to know it, like the smell from a butcher's shop in summer twilight.

What was there about the illustrated carnival owner's silences that spoke thousands of violent, corrupt, and crippling words?

What was there in that old man he had seen through a tent

flap late this afternoon, seated in a chair with the words MR. ELECTRICO bannered over him, power webbing and crawling on his flesh like green lizards?

All, all, all of it. And now, these books. This. He touched *Physiognomonie. The secrets of the individual's character as found in his face.*

Were Jim and Will, then, featured all angelic, pure, half-innocent, peering up through the sidewalk at marching terror? Did the boys represent the ideal for your Woman, Man, or Child of Excellent Bearing, Color, Balance, and Summer Disposition?

Conversely . . . Charles Halloway turned a page . . . did the scurrying freaks, the Illustrated Marvel, bear the foreheads of the Irascible, the Cruel, the Covetous, the mouths of the Lewd and Untruthful? the teeth of the Crafty, the Unstable, the Audacious, the Vainglorious, and your Murderous Beast?

No. The book slipped shut. If faces were judged, the freaks were no worse than many he'd seen slipping from the library late nights in his long career.

There was only one thing sure.

Two lines of Shakespeare said it. He should write them in the middle of the clock of books, to fix the heart of his apprehension:

By the pricking of my thumbs,
Something wicked this way comes.

So vague, yet so immense.

He did not want to live with it.

Yet he knew that, during this night, unless he lived with it very well, he might have to live with it all the rest of his life.

At the window he looked out and thought, Jim, Will, are you coming? will you *get* here?

Waiting, his flesh took paleness from his bones.

Chapter Thirty-Eight

THE LIBRARY, then, at seven-fifteen, seven-thirty, seven-forty-five of a Sunday night, cloistered with great drifts of silence and transfixed avalanche of books poised like the cuneiform stones of eternity on shelves, so high the unseen snows of time fell all year there.

Outside, the town breathed back and forth to the carnival, hundreds of people passing near where Jim and Will lay strewn in bushes to one side of the library, now ducking up, now ducking down to nose raw earth.

"Cheezit!"

Both smothered in grass. Across the street there passed what could have been a boy, could have been a dwarf, could have been a boy-with-dwarf-mind, could have been anything blown along like the scuttle-crab leaves on the frost-mica sidewalks. But then whatever it was went away; Jim sat up, Will still lay face buried in good safe dirt.

"Come on, what's wrong?"

"The library," said Will. "I'm even afraid of *it*, now." All the books, he thought, perched there, hundreds of years old, peeling skin, leaning on each other like ten million vultures. Walk along the dark stacks and all the gold titles shine their eyes at you. Between old carnival, old library and his own father, everything old . . . well . . .

"I know Dad's in there, but *is* it Dad? I mean, what if *they* came, changed him, made him bad, promised him something they can't give but he thinks they can, and we go in there and some day fifty years from now someone opens a book in there and you and me drop out, like two dry moth wings on the floor, Jim, someone pressed and hid us between pages, and no one ever guessed where we went—"

This was too much for Jim, who had to do something to flog his spirits. Next thing Will knew, Jim was hammering on the library door. Both hammered, frantic to jump from this night to that warmer book-breathing night inside. Given a choice of darknesses, this one was the better: the oven smell of books, as the door opened and Dad stood with his ghost-colored hair. They tiptoed back through the deserted corridors, Will feeling a crazy urge to whistle as he often did past the graveyard at sundown, Dad asking what made them late, and they trying to remember all the places they hid in one day.

They had hid in old garages, they had hid in old barns, they had hid in the highest trees they could climb and got bored and boredom was worse than fear so they came down and reported in to the Police Chief and had a fine chat which gave them twenty safe minutes right in the station and Will got the idea of touring churches and they climbed all the steeples in town and scared pigeons off the belfries and whether or not it was safer in churches and especially up with the bells or not, no one could claim, but it *felt* safe. But there again they began to get starchy with boredom and fatigued with sameness, and were almost on the point of giving themselves up to the carnival in order to have something to do, when quite fortunately the sun went down. From sundown to now it had taken a wonderful time, creeping upon the library, as if it were a once friendly fort that might now be manned by Arabs.

"So here we are," whispered Jim, and stopped.

"Why am I whispering? It's after hours. Heck!"

He laughed, then stopped.

For he thought he heard a soft tread off in the subterranean vaults.

But it was only his laughter walking back through the deep stacks on panther feet.

So when they talked again, it was still in whispers. Deep forests, dark caves, dim churches, half-lit libraries were all the same, they tuned you down, they dampened your ardor, they brought you to murmurs and soft cries for fear of raising up phantom twins of your voice which might haunt corridors long after your passage.

They reached the small room and circled the table on which Charles Halloway had laid out the books, where he had read many hours, and for the first time looked in each other's faces and saw a dreadful paleness, so did not comment.

"From the beginning." Will's father pulled out chairs. "Please."

So, each taking his part, in their own good time, the boys

told of the wandering-by lightning-rod salesman, the predictions of storms to come, the long-after-midnight train, the suddenly inhabited meadow, the moonblown tents, the untouched but full-wept calliope, then the light of noon showering over an ordinary midway with hundreds of Christians wandering through but no lions for them to be tossed to, only the maze where time lost itself backward and forward in waterfall mirrors, only the OUT OF ORDER carousel, the dead supper hour, Mr. Cooger, and the boy with the eyes that had seen all the glistery tripes of the world shaped like hung-and-dripping sins and all the sins tenterhooked and running red and verminous, this boy with the eyes of a man who has lived forever, seen too much, might like to die but doesn't know how. . . .

The boys stopped for breath.

Miss Foley, the carnival again, the carousel run wild, the ancient Cooger mummy gasping moonlight, exhaling silver dust, dead, then resurrected in a chair where green lightning struck his skeleton alight, all of it a storm minus rain, minus thunder, the parade, the cigar store basement, the hiding, and at last them here, finished, done with the telling.

For a long moment, Will's father sat staring blindly into the center of the table. Then, his lips moved.

"Jim. Will," he said. "I believe."

The boys sank in their chairs.

"All of it?"

"All."

Will wiped his eyes. "Boy," he said gruffly. "I'm going to start bawling."

"We got no time for that!" said Jim.

"No time." And Will's father stood up, stuffed his pipe with tobacco, rummaged his pockets for matches, brought out a battered harmonica, a penknife, a cigarette lighter that wouldn't work, and a memo pad he had always meant to write great thoughts down on but never got around to, and lined up these weapons for a pygmy war that could be lost before it even started. Probing this idle refuse, shaking his head, he finally found a tattered matchbox, lit his pipe and began to muse, pacing the room.

"Looks like we're going to do a lot of talking about one particular carnival. Where's it come from, where's it going, what's it up to? We thought it never hit town before. Yet, by God, look here."

He tapped a yellowed newspaper ad dated October 12, 1888, and ran his fingernail along under this:

J. C. COOGER AND G. M. DARK PRESENT THE PANDEMONIUM THEATER CO. COMBINED SIDE SHOWS AND UNNATURAL MUSEUMS, INTERNATIONAL!

"J.C. G.M." said Jim. "Those are the same initials as on the throwaways around town this week. But—it couldn't be the *same* men. . . ."

"No?" Will's father rubbed his elbows. "My goose pimples run counter to that."

He laid forth other old newspapers.

"1860. 1846. Same ad. Same names. Same initials. Dark and Cooger, Cooger and Dark, they came and went, but only once every twenty, thirty, forty years, so people forgot. Where were they all the other years? Traveling. And *more* than traveling. Always in October: October 1846, October 1860, October 1888, October 1910, and October now, tonight." His voice trailed off. ". . . Beware the autumn people. . . ."

"What?"

"An old religious tract. Pastor Newgate Phillips, I think. Read it as a boy. How does it go again?"

He tried to remember. He licked his lips. He did remember.

"'For some, autumn comes early, stays late through life where October follows September and November touches October and then instead of December and Christ's birth, there is no Bethlehem Star, no rejoicing, but September comes again and old October and so on down the years, with no winter, spring, or revivifying summer. For these beings, fall is the ever normal season, the only weather, there be no choice beyond. Where do they come from? The dust. Where do they go? The grave. Does blood stir their veins? No: the night wind. What ticks in their head? The worm. What speaks from their mouth? The toad. What sees from their eye? The snake. What hears with their ear? The abyss between the stars. They sift the human storm for souls, eat flesh of reason, fill tombs with sinners. They frenzy forth. In gusts they beetle-scurry, creep, thread, filter, motion, make all moons sullen, and surely cloud all clear-run waters.

The spider-web hears them, trembles—breaks. Such are the autumn people. Beware of them.'"

After a pause, both boys exhaled at once.

"The autumn people," said Jim. "That's them. *Sure!*"

"Then—" Will swallowed—"does that make us . . . *summer* people?"

"Not quite." Charles Halloway shook his head. "Oh, you're nearer summer than me. If I was ever a rare fine summer person, that's long ago. Most of us are half-and-half. The August noon in us works to stave off the November chills. We survive by what little Fourth of July wits we've stashed away. But there are times when we're all autumn people."

"Not you, Dad!"

"Not *you*, Mr. Halloway!"

He turned quickly to see both appraising him, paleness next to paleness, hands on knees as if to bolt.

"It's a way of speaking. Easy, boys. I'm after the facts. Will, do you really *know* your Dad? Shouldn't you know me, and me you, if it's going to be us'ns against them'ns?"

"Hey, yeah," breathed Jim. "Who *are* you?"

"We *know* who he is, darn it!" Will protested.

"Do *we*?" said Will's father. "Let's see. Charles William Halloway. Nothing extraordinary about me except I'm fifty-four, which is always extraordinary to the man inside it. Born in Sweet Water, lived in Chicago, survived in New York, brooded in Detroit, floundered in lots of places, arrived here late, after living in libraries around the country all those years because I liked being alone, liked matching up in books what I'd seen on the roads. Then in the middle of all the running-away, which I called travel, in my thirty-ninth year, your mother fixed me with one glance, been here ever since. Still most comfortable in the library nights, in out of the rain of people. Is this my last stop? Chances are. Why am I here at all? Right now, it seems, to help you."

He paused and looked at the two boys and their fine young faces.

"Yes," he said. "Very late in the game. To help you."

Chapter Thirty-Nine

EVERY NIGHT-BLIND library window chattered with cold. The man, the two boys, waited for the wind to pass away.

Then Will said: "Dad. You've always helped."

"Thanks, but it's not true." Charles Halloway examined one very empty hand. "I'm a fool. Always looking over your shoulder to see what's coming instead of right at you to see what's *here*. But then, for what salve it gives me, every man's a fool. Which means you got to pitch in all your life, bail out, board over, tie rope, patch plaster, pat cheeks, kiss brows, laugh, cry, make do, against the day you're the worst fool of all and shout 'Help!' Then all you need is one person's answer. I see it so clear, across the country tonight lie cities, towns and mere jerkwater stops of fools. So the carnival steams by, shakes *any* tree: it rains jackasses. Separate jackasses, I should say, individuals with no one, they think, or no one actual, to answer their 'Help!' Unconnected fools, that's the harvest the carnival comes smiling after with its threshing machine."

"Oh gosh," said Will. "It's hopeless!"

"No. The very fact we're here worrying about the difference between summer and autumn, makes me sure there's a way out. You don't have to *stay* foolish and you don't *have* to be wrong, evil, sinful, whatever you want to call it. There's more than three or four choices. *They*, that Dark fellow and his friends don't hold all the cards, I could tell that today, at the cigar store. I'm afraid of him but, I could see, he was afraid of me. So there's fear on both sides. Now *how* can we use it to advantage?"

"How?"

"First things first. Let's bone up on history. If men had wanted to stay bad forever, they could have, agreed? Agreed. *Did* we stay out in the fields with the beasts? No. In the water with the barracuda? No. Somewhere we let go of the hot gorilla's paw. Somewhere we turned in our carnivore's teeth and started chewing blades of grass. We been working mulch as much as blood, into our philosophy, for quite a few lifetimes. Since then we measure ourselves up the scale from apes, but not half so high as angels. It was a nice new idea and we were afraid we'd lose it, so we put it on paper and built buildings like this one around it. And we been going in and out of these buildings chewing it over, that one new sweet blade of grass, trying to figure how it all started, when we made the move, when we decided to be different. I suppose one night hundreds of thousands of years ago in a cave by a night fire when one of those shaggy men wakened to gaze over the banked coals at his woman, his children, and thought of their being cold, dead, gone forever. Then he must have wept. And he put out his hand in the night to the woman who must die some day and to the children who must follow her. And for a little bit next morning, he treated them somewhat better, for he saw that they, like himself, had the seed of night in them. He felt that seed like slime in his pulse, splitting, making more against the day they would multiply his body into darkness. So that man, the first one, knew what we know now: our hour is short, eternity is long. With this knowledge came pity and mercy, so we spared others for the later, more intricate, more mysterious benefits of love.

"So, in sum, what are we? We are the creatures that know and know too much. That leaves us with such a burden again we have a choice, to laugh or cry. No other animal does either. We do both, depending on the season and the need. Somehow, I feel the carnival watches, to see which we're doing and how and why, and moves in on us when it feels we're ripe."

Charles Halloway stopped, for the boys were watching him so intently he suddenly had to turn, flushing, away.

"Boy, Mr. Halloway," cried Jim, softly. "That's great. Go on!"

"Dad," said Will, amazed. "I never knew you could *talk*."

"You should hear me here late nights, nothing *but* talk!" Charles Halloway shook his head. "Yes, you should've heard. I should've said more to you any day you name in the past. Hell. Where *was* I? Leading up to love, I think. Yes . . . love."

Will looked bored, Jim looked wary of the word.

And these looks gave Charles Halloway pause.

What could he say that might make sense to them? Could he say love was, above all, common cause, shared experience? That *was* the vital cement, wasn't it? Could he say how he felt about their all being here tonight on this wild world running around a big sun which fell through a bigger space falling through yet vaster immensities of space, maybe toward and maybe away from Something? Could he say: we share this billion-mile-an-hour ride. We have common cause against the night. You start with little common causes. Why love the boy in a March field with his kite braving the sky? Because our fingers burn with the hot string singeing our hands. Why love some girl viewed from a train, bent to a country well? The tongue remembers iron water cool on some long lost noon. Why weep at strangers dead by the road? They resemble friends unseen in forty years. Why laugh when clowns are hit by pies? We taste custard, we taste life. Why love the woman who is your wife? Her nose breathes in the air of a world that I know; therefore I love that nose. Her ears hear music I might sing half the night through; therefore I love her ears. Her eyes delight in seasons of the land; and so I love those eyes. Her tongue knows quince, peach, chokeberry, mint and lime; I love to hear it speaking. Because her flesh knows heat, cold, affliction, I know fire, snow, and pain. Shared and once again shared experience. Billions of prickling textures. Cut one sense away, cut part of life away. Cut two senses; life halves itself on the instant. We love what we know, we love what we are. Common cause, common cause, common cause of mouth, eye, ear, tongue, hand, nose, flesh, heart, and soul.

But . . . how to say it?

"Look," he tried, "put two men in a rail car, one a soldier, the other a farmer. One talks war, the other wheat; and bore each other to sleep. But let one spell long-distance running, and if the other once ran the mile, why, those men will run all night, like boys, sparking a friendship up from memory. So, all men have *one* business in common: women, and can talk that till sunrise and beyond. Hell."

Charles Halloway stopped, flushed, self-conscious again, knowing vaguely there was a target up ahead but not quite how to get there. He chewed his lips.

Dad, don't stop, thought Will. When you talk, it's swell in here. You'll save us. Go on.

The man read his son's eyes, saw the same look in Jim, and walked slowly around the table, touching a night beast here, a clutch of ragged crones there, a star, a crescent moon, an antique sun, an hourglass that told time with bone dust instead of sand.

"Have I said anything I started out to say about being good? God, I don't know. A stranger is shot in the street, you hardly move to help. But if, half an hour before, you spent just ten minutes with the fellow and knew a little about him and his family, you might just jump in front of his killer and try to stop it. Really knowing is good. Not knowing, or refusing to know, is bad, or amoral, at least. You can't act if you don't know. Acting without knowing takes you right off the cliff. God, God, you must think I'm crazy, this talk. Probably think we should be out duck-shooting, elephant-gunning balloons, like you did, Will, but we got to know all there is to know about those freaks and that man heading them up. We can't be good unless we know what bad is, and it's a shame we're working against time. Show'll close and the crowds go home early on a Sunday night. I feel we'll have a visit from the autumn people, then. That gives us maybe two hours."

Jim was at the window now, looking out across the town to the far black tents and the calliope that played by the turning of the world in the night.

"*Is* it bad?" he asked.

"Bad?" cried Will, angrily. "Bad! You ask that!?"

"Calmly," said Will's father. "A good question. Part of that show looks just great. But the old saying really applies: you can't get something for nothing. Fact is, from them, you get nothing for something. They make you empty promises, you stick out your neck and—wham!"

"Where'd they come from?" asked Jim. "Who are they?"

Will went to the window with his father and they both looked out and Charles Halloway said, to those far tents:

"Maybe once it was just one man walking across Europe, jingling his ankle bells, a lute on his shoulder making a hunchbacked shadow, before Columbus. Maybe a man walked around in a monkey skin a million years ago, stuffing himself with other people's unhappiness, chewed their pain all day like spearmint gum, for the sweet savor, and trotted faster, revivified by personal disaster. Maybe his son after him refined his father's deadfalls, mantraps, bone-crunchers, head-achers, flesh-twitchers, soul-skinners. These laid the scum on lonely ponds from which came vinegar gnats to snuff up noses, mosquitoes to ride summer-night flesh and sting forth those bumps that carnival phrenologists dearly love to fondle and prophesy upon. So from one man here, one man there, walking as swift as his oily glances, it became scuttles of dogmen begging gifts of trouble, pandering misery, seeking under carpets for centipede treads, watchful of night sweats, harkening by all bedroom doors to hear men twist basting themselves with remorse and warm-water dreams.

"The stuff of nightmare is their plain bread. They butter it with pain. They set their clocks by death-watch beetles, and thrive the centuries. They were the men with the leather-ribbon whips who sweated up the Pyramids seasoning it with other people's salt and other people's cracked hearts. They coursed Europe on the White Horses of the Plague. They whispered to Caesar that he was mortal, then sold daggers at half-price in the grand March sale. Some must have been lazing clowns, foot props for emperors, princes, and epileptic popes. Then out on the road, Gypsies in time, their populations grew as the world grew, spread, and there was more delicious variety of pain to thrive on. The train put wheels under them and here they run down the long road out of the Gothic and baroque; look at their wagons and coaches, the carving like medieval shrines, all of it stuff once drawn by horses, mules, or, maybe, men."

"All those years." Jim's voice swallowed itself. "The *same* people? You think Mr. Cooger, Mr. Dark are both a couple hundred years old?"

"Riding that merry-go-round they can shave off a year or two, any time they want, right?"

"Why, then—" The abyss opened at Will's feet—"they could live *forever*!"

"And *hurt* people." Jim turned it over, again and again. "But why, why all the hurt?"

"Because," said Mr. Halloway. "You need fuel, gas, something to run a carnival on, don't you? Women live off gossip, and what's gossip but a swap of headaches, sour spit, arthritic bones, ruptured and mended flesh, indiscretions, storms of madness, calms after the storms? If some people didn't have something juicy to chew on, their choppers would prolapse, their souls with them. Multiply *their* pleasure at funerals, their chuckling through breakfast obituaries, add all the cat-fight marriages where folks spend careers ripping skin off each other and patching it back upside around, add quack doctors slicing persons to read their guts like tea leaves, then sewing them tight with fingerprinted thread, square the whole dynamite factory by ten quadrillion, and you got the black candlepower of this one carnival.

"All the meannesses we harbor, they borrow in redoubled spades. They're a billion times itchier for pain, sorrow, and sickness than the average man. We salt our lives with other people's sins. Our flesh to us tastes sweet. But the carnival doesn't care if it stinks by moonlight instead of sun, so long as it gorges on fear and pain. That's the fuel, the vapor that spins the carousel, the raw stuffs of terror, the excruciating agony of guilt, the scream from real or imagined wounds. The carnival sucks that gas, ignites it, and chugs along its way."

Charles Halloway took a breath, shut his eyes, and said:

"How do I know this? I don't! I *feel* it. I *taste* it. It was like old leaves burning on the wind two nights ago. It was a smell like mortuary flowers. I hear that music. I hear what you tell me, and half what you *don't* tell me. Maybe I've *always* dreamt about such carnivals, and was just waiting for it to come so's to see it once, and nod. Now, that tent show plays my bones like a marimba.

"My skeleton *knows.*

"*It* tells me.

"*I* tell you."

Chapter Forty

"CAN THEY . . ." said Jim. "I mean . . . do they . . . buy souls?"

"Buy, when they can get them free?" said Mr. Halloway. "Why, most men jump at the chance to give up everything for nothing. There's nothing we're so slapstick with as our own immortal souls. Besides, you're inferring that's the Devil out there. I only say it's a type of creature has learned to live off souls, not the souls themselves. That always worried me in the old myths. I asked myself, why would Mephistopheles want a soul? What does he *do* with it when he gets it, of what use is it? Stand back while I throw my own theory over the plate. Those creatures want the flaming gas off souls who can't sleep nights, that fever by day from old crimes. A dead soul is no kindling. But a live and raving soul, crisped with self-damnation, oh that's a pretty snoutful for such as them.

"How do I know this? I observe. The carnival is like people, only more so. A man, a woman, rather than walk away from, or kill, each other, ride each other a lifetime, pulling hair, extracting fingernails, the pain of each to the other like a narcotic that makes existence worth the day. So the carnival feels ulcerated egos miles off and lopes to toast its hands at that ache. It smells boys ulcerating to be men, paining like great unwise wisdom teeth, twenty thousand miles away, summer abed in winter's night. It feels the aggravation of middle-aged men like myself, who gibber after long-lost August afternoons to no avail. Need, want, desire, we burn those in our fluids, oxidize those in our souls, which jet streams out lips, nostrils, eyes, ears, broadcasts from antennae-fingers, long or short wave, God only knows, but the freak-masters perceive Itches and come crab-clustering to Scratch. It's traveled a long way on an easy map, with people handy by every crossroad to lend it lustful pints of agony to power it on. So maybe the carnival survives, living off the poison of the sins we do each other, and the ferment of our most terrible regrets."

Charles Halloway snorted.

"Good grief, how much have I said out loud, how much to myself, the last ten minutes?"

"You," said Jim, "talk a lot."

"In what language, dammit!?" cried Charles Halloway, for suddenly it seemed he had done no more than other nights walking exquisitely alone, deliciously propounding his ideas to halls which echoed them once, then made them vanish forever. He had written books a lifetime, on the airs of vast rooms in vast buildings, and had it all fly out the vents. Now it all seemed fireworks, done for color, sound, the high architecture of words, to dazzle the boys, powder his ego, but with no mark left on retina or mind after the color and sound faded; a mere exercise in self-declamation. Sheepishly he accosted himself.

"How much of all this got through? One sentence out in five, two out of eight?"

"Three in a thousand," said Will.

Charles Halloway could not but laugh and sigh in one.

Then Jim cut across with:

"Is . . . is it . . . Death?"

"The carnival?" The old man lit his pipe, blew smoke, seriously studied the patterns. "No. But I think it uses Death as a threat. Death doesn't exist. It never did, it never will. But we've drawn so many pictures of it, so many years, trying to pin it down, comprehend it, we've got to thinking of it as an entity, strangely alive and greedy. All it is, however, is a stopped watch, a loss, an end, a darkness. Nothing. And the carnival wisely knows we're more afraid of Nothing than we are of Something. You can fight Something. But . . . Nothing? Where do you hit it? Has it a heart, soul, butt-behind, brain? No, no. So the carnival just shakes a great croupier's cupful of Nothing at us, and reaps us as we tumble back head-over-heels in fright. Oh, it shows us Something that might eventually lead to Nothing, all right. That flourish of mirrors out there in the meadow, that's a raw Something, for sure. Enough to knock your soul sidewise in the saddle. It's a hit below the belt to see yourself ninety years gone, the vapors of eternity rising from you like breath off dry ice. Then, when it's frozen you stiff, it plays that fine sweet soul-searching music that smells of fresh-washed frocks of women dancing on back-yard lines in May, that sounds like haystacks trampled into wine, all that blue sky and summer night-on-the-lake kind of tune until your head bangs with the drums that look like full moons beating around the calliope. Simplicity. Lord, I do admire their direct approach. Hit an old man with mirrors, watch his pieces fall in jigsaws of ice only the carnival can put together again. How? Waltz around back on the carousel to 'Beautiful Ohio' or 'Merry Widow.' But they're careful not to tell one thing to people who go riding to its music."

"What?" asked Jim.

"Why, that if you're a miserable sinner in one shape, you're a miserable sinner in another. Changing size doesn't change the brain. If I made you twenty-five tomorrow, Jim, your thoughts would still be boy thoughts, and it'd show! Or if they turned *me* into a boy of ten this instant, my brain would still be fifty and that boy would act funnier and older and weirder than any boy ever. Then, too, time's out of joint another way."

"Which way?" asked Will.

"If I became young again, all my friends would still be fifty, sixty, wouldn't they? I'd be cut off from them, forever, for I couldn't tell them what I'd up and done, could I? They'd resent it. They'd hate me. Their interests would no longer be mine, would they? Especially their worries. Sickness and death for them, new life for me. So where's the place in this world for a man who looks twenty but who is older than Methuselah, what man could stand the shock of a change like that? Carnival won't warn you it's equal to postoperative shock, but, by God, I bet it is, and more!

"So, what happens? You get your reward: madness. Change of body, change of personal environment, for one thing. Guilt, for another, guilt at leaving your wife, husband, friends to die the way all men die—Lord, that alone would give a man fits. So more fear, more agony for the carnival to breakfast on. So with the green vapors coming off your stricken conscience you say you want to go back the way you were! The carnival nods and listens. Yes, they promise, if you behave as they say, in a short while they'll give you back your twoscore and ten or whatever. On the promise alone of being returned to normal old age, that train travels with the world, its side show populated with madmen waiting to be released from bondage, meantime servicing the carnival, giving it coke for its ovens."

Will murmured something.

"What?"

"Miss Foley," mourned Will. "Oh, poor Miss Foley, they got her now, just like you say. Once she got what she wanted it scared her, she didn't like it, oh, she was crying so hard, Dad, so hard; now I bet they promise her someday she can be fifty again if she'll mind. I wonder what they're doing with her, right now, oh, Dad, oh, Jim!"

"God help her." Will's father put a heavy hand out to trace the old carnival portraits. "They've probably thrown her in with the freaks. And what are they? Sinners who've traveled so long, hoping for deliverance, they've taken on the shape of their original sins? The Fat Man, what was he once? If I can guess the carnival's sense of irony, the way they like to weight the scales, he was once a ravener after all kinds and varieties of lust. No matter, there he lives now, anyway, collected up in his bursting skin. The Thin Man, Skeleton, or whatever, did he starve his wife's, children's spiritual as well as physical hungers? The Dwarf? Was he or was he not your friend, the lightning-rod salesman, always on the road, never settling, ever-moving, facing no encounters, running ahead of the lightning and selling rods, yes, but leaving others to face the storm, so maybe, through accident, or design, when he fell in with the free rides, he shrank not to a boy but a mean ball of grotesque tripes, all self-involved. The fortune-telling Gypsy Dust Witch? Maybe someone who lived always tomorrow and let today slide, like myself, and so wound up penalized, having to guess other people's wild sunrises and sad sunsets. You tell me, you've seen her *near*. The Pinhead? The Sheep Boy? The Fire Eater? The Siamese Twins, good God, what were they? twins all bound up in tandem narcissism? We'll never know. They'll never tell. We've guessed, and probably guessed wrong, on ten dozen things the last half hour. Now—some plan. Where do we go from here?"

Charles Halloway placed forth a map of the town and drew in the location of the carnival with a blunt pencil.

"Do we keep hiding out? No. With Miss Foley, and so many

others involved, we just can't. Well, then, how do we attack so we won't be picked off first thing? What kind of weapons—"

"Silver bullets!" cried Will, suddenly.

"Heck, no!" snorted Jim. "They're not vampires!"

"If we were Catholic, we could borrow church holy water and—"

"Nuts," said Jim. "Movie stuff. It don't happen that way in real life. Am I wrong, Mr. Halloway?"

"I wish you were, boy."

Will's eyes glowed fiercely. "Okay. Only one thing to do: trot down to the meadow with a couple gallons of kerosene and some matches—"

"That's against the law!" Jim exclaimed.

"Look who's *talking*!"

"Hold on!"

But everyone stopped right then.

Whisper.

A faint tide of wind flowed up along through the library corridors and into this room.

"The front door," Jim whispered. "Someone just opened it."

Far away, a gentle click. The draft that had for a moment stirred the boys' trouser cuffs and blown the man's hair, ceased.

"Someone just *closed* it."

Silence.

Just the great dark library with its labyrinths and hedgerow mazes of sleeping books.

"Someone's *inside.*"

The boys half rose, bleating in the backs of their mouths.

Charles Halloway waited, then said one word, softly:

"Hide."

"We can't leave you—"

"Hide."

The boys ran and vanished in the dark maze.

Charles Halloway then rigidly, slowly, breathing in, breathing out, forced himself to sit back down, his eyes on the yellowed newspapers, to wait, to wait, then again . . . to wait some more.

Chapter Forty-One

A SHADOW moved among shadows.

Charles Halloway felt his soul submerge.

It took a long time for the shadow and the man it escorted to come stand in the doorway of the room. The shadow seemed deliberate in its slowness so as to shingle his flesh and cheese-grate his steadily willed calm. And when at last the shadow reached the door it brought not one, not a hundred, but a thousand people with it to look in.

"My name is Dark," said the voice.

Charles Halloway let out two fistfuls of air.

"Better known as the Illustrated Man," said the voice. "Where are the boys?"

"Boys?" Will's father turned at last to appraise the tall man who stood in the door.

The Illustrated Man sniffed the yellow pollen that whiffed up from the ancient books as quite suddenly Will's father saw them laid out in full sight, leaped up, stopped, then began to close them, one by one, as casually as possible.

The Illustrated Man pretended not to notice.

"The boys are not home. The two houses are empty. What a shame, they'll miss those free rides."

"I wish I knew where they were." Charles Halloway started carrying the books to the shelves. "Hell, if they knew you were here with free tickets, they'd shout for joy."

"Would they?" Mr. Dark let his smile melt like a white and pink paraffin candy toy he no longer had appetite for. Softly, he said, "I could kill you."

Charles Halloway nodded, walking slowly.

"Did you hear what I said?" barked the Illustrated Man.

"Yes." Charles Halloway weighed the books, as if they were his judgment. "But you won't kill now. You're too smart. You've kept the show on the road a long time, being smart."

"So you've read a few papers and think you know all about us?"

"No, not all. Just enough to scare me."

"Be more scared, then," said the crowd of night-crawling

illustrations locked under black suiting, speaking through the thin lips. "One of my friends, outside, can fix you so it seems you died of most natural heart failure."

The blood banged at Charles Halloway's heart, knocked at his temples, tapped twice at his wrists.

The Witch, he thought.

His lips must have formed the words.

"The Witch." Mr. Dark nodded.

The other shelved the books, withholding one.

"Well, what have you there?" Mr. Dark squinted. "A Bible? How very charming, how childish and refreshingly old-fashioned."

"Have you ever read it, Mr. Dark?"

"Read it! I've had every page, paragraph, and word read *at* me, sir!" Mr. Dark took time to light a cigarette and blow smoke toward the NO SMOKING sign, then at Will's father. "Do you really imagine that book can harm me? Is naiveté *really* your armor? Here!"

And before Charles Halloway could move, Mr. Dark ran lightly forward and took the Bible. He held it in his two hands.

"Aren't you surprised? See, I touch, hold, even *read* from it."

Mr. Dark blew smoke on the pages as he riffled them.

"Do you expect me to fall away into so many Dead Sea scrolls of flesh before you? Myths, unfortunately, are just that. Life, and by life I could mean so many fascinating things, goes on, makes shift for itself, survives wildly, and I not the least wild among many. Your King James and his literary version of some rather stuffy poetic materials is worth just about *this* much of my time and sweat."

Mr. Dark hurled the Bible into a wastepaper basket and did not look at it again.

"I hear your heart beating rapidly," said Mr. Dark. "My ears are not so finely tuned as the Gypsy's, but they hear. Your eyes jump beyond my shoulder. The boys hide out there in the warrens? Good. I would not wish for their escape. Not that anyone will believe their gibberings, in fact it's good advertisement for our shows, people titillate, night-sweat, then come prowling down to look us over, lick their lips, and wonder about investing in our special securities. You came, you prowled, and it wasn't just for curiosity. How old are you?"

Charles Halloway pressed his lips shut.

"Fifty?" purred Mr. Dark. "Fifty-one?" he murmured. "Fifty-two? Like to be younger?"

"No!"

"No need to yell. Politely, please." Mr. Dark hummed, strolling the room, running his hand over the books as if they were years to be counted. "Oh, it's nice to be young, really. Wouldn't forty be nice, again? Forty's ten years nicer than fifty, and thirty's twenty years nicer by an incredible long shot."

"I won't listen!" Charles Halloway shut his eyes.

Mr. Dark tilted his head, sucked on his cigarette, and observed. "Strange, you shut your eyes, not to listen. Clapping your hands over your ears would be better—"

Will's father clapped his hands to his ears, but the voice came through.

"Tell you what," said Mr. Dark, casually, waving his cigarette. "If you help me within fifteen seconds I'll give you your fortieth birthday. Ten seconds and you can celebrate thirty-five. A rare young age. A stripling, almost, by comparison. I'll start counting by my watch and by God, if you should jump to it, lend a hand, I might just cut thirty years off your life! Bargains galore, as the posters say. Think of it! Starting all over again, everything fine and new and glorious, all the things to be done and thought and savored again. Last chance! Here goes. One. Two. Three. Four—"

Charles Halloway hunched away, half crouched, propped hard against the shelves, grinding his teeth to drown the sound of counting.

"You're losing out, old man, my dear old fellow," said Mr. Dark. "Five. Losing. Six. Losing very much. Seven. Really losing. Eight. Frittering away. Nine. Ten. My God, you fool! Eleven. Halloway! Twelve. Almost gone. Thirteen! Gone! Fourteen! Lost! Fifteen! Lost forever!"

Mr. Dark put down his arm with the watch on it.

Charles Halloway, gasping, had turned away to bury his face in the smell of ancient books, the feel of old and comfortable leather, the taste of funeral dust and pressed flowers.

Mr. Dark stood in the door now, on his way out.

"Stay there," he directed. "Listen to your heart. I'll send someone to fix it. But, first, the boys . . ."

The crowd of unsleeping creatures, saddled upon tall flesh, strode quietly forth into darkness, borne with and all over upon Mr. Dark. Their cries and whines and utterances of vague but excruciating excitements sounded in his husky summoning:

"Boys? Are you there? Wherever you are . . . answer."

Charles Halloway sprang forward, then felt the room spin and whirl him, as that soft, that easy, that most pleasant voice of Mr. Dark went calling through the dark. Charles Halloway fell against a chair, thought: Listen, my heart! sank down to his knees, he said, Listen to my heart! it explodes! Oh God, it's tearing free!—and could not follow.

The Illustrated Man trod cat-soft in the labyrinths of shelved and darkly waiting books.

"Boys . . . ? Hear me . . . ?"

Silence.

"Boys . . . ?"

Chapter Forty-Two

SOMEWHERE IN the recumbent solitudes, the motionless but teeming millions of books, lost in two dozen turns right, three dozen turns left, down aisles, through corridors, toward dead ends, locked doors, half-empty shelves, somewhere in the literary soot of Dickens's London, or Dostoevsky's Moscow or the steppes beyond, somewhere in the vellumed dust of atlas or *Geographic*, sneezes pent but set like traps, the boys crouched, stood, lay sweating a cool and constant brine.

Somewhere hidden, Jim thought: *He's coming!*

Somewhere hidden, Will thought: *He's near!*

"Boys . . . ?"

Mr. Dark came carrying his panoply of friends, his jewel-case assortment of calligraphical reptiles which lay sunning themselves at midnight on his flesh. With him strode the stitch-inked *Tyrannosaurus rex*, which lent to his haunches a machined and ancient wellspring mineral-oil glide. As the thunder lizard strode, all glass-bead pomp, so strode Mr. Dark, armored with vile lightning scribbles of carnivores and sheep blasted by that thunder and arun before storms of juggernaut flesh. It was the pterodactyl kite and scythe which raised his arms almost to fly the marbled vaults. And with the inked and stencilled flash-burnt shapes of pistoned or bladed doom came his usual crowd of hangers-on, spectators gripped to each limb, seated on shoulder blades, peering from his jungled chest, hung upside down in microscopic millions in his armpit vaults screaming bat-screams for encounters, ready for the hunt and if need be the kill. Like a black tidal wave upon a bleak shore, a dark tumult infilled with phosphorescent beauties and badly spoiled dreams, Mr. Dark sounded and hissed his feet, his legs, his body, his sharp face forward.

"Boys . . . ?"

Immensely patient, that soft voice, ever the warmest friend to chilly creatures burrowed away, nested amongst dry books; so he scuttered, crept, scurried, stalked, tiptoed, wafted, stood immensely still among the primates, the Egyptian monuments to bestial gods, brushed black histories of dead Africa, stayed awhile in Asia, then sauntered on to newer lands.

"Boys, I know you hear me! The sign reads: SILENCE! So, I'll whisper: one of you still wants what we offer. Eh? *Eh?*"

Jim, thought Will.

Me, thought Jim. No! oh, no! not still! not me!

"Come out." Mr. Dark purred the air through his teeth. "I guarantee rewards! Whoever turns himself in wins it *all*!"

Bangity-bang!

My heart! thought Jim.

Is that me? thought Will, *or Jim!!?*

"I hear you." Mr. Dark's lips quivered. "Closer now. Will? Jim? Isn't it Jim who's the *smart* one? Come along, boy . . . !"

No! thought Will.

I don't know anything! thought Jim, wildly.

"Jim, yes . . ." Mr. Dark wheeled in a new direction. "Jim, show me where your friend is." Softly. "We'll shut him up, give you the ride that would have been his if he'd used his head. Right, Jim?" A dove voice, cooing. "Closer. I hear your heart jump!"

Stop! thought Will to his chest.

Stop! Jim clenched his breath. *Stop!!*

"I wonder . . . are you in this alcove . . . ?"

Mr. Dark let the peculiar gravity of a certain group of stacks tug him forward.

"You *here*, Jim . . . ? Or . . . over behind . . . ?"

He shoved a trolley of books mindlessly off on rubber rollers to bump through the night. A long way off, it crashed and spilled its contents to the floor like so many dead black ravens.

"Smart hide-and-seekers, both," said Mr. Dark. "But someone's smarter. Did you hear the carousel calliope tonight? Did you know, someone dear to you was down to the carousel? Will? Willy? William. William Halloway. Where's your mother tonight?"

Silence.

"She was out riding the night wind, Willy-William. Around. We put her on. Around. We left her on. Around. You *hear*, Willy? Around, a year, another year, another, around, around!

Dad! thought Will. *Where are you!*

In the far room, Charles Halloway, seated, his heart

pounding, heard and thought, He won't find them, I won't move unless he does, he can't find them, they won't listen! they won't believe! he'll go away!

"Your mother, Will," called Mr. Dark, softly. "Around and around, can you guess *which* direction, Willy?"

Mr. Dark circled his thin ghost hand in the dark air between the stacks.

"Around, around, and when we let your mother off, boy, and showed her herself in the Mirror Maze, you should have heard the *one single sound* she made. She was like a cat with a hair ball in her so big and sticky there was no way to gag it out, no way to scream around the hair coming out her nostrils and ears and eyes, boy, and her old old old. The last we saw of her, boy Willy, she was running off away from what she saw in the mirrors. She'll bang Jim's house door but when his ma sees a thing two hundred years old slobbering at the keyhole, begging the mercy of gunshot death, boy, Jim's ma will gag the same way, like a hairballed cat sick but can't be sick, and beat her away, send her beggaring the streets, where no one'll believe, Will, such a kettle of bones and spit, no one'll believe this was a rose beauty, your kind relation! So Will, it's up to us to run find, run save her, for we know who she is—right, Will, right, Will, right, right, *right*?!"

The dark man's voice hissed away to silence.

Very faintly now, somewhere in the library, someone was sobbing.

Ah . . .

The Illustrated Man gassed the air pleasantly from his dank lungs.

Yesssssssssss . . .

"Here . . ." he murmured. "What? Filed under B for Boys? A for Adventure? H for Hidden. S for Secret. T for Terrified? Or filed under J for Jim or N for Nightshade, W for William, H for Halloway? Where are my two precious human books, so I may turn their pages, eh?"

He kicked a place for his right foot on the first shelf of a towering stack.

He shoved his right foot in, put his weight there, and swung his left foot free.

"*There*."

His left foot hit the second shelf, knocked space. He climbed. His right foot kicked a hole on the third shelf, plunged books back, and so up and up he climbed, to fourth shelf, to fifth, to sixth, groping dark library heavens, hands clutching shelf-boards, then scrabbling higher to leaf night to find boys, if boys there were, like bookmarks among books.

His right hand, a princely tarantula, garlanded with roses, cracked a book of Bayeaux tapestries aspin down the sightless abyss below. It seemed an age before the tapestries struck, all askew, a ruin of beauty, an avalanche of gold, silver, and sky-blue thread on the floor.

His left hand, reaching the ninth shelf as he panted, grunted, encountered empty space—no books.

"Boys, are you here on Everest?"

Silence. Except for the faint sobbing, nearer now.

"Is it cold here? Colder? Coldest?"

The eyes of the Illustrated Man came abreast of the eleventh shelf.

Like a corpse laid rigid out, face down just three inches away, was Jim Nightshade.

One shelf further up in the catacomb, eyes trembling with tears, lay William Halloway.

"Well," said Mr. Dark.

He reached a hand to pat Will's head.

"Hello," he said.

Chapter Forty-Three

TO WILL, the palm of the hand that drifted up was like a moon rising.

Upon it was the fiery blue-inked portrait of himself.

Jim, too, saw a hand before his face.

His own picture looked back at him from the palm.

The hand with Will's picture grabbed Will.

The hand with Jim's picture grabbed Jim.

Shrieks and yells.

The Illustrated Man heaved.

Twisting, he fell-jumped to the floor.

The boys, kicking, yelling, fell with him. They landed on their feet, toppled, collapsed, to be held, reared, set right, fistfuls of their shirts in Mr. Dark's fists.

"Jim!" he said. "Will! What were you doing up there, boys? Surely not reading?"

"Dad!"

"Mr. Halloway!"

Will's father stepped from the dark.

The Illustrated Man rearranged the boys tenderly under one arm like kindling, then gazed with genteel curiosity at Charles Halloway and reached for him. Will's father struck one blow before his left hand was seized, held, squeezed. As the boys watched, shouting, they saw Charles Halloway gasp and fall to one knee.

Mr. Dark squeezed that left hand harder and, doing this, slowly, certainly, pressured the boys with his other arm, crushing their ribs so air gushed from their mouths.

Night spiraled in fiery whorls like great thumbprints inside Will's eyes.

Will's father, groaning, sank to both knees, flailing his right arm.

"Damn you!"

"But," said the carnival owner quietly, "I am already."

"Damn you, damn you!"

"Not words, old man," said Mr. Dark. "Not words in books

or words you say, but real thoughts, real actions, quick thought, quick action, win the day. So!"

He gave one last mighty clench of his fist.

The boys heard Charles Halloway's finger bones crack. He gave a last cry and fell senseless.

In one motion like a solemn pavane, the Illustrated Man rounded the stacks, the boys, kicking books from shelves, under his arms.

Will, feeling walls, books, floors fly by, foolishly thought, pressed close, Why, why, Mr. Dark smells like . . . calliope steam!

Both boys were dropped suddenly. Before they could move or regain their breath, each was gripped by the hair on their head and roused marionettes-wise to face a window, a street.

"Boys, you read Dickens?" Mr. Dark whispered. "Critics hate his coincidences. But we know, don't we? life's *all* coincidence. Turn death and happenstance flakes off him like fleas from a killed ox. Look!"

Both boys writhed in the iron-maiden clutch of hungry saurians and bristly apes.

Will did not know whether to weep with joy or new despair.

Below, across the avenue, passing from church, going home, was his mother and Jim's mother.

Not on the carousel, not old, crazy, dead, in jail, but freshly out in the good October air. She had been not a hundred yards away in church during all the last five minutes!

Mom! screamed Will, against the hand which, anticipating his cry, clamped tight to his mouth.

"Mom," crooned Mr. Dark, mockingly. "Come save me!"

No, thought Will, save *yourself*, run!

But his mother and Jim's mother simply strolled content, from the warm church through town.

Mom! screamed Will again, and some small muffled bleat of it escaped the sweaty paw.

Will's mother, a thousand miles away over on that sidewalk, paused.

She *couldn't* have heard! thought Will. Yet—

She looked over at the library.

"Good," sighed Mr. Dark. "Excellent, fine."

Here! thought Will. See us, Mom! Run call the police!

"Why doesn't she look at this window?" asked Mr. Dark quietly. "And see us three standing as for a portrait. Look over. Then, come running. We'll let her *in*."

Will strangled a sob. No, no.

His mother's gaze trailed from the front entrance to the first-floor windows.

"Here," said Mr. Dark. "Second floor. A proper coincidence, let's make it proper."

Now Jim's mother was talking. Both women stood together at the curb.

No, thought Will, oh, no.

And the women turned and went away into the Sunday-night town.

Will felt the Illustrated Man slump the tiniest bit.

"Not much of a coincidence, no crisis, no one lost or saved. Pity. Well!"

Dragging the boys' feet, he glided down to open the front door.

Someone waited in the shadows.

A lizard hand scurried cold on Will's chin.

"Halloway," husked the Witch's voice.

A chameleon perched on Jim's nose.

"Nightshade," whisked the dry-broom voice.

Behind her stood the Dwarf and the Skeleton, silent, shifting, apprehensive.

Obedient to the occasion, the boys would have given their best stored yells air, but again, on the instant recognizing their need, the Illustrated Man trapped the sound before it could issue forth, then nodded curtly to the old dust woman.

The Witch toppled forward with her seamed black wax sewn-shut iguana eyelids and her great proboscis with the nostrils caked like tobacco-blackened pipe bowls, her fingers tracing, weaving a silent plinth of symbols on the mind.

The boys stared.

Her fingernails fluttered, darted, feathered cold winter-water air. Her pickled green frog's breath crawled their flesh in pimples as she sang softly, mewing, humming, glistering her babes, her boys, her friends of the slick snail-tracked roof, the straight-flung arrow, the stricken and sky-drowned balloon.

"Darning-needle dragonfly, sew up these mouths so they not speak!"

Touch, sew, touch, sew her thumbnail stabbed, punched, drew, stabbed, punched, drew along their lower, upper lips until they were thread-pouch shut with invisible thread.

"Darning-needle dragonfly, sew up these ears, so they not hear!"

Cold sand funneled Will's ears, burying her voice. Muffled, far away, fading, she chanted on with a rustle, tick, tickle, tap, flourish of caliper hands.

Moss grew in Jim's ears, swiftly sealing him deep.

"Darning needle-dragonfly, sew up these eyes so they not see!"

Her white-hot fingerprints rolled back their stricken eyeballs to throw the lids down with bangs like great tin doors slammed shut.

Will saw a billion flashbulbs explode, then suck to darkness while the unseen darning-needle insect out beyond somewhere pranced and fizzed like insect drawn to sun-warmed honeypot, as closeted voice stitched off their senses forever and a day beyond.

"Darning-needle dragonfly, have done with eye, ear, lip and tooth, finish hem, sew dark, mound dust, heap with slumber sleep, now tie all knots ever so neat, pump silence in blood like sand in river deep. So. So."

The Witch, somewhere outside the boys, lowered her hands.

The boys stood silent. The Illustrated Man took his embrace from them and stepped back.

The woman from the Dust sniffed at her twin triumphs, ran her hand a last loving time over her statues.

The Dwarf toddled madly about in the boys' shadows, nibbling daintily at their fingernails, softly calling their names.

The Illustrated Man nodded toward the library.

"The janitor's clock. Stop it."

The Witch, mouth wide, savoring doom, wandered off into the marble quarry.

Mr. Dark said: "Left, right. One, two."

The boys walked down the steps, the Dwarf at Jim's side, the Skeleton at Will's.

Serene as death, the Illustrated Man followed.

Chapter Forty-Four

SOMEWHERE NEAR, Charles Halloway's hand lay in a white-hot furnace, melted to sheer nerve and pain. He opened his eyes. At the same moment he heard a great breath as the front door swung shut and a woman's voice came singing in the hall:

"Old man, old man, old man, old man . . . ?"

Where his left hand should be was this swelled blood pudding which pulsed with such ecstasies of pain it fed forth his life, his will, his whole attention. He tried to sit up, but the pain hammerblowed him down again.

"Old man . . . ?"

Not old! Fifty-four's not old, he thought wildly.

And here she came on the worn stone floors, her moth-fingers tapping, scanning braille book titles, as her nostrils siphoned the shadows.

Charles Halloway hunched and crawled, hunched and crawled, toward the nearest stack, cramming pain back with his tongue. He must climb out of reach, climb where books might be weapons flung down upon any night-crawling pursuer. . . .

"Old man, hear you breathing. . . ."

She drifted on his tide, let her body be summoned by every sibilant hiss of his pain.

"Old man, feel your *hurt*. . . ."

If he could fling the hand, the pain, out the window! where it might lie beating like a heart, summoning her away, tricked, to go seek this awful fire. Bent in the street, he imagined her brisking her palms at this throb, an abandoned chunk of delirium.

But no, the hand stayed, glowed, poisoned the air, hurrying the strange nun-Gypsy's tread as she gasped her avaricious mouth most ardently.

"Damn you!" he cried. "Get it over with! I'm here!"

So the Witch wheeled swift as a black clothes dummy on rubber rollers and swayed over him.

He did not even look at her. Such weights and pressures of despair and exertion fought for his attention, he could only free his eyes to watch the inside of his lids upon which multiple and everchanging looms of terror jigged and gamboled.

"Very simple." The whisper bent low. "Stop the heart."

Why not, he thought, vaguely.

"Slow," she murmured.

Yes, he thought.

"Slow, very slow."

His heart, once bolting, now fell away to a strange dis-ease, disquiet, then quiet, then ease.

"Much more slow, slow . . ." she suggested.

Tired, yes, you hear that, heart? he wondered.

His heart heard. Like a tight fist it began to relax, a finger at a time.

"Stop all for good, forget all for good," she whispered.

Well, why not?

"Slower . . . slowest."

His heart stumbled.

And then for no reason, save perhaps for a last look around, because he *did* want to get rid of the pain, and sleep was the way to do that . . . Charles Halloway opened his eyes.

He saw the Witch.

He saw her fingers working at the air, his face, his body, the heart within his body, and the soul within the heart. Her swamp breath flooded him while, with immense curiosity, he watched the poisonous drizzle from her lips, counted the folds in her stitch-wrinkled eyes, the Gila monster neck, the mummy-linen ears, the dry-rivulet river-sand brow. Never in his life had he focused so nearly to a person, as if she were a puzzle, which once touched together might show life's greatest secret. The solution was in her, it would all spring clear this moment, no, the next, no, the next, watch her scorpion fingers! hear her chant as she diddled the air, yes, diddled was it, tickling, tickling, "Slow!" she whispered. "Slow!" And his obedient heart pulled rein. Diddle-tickle went her fingers.

Charles Halloway snorted. Faintly, he giggled.

He caught this. Why? Why am I . . . giggling . . . at such a time!?

The Witch pulled back the merest quarter inch as if some strange but hidden electric light socket, touched with wet whorl, gave shock.

Charles Halloway saw but did not see her flinch, sensed but seemed in no way to consider her withdrawal, for almost immediately, seizing the initiative, she flung herself forward, not touching, but mutely gesticulating at his chest as one might try to spell an antique clock pendulum.

"Slow!" she cried.

Senselessly, he permitted an idiot smile to balloon itself up from somewhere to attach itself with careless ease under his nose.

"Slowest!"

Her new fever, her anxiety which changed itself to anger was even more of a toy to him. A part of his attention, secret until now, leaned forward to scan every pore of her Halloween face. Somehow, irresistibly, the prime thing was: nothing mattered. Life in the end seemed a prank of such size you could only stand off at this end of the corridor to note its meaningless length and its quite unnecessary height, a mountain built to such ridiculous immensities you were dwarfed in its shadow and mocking of its pomp. So with death this near he thought numbly but purely upon a billion vanities, arrivals, departures, idiot excursions of boy, boy-man, man and old-man goat. He had gathered and stacked all manner of foibles, devices, playthings of his egotism and now, between all the silly corridors of books the toys of his life swayed. And none more grotesque than this thing named Witch Gypsy Reader-of-Dust, tickling, that's what! just *tickling* the air! Fool! Didn't she know what she was *doing*!

He opened his mouth.

Of itself, like a child born of an unsuspecting parent, one single raw laugh broke free.

The Witch swooned back.

Charles Halloway did not see. He was far too busy letting the joke rush through his fingers, letting hilarity spring forth of its own volition along his throat, eyes squeezed shut; there it flew, whipping shrapnel in all directions.

"You!" he cried, to no one, everyone, himself, her, them, it, all. "Funny! You!"

"No," the Witch protested.

"Stop tickling!" he gasped.

"Not!" she lunged back, frantically. "Not! Sleep! Slow! Very slow!"

"No, tickling is all it is, for sure!" he roared. "Oh, ha! Ha, stop!"

"Yes, *stop* heart!" she squealed. "*Stop* blood." Her own heart must have shaken like a tambourine; her hands shook. In mid-gesticulation she froze and became aware of the silly fingers.

"Oh, my God!" He wept beautiful glad tears. "Get off my ribs, oh, ha, go on, my heart!"

"Your *heart*, yesssssss!"

"God!" He popped his eyes wide, gulped air, released more soap and water washing everything clear, incredibly clean. "Toys! The key sticks out your back! Who wound you up!?"

And the largest roar of all, flung at the woman, burnt her hands, seared her face, or so it seemed, for she seized herself as from a blast furnace, wrapped her fried hands in Egyptian rags, gripped her dry dugs, skipped back, gave pause, then started a slow retreat, nudged, pushed, pummeled inch by inch, foot by foot, clattering bookracks, shelves, fumbling for handholds on volumes that thrashed free as she scrambled them down. Her brow knocked dim histories, vain theories, duned-up time, promised but compromised years. Chased, bruised, beaten by his laugh which echoed, rang, swam to fill the marble vaults, she whirled at last, claws razoring the wild air and fled to fall downstairs.

Moments later, she managed to cram herself through the front door, which *slammed*!

Her fall, the door slam, almost broke his frame with laughter.

"Oh God, God, please stop, stop yourself!" he begged of his hilarity.

And thus begged, his humor let be.

In mid-roar, at last, all faded to honest laughter, pleasant chuckling, faint giggling, then softly and with great contentment receiving and giving breath, shaking his happy-weary head, the good ache of action in his throat and ribs, gone from his crumpled hand. He lay against the stacks, head leaned to some dear befriending book, the tears of releaseful mirth salting his cheeks, and suddenly knew her gone.

Why? he wondered. *What did I do?*

With one last bark of mirth, he rose up, slow.

What's happened? Oh, God, let's get it clear! First, the drug store, a half-dozen aspirin to cure this hand for an hour, then, *think*. In the last five minutes you did win something, ***didn't*** you? What's victory taste like? Think! Try to remember!

And smiling a new smile at the ridiculous dead-animal left hand nested in his right crooked elbow, he hurried down the night corridors, and out into town. . . .

III. DEPARTURES

Chapter Forty-Five

THE SMALL parade moved, soundless, past the eternally revolving, ending-but-unending candy serpentine of Mr. Crosetti's barber pole, past all the darkening or darkened shops, the emptying streets, for people were home now from the church suppers, or out at the carnival for the last side show or the last high-ladder diver floating like milkweed down the night.

Will's feet, far away below, clubbed the sidewalk. One, two, he thought, someone tells me left, right. Dragonfly whispers: one-two.

Is Jim in the parade?! Will's eyes flicked the briefest to one side. Yes! But who's the other little one? The gone-mad, everything's-interesting-so-touch-it, everything's red-hot, pull-back, Dwarf! Plus the Skeleton. And then behind, who were all those hundreds, no, thousands of people marching along, breathing down his neck?

The Illustrated Man.

Will nodded and whined so high and silently that only dogs, dogs who were no help, dogs who could not speak, might hear.

And sure enough, looking obliquely over, he saw not one, not two, but three dogs who, smelling the occasion, their own parade, now ran ahead, now fell behind, their tails like guidons for the platoon.

Bark! thought Will, like in the movies! Bark, bring the police!

But the dogs just smiled and trotted.

Coincidence, please, thought Will. Just a *small* one!

Mr. Tetley! Yes! Will saw-but-did-not-see Mr. Tetley! Rolling the wooden Indian back into his shop, closing for the night!

"Turn heads," murmured the Illustrated Man.

Jim turned his head. Will turned his head.

Mr. Tetley smiled.

"Smile," murmured Mr. Dark.

The two boys smiled.

"Hello!" said Mr. Tetley.

"Say hello," someone whispered.

"Hello," said Jim.

"Hello," said Will.

The dogs barked.

"A free ride at the carnival," murmured Mr. Dark.

"Free ride," said Will.

"At the carnival!" clacked Jim.

Then, like good machines, they shut up their smiles.

"Have fun!" called Mr. Tetley.

The dogs barked joy.

The parade marched on.

"Fun," said Mr. Dark. "Free rides. When the crowds go home, half an hour from now. We'll ride Jim round. You still *want* that, Jim?"

Hearing but not hearing, locked away in himself, Will thought, Jim, don't listen!

Jim's eyes slid: wet or oily, it was hard to tell.

"You'll travel with us, Jim, and if Mr. Cooger doesn't survive (it's a near thing for him, we haven't saved him yet, we'll try again now) but if he doesn't make it, Jim, how would you like to be partners? I'll grow you to a fine strong age, eh? Twenty-two? twenty-five?! Dark and Nightshade, Nightshade and Dark, sweet lovely names for such as we with such as the side shows to run around the world! What say, Jim?"

Jim said nothing, sewn up in the Witch's dream.

Don't listen! wailed his best friend, who heard nothing but heard it all.

"And Will?" said Mr. Dark. "Let's ride *him* back and back, eh? Make him a babe in arms, a babe for the Dwarf to carry like a clown-child, roundabout in parades, every day for the next fifty years, would you like that, Will? to be a babe forever? not able to talk and tell all the lovely things you know? Yes, I think that's best for Will. A plaything, a little wet friend for the Dwarf!"

Will must have screamed.

But not out loud.

For only the dogs barked, in terror; yipping, off they ran, as if pelted with rocks.

A man came around the corner.

A policeman.

"Who's this?" muttered Mr. Dark.

"Mr. Kolb," said Jim.

"Mr. Kolb!" said Will.

"Darning-needle," whispered Mr. Dark. "Dragonfly."

Pain stabbed Will's ears. Moss stuffed his eyes. Gum glued his teeth. He felt a multitudinous tapping, shuttling, weaving, about his face, all numb again.

"Say hello to Mr. Kolb."

"Hello," said Jim.

". . . Kolb . . ." said the dreaming Will.

"Hello, boys. Gentlemen."

"Turn here," said Mr. Dark.

They turned.

Away toward meadow country, away from warm lights, good town, safe streets, the drumless march progressed.

Chapter Forty-Six

STRETCHED OUT over a mile of territory the straggling parade now moved as follows:

At the edge of the carnival midway, stumping the grass with their dead feet, Jim and Will paced friends who constantly retold the wondrous uses of darning-needle dragonflies.

Behind, a good half mile, trying to catch up, walking mysteriously wounded, the Gypsy, who whorl-symboled the dust.

And yet farther back came the janitor-father, now slowing himself with remembrances of age, now pacing swiftly young with thoughts of the brief first encounter and victory, carrying his left hand patted to his chest, chewing medicines as he went.

At the midway rim, Mr. Dark looked back as if an inner voice had named the stragglers in his widely separated maneuver. But the voice failed, he was unsure. He nodded briskly, and Dwarf, Skeleton, Jim, Will thrust through the crowd.

Jim felt the river of bright people wash by all around but not touching. Will heard waterfall laughter here, there, and him walking through the downpour. An explosion of fireflies blossomed on the sky; the ferris wheel, exultant as a titanic fireworks, dilated above them.

Then they were at the Mirror Maze and sidling, colliding, bumping, careening through the unfolded ice ponds where stricken spider-stung boys much like themselves appeared, vanished a thousand times over.

That's *me*! thought Jim.

But I can't help me, thought Will, no matter how many of me there are!

And crowd of boys, plus crowd of reflected Mr. Dark's illustrations, for he had taken off his coat and shirt now, crammed and crushed through to the Waxworks at the end of the maze.

"Sit," said Mr. Dark. "Stay."

Among the wax figures of murdered, gunshot, guillotined, garroted men and women the two boys sat like Egyptian cats, unblinked, untwitched, unswallowing.

Some late visitors passed through, laughing. They commented on all the wax figures.

They did not notice the thin line of saliva crept from the corner of one "wax" boy's mouth.

They did not see how bright was the second "wax" boy's stare, which suddenly brimmed and ran clear water down his cheek.

Outside, the Witch limped in through back alleys of rope and peg between the tents.

"Ladies and gentlemen!"

The last crowd of the night, three or four hundred strong, turned as a body.

The Illustrated Man, stripped to the waist, all nightmare viper, sabertooth, libidinous ape, clotted vulture, all salmon-sulphur sky rose up with annunciations:

"The last free event this evening! Come one! Come all!"

The crowd surged toward the main platform outside the freak tent, where stood Dwarf, Skeleton, and Mr. Dark.

"The Most Amazingly Dangerous, ofttimes Fatal—World Famous BULLET TRICK!"

The crowd gasped with pleasure.

"The rifles, if you please!"

The Thin One cracked wide a racked display of bright artillery.

The Witch, hurrying up, froze when Mr. Dark cried: "And here, our death-defier, the bullet-catcher who will stake her life—Mademoiselle Tarot!"

The Witch shook her head, bleated, but Dark's hand swept down to swing her like a child to the platform, still protesting, which gave Dark pause, but, in front of everyone now, he went on:

"A volunteer, please, to fire the rifle!"

The crowd rumbled softly, daring itself to speak up.

Mr. Dark's mouth barely moved. Under his breath he asked, "Is the clock stopped?"

"Not," she whined, "stopped."

"No?" he almost burst out.

He burnt her with his eyes, then turned to the audience and let his mouth finish the spiel, his fingers rapping over the rifles.

"Volunteers, please!"

"Stop the act," the Witch cried softly, wringing her hands.

"It goes on, damn you, *worse* than double-damn you," he whispered, whistled fiercely.

Secretly, Dark gathered a pinch of flesh on his wrist, the illustration of a black-nun blind woman, which he bit with his fingernails.

The Witch spasmed, seized her breast, groaned, ground her teeth. "Mercy!" she hissed, half aloud.

Silence from the crowd.

Mr. Dark nodded swiftly.

"Since there are no volunteers—" He scraped his illustrated wrist. The Witch shuddered. "We will cancel our last act and—"

"Here! A volunteer!"

The crowd turned.

Mr. Dark recoiled, then asked: "Where?"

"Here."

Far out at the edge of the crowd, a hand lifted, a path opened.

Mr. Dark could see very clearly the man standing there, alone.

Charles Halloway, citizen, father, introspective husband, night-wanderer, and janitor of the town library.

Chapter Forty-Seven

THE CROWD's appreciative clamor faded.

Charles Halloway did not move.

He let the path grow leading down to the platform.

He could not see the expression on the faces of the freaks standing up there. His eyes swept the crowd and found the Mirror Maze, the empty oblivion which beckoned with ten times a thousand million light years of reflections, counter-reflections, reversed and double-reversed, plunging deep to nothing, face-falling to nothing, stomach-dropping away to yet more sickening plummets of nothing.

And yet, wasn't there an echo of two boys in the powdered silver at the back of each glass? Did or did he not perceive, with the tremulous tip of eyelash if not the eye, their passage through, their wait beyond, warm wax amongst cold, waiting to be key-wound by terrors, run free in panics?

No, thought Charles Halloway, don't think. Get on with this!

"Coming!" he shouted.

"Go get 'em, Pop!" a man said.

"Yes," said Charles Halloway. "I will."

And he walked down through the crowd.

The Witch spun slowly, magnetized at the night-wandering volunteer's approach. Her eyelids jerked at their sewn black-wax threads behind dark glasses.

Mr. Dark, the illustration-drenched, superinfested civilization of souls, leaned from the platform, gladly whetting his lips. Thoughts spun fiery Catherine wheels in his eyes, quick, quick, what, what, *what*!

And the aging janitor, fixing a smile to his face like a white celluloid set of teeth from a Cracker Jack box, strode on, and the crowd opened as the sea before Moses and closed behind, and him wondering what to do? why was he here? but on the move, steadily, nevertheless.

Charles Halloway's foot touched the first step of the platform.

The Witch trembled secretly.

Mr. Dark felt this secret, glanced sharply. Swiftly he put his hand out to grab for the good right hand of this fifty-four-year-old man.

But the fifty-four-year-old man shook his head, would not give his hand to be held, touched, or helped up. "Thanks, no."

On the platform, Charles Halloway waved to the crowd.

The people set off a few firecrackers of applause.

"But—" Mr. Dark was amazed—"your left hand, sir, you can't hold and fire a rifle if you have only the use of one hand!"

Charles Halloway paled.

"I'll do it," he said. "With one hand."

"Hoorah!" cried a boy, below.

"Go it, Charlie!" a man called, out beyond.

Mr. Dark flushed as the crowd laughed and applauded even louder now. He lifted his hands to ward off the wave of refreshing sound, like rain that washed in from the people.

"All right, all right! Let's see if he *can* do it!"

Brutally, the Illustrated Man snapped a rifle from its locks, hurled it through the air.

The crowd gasped.

Charles Halloway ducked. He put up his right hand. The rifle slapped his palm. He grabbed. It did not fall. He had it good.

The audience hooted, said things against Mr. Dark's bad manners which made him turn away for a moment, damning himself, silently.

Will's father lifted the rifle, beaming.

The crowd roared.

And while the wave of applause came in, crashed, and went back down the shore, he looked again to the maze, where the sensed but unseen shadow-shapes of Will and Jim were filed among titanic razor blades of revelation and illusion, then back to the Medusa gaze of Mr. Dark, swiftly reckoned with, and on to the stitched and jittering sightless nun of midnight, sidling back still more. Now she was as far as she could sidle, at the far end of the platform, almost pressed to the whorled red-black rifle bull's-eye target.

"Boy!" shouted Charles Halloway.

Mr. Dark stiffened.

"I need a boy volunteer to help me hold the rifle!" shouted Charles Halloway.

"Someone! Anyone!" he shouted.

A few boys in the crowd shifted around on their toes.

"Boy!" shouted Charles Halloway. "Hold on. My son's out there. He'll volunteer, *won't* you, Will?"

The Witch flung one hand up to feel the shape of this audacity which came off the fifty-four-year-old man like a fever. Mr. Dark was spun round as if hit by a fast-traveling gunshot.

"Will!" called his father.

In the Wax Museum, Will sat motionless.

"Will!" called his father. "Come on, boy!"

The crowd looked left, looked right, looked back.

No answer.

Will sat in the Wax Museum.

Mr. Dark observed all of this with some respect, some degree of admiration, some concern; he seemed to be waiting, just as was Will's father.

"Will, come help your old man!" Mr. Halloway cried, jovially.

Will sat in the Wax Museum.

Mr. Dark smiled.

"Will! Willy! Come here!"

No answer.

Mr. Dark smiled more.

"Willy! Don't you hear your old man?"

Mr. Dark stopped smiling.

For this last was the voice of a gentleman in the crowd, speaking up.

The crowd laughed.

"Will!" called a woman.

"Willy!" called another.

"Yoohoo!" A gentleman in a beard.

"Come on, William!" A boy.

The crowd laughed more, jostled elbows.

Charles Halloway called. *They* called. Charles Halloway cried to the hills. *They* cried to the hills.

"Will! Willy! William!"

A shadow shuttled and wove in the mirrors.

The Witch broke out chandeliers of sweat.

"There!"

The crowd stopped calling.

As did Charles Halloway, choked on the name of his son now, and silent.

For Will stood in the entrance of the Maze, like the wax figure that he almost was.

"Will," called his father, softly.

The sound of this chimed the sweat off the Witch.

Will moved, unseeing, through the crowd.

And handing the rifle down like a cane for the boy to grasp, his father drew him up onto the stand.

"Here's my good left hand!" announced the father.

Will neither saw nor heard the crowd sound forth a solid and offensive applause.

Mr. Dark had not moved, though Charles Halloway could see him, during all this, lighting and setting off cannon crackers in his head; but each, one by one, fizzled and died. Mr. Dark could not guess what they were up to. For that matter, Charles Halloway did not know or guess. It was as if he had written this play for himself, over the years, in the library, nights, torn up the play after memorizing it, and now forgotten what he had set forth to remember. He was relying on secret discoveries of self, moment by moment, playing by ear, no! heart and soul! And . . . *now*?!

The brightness of his teeth seemed to strike the witch blinder! Impossible! She flung one hand to her glasses, her sewn eyelids!

"Closer, everyone!" called Will's father.

The crowd gathered in. The platform was an island. The sea was people.

"Watch the bull's-eye targeteer!"

The Witch melted in her rags.

The Illustrated Man looked left, found no pleasure in the Skeleton, who simply looked thinner; found no pleasure looking right to a Dwarf who blandly dwelt in squashed idiot madness.

"The bullet, please!" Will's father said, amiably.

The thousand illustrations on his jerking horseflesh frame did not hear, so why should Mr. Dark?

"If you please," said Charles Halloway. "The bullet? So I may knock that flea off the old Gypsy's wart!"

Will stood motionless.

Mr. Dark hesitated.

Out in the choppy sea, smiles flashed, here, there, a hundred, two hundred, three hundred whitenesses, as if a vast titillation of water had been provoked by a lunar gravity. The tide ebbed.

The Illustrated Man, in slow motion, proffered the bullet. His arm, a long molasses undulation, lazed to offer the bullet to the boy, to see if he would notice; he did not notice.

His father took the missile.

"Mark it with your initials," said Mr. Dark, by rote.

"No, with more!" Charles Halloway raised his son's hand and made him hold the bullet, so he could take a penknife with his one good hand and carve a strange symbol on the lead.

What's happening? Will thought. I know what's happening. I don't know what's happening? What!?

Mr. Dark saw a crescent moon on the bullet, saw nothing wrong with such a moon, rammed it in the rifle, slapped the rifle back at Will's father, who once more caught it deftly.

"Ready, Will?"

The boy's peach face drowsed in the slightest nod.

Charles Halloway flicked a last glance at the maze, thought, Jim, you there still? Get ready!

Mr. Dark turned to go pat, conjure, calm his dust-crone friend, but cracked to a halt at the crack of the rifle being reopened, the bullet ejected by Will's father, to assure the audience it was there. It seemed real enough, yet he had read long ago that this was a substitute bullet, shaped of a very hard steel-colored crayon wax. Shot through the rifle it would dissolve out the barrel as smoke and vapor. At this very moment, having somehow switched bullets, the Illustrated Man was slipping the real marked bullet into the Witch's jerking fingers. She would hide it in her cheek. At the shot, she would pretend to jolt under the imagined impact, then reveal the bullet caught by her yellow rat teeth. Fanfare! Applause!

The Illustrated Man, glancing up, saw Charles Halloway with the opened rifle, the wax bullet. But instead of revealing what he knew, Mr. Halloway simply said, "Let's cut our mark more clearly, eh, boy?" And with his penknife, the boy holding the bullet in his senseless hand, he marked this fresh new wax unmarked bullet with the same mysterious crescent moon, then snapped it back into the rifle.

"Ready?!"

Mr. Dark looked to the Witch.

Who hesitated, then nodded, once, faintly.

"Ready!" announced Charles Halloway.

And all about lay the tents, the breathing crowd, the anxious freaks, a Witch iced with hysteria, Jim hidden to be found, an ancient mummy still seated glowing with blue fire in his electric chair, and a merry-go-round waiting for the show to cease, the crowd to go, and the carnival to have its way with boys and janitor trapped, if possible, and alone.

"Will," said Charles Halloway conversationally, as he lifted the now suddenly heavy rifle. "Your shoulder here is my brace. Take the middle of the rifle, gently, with one hand. Take it, Will." The boy raised a hand. "That's it, son. When I say 'hold,' hold your breath. Hear me?"

The boy's head tremored with the slightest affirmation. He slept. He dreamed. The dream was nightmare. The nightmare was *this.*

And the next part of this was his father shouting:

"Ladies! Gentlemen!"

The Illustrated Man clenched his fist. Will's picture, lost in it, like a flower, was crushed.

Will twisted.

The rifle fell.

Charles Halloway pretended not to notice.

"Me and Will here will now, together, him being the good left arm I can't use, do the one and only most dangerous, sometimes fatal, Bullet Trick!"

Applause. Laughter.

Quickly the fifty-four-year-old janitor, denying each year, laid the rifle back on the boy's jerking shoulder.

"Hear that, Will? Listen! That's for *us*!"

The boy listened. The boy grew calm.

Mr. Dark tightened his fist.

Will was taken with slight palsy.

"We'll hit 'em bull's-eye on, won't we, boy!" said his father.

More laughter.

And the boy grew very calm indeed, with the rifle on his shoulder, and Mr. Dark squeezed tight on the peach-fuzz face nestled in the flesh of his hand, but the boy was serene in the laughter which still flowed and his father kept the hoop rolling thus:

"Show the lady your teeth, Will!"

Will showed the woman against the target his teeth.

The blood fell away from the Witch's face.

Now Charles Halloway showed her his teeth, too, such as they were.

And winter lived in the Witch.

"Boy," said someone in the audience, "she's great. Acts scared! Look!"

I'm looking, thought Will's father, his left hand useless at his side, his right hand up to the rifle trigger, his face to the sight as his son held the rifle unswervingly pointed at the bull's-eye and the Witch's face superimposed there, and the last moment come, and a wax bullet in the chamber, and what could a wax bullet do? A bullet that dissolved in transit, what use? why were they here, what could they do? silly, silly!

No! thought Will's father. Stop!

He stopped the doubts.

He felt his mouth shape words with no sound.

But, the Witch heard what he said.

Above the dying laughter, before the warm sound was completely gone, he made these words, silently with his lips:

The crescent moon I have marked on the bullet is not a crescent moon.

It is my own smile.

I have put my smile on the bullet in the rifle.

He said it once.

He waited for her to understand.

He said it, silently, again.

And in the moment before the Illustrated Man himself translated the mouthings, quickly, Charles Halloway cried, faintly, "Hold!" Will held his breath. Far back among wax statues, Jim, hid away, dripped saliva from his chin. Strapped in electric chair a dead-alive mummy hummed power in its teeth. Mr. Dark's illustrations writhed with sick sweat as he clenched his fist a final time, but—too late! Serene, Will held breath, held weapon. Serene, his father said, "*Now.*"

And fired the rifle.

Chapter Forty-Eight

ONE SHOT!

The Witch sucked breath.

Jim, in the Wax Museum, sucked breath.

As did Will, asleep.

As did his father.

As did Mr. Dark.

As did all the freaks.

As did the crowd.

The Witch screamed.

Jim, among the wax dummies, blew all the air from his lungs.

Will shrieked himself awake, on the platform.

The Illustrated Man let the air from his mouth in a great angry bray, whipping up his hands to stop all events. But the Witch fell. She fell off the platform. She fell in the dust.

The smoking rifle in his one good hand, Charles Halloway let his breath go slow, feeling every bit of it move from him. He still stared along the rifle sights at the target where the woman had been.

At the platform rim, Mr. Dark looked down at the screaming crowd and what they were screaming about.

"She's fainted—"

"No, she slipped!"

"She's . . . shot!"

At last Charles Halloway came to stand by the Illustrated Man, looking down. There were many things in his face: surprise, dismay, and some small strange relief and satisfaction.

The woman was lifted and put on the platform. Her mouth was frozen open, almost with a look of recognition.

He knew she was dead. In a moment, the crowd would know. He watched the Illustrated Man's hand move down to touch, trace, feel for life. Then Mr. Dark lifted both her hands, like a doll, in some marionette strategy, to give her motion. But the body refused.

So he gave one of the Witch's arms to the Dwarf, the other to the Skeleton, and they shook and moved them in a ghastly semblance of reawakening as the crowd backed.

"... dead ..."

"But ... there's no wound."

"Shock, you think?"

Shock, thought Charles Halloway, my God, did *that* kill her? Or the other bullet? When I fired the shot, did she suck the *other* bullet down her throat? Did she ... choke on my smile! Oh, Christ!

"It's all right! Show's over! Just fainted!" said Mr. Dark. "All an act! All part of the show," he said, not looking at the woman, not looking at the crowd, but looking at Will, who stood blinking around, out of one nightmare and fresh into the next as his father stood with him and Mr. Dark cried: "Everyone home! Show's over! Lights! Lights!"

The carnival lights flickered.

The crowd, herded before the failing illumination, turned like a great carousel, and as the lamps dimmed, hustled toward the few remaining pools of light as if to warm themselves there before braving the wind. One by one, one by one, the lights indeed were going off.

"Lights!" said Mr. Dark.

"Jump!" said Will's father.

Will jumped. Will ran with his father who still carried the weapon that had fired the smile that had killed the Gypsy and put her to dust.

"Is Jim in there?"

They were at the maze. Behind them, on the platform, Mr. Dark bellowed: "Lights! Go home! All over! Done!"

"*Is* Jim in there?" wondered Will. "Yes. Yes, he is!"

Inside the Wax Museum, Jim still had not moved, had not blinked.

"Jim!" The voice came through the maze.

Jim moved. Jim blinked. A rear exit door stood wide. Jim blundered toward it.

"I'm coming for you, Jim!"

"No, Dad!"

Will caught at his father, who stood at the first turn of the mirrors with the pain come back to his hand, racing up along the nerves to strike a fireball near his heart. "Dad, don't go in!" Will grabbed his good arm.

Behind them, the platform was empty, Mr. Dark was running

. . . where? Somewhere as the night shut in, the lights went off, went off, went off, the night sucked around, gathering, whistling, simpering, and the crowd, like a shake of leaves from one huge tree, blew off the midway, and Will's father stood facing the glass tides, the waves, the gauntlet of horror he knew waited for him to swim through, stride through to fight the desiccation, the annihilation of one's self that waited there. He had seen enough to know. Eyes shut, you'd be lost. Eyes open, you'd know such utter despair, such gravities of anguish would weight you, you might never drag past the twelfth turn. But Charles Halloway took Will's hands away. "Jim's there. Jim, wait! I'm coming in!"

And Charles Halloway took the next step into the maze.

Ahead flowed sluices of silver light, deep slabs of shadow, polished, wiped, rinsed with images of themselves and others whose souls, passing, scoured the glass with their agony, curried the cold ice with their narcissism, or sweated the angles and flats with their fear.

"Jim!"

He ran. Will ran. They stopped.

For the lights in here were going blind, one by one, going dim, changing color, now blue, now a color like lilac summer lightning which flared in haloes, then a flickerlight like a thousand ancient windblown candles.

And between himself and Jim in need of rescue, stood an army of one million sick-mouthed, frost-haired, white-tine-bearded men.

Them! all of them! he thought. That's *me*!

Dad! thought Will, at his back, don't be afraid. It's only you. All only my father!

But he did not like their look. They were so old, so very old, and got much older the farther away they marched, wildly gesticulating, as Dad threw up his hands to fend off the revelation, this wild image repeated to insanity.

Dad! he thought, it's you!

But, it was more.

And all the lights went out.

And both, squeezed still, in muffle-gasping silence, stood afraid.

Chapter Forty-Nine

A HAND dug like a mole in the dark.

Will's hand.

It emptied his pockets, it delved, it rejected, it dug again. For while it was dark he knew those million old men might march, hustle, rush, leap, smash Dad with what they *were*! In this shut-up night, with just four seconds to think of them, they might do *anything* to Dad! If Will didn't hurry, these legions from Time Future, all the alarms of coming life, so mean, raw, and true you couldn't deny that's how Dad'd look tomorrow, next day, the day after the day after that, that cattle run of possible years might sweep Dad under!

So, quick!

Who has more pockets than a magician?

A boy.

Whose pockets contain *more* than a magician's?

A boy's.

Will seized forth kitchen matches!

"Oh God, Dad, here!"

He struck the match.

The stampede was close!

They had come running. Now, fixed by light, they widened their eyes, as did Dad, amazed their mouths at their own ancient quakes and masquerades. Halt! the match had cried. And platoons left, squads right, had stilt-muscled themselves to fitful rest, to baleful glare, itching for the match to whiff out. Then, given lease to run next time, they'd hit this old, very old, much older, terribly old man, suffocate him with Fates in one instant.

"No!" said Charles Halloway.

No. A million dead lips moved.

Will thrust the match forward. In the mirrors, a wizened multiplication of boy-apes did likewise, posing a single rosebud of blue-yellow flame.

"No!"

Every glass threw javelins of light which invisibly pierced, sank deep, found heart, soul, lungs, to frost the veins, cut nerves, send Will to ruin, paralyze and then kick-football heart. Hamstrung, the old old man foundered to his knees, as did his suppliant images, his congregation of terrified selves one week, one month, two years, twenty, fifty, seventy, ninety years from now! every second, minute, and long-after-midnight hour of his possible survival into insanity, there all sank grayer, more yellow as the mirrors ricocheted him through, bled him lifeless, mouthed him dry, then threatened to whiff him to skeletal dusts and litter his moth ashes to the floor.

"No!"

Charles Halloway struck the match from his son's hand.

"Dad, don't!"

For in the new dark, the restive herd of old men shambled forward, hearts hammering.

"Dad, we gotta *see*!"

He struck his second and final match.

And in the flare saw Dad sunk down, eyes clenched, fists tight, and all those other men who would have to shunt, crawl, scramble on knees once this last light was gone. Will grabbed his father's shoulder and shook him.

"Oh, Dad, Dad, I don't care how old you are, ever! I don't care what, I don't care anything! Oh, Dad," he cried, weeping. "I love you!"

At which Charles Halloway opened his eyes and saw himself and the others like himself and his son behind holding him, the flame trembling, the tears trembling on his face, and suddenly, as before, the image of the Witch, the memory of the library, defeat for one, victory for another, swam before him, mixed with sound of rifle shot, flight of marked bullet, surge of fleeing crowd.

For only a moment longer he looked at all of himselves, at Will. A small sound escaped his mouth. A little larger sound escaped his mouth.

And then, at last, he gave the maze, the mirrors, and all Time ahead, Beyond, Around, Above, Behind, Beneath or squandered inside himself, the only answer possible.

He opened his mouth very wide, and let the loudest sound of all free.

The Witch, if she were alive, would have known that sound, and died again.

Chapter Fifty

JIM NIGHTSHADE, out the back door of the maze, lost on the carnival grounds, running, stopped.

The Illustrated Man, somewhere among the black tents, running, stopped.

The Dwarf froze.

The Skeleton turned.

All had heard.

Not the sound that Charles Halloway made, no.

But the terrific sounds that followed.

One mirror alone, and then a second mirror, followed by a pause, and then a third mirror, and a fourth and another after that and another after that and still another and another after that, in domino fashion, they formed swift spiderwebs over their fierce stares and then with faint tinkles and sharp cracks, fell.

One minute there was this incredible Jacob's ladder of glass, folding, refolding and folding away yet again images pressed in a book of light. The next, all shattered to meteor precipitation.

The Illustrated Man, halted, listening, felt his own eyes, crystal, almost spiderweb and splinter with the sounds.

It was as if Charles Halloway, once more a choirboy in a strange sub-sub-demon church had sung the most beautiful high note of amiable humor ever in his life which first shook moth-silver from the mirror backs, then shook images from glass faces, then shook glass itself to ruin. A dozen, a hundred, a thousand mirrors, and with them the ancient images of Charles Halloway, sank earthward in delicious moonfalls of snow and sleety water.

All because of the sound he had let come from his lungs through his throat out his mouth.

All because he accepted everything at last, accepted the carnival, the hills beyond, the people in the hills, Jim, Will, and above all himself and all of life, and, accepting, threw back his head for the second time tonight and showed his acceptance with sound.

And lo! like Jericho and the trump, with musical thunders

the glass gave up its ghosts, Charles Halloway cried out, released. He took his hands from his face. Fresh starlight and dying carnival glow rushed in to set him free. The reflected dead men were gone, buried under the cymbaled slide, the splash and surfing of glass at his feet.

"Lights . . . lights!"

A far voice cried away more warmth.

The Illustrated Man, unfrozen, vanished among the tents.

The crowd was now gone.

"Dad, what'd you *do*?"

But the match burned Will's fingers, he dropped it, but now there was dim light enough to see Dad shuffle the trash, stir the mess of mirrored glass, heading back through the empty places where the maze had been and was no more.

"Jim?"

A door stood open. Pale carnival illumination, fading, poured through to show them wax figures of murderers and murderees.

Jim did not sit among them.

"Jim!"

They stared at the open door through which Jim had run to be lost in the swarms of night between black canvases.

The last electric light bulb went out.

"We'll *never* find him now," said Will.

"Yes," said his father, standing in the dark. "We'll find him."

Where? Will thought, and stopped.

Far down the midway, the carousel steamed, the calliope tortured itself with musics.

There, thought Will. If Jim's anywhere, it's there, to the music, old funny Jim, the free-ride ticket hid in his pocket still, I bet! Oh, damn Jim, damn him, damn him! he cried, and then thought, no! don't *you*, he's damned already, or near it! So how do we find him in the dark, no matches, no lights, just the two of us, all of them, and us alone in their territory?

"How—" said Will, aloud.

But his father said "There," very softly. With gratitude.

And Will stepped to the door, which was lighter now.

The moon! Thank God.

It was rising from the hills.

"The police . . . ?"

"No time. It's the next few minutes or nothing. Three people we got to worry about—"

"The freaks!"

"Three people, Will. Number one, Jim, number two, Mr. Cooger frying in his Electric Chair. Number three, Mr. Dark and his skinful of souls. Save one, kick the other two to hell and gone. Then I think the freaks go, too. You ready, Will?"

Will eyed the door, the tents, the dark, the sky with new light paling it.

"God bless the moon."

Hands tight together, they stepped out the door.

As if to greet them, the wind flung up and down all the tent canvases in a great prehistoric thunder-kite display of leprous wings.

Chapter Fifty-One

THEY RAN in urine smell of shadow, they ran in clean ice smell of moon.

The calliope steam-throb whispered, tatted, trilled.

The music! thought Will, is it running backward or forward?

"Which way?" Dad whispered.

"Through here!" Will pointed.

A hundred yards off, beyond a foothill of tents, there was a flare of blue light, sparks jumped up and fell away, then dark again.

Mr. Electrico! thought Will. They're trying to move him, sure! Get him to the merry-go-round, kill or cure! And if they cure him, then, oh gosh, then, it's angry him and angry Illustrated Man against just Dad and me! And Jim? Well, where was Jim? This way one day, that way the next, and . . . tonight? Whose side would he wind up on? Ours! Old friend Jim! Ours, of course! But Will trembled. Did friends last forever, then? For eternity, could they be counted to a warm, round, and handsome sum?

Will glanced left.

The Dwarf stood half enfolded by tent flaps, waiting, motionless.

"Dad, look," cried Will, softly. "And there—the Skeleton."

Further over, the tall man, the man all marble bone and Egyptian papyrus stood like a dead tree.

"The freaks—why don't they stop us?"

"Scared."

"Of *us*?!"

Will's father crouched and squinted out from around an empty cage.

"They're walking wounded, anyway. They saw what happened to the Witch. That's the only answer. Look at them."

And there they stood, like uprights, like tent poles spotted all through the meadow grounds, hiding in shadow, waiting. For what? Will swallowed, hard. Maybe not hiding at all, but spread out for the running fight to come. At the right time,

Mr. Dark would yell and—they'd just circle in. But the time wasn't right. Mr. Dark was busy. When he'd done what must be done, then he'd give that yell. So? So, thought Will, we got to see he never yells at all.

Will's feet slithered in the grass.

Will's father moved ahead.

The freaks watched with moon-glass eyes as they passed.

The calliope changed. It whistled sadly, sweetly, around a curve of tents, around a riverflow of darkness.

It's going ahead! thought Will. Yes! It *was* going backward. But now it stopped and started again, and this time forward! What's Mr. Dark *up* to?

"Jim!" Will burst out.

"Sh!" Dad shook him.

But the name had tumbled from his mouth only because he heard the calliope summing the golden years ahead, felt Jim isolate somewhere, pulled by warm gravities, swung by sunrise notes, wondering what it could be like to stand sixteen, seventeen, eighteen years tall, and then, oh then, nineteen and, most incredible!—twenty! The great wind of time blew in the brass pipes, a fine, a jolly, a summer tune, promising everything and even Will, hearing, began to run toward the music that grew up like a peach tree full of sun-ripe fruit—

No! he thought.

And instead made his feet step to his own fear, jump to his own tune, a hum cramped back by throat, held fast by lungs, which shook the bones of his head and drowned the calliope away.

"There," said Dad softly.

And between the tents, ahead, in transit, they saw a grotesque parade. Like a dark sultan in a palanquin, a half-familiar figure rode a chair borne on the shoulders of assorted sizes and shapes of darkness.

At Dad's cry, the parade jolted, then broke into a run!

"Mr. Electrico!" said Will.

They're taking him to the carousel!

The parade vanished.

A tent lay between them.

"Around here!" Will jumped, pulling his father.

The calliope played sweet. To pull Jim, to draw Jim.

And when the parade arrived with Electrico?

Back the music would spin, back the carousel run, to shard away his skin, to freshen forth his years!

Will stumbled, fell. Dad picked him up.

And then . . .

There arose a human barking, yapping, baying, whining, as if *all* had fallen. In a long-drawn moan, a gasp, a shuddering sigh, an entire crowd of people with crippled throats made chorus together.

"Jim! They've got Jim!"

"No . . ." murmured Charles Halloway, strangely. "Maybe Jim . . . or us . . . got *them*."

They stepped around the last tent.

Wind blew dust in their faces.

Will clapped his hand up, squinched his nose. The dust was antique spice, burnt maple leaves, a prickling blue that teemed and sifted to earth. Swarming its own shadows, the dust filtered over the tents.

Charles Halloway sneezed. Figures jumped and scurried away from an upended, half-tilted object abandoned halfway between one tent and the carousel.

The object was the electric chair, capsized, with straps dangling from wooden arms and legs, and a metal head-cap hanging from its top.

"But," said Will. "Where's Mr. Electrico!? I mean . . . Mr. Cooger!?"

"*That* must have been him."

"*What* must have been him?"

But the answer was there, sifting down the midway in the whorling wind devils . . . the burnt spice, the autumn incense that had floured them when they turned this corner.

Kill or cure, Charles Halloway thought. He imagined them rushed in the last few seconds, toting the ancient dustsack boneheap over starched grasses in his disconnected chair, perhaps only one in a running series of attempts to foster, encourage, preserve life in what was really nothing but a mortuary junkpile, rust-flakes and dying coals that no wind could blow alight again. Yet they must try. How many times in the last twenty-four hours had they run out on such excursions, only, in panic, to cease activity because the merest jolt, the slightest breath, threatened to shake old ancient Cooger down to meal-mush and chaff? Better to leave him propped in electric-warm chair, a continual exhibit, an ever-going-on performance for gaping audiences, and try again, but especially try now, when, lights out, and crowds herded off in the dark, all threatened by one smile on a bullet, there was need of Cooger as he once was, tall, flame-headed, and riven with earthquake violence. But somewhere, twenty seconds, ten seconds ago, the last glue crumbled, the last bolt of life fell free, and the mummy-doll, the Erector-set grotesque disencumbered itself in smoke puffs and November leaflets, a broadcast of mortality along the wind. Mr. Cooger, threshed in a final harvest, was now a billion parchment flecks, tumbled sea-scrolls capered in meadows. A mere dust explosion in a silo of ancient grain: gone.

"Oh, no, no, no, no, no," someone murmured.

Charles Halloway touched Will's arm.

Will stopped saying "Oh, no, no, no." He, too, in the last few moments, had thought the same as his father, of the toted corpse, the strewn bone-meal, the mineral-enriched hills of grass. . . .

Now there was only the empty chair and the last particles of mica, the radiant motes of peculiar dirt crusting the straps. And the freaks, who had been toting the baroque dump, now fled to shadows.

We made them run, thought Will, but something made them drop it!

No, not something. Someone.

Will flexed his eyes.

The carousel, deserted, empty, traveled on its way through its own special time, forward.

But between the fallen chair and the carousel, standing alone, was that a freak? No . . .

"Jim!"

Dad knocked his elbow and Will shut up.

Jim, he thought.

And where, now, was Mr. Dark?

Somewhere. For he had started the carousel, hadn't he? Yes! To draw them, to draw Jim, and—what else? Right now there was no time, for—

Jim turned from the spilled chair, turned and walked slowly toward the free, free ride.

He was going where he had always known he must go. Like a weather vane in wild seasons he had tremored this way, wandered that, hesitated upon bright horizons and warm directions, only at last now to tilt and, half sleepwalking, tremble about in the bright brass pull and summer march of music. He could not look away.

Another step, and then another, toward the merry-go-round, there went Jim.

"Go get him, Will," said his father.

Will went.

Jim raised his right hand.

The brass poles flashed by into the future, pulling the flesh like syrup, stretching the bones like taffy, the sun-metal color burning Jim's cheeks, flinting his eyes.

Jim reached. The brass poles flick-knocked his fingernails, tinkling their own small tune.

"Jim!"

The brass poles chopped by in a yellow sunrise at night.

The music leaped in a clear fountain, high.

Eeeeeeeeeeeeee.

Jim opened his mouth with the same cry:

"Eeeeeeeeeeeee!"

"Jim!" cried Will, running.

Jim's palm slapped one brass pole. The pole whipped on.

He slapped another brass pole. This time, his palm glued itself tight.

Wrist followed fingers, arm followed wrist, shoulder and body followed arm. Jim, sleepwalked, was torn from his roots in the earth.

"Jim!"

Will reached, felt Jim's foot flick from his grasp.

Jim swung round the wailing night in a great dark summer circle, Will racing after.

"Jim, get off! Jim, don't leave me *here*!"

Flung by centrifuge, Jim grasped the pole with one hand, spun, and, as if by some lone lost and final instinct, gestured his other hand free to trail on the wind, the one part of him, the small white separate part that still remembered their friendship.

"Jim, *jump*!!"

Will snatched for that hand, missed, stumbled, almost fell. The first race was lost. Jim must circle once, alone. Will stood waiting the next charge of horses, the fling-about of boy not-so-much boy—

"Jim! Jim!"

Jim awoke! Circled half round, his face showed now July, now December. He seized the pole, bleating out his despair. He wanted, he did not want. He wished, he rejected, he ardently wished again, in flight, in heat-spell river of wind and blaze of metal, in jog of July and August horses whose hoofs thudded the air like thrown fruit, his eyes blazed. Tongue clamped in teeth, he hissed his frustration.

"Jim! Jump! Dad, stop the machine!"

Charles Halloway turned to see where the control box stood, fifty feet off.

"Jim!" Will's side was stabbed with pain. "I need you! Come back!"

And, far over away on the far side of the carousel, traveling, fast-traveling, Jim fought with his own hands, the pole, the empty wind-whipped journey, the growing night, the wheeling stars. He let go the pole. He grabbed it. And still his right hand trailed down and out, begging Will's last full ounce of strength.

"Jim!"

Jim came around. There, below, in the black-night station from which this train pulled away forever in a flurry of ticket-punch confetti, he saw Will—Willy—William Halloway, young pal, young friend who would seem younger still at the end of this journey, and not just young but unknown! vaguely remembered from some other time in some other year . . . but now that boy, that friend, that younger friend, ran along by the train, reached up, asking passage? or demanding he get off? which?!

"Jim! Remember *me*?"

Will lunged his final lunge. Fingers touched fingers, palm touched palm.

Jim's face, white cold, stared down.

Will trot-paced the circling machine.

Where was Dad? Why didn't he shut it *off*?

Jim's hand was a warm hand, a familiar, a good hand. It closed on his. He gripped it yelling.

"Jim, please!"

But still they spun on the journey, Jim borne, Will dragged in a jog-crazy-trot.

"Please!"

Will jerked. Jim jerked. Trapped by Jim, Will's hand was shot with July heat. It went, like a kept animal, held and fondled by Jim, along, around, into older times. So his hand, far-traveling, would be alien to himself, knowing things by night that he himself, abed, might only guess. Fourteen-year boy, fifteen-year hand! Jim had it, yes! cramped it tight, would not let go! And Jim's face, was it older, from the journey round? Was he fifteen now, going on sixteen!?

Will pulled. Jim pulled opposite.

Will fell on the machine.

Both rode the night.

All of Will rode with friend Jim now.

"Jim! Dad!"

How easy it might be to just stand, ride, go round with Jim, if he couldn't pull Jim off, just leave him on and, dear pals, travel! The juices of his body swam, blinding his sight, they drummed his ears, shot electric jolts through his loins. . . .

Jim shouted. Will shouted.

They traveled half a year in slithering orchard-warm dark before Will seized Jim's arm tight and dared to leap from so much promise, so many fine tall-growing years, flail out, off, down, pull Jim with. But Jim could not let go the pole, could not give up the ride.

"Will!"

Jim, half between machine and friend, one hand on each, screamed.

It was like a great tearing of cloth or flesh.

Jim's eyes went blind as a statue's.

The carousel whirled.

Jim screamed, fell, spun crazily, on the air.

Will tried to break his fall, but Jim struck earth rolling. He lay, silent.

Charles Halloway hit the carousel control switch.

Empty, the machine slowed. Its horses paced themselves down from their trot toward some far midsummer night.

Together, Charles Halloway and his son knelt by Jim to touch his wrist, to put ear to his chest. Jim's eyes, skinned white, were fixed on the stars.

"Oh, God," cried Will. "Is he dead?"

Chapter Fifty-Two

"DEAD . . . ?"

Will's father moved his hand over that cold face, the cold chest.

"I don't feel . . ."

A long way off, someone cried for help.

They looked up.

A boy came running down the midway, bumping into ticket booths, falling over tent ropes, looking back over his shoulder.

"Help! He's after me!" the boy cried. "The terrible man! The terrible man! I want to go home!"

The boy flung himself forward, and grabbed at Will's father.

"Oh, help, I'm lost, I don't like it. Take me home. That man with the tattoos!"

"Mr. Dark!" gasped Will.

"Yes!" gibbered the boy. "He's down that way! Oh, stop him!"

"Will—" his father rose—"take care of Jim. Artificial respiration. All right, boy."

The boy trotted off. "This way!"

Following, Charles Halloway watched the distraught boy who led him; observed his head, his frame, the way his pelvis hung from his spine.

"Boy," he said, by the shadowed merry-go-round, twenty feet around from where Will bent to Jim. "What's your name?"

"No time!" cried the boy. "Jed. Quick, quick!"

Charles Halloway stopped.

"Jed," he said. The boy no longer moved, but turned, chafing his elbows. "How old are you, Jed?"

"Nine!" said the boy. "My gosh, this is no time! We—"

"This is a fine time, Jed," said Charles Halloway. "Only nine? So young. I was *never* that young."

"Holy cow!" shouted the boy, angrily.

"Or unholy something," said the man, and reached out. The boy backed away. "You're only afraid of one man, Jed. Me."

"You?" The boy still backed off. "Cut it out! Why, why?"

"Because, sometimes good has weapons and evil none.

Sometimes tricks fail. Sometimes people can't be picked off, led to deadfalls. No divide-and-conquer tonight, Jed. Where were you taking me, Jed? To some lion's cage you got fixed and ready? To some side show, like the mirrors? To someone like the Witch? What, what, Jed, what? Let's just roll up your right shirt sleeve, shall we, Jed?"

The great moonstone eyes flashed at Charles Halloway.

The boy leaped back, but not before the man had leaped with him, seized his arm, grabbed the back of his shirt and instead of simply rolling up the sleeve as first suggested, tore the entire shirt off the boy's body.

"Why, yes, Jed," said Charles Halloway, almost quietly. "Just as I thought."

"You, you, you, you!"

"Yes, Jed, me. But especially you, look at you."

And look he did.

For there, on the back of the small boy's hand, on the fingers, and up along the wrist scrambled blue serpents, blue-venomed snake eyes, blue scorpions scuttling about blue shark maws which gaped eternally hungry to feed upon all the freaks crammed and stung-sewn cheek by jowl, skin to skin, flesh to flesh all up and down the chest, the tiny torso, and tucked in the secret gathering places on this small small very small body, this cold and now shocked and trembling body.

"Why, Jed, that's fine artwork, that is."

"You!" The boy struck.

"Yes, still me." Charles Halloway took the blow in the face and clamped a vise on the boy.

"No!"

"Oh, yes," said Charles Halloway, using just his good right hand, his ruined left hand hanging limp. "Yes, Jed, jump, squirm, go ahead. It was a fine idea. Get me off alone, fix me, then go back and get Will. And when the police come, why, you're just a boy nine or ten and the carnival, oh, no, it's not yours, doesn't belong to you. Stay here, Jed. Why you trying to get out from under my arm? The police look and the owners of the show have vanished, isn't that it, Jed? A fine escape."

"You can't hurt me!" the boy shrieked.

"Funny," said Charles Halloway. "I think I can."

He pressed the boy, almost lovingly, close, very close.

"Murder!" wailed the boy. "Murder."

"I'm not going to murder you, Jed, Mr. Dark, whoever, whatever you are. You're going to murder yourself because you can't stand being near people like me, not this close, *close*, not this *long*."

"Evil!" groaned the boy, writhing. "You're evil!"

"Evil?" Will's father laughed, which made the boy, wasp-stung and brambled by the sound, jerk all the more violently. "Evil?" The man's hands were flypaper fastened to the small bones. "Strange hearing that from you, Jed. So it must seem. Good to evil seems evil. So I will do only good to you, Jed, I will simply hold you and watch you poison yourself. I will do good to you, Jed, Mr. Dark, Mr. Proprietor, boy, until you tell what's wrong with Jim. Wake him up. Let him free. Give him life!"

"Can't . . . can't. . . ." The boy's voice fell down a well inside his body, fading away, away . . . "can't. . . ."

"You mean you won't?"

". . . can't . . ."

"All right, boy, all right then here and here and this and this . . ."

They looked like father and son long apart, passionately met, embraced, yet more embraced, as the man lifted his wounded hand to gently touch the stricken face as the crowd, the teem, of illustrations shivered and fled now this way and that in microscopic forays quickly abandoned. The boy's eyes swiveled wildly, fixed upon the man's mouth. He saw there the strange and somehow lovely smile once flung as beatification to the Witch.

He gathered the boy somewhat closer and thought, Evil has only the power that we give it. I give you nothing. I take back. Starve. Starve. Starve.

The two matchstick lights in the boy's affrighted eyes blew out.

The boy, and his stricken and bruised conclave of monsters, his felt but half-seen crowd, fell to earth.

There should have been a roar like a mountain slid to ruin.

But there was only a rustle, like a Japanese paper lantern dropped in the dust.

Chapter Fifty-Three

CHARLES HALLOWAY stood for a long while, breathing deep, lungs aching, looking down at the body. The shadows swooned and fluttered in all the canvas alleys where odd assorted sizes of freaks and people, fleshed in their own terrors and sins, held to poles, moaning in disbelief. Somewhere, the Skeleton moved out in the light. Somewhere else, the Dwarf *almost* knew who he was, and scuttled forth like a crab from a cave to blink and blink again at Will bent working over Jim, at Will's father bent to exhaustion over the still form of the silent boy, while the merry-go-round, at last, slow, slow, came to a stop, rocking like a ferryboat in the watery-blowing grass.

The carnival was a great dark hearth lit with gathered coals, as shadows came to stare and fire their gaze with the tableau by the carousel.

There in the moonlight lay the illustrated boy named Dark.

There lay dragons slaughtered, towers ruined, monsters from dim ages toppled into rusted coinage, pterodactyls smashed like biplanes from old and always meaningless wars, crustacea the color of emeralds abandoned on a white sand shore where the tide of life was going out, all, all the illustrations changing now, shifting, shriveling as the small flesh cooled. There the obscene wink of the navel eye gasped in on itself, there the nipple-iris of a trumpeting mastodon went blind and raved at its blindness; each and every picture remembered from the tall Mr. Dark now rendered down to miniature canvas pronged and forked over a boy's tennis-racket bones.

More freaks, with faces the color of beds where so many had lost the battle of souls, emerged from the shadows to glide in a great and ever more curious carousel motion about Charles Halloway and his dropped burden.

Will paused in his desperate push and relaxation, push and relaxation, trying to shape Jim back to life, unafraid of the watchers in the dark, no time for that! Even if there were time, these freaks, he sensed, were breathing the night as if they had not been fed on such rare fine air in years!

And as Charles Halloway watched, and the fox-fire,

lobster-moist, phlegm-trapped eyes watched from distances, the boy-who-had-been-Mr.-Dark grew yet colder, as death cut the timbers of nightmares, and the calligraphies, the smoky lightnings of sketch that coiled and crouched and soared like terrible banners of a lost war, began to vanish one by one from the strewn small body.

A score of freaks glanced fearfully round as if the moon had suddenly filled itself full and they could see; they chafed their wrists as if chains had fallen from them, chafed their necks as if weights had crumbled from their bowed shoulders. Stumbled forth after long entombments, they blinked swiftly, disbelieving the packet of their misery sprawled near the spent carousel. If they dared they might have bent to tremble their hands over that suddenly death-sweet mouth, the marbling brow. As it was they watched, benumbed, as their portrait pictures, the vital stuffs of their mortal greed, rancor, and poisonous guilt, the emerald abstracts of their self-blinded eyes, self-wounded mouths, self-trapped bodies melted one by one from this insignificant mound of snow. There melted the Skeleton! there the sidewise-scuttling crayfish Dwarf! Now the Lava Sipper took leave of autumn flesh, followed by the black Executioner from London Dock, there soared off and gone went the Human Montgolfier, the Balloon Man, Avoirdupois the Magnificent! deflated to purest air, there! there fled mobs and bands, as death washed the drawing board clean!

Now there lay just a plain dead boy, unbruised by pictures, staring up at the stars with Mr. Dark's empty eyes.

"Ahhhh . . ."

In a chorus of release, the strange people in the shadows sighed.

Perhaps the calliope gave a last ringmaster's bark. Perhaps thunder turned, sleeping, in the clouds. Suddenly all wheeled about. The freaks stampeded. North, south, east, west, free of tent, master, dark law, free above all of each other, they ran like albino pigs, tuskless boars, and stricken sloths before storms.

It must have been, it seemed, each yanked a rope, loosed a tent-peg, running.

For now the sky was shaken with a fatal respiration, the breathing down, the insunk rattle and pule of collapsing darkness as the tents gave way.

With hiss of viper, swirl of cobra, the ropes insanely raveled, slithered, snapped, cut grass with frictioned whips.

The networks of the vast Main Freak Tent convulsed, parted bones, small from medium, and medium from brontosaur magnificent. All swayed with impending fall.

The menagerie tent shut up like a dark Spanish fan.

Other small tents, caped figures in the meadow, fell down at the wind's command.

Then at last, the Freak Tent, the great melancholy mothering reptile bird, after a moment of indecision, sucked in a Niagara of blizzard air, broke loose three hundred hempen snakes, crack-rattled its black sidepoles so they fell like teeth from a cyclopean jaw, slammed the air with acres of moldered wing as if trying to kite away but, earth-tethered, must succumb to plain and most simple gravity, must be crushed by its own locked bulk.

Now this greatest tent staled out hot raw breaths of earth, confetti that was ancient when the canals of Venice were not yet staked, and wafts of pink cotton candy like tired feather boas. In rushing downfalls, the tent shed skin; grieved, soughed as flesh fell away until at last the tall museum timbers at the spine of the discarded monster dropped with three cannon roars.

The calliope simmered, moronic with wind.

The train stood, an abandoned toy, in a field.

The freak oil paintings clapped hands high on the last standing pennant poles, then plummeted to earth.

The Skeleton, the only strange one left, bent to pick up the body of the porcelain boy-who-was-Mr.-Dark. He moved away into the fields.

Will, in a swift moment, saw the thin man and his burden go over a hill among all the footprints of the vanished carnival race.

Will's face shadowed this way, then that, pulled by the swift concussions, the tumults, the deaths, the fleeing away of souls. Cooger, Dark, Skeleton, Dwarf-who-was-Lightning-Rod-Salesman, don't run, come back! Miss Foley, where are you? Mr. Crosetti! it's over! Be still! Quiet! It's all right. Come back, come back!

But the wind was blowing their footprints out of the grass and they might run forever now trying to outflee themselves.

So Will turned back astride Jim and pushed the chest and let go, pushed and let go, then, trembling, touched his dear friend's cheek.

"Jim . . . ?"

But Jim was cold as spaded earth.

Chapter Fifty-Four

BENEATH THE cold was a fugitive warmness, in the white skin lay some small color, but when Will felt Jim's wrist there was nothing and when he put his ear to the chest there was nothing.

"He's *dead*!"

Charles Halloway came to his son and his son's friend and knelt down to touch the quiet throat, the unstirred rib cage.

"No." Puzzled. "Not quite . . ."

"Dead!"

The tears burst from Will's eyes. But then, as swiftly, he felt himself knocked, struck, shaken.

"Stop that!" cried his father. "You want to save him?!"

"It's too late, oh, Dad!"

"Shut up! Listen!"

But Will wept.

And again his father hauled off and hit him. Once on the left cheek. Once on the right cheek, hard.

All the tears in him were knocked flying; there were no more.

"Will!" His father savagely jabbed a finger at him and at Jim. "Damn it, Willy, all this, all these, Mr. Dark and his sort, they *like* crying, my God, they *love* tears! Jesus God, the more you bawl, the more they drink the salt off your chin. Wail and they suck your breath like cats. Get up! Get off your knees, damn it! Jump around! Whoop and holler! You hear! Shout, Will, sing, but most of all laugh, you got that, laugh!"

"I can't!"

"You must! It's all we got. I *know*! In the library! The Witch ran, my God, *how* she ran! I shot her dead with it. A single smile, Willy, the night people can't stand it. The sun's there. They hate the sun. We *can't* take them seriously, Will!"

"But—"

"But hell! You saw the mirrors! And the mirrors shoved me half in, half out the grave. Showed me all wrinkles and rot! Blackmailed me! Blackmailed Miss Foley so she joined the grand march Nowhere, joined the fools who wanted everything! Idiot thing to want: everything! Poor damned fools. So wound up with nothing like the dumb dog who dropped his bone to go after the reflection of the bone in the pond. Will, you saw: *every* mirror fell. Like ice in a thaw. With no rock or rifle, no knife, just my teeth, tongue and lungs, I gunshot those mirrors with pure contempt! Knocked down ten million scared fools and let the *real* man get to his feet! Now, on *your* feet, Will!"

"But Jim—" Will faltered.

"Half in, half out. Jim's been that, always. Sore-tempted. Now he went too far and maybe he's lost. But he fought to save himself, right? Put his hand out to you, to fall free of the machine? So we finish that fight *for* him. Move!"

Will sailed up, giddily, yanked.

"Run!"

Will sniffed again. Dad slapped his face. Tears flew like meteors.

"Hop! Jump! Yell!"

He banged Will ahead, shuffled with him, shoved his hand in his pockets, tearing them inside out until he pulled forth a bright object.

The harmonica.

Dad blew a chord.

Will stopped, staring down at Jim.

Dad clouted him on the ear.

"Run! Don't look!"

Will ran a step.

Dad blew another chord, yanked Will's elbow, flung each of his arms.

"Sing!"

"What?"

"God, boy, anything!"

The harmonica tried a bad "Swanee River."

"Dad." Will shuffled, shaking his head, immensely tired. "Silly . . . !"

"Sure! We *want* that! Silly damn fool man! Silly harmonica! Bad off-key tune!"

Dad whooped. He circled like a dancing crane. He was not *in* the silliness yet. He *wanted* to crack through. He had to *break* the moment!

"Will: louder, funnier, as the man said! Oh, hell, don't let them drink your tears and want more! Will! Don't let them take your crying, turn it upside down and use it for their own smile! I'll be damned if death wears *my* sadness for glad rags. Don't feed them one damn thing, Willy, loosen your bones! Breathe! Blow!"

He seized Will's hair, shook him.

"Nothing . . . funny . . ."

"*Sure* there is! Me! You! Jim! All of us! The whole shooting works! Look!"

And Charles Halloway pulled faces, popped his eyes, mashed his nose, winked, cavorted like chimpanzee-ape, waltzed with the wind, tap-danced the dust, threw back his head to bay at the moon, dragging Will with him.

"Death's funny, God damn it! Bend, two, three, Will. Soft-shoe. Way down upon the Swanee River—what's *next*, Will? . . . Far far away! Will, your God-awful voice! Damn girl soprano. Sparrow in a tin can. Jump, boy!"

Will went up, came down, cheeks hotter, a wincing like lemons in his throat. He felt balloons grow in his chest.

Dad sucked the silver harmonica.

"That's where the old folks—" Will spoke.

"Stay!" bellowed his father.

Shuffle, tap, bounce, jog.

Where was Jim? Jim was forgotten.

Dad jabbed his ribs, tickling.

"De Camptown ladies sing this song!"

"Doo-dah!" yelled Will. "Doo-dah!" he sang it now, with a tune. The balloon grew. His throat tickled.

"Camptown race track, five miles long!"

"Oh, doo-dah day!"

Man and boy did a minuet.

And in midstep *it* happened.

Will felt the balloon grow huge within him.

He smiled.

"What?" Dad was surprised by those teeth.

Will snorted. Will giggled.

"What *say*?" asked Dad.

The force of the exploding warm balloon alone shoved Will's teeth apart, kicked his head back.

"Dad! Dad!"

He bounded. He grabbed his Dad's hand. He raced crazily, hollering, quacking like a duck, clucking like a chicken. His palms hit his throbbing knees. Dust flew off his soles.

"Oh, Susanna!"

"Oh, don't you cry—"

"—for me!"

"For I come from—"

"Alabama with my—"

"Banjo on my—"

Together. "Knee!"

The harmonica knocked teeth, wheezing, Dad hocked forth great chords of squeeze-eyed hilarity, turning in a circle, jumping up to kick his heels.

"Ha!" They collided, half-collapsed, knocked elbows, cracked heads, which blew the air out faster. "Ha! Oh God, ha! Oh God, Will, ha! Weak! Ha!"

In the middle of wild laughter—

A sneeze!

They spun. They stared.

Who lay there on the moonlit earth?

Jim? Jim Nightshade?

Had *he* stirred? *Was* his mouth wider, his eyelids quivering? *Were* his cheeks pinker?

Don't look! Dad swung Will handily round in a further reel. They do-si-do'ed, hands extended, the harmonica seeping and guzzling raw tunes from a father who storked his legs and turkeyed his arms. They hopped Jim one way, hopped back, as if he were but a lump-stone on the grass.

"Someone's in the kitchen with Dinah! Someone's in the kitchen—"

"—I know-oh-oh-*oh*!"

Jim's tongue slid out on his lips.

No one saw this. Or if they saw, ignored it, fearing it might pass.

Jim did the final things himself. His eyes opened. He watched the dancing fools. He could not believe. He had been off on a journey of years. Now, returned, no one said "Hi!" All jigged Sambo-style. Tears might have jumped to his eyes. But before they could start, Jim's mouth curved. He gave up a ghost of laughter. For, after all, there indeed was silly Will and his silly old janitor dad racing like gorillas knuckle-dusting the meadows, their faces a puzzlement. They toppled above him, clapped hands, wiggled ears, bent to wash him all over with their now bright full-river flowing laughter that could not be stopped if the sky fell or the earth rent open, to blend their good mirth with his, to fuse-light and set him off in a detonation which could not stop exploding from ladyfingers to four-inchers to doomsday cannon crackers of delight!

And looking down, jolt-dancing his bones loose and delicious, Will thought: Jim don't remember he was dead, so we won't tell, not now—some day, sure, but not . . . Doo-dah! Doo-dah!

They didn't even say "Hello, Jim" or "Join the dance," they just put out hands as if he had fallen from their swung pandemonium commotion and needed a boost back into the swarm. They yanked Jim. Jim flew. Jim came down dancing.

And Will knew, hand in hand, hot palm to palm, they had truly yelled, sung, gladly shouted the live blood back. They had slung Jim like the newborn, knocked his lungs, slapped his back, shocked joyous breath to where it made room.

Then Dad bent and Will leaped over him and Will bent and Dad jumped him and they both waited, crouched in a line, wheezing songs, deliciously tired, while Jim swallowed spit, and ran full tilt. He got half over Dad when they all fell, rolled in the grass, all hoot-owl and donkey, all brass and cymbal as it must have been the first year of Creation, and Joy not yet thrown from the Garden.

Until at last they drew up their feet, socked each other's shoulders, embraced knees tight, rocking, and looking with swift bright happiness at each other, growing wine-drunkenly quiet.

And when they were done smiling at each other's faces as at burning torches, they looked away across the field.

And the black tent poles lay in elephant boneyards with the dead tents blowing away like the petals of a great black rose.

The only three people in a sleeping world, a rare trio of tomcats, they basked in the moon.

"What happened?" asked Jim, at last.

"What *didn't*!" cried Dad.

And they laughed again, when suddenly Will grabbed Jim, held him tight and wept.

"Hey," Jim said, over and over, quietly. "Hey . . . hey . . ."

"Oh, Jim, Jim," Will said. "We'll be pals forever."

"Sure, hey sure." Jim was very quiet now.

"It's all right," said Dad. "Have a small cry. We're out of the woods. Then we'll laugh some more, going home."

Will let Jim go.

They got to their feet and stood looking at each other. Will examined his father, with fierce pride.

"Oh, Dad, Dad, you *did* it, you did it!"

"No, we did it together."

"But without you it'd all be over. Oh, Dad, I never knew you. I sure know you now."

"Do you, Will?"

"Darn right!"

Each, to the other, shimmered in bright halos of wet light.

"Why then, hello. Reply, son, and curtsey."

Dad held out his hand. Will shook it. Both laughed and wiped their eyes, then looked quickly at the footprints scattered in the dew over the hills.

"Dad, will they ever come back?"

"No. And yes." Dad tucked away his harmonica. "No, not them. But yes, other people like them. Not in a carnival. God knows what shape they'll come in next. But sunrise, noon, or at the latest, sunset tomorrow they'll show. They're on the road."

"Oh, no," said Will.

"Oh, yes," said Dad. "We got to watch out the rest of our lives. The fight's just begun."

They moved around the carousel slowly.

"What will they look like? How will we know them?"

"Why," said Dad, quietly, "maybe they're already here."

Both boys looked around swiftly.

But there was only the meadow, the machine, and themselves.

Will looked at Jim, at his father, and then down at his own body and hands. He glanced up at Dad.

Dad nodded, once, gravely, and then nodded at the carousel, and stepped up on it, and touched a brass pole.

Will stepped up beside him. Jim stepped up beside Will.

Jim stroked a horse's mane. Will patted a horse's shoulders.

The great machine softly tilted in the tides of night.

Just three times around, ahead, thought Will. Hey.

Just four times around, ahead, thought Jim. Boy.

Just ten times around, back, thought Charles Halloway. Lord.

Each read the thoughts in the other's eyes.

How easy, thought Will.

Just this once, thought Jim.

But then, thought Charles Halloway, once you start, you'd always come back. One more ride and one more ride. And, after awhile, you'd offer rides to friends, and more friends until finally . . .

The thought hit them all in the same quiet moment.

. . . finally you wind up owner of the carousel, keeper of the freaks . . . proprietor for some small part of eternity of the traveling dark carnival shows. . . .

Maybe, said their eyes, *they're already here.*

Charles Halloway stepped back into the machinery of the merry-go-round, found a wrench, and knocked the flywheels and cogs to pieces. Then he took the boys out and he hit the control box one or two times until it broke and scattered fitful lightnings.

"Maybe this isn't necessary," said Charles Halloway. "Maybe it wouldn't run anyway, without the freaks to give it power. But—" He hit the box a last time and threw down the wrench.

"It's late. Must be midnight straight up."

Obediently, the City Hall clock, the Baptist church clock, the Methodist, the Episcopalian, the Catholic church, all the clocks, struck twelve. The wind was seeded with Time.

"Last one to the railroad semaphore at Green Crossing is an old lady!"

The boys fired themselves off like pistols.

The father hesitated only a moment. He felt the vague pain in his chest. If I run, he thought, what will happen? Is Death important? No. Everything that happens before Death is what counts. And we've done fine tonight. Even Death can't spoil it. So, there went the boys . . . and why not . . . *follow*?

He did just that.

And Lord! it was fine printing their life in the dew on the

cool fields that new dark suddenly-like-Christmas morning. The boys ran as tandem ponies, knowing that someday one would touch base first, and the other second or not at all, but now this first minute of the new morning was not the minute or the day or morning of ultimate loss. Now was not the time to study faces to see if one was older and the other too much younger. Today was just another day in October in a year suddenly better than anyone supposed it could ever be just a short hour ago, with the moon and the stars moving in a grand rotation toward inevitable dawn, and them loping, and the last of this night's weeping done, and Will laughing and singing and Jim giving answer line by line, as they breasted the waves of dry stubble toward a town where they might live another few years across from each other.

And behind them jogged a middle-aged man with his own now solemn, now amiable, thoughts.

Perhaps the boys slowed. They never knew. Perhaps Charles Halloway quickened his pace. He could not say.

But, running even with the boys, the middle-aged man reached out.

Will slapped, Jim slapped, Dad slapped the semaphore signal base at the same instant.

Exultant, they banged a trio of shouts down the wind.

Then, as the moon watched, the three of them together left the wilderness behind and walked into the town.

APPENDIX

A Few Notes on The Martian Chronicles

IN 1944, after a long summer of reading John Steinbeck, Sinclair Lewis, Jean Giono, and Sherwood Anderson, I put down a few sentences on a piece of yellow paper. I came across those notes the other day. "Do a book," I said, "about all the people on Mars."

I think now that I was being a bit optimistic, and not a little preposterous. If I can believe the readers of the s-f magazines, I have already written about too many people on Mars. I don't see how this can be, for I haven't run out of people yet, but never the less, there it is. I think I'll be writing about Venus and a few other planets for a while now.

But at least I do have a book to show for the last six years of thinking about Mars—not the book that I had planned back in 1944, no, but another book entirely. I had the idea then that I wanted to do something of a *Winesburg, Ohio*, on Mars. Well, I didn't do that, fortunately, for it would have been doing something over that had already been done and done beautifully. But out of reading Anderson and Steinbeck and a lady named Jessamyn West, and a gentle and understanding book which nobody seems to have heard of, *The Friendly Persuasion*, I realized that if I did not know what my book was going to be about, I at least knew what it was *not* going to be about. It was not going to be about bug-eyed-monsters or rockets or intricate inventions, or Esperanto, or Semantics, or—well—rhodomagnetics. It was going to be about people and they were going to be lonely people. They could not help being lonely, for they were doubly damned; once by a civilization that yanked the base out from under their God, and tried to take their mind off their loss with nylon toothbrushes and V-8 engines, and again by the impossible total of miles between Earth and Mars.

It is all very well to say that one would like to be one of the first Martian colonials, but quite another thing to awaken at midnight and find yourself, in reality, on the red planet, sixty million miles from everything that means anything. It'll take a little adjustment. How much nicer if the colonials could look upon space as a Cathredal, with God in His place, and all right with the universe, except that these colonials would be going into space that they had carefully sprayed with equal parts of philosophical cyanide and scientific DDT.

Long before Mr. Steig, the illustrator, in my home in Illinois there was a man who prowled the streets in the year 1928, who was known as "the lonely one." I have never forgotten him. Some day his sons, or the sons of his sons, will go to Mars. Eliot calls them The Hollow Men. Call them what you will, but there they go, off to Mars, just for the ride, thinking they will find a planet like a seer's crystal, in which to read a miraculous future. What they'll find, instead, is the somewhat shopworn image of themselves. Mars is a mirror, not a crystal.

I imagine this idea grew over the years until all of my Martian stories were finished and fitted into a book. From extreme excitement at an early age over the prospect of space travel, I have simmered down to a quiet interest in such possibilities. If we have nothing to offer Mars but bubble-gum and atom-bombs, I think we should wait another century or so. Whether or not this attitude is apparent in *The Martian Chronicles*, I leave it to you to discover. As for myself, I have just purchased an Al Jolson record, parts of which sound pretty fine to me:

"Go to the East, go to the West,
Some day you'll come,
Weary of heart, back where you started from."

The title of the song, which might be prophetic for those rocket-men trying to travel in Mr. Einstein's curved space, is "Back in Your Own Backyard." Enough said.

Day After Tomorrow: Why Science Fiction?

THREE years ago I wrote a short novel entitled "The Fire Man" which told the story of a municipal department in the year 1999 that came to your house to *start* fires, instead of to put them out. If your neighbors suspected you of reading a mildly subversive book, or any book at all for that matter, they simply turned in an alarm. The hose-bearing censors then thundered up in their red engines and squirted kerosene on your books, your house, and sometimes on you. Then a match was struck. This short novel was intended as science fiction.

Elsewhere in the narrative I described my Fire Man arriving home after midnight and finding his wife in bed afflicted with two varieties of stupor. She is in a trance, a condition so withdrawn as to resemble catatonia, compounded of equal parts of liquor and a small Seashell thimble-radio tucked in her ear. The Seashell croons and murmurs its music and commercials and private little melodramas for her alone. The room is silent. The husband cannot even try to guess the communion between Seashell and wife. Awakening her is not unlike applying shock to a cataleptic.

I thought I was writing a story of prediction, describing a world that might evolve in four or five decades. But only a month ago, in Beverly Hills one night, a husband and wife passed me, walking their dog. I stood staring after them, absolutely stunned. The woman held in one hand a small cigarette-package-sized radio, its antenna quivering. From this sprang tiny copper wires which ended in a dainty cone plugged into her right ear. There she was, oblivious to man and dog, listening to far winds and whispers and soap-opera cries, sleep-walking, helped up and down curbs by a husband who might just as well not have been there. This was *not* science fiction. This was a new fact in our changing society.

As you can see, I must start writing very fast indeed about our future world in order to stand still. I thought I had raced ahead of science, predicting the radio-induced semi-catatonic. In the long haul, science pulled abreast, tipped its hat, and fed me the dust. The woman with the radio-thimble crammed in her ear the other night symbolized my failure to count on certain psychological needs which demanded satisfaction earlier than I supposed.

Whether or not my ideas on censorship via the fire department will be old hat by this time next week, I dare not predict. When the wind is right, a faint odor of kerosene is exhaled from Senator McCarthy.

All of the above long prologue leads up to the simple fact that I very much enjoy, I *relish*, writing science fiction.

There is great serious fun for the writer in asking himself when does an invention stop being a reasonable escape mechanism—for we must all evade the world and its crushing responsibilities at times—and start being a paranoiacally dangerous device? How much of any one such invention is good for a person, bad for a person, fine for this man, fatal to the next?

So much depends, of course, on what the individual *hears* when he gives himself over to the electronic tides breaking on the shore of his Seashell. The voice of conscience and reason? An echo of morality? A new thought? A fresh idea? A morsel of philosophy? Or bias, hatred, fear, prejudice, nightmare, lies, half-truths, and suspicions? Or, perhaps even worse, the sound of one emptiness striking hollowly against yet another and another emptiness, broken at two-minute intervals by a jolly commercial, preferably in rhymed quatrains or couplets?

In writing a science-fiction story around such an idea, the author must consider many things. Is there, for instance, a delicate interplay where the society does not crush the individual but where the individual realizes that without his cooperation society would fly to pieces through the centrifugal force of anarchy? Is the programming on such an ear-button receiver of a caliber to enable a man to be a gyroscope, both taking from and giving to society, beautifully balanced? Does it tell him what to do *every* hour and *every* minute of *every* day? Or, fearing knowledge of any sort, tell him nothing, and spoonfeed him mush? The challenge and the fun come in handling all the above ideas and materials in such a way as to predict how perversely or how well man will use himself, and therefore his mechanical extensions, in the coming time of our lives.

It is both exciting and disconcerting for a writer to discover that man's machines are *indeed* symbols of his own most secret cravings and desires, extra hands put out to touch and reinterpret the world. The machines themselves are empty gloves into which a hand, either cold and excessively bony, or warm, full-fleshed, and gentle, can be inserted. The hand is always the hand of man, and the hand of man can be good or evil, while the gloves themselves remain amoral.

The problem of good and evil fascinates, then, especially when it is to be found externalized and purified in the thousands of semi-robots we are using and will use in the coming century. Our atomic knowledge destroys cancer or men. Our airplanes carry passengers or jellied gasoline bombs. The hairline, the human, choice is there. Before us today we see the aluminum and steel and uranium chess pieces which the interested science-fiction writer can hope to move about, trying to guess how man will play out the game.

This, I think, should answer why I have more often than not written stories which, for a convenient label, are called science fiction. There are few literary fields, it seems to me, that deal so strikingly with themes that concern us all today, there are few more exciting genres, there are none fresher or so full of continually renewed and renewable concepts.

It is, after all, the fiction of ideas, the fiction where philosophy can be tinkered with, torn apart, and put back together again, it is the fiction of sociology and psychology and history compounded and squared by time. It is the fiction where you may set up and knock down your own political and religious and moral states. It can be a high form of Swiss watch-making. It *can* be poetry. It *has* resulted in some of the greatest writing in our past, from Plato and Lucian to Sir Thomas More and François Rabelais and on down through Jonathan Swift and Johannes Kepler to Poe and Edward Bellamy and George Orwell.

If you try to cram philosophical and sociological theories into the non-science-fiction tale, you more often than not wind up with more crust than filling. It takes a very agile writer indeed to keep a book together under such conditions. But in the story of prediction, at its best, you are given leave to act out your problem in easily stage-managed symbols, in allegories, if you wish. It isn't necessary to stop for long-winded explanations of philosophical or sociological climates. Simply by showing your real characters living and dying against your fresh background, the reader can guess an entire and different world, can feel it come alive through an osmotic literary pròcess which is often exceptionally subtle. Science fiction, then, does one the favor of making outsize images of problems so they can be seen and handled from all sides like those Easter balloons strung along the avenue by Macy's each year.

Over and above everything, the writer in this field has a sense of being confronted by dozens of paths that move among the thousand mirrors of a carnival maze, seeing his society imaged and re-imaged and distorted by the light thrown back at him. Without moving anything but his typewriter, that immensely dependable Time Machine, the writer can take those paths and examine those billion images. Where are we going? Well, first let us see where we've *been*. And let us ask ourselves what we *are* at this very hour. Fortified with this knowledge, nebulous at most, the writer's imagination selects the first path.

Would you like to know how a Communist government might run the United States? A fascist clique? A government of matriarchs? Novels exist covering all these subjects. What if all parents gave over the education of their children entirely to machines? Or if a law was passed forbidding pedestrians in the year 2001? Why travel to the Moon or Mars if we only continue our wars there with Russia or Britain or Africa? Why build rockets at all? For fun? For adventure? Or is this the same process which sends the salmons back upstream year after year to spawn and die—a subliminal urge in mankind to spread, in self-preservation, to the stars? Are we then secretly fearful that one day the sun might freeze and the earth grow cold or the sun explode in a terrific thermal cataclysm and burn down our house of cards? And is all this space-travel talk nothing more than the human race itself seeing to it that it survives when survival means getting off a single, unstable planet and seeding space to its farthest boundaries, where no natural catastrophe, no congealing of sun or passing comet, can destroy man? Is self-preservation, then, our prime mover, and all our speechifying about adventure and fun and a New West in the Sky so much rationalization?

I know I cannot answer the above questions. But I also know I am endlessly fascinated with these questions, minor as they may seem to some, or pompous as they may seem to others. And many, including myself, are having a go at answering them, in the science-fiction field. Here are a few more:

How do you go about converting a group of non-materialist utterly alien Martians to the Methodist conviction? If you find a race of dogs or cows on Venus with I.Q.'s verging on 190, capable of carrying on highly enlightened and logical conversations on social and metaphysical topics, where does this put the Christian faith relative to their dictum that canines and cows do not have souls of transferable value? If these dogs and cows are morally aware and *responsible for their actions*, that is supposedly the test one must pass in order to be credited with a soul. Well, then, one is tempted to ask the Christian religion to point out that exact moment in the history of dogdom and cowdom on Venus when they stopped being brutes without souls and became equal and perhaps superior to man, thus inheriting the soul as a blessed gift?

I ask these questions both in good humor and in all seriousness. I ask them simply because some time soon they must be answered. The day of the rocket is not so distant that we can delay longer in answering some of them. It will be very embarrassing if we discover on Mars not only that the Adam and Eve legend is the myth we suspected it to be but that Mr. Darwin, too, has been thrown bodily out the window by the things we find on that far world. Science and religion might *both* run in circles, like broken toys, momentarily, confronted with such factual heresy.

Not that we won't be able to adjust to any problems met at home or abroad in the solar system in 1999. We *will* adjust. But I also think our adjustment will derive in part from our practicality in both entertaining ourselves with science fiction and looking to our answers now, while still it is afternoon. These problems are human problems, which all too soon will no longer be science-fictional but part of a past history our children will read. I consider none of the above questions improbable or impossible. I consider them very probable and possible indeed.

Consider the similarity of two books—Koestler's *Darkness at Noon*, laid in our recent past, and George Orwell's *1984*, set in our immediate future. And here *we* are, poised between the two, between a dreadful reality and an unformed terror, trying to make such decisions as will avoid the tyranny of the very far right and the tyranny of the very far left, the two of which can often be seen coalescing into a tyranny pure and simple, with no qualifying adjective in front of it at all.

Space, which is very large indeed, is not the only huge thing which stands before man. Bigness in all its forms towers above us—bigness in religion, bigness in the fields of communication, labor, corporative enterprise, and government. No sooner has the private citizen warded off the millstone wheel of one Juggernaut than another lumbers on stage. Compared to other ages, in which man hid from a single Giant here or a Titan there, we are living, it cannot be denied, in a year when every one of us must stand ready, alone, ax in hand, by the Beanstalk.

Science fiction, it has been suggested, could possibly be the ax which on occasion might hew as much as half an inch of fibrous material from certain Beanstalks. I do not know whether it has ever killed, maimed, or even bruised a Giant. I do not know whether it can be a sling to send the pebble against the brow of Goliath for the millions of Davids alive and put-upon today. I would not dare to say that it is probably the literature of warning or that it might be the dream which can help ward off the nightmare. Too many have claimed too much for science fiction already. And there is no charting agency available to show how much literature goes into the minds and, years later, works down and comes out through the hands of acting individuals.

I know only that there isn't a time, when I've had a really good night's sleep and am clear-headed, that I haven't thought of science fiction and been excited and concerned with its function, minor if you wish, both as fresh entertainment and as morality cloaked in symbol and allegory.

Certainly I have often wished that a new name might be applied to this field, since the old name has grown shopworn in the service of bug-eyed monsters and half-naked space women.

But there seems to be no way to avoid that, and new writers coming into the field will have to carry the burden of the old label until someone provides a better one, in this land where everything must *absolutely* have a label.

Even as I finish this article, our civilization is thinking about the future and pouring it into molds to harden and become the newer machines which will further prove that, in motion, mankind's ability to externalize his loves and hates, thus more quickly building or destroying his culture, is seemingly inexhaustible. As long as "science fiction" can keep me alert to all this, I'll go on writing it. And I'll go on as long as there is gusto and zest in the writing; for if it should ever become completely and bodily nothing but self-important social and political prediction, I think I would become bored, and my reader bored, too.

I once strongly suspected that fun was the handmaiden, if not the progenitor, of the arts; now I *know* this for certain. And with a great sense of pleasure and personal well-being I intend to continue in the field for a good many years along with those others who are interested in trying to find a bridge to cross that vast gulf of communication permanently for all of us. I do not know whether tomorrow's street will be full of human beings with Seashell thimble-radios whispering in their ears and all the world and its problems moved away from and neglected. Or whether by some miracle we may all carry supersonic stethoscopes with us on our rounds, so that each may know the sound of every other human heart. I only know that it would be interesting to walk on that street and think about it and write about it, before that evening sun goes down.

No Man Is An Island

It is good to confront a group of people who are planning to build a library rather than burn one.

It is good, because I am reminded of our recent past, when Adolf Hitler conceived his wonderfully insidious plan to destroy the mind of Europe and kill its civilized thought. His idea was in turn simple and practical: if you burn the libraries utterly, down to the last stick of type on the last page, you burn the mind and memory of man. History and culture are smoke blown off in the first storm. At your leisure, you can rewrite and reform this history and that culture.

Ideas, what are they? Winds that rush here and there, to be caught and bottled by your own thinkers, your own German Elite. With their libraries furnaced, Poland, Czechoslovakia, France and Hungary would simply have no past at all. How easy then to shape the future of a country that cannot clearly remember the day before yesterday.

That was Hitler's impressive idea.

In still more ancient times, a Chinese poet declaiming verses dedicated to a dead Emperor, might find himself seized, tried on the spot, and buried alive, his poems crammed in his mouth. Living Emperors thus easily disposed of anyone speaking well of their predecessors.

In George Orwell's remarkable novel *1984* the destruction of books is unbelievably proficient. By comparison, the burnings of the past are so many sparks and flickers; mere kindling. As often as is deemed necessary during the year, Orwell's future government hurls everything down the incinerator-chute and reprints fresh histories wherein circumstances reverse, white turns black, bad is good, and war is declared to be nothing else but peace!

Three examples: one from antiquity, one from our immediate past, and one from the literature of our fast-arriving future. Any of them enough to give us pause, all of them cause to make me glad I am here today speaking to a group whose purpose is to build that particularly quiet fortress known in our society as a library.

I think this is a wonderful and a good thing. I think it is wonderful because you are building an asylum for all the ideas that have been and that *are* and that ever will be. Doubtless, you might even be building some manner of church, a meetinghouse of the spirit of everyone everywhere, a place where we can make our proper study of mankind which, as you know, is man.

There are many pompous and sentimental things I could say about libraries and books, I suppose. And I also suppose I will not quite be able to avoid these before I finish here.

It is good, first of all, that you are building at a time when many people are tearing down. How fine to see that you are calm and quiet with your undertaking in a year when thousands are screaming and running from shadows as well as realities. It is good that you will allow entrance to your library ideas of such diverse natures that often it would seem the deserted corridors at midnight might absolutely howl with converse, declamation, and the scrapings and scratchings of philosophies and prejudicial viewpoints.

In the battle of ideas, you show great courage. Here you have a roomful of capitalist cocker spaniels and terriers into which you are not afraid to toss a Communist cat. On one shelf together sit the teachings of Buddha and Christ, of Locke and Marx and Philip Wylie, of Freud and St. Thomas Aquinas. Here sit the Communist Manifesto and the Declaration of Independence, here is the Talmud and the Catholic Bible. Here is Socrates and Plato, and Dale Carnegie.

You are not, then, afraid of ideas, or you would not be here today, and you would not be furnishing a library. You are not afraid in a century of fear, and this is the most wonderful thing of all. You are not ashamed to be seen in the company of Judas and Genghis Khan and Oscar Wilde and Hitler and Lenin and Cotton Mather and Torquemada and John Wilkes Booth. You are willing to tolerate Tom Swift for boys in order to introduce Dean Swift at a later date. You are completely unruffled at seeing Henry James and Jesse James brush elbows.

I say it takes courage to build a library and leave it alone. I say it takes courage to throw wide the doors and declare to every citizen: enter, the world is yours, make what you will of it, have it out; this is your Forum, your Union Square, your silent soap-box, your confessional, your prison, or your Garden of Eden, see what you can do!

It also takes faith to build a library. Above all, faith in civilized man who, entering like a reader of Braille, his blind mind and fingers groping, may somehow grasp those books which shape thinking and thus history. It is, of course, a gamble, but a gamble that absolutely must be taken, with the results always in doubt, with ten thousand exciting possibilities straight ahead. The future is always exciting to the free man with a free choice of discovering and doing. When you limit curiosity, when you prune educational selectivity, excitement dies, and all days know the same gray weather.

Therefore it is amazing when a library or a culture resists the temptation to snatch the kaleidoscope from the hands of the curious who are holding it up to the sun, shaking it, twisting it, and crying, "Look! Look at the patterns!" How natural to want to seize the kaleidoscope and freeze the pattern, declaring that *this* and this *only* is life! That's what Hitler and the ancient Chinese Emperor sought after, that's what you'll find in Orwell's nightmare: *1984*.

A library's efficiency is best tested by noting how actively it makes the hand of the local tyrant itch and perspire. Dictators have night-sweats when they perceive the power of the gentle library towering above them. They *must* cut it down to size.

Nor are dictators the only people whose most loved occupation is playing with matches. You will undoubtedly be attacked, at one time or another, by pressure groups whose constitutional rights fairly and certainly allow them to scream, Go here, go there, do this, do that, turn about, go up, go down, go around, go in, go out! The Legion says yes, the Mormons say no, the Klan says boo! the Baptists say "But—," the Doctors say, "Ah!," the N.A.M. says "Uh-uh," the Unions shake their heads and the Society For The Prevention of Naked Women in Books will bite your heels.

Then, the one thing you can do is tap the sign which says "Talk quietly," swing wide the library doors and invite them to "Come in, fight it out, let's boil over, simmer down, and hope that out of all the steam, we can precipitate a few clear drops of sanity."

I say this takes courage, and I say this is fine.

I suppose the reason why you are remarkably unafraid, as a group, is because you know that books can crystallize our thoughts, help us pin them like butterflies in amber, so we can look at them saying, "This is this, and that's that, and this other thing seems to be what we always said it was."

I suppose you are unafraid because you know books can help us to see the things that were right at one time and wrong at another, and right yet again in a later year. Print it, and if a lie is there it is trapped for anyone to see, down the years.

How familiar the spectacle of governments, politicians, and military men in the last twenty centuries who suffered the severest forms of insomnia because books were the blueprints of their souls and the irrevocable evidences of their pasts.

No man enjoys being held up, shaken, turned over, and squinted at, to see what makes him tick. Therefore, remember: books are dangerous, celebrities detest these handy memory courses which recollect their promises at midnight and their absentmindedness at dawn. They would rather life be lived and forgotten. How lovely, without books, when experience vanishes in stale air, in mouth-to-mouth mythology, and bed-time tales.

But, enter Mr. Gutenberg! The competition begins! The marketplace of ideas swarms with versions and focuses of historical events. There seem, for instance, as many books about the Civil War as there were soldiers fighting it. Each claims omniscience, each book partakes, if only peripherally, of the whole truth, each represents a single mind rationalizing itself into history. It would probably be impossible to touch any one book and say this is it, this is the truth, this is the whole. But when we aggregate all of the books that have been written on the Civil War, we can point to the impressive hill and say, This is pretty nearly the whole, from this we can "make do," we can patch and sew, we can plant and transplant, from *all* of this we can learn. Without these books, the Civil War would be a vapor on the tongues of sleepy old men.

I imagine then that we can describe books as being important in two ways. First, they can help us to lay away those dreams which might hurt us, they can tell us that we are not so good as we think we are. They can remind us that this country was settled, in many places, from 1620 to 1650, by English debtors and criminals. They can remind us that this country was founded not on religious tolerance as some of us like to think, but on religious *in*tolerance. For many years you could not live in some parts of this country if you were a Catholic; you could not survive in one community unless you were a Quaker, or live in another without being a Puritan. Men were often killed for doing otherwise.

That is the real side of the coin that books can show us. That is the way books can stop the dreams we dream that might harm us. When we lie to ourselves that we are what we are not, then it is a comfort to have a weapon nearby that rides so easily and fits so well in the hand as does a book.

Now the second thing books can give us are new and better dreams to replace the old bad ones. Books can recall the journey we have made from the days of intolerance after the Pilgrims arrived, to this day when a thousand different sects, cultures, racial strains, political beliefs and religious cross-currents mix and intermix through our country.

Intolerance is not by any means gone, but it is on the wane. You cannot hate what you are. And if finally there is something of the Cherokee Indian and the Jew and the Irish and the English and the German and the Italian and the Negro in all of us, we will have to find other things to hate beyond race and nationality.

Books can show us that we have moved closer to this ideal. And they can help us dream a larger dream to achieve this ideal. They can allow us to confess error and change our lives. But the second cannot be done properly without the first. Without a knowledge of our lies, our deceits, our greed, through which runs a narrow vein of thoughtfulness and good, we would go on forever repeating the same mistakes in the same way. Making the same mistake in a *new* way might not be immensely encouraging, but at least it shows progress and experimentation, if only of an ironic sort.

The hardest thing in the world for an individual to do is imagine himself another person. What must it be like to look from the eyes of a Chinese or a Russian or a Moslem or a Jew, one wonders? What can it be like to sit within the head of an Eskimo and see the winter sun and smell the perpetual snows of a lifetime? Most of us are unable to move our minds into the heads of other people, smell with their noses, see with their eyes, taste with their tongues. How then to achieve this massive effort of the imagination?

The answer is as simple as it is obvious.

Books.

A book is a body, a book is a house. And you are the ghost come to haunt that body, to peer from the high windows of that house, to live in its attic. You move into a book and you exist there and you see what the author wants you to see: Look! *Here! Feel* the cold! Feel how *hungry* I am! How *warm*. How remote. How overjoyed! How tired. How sad. How happy! See, there's Mt. Everest! And *that*? Stone Henge! The Leaning Tower! The Via Roma on a summer's noon!

For a few pennies you are not Mrs. Smith of Los Angeles or Mr. Jenkins of Chicago. For a few pennies you are Mr. Shakespeare of Avon or Mr. Hemingway of Cuba, or even, God bless us, Mr. Mickey Spillane from the other side of town.

For a few hours then you have tolerated the body and the mind of another. You have discovered that the act of reading is the act of identification with another man's problems. You have discovered that reading a book cannot but spread your horizons, if only the smallest bit. And if you can sit for only a few hours each year and be a Jew when you are not a Jew, and be a Catholic while reading under a parasol at a Baptist picnic, and be a Chinese in Shanghai, dying of starvation even while supper waits on your own plate, then I think you are well on toward being a sympathetic and understanding member of the human race.

The act of reading is the act of insemination. Any man who has read the history of the Jews cannot but be in some small part a Jew. The man who reads narrowly, who confines his selections to those books that will reaffirm his prejudices so that he can keep them in a conveniently small, concretous mass, is refusing to be a Buddhist for an hour, a Moslem for ten minutes, a Bushman for sixty seconds, and, finally, a human being for the rest of his life. Books can be used, as all of the inventions of mankind are used, in good ways and bad. The good way lies in reading many books of many colors and varieties, thus becoming, I believe, part of that fabulous land spoken of so eloquently by John Donne when he said that no man is an island unto himself. Books help us to cure our insufferable tendency toward isolation so we may never have to send to ask for whom the bell tolls.

Comprehension, identification, understanding, pity, mercy, love. To put out your hand, *freely*, in a library, is to put out your blind hand and touch humanity.

It is a bad thing if a man in the city of Delhi dies of malnutrition. It is a terrible thing indeed if he dies alone, and we forget. But it can be a good thing if, through a book, we can die with him over and over and over, as many times as are necessary, until our spirit is moved to finding ways to prevent his or his children's children ever dying in such a fashion again.

Books are fairly new things in the history of man. I do not for an instant claim they are a cure-all or that they can save us. Man, after all, is his own salvation. But I think that as long as we are building *uncensored* libraries, even as you people are now building a library instead of systematically destroying one, we are at least halfway down the road to knowing that when the bell tolls it most certainly tolls for each and every one of us.

Just This Side Of Byzantium (*An Introduction to* Dandelion Wine)

THIS BOOK, like most of my books and stories, was a surprise. I began to learn the nature of such surprises, thank God, when I was fairly young as a writer. Before that, like every beginner, I thought you could beat, pummel, and thrash an idea into existence. Under such treatment, of course, any decent idea folds up its paws, turns on its back, fixes its eyes on eternity, and dies.

It was with great relief, then, that in my early twenties I floundered into a word-association process in which I simply got out of bed each morning, walked to my desk, and put down any word or series of words that happened along in my head.

I would then take arms against the word, or for it, and bring on an assortment of characters to weigh the word and show me its meaning in my own life. An hour or two hours later, to my amazement, a new story would be finished and done. The surprise was total and lovely. I soon found that I would have to work this way for the rest of my life.

First I rummaged my mind for words that could describe my personal nightmares, fears of night and time from my childhood, and shaped stories from these.

Then I took a long look at the green apple trees and the old house I was born in and the house next door where lived my grandparents, and all the lawns of the summers I grew up in, and I began to try words for all that.

What you have here in this book then is a gathering of dandelions from all those years. The wine metaphor which appears again and again in these pages is wonderfully apt. I was gathering images all of my life, storing them away, and forgetting them. Somehow I had to send myself back, with words as catalysts, to open the memories out and see what they had to offer.

So from the age of twenty-four to thirty-six hardly a day passed when I didn't stroll myself across a recollection of my grandparents' northern Illinois grass, hoping to come across some old half-burnt firecracker, a rusted toy, or a fragment of letter written to myself in some young year hoping to contact the older person I became to remind him of his past, his life, his people, his joys, and his drenching sorrows.

It became a game that I took to with immense gusto: to see how much I could remember about dandelions themselves, or picking wild grapes with my father and brother, rediscovering the mosquito-breeding ground rain barrel by the side bay window, or searching out the smell of the gold-fuzzed bees that hung around our back porch grape arbor. Bees do have a smell, you know, and if they don't they should, for their feet are dusted with spices from a million flowers.

And then I wanted to call back what the ravine was like, especially on those nights when walking home late across town, after seeing Lon Chaney's delicious fright *The Phantom of the Opera*, my brother Skip would run ahead and hide under the ravine-creek bridge like the Lonely One and leap out and grab me, shrieking, so I ran, fell, and ran again, gibbering all the way home. That was great stuff.

Along the way I came upon and collided, through word-association, with old and true friendships. I borrowed my friend John Huff from my childhood in Arizona and shipped him East to Green Town so that I could say goodbye to him properly.

Along the way, I sat me down to breakfasts, lunches, and dinners with the long dead and much loved. For I was a boy who did indeed love his parents and grandparents and his brother, even when that brother "ditched" him.

Along the way, I found myself in the basement working the wine-press for my father, or on the front porch Independence night helping my Uncle Bion load and fire his homemade brass cannon.

Thus I fell into surprise. No one told me to surprise myself, I might add. I came on the old and best ways of writing through ignorance and experiment and was startled when truths leaped out of bushes like quail before gunshot. I blundered into creativity as blindly as any child learning to walk and see. I learned to let my senses and my Past tell me all that was somehow true.

So, I turned myself into a boy running to bring a dipper of clear rainwater out of that barrel by the side of the house.

And, of course, the more water you dip out the more flows in. The flow has never ceased. Once I learned to keep going back and back again to those times, I had plenty of memories and sense impressions to play with, not work with, no, play with. *Dandelion Wine* is nothing if it is not the boy-hid-in-the-man playing in the fields of the Lord on the green grass of other Augusts in the midst of starting to grow up, grow old, and sense darkness waiting under the trees to seed the blood.

I was amused and somewhat astonished at a critic a few years back who wrote an article analyzing *Dandelion Wine* plus the more realistic works of Sinclair Lewis, wondering how I could have been born and raised in Waukegan, which I renamed Green Town for my novel, and not noticed how ugly the harbor was and how depressing the coal docks and railyards down below the town.

But, of course, I had noticed them and, genetic enchanter that I was, was fascinated by their beauty. Trains and boxcars and the smell of coal and fire are not ugly to children. Ugliness is a concept that we happen on later and become self-conscious about. Counting boxcars is a prime activity of boys. Their elders fret and fume and jeer at the train that holds them up, but boys happily count and cry the names of the cars as they pass from far places.

And again, that supposedly ugly railyard was where carnivals and circuses arrived with elephants who washed the brick pavements with mighty steaming acid waters at five in the dark morning.

As for the coal from the docks, I went down in my basement every autumn to await the arrival of the truck and its metal chute, which clanged down and released a ton of beauteous meteors that fell out of far space into my cellar and threatened to bury me beneath dark treasures.

In other words, if your boy is a poet, horse manure can only mean flowers to him; which is, of course, what horse manure has always been about.

Perhaps a new poem of mine will explain more than this introduction about the germination of all the summers of my life into one book.

Here's the start of the poem:

Byzantium, I come not from,
But from another time and place
Whose race was simple, tried and true;
As boy
I dropped me forth in Illinois.
A name with neither love nor grace
Was Waukegan, there I came from
And not, good friends, Byzantium.

The poem continues, describing my lifelong relationship to my birthplace:

And yet in looking back I see
From topmost part of farthest tree
A land as bright, beloved and blue
As any Yeats found to be true.

Waukegan, visited by me often since, is neither homelier nor more beautiful than any other small midwestern town. Much of it is green. The trees *do* touch in the middle of streets. The street in front of my old home is still paved with red bricks. In what way then was the town special? Why, I was born there. It was my life. I had to write of it as I saw fit:

So we grew up with mythic dead
To spoon upon midwestern bread
And spread old gods' bright marmalade
To slake in peanut-butter shade,
Pretending there beneath our sky
That it was Aphrodite's thigh . . .
While by the porch-rail calm and bold
His words pure wisdom, stare pure gold
My grandfather, a myth indeed,
Did all of Plato supersede
While Grandmama in rockingchair
Sewed up the raveled sleeve of care
Crocheted cool snowflakes rare and bright
To winter us on summer night.
And uncles, gathered with their smokes
Emitted wisdoms masked as jokes,
And aunts as wise as Delphic maids

Dispensed prophetic lemonades
To boys knelt there as acolytes
To Grecian porch on summer nights;
Then went to bed, there to repent
The evils of the innocent;
The gnat-sins sizzling in their ears
Said, through the nights and through the years
Not Illinois nor Waukegan
But blither sky and blither sun.
Though mediocre all our Fates
And Mayor not as bright as Yeats
Yet still we knew ourselves. The sum?
Byzantium.
Byzantium.

Waukegan/Green Town/Byzantium.

Green Town *did* exist, then?

Yes, and again, yes.

Was there a real boy named John Huff?

There was. And that was truly his name. But he didn't go away from me, I went away from him. But, happy ending, he is still alive, forty-two years later, and remembers our love.

Was there a Lonely One?

There was, and that was *his* name. And he moved around at night in my home town when I was six years old and he frightened everyone and was never captured.

Most importantly, did the big house itself, with Grandpa and Grandma and the boarders and uncles and aunts in it exist? I have already answered that.

Is the ravine real and deep and dark at night? It was, it is. I took my daughters there a few years back, fearful that the ravine might have gone shallow with time. I am relieved and happy to report that the ravine is deeper, darker, and more mysterious than ever. I would not, even now, go home through there after seeing *The Phantom of the Opera.*

So there you have it. Waukegan was Green Town was Byzantium, with all the happiness that that means, with all the sadness that these names imply. The people there were gods and midgets and knew themselves mortal and so the midgets walked tall so as not to embarrass the gods and the gods crouched so as to make the small ones feel at home. And, after all, isn't that what life is all about, the ability to go around back and come up inside other people's heads to look out at the damned fool miracle and say: oh, so that's how you see it!? Well, now, I must remember that.

Here is my celebration, then, of death as well as life, dark as well as light, old as well as young, smart and dumb combined, sheer joy as well as complete terror written by a boy who once hung upside down in trees, dressed in his bat costume with candy fangs in his mouth, who finally fell out of the trees when he was twelve and went and found a toy-dial typewriter and wrote his first "novel."

A final memory.

Fire balloons.

You rarely see them these days, though in some countries, I hear, they are still made and filled with warm breath from a small straw fire hung beneath.

But in 1925 Illinois, we still had them, and one of the last memories I have of my grandfather is the last hour of a Fourth of July night forty-eight years ago when Grandpa and I walked out on the lawn and lit a small fire and filled the pear-shaped red-white-and-blue-striped paper balloon with hot air, and held the flickering bright-angel presence in our hands a final moment in front of a porch lined with uncles and aunts and cousins and mothers and fathers, and then, very softly, let the thing that was life and light and mystery go out of our fingers up on the summer air and away over the beginning-to-sleep houses, among the stars, as fragile, as wondrous, as vulnerable, as lovely as life itself.

I see my grandfather there looking up at that strange drifting light, thinking his own still thoughts. I see me, my eyes filled with tears, because it was all over, the night was done, I knew there would never be another night like this.

No one said anything. We all just looked up at the sky and we breathed out and in and we all thought the same things, but nobody said. Someone finally had to say, though, didn't they? And that one is me.

The wine still waits in the cellars below.

My beloved family still sits on the porch in the dark.

The fire balloon still drifts and burns in the night sky of an as yet unburied summer.

Why and how?

Because I say it is so.

Summer, 1974

Dandelion Wine *Revisited*

SOME TEN years ago I walked through the streets of Waukegan, Illinois, renamed Green Town in my novel *Dandelion Wine*, and I came to the old house at the corner of St. James and Washington where my grandparents had lived and where I had thrived as a child.

The lawn was a pure green carpet, starred with a multitude of dandelions. I stood on its edge like one about to dive in and swim out to the middle of summer. Then, prompted by a whim, I walked to the center of all that green and bent to select a single huge dandelion.

As I did this, a voice called from my grandparents' front porch. An old woman had come out of the door and was gazing down at me.

"If I see a stranger standing in the middle of my lawn picking a dandelion," she said, "it must be Ray Bradbury."

"Yes'm," I said, and blushed.

"Well, now, come in," she said. "Let me show you where you used to live."

Obediently, I climbed the porch stairs to pass into the hall, where bright panels of stained glass—cherry, lemon, grape, and summer green—framed the clear central window. Through them I had once stared, moving from pane to pane, causing pedestrians, dogs, and cats to change complexions as they strolled or ran by; here a tangerine cat, there a pink mongrel, and just beyond a man mysteriously colored by my shifting gaze.

From there to the library, where my grandfather sat for years, enchanted with the nightly newspaper, his golden specs on the tip of his nose; thence into the dining room, where a tidal wave of relatives had once roared on the shoreline of Thanksgiving; and into the kitchen, where the ghosts of a thousand turkeys and chickens withstood being plucked, singed, and stuffed.

And from there to the steps leading down to the cellar, where, perhaps, bright bottles of dandelion wine without number had been pressed and stashed in August to warm the long cold days of February.

I say perhaps, for memory is as fragile as the frosted windows of full winter, which a single breath steamed forth from a boy's nostrils can melt, erasing the no-two-alike patterns.

"Has much changed?" the old lady said behind me.

"In most of the house, yes," I said. "But here?" I took a deep breath of the dank air rising from the basement. "Nothing. Or almost nothing."

I did not descend to the cellar. I wanted to believe that what was down there had remained, waiting for me, for more than half a lifetime.

I took coffee with the nice old woman and then walked downtown (only three blocks away—we did not drive places in the twenties, we made it around our small town on foot). When I reached the Main Street barber shop, which I had not invaded since I was thirteen, I stopped. The name above the door was still the same Lee Wyneski, who had been my grandma's boarder and came to have soup and chicken or a sandwich at noon every day for ten years. I remembered his crisp-as-cornflakes straw hat and his sharply pressed suits. Years later I wrote a story in which I turned him into a most peculiar vampire in the summer of 1929.

But now here was his shop. I touched the screen door and, still following impulse, stepped in.

The town barber, a man somewhere in his seventies, was in the midst of a long-on-the-sides, short-in-back. He glanced up, squinted, then gave a great shout.

"My God!" he cried. "I been waiting for you to come through that door for forty years!" Whereupon he threw his comb and shears on the hair-strewn floor for emphasis.

"My God," I cried in response. "Who are *you*?"

"Your grandma's boarder when you were three years old!"

"Not—"

"Lee Wyneski? No. He's been dead five years. I'm Ben Powell."

"Yes, yes," I said. "Now I remember. Last time I saw you, you were twenty years old!"

"Time *does* pass." He turned to his shorn customer. "You're done," he advised him. "Out." The man paid up and left.

"Sit!" said the barber.

I climbed up in the chair and was a boy once again, three feet high and the center of an embarrassing universe.

"You know the one dead certain thing I remember about you and your brother when you were three?" said the barber.

"What?" I said.

"Hold on." He bent to pick up his comb and scissors. "Can't talk without my equipment. I won't skin you. Just a light touch. Where was I?" He began to snip—a bit here, a bit there, around my ears—and his warm breath perambulated along with the scissors. "Oh, yeah. The one thing I remember is your grandpa giving you and your brother, Skip, a nickel apiece and two gunnysacks and saying, 'Skedaddle to the empty lot across the street. It's full of dandelions. Pick 'em. Fill the sacks. Drag 'em down in the basement and dump 'em in the winepress. Then the three of us'll wind the press down, and what'll come out will be dandelion wine!'"

No sooner had he stopped talking than he switched on his silver Bumblebee Electric Clippers. His last two words and the buzzing tickle of the hovering machine roused up every hair on my head, down my neck, and along my spine. I sat upright, shocked with Revelation.

"Say that *again*!" I said.

"You didn't hear?"

"Yes," I said. "But, oh God, say that again."

He said it again, and I took a fever and then grew very cold. His voice stopped as he buzzed the Bumblebee Electric Clippers on the peach fuzz inside my left ear. I shivered with joy and remembrance.

No tears fell, but my eyes were wet.

"My God," I said, slumping back in the barber chair.

"My God, what?" said the barber.

"It really *happened*!"

"It?"

"The dandelions. The winepress. The wine."

"Twenty or thirty bottles, give or take a few, over the years. Till your grandpa died, when you were five. Then, somehow, the harvest got lost. The winepress was used for grapes. Your dad did that."

"Yeah," I said, "and all these years, I wasn't sure. Whether it was a real memory or something I made up. I wrote it down in a novel anyway, hoping it was real, along with the rain barrel outside the dining room window."

"*It* was there."

"And the front porch on July 4 nights, when we got all the family and boarders there until midnight, shooting off fireworks."

"*We* were there."

"Five bucks' worth of fireworks from each aunt, uncle, and grandpa. Seventy, eighty dollars' worth of skyrockets and ladyfingers."

"A lot of money in 1923."

"And Halloweens, when we laid table extensions on the steps and slid people down in the dark, past the wine, into the coal bin."

"I helped lay the table extensions."

I leaned forward.

"What does the wine taste like?" I asked. "No, forget it, I don't want to know—"

"Your grandpa gave you a sip once."

"That's a long time back—"

"Well, it's not the taste, anyway, it's the idea." The Bumblebee found and sifted the nape of my neck. "You consider how long winter is, and you keep the bottle handy. You may never uncork it. It's just knowing it's there, left over from the last picnic before October. I've kept a bottle around ten years sometimes. Just a sip. A trifle bitter. Adding orange juice takes the edge off. . . . You didn't want to hear. Sorry I told."

"It's okay," I said. "I don't suppose—"

"What?"

"You happen to remember the recipe?"

"Why wouldn't I?" He laughed quietly. "Lean back. Relax. Let me finish around your other ear."

He turned on the Bumblebee.

It hovered and touched my neck.

I shivered.

"Well," said the town barber. "First." Another touch. Another shiver. Then he recited, eyes shut:

"One gallon blossoms put through the press, add one gallon boiling water, let stand twenty-four hours, strain two or three times through cloth, add three pounds white sugar, one yeast cake, juice of one lemon, three oranges, when finished add orange peels, let stand three weeks, strain, and bottle tight."

He opened his eyes.

"But first—" He reapplied the summer Bee to my close-to-autumn neck. "Find the flowers," he said.

I tapped at the back screen door of my grandparents' house. A smell of baking pies drifted out to me. The old woman in the doorway glanced at the oven behind her and said, "I bet that's why you came back."

"I wouldn't mind," I said. "Is it apricot?"

"You got a good nose. What else?"

"I'd . . ." I hesitated. "I'd like, this time, to actually go into my grandparents'—into *your* cellar."

At the top of the stairs I looked down in darkness.

I was no longer afraid to go down there. It was empty, but it was no longer empty. I could fill it with a glance.

I went down the stairs and did not turn on the light.

I stood looking at the cellar windows where once ketchup bottles had been placed. In them the sun had been caught, capped, and labeled:

Summer 1921.

Summer 1922.

Summer 1923.

I put them there, one by one, without touching or seeing but only with the sort of recall that values absence.

I can drink you, too, I thought, without touching a bottle or filling a glass.

I did just that and was drunk with Time.

"Come up," the old lady's voice called from the top of the stairs. "Your pie is waiting."

Carnivals, Near and Far (An Afterword to Something Wicked This Way Comes)

WHERE IDEAS come from and how they finally arrive are the largest mystery in a life of writing.

I imagine you would describe *Something Wicked This Way Comes* as a carnival far-traveling from childhood to reach me in my almost middle years.

It may well have begun when I was four and my mother lugged me onto a merry-go-round for an hysterical spin. For no sooner had the calliope sounded and the horses plunged into a gallop than small Ray shrieked. My screams continued until the carousel operator, murderous, stopped the horses and let us flee.

Not long after that I saw Lon Chaney, with a roller skate on his head, slide down a high-wire, fall and die in the arms of a beautiful young dancer, Loretta Young. That film, *Laugh, Clown, Laugh*, taught me what went on behind a clown's mask.

Charlie Chaplin's *The Circus* came next, but I didn't want to run away and join it; I only became more curious about the strange life within the tents.

In those same years Lon Chaney filmed *He Who Gets Slapped* and let some lions loose in a house to devour his fiancée's lover.

With these events and films my carnival was well on its way.

I was twelve years old when it got its biggest jolt when Mr. Electrico arrived on Labor Day weekend, 1932, sat in his electric chair to be "electrocuted," dubbed me with his fiery sword until my hair rose and sparks jumped from my nostrils, and cried, "Live forever!" Next day, I ran back to the carnival grounds to find out just how to *do* that. Mr. Electrico introduced me to all the carnival freaks behind the scenes, including the Hippo Lady, the Human Skeleton, and the Illustrated Man. We sat on the beach and he listened to my grand ideas about my irresistible future.

When I had run out of gas, Mr. Electrico said, "We've met before." "Oh, no, sir," I said, "this is the first time I've ever talked to you." "No, no," he said, "you were my best friend at the battle of the Ardennes Forest outside Paris in October 1918, were wounded, and died in my arms. And here you are with a new face, new name, but the light coming from your eyes is the soul of my lost friend. Welcome back to the world."

I wandered out of the carnival, stunned, and stood by the rushing horses of the carousel listening to the calliope wheezing "Beautiful Ohio," and wept. I knew that something amazing had struck me with electric fire and changed me forever.

Within eight weeks I began to write. I wrote every day after that, for the next sixty-five years.

So I imagine you could say it was only natural that when Gene Kelly invited me and my wife, Maggie, to a screening of his motion picture musical *Invitation to the Dance*, the carnival sequence in it would strike a final bolt.

Walking home from the film, feeling much like that boy by the carousel on the long-ago September day in 1932, I said:

"I'd give my right arm to write a screenplay for Gene Kelly."

"Well, go through your files," Maggie said. "There are lots of clowns in there that smell funny and circuses that only come alive at three A.M."

She was right. I found a story, "The Black Ferris," that I had planned to use under the name "Dark Carnival" in my first book. The story was never finished, and the book *Dark Carnival* was published minus its title fantasy.

And so I wrote an eighty-page screenplay based on that unpublished tale and my far-traveling long-after-midnight carnival truly arrived.

Kelly loved it, wanted to direct and produce it, but could find no money, and handed my carnival back to me. With the screen treatment dead, the novel came alive. I spent five years putting the dark train on track; the novel, now titled *Something Wicked This Way Comes*, was published in 1962. It then became a series of screenplays *again* and culminated in the 1983 Disney film.

So there you have the long journey from carousel to carousel, circus to carnival, and my suspicion, shared by Walt Disney, that something was rotten in the Denmark behind the freak tent canvas. Disney created Disneyland as a bright antidote. He made a new world. I finished a novel, with Mr. Electrico at its center, changed from a kind Christian mystic into an unfailingly evil Cooger of Cooger & Dark's Pandemonium Shadow Show.

If Mr. Electrico ever read this novel a long time back, I hope he forgave me for turning him inside out and upside down, from high noon to an eternal night.

Part of me is still on that hideous carousel when I was four. I seem never to have found a way to get off.

Los Angeles
December 1998

CHRONOLOGY

NOTE ON THE TEXTS

NOTES

Chronology

1920–25 Born Ray Douglas Bradbury in Waukegan, Illinois, on August 22, 1920, the third of four children of Leonard Spaulding Bradbury, age twenty-nine, and Esther Moberg Bradbury, age thirty-two. Mother, a native of Sweden raised in Waukegan with five siblings, works as a supervisor in an envelope factory in North Chicago before becoming a full-time homemaker and mother. Father, the son and grandson of Waukegan newspaper publishers, travels in the western United States as a young man before returning home and marrying. He is briefly a deputy sheriff and serves in the Navy at nearby Great Lakes Naval Station, eventually settling into work as a lineman with the Waukegan telephone company. Twin boys were born in 1916, but one, Samuel, died at age two. Leonard, Jr. (known as "Skip") survives. In later years Ray Bradbury claims to retain memories of his own birth; theater encounters with Lon Chaney's *Hunchback of Notre Dame* at age three and *The Phantom of the Opera* at age five become lifelong memories.

1926–27 For most of his first fourteen years, lives with his family in a home rented from his Bradbury grandparents, who live next door and take in boarders. Learns about radio from his paternal grandfather, who dies in 1926. His aunt Neva Bradbury, an artist-designer who studied at the Chicago Art Institute, keeps a studio in the house where Ray lives; she reads to him from the Oz books of L. Frank Baum. His parents help him learn to read from the newspaper comics. Grandfather Bradbury gives him pictures of the 1892 and 1903 World's Fairs and the 1899 *Harper's Weekly* serial illustrations of H. G. Wells's *When the Sleeper Wakes.* These readings and images, along with the sensational color photographs of King Tutankhamen's mask and treasures, inspire a lifetime of fascination with the fantastic. Begins first grade at Waukegan's Central School, but father moves the family to Roswell, New Mexico, in October 1926, and then to Tucson, Arizona, looking for work during much of the school year. A sister, Elizabeth

Jane Bradbury, is born in Tucson. Family moves back to Waukegan in May 1927.

1928 Sister Elizabeth, known as Betty Jane, dies of pneumonia or influenza in February. Misses three months of school during the fall term while sick in bed with whooping cough. Aunt Neva reads him Edgar Allan Poe's works. Discovers *Amazing Stories Quarterly*, one of the earliest science fiction pulps, in Grandmother Bradbury's parlor next door, among her boarders' reading materials. Attends his first of several local performances by Blackstone the Magician.

1929–30 Discovers the romances of Edgar Rice Burroughs and begins to read Burroughs's John Carter of Mars series in the home library of his uncle Bion Bradbury, who lives on the same block; also reads fantasy adventures serialized in *Blue Book* and *Argosy* magazines. Plays during the daytime in the deep ravine that separates his neighborhood from Central School and the Carnegie Library.

1931 For his eleventh birthday, receives a copy of Walter B. Gibson's *The Book of Secrets: Miracles Ancient and Modern with Chapters on Easy Magic You Can Do*, which becomes his amateur magician's bible. Performs his own magic act for various service clubs and lodges and on Christmas Eve at the Veterans of Foreign Wars Hall.

1932 As the Great Depression deepens, father Leo loses his job with the telephone company and in October moves the family back to Tucson. Receives a toy dial-a-letter typewriter for Christmas from his parents and begins to type a sequel to *The Gods of Mars*, the second John Carter of Mars novel. Makes himself useful at local radio station KGAR and is allowed to broadcast the newspaper comics to children on Saturday nights; eventually gets juvenile reading parts on radio programs and handles sound effects for a young-listener version of "Tailspin Tommy." Discovers the novels of Jules Verne.

1933 Father moves the family from the desert outskirts of Tucson into rooms in a railroad boardinghouse near downtown, requiring Ray to transfer from the seventh grade at Amphitheatre to Roskruge School. Continues working at KGAR. Sees the newly released film *King Kong* for the first time just before leaving Tucson. Father moves family back to Waukegan in the spring. Returns to Central School, where he had started his seventh-grade year the previous fall. Makes two trips to the Century of Progress Exposition (the Chicago World's Fair) that summer, once with his parents and again with his aunt Neva; he is fascinated by "The City of the Future" and the dinosaurs of the "Sinclair Prehistoric Exhibit." Reads borrowed copies of the early genre pulps *Wonder Stories* and *Amazing Stories* and will read an ever-widening range of pulps for the next ten years, eventually publishing stories in many of them throughout the 1940s.

1934 Near the end of Ray's eighth-grade year at Central School, father once again loses his lineman's job and moves the family to California, following Ray's favorite uncle Inar Moberg, who has moved there with his family. Spends the summer in a new world of cinema and radio, talking his way into live broadcasts and studio gates to get autographs of the stars. In the fall he begins the ninth grade at Berendo Junior High. Resumes his grade school compilation of *Flash Gordon* and *Buck Rogers* comic strips.

1935 Family lives in a succession of rented rooms and subdivided houses for the next seven years on the near west and southwest side of Los Angeles. In the fall, begins tenth grade at Los Angeles High School, where he will work on one of the few high school daily newspapers published in the United States. Submits stories to *The Saturday Evening Post* and other magazines but is unsuccessful.

1936 Joins the drama club; he takes no significant roles until his senior year, but his passion to act soon rivals his passion for writing. Also joins the poetry club, known as "The Ink Beasts"; his poem "In Memory of Will Rogers" is printed back home in the Waukegan *News-Sun*. Two L.A. High teachers, Snow Longley Housh (poetry) and Stanford graduate Jennet Johnson (fiction), encourage his creative development.

1937 Discovers the novels of Thomas Wolfe. His poem "Death's Voice" is published in *Anthology of Student Verse* in March. Buys his first portable typewriter secondhand for $10. In early October, joins the Los Angeles chapter of the Science Fiction League (LASFL), and begins to illustrate for and contribute to their fan publications. Meets Robert Heinlein and future mentors Henry Kuttner and Leigh Brackett through LASFL. Enjoys his senior-year class in classical astronomy, and does well in his biology and physiology classes, but shows no deeper interest in scientific studies. Develops competence in his ceramics class, and experiments widely with weird tales and science fiction under the instruction of Jennet Johnson, who encourages him to write descriptive mood pieces and lets him work through his continuing impulse to imitate genre masters.

1938 In January, his first amateur story, "Hollerbochen's Dilemma," is printed in the LASFL fan magazine, *Imagination!* Poem "Truck Driver After Midnight" appears in citywide school anthology *Morning Song*. Contributes reviews and commentary to *Blue and White Daily*, the Los Angeles High School student newspaper. Scripts and acts in the annual high school talent show, the *1938 Roman Review*. Graduates in June; starts selling the late-afternoon edition of the *Herald and Express* in September from the corner of Olympic and Norton, providing his principal income for the next four years.

1939 Launches his own fanzine, *Futuria Fantasia*, which runs for four issues through 1940. Attends the first World Science Fiction Convention in New York, where he meets writers Jack Williamson and Isaac Asimov, a number of pulp editors, and his future genre agent, Julius Schwartz. Takes artist Hannes Bok's art portfolio with him to New York and wins Bok a commission from *Weird Tales*. Reads Hemingway, Steinbeck, Wolfe, and other American novelists.

1940 Sees Disney's *Fantasia* multiple times, initially with Aunt Neva, who has moved to Los Angeles. Receives advice from Robert Heinlein, resulting in the publication of "It's Not the Heat, It's the Hu—" in the

November 2 issue of the nonpaying but professional *Script* magazine; this is his first professional story publication. Active in amateur productions of Laraine Day's Wilshire Players Guild.

1941 "The Pendulum," written with Henry Hasse, appears in the November issue of *Super Science Stories*; it is his first professional story sale, negotiated by his first agent, Julius Schwartz, who places two additional stories before year-end. As the U.S. enters World War II, receives a medical draft deferment because of his poor eyesight; during the war years he writes Red Cross blood drive announcements for print and radio.

1942 In March, the family moves to a rental house in Venice Beach owned by the power and light company, where his father Leo now works as a troubleshooter. Begins to spend many Sundays at Muscle Beach with Leigh Brackett, critiquing and revising stories. Publishes "The Candle," his first of many sales to *Weird Tales.* Quits selling newspapers and begins to write full-time from a day office near Temple and Figueroa in Los Angeles, and at home in the detached garage, inspired by the nighttime glow and sounds of the adjacent power substation.

1943 Publishes supernatural stories in four of the six bimonthly issues of *Weird Tales*, and his first significant science fiction story, "King of the Gray Spaces" (later revised as "R Is for Rocket"), in the December issue of *Famous Fantastic Mysteries.*

1944 Places seven stories in the detective pulps, as well as stories in all six bimonthly issues of *Weird Tales.* Undertakes extensive readings of contemporary American and British fiction writers in libraries and bookstores, as well as literary criticism in a wide range of periodicals. Anxiety of influence leads him to diminish his reading of the genre magazines from this time forward.

1945 His success in the science fiction pulps lags behind his weird and detective fiction works, but he successfully completes the second half of Leigh Brackett's novella "Lorelei of the Red Mist" while she coauthors the screenplay of *The Big Sleep* for director Howard Hawks. His first anthology sale, "The Lake," appears in August

Derleth's *Who Knocks.* Sells his first major market story, "The Big Black and White Game," to *American Mercury.* Begins to correspond with Don Congdon, then an editor with Simon & Schuster. Three more major market magazine sales enable him to travel by automobile through Mexico with his friend Grant Beach to purchase masks for the Los Angeles County Museum. This trip results in a number of dark tales, including his classic mummies of Guanajuato story "The Next in Line."

1946 Gives up his day office in downtown Los Angeles. Meets his future wife Marguerite "Maggie" McClure at Fowler's Book Shop, where she clerks. "The Million Year Picnic" appears in *Planet Stories*; it is the earliest published story that he will eventually bring into *The Martian Chronicles.* "The Big Black and White Game" is selected for *Best American Short Stories 1946.* A radio adaptation of "Killer Come Back to Me!" for NBC's *Mollé Mystery Theatre* becomes the first Bradbury story on air. Visits future literary agent Don Congdon during a fall train trip to New York, where Congdon introduces him to major market book and magazine editors.

1947 His original radio play *The Meadow*, broadcast on *World Security Workshop* in January, later appears in *Best One-Act Plays 1947–48.* His first story collection, *Dark Carnival*, containing supernatural and suspense tales from both pulp and mainstream magazines, is published by August Derleth's Arkham House in May. Julius Schwartz transitions out as Bradbury's representative in the pulp magazine market. Don Congdon, now with the Harold Matson Agency in New York, becomes his literary agent in all markets. In September he marries Maggie McClure. In November, his as-yet-unpublished story "Riabouchinska" becomes the first of a dozen stories adapted and broadcast on the CBS Radio programs *Suspense* and *Escape* over the next decade. His story "Homecoming" is selected for *O. Henry Memorial Award: Prize Stories 1947.*

1948 Awarded third place in the *O. Henry Memorial Award: Prize Stories 1948* anthology for "Powerhouse." "I See You Never" is selected for *Best American Short Stories 1948. Dark Carnival* is reprinted in abridged form in

Great Britain. Various story collection concepts are turned down by major trade publishing houses in New York. Begins to write cautionary tales of censorship and book burning in reaction to the Cold War climate of fear slowly rising in America.

1949 Arrives in New York to visit book publishers with Don Congdon. Meets Walter Bradbury at Doubleday. They conceive the idea for *The Martian Chronicles.* Applies (unsuccessfully) for a Guggenheim grant to work on a novel, *The Masks.* First daughter Susan is born. Named the year's Best Author of Science Fiction by the National Fantasy Fan Federation.

1950 Publishes regularly in major market magazines, including some of his Martian stories. *The Martian Chronicles* appears in May. Gives a copy to Christopher Isherwood in a Los Angeles bookstore; Isherwood writes a significant review in *Tomorrow* and introduces Bradbury to Aldous Huxley and other British expatriate writers in Hollywood. In May, NBC Radio's *Dimension X* broadcasts the first of ten adaptations of Bradbury stories for the 1950 and 1951 seasons.

1951 "The Fireman" is published as a novella in the February issue of *Galaxy*; he will later revise and expand it into *Fahrenheit 451.* The same month, Doubleday releases his story collection *The Illustrated Man.* Ramona, his second daughter, is born in May. *The New York Times Book Review* publishes a "Talk with Mr. Bradbury" in August.

1952 *The Illustrated Man* is runner-up for the International Fantasy Award. Becomes president of the newly formed Science Fantasy Writers of America; attends Westercon 5 in San Diego as guest of honor. "The Other Foot" is selected for *Best American Short Stories 1952.* Edits the multi-author anthology *Timeless Stories for Today and Tomorrow* for Bantam. Publishes his anti-authoritarian "Letter to the Republican Party" in *Variety* immediately after the 1952 elections; it is subsequently reprinted in *The Nation.* Begins to expand "The Fireman" into what will become *Fahrenheit 451.*

1953 In March, *The Golden Apples of the Sun*, a mixture of science fiction, magical realism, and fantasy stories, becomes his third Doubleday title. Bradbury's "The Beast From 20,000 Fathoms" inspires the Warner Brothers film of that title; *It Came from Outer Space*, a Universal film based on his original screen treatment, reaches theaters. Publishes "Day After Tomorrow: Why Science Fiction?" in *The Nation* in May; the essay attracts the interest of art historian Bernard Berenson. In August, film director John Huston asks Bradbury to write the *Moby Dick* screenplay for Warner Brothers; in September he and his family travel by train and ocean liner to Europe, where Bradbury will spend the next eight months in Ireland and London writing the script for Huston. His first novel, *Fahrenheit 451*, is published by Ballantine Books in October.

1954 With Maggie, visits Bernard Berenson in Florence; he guides their journey through the art history of northern Italy. Returns to the United States in June. Wins the Benjamin Franklin magazine award for best short story, "Sun and Shadow"; receives a gold medal from Commonwealth Club of California and a $1,000 grant from the National Institute of Arts and Letters for *Fahrenheit 451*.

1955 In March, Pantheon publishes *Switch on the Night*, his first children's book. NBC Radio's *X Minus 1* broadcasts the first of eight new productions of Bradbury stories for the 1955–56 seasons. Third daughter, Bettina, is born in July. *The October Country*, containing revised versions of fifteen of his *Dark Carnival* weird tales and four new stories, is released in October by Ballantine Books and becomes the enduring showcase for his dark fantasy legacy. "Shopping for Death" is picked for *Best Detective Stories of the Year.* His stage adaptation of *Fahrenheit 451* for film star Charles Laughton fails to reach production, but Laughton becomes a mentor and friend.

1956 *Alfred Hitchcock Presents* broadcasts teleplays of two Bradbury stories; others appear regularly on this series through 1964. Wins Boys Club of America Award for *Switch on the Night.* Edits Bantam's multi-author anthology *The Circus of Dr. Lao and Other Improbable Stories.* Writes "Happy Birthday 2115 A.D.," an unproduced operetta, for Charles Laughton and his wife Elsa

Lanchester. John Huston's production of *Moby Dick*, filmed from Bradbury's screenplay, is released as a feature film by Warner Brothers.

1957 Travels to London over the summer to write a screenplay based on his story "And the Rock Cried Out" for independent filmmakers Hecht-Hill-Lancaster and director Sir Carol Reed. Proceeds with family to Paris and then to Florence, where they visit Bernard Berenson a final time before returning home. Doubleday publishes *Dandelion Wine* in September. Father Leo dies in October at age sixty-six.

1958 "The Day It Rained Forever" is included in *Best American Short Stories.* The Bradburys' fourth daughter, Alexandra, is born in August. The family moves to a larger home in the Cheviot Hills neighborhood of Los Angeles in November.

1959 New story collection *A Medicine for Melancholy* is published by Doubleday in February. Rupert Hart-Davis, his longtime British publisher, follows with *The Day It Rained Forever*, containing a slightly different mix of stories.

1960 Article "A Serious Search for Weird Worlds" appears in the October issue of *Life*, beginning a relationship with the magazine that continues through the 1960s, giving him access to NASA scientists, administrators, and astronauts.

1961 In January wins a federal appellate court decision against CBS television for a 1957 *Playhouse 90* plagiarism of *Fahrenheit 451.* Co-founds the Writers Guild Film Society and guides its development with other writers and film critic Arthur Knight. Is hired to write a screen treatment of *The Martian Chronicles* for MGM; the project is never produced, but before his contract ends, he writes the voice-over narration (without screen credit) for MGM's *King of Kings.*

1962 His original teleplay, "The Jail," appears on *Alcoa Premier* in February and is nominated for a Writers Guild award. In the fall, *Life* publishes his article "Cry the Cosmos." Simon & Schuster publishes his long-awaited novel *Something Wicked This Way Comes*, and

Doubleday a compilation of his stories for young readers, *R Is for Rocket.*

1963 Receives Academy Award nomination for the 1962 animated short film *Icarus Montgolfier Wright*, adapted from his story; George Clayton Johnson and illustrator Joseph Mugnaini share the nomination. In October, Dial publishes Bradbury's dramatic adaptations of his own Irish stories as *The Anthem Sprinters and Other Antics.*

1964 His "American Journey" narrative opens at the U.S. Pavilion of the World's Fair in New York. Simon & Schuster publishes short story collection *The Machineries of Joy.* Produces three of his own one-act science fiction plays as *The World of Ray Bradbury*, which has a successful four-month run in Los Angeles.

1965 *Life* publishes "The Kilimanjaro Machine," a fictional tribute to Hemingway, in January. He produces his play *The Wonderful Ice Cream Suit* in Los Angeles. "The Other Foot" is selected for *Best American Short Stories 1915–1965.* Random House publishes *The Vintage Bradbury*, and Ballantine *The Autumn People*, the first of two mass-market paperbacks featuring the early 1950s EC Comics graphic adaptations of Bradbury stories. Receives the first of two Ann Radcliffe Awards for contributions to Gothic Literature from the Count Dracula Society, precursor to the Academy of Science Fiction, Fantasy, and Horror Films. *The World of Ray Bradbury* has a short New York run at the Orpheum Theatre.

1966 Doubleday publishes *S Is for Space*, a companion to *R Is for Rocket*; Ballantine collects early 1950s EC Comics versions of Bradbury stories as *Tomorrow Midnight*, a companion to *The Autumn People.* François Truffaut's *Fahrenheit 451* premieres at the Venice Film Festival in September, followed by a November U.S. release. In November, mother dies in Los Angeles at age seventy-eight.

1967 Musical production of *Dandelion Wine* opens at Lincoln Center in April. In November, *Life* publishes his celebration of the Apollo space program, "An Impatient Gulliver above Our Roofs." Begins to script an animated history of Halloween for MGM producer Chuck Jones, titled *The Halloween Tree.*

1968 Wins Aviation Space Writers Association's Robert Ball Memorial Award for "An Impatient Gulliver above Our Roofs." *Leviathan '99*, his space-age adaptation of *Moby-Dick*, is broadcast as a BBC radio play. Is named president of the Chamber Symphony Society of California. "Any Friend of Trains Is a Friend of Mine" is published in *Life* in August. *Christus Apollo*, a cantata based on his poem of the same title, is performed at UCLA with music by Jerry Goldsmith and Charlton Heston as narrator.

1969 *The Illustrated Man*, a movie based on three stories from his 1951 collection of the same title, premieres in March. Lectures at the newly founded American Film Institute. Story collection *I Sing the Body Electric!* is published by Knopf in October.

1970 As funding fails to materialize for an animated *Halloween Tree*, begins to transform the work into a short novel. Collaborates with WED, a Disney Imagineering think tank, on Robot Factory exhibits. "Mars Is Heaven!" ("The Third Expedition," 1948) is selected for the first volume of Doubleday's *Science Fiction Hall of Fame* anthology.

1971 Apollo 15 crew names a lunar impact feature Dandelion Crater in honor of Bradbury; it becomes a navigational point during the longest of Apollo 15's three Lunar Rover excursions. Participates in a panel discussion, "Mars and the Mind of Man," at California Institute of Technology. Witnesses Mariner 9's successful insertion into Martian orbit from Caltech's mission control room; meets space pioneer Wernher von Braun.

1972 *The Wonderful Ice Cream Suit and Other Plays* is published by Bantam. The Warner Brothers film *Picasso Summer*, based on his story "In a Season of Calm Weather," released directly to CBS as a late-night movie. *The Screaming Woman*, a feature-length adaptation of an early Bradbury story, airs as a CBS Movie of the Week. *The Halloween Tree* fully evolves from unproduced screenplay to novel and is published by Knopf in August. Essay "From Stonehenge to

Tranquility Base" appears in *Playboy*, paving the way for similar major-market magazine speculative articles over the next decade.

1973 *When Elephants Last in the Dooryard Bloomed* becomes the first of three Bradbury poetry volumes published by Knopf.

1974 Receives Valentine Davies Career Award from the Writers Guild of America West for contributions to motion picture screenwriting. Records *Bradbury Reads Bradbury* with the Listening Library for high school use.

1975 *Pillar of Fire and Other Plays* becomes his second trio of stage adaptations published by Bantam. Bradbury's 1972 *Madrigals for the Space Age*, with music by Lalo Schifrin, is reprised for an American bicentennial concert in Los Angeles conducted by Aaron Copland and narrated by actor Jimmy Stewart.

1976 Witnesses the Viking 1 landing on Mars from mission control at Caltech's Jet Propulsion Lab. *Long After Midnight*, his first story collection in seven years, is published by Knopf in August. *Fahrenheit 451* (as read by Bradbury) is nominated for Best Spoken Word Recording by the National Academy of Recording Arts and Sciences.

1977 Selected as the Life Achievement Award winner (for 1976) by jurors of the World Fantasy Awards. Knopf publishes his second book of verse, *Where Robot Mice and Robot Men Run Round in Robot Towns.* Essay "The God in Science Fiction" appears in the December 10 issue of *The Saturday Review of Literature.*

1978 Travels to Paris with Maggie as a guest of the French government to speak during the 150th anniversary of Jules Verne's birth. They tour northern Italy and spend a week visiting with film director Federico Fellini in Rome. Abrams publishes *The Mummies of Guanajuato*, a book of photos by Archie Lieberman built around Bradbury's Mexican tale "The Next in Line."

1979 Receives an honorary Doctor of Literature degree from Whittier College. Hosts and co-writes the ABC hour-long special broadcast *Infinite Horizons: Space Beyond*

Apollo; wins an Emmy with his co-writer and director Malcolm Clarke.

1980 Selected as the Gandalf Grand Master of Fantasy Award winner during the annual Hugo Award competition. NBC's television miniseries *The Martian Chronicles* airs in January with a script by Richard Matheson and a distinguished cast. "Beyond Eden," his speculative preview of the Space Shuttle era, appears in the April issue of *Omni*. Traveling by rail and sea, spends late summer and early fall in Paris with Maggie, who is fluent in French. Knopf publishes the hundred-story retrospective collection *The Stories of Ray Bradbury*.

1981 Gives lecture on screenwriting at the American Film Institute in April, and again the following year. His third collection of verse, *The Haunted Computer and the Android Ape*, is published by Knopf.

1982 After a dozen years of work with Disney Imagineers on the concept and narrative for the Spaceship Earth geodome ride, appears at the opening of Disney World and EPCOT in October. Returns to Los Angeles by plane, conquering a lifelong fear of flying; subsequently travels by air overseas. Release of the Disney feature film adaptation of *Something Wicked This Way Comes* is delayed after a studio screening.

1983 *Dinosaur Tales*, an illustrated collection of stories for young readers, is published by Bantam. After significant reshooting and editing, *Something Wicked This Way Comes* is released by Disney in April; Bradbury's screenplay receives the Saturn Award for Writing from the Academy of Science Fiction, Fantasy, and Horror Films.

1984 Occasional unpublicized visits home to Waukegan, Illinois, culminate in an official visit, during which he receives the "Key to the City." The omnibus volume *Novels of Ray Bradbury* published by Granada in Great Britain. Dell releases a collection of Bradbury's early detective stories as *A Memory of Murder* in February. *Fahrenheit 451* receives Prometheus Award for best Hall of Fame Classic Fiction from the Libertarian Futurist Society; co-winner is George Orwell's *1984*. Chairs the newly formed World Interdependence Fund and its efforts to provide technological help to the disabled and disadvantaged.

1985 Testifies before the National Commission on Space, convened by President Reagan and the United States Congress to plan the next fifty years of space exploration. In its first season, *The Ray Bradbury Theater* receives an ACE (Award for Cable Excellence); by its final season (1993) the series will earn a total of ten ACE nominations and net six wins, as well as two Emmy nominations. *Death Is a Lonely Business*, the first of his three late-life autobiographical mystery novels, published by Knopf in October. Receives the Body of Work Award for lifetime achievement from the writers' group PEN USA.

1986 Serves as guest of honor at the World Science Fiction Convention. Dramatic Publishing releases a series of his plays for theatrical use. "There Is Life on Mars, and It Is Us!," expressing his settled views on the human desire to explore the cosmos, appears in the summer issue of *The Planetary Report*.

1987 Honored as keynote speaker at NASA's thirtieth annual Goddard Memorial Dinner in Washington, D.C.

1988 In May, Knopf releases his first story collection in twelve years, *The Toynbee Convector*.

1989 Named a Grand Master by the Science Fiction and Fantasy Writers of America for his lifetime achievement in these fields. Joshua Odell Editions publishes *Zen in the Art of Writing* in March; over time, it becomes his best-selling nonfiction work. *The Toynbee Convector* is nominated for a 1988 Bram Stoker Award by the Horror Writers Association.

1990 Attends a state luncheon at the Soviet Embassy in Washington, D.C., in June. A portion of the Yeoman Creek ravine near his childhood home in Waukegan, Illinois, is named the Ray Bradbury section of Powell Park. In July, Knopf publishes his second mystery novel, *A Graveyard for Lunatics*, based on his occasional stints as a contract writer in Hollywood during the 1950s and early 1960s.

1991 Selected with other internationally prominent writers to judge the Turner Tomorrow Award. Travels to France, Italy, and Spain over the summer, giving the opening address for the Spoleto *Festival dei Due Mondi* and visiting Federico Fellini in Rome. *Ray Bradbury on Stage*, a compilation of his published stage plays, is released under the Donald I. Fine imprint. His essay collection *Yestermorrow!* is published by Joshua Odell Editions.

1992 In May, Knopf publishes *Green Shadows, White Whale*, a novelization of his Irish stories and his 1953–54 experiences in Ireland writing the screenplay for *Moby Dick*. The Science Fiction and Fantasy Writers of America establish The Ray Bradbury Award for excellence in screenwriting. Receives Mark Twain Award from the Society for the Study of Midwestern Literature, and honorary degrees from the California Institute of the Arts and West Coast University. Television documentary *Ray Bradbury: An American Icon* airs, with narration by actor and friend Rod Steiger.

1993 Bradbury's feature-length animated teleplay of his 1972 novel, *The Halloween Tree*, is aired October 20, 1993, on the Turner Broadcasting Channel. Bradbury shares a Cable ACE award for *The Ray Bradbury Theater* as Best Dramatic Series; this is the last of ten ACE nominations (and six wins) for the Bradbury series.

1994 Wins an Emmy for his animated screenplay adaptation of *The Halloween Tree*. Works through much of his annual summer stay in Paris on early drafts of a *Fahrenheit 451* screenplay for Mel Gibson, who has elicited interest from Warner Brothers.

1995 Is named Los Angeles Citizen of the Year for his contributions to city planning. Works on a screenplay of his story and stage play *The Wonderful Ice Cream Suit* for a possible Disney film production. Plans for the *Fahrenheit 451* screenplay-in-progress shift from Warner Brothers to Universal Studios.

1996 Receives an Honorary Doctorate of Humane Letters from California Lutheran University, and is nominated for the First Fandom Hall of Fame Award, a Hugo ceremony honor recognizing original fans from the days of the first World Science Fiction Convention of 1939. Avon Books publishes *Quicker Than the Eye* (a story collection) in November. Los Angeles names a room in its main library for Ray Bradbury.

1997 *Driving Blind*, a collection of stories, is published in September by Avon. Under an option with Mel Gibson and Universal Studios, completes the final draft of his *Fahrenheit 451* screenplay; despite a long series of options, it is never produced.

1998 Publishes his second children's picture book, *Ahmed and the Oblivion Machines. Driving Blind* is nominated for a World Fantasy Award. Disney releases the feature film version of *The Wonderful Ice Cream Suit*, but distribution is limited to home video through Disney's Touchstone subsidiary.

1999 Receives the George Pal Memorial Award from the Academy of Science Fiction, Fantasy, and Horror Films, and is inducted (along with Robert Silverberg and posthumous inductees A. Merritt and Jules Verne) into the Science Fiction Hall of Fame. In November, suffers a stroke in Palm Springs that permanently limits his mobility and ability to type. Most of his subsequent writing will be initially recorded by dictation and transcribed by his daughter Alexandra.

2000 Receives the National Book Foundation Medal for Distinguished Contribution to American Letters on November 15. In spite of his limited mobility and the sudden permanent loss of vision in his left eye, attends the award ceremony in New York. Spacewatch project astronomers at Kit Peak observatory rename asteroid 1992DZ2 as 9766 Bradbury, in honor of the author.

2001 The World Horror Convention names Bradbury a Grand Master. July sees publication of *A Chapbook for Burnt-Out Priests, Rabbis, and Ministers* (published by Cemetery Dance), a collection of Bradbury's speculative writings on the cosmos and faith. *From the Dust Returned*, a novelized story cycle started more than fifty years earlier, published by Morrow. *Ray Bradbury, His Life and Work* printed by Book-of-the-Month Club in conjunction with its rerelease of four Bradbury classics. Mayor James Hahn of Los Angeles proclaims Ray Bradbury Day for Friday, December 14.

2002 *From the Dust Returned* is nominated for a Bram Stoker Award and a World Fantasy Award. *One More for the Road*, a story collection, is published in March by Morrow. *Fahrenheit 451* is named the "One Book, One City" selection for Los Angeles; other cities eventually select *Fahrenheit 451* for subsequent reading programs. Recognized for his contributions to film with the 2,193rd star on the Hollywood Walk of Fame in April.

2003 *One More for the Road* receives the Bram Stoker Award for best fiction collection. *Bradbury Stories*, his second hundred-story compilation, is published by Morrow. Receives an Honorary Doctorate from Woodbury University. Maggie Bradbury passes away in November after a brief illness. His third and final mystery novel, *Let's All Kill Constance!*, is published by Morrow.

2004 Addresses the Presidential Commission on Moon, Mars, and Beyond in April. His older brother and sole surviving sibling, Leonard, Jr. ("Skip"), passes away the same month. The 62nd World Science Fiction Convention awards *Fahrenheit 451* the Retro-Hugo as best novel fifty years after its 1953 publication. *The Cat's Pajamas*, a story collection with a cover illustration by Bradbury, is published by Morrow. Receives the National Medal of Arts from President Bush in November at a White House ceremony.

2005 *Bradbury Speaks*, a collection of articles and essays, is published in July by Morrow. *Maggie Remembered*, a tribute from Bradbury to his late wife, published by Hill House. Receives an honorary degree from the University of Ireland, Galway, presented in Los Angeles.

2006 The National Endowment for the Arts selects *Fahrenheit 451* for "The Big Read" national reading program. *The Homecoming* appears as a children's book, illustrated by Dave McKean for Collins Design. Deferred for a half century, *Farewell Summer*, the original novel from which the story-chapters of *Dandelion Wine* were extracted, is published by Morrow in October. Along with *Dandelion Wine* and *Something Wicked This Way Comes*, *Farewell Summer* completes his "Green Town"

Illinois trilogy, based on memories of his childhood adventures in Waukegan.

2007 Is awarded a Pulitzer Prize special citation in April for his "prolific and deeply influential" career. Gauntlet Press gathers early versions of *Fahrenheit 451* and related stories as *Match to Flame*, later retitled *A Pleasure to Burn*. Receives the French Ordre des Arts et des Lettres (Commandeur) Medal from the French ambassador to the United States, and a National Olympus Award from the Russian Academy of Sciences. In September *Now and Forever*, a pairing of the long-deferred short novels *Somewhere a Band Is Playing* and *Leviathan '99*, is published by Morrow.

2008 Is named Grand Master Poet at the Rhysling Awards for science fiction and fantasy verse, and receives the first J. Lloyd Eaton Award for Lifetime Achievement in Science Fiction, from the University of California, Riverside. *Masks*, a gathering of materials from an unpublished novel of the late 1940s, is published by Gauntlet Press; Subterranean Press releases *Moby Dick: A Screenplay* from his submitted 1954 script of the 1956 Warner Brothers film. His final story collection, *We'll Always Have Paris*, appears in December.

2009 Hill & Wang publishes a graphic novel adaptation of *Fahrenheit 451*. Receives an honorary doctorate from Columbia College, Chicago. Don Congdon, his agent for sixty-two years, dies in November.

2010 Receives the Comic Con Icon Award during the Scream Awards, celebrating the history of horror, science fiction, and fantasy feature films. His ninetieth birthday is celebrated in and around Los Angeles through various events coordinated by writer Steven Paul Leiva; the Los Angeles City Council passes a resolution declaring August 22–28 to be Ray Bradbury Week.

2011 Contracts pneumonia in January and a subsequent MRSA infection in the spring; suffers what may be a minor stroke late in the year. He remains lucid and works on a few incomplete stories from earlier times.

2012 William Morrow publishes the Bradbury tribute volume *Shadow Show*, with stories by a wide range of contemporary writers. "Take Me Home," a short essay, appears in a June special science fiction issue of *The New Yorker.* Dies on June 5 at Cedars Sinai Hospital in Los Angeles and is buried in Westwood Memorial Park. The Jet Propulsion Laboratory and NASA name the Mars rover Curiosity's landing zone after Bradbury on what would have been his ninety-second birthday, August 22. In September, a Los Angeles City Council resolution renames the intersection of Fifth and Flower, adjacent to the Los Angeles Central Library, as Ray Bradbury Square.

Note on the Texts

This volume is the first of a two-volume set of Ray Bradbury's fiction. It presents the complete texts of the major book-length works from the earliest decades of his career—*The Martian Chronicles* (1950), *Fahrenheit 451* (1953), *Dandelion Wine* (1957), and *Something Wicked This Way Comes* (1962)—along with an appendix of several related short articles and introductions by Bradbury. The second volume in the set, *Selected Stories*, will present *The Illustrated Man* (1951) and *The October Country* (1955), followed by additional stories from these early decades. The texts of the books included in this volume have been taken from first printings, with the exception of *The Martian Chronicles*, to be discussed below; texts of the short articles and introductions have been taken from the earliest published versions.

The Martian Chronicles. Bradbury's broad range of Martian stories dates from the beginning of his professional career in the early 1940s and stretches well beyond the initial publication of *The Martian Chronicles* on May 4, 1950. He first had the idea to present some of these stories within a larger framework after his friend and fellow genre writer Henry Kuttner suggested in 1944 that he read Sherwood Anderson's story cycle *Winesburg, Ohio* (1919). The resulting single-page list of stories about migration to Mars was soon forgotten, but variations on Martian themes surfaced frequently within the 120 stories he would publish in both pulp and major market magazines by the end of the 1940s.

In 1948, among a number of outlines for story collections that he proposed to various publishers with the assistance of his agent Don Congdon, Bradbury envisioned two potential books of Martian stories to be titled *The Martian Chronicles*: one would have gathered his own work; and the other, stories by a variety of authors. Neither project found a publisher, but during a trip to New York in June 1949, Bradbury's ideas about possible Mars books prompted an alternative proposal, and an offer, from Walter I. Bradbury (no relation), an editor at Doubleday: if Ray Bradbury would consider making a kind of novel out of his Martian stories, linking them into a unified whole, Doubleday would offer him a contract. By the time he left New York, he had accepted this offer and presented a new outline, arranging some of his Martian stories in a chronological sequence that imagined a history of future Mars colonization.

Throughout the summer of 1949 Bradbury focused on seventeen

of the nearly thirty Martian stories, published and unpublished, that he had in hand, revising them in varying degrees to fit a new *Chronicles* timeline. He added a date prefix to each story's title, and wrote thirteen titled bridges (also with date prefixes) to serve as transitions between the revised tales. For three of the new bridges he borrowed titles from unrelated, previously published stories: "Rocket Summer," "Interim," and "The Naming of Names" were all repurposed. Fifteen of the seventeen stories remained in the final contents, and all but three had earlier magazine or anthology versions. Information about the prior publication history of individual story-chapters included in the May 1950 first edition of *The Martian Chronicles* is provided below:

February 1999: Ylla. *Maclean's*, January 1, 1950 (as "I'll Not Ask for Wine").

August 1999: The Summer Night. *Arkham Sampler*, Winter 1949 (as "The Spring Night").

August 1999: The Earth Men. *Thrilling Wonder Stories*, August 1948; *The Other Side of the Moon*, ed. August Derleth (New York: Pellegrini & Cudahy, 1949).

April 2000: The Third Expedition. *Planet Stories*, Fall 1948 (as "Mars Is Heaven!"); *The Best Science Fiction Stories 1949*, ed. Everett F. Bleiler and T. E. Dikty (New York: Frederick Fell, 1949; as "Mars Is Heaven!"); *Shot in the Dark*, ed. Judith Merril (New York: Bantam 1950; as "Mars Is Heaven!"); *Argosy* (UK), April 1950 (as "Circumstantial Evidence").

June 2001: —And the Moon Be Still as Bright. *Thrilling Wonder Stories*, June 1948 (as ". . . And the Moon Be Still as Bright"); *The Best Science Fiction Stories 1949*, ed. Everett F. Bleiler and T. E. Dikty (New York: Frederick Fell, 1949).

April 2005: Usher II. *Thrilling Wonder Stories*, April 1950 (as "Carnival of Madness").

September 2005: The Martian. *Super Science Stories*, November 1949 (as "Impossible").

November 2005: The Off Season. *Thrilling Wonder Stories*, December 1948.

December 2005: The Silent Towns. *Charm*, March 1949.

April 2026: The Long Years. *Maclean's*, September 15, 1948; *Planet Stories*, Spring 1949 (as "Dwellers in Silence"); *Argosy* (UK), March 1949.

August 2026: There Will Come Soft Rains. *Collier's*, May 6, 1950.

October 2026: The Million Year Picnic. *Planet Stories*, Summer 1946; *Strange Ports of Call*, ed. August Derleth (New York: Pellegrini

& Cudahy, 1948); *Invasion from Mars: Interplanetary Stories*, ed. Orson Welles (New York: Dell, 1949); *Argosy* (UK), February 1950 (as "The Long Weekend").

Bradbury's revisions progressed slowly, and he missed two deadlines. ("I think you should strive to free yourself of the perfectionistic reins you hold on yourself," Don Congdon told him; "let the stories get away from you more easily.") On October 8, he finally sent Congdon a fair copy typescript, prepared by his wife Maggie while she was pregnant with their first daughter. Yet he continued to make changes in his work up to its first publication and beyond.

Early in the winter of 1949–50, Bradbury asked that Doubleday cut one story ("They All Had Grandfathers") and two bridges ("The Disease" and "The Wheel") that he decided were not right for the book; he soon cut a second tale, "The Fire Balloons," leaving fifteen stories and eleven bridges. During late January and early February he carefully read galley proofs of this twenty-six-chapter text, and it was with twenty-six chapters that Doubleday published his work in May 1950. New printings of the Doubleday first edition continued to appear until 1978; in other American editions, published with his consent, the twenty-six-chapter contents have remained in print up to the present. In spite of this consistency, however, Bradbury came to feel that the "complete" *Martian Chronicles* should include two additional stories: "The Fire Balloons" and "The Wilderness."

His first alteration to the published contents of *The Martian Chronicles* appeared in *The Silver Locusts*, the first British edition of his work, published by Rupert Hart-Davis in London in 1951 and retitled at the publisher's request. Regretting his decision to cut "The Fire Balloons," he restored the story, while also omitting "Usher II"—an omission common to all British editions. Bradbury added another story to his second British edition (titled *The Martian Chronicles* and published by The Science Fiction Book Club in 1953): "The Wilderness," first printed in the *Philadelphia Inquirer*'s *Today* magazine on April 6, 1952, and collected separately, in the United States, in *The Golden Apples of the Sun*, published by Doubleday in 1953.

The first "complete" *Martian Chronicles*—retaining "Usher II" and adding "The Fire Balloons" and "The Wilderness"—was published by Time, Inc., in New York in 1963; Bradbury approved this revision of the contents of his work but is not believed to have reviewed the reset Time, Inc., text. Doubleday published a second "complete" edition in 1973; it reproduces the typesetting of the 1950 first edition, interpolating "The Fire Balloons" and "The Wilderness" from the first U.S. editions in which they appeared, both also published by Doubleday and carefully revised and proofread by the author: *The Illustrated Man* (1951) and *The Golden Apples of the Sun* (1953).

Many of the individual story-chapters in *The Martian Chronicles* have also appeared separately, after their initial book publication and sometimes under different titles, in magazines, anthologies, and Bradbury collections such as *The Vintage Bradbury* (1965), *S Is for Space* (1966), *The Stories of Ray Bradbury* (1980), *Classic Stories 2* (1990), and *Bradbury Stories* (2003). In 1997, for an edition published by Avon/Morrow, Bradbury permitted an update to his chronology, which originally commenced in 1999: advancing his date-prefixes into the middle of the twenty-first century, this edition also omitted the story-chapter "Way in the Middle of the Air." In 2009, Subterranean Press published *The Martian Chronicles: The Complete Edition*, which along with other ancillary material included the previously unpublished story-chapter "They All Had Grandfathers" and bridge-chapters "The Disease" and "The Wheel," which Bradbury discarded in the process of revision.

Bradbury's submitted typescript, which served as setting copy for the Doubleday galleys, is preserved in Special Collections at UCLA. Separate typescripts of individual story-chapters are also known to survive. The text of *The Martian Chronicles* in the present volume is that of the 1973 Doubleday second "complete" edition, which reproduces the typesetting of the 1950, 1951, and 1953 Doubleday first editions in which its contents originally appeared.

Fahrenheit 451. First published by Ballantine Books in New York on October 19, 1953, in an edition that also included his short stories "And the Rock Cried Out" and "The Playground," Bradbury's novel *Fahrenheit 451* had its beginnings in a story draft titled "The Fireman," the earliest known fragments of which date to 1946–47. In 1944, Bradbury read Arthur Koestler's novel *Darkness at Noon* (1940), an exposé of Stalinist authoritarianism that galvanized his attention and concern: "The Fireman" was one of several stories he worked on prior to *Fahrenheit 451* dramatizing various threats to freedom, imaginative and otherwise, including "Pillar of Fire" (1948), "The Mad Wizards of Mars" (1949, later titled "The Exiles"), "Carnival of Madness" (1950, later titled "Usher II"), and "The Pedestrian" (1951), the last of these written after an incident in 1949 when he was stopped by the police while taking a late-night walk with a friend.

In the summer of 1950, working in a basement typing room of the Powell Library at UCLA, where his breaks included walks through the book stacks for inspiration, Bradbury returned to the unfinished story. Within a week or two, he was able to recast "The Fireman" as a 25,000-word novella, titled *Long After Midnight.* In September, having revised his first draft of the novella and having restored his original title, he sent it to his agent, Don Congdon; Doubleday declined to include it in his collection *The Illustrated Man*, published in February 1951, and several magazines turned it down before Horace Gold bought it for *Galaxy Science Fiction*, where it appeared in the same month as *The Illustrated Man.*

During the summer of 1951, while in New York consulting with Congdon and various editors, Bradbury attended a first-run Broadway production of *Darkness at Noon*, adapted for the stage by Koestler and Sidney Kingsley. By late 1952, he was expanding "The Fireman" once again, now as the anchor for a new story collection he was preparing for Ballantine Books. In January 1953, his search for the temperature at which book paper burns led him to a new title, *Fahrenheit 451.* In June, having missed his submission deadlines, he returned to the Powell Library, completing a novel draft of approximately 50,000 words.

In order to accommodate *Fahrenheit 451*, Ballantine revised their original eight-story publication plan: the novel would be followed only by "And the Rock Cried Out" and "The Playground." To save time, the Ballantine editor Stanley Kauffmann traveled to Los Angeles in early August to assist during several days of galley revisions and corrections; Bradbury took the lead in these sessions, making final cuts to two dreamlike reveries in the final section of the novel, "Burning Bright." With the revised galleys in hand, Kauffmann was able to drop them off with the printer in Chicago on his way back to New York.

Fahrenheit 451 appeared in numerous printings and editions after its October 1953 Ballantine debut. The first of these, published by Rupert Hart-Davis in London in 1954, omitted the two stories originally included with the novel, an omission that persisted in the novel's subsequent British publication history, and that characterizes many of its subsequent American appearances as well. Bradbury did not believe that the stories necessarily belonged with the novel, and he is not known to have been involved in any subsequent alteration to the text of the novel, with two possible exceptions. In 1966, Ballantine prepared a special "Bal-Hi" issue for school adoption that silently removed profanity and references to sexuality, drugs, alcohol, insanity, and God, at about one hundred points. Though he had been informed about the special imprint, Bradbury did not realize the extent of these bowdlerizations until high school English classes contacted him. His strong recommendation to restore the text influenced

Ballantine's decision to discontinue the Bal-Hi printings in 1978, and to restore the unaltered text. He may also have consented to a change in the novel's chronology: a reference to "atomic wars since 1960" in the first edition (see page 291, lines 1–2 in the present volume) was updated to "1990" in Ballantine printings beginning in 1979, and to "2022" in Simon & Schuster printings beginning in 1993.

Bradbury's submitted typescript is preserved in the William F. Nolan Collection at Bowling Green State University, but his revised galleys remain unlocated. The text of *Fahrenheit 451* in the present volume is that of the October 1953 Ballantine first printing.

Dandelion Wine. First published by Doubleday in New York on September 5, 1957, *Dandelion Wine* had its origins in a book project Bradbury began in the mid-1940s under the working titles *The Winds of Time* and *Summer Morning, Summer Night.* This slowly evolving "Illinois novel," drawing on his childhood memories of Waukegan, Illinois, in the 1920s and early 1930s, proved both troublesome and rewarding: Bradbury found it difficult to sustain an effective, novel-length story line and to complete the book, and yet the individual "Green Town" stories he wrote along the way won him increasing popularity in major market magazines. His Doubleday editor Walter Bradbury hoped the Illinois novel would help to ensure his transition into the literary mainstream, and in June 1951 offered him a contract for the book, but his struggle with it continued.

In place of the promised but still-unfinished novel, Bradbury first persuaded Doubleday to accept *The Golden Apples of the Sun*, a short story collection; it appeared in March 1953. By this time, he was deep in the process of transforming "The Fireman" into *Fahrenheit 451*, published by Ballantine Books in October 1953. After a nine-month screenwriting sojourn in Europe, he turned next to gathering his earlier weird tales in *The October Country*, published in November 1955, again by Ballantine. Sensing an impasse, Walter Bradbury advised him to extract what he could from the larger project, and to publish a collection of linked stories as a prelude to the novel itself. Changing his working title from *Green Town, Illinois* to *Dandelion Wine* in early 1956, he worked on the reconceived book throughout the year and into the spring of 1957.

On August 14, 1956, he sent Doubleday a revised outline, and by October he was able to hand a first full draft to Walter Bradbury, during his editor's annual visit to Doubleday's West Coast office. He revised, expanded, and rearranged this draft before it was typeset, adding two previously unpublished carnivalesque adventures, "Exorcism" and "The Tarot Witch" (see pages 459–71 and 526–40 of the present volume), and making many other changes. He continued to revise in galley proofs, which arrived in February 1957, and carefully reviewed page proofs in late March and early April.

Many of the individual, unnumbered, and untitled story-chapters in *Dandelion Wine* had appeared in print before the book's publication, as described in the list below. Bringing them together, Bradbury removed their titles and rewrote freely, making substantial alterations:

PAGES 367–73 IN THIS VOLUME. "Illumination," *The Reporter*, May 16, 1957.

374–76. "Dandelion Wine," *Gourmet*, June 1953.

379–84. "Summer in the Air," *The Saturday Evening Post*, February 18, 1956; *Argosy* (UK), September 1956.

387–89. "The Season of Sitting," *Charm*, August 1951 (as a nonfiction article).

390–91. "The Happiness Machine," *Saturday Evening Post*, September 14, 1957 (parts 1 and 2 of 4).

392–99. "The Night," *Weird Tales*, July 1946 (US) and September 1946 (Canada); *Dark Carnival* (Sauk City, Wisconsin: Arkham House, 1947).

400–01. "The Happiness Machine," *Saturday Evening Post*, September 14, 1957 (part 3 of 4).

402–06. "The Lawns of Summer," *Nation's Business*, May 1952.

407–16. "The Happiness Machine," *Saturday Evening Post*, September 14, 1957 (part 4 of 4).

420–28. "Season of Disbelief," *Collier's*, November 25, 1950.

430–36. "The Last, the Very Last," *Reporter*, June 2, 1955.

439–44. "The Green Machine," *Argosy* (UK), March 1951.

445–48. "The Trolley," *Good Housekeeping*, July 1955; "The Enchanted Trolley," *Argosy* (UK), March 1956.

473–78. "The Window," *Collier's*, August 5, 1950; "Calling Mexico," *Argosy* (UK), May 1952; *The New York Post*, December 11, 1955.

483–95. "The Swan," *Cosmopolitan*, September 1954; "Lime-Vanilla Ice," *Argosy* (UK), June 1955.

499–514. "The Whole Town's Sleeping," *McCall's*, September 1950; *Woman's Journal* (UK), December 1950; *Argosy* (UK), July 1951; *Ellery Queen's Mystery Magazine*, June 1954. Adapted for radio and broadcast on *Suspense* (CBS, July 15, 1948), as "Summer Night."

518–22. "Good-by, Grandma," *Saturday Evening Post*, May 25, 1957.

558–68. "Dinner at Dawn," *Everywoman's*, February 1954; *Everybody's Magazine* (UK), August 28, 1954.

Dandelion Wine appeared in many new printings and editions during Bradbury's lifetime, beginning with a Hart-Davis edition in the United Kingdom in the month after its U.S. release, and continuing with a much reprinted Bantam paperback (1959). Several omnibus editions incorporated the book. In contrast to *The Martian Chronicles*, Bradbury is not known to have sought any change in its contents and is unlikely to have revisited its text on the occasion of any of these subsequent publications. In November 1974, while Alfred A. Knopf was preparing a new hardbound edition, he asked his editor Nancy Nicholas to attend to the details. "Proofing has always been one darned awful chore to me," he told her; "I've read *Wine* so many times now I just couldn't do it again." Nicholas corrected a long-standing date error in "The Swan" with his concurrence (see page 491, lines 37–38 in the present volume, and the corresponding note). Though he left his work as a whole untouched, Bradbury selected or consented to the selection of some of the story-chapters in *Dandelion Wine* for inclusion in later collections of his short fiction, among them *R Is for Rocket* (1960), *The Vintage Bradbury* (1965), *S Is for Space* (1966), *The Stories of Ray Bradbury* (1980), *Classic Stories 1* and *2* (1990) and *Bradbury Stories* (2003). These story-chapters sometimes restore earlier magazine titles and sometimes bear new titles, which he may have supplied.

Nearly fifty years after the first appearance of *Dandelion Wine*, Bradbury was able to complete his original novel, publishing it as *Farewell Summer* (2006). He wrote many other "Green Town" stories at midcentury, including "One Timeless Spring" (1946) and "At Midnight, in the Month of June" (1954), which were not included in either book. His October 1956 typescript, revised galleys, and corrected page proofs were all returned to him in February 1958 and are now in the private collection of his friend and principal bibliographer, Donn Albright; photocopies are preserved in The Center for Ray Bradbury Studies at Indiana University. Separate typescripts of individual story-chapters are also known to survive. The text of *Dandelion Wine* in the present volume is that of the September 1957 Doubleday first printing.

Something Wicked This Way Comes. First published by Simon & Schuster in New York on September 17, 1962, *Something Wicked This Way Comes* evolved slowly, like *Dandelion Wine*, from memories of Bradbury's Waukegan childhood. As early as 1944–45, he began to envision a collection of related stories, to be titled *A Child's Garden of Terror*, about a mysterious carnival much like the carnival in the novel; some of these stories ultimately appeared in a 1947 Arkham House collection, as *Dark Carnival.* Yet another story, "The Black Ferris," anticipates the devices and themes of *Something Wicked This Way Comes* even more directly. Published in the May 1948 issue of *Weird Tales*, it continued to occupy Bradbury's imagination: in 1949, he suggested to Mel Dinelli, a Hollywood writer who went on to adapt the story for the local television show *Starlight Summer Theater* in 1954 or 1955, that the story's Ferris wheel might be made into a carousel; in 1952, he collaborated with the illustrator Joe Mugnaini on an unfinished picture version of the story; in July 1956, Dinelli's version was broadcast again as "Merry-Go-Round," the pilot episode of the NBC television series *Sneak Preview*, produced by Sam Goldwyn, Jr.; and also in 1956 Bradbury finished his own screenplay version, *Dark Carnival*, which won the strong support of his friend Gene Kelly, the actor-director, but which failed to find immediate backing.

From 1957 to 1962, while he continued to shop the screenplay, Bradbury wrote a novel that drew on these related works. Discarding an early, first-person draft titled *Jamie and Me* (1958–59), he submitted a revised, third-person version to Doubleday in 1960, but it met with an unenthusiastic reception, his editor and chief advocate Walter Bradbury having left the firm. Working instead with Robert Gottlieb at Simon & Schuster, he continued to revise the novel, changing its title to *The Autumn People* and then to *Something Wicked This Way Comes.* Acting on comments from Don Congdon and from his friend Jack Guss, among others, he drew clearer distinctions between Will Halloway and Jim Nightshade, the two boys at the novel's center, while combining two other principal characters, Will's aging father, Charles Halloway, and the library custodian who helps to save the boys. Four largely complete drafts of the novel are now preserved in the private collection of Donn Albright: Bradbury's initial 377-page Doubleday submission, a 425-page revision for Simon & Schuster, a 380-page third draft dated December 1961, and his final, 340-page typescript, received by Gottlieb at the end of February 1962. (Copies of these drafts, along with discarded pages, are held at The Center for Ray Bradbury Studies.)

While Bradbury revised, Congdon submitted excerpts of the novel to magazines, including *Life*, *Harper's*, *Good Housekeeping*, *The Saturday Evening Post*, and *Mademoiselle*; the last published "Nightmare Carousel," combining parts of chapters 16, 18, 19, and 21 of Bradbury's second draft, in January 1962. Bradbury continued to make changes in the novel, working on his carbon copy, even after Simon &

Schuster began typesetting. He transferred these late alterations onto galley proofs, which he read with care from April 21 to May 14, 1962. Postponing a planned summer publication date to the fall, Simon & Schuster published the novel on September 17.

Something Wicked This Way Comes has subsequently appeared in multiple printings and editions on both sides of the Atlantic, but Bradbury is not believed to have corrected or further altered it. The text of *Something Wicked This Way Comes* in the present volume is that of the September 1962 Simon & Schuster first printing.

Appendix. This volume concludes with a selection of six short items associated with the novels and story cycles it presents. The texts of these items have been taken from their first known appearances in print, as listed below:

A Few Notes on *The Martian Chronicles. Rhodomagnetic Digest*, May 1950.

Day After Tomorrow: Why Science Fiction? *The Nation*, May 2, 1953.

No Man Is an Island. *No Man Is an Island* (Los Angeles: National Women's Committee of Brandeis University, 1952).

Just This Side of Byzantium: An Introduction. *Dandelion Wine* (New York: Alfred A. Knopf, 1975).

Dandelion Wine Revisited. *Gourmet*, June 1991.

Carnivals, Near and Far. *Something Wicked This Way Comes* (New York: Harper Voyager, 1998).

This volume presents the texts of the original printings chosen for inclusion here, but it does not attempt to reproduce features of their design and layout. The texts are presented without change, except for the correction of typographical errors. Spelling, punctuation, and capitalization are often expressive features and they are not altered, even when inconsistent or irregular. The following is a list of errors corrected, cited by page and line number: 38.5, Sight Smell.; 108.7, paramecium; 138.8, antilynchin'; 153.5, roils; 216.19, gone; 235.3, RAMÒN JIMÈNEZ; 248.20, men disposable; 320.13, how I can; 325.15, it on; 359.9, days; 370.5, Adolph; 545.5, horde; 562.21, blessing devoted; 666.3, floor,; 668.12, racheted; 682.2, "Tomorow,; 741.28, fortune-telling,; 748.8, *all*!; 764.36, yiping,; 822.33, progresss.

Notes

In the notes below, the reference numbers denote page and line of this volume (the line count includes chapter headings but not blank lines). No note is generally made for material included in standard desk-reference works. Quotations from Shakespeare are keyed to *The Riverside Shakespeare*, ed. G. Blakemore Evans (Boston: Houghton Mifflin, 1974), and biblical references to the King James Version. For further information about Bradbury's life and works, and references to other studies, see Jonathan R. Eller, *Becoming Ray Bradbury*, *Ray Bradbury Unbound*, and *Bradbury Beyond Apollo* (Urbana: University of Illinois Press, 2011, 2014, 2020, respectively); Jonathan R. Eller and William F. Touponce, *Ray Bradbury: The Life of Fiction* (Kent, OH: The Kent State University Press, 2004); William F. Nolan, *The Bradbury Companion* (Detroit: Gale, 1975); and Sam Weller, *The Bradbury Chronicles* (New York: William Morrow, 2005).

THE MARTIAN CHRONICLES

8.5 cleaning . . . dust] Bradbury's early circulating draft of "Ylla" (c. 1948) reads "sweeping the floor with soft fluffs of spider web."

11.13–16 "'Drink to me . . . wine.'"] See Ben Jonson, "To Cecilia" (1616).

12.1 flame birds] The earliest typescript version of "Ylla" reads "sand ships" here.

21.30–33 "She walks . . . eyes . . ."] See George Gordon, Lord Byron, "She Walks in Beauty" (1814, first published in *Hebrew Melodies*, 1815).

41.21 Navigator Lustig] Bradbury's use of the names of family, friends, and acquaintances in his fiction extends here to New Directions cover designer Alvin Lustig, whose work he knew as early as 1945; in 1946, he met Lustig in New York.

41.22 Samuel Hinkston] Bradbury was related to the Hinkston family of Waukegan, Illinois, his hometown; his grandfather was Samuel Hinkston Bradbury.

41.33–34 "Beautiful Ohio"] The state song of Ohio, written in 1918 by Robert A. King (1862–1932) under the pseudonym Mary Earl, with lyrics by Ballard MacDonald (1882–1935).

44.36–37 "Beautiful Dreamer."] Song by Stephen Foster (1826–1864), first published posthumously in 1864.

44.38–39 "Roamin' . . . Harry Lauder.] Lauder (1870–1950), a Scottish music hall performer, recorded "Roamin' in the Gloamin'" in 1912.

45.4–6 the phonograph record . . . *and you* . . ."] "June Night," a popular 1924 foxtrot dance song written by Abel Baer (1893–1976) and Cliff Friend (1893–1974), has been recorded by numerous orchestras and performers.

46.12 Maxfield Parrish] American painter and illustrator (1870–1966) whose works were widely reproduced.

46.13 Morris chair] A type of reclining chair first manufactured by Morris & Company in England in the 1860s and widely reproduced.

57.21 "Columbia, the Gem of the Ocean,"] American patriotic song composed by Thomas A'Beckett (1808–1890) around 1843.

58.1–2 AND THE MOON . . . BRIGHT] See George Gordon, Lord Byron's poem "So, We'll Go No More A-Roving," written in 1817 and first published posthumously, in Thomas Moore, ed., *Letters and Journals of Lord Byron* (1830). Bradbury quotes the entire poem later in this chapter. In the typescript of *The Martian Chronicles* that Bradbury submitted to his publisher, a brief narrative bridge ("The Disease") preceded this chapter; it described how the Martians died from germs unknowingly carried by the first three expeditions. He deleted "The Disease" and substituted Doc Hathaway's explanation of this tragedy (59.27–61.11) prior to publication.

67.33 McClure] Bradbury's wife's maiden name was Marguerite S. McClure.

100.15 the Episcopal Fathers] Traditionally, members of a communal and celibate religious order within the Anglican Communion, under the See (or Diocese) of Canterbury.

104.2 black Irish] A term sometimes associated with immigrant Irish down through history, including those who left Ireland during the potato famine of 1847, known as "the black '47." More broadly attributed to Irish descendants of successive invaders or applied descriptively to Irish with black hair but fair skin and blue eyes.

109.7 St. Anthony's fire] Bradbury may have intended a reference to St. Elmo's fire, the glow or balls of light generated during electrical storms at sea, often seen by sailors as a good omen, rather than St. Anthony's fire, a medieval name for the burning sensations and hallucinations caused by consumption of ergot-poisoned grain.

116.18–19 lilies . . . spin] See Matthew 6:28, Luke 12:27.

118.13–15 whirlwind twister . . . bump.] See the opening chapters of L. Frank Baum's novel *The Wonderful Wizard of Oz* (1900).

121.20–24 *Oh, the Good Time* . . . an old Wyoming song,"] Possibly inspired by R. V. Sankey's "The Good Time's Come at Last, or The Race to California" (c. 1849), a British music hall song of the California Gold Rush.

121.31–32 Fort Laramie to Hangtown,] Fort Laramie, Wyoming, to the Gold Rush fields at Placerville, California, originally known as "Hangtown."

134.21–22 that song . . . middle of the air'] See "Ezekiel Saw the Wheel," a spiritual by William L. Dawson (1899–1990), adapted from Ezekiel 1:15–22.

140.37 Elijah and the Chariot,] See 2 Kings 2:11–12.

140.37–38 The Big Wheel and the Little Wheel] From the repeating chorus in various versions of the spiritual, "Ezekiel Saw the Wheel."

140.38 Faith, Hope, and Charity] The three theological virtues of St. Paul, identified in 1 Cor. 13:13 and 1 Thess. 5:8 as Faith, Hope, and Love.

146.20–31 *desolate* and *terrible* . . . dreariness of thought'?] See the opening paragraph of Edgar Allan Poe's story "The Fall of the House of Usher," first collected in *Tales of the Grotesque and Arabesque*, vol. 1 (1840).

148.25 Once Upon a Time] Bradbury's first book, given to him for Christmas 1925 by his aunt Neva Bradbury, was the fairy tale collection *Once Upon a Time* (1921), with illustrations by Margaret Evans Price.

148.26 the Phantom Rickshaw] Rudyard Kipling's *The Phantom 'Rickshaw & Other Eerie Tales* (1888).

148.27–29 Glinda . . . Jack Pumpkinhead] L. Frank Baum's Oz characters: Glinda the Good Witch of the South (appearing in almost all titles of the fourteen-book Oz series), Princess Ozma, the true heir to Oz (beginning in volume 2, *The Land of Oz*), the sky fairy Polychrome (beginning in volume 4, *The Road to Oz*), and Jack Pumpkinhead (featured in *The Land of Oz*).

150.14 Babbitts] Conformists, as personified by the title character of the Sinclair Lewis novel *Babbitt* (1922).

152.36 Karloff?] Boris Karloff (William Henry Pratt, 1887–1969), English actor who played Frankenstein's monster in *Frankenstein* (1931), *Bride of Frankenstein* (1935), and *Son of Frankenstein* (1939).

152.38 Lugosi?] Bela Lugosi (1882–1956), Hungarian American actor known for roles in horror films, including *Dracula* (1931), *Murders in the Rue Morgue* (1932), *The Raven* (1935), and *Son of Frankenstein* (1939).

153.25 F.O.B.] "Free on Board," a commercial term used to describe the location at which a buyer or seller is liable for shipping costs and risks.

153.33–34 Tweedledum . . . Dormouse] See Lewis Carroll's *Through the Looking-Glass and What Alice Found There* (1871).

153.37–38 Tik-Tok, Ruggedo] Tik-Tok is the mechanical title character of *Tik-Tok of Oz* (1914), the eighth book in the Land of Oz series by L. Frank Baum (1856–1919); Ruggedo, also known as Roquat the Red and the Nome King, appears in several Oz books, beginning with *Ozma of Oz* (1907).

159.23–24 'For the love . . . Montresor!'] See Poe's story "The Cask of Amontillado," first published in *Godey's Lady's Book* in November 1846.

169.25 Joe Spaulding?] Bradbury's father, Leo Spaulding Bradbury, was a Spaulding on his mother's side.

170.30 'The Bonnie . . . Lomond'] Scottish traditional song, first published in 1841.

188.10–11 Send me your hungry . . . poem go?] See Emma Lazarus's sonnet "The New Colossus," written in 1883 to help raise funds for the construction of a pedestal for the Statue of Liberty.

193.23–24 "That Old Gang of Mine."] Popular song composed by Ray Henderson (1896–1970) in 1923, with lyrics by Mort Dixon (1892–1956) and Billy Rose (1899–1966); it was recorded by multiple artists and sold over a million copies.

197.39–198.1 *Oh, Genevieve, . . . years may go.*] See "Sweet Genevieve," an 1869 song composed by Henry Tucker (1826–1882) with lyrics by George Cooper (1840–1927).

200.12–13 a fifty-year-old film of Clark Gable.] Possibly one of the three romantic dramas that Gable (1901–1960) made after his return from World War II service and before Bradbury's 1945–48 composition of the story: *Adventure* (1945), *The Hucksters* (1947), and *Homecoming* (1948).

200.27 the life of Reilly] A life of unexpected ease and luxury; the phrase may have originated with a comic song of 1883, "Is That Mr. Reilly?" by Pat Rooney (1844–1892), and later provided the title for a popular 1945–51 radio show, *The Life of Riley.*

205.34 Lazarus come forth] See John 11:43. Bradbury published a story titled "Lazarus Come Forth" in *Planet Stories* in 1944.

208.6–7 Marguerite and Susan.] Bradbury's wife Maggie was Marguerite Susan McClure Bradbury; their first child, Susan Marguerite, was born just after Bradbury completed revisions for *The Martian Chronicles.*

217.22–34 "Sara Teasdale . . . *gone.*"] See Teasdale's poem "There Will Come Soft Rains," first published in *Harper's Monthly* in July 1918.

227.18 a family outing,] Bradbury's early working title for "The Million Year Picnic" was "Family Outing."

FAHRENHEIT 451

232.3 DON CONGDON] Congdon (1918–2009) served as Bradbury's literary agent beginning in 1947.

235.1–3 *If they* . . . JIMÉNEZ] From "Estética y Etica Estética," a collection of aphorisms by Juan Ramón Jiménez (1881–1958) first published in *España: Semanario de la Vida Nacional* on November 20, 1920.

259.33 The flutter of cards,] The opening scene of "The Fireman" (1951), the novella that preceded *Fahrenheit 451*.

262.29–31 'Play the man, Master Ridley . . . put out.'] Reportedly spoken by Protestant reformer Hugh Latimer to Anglican bishop Nicholas Ridley, on the point of execution by burning; a consequence of the accession of the Catholic Mary I to the English throne and her vigorous persecution of Anglicans.

263.35–36 "Time has fallen . . . sunshine."] From Alexander Smith's *Dreamthorp: Essays Written in the Country* (1863).

281.22 Colored people . . . *Little Black Sambo*.] Numerous efforts have been made to remove *The Story of Little Black Sambo* (1899), a children's book by Scottish author Helen Bannerman (1862–1946), from school libraries; in 1932, Langston Hughes described the book as "amusing undoubtedly to the white child, but like an unkind word to one who has known too many hurts to enjoy the additional pain of being laughed at."

281.23 White people . . . *Uncle Tom's Cabin*.] Harriet Beecher Stowe's best-selling 1852 antislavery novel provoked outrage among slaveholders and their supporters.

283.7 the Happiness Boys] Radio show of the 1920s and 1930s featuring singers Billy Jones (1889–1940) and Ernie Hare (1883–1939) and their popular comic songs satirizing events of the times.

283.7 the Dixie Duo] Eubie Blake (1887–1983) and Noble Sissle (1889–1975) began to perform ragtime and jazz concerts together around 1919 and were eventually billed as "The Dixie Duo."

288.16–18 "'It is computed, . . . smaller end.'"] See Jonathan Swift's *Gulliver's Travels* (1726), part I, chapter IV, where the cause of the war between Lilliput and Blefuscu is revealed as disagreement over which end of an egg to break at breakfast.

289.12–15 "'We cannot . . . run over.'"] See Dr. Johnson's September 19, 1777, observations on friendship in *The Life of Samuel Johnson* (1791) by James Boswell (1740–1795).

289.26 "'That favorite subject, Myself.'"] From a letter of July 26, 1763, written by James Boswell to essayist and cleric William Johnson Temple (1739–1796).

292.25 copies of the Bible] In "Long After Midnight" (1950), Bradbury's first complete draft of what would become *Fahrenheit 451*, Montag takes Faber the works of Shakespeare rather than the Bible.

295.1 Consider the lilies of the field.] See Matthew 6:28 (the Sermon on the Mount) and Luke 12:27.

311.37 "*Dover Beach.*"] A poem by Matthew Arnold (1822–1888), first published in his *New Poems* (1867).

316.9–10 "here comes . . . called a fool."] See Shakespeare, *As You Like It*, V.iv.36–38.

316.13–14 'Who are a little . . . fools be.'] See John Donne's "The Triple Fool," first published posthumously in 1633.

316.37 Truth is . . . end of reckoning,] See Shakespeare, *Measure for Measure*, V.i.45.

316.37–39 They are never . . . ourselves.] See Sir Philip Sidney, *Arcadia* (1593).

316.39–40 'Sweet food . . . Sidney said.] See Sir Philip Sidney, *The Defense of Poesy* (c. 1580).

316.40–317.2 'Words are like leaves . . . Pope.] See Alexander Pope, *An Essay on Criticism* (1711), part II, 215–18.

317.7–9 'A little learning . . . sobers us again.'] See Pope, *An Essay on Criticism*, II, 309–10.

317.22–23 Dr. Johnson . . . equivalent to force!'] See Samuel Johnson, *The History of Rasselas, Prince of Abyssinia* (1759), chapter 13.

317.24–25 "He is no wise man . . . uncertainty."'] See Samuel Johnson, *The Idler* 57 (May 19, 1757).

317.29–30 'Truth will come . . . hid long!'] See Shakespeare, *The Merchant of Venice*, II.ii.79.

317.31 'Oh God, . . . horse!'] See Shakespeare, *The Merchant of Venice*, I.ii.40–41.

317.31–32 'The Devil . . . purpose.'] See Shakespeare, *The Merchant of Venice*, I.iii.98.

317.32–34 'This age . . .school!'] See Thomas Dekker, "The Choice of Fortunatus" (from *Old Fortunatus*, c.1598), 8–9.

317.34–35 'The dignity . . . protesting.'] See Ben Jonson, *Catiline's Conspiracy* (1611), III.ii.

317.35–36 'Carcasses . . . murderer!'] See Robert Burton, *The Anatomy of Melancholy* (1621), part 1, section 1, member 2, subsection 5.

317.38 'Knowledge is power!'] See Sir Francis Bacon, *Advancement of Learning* (1605), I.i.3.

317.38–39 'A dwarf . . . two!'] See Robert Burton's introduction to *The Anatomy of Melancholy* (1621), "Democritus Junior to the Reader."

317.40–318.2 'The folly . . . once said.'] See Paul Valery, *Introduction to the Method of Leonardo da Vinci* (1895).

318.11 A kind of excellent . . . Willie!"] See Shakespeare, *The Tempest*, III. iii.38.

318.24 "All's well that is well in the end."] See Shakespeare, *All's Well That Ends Well*, IV.iv.35.

321.2 *Burning Bright*] See William Blake's poem "The Tyger," from *Songs of Experience* (1794). This section title evolved from "Books without Pages" (in Bradbury's "Long After Midnight" typescript) and "Water, Water, Quench Fire" (in his novella "The Fireman").

325.29–31 'There is . . . respect not!'] See Shakespeare, *Julius Caesar*, IV.iii.66–69.

340.19 Keystone Comedy,] Silent film era "Keystone Cops" comedies produced by Mack Sennett from 1914 to 1920.

349.36 Ortega y Gasset] José Ortega y Gasset (1883–1965), Spanish philosopher.

361.19–21 To everything . . . to speak.] See Ecclesiastes 3:1–3.

361.23–25 *And on . . . the nations.*] See Revelation 22:2.

361.28 When we reach the city.] Bradbury's novella "The Fireman" closes with the men reciting fragments of literature as they eat their breakfast:

> The forks moved in the pink light. Now each of the men remembered a separate and different thing, a bit of poetry, a line from a play, an old song. And they spoke these little bits and pieces in the early morning air:
>
> "Man that is born of a woman
> Is of few days and full of trouble . . ."
> A wind blew in the trees.
> "To be or not to be, that is the question . . ."
> The sun was fully up.
> "Oh do you remember, Sweet Alice, Ben Bolt . . . ?"
> Montag felt fine.

DANDELION WINE

364.1 Walter I. Bradbury] Bradbury (1914–1996), not a relation, was an editor at Doubleday in New York.

369.39–370.7–8 Matinees I seen . . . *The Bat*,] Jones (1891–1942), Hoxie (1885–1965), Mix (1880–1940), and Gibson (1892–1962) were silent Western stars. Fairbanks, Sr., (1883–1939) was known for his swashbuckling roles in films such as *The Thief of Bagdad* (1924); Sills (1882–1930) and Menjou

(1890–1963) starred in films of several genres. *The Phantom of the Opera* (1925), *The Cat and the Canary* (1927) and *The Bat* (1926) were silent horror films.

While reading *Dandelion Wine* galleys, Bradbury realized that Tom's encyclopedic list of movie matinees had carried over from the May 16, 1957, publication of the berry-picking story in *Reporter* (as "Illumination"), set in the mid-1950s. He hand-revised this anachronistic passage, which originally read as follows:

> Matinees I seen: forty Roy Rogerses, thirty Hopalongs, forty-two Gene Autrys, thirty-five Walt Disneys, one hundred and ninety-two single and separate Bugs Bunnys, ten Burt Lancasters, eight repeats on Davey Crockett, and one Robert Taylor thing about love where I spent ninety hours in the theater toilet waiting for it to be over so I could see "The Mummy Creeps" or "The Bride of Frankenstein."

376.17 the boarders] During Bradbury's childhood, his Bradbury grandparents rented rooms to boarders, who inspired characters in *Dandelion Wine* and such stories as "The Man Upstairs" (1947), "All on a Summer's Night" (1950), and "Any Friend of Nicholas Nickleby Is a Friend of Mine" ("The Best of Times," 1966).

378.1 John Huff] Inspired by a real John Huff, Bradbury's best friend during his family's seven-month stay in Tucson in 1932–33.

382.16 United Cigar Store] During Bradbury's childhood, the United Cigar Store chain had thousands of outlets and sold many non-tobacco items. They were often located in or adjacent to bus stations and rail terminals.

387.8–9 Ahab surveying . . . mild-looking sky,] See "The Symphony," chapter 132 of Herman Melville's novel *Moby-Dick* (1851).

393.34–35 Knickerbocker . . . Crows] Recordings by these artists from the mid- to late 1920s remained fond Bradbury memories, including the comic novelty song "Two Black Crows Part 1" and sequels, by Moran and Mack (1927–28), and many Al Jolson records. Jolson sang on the Knickerbocker Quartet's enduring single, "Pack Up Your Troubles in Your Old Kit Bag" (1917); as a teenager, Bradbury would later attend broadcasts of Jolson's *Shell Chateau* radio show.

395.15 The Lonely One's] Orvel Weyant (1909–1986) robbed almost forty businesses in Waukegan, Illinois, from February through October 1928 before he was captured and sentenced to prison; during this crime spree he wrote taunting letters to newspapers, the police, and his victims, signed "The Lonely One."

395.31–32 when he was six and Great-grandfather passed away,] Grandfather Samuel H. Bradbury (1858–1926) passed away when Ray Bradbury was six; none of his great-grandfathers had lived into his lifetime.

395.35 Death was his little sister] In February 1928, when Bradbury was seven, his baby sister Elizabeth (Betty) Jane died at home from influenza or pneumonia.

404.26 Socrates . . . hemlock.] For politicizing his teachings, an Athenian jury sentenced Socrates to death administered by a drink of hemlock in 399 B.C.E.

405.28 Whittier,] John Greenleaf Whittier (1807–1892), American poet.

408.29 the Red Death] See Edgar Allan Poe's story "The Mask of the Red Death" (1842).

411.14–15 "*A Tale . . . Expectations*?] Novels by Charles Dickens (1812–1870) first published in 1859, 1841, and 1861.

411.25 *Tom Swift and his Electric Annihilator*] Bradbury read many titles in the first series of Tom Swift juvenile novels (1910–40) through copies in Waukegan's Carnegie Library. This title recalls *Tom Swift and his Electric Rifle* (1911).

420.15 Caruso] Italian operatic tenor Enrico Caruso (1873–1921).

431.27 Ching Ling Soo] William Ellsworth Robinson (1861–1918), an American magician who performed under the name Chung Ling Soo, died accidentally onstage during the "bullet" trick Colonel Freeleigh recalls in *Dandelion Wine*; Robinson's act imitated that of Chinese magician Ching Ling Foo (1854–1922), who toured the United States beginning in 1898. Bradbury had previously used the bullet trick in an unpublished story adapted for television as "The Marked Bullet," which aired on the NBC series *Jane Wyman Presents* on November 20, 1956.

432.21 Pawnee Bill?"] Wild West show entrepreneur Gordon William Lillie (1860–1942), creator of several iterations of his "Pawnee Bill" traveling shows and exhibitions. His 1908 tour was briefly combined with William F. Cody and his "Buffalo Bill" traveling Western show.

434.23 Green Town] A thinly veiled Waukegan, Illinois, Bradbury's hometown.

435.11–435.31 'All's quiet . . . free . . .'] See Ethel Lynn Beers, "The Picket-Guard" (1861), a poem set to music by John Hill Hewett as "All Quiet Along the Potomac Tonight" (1863). Colonel Freeleigh's reverie includes Union and Confederate song fragments from "Dixie" (Emmett and Snowden), "The Battle Hymn of the Republic" (Julia Ward Howe, to the melody of "John Brown's Body"), "Ye Cavaliers of Dixie" (Benjamin F. Porter, to the melody of "Ye Mariners of England"), "Tenting on the Old Camp Ground" (Walter Kittredge), and "Marching Through Georgia" (Henry Clay Work).

437.22 Appomattox the summer of 1865.] Confederate general Robert E. Lee's surrender of the Army of Northern Virginia took place at Appomattox on April 9, 1865.

447.26 the seats were turned] At the end of a trolley street line in many cities, the conductor or motorman would turn or flip the seats to face the return direction of travel.

459.22 *Albertus Magnus*] German scholar and theologian (c. 1200–1280), canonized as a Catholic saint, to whom numerous works on alchemy have falsely been attributed.

459.34–35 a head like a box Brownie.] A photographic memory. Bradbury used his father's box Brownie camera to photograph stars in Hollywood after the family moved to Los Angeles in 1934.

460.24 the blood of the Lamb] A reference to the Jewish Passover and Christianity's substitutional sacrifice of Christ.

461.22 Got a nose out to *here*!"] See Carlo Collodi's *Adventures of Pinocchio*, first published in its entirety in Italian in 1883; the 1940 Walt Disney film adaptation was a Bradbury favorite.

465.12 SHE] The immortal lost-world queen Ayesha in H. Rider Haggard's novel *She: A History of Adventure* (1886–87) and its sequels.

491.37–38 one early September afternoon] In 1975, when *Dandelion Wine* was published in a new edition by Alfred A. Knopf, Bradbury's Knopf editor caught an error here, correcting the text to read "early August afternoon" to align with the calendar reference ("August 27, 1928") established a few pages later.

497.28–29 "The Snow Queen.] See Hans Christian Andersen's original fairy tale "The Snow Queen" (1844).

508.1 Electric Park] Now known as Weiss Field, the football stadium for the present Waukegan High School at 100 N. Lewis Avenue. During Bradbury's childhood, this location was also the western terminus of the Washington Street trolley tracks, a line that, for many years, passed close to Bradbury's home and his grandparents' house at 619 Washington Street.

508.14 "Shine On . . . Moon . . ."] 1908 popular song credited on first publication to Nora Bayes (1880–1928) and Jack Norworth (John Godfrey Knauff, 1879–1959) but since attributed to others.

510.22 "Oh, give me . . . you . . ."] See note 45.4–6.

515.35 vanilla junket] An old-fashioned milk and rennet-based dessert; curds and whey.

529.7–15 *"Hey, nonny . . . nonny no!"*] An anonymous sixteenth-century English song.

530.13 Keystone Kops] See note 340.19.

530.23 San Francisco was built and burned] A reference to the extensive fires following the San Francisco earthquake of April 18, 1906.

532.9 Charlie Chase Comedy] Many of the Hal Roach comedy shorts and films of the 1920s (including the first Our Gang films) were directed by Charles Joseph Parrott (1893–1940), who also starred in some of the Roach films in the comic lead role of Charley Chase.

532.21 Mme. Tarot's real] Bradbury may have based his Mme. Tarot on Marie Anne Adelaide Lenormand (1772–1843), a famous French card reader; various decks of tarot cards evolved from her influence.

537.35–36 Washington Street] Bradbury's home was just south of Washington Street on South St. James, several blocks west of downtown Waukegan and the Yeoman Creek branch of the ravine where Mr. Black dumped the mechanical Tarot Witch.

543.3 twenty-six thousand . . . inhabitants] A fair estimate of the population of Waukegan during this period, as reported in the U.S. Censuses of 1920 (19,226) and 1930 (33,499).

544.6 before Manila Bay] The U.S. naval victory over the Spanish fleet in Manila Bay occurred on May 1, 1898.

545.25 bumbershoots] Umbrellas.

549.35–37 "*Yes, we'll gather . . . God . . .*"] See "Shall We Gather at the River?" (also titled "Beautiful River" or "Hanson Place"), a hymn written by Robert Lowry (1826–1889) in 1864. Bradbury later published a story titled "Yes, We'll Gather at the River" in *I Sing the Body Electric!* (1969).

551.22 the book of magic tricks] Bradbury's parents bought him his first book on magic in 1931 for his eleventh birthday, Walter B. Gibson's *The Book of Secrets: Miracles Ancient and Modern with Chapters on Easy Magic You Can Do* (1927).

555.25–26 the Aran Isles] An island archipelago off the west coast of Ireland, known for preserving the Irish language and traditions.

SOMETHING WICKED THIS WAY COMES

576.9 *JACK GUSS*] A writer and longtime member of Ray Bradbury's writing group, Guss (1919–1987) suggested that Bradbury combine the parallel characters of Charles Halloway (originally a timid librarian) and the fast-thinking and courageous library janitor.

579.1–2 Man is . . . YEATS] See Yeats's poem "Nineteen Hundred and Nineteen," written in 1921 and collected in *The Tower* (1928).

579.8–10 I know . . . *Moby Dick*] See "First Night Watch," chapter 39 of Herman Melville's *Moby-Dick* (1851).

585.2 Green Town] See note 434.23.

588.34–35 Indian-heads . . . quarters,] Indian Head cents, minted through 1909, and Lincoln cents, which succeeded them. "Miss Columbia" is a nickname for the female personification of Liberty featured on quarters minted until 1930, and on other coins.

590.8 Cabbage Night] Traditionally October 30, the prank night before Halloween, also known as Devil's Night.

591.18 Peiping] Beijing, China.

591.18 Celebes.] Sulawesi, the third most populous island of Indonesia.

591.27 20,000-fathoms-deep] An allusion to Jules Verne's novel *20,000 Leagues Under the Sea*, originally published in French in 1869–70; Bradbury wrote an introduction to the novel, "The Ardent Blasphemers," for a newly translated edition in 1962.

592.2 Mister Doré] Gustave Doré (1832–1883), French illustrator of Dante.

592.31 Moriarty,] Professor James Moriarty, archvillain in a number of the Sherlock Holmes tales of Arthur Conan Doyle (1859–1930).

592.32 Fu Manchu] The super-villainous title character of more than a dozen novels by Sax Rohmer (Arthur Henry Ward, 1883–1959), beginning with *The Mystery of Dr. Fu-Manchu* in 1913; also featured in numerous film, television, and comic book adaptations.

592.37–38 *The Mysterious Island*] Novel by Jules Verne (1828–1905), originally published in French in 1875.

594.18 Caesar's lean and hungry friends.] See Shakespeare, *Julius Caesar*, I.ii.194: "Yond Cassius has a lean and hungry look."

594.18–19 They eat . . . breathe.] See the final line of John Milton's sonnet "When I Consider How My Light Is Spent," published in 1673.

595.30 bons] An apparent neologism from *bonfire*, which was originally formed in English by the combination of *bone* and *fire.*

599.19–35 I heard . . . to men!"] The first and final stanzas of Henry Wadsworth Longfellow's 1863 poem "I Heard the Bells on Christmas Day," which became a popular Christmas carol.

600.27 Fantoccini,] Italian for "hand puppet."

601.27 Star of India] One of the largest blue star sapphires in the world, now in the American Museum of Natural History.

647.31–33 the 'Funeral March' . . . Chopin] Chopin's "Funeral March" ("Marche Funèbre"), the third movement of his Piano Sonata No. 2, was composed two years prior to its incorporation within the Sonata in 1839, and remains a popular piece in solo performance.

648.3 "Oh, Susanna."] 1848 popular song by Stephen Foster (1826–1864).

651.30–31 "Way Down . . . Swanee River,"] See "Old Folks at Home," also known as "Swanee River," an 1851 minstrel song by Stephen Foster.

651.34–35 "Marching Through Georgia,"] 1865 marching song by Henry Clay Work (1832–1884).

725.9 *Bizarie* . . . Bracelli,] Bracelli (fl. 1616–1650) published *Bizzarie di varie figure* in 1624.

725.12–22 *Dr. Faustus* . . . *Pacts With Demons*] With the exception of *Dr. Faustus*—either the 1592 play by Christopher Marlowe (1564–1593) or the 1806–32 plays by Johann Wolfgang von Goethe (1749–1832)—these appear to be imaginary or partial titles.

726.24–25 *By the pricking . . . comes.*] See Shakespeare, *Macbeth*, IV.i.45.

731.25 Sweet Water] A town in central Illinois north of Springfield.

736.16–17 Caesar . . . grand march sale.] See Plutarch's *Lives of the Noble Greeks and Romans*, "Julius Caesar" (c. 100 C.E.), which apparently originated the story of the prediction that harm would befall the newly crowned Emperor Julius Caesar on the Ides of March, 44 B.C.E.; Caesar was stabbed by Senators armed with knives in the Roman Senate on March 15.

740.7 'Beautiful Ohio'] See note 41.33–34.

740.7 'Merry Widow.'] The "Merry Widow Waltz," from Franz Lehár's Austrian operetta *The Merry Widow* (1905).

747.20 arun] Running.

767.20 BULLET TRICK!"] See note 431.27.

769.28 Catherine wheels] Also known as pinwheels, a type of firework.

781.37 Jericho and the trump] See Joshua 6.1–27; *trump* is an archaic and poetic form of *trumpet.*

796.23 Avoirdupois] The thirteenth-century pounds-and-ounces weight system (Anglo-Norman French, "goods of weight") still in use in the United States and, to a lesser extent, in Great Britain and British Commonwealth countries.

800.32 "Swanee River."] See note 651.30–31.

801.26–30 "De Camptown . . . doo-dah day!"] From "Gwine to Run All Night, or De Camptown Races," an 1850 minstrel song by Stephen Foster.

805.31 railroad semaphore] Pivoting arms used to give flag signals and instructions to railroad engineers.

APPENDIX

809.16 *Winesburg, Ohio*] 1919 short story sequence by Sherwood Anderson (1876–1941) subtitled *A Group of Tales of Ohio Small Town Life.*

809.20–21 Jessamyn West . . . *Friendly Persuasion*] West (1902–1984) published *The Friendly Persuasion*, a novelized story cycle about an Indiana Quaker farming family, in 1945.

809.26 rhodomagnetics.] "A Few Notes on *The Martian Chronicles*" was originally published in the May 1950 *Rhodomagnetic Digest*, a fanzine that borrowed its title from the fictional science of rhodomagnetism, described by Jack Williamson (1908–2006) in his 1947 novelette "With Folded Hands" and his 1949 novel *The Humanoids.*

810.7–9 Mr. Steig . . . lonely one."] American illustrator William Steig (1907–2003) published *The Lonely Ones*, a collection of humorous portraits, in 1942; see also note 395.15.

810.11 Eliot . . . Hollow Men.] See T. S. Eliot's poem "The Hollow Men," first published in *Poems: 1909–1925* (1925).

810.24–30 Al Jolson . . . Backyard."] Jolson (1886–1950) recorded the song in 1928 and again in 1947; it was composed by Dave Dreyer (1894–1967) with lyrics by Billy Rose (1899–1966).

819.6–7 proper study . . . is man.] See the opening couplet of Alexander Pope's *Essay on Man* (1733), epistle II.

819.24 Philip Wylie] American author (1902–1971) known for both his science fiction and works of social criticism.

819.27 Dale Carnegie] Carnegie (1888–1955) wrote the 1936 best seller *How to Win Friends and Influence People.*

819.34–35 Tom Swift . . . Dean Swift] Tom Swift is the main character, conceived by writer and publisher Edward Stratemeyer (1862–1930), of many juvenile adventure and science fiction novels beginning with *Tom Swift and His Motorcycle* in 1910, usually credited to the pseudonymous Victor Appleton but written by many hands; "Dean Swift" is a common reference to Anglo-Irish satirist Jonathan Swift (1667–1745), for many years the dean of St. Patrick's Cathedral, Dublin.

820.30 The Legion] The National Legion of Decency, a Catholic organization established in 1933 to evaluate the moral content of motion pictures.

820.32 the N.A.M.] The National Association of Manufacturers, an advocacy organization founded in 1895.

823.17 Mr. Mickey Spillane] American crime novelist (1918–2006).

823.40–824.1 Donne . . . unto himself.] See Meditation 17 in Donne's *Devotions upon Emergent Occasions* (1624).

827.9–15 a critic . . . below the town.] See Paul A. Carter, "Of Towns and Roads, Three Novelists, and George McGovern," *The Columbia Forum*, Spring 1973.

828.1–14 *Byzantium . . . any Yeats*] Yeats wrote two well-known Byzantine poems, "Sailing to Byzantium" in 1926 and "Byzantium" in 1930.

833.19–21 Years later . . . 1929.] "The Man Upstairs," first published in *Harper's* in March 1947 and subsequently collected in *Dark Carnival* (1947) and (with revisions) in *The October Country* (1955).

838.21–24 "The Black Ferris" . . . fantasy.] A version of "The Black Ferris" appeared in the May 1948 issue of *Weird Tales*, a year after *Dark Carnival* was published. Bradbury changed the Ferris wheel to a carousel, but the plot of the original story remained a pivotal adventure in the screenplay and novel.

This book is set in 10 point ITC Galliard, a face designed for digital composition by Matthew Carter and based on the sixteenth-century face Granjon. The paper is acid-free lightweight opaque that will not turn yellow or brittle with age. The binding is sewn, which allows the book to open easily and lie flat. The binding board is covered in Brillianta, a woven rayon cloth made by Van Heek–Scholco Textielfabrieken, Holland. Composition by Publishers' Design and Production Services, Inc. Printing by Sheridan, Grand Rapids, MI. Binding by Dekker Bookbinding, Wyoming, MI. Designed by Bruce Campbell.